CET-4

大学

4级 阅读简答 与简答

U0133139

新题型
NEW

内容提要

　　本书根据《大学英语教学大纲》(修订本)和《大学英语课程教学要求》(试行)对阅读的要求以及大学英语教材的难易度编写而成。全书分为两大部分,第一部分为阅读技巧简介;第二部分为阅读实践,包括 150 篇阅读文章,分成 30 个单元,每单元包括 5 篇阅读文章,其中,1 篇快速阅读理解、1 篇篇章词汇理解、2 篇篇章阅读理解、1 篇篇章问答,每篇文章后有阅读练习题和问答练习题,每单元后有难点(包括词汇、搭配、语法结构)注释以及练习题答案解析。

　　本书内容详实,编排合理,注释与解析深入浅出,有助于读者阅读能力及英语水平的全面提高。

　　本书适用于准备参加全国大学英语 4 级统考的考生以及同等水平的读者学习使用。

本书编委会

主　　编　刘宇慧　张俊梅
副主编　张俊英　孔延红　张玉娟
编　　者　梁梅红　郭　玮　周江源
　　　　　邢　芳　殷红梅

前言

《大学英语课程教学要求》(试行)强调培养学生的英语听说能力,以及读写译等英语综合应用能力,其中听说培养的是口头交流能力,读写译培养的是书面交流能力。读、写、译三项能力中,阅读是基础。只有通过大量的阅读,不断地输入与积累,才有可能不断提高写和译的能力。因此,在掌握了一定词汇量的基础上,阅读就成了提高英语书面交流能力的关键。本书旨在帮助和促进读者阅读能力及英语水平的全面提高。

本书具有以下特点:

选材广泛,可读性强　书中文章多选自国内外各类英语刊物、专著、同等水平的英文教材等资料。题材广泛,包括社会、文化、日常生活知识、人物传记等社会科学领域和科普常识、地理等自然科学领域的知识内容;体裁多样,包括叙事、描述、议论、说明文等形式,为读者提供具有可读性与趣味性的读物。

紧扣大纲,针对性强　本书所选的文章在语言和内容上的难易度以及每篇文章和每个单元的阅读量符合大纲的要求;练习题的编写既考虑到了对文章有关细节和主要事实的理解,更注重对理解文章的主旨及作者的观点和态度的考查;阅读技巧部分也是从以上几个方面入手,并把重点放在了概括中心思想、预见、推理和推论方面,有助于培养学生理解文章深层意义的能力。

配有解析,指导性强　每单元后有难点(包括词汇、搭配、语法结构)注释以及练习题答案解析,有助于读者充分理解文章内容,并在提高阅读理解能力的同时扩大词汇量、巩固语法知识、全面提高英语水平;这种编排也便于读者自学、自测。

另外,每单元的5篇阅读文章(包括1篇简答)和练习题编排在一起,其后是文章注释和练习题答案解析。这种编排有助于读者计时阅读以及教师课堂测验使用(1篇快速阅读理解需15分钟、1篇篇章词汇理解和2篇篇章阅读理解需25分钟、1篇篇章问答需15分钟,每单元阅读时间共需55分钟)。

本书编写工作由刘宇慧、张俊梅主持,参加编写工作的还有张俊英、孔延红、张玉娟、梁梅红、郭玮、周江源、邢芳、殷红梅。全书由刘宇慧、张俊梅统编、修改、补充、定稿,张俊英、孔延红、张玉娟协助校对与修改工作,在编写过程中,我们参阅了大量的文献、杂志、教材等,得到了许多专家和同仁的支持与帮助,使我们受益匪浅。在此表示衷心感谢。

由于编者水平有限,书中谬误疏漏之处在所难免,望广大读者及同行专家批评指正。

目录

第一部分　阅读与简答技巧简介

要提高阅读能力,首先要学好基本的语言知识,不断扩大词汇量,熟练掌握特殊语言现象、惯用法等;同时,大量的阅读实践也是必不可少的,只有在大量的阅读实践中,才能培养语感,不断扩大知识面。此外,正确的阅读方法与技巧也不失为提高阅读能力的有效辅助手段。

一、掌握正确阅读方法,摒弃不良阅读习惯,提高阅读速度

要达到一定的阅读速度,平时训练就应该模拟考试,在规定时间内完成一定的阅读量,反复练习阅读技巧,养成熟练的解题习惯。因此,平时做题时就应采取正确的阅读方法,摒弃不良阅读习惯。

1. 正确阅读方法

1) 成组视读

成组视读是以"意群"(有意义的语法结构)为单位,一组单词一组单词地阅读,这样避免了逐词阅读,大大提高了阅读速度。

2) 略读

略读是指跳过细节,跳过不重要的描述与例子,进行快速阅读,以求抓住文章梗概。这种方法的主要目的是通过略读,了解所读材料的体裁、结构和逻辑关系,了解文章的大意和主旨。为了更好地抓住全文的中心思想,略读时要留心文章中某些反复出现的词语,这些往往与文章的主题有关。还应特别注意文章的开始段和结束段以及每一段的段首句和结尾句,这些往往是对文章内容最好的概括。

3) 查读

查读是用眼睛快速扫视,以最快的速度找到你所要的信息。使用这种方法时,首先弄清你要寻找什么信息,然后,估测一下它大概会以什么形式在什么地方出现,达到目的后,就不要再接着往下读,以节约时间。例如:你想了解事件发生的时间、地点,你就得留心查阅日期、地点;你如果想了解谁做了什么事,就要留心查阅人名。

4) 细读

细读即阅读时,先浏览全文,然后再根据需要,在特定范围内逐句阅读,特别对关键词句要仔细推敲,以便对其有较深刻、较准确的理解和把握。不仅要理解其字面意思,而且要通过判断和推理,弄清文章中"字里行间"所隐含的意思。在细读中,对生词,可根据上下文或背景知识等来推测其意义;对难以看懂的长句,可借助语法手段对其加以分析,以达到透彻的理解。

5) 计时阅读

计时阅读,是指平时进行一定时间的快速阅读,阅读时记住起止时间,再计算一下本次的阅读速度(每分钟所读词数),这样,就有明确的时间观念,每次读完之后对自己的阅读速度有所了解,经过一段时间刻苦

训练，一定会达到满意的阅读速度。

2. 不良阅读习惯

1）频繁复读

有些读者担心忘掉已读的内容，读完了一句要读下一句时，又回过头重读一遍上一句，这样循环前进，频繁复读，大大降低了阅读速度。克服这种毛病的方法是：充分相信自己能记住已读过的内容，一直往下读完全文。

2）出声阅读

另一种常见的不良阅读习惯，是在阅读时读出声来，有时还边读边摇头晃脑。有时尽管声音很小，近乎喃喃自语，也是不可取的。出声阅读使阅读速度受到很大限制。为了克服这种不良阅读习惯，一种方法是在嘴唇之间叼一支铅笔，嘴唇动作时，铅笔就会掉下来，保持铅笔不掉，就能克服这一习惯；另一方法是用手指触摸颈部声带部位，如果觉察不到声带的振动，就是克服了出声阅读的习惯。

3）心读

这是一种广泛的、较难克服的不良阅读习惯。因为心读时，觉察不到嘴唇、舌头或声带的活动，只存在一种说话的内在形式，就像电影或电视中的字幕在脑海中浮现出来一样。这种毛病与初学英语时必须经过逐字、逐句大声朗读方能把课文和单词记住有关。要克服这一毛病，必须大大提高阅读速度，因为速度很快时，你就无暇顾及心读了。

4）读速太慢

有些人习惯于一个词一个词地阅读，而不能将词连成词组按意群连贯地进行阅读。有人认为读得越慢，记得越牢，理解也越好。其实不然，读得太慢，不易引起大脑皮层高度兴奋，精力不易高度集中。如果拘泥于个别词的理解与记忆，往往会"见木不见林"，忽视对文章的大意及个别重要细节的理解。反之，保持一定的阅读速度则会加强对全篇大意和细节的理解与记忆。

5）边读边译

在阅读过程中进行翻译（心译），是直接影响阅读速度的重要原因之一。有的读者一面阅读英文句子，脑海里马上浮现出相应的中文句子。这种习惯可能与平时一边阅读英语，一边查阅中文译文的习惯有关。用这种方式进行阅读无疑要耗费过多的时间与精力，必然大大降低阅读速度。要提高阅读速度，我们就得克服在快速阅读时进行心译的不良习惯，学会用英文进行思维，将原文直接吸收和消化。

二、运用不同的阅读方法达到不同的阅读目的

阅读的最终目的是为了获取信息，有效地利用不同的阅读方法获取不同的信息，对于达到不同的阅读目的，可起到事半功倍的效果。

1. 略读概括主题思想

概括主题思想可用"略读"或"浏览总结"法，即：跳过细节，把阅读重点放在与中心思想有关的关键词、句子上。阅读时应注意以下三点：

（1）首先要学会识别文章中那些最根本、最有概括性的信息。这种信息应能归纳和概括文中其他信息所具有的共性。

（2）主题思想应能恰如其分地概括文中所阐述的内容。面不能太窄，即：不足以概括全部内容；但是面也不能太宽，即：包含了文中没有阐述的内容。

（3）一段文章的中心思想常常由主题句表达。主题句常常位于段首或段尾处，间或出现在段落中间。同样，一篇文章的中心思想也常常在开始段或结尾段点出。因此在阅读中，要特别注意文章的开头及结尾。

在阅读理解测试中，常见的用于考查对主题思想的掌握的题型有：

1) 要求概括主题思想

这类问题要求考生理解文章的主题思想。一般来说，这类文章中都有概括主题思想的主题句或主题段以及说明主题句或主题段的细节。例如：

2000 年 1 月试题第二篇文章：

Believe it or not, optical *illusion*（错觉）can cut highway crashes.

Japan is a case in point. It has reduced automobile crashes on some roads by nearly 75 percent using a simple optical illusion. Bent stripes, called *chevrons*（人字形）, painted on the roads make drivers think that they are driving faster than they really are, and thus drivers slow down.

Now the American Automobile Association Foundation for Traffic Safety in Washington D. C. is planning to repeat Japan's success. Starting next year, the foundation will paint chevrons and other patterns of stripes on selected roads around the country to test how well the patterns reduce highway crashes.

Excessive speed plays a major role in as much as one fifth of all fatal traffic accidents, according to the foundation. To help reduce those accidents, the foundation will conduct its tests in areas where speed-related hazards are the greatest—curves, exit slopes, traffic circles, and bridges.

Some studies suggest that straight, horizontal bars painted across roads can initially cut the average speed of drivers in half. However, traffic often returns to full speed within months as drivers become used to seeing the painted bars.

Chevrons, scientists say, not only give drivers the impression that they are driving faster than they really are but also make a lane appear to be narrower. The result is a longer lasting reduction in highway speed and the number of traffic accidents.

▲ The passage mainly discusses _____.

   A) a new way of highway speed control

   B) a new pattern for painting highways

   C) a new approach to training drivers

   D) a new type of optical illusion

解析 该文第一段就道出了主题，即"视觉错觉可以减少高速公路上的车祸"。在接下来的几段中，作者具体讨论了如何在高速公路上用不同的视觉错觉图形来减少车祸的发生，其中人字形图形效果最好。因此正确答案为 A。

2) 要求归纳文章的主题或中心思想

与第一类问题不同的是，这一类文章没有明显的主题句，因此，理解文章的主题或中心思想有赖于对文章中的信息进行高度的综合和概括。例如：

2001 年 1 月试题第四篇文章：

In 1993, New York State ordered stores to charge a deposit on *beverage*（饮料）containers. Within a year, consumers had returned millions of aluminum cans and glass and plastic bottles. Plenty of companies were eager to accept the aluminum and glass as raw materials for new products, but because few could figure out what to do with the plastic, much of it wound be buried in *land fills* （垃圾填埋场）. The problem was not limited to New York. Unfortunately, there were too few uses for second-hand plastic.

Today, one out of five plastic soda bottles is *recycled* （回收利用） in the United States. The reason for the change is that now there are dozens of companies across the country buying discarded plastic soda bottles and turning them into fence posts, paint brushes, etc.

As the New York experience shows, recycling involves more than simply separating valuable materials from the rest of the rubbish. A discard remains a discard until somebody figures out how to give it a second life—and until economic arrangements exist to give that second life value. Without adequate markets to absorb materials collected for recycling, throwaways actually depress prices for used materials.

Shrinking landfill space, and rising costs for burying rubbish are forcing local governments to look more closely at recycling. In many areas, the East Coast especially, recycling is already the least expensive waste-management option. For every ton of waste recycled, a city avoids paying for its disposal, which, in parts of New York, amounts to savings of more than $100 per ton. Recycling also stimulates the local economy by creating jobs and trims the pollution control and energy costs of industries that make recycled products by giving them a more refined raw material.

▲ It can be concluded from the passage that _____.

   A) rubbish is a potential remedy for the shortage of raw materials

   B) local governments in the U. S. can expect big profits from recycling

   C) recycling is to be recommended both economically and environmentally

   D) landfills will still be widely used for waste disposal

解析 根据第一段，虽然饮料罐得到回收利用，但存在的问题是塑料瓶仍然被埋入垃圾填埋场；根据第二、三段，如今部分的塑料瓶得以回收利用，是因为存在着消化废旧物品的市场，一些公司愿意回购废旧塑料瓶并将它们回收利用；如果废旧物品得不到回收利用，就会压制废旧物品的价格；根据第四段，随着垃圾填埋场面积的逐步缩小以及垃圾填埋费用的增加，地方政府越来越重视回收利用，而且回收利用可以节约费用、振兴经济。从以上各段可以归纳出以下的结论：废物的回收利用有利于经济发展和环境保护。因此正确答案为 C。

3) 要求给出文章标题

这一类问题要求用文章的标题形式来表达文章的中心思想。和上一类问题不同的是，这一类问题是将命题进行浓缩，也就是说问题的选项包含了对主题进行某种判断，纳入了某种观点和立场。例如：

2000 年 6 月试题第三篇文章：

Americans are proud of their variety and individuality, yet they love and respect few things more than a uniform, whether it is the uniform of an elevator operator or the uniform of a five-star general. Why are uniforms so popular in the United States?

Among the arguments for uniforms, one of the first is that in the eyes of most people they look more professional than *civilian* （百姓的） clothes. People have become conditioned to expect superior quality from a man who wears a uniform. The television repairman who wears a uniform tends to inspire more trust than one who appears in civilian clothes. Faith in the skill of a garage mechanic is increased by a uniform. What easier way is there for a nurse, a policeman, a barber, or a waiter to lose professional identity than to step out of uniform?

Uniforms also have many practical benefits. They save on other clothes. They save on laundry bills. They are *tax-deductible*（可减税的）. They are often more comfortable and more durable than civilian clothes.

Primary among the arguments against uniforms is their lack of variety and the consequent loss of individuality experienced by people who must wear them. Though there are many types of uniforms, the wearer of any particular type is generally stuck with it, without change, until retirement. When people look alike, they tend to think, speak, and act similarly, on the job at least.

Uniforms also give rise to some practical problems. Though they are long-lasting, often their initial expense is greater than the cost of civilian clothes. Some uniforms are also expensive to maintain, requiring professional dry cleaning rather than the home laundering possible with many types of civilian clothes.

▲ The best title for this passage would be _____.

　A) Uniforms and Society

　B) The Importance of Wearing a Uniform

　C) Practical Benefits of Wearing a Uniform

　D) Advantages and Disadvantages of Uniform

解析 该题的主题是工作服,但作者的笔墨涉及了工作服的外延。解题的关键在于理解各段落的主题句。第二、三段的主题句归纳了工作服的优点,但第四、五段的主题句则归纳了工作服的缺点。如果只根据第二、三段的内容来做出判断,就不免会以偏概全,落入选项 B 所设下的陷阱。因此正确答案为 D。

4) 要求理解作者的目的和意图

这一类问题要求理解作者的目的和意图。例如:

2001 年 6 月试题第二篇文章:

Sport is not only physically challenging, but it can also be mentally challenging. Criticism from coaches, parents, and other teammates, as well as pressure to win can create an excessive amount of anxiety or stress for young *athletes*（运动员）. Stress can be physical, emotional, or psychological and research has indicated that it can lead to burnout. Burnout has been described as dropping or quitting of an activity that was at one time enjoyable.

The early years of development are critical years for learning about oneself. The sport setting is one where valuable experiences can take place. Young athletes can, for example, learn how to cooperate with others, make friends, and gain other social skills that will be used throughout their lives. Coaches and parents should be aware, at all times, their feedback to youngsters can greatly affect their children. Youngsters may take their parents' and coaches' criticisms to heart and find a *flaw*（缺陷）in themselves.

Coaches and parents should also be cautious that youth sport participation does not become work for children. The outcome of the game should not be more important than the process of learning the sport and other life lessons. In today's youth sport setting, young athletes may be worrying more about who will win instead of enjoying themselves and the sport. Following a game many parents and coaches focus on the outcome and find fault with youngsters' performances. Positive reinforcement should be provided regardless of the outcome. Research indicates that positive reinforcement motivates and has a greater effect on learning than criticism. Again, criticism can create high levels of stress, which can lead to burnout.

▲ The author's purpose in writing the passage is _____.

A) to teach young athletes how to avoid burnout

B) to persuade young children not to worry about criticism

C) to stress the importance of positive reinforcement to children

D) to discuss the skill of combining criticism with encouragement

解析 在第一段中作者首先提出一个问题,即年轻运动员由于受到教练、家长和队友的批评而感到精神压抑,从而有可能导致精神完全崩溃。接着在第二、三段,作者讨论了解决这一问题的方法,即运动员从小就应该有一个良好的环境,这其中包括教练和家长应该给运动员更多的正面鼓励。在最后一段,作者用几个 should 来强调正面鼓励的重要性。因此正确答案为 C。

2. 细读全文或部分内容进行判断和推理

对篇章的理解涉及语义学和语用学的范畴。语义学研究的是语言结构,即语句本身的意义;语用学研究的是信息结构,是对语言运用进行整体研究,反映话语和环境的关系,也可以说语用学研究的对象是超出语句本身意义范围的意义。根据以上原则,对一篇文章的理解应该是分层次的,即表层意义、深层意义以及外延意义。表层意义即字面意义,是可以直接从阅读文章中得到的信息。然而,语言所表达的内容常常超过其字面意义。在许多文章中,作者对所论述的问题的观点、态度、语气、情绪以及问题的结论不是直接表述出来,而是通过大量的有说服力的论证、事实或细节反映出来。要获取这种信息,需要读者读懂字里行间的意思(to read between the lines)。这是对文章深层意义的理解。可以说,阅读是读者与作者之间进行的书面交际,一篇好文章会对读者产生影响,引起读者的反应。这种影响和反应也是双向的,读者对文章的深层意义理解得越透彻,文章对读者产生的影响和反应越大。而读者对文章及作者的背景或与此相关的内容产生兴趣,有了继续阅读的动力,从而扩大了这方面的知识面,这应该说是对文章外延意义的理解。

对文章深层意义和外延意义的理解均需要掌握逻辑判断和推理的方法。判断是对文章中所阐述的事实或细节按照逻辑发展的规律进行分析和概括,并以此为依据得出结论;推理是以已知的事实为依据,来获取未知的信息。因此,利用判断和推理的方法,根据事物发展的自然规律以及语言本身的内在联系,可以从一定的文字符号中获取尽可能多的信息。

在阅读中训练判断和推理能力时,应注意以下几点:

(1) 在阅读中,要善于利用文章中明确表示的内容,进行正确的推理,以此为基础挖掘作者的隐含意思。

(2) 有时作者先介绍了某一种观点,却接着在后面提出了相反的观点。因此,要正确判断作者的态度或观点,必须将上下文联系起来看。要注意文章中所陈述的内容并非都代表了作者的观点。

(3) 有时作者通过使用词汇的手段,暗示了自己对文中某一具体问题所持的态度和观点。这时要特别注意文中所用词汇的特点,弄清作者的态度是赞成还是反对,是肯定还是否定。

(4) 如果要理解某句或某段的含蓄意义,必须在文中找到所涉及的关键词语,仔细阅读,吃透意思,并以此为依据,进行判断和推理。如果需要进行推理判断的内容涉及全文,则必须在理解全文中心思想、掌握全文逻辑发展过程的基础上,进行正确的推理判断。

(5) 做这类阅读理解题时,要认真审题,注意分析、对比,排除干扰项。特别要注意原文中的意思在题目中的表达形式,准确理解题目的意思和要求。

在阅读理解测试中,判断和推理题型的常见形式有:

1) 言外之意题

这类问题要求通过文章的表层意义,借助常识或上下文逻辑关系来推断无法直接得到的、具有深层含义的某种结论。该类问题的句式通常是:

It can be inferred from the passage that _____.

It is implied in the passage that _____.

The author suggests that _____.

2000 年 1 月试题第三篇文章中的一段：

At one time, trains were the only practical way to cross the vast areas of the west. Trains were fast, very luxurious, and quite convenient compared to other forms of transportation existing at the time. However, times change and the automobile became America's standard of convenience. Also, air travel had easily established itself as the fastest method of traveling great distances.

▲ It can be inferred from the passage that the drop in Amtrak ridership was due to the fact that _____.

A) trains were not suitable for short distance passenger transportation

B) trains were not the fastest and most convenient form of transportation

C) trains were not as fast and convenient as they used to be

D) trains could not compete with planes in terms of luxury and convenience

解析 该题要求推断美国铁路公司客源下降的原因。虽然作者没有对此加以直接陈述，但却提到汽车的便利和飞机的速度。因此正确答案为 B。

有时，有些推断题并不用上面的句式，但出题者仍然要求考生用推断的方法来解题。例如：

2001 年 6 月试题第一篇文章第三段中：

Meanwhile, if you want to buy a cheap house with an uncertain future, apply to a house agent in one of the threatened areas on the south coast of England. You can get a house for a knockdown price but it may turn out to be a knockdown home.

▲ According to the author, when buying a house along the south coast of England, people should _____.

A) take the quality of the house into consideration

B) guard against being cheated by the house agent

C) examine the house carefully before making a decision

D) be aware of the potential danger involved

解析 作者没有直接说应该买什么样的房子，但通过最后一句（你可以用十分便宜的价格买一座房子，但那也许是一座危房），作者暗示了买房时应该注意的问题。因此正确答案为 D。

2) 理解作者态度题

在日常生活中，人们可以通过手势、语调、脸部表情等来表露自己的态度，同样，解决该类问题要求注意把握作者的措词、阐述问题的角度和倾向以及文章中能够表露作者态度和情感的修饰性词语。要把握作者对某一问题所持的态度，理解作者对某一问题是主观还是客观，是支持、反对还是中立，是高兴还是愤怒，是幽默还是讽刺等。如果所涉及的是作者对某个问题的态度，题干中的关键词用 attitude；如果涉及的是通篇的基调，关键词用 tone。例如：

2002 年 1 月试题第一篇文章第二、三段：

The motorcar will undoubtedly change significantly over the next 30 years. It should become smaller, safer, and more economical, and should not be powered by the gasoline engine. The car of the future should be far more pollution-free than present types.

Regardless of its power source, the auto in the future will still be the main problem in urban traffic *congestion*（拥挤）. One proposed solution to this problem is the automated highway system.

大学英语 4 级阅读与简答（新题型）

▲ What is the author's attitude toward the future of autos?

A) Enthusiastic.　　　　　　　　　　B) Pessimistic.

C) Optimistic.　　　　　　　　　　　D) Cautious.

　　解析　在上面第一段中,作者认为未来的汽车会发生很大的变化,例如汽车的驱动不再依靠汽油。值得注意的是,作者用 undoubtedly、significantly、should 等词来表达自己对未来汽车变化所持的肯定态度。在第二段,作者认为未来汽车仍然要克服交通拥挤的问题,并提出了解决这一问题的方法。选项 A 夸大了作者对未来汽车的信心,因为在作者看来,未来汽车不是十全十美的,还有问题需要解决。因此正确答案为 C。

　　2000 年 1 月试题第一篇文章：

Unless we spend money to spot and prevent *asteroids*（小行星）now, one might crash into Earth and destroy life as we know it, say some scientists.

Asteroids are bigger versions of the *meteoroids*（流星）that race across the night sky. Most orbit the sun far from Earth and don't threaten us. But there are also thousands of asteroids whose orbits put them on a collision course with Earth.

Buy $50 million worth of new telescopes right now. Then spend $10 million a year for the next 25 years to locate most of the space rocks. By the time we spot a fatal one, scientists say, we'll have a way to change its course.

Some scientists favor pushing asteroids off course with nuclear weapons. But the cost wouldn't be cheap.

Is it worth it? Two things experts consider when judging any risk are: 1) How likely the event is; and 2) How bad the consequences are if the event occurs. Experts think an asteroid big enough to destroy lots of life might strike Earth once every 500,000 years. Sounds pretty rare— but if one did fall, it would be the end of the world. "If we don't take care of these big asteroids, they'll take care of us," says one scientist. "It's that simple."

The cure, though, might be worse than the disease. Do we really want fleets of nuclear weapons sitting around on Earth? "The world has less to fear from *doomsday*（毁灭性的）rocks than from a great nuclear fleet set against them," said a New York Time article.

▲ Which of the following best describes the author's tone in this passage?

A) Optimistic.　　　　　　　　　　B) Critical.

C) Objective.　　　　　　　　　　　D) Arbitrary.

　　解析　在这篇文章中,作者没有留下自己的一丝痕迹,也就是说,作者对陨石有可能撞击地球没有表露自己的看法。整篇文章作者大量引述他人的话,使用了 say some scientists, scientists say, Some scientists favor, Experts think, says one scientist, said a New York Time article 等客观报道的结构。因此正确答案为 C。

　　3）是非判断题

　　是非判断题也是常见的测试题型之一。这类题主要是问"什么是真实(...true?)的",或"什么是不真实(...not true / false?)的",其特点是：对文章中具体的事实和依据进行提问,确定或证实某一种说法是否真实。其内容可能涉及整篇文章,也可能只涉及文章的一部分。所以,在做这类题时,首先应弄清楚题目的要求和涉及面。进行正确的判断是解答这类的出发点,应找出问句中的关键词语,从而找到答案所在的段和句。在此基础上,再力求明确整体和局部、局部和局部间的关系和概念,根据有关方面的信息做出正确的选择。

　　一般说来,做这类题的技巧是推断和排除手法相结合,尤其是回答"哪种说法是不真实的"这种问题时,排除掉真实的信息即得出正确的答案。例如：

2002 年 6 月第三篇文章：

It is hard to track the blue whale, the ocean's largest creature, which has almost been killed off by commercial whaling and is now listed as an endangered species. Attaching radio devices to it is difficult, and visual sightings are too unreliable to give real insight into its behavior.

So biologists were delighted early this year when, with the help of the Navy, they were able to track a particular blue whale for 43 days, monitoring its sounds. This was possible because of the Navy's formerly top-secret system of underwater listening devices spanning the oceans.

Tracking whales is but one example of an exciting new world just opening to civilian scientists after the cold war as the Navy starts to share and partly uncover its global network of underwater listening system built over the decades to track the ships of potential enemies.

Earth scientists announced at a news conference recently that they had used the system for closely monitoring a deep-sea volcanic *eruption* (爆发) for the first time and that they plan similar studies.

Other scientists have proposed to use the network for tracking ocean currents and measuring changes in ocean and global temperatures.

The speed of sound in water is roughly one mile a second—slower than through land but faster than through air. What is most important, different layers of ocean water can act as channels for sounds, focusing them in the same way a *stethoscope* (听诊器) does when it carries faint noises from a patient's chest to a doctor's ear. This focusing is the main reason that even relatively weak sounds in the ocean, especially low-frequency ones, can often travel thousands of miles.

▲ Which of the following is true about the U. S. Navy underwater listening network?

A) It is now partly accessible to civilian scientists.

B) It has been replaced by a more advanced system.

C) It became useless to the military after the cold war.

D) It is indispensable in protecting endangered species.

解析　本题属是非判断题。根据第三段(在冷战后,海军开始把几十年来建立的水下监听系统部分作为民用,而这一系统本来是用于追踪潜伏的敌舰船的,用这个系统来追踪蓝鲸不过是科学家把军事系统转为民用的新领域的一个例子而已。)题干加选项 A 与本句意思吻合。通读全文,其他几个选项信息都不对。因此正确答案为 A。

3. 查读有关内容,猜测词义或寻找特定细节

词义及细节这类信息,常常可从文章中直接找到,属于表层意义上的理解,比较容易。但在猜测词义时,应注意有些词在特定的语言环境中产生的不同于本义的特定含义。要猜出这类词的词义,也需要对文章的内容作深层理解。

做阅读理解细节题时,需注意的是,问题的表述常常不是采用文章中的原话,而是用同义词语进行提问。因此做题时,首先要认真审题,读懂问题。然后,根据所涉及的问题,快速扫视到文章中相应的部分,找到与问题相关的关键词或短语,在确信理解了原文的基础上,来确定答案。

词义和细节题主要有以下几类：

1) 词义题

当遇到生词时,理解会发生障碍,这就好像完整的意思形成了一个缺口。这时要根据上下文的信息以

及常识来确定该词的特定含义,使其能够弥补缺口,使意思完整,然后选择四个选项中和该特定含义最接近的一个。例如:

2000 年 6 月试题第四篇文章第二段:

Social support cushions stress in a number of ways. First, friends, relatives, and co-workers may let us know that they value us. Our self-respect is strengthened when we feel accepted by others despite our faults and difficulties. Second, other people often provide us with informational support. They help us to define and understand our problems and find solutions to them. Third, we typically find social companionship supportive. Engaging in leisure-time activities with others helps us to meet our social needs while at the same time *distracting*(转移……注意力) us from our worries and troubles. Finally, other people may give us instrumental support—financial aid, material resources, and needed services—that reduces stress by helping us resolve and cope with our problems.

▲ Which of the following is closest in meaning to the word "cushions"?

A) Adds up to.   B) Does away with.

C) Lessens the effect of.   D) Lays the foundation for.

解析 该段第一句是主题句,其余部分是说明该主题句的细节,细节从四个方面说明了他人的关心和帮助可以减轻精神压力。因此正确答案为 C。

2) 复述题

这一类题是把文章中的内容通过不同的词语或结构重新表达出来。例如:

2002 年 1 月试题第四篇文章中有这样一句话:

Data show that Americans are struggling with problems unheard of in the 1950s, such as classroom violence and a high rate of births to unmarried mothers.

▲ In the 1950s, classroom violence _____.

A) was something unheard of   B) was by no means a rare occurrence

C) attracted a lot of public attention   D) began to appear in analysts' data

解析 该句意思是说,有数据表明,美国人正面临着在 20 世纪 50 年代从未听说过的问题,如教室暴力,未婚妈妈中的高分娩率等。题干加选项 A 通过语言的重新组织复述了文章中的这句话。

有时复述题依赖对某个词、词组或句法的理解。例如:

2002 年 1 月试题第二篇文章的部分内容是:

People who take part in hunting think of it as a sport; they wear a special uniform of red coats and white trousers, and follow strict codes of behavior. But owning a horse and hunting regularly is expensive, so most hunters are wealthy.

▲ What is special about fox hunting in Britain?

A) It involves the use of a deadly poison.

B) It is a costly event which rarely occurs.

C) The hunters have set rules to follow.

D) The hunters have to go through strict training.

解析 该题的关键在于理解短语 codes of behavior(行为准则),并把它和选项 C 中的 set rules 相对应。

3) 因果题

该类题出现频率很高,几乎每篇文章都有两三道这样的题。解决这类题关键在于理解句子内部以及上下文之间存在的因果关系。例如：

2001 年 1 月试题第三篇文章有这样一句话：

Back in the days when energy was cheap, home builders didn't worry much about unsealed cracks.

▲ Why were cracks in old houses not a big concern?

A) Because indoor cleanness was not emphasized.

B) Because energy used to be inexpensive.

C) Because environmental protection was given top priority.

D) Because they were technically unavoidable.

解析 该句虽然没有显性的因果连接词，但还是能够看出该句内部的因果关系，即廉价的能源使房屋建造者对房屋的缝隙不很在乎。因此正确答案为 B。

1999 年 6 月试题第四篇文章中的一段：

In the ancient world, as is today, most boys played with some kinds of toys and most girls with another. In societies where social roles are rigidly determined, boys pattern their play after the activities of their fathers and girls after the tasks of their mothers. This is true because boys and girls are being prepared, even in play, to step into the roles and responsibilities of the adult world.

▲ The reason why the toys most boys play with are different from those that girls play with is that _____.

A) their social roles are rigidly determined

B) most boys would like to follow their fathers' professions

C) boys like to play with their fathers while girls with their mothers

D) they like challenging activities

解析 该题要求理解该段上下文之间的因果关系。第二、三句解释了第一句中的现象，即男孩和女孩有不同的玩具是因为他们生活在社会责任分工十分严谨的社会里，他们的玩耍是为他们将来承担大人的职责和义务在做准备。因此正确答案为 A。

4) 例证题

言而有据是写作应该遵守的原则，而且例证法是英语文章展开论述的主要模式之一。因此，理解例证的方法、内容和目的是阅读的一个重要内容。例如：

2001 年 6 月试题第四篇文章第二段：

The importance of the product life cycle to marketers is this: Different stages in the product life cycle call for different strategies. The goal is to extend product life so that sales and profits do not decline. One strategy is called market modification. It means that marketing managers look for new users and market sections. Did you know, for example, that the backpacks that so many students carry today were originally designed for the military?

▲ The author mentions the example of "backpacks" to show the importance of _____.

A) increasing usage among students

B) exploring new market sections

C) pleasing the young as well as the old

D) serving both military and civil needs

解析 该题要求理解例证的目的。该段主要谈的是关于延长产品寿命的一种方法——市场转换法，即将某一市场的产品投放到另一市场,从而延长产品的寿命。背包原来是军用品,但现在成为学生广泛使用的产品。作者用背包这个例子来说明市场转换的重要性。因此正确答案为 B。

三、快速阅读理解正误或未提及判断题答题技巧

1. 正误或未提及判断题的特点

大学英语 4 级考试新增加的快速阅读理解采用了正误或未提及判断题,该题型属于主观判断题,旨在测试考生对作者观点、态度等的理解以及对这些观点的灵活运用程度。其形式是给出一些完整的陈述,要求考生根据文章内容判断这些陈述是正确(True/Yes)、错误(False/No)还是未提及(Not Given)。如果一个陈述和文章中的相关陈述意思一致,则是正确的陈述。如果一个陈述和文章中的陈述意思不一致或相反,该陈述则是错误的陈述。如果某一陈述在文章中没有对应的阐述,则该陈述为未提及的陈述。

有时很难判断某一陈述是错误的陈述还是未提及的陈述,这时需分清什么是错误的陈述:

1)错误的陈述的意思与原文恰恰相反。例如原文的陈述是 Four times as many children are driven to school in Britain as in Germany because of road dangers. 意思是"乘车上学的英国孩子是德国孩子的四倍"。试题的陈述是 More German children go to school by car than British Children. 意思是"德国乘车上学的孩子比英国多"。两句话的意思正好相反,所以试题的陈述是错误的陈述。

2)错误的陈述表达的情形与原文中列举的情形在数量上不一致,即原文中列举了几种情形,但试题中的陈述只提到一种情形,这样就间接否定了原文中其他几种正确的情形。例如原文的陈述是 You can join the association for as little as one month and for up to one year at a time. 意思是"加入协会的时间最短可以是一个月,最长可以是十二个月"。如果试题的陈述是 Membership must be renewed monthly. 那么这个陈述只肯定了一个月的情况,同时否定了其他十一个月的情况,所以这样的陈述是错误的陈述。

3)错误的陈述表达的程度、范围、频率或可能性大于原文中的程度、范围、频率或可能性。例如原文的陈述是 Of the representatives in the House of Commons, many are from south states. 意思是"众议院的代表中很多来自南部各州"。如果试题的陈述是 All the representatives in the House of Commons are elected from south states. 意思是"所有众议院的代表都来自南部各州"。试题陈述的范围超出了原文陈述的范围,那么试题的陈述就是错误的陈述。

4)原文是理论陈述,试题则是客观事实,这样的陈述也是错误的陈述。例如原文 Another theory is that worldwide temperature increases are upsetting the breeding cycles of frogs. 陈述的是一种理论,如果试题 It is a fact that frog's breeding cycles are upset by worldwide increases in temperature. 陈述的是一个客观事实,那么试题的陈述就是错误的陈述。

还需分清什么样的陈述是未提及的陈述:

1)试题的陈述在原文中根本找不到。

2)试题的陈述是具体的概念,原文的陈述是较大较模糊的范畴。例如原文的陈述是 The tourists mainly come from Europe. 试题的陈述是 The tourist come mainly from Britain. 意思是"游客主要来自英国"。原文的意思是游客主要来自欧洲,但没有具体说哪一个国家,因此试题的陈述应该是原文中未提到。

3)试题的陈述是确定的,原文的陈述是不确定的。例如原文的陈述是 The conservative Rally for the Republic appealed to the ministers responsible for early action to double the size of A4 highway that links the capital and the park. 意思是"代表共和党的保守派要求负责前期工程的大臣们将连接首都和公园的 A4 号公路加宽一倍"。大臣们是否真的要扩建 A4 号公路文中并未提及。而试题的陈述是 The A4 highway leading to the park will be widened. 意思是"A4 号公路将被扩建",所以试题的陈述文中并未提到。

4)试题的陈述是对原文事实的评论。例如原文的陈述是 In a five-year period between 1985 and 1989 the community's female workforce grew by almost six million. As a result, 51% of all women aged 14 to 64 are now economically active in the labor market compared with 78% of men. 试题的陈述 The rise in the female workforce in the European community is a positive trend. 是对原文陈述的评论,原文中并未提及,所以试题的陈述是未提及的陈述。

2.正误或未提及判断题的答题步骤

做 Y/N/NG 题之前不必先看试题,以避免试题与文章中相矛盾的陈述带来的负面影响。正确的做法是:

1)浏览文章,划出段落中的关键词。

2)阅读试题的陈述,透彻理解并划出其中的关键词。

3)根据关键词的提示迅速找到原文中和试题陈述对应的句子。

4)仔细比较两个句子的意思并做出判断。

四、篇章词汇理解填充题答题技巧

1.填充题(Gap Filling)的特点

大学英语4级考试新增加的篇章词汇理解采用了词汇填充题的形式,其考察方式是阅读文章之后利用所给单词或短语进行填空。这种题型既测试考生对文章内容的理解能力又测试考生正确运用语法知识的能力。填空时涉及的语法知识包括词类、词性、词义、名词单复数、形容词和副词比较级和最高级、介词短语、动词短语、动词时态、语态、虚拟语气、非谓语动词、主谓一致、倒装句、强调句以及引导各种从句的关系代词、关系副词和连词等等。因此填充题是一种测试考生综合能力的题型。

2.填充题的答题步骤

1)快速阅读文章,了解文章大意。

2)阅读、分析并理解横线所在句子的意思及其和上下文的关系。

3)查看横线前后的单词或短语,确定所填词汇在句子中的语法成分、形式、词义和词性。

4)确定所给单词的词性、词义和短语的意思。

5)根据以上分析确定所填词汇的范围。

6)从所给单词中选出符合横线所在句子意思的单词。

7)运用语法知识确定所填单词的形式。

8)阅读全文,根据文章意思和句子含义以及上下文检查确定所填单词的准确性。

五、简答技巧

1.简答题的特点

除了要求考生具有较强的阅读能力,即"阅读理解"部分所考核的全部能力以外,简答题"主要考查考生对英语书面材料的确切理解能力"。我们都知道,"阅读理解"部分的出题形式是在每篇文章的后面出若干问题,每个问题有 4 个供考生选择的项目 A、B、C 和 D。但简答题没有选择项,答案也不是现成的,考生必须在确切理解原文的基础上,用恰当的书面语自己写出答案,其难度显然高于"阅读理解"部分。

简答题除了考查考生的阅读理解能力外,还考查考生对词汇的掌握,对语法规则的应用以及是否具有在吃透原文、正确判断推理的基础上,用最简洁的书面语言概述作者的思想、观点、态度,归纳总结文章中心思想的能力。

简答题虽然在题材、篇幅和难易程度上和"阅读理解"部分基本相同,但由于其出题形式不一样,因而对考生提出了更高的要求。因此,考生在平时的学习过程中首先应扎扎实实地打好语言基础,如,全面熟练地掌握语法、词汇知识,特别是常用词汇的拼写、词义的辨析等。其次,在英语学习中,不但要重视提高自己的语言能力,重视不同层次上的阅读技能的训练,还要不断提高自己语言的实际运用能力,尤其是书面表达的能力,这是做好简答题的基础。

2．应试技巧

简答题是以"阅读理解"为基础,或者说是"阅读理解"部分的延伸。因此,凡是在"阅读理解"部分讲的应试技巧,除个别例外,都适应"简答题"部分,在此就不再赘述,只简述一下做简答题时,一般应注意遵循的几个步骤:

(1) 做题前,不要急着看文章,可先用 1 分钟时间,浏览一下文后给出的 5 个问题,了解各题所问的内容,以便在阅读文章时,有的放矢,这样既可节省时间,又能提高答对率。

(2) 用大约 6～7 分钟的时间(阅读速度每分钟 50 个单词,略低于做"阅读理解"部分的速度)仔细阅读原文,阅读时凭借大脑中对各题所问内容的印象或语感,捕捉与问题有关的信息,在原文上对关键词、与问题有关的句子、短语做个记号。但记号不要做得太多,其代表意义自己要清楚明白,以免混淆。

(3) 读一遍原文后即可试着答题。可先回答自己确有把握的题目。自己还拿不准的题目可再仔细阅读原文中与该题目有关的部分,弄清楚后再回答。

(4) 回答问题时,可先草拟出答案,经检查、核实,所选答案有可靠的根据,经得起逻辑推理,而且无语法、拼写、用词不当等错误后,再把答案按要求抄写在试卷上。

(5) 答案以简洁为好,切忌啰嗦,能用单词说清楚的不用短语,能用短语说清楚的不用句子。答案不能超过 10 个单词。

(6) 抄写答案时,尽量保持书写工整、卷面干净整洁,给阅读者一个良好的印象。

六、常见文章类型及其阅读方法

1．自然科学类

1) 专业性很强的文章

此类文章语气上总是很客观,常常论述科学"事实",描述某生物体、实验过程,讨论某种自然现象、普通的认识错误,等等。一般没有复杂的主题和独特的观点;有时也会有不少复杂术语,专业词汇,但问题往往并不难。对这类文章不必通读,可以边读文章边做题,按顺序解答各个具体问题,最后回答概括性问题。需要注意的是近年来能直接在原文中找到答案的问题越来越少了。做这类题时,对细节部分一定要多加注意,认真读题,不要掉进出题者的"陷阱"。

2) 科普类文章

此类文章论述科学发展史,科学方法的发展,以及其他类似的"软性"主题,文章的语气并不一定客观,往往带有主观性,因而其问题可能比上一类文章的问题难度更大。例如作者对某种现代研究领域发表自己的见解或对某种研究方法提出警告。遇到这类文章要先略读,掌握其主旨及大概结构,同时注意各段的中心及其论证方法,这对于我们做出正确判断很有帮助。

2. 非自然科学类

1) 人文科学类文章

此类文章涉及艺术、文学、哲学等领域的内容,例如艺术形式的新技巧、不同流派的差异等等。用自己的语言来概括这类文章甚为重要,因其语言抽象晦涩,长难的句子、抽象的词汇往往使读者望而生畏。阅读这类文章的第一步仍是略读,在略读时标出关键词,排除自己的主观干扰,牢牢抓住作者的观点。

2) 社会科学类文章

此类文章有关历史、经济、法律等方面的内容,其语气常常具有个性,也有一些较为客观。有关人物、事物的文章看起来明白易懂、颇吸引人,但其问题往往比较刁钻,需要仔细推敲、判断。

综上所述,要提高阅读理解能力,必须有扎实的语言基础,有足够的词汇量和语法知识。同时,还应有较宽的知识面。如果在提高阅读理解能力的基础上,再掌握一些阅读方法和技巧,则会在获取信息方面取得事半功倍的效果。

第二部分　阅读与简答实践

Section A　Skimming and Scanning

Directions：*In this part，you will have 15 minutes to go over the passage quickly and answer the questions.*

For questions 1－7，mark

Y（*for YES*）　　　　*if the statement agrees with the information given in the passage*；

N（*for NO*）　　　　*if the statement contradicts the information given in the passage*；

NG（*for NOT GIVEN*）　*if the information is not given in the passage*.

For questions 8－10，complete the sentences with the information given in the passage.

Passage 1

Finding the Lost Freedom

1. The private car is assumed to have widened our horizons and increased our mobility. When we consider our children's mobility, they can be driven to more places（and more distant places）than they could visit without access to a motor vehicle. However, allowing our cities to be dominated by cars has progressively eroded children's independent mobility. Children has lost much of their freedom to explore their own neighborhood or city without adult supervision. In recent surveys, when parents in some cities were asked about their own childhood experiences, the majority remembered having more, or far more opportunities for going out on their own, compared with their own children today. They had more freedom to explore their own environment.

2. Children's independent access to their local streets may be important for their own personal, mental and psychological development. Allowing them to get to know their own neighborhood and community gives them a "sense of place". This depends on "active exploration", which is not provided for when children are passengers in cars.（Such children may see more, but they learn less.）Not only is it important that children be able to get to local play areas by themselves, but walking and cycling journeys to school and to other destinations provide genuine play activities in themselves.

3. There are very significant time and money costs for parents associated with transporting their children to school, sport and to other locations.

4. The reduction in children's freedom may also contribute to a weakening of the sense of

local community. As fewer children and adults use the streets as pedestrians, these streets become less sociable places. There is less opportunity for children and adults to have the spontaneous exchanges that help to engender a feeling of community. This in itself may *exacerbate*（加重,使恶化）fears associated with assault and *molestation*（骚扰）of children, because there are fewer adults available who know their neighbor's children, and who can look out for their safety.

5. The extra traffic involved in transporting children results in increased traffic congestion, pollution and accident risk. As our roads become more dangerous, more parents drive their children to more places, thus contributing to increased levels of danger for the remaining pedestrians. Anyone who has experienced either the reduced volume of traffic in peak hour during school holidays, or the traffic jams near school at the end of a school day, will not need convincing about these points. Thus, there are also important environmental implications of children's loss of freedom.

6. As individuals, parents strive to provide the best upbringing they can for their children. However, in doing so, (e. g. by driving their children to sport, school or recreation) parents may be contributing to a more dangerous environment for children generally. The idea that streets are for cars and backyards and playgrounds are for children is a strongly held belief, and parents have little choice as individuals but to keep their children off the streets if they want to protect their safety.

7. In many parts of Dutch cities, and some traffic-calmed *precincts*（地区）in Germany, residential streets are now places where cars must give way to pedestrians. In these areas, residents are accepting the view that the function of streets is not solely to provide mobility for cars. Streets may also be for social interaction, walking, cycling and playing. One of the most important aspects of these European cities, in terms of giving cities back to children, has been a range of "traffic calming" initiatives, aimed at reducing the volume speed of traffic. These initiatives have had complex interactive effects, leading to a sense that children have been able to "rapture" their local neighborhood, and more importantly, that they have been able to do this in safety. Recent research has demonstrated that children in many Germany cities have significantly higher levels to freedom to travel to places in their own neighborhood or city than children in other cities in the world.

8. Modifying cities in order to enhance children's freedom will not only benefit children. Such cities will become more environmentally sustainable, as well as more sociable and more livable for all city residents. Perhaps it will be our concern for our children's welfare that convinces us that we need to challenge the dominance of the car in our cities.

1. The private car has helped children have more opportunities to learn.
2. Children are more independent today than they used to be.
3. Walking and cycling to school allows children to learn more.
4. Children usually walk or cycle to school.
5. Parents save time and money by driving Children to school.
6. The low sense of community feeling was due to the reduced freedom for children.
7. More children driven to school will surely bring about lower accident risk.
8. In some German towns, pedestrians have right of way on _____.
9. Reducing the amount of traffic and the speed is _____.

10. All people who live in the city will benefit if cities are _____.

Section B Discourse Vocabulary Test

Directions: *In this section, there is a passage with ten blanks. You are required to select one word for each blank from a list of choices given in a word bank following the passage. Read the passage through carefully before making your choices. Each choice in the bank is identified by a letter. Please mark the corresponding letter for each item on Answer Sheet with a single line through the centre.* **You may not use any of the words in the bank more than once.**

Passage 2

To most of us, the word "speech" means a __11__ of communication based on the use of sounds __12__ by the throat, tongue, lips, etc. Of course, other communicative processes can be substituted under given conditions; writing, for instance, and __13__ may adequately replace vocal intercourse when hearing is prevented and sounds cannot be received.

Besides speech as we know it, and its substitutes, there exist a number of languages which have *acoustic* (有关声音的) bases but which nevertheless do not use *vowels* (元音) and *consonants* (辅音) as the sound material of speech.

For example in La Gomera (one of the small and less-developed islands of the Canary Archipelago) the inhabitants can __14__ by means of *articulated* (发音的) whistles. For __15__ conversation they use normal spoken Spanish, but whenever __16__ makes speech __17__ or impossible, they resort to the silbo, as this whistled form of speech is called.

Gomera is of volcanic origin and exceedingly mountainous, and moving over such ground involves the expenditure of much time and energy. For this reason, the silbo is of constant utility to Gomeros. A good whistler (silbador) will be heard and understood five miles or more away when conditions are __18__, that is, when there is little or no wind.

The point is that a whistle is __19__ a pure tone of unchanging quality (the only significant variables are pitch and duration, so there are no weak overtones and transients to be lost) which, if perceived at all, will be understood. So the silbo scores over shouted speech in two major respects: articulation does not suffer in any way when an effort is made to increase loudness, as easily heard a thousand yards away as at close quarters; and it is superior to visual "codes" in that it is as rapid as __20__ Spanish.

A) produced	I) practically
B) technique	J) principle
C) method	K) gestures
D) distance	L) ordinary
E) manufacture	M) spoken
F) inconvenient	N) individual
G) conscious	O) favorable
H) converse	

Section C Reading in Depth

Directions: *There are 2 passages in this section. Each passage is followed by some questions or unfinished statements. For each of them there are four choices marked A), B), C), and D). You should decide on the best choice and mark the corresponding letter on Answer Sheet with a single line through the center.*

Passage 3

1991 was not one of the best years financially for the company. The *recession*（衰退）from which the country was suffering affected us as well as other business.

The three London hotels fared the worst. Their business was down by as much as forty per cent on the previous year. These hotels were used by fewer businessmen and women than usual—obviously because many businesses closed down. The number of overseas visitors particularly Americans was down by thirty per cent on 1990. The companies that used the London hotels for conferences were more than satisfied with the service they received, but their number was down by twenty nine per cent. A number of letters of praise for our services were received from several companies who used these hotels. Bong Brothers, makers of harps, who used our London hotels for their annual staff conference for the last fifteen years, *whet*（促使）into *liquidation*（清算）: a particularly sad loss as they were a charming, friendly bunch of people.

Our eighteen seaside hotels, which are usually fully booked in spring and summer, had an average of twenty per cent vacancies through these seasons. It would appear that many people gave up the luxury of a hotel holiday for guest house or other types of accommodation. For the remainder of the year business was much quieter than usual.

The nine hotels situated in country areas did slightly better than London and seaside ones, their business being down fifteen per cent only. The introduction of cheap weekend breaks helped here.

From the information we have, our rivals were also hit by about the same amount. It is reported that the Pickett Hotel Group is in financial difficulties and it is doubtful if it will remain in business.

However, all is not bad news. We have not reduced staffing levels at any of the hotels and do not have plans to do so, although staff at Head Office will be reduced by eight.

Although overall we have fewer guests than usual, we have received many more letters of praise for our service, courteous stall, *hygiene*（卫生保健）standards, and so on.

21. Which of the following is true according to the report?

A) The 1990s recession in Britain has brought passive effects to the entire line.

B) The profit of GHO in 1991 was the worst one, compared with the previous years.

C) There are many people going to be unemployed as the result of the loss of benefits.

D) As a rule, British people tend to prefer hotels in the country to those at the seaside.

22. We may infer from the report that GHO has _____ hotels in all.

  A) 12   B) 17   C) 21   D) 30

23. The reason why people would give up luxury hotel holiday for guest house or other types of accommodation probably is that _____.

    A) guest house and other types of accommodation provide better services

    B) luxury hotels at the seaside cost more than other types of accommodation

    C) British people do not enjoy staying at luxury seaside hotels

    D) the high cost of settling in a luxury hotel does not match the poor service provided

24. Which of the following percentages does NOT show a rate down?

    A) 30%　　　　　B) 15%　　　　　C) 20%　　　　　D) 40%

25. Which of the following statements is not covered in the passage?

    A) Competitors were affected in the same way.

    B) There were fewer guests but more praise than ever before.

    C) There was no job losses at Head Office, but hotels will lose 8.

    D) Pickett Hotel Group was in financial difficulties.

Passage 4

Joseph Weizenbaum, professor of computer science at *MIT*（麻省理工学院）, thinks that the sense of power over the machine *ultimately*（根本上）corrupts the computer *hacker*（黑客）and makes him into a not very desirable sort of programmer. The hackers are so involved with designing their program, making it more and more complex and bending it to their will, that they don't bother trying to make it understandable to other users. They rarely keep records of their programs for the benefit of others, and they rarely take time to understand why a problem occurred.

Computer science teachers say they can usually pick out the *prospective*（将来的）hackers in their courses because these students make their homework assignments more complex than they need to be. Rather than using the simplest and most direct method, they take joy in adding extra steps just to prove their *ingenuity*（心灵手巧）.

But perhaps those hackers know something that we don't know about the shape of things to come. "That hacker who had to be literally dragged off his chair at MIT is now a multimillionaire of the computer industry." says MIT professor Michael Dertouzos. "And two former hackers become the founders of the highly successful Apple home computer company."

When seen in this light, the hacker phenomenon may not be so strange after all. If, as many *psychiatrists*（精神病学家）say, play is really the basis for all human activity, then the hacker games are really the preparation for future developments. Sherry Turkic, a professor of sociology at MIT, has for years been studying the ways computers fit into people's lives. She points out that the computer, because it seems to us to be so "intelligent", so "capable", so "human", affects the way we think about ourselves and our ideas about what we are. She says that computers and computer toys, already, play an important role in children's efforts to develop an identity by allowing them to test about what is alive and what isn't. "The youngsters can form as many subtle *nuances*（细微差别）and *textured*（密切的）relationships with the computers as they can with people." Turkic points out.

26. The passage tells about _____.

    A) what has caused the emergence of computer hackers

    B) the strange behavior of the computer hackers

    C) the ultimate importance of bringing up computer hackers

    D) different opinions concerning the hacker phenomenon

27. According to Prof. Weizenbaum，what led to the hackers' strange behavior is _____.

    A) their deliberate attempts to make their problems complex and impracticable

    B) their incompetence in making new computer program

    C) their ignorance of the responsibility of a programmer

    D) their strong desire to control the computer

28. We can guess from the context clues that the phrase "to develop an identity" (Line 7，Para. 4) means _____.

    A) to build a creative ability   B) to seek an answer

    C) to become distinguished   D) to form a habit

29. The passage tries to convey to its readers the idea that _____.

    A) perhaps the hacker phenomenon is not bad at all

    B) the computer hackers are the hope of the computer industry of tomorrow

    C) the computer hackers could be useful if under proper guidance

    D) though the hackers are in fact playing with the computer，there may be some benefits

30. According to Prof. Turkic, teenagers play computer games _____.

    A) to form closer relationship with computer than with people

    B) to become computer hackers

    C) to show off their intelligence，capability and humanity

    D) to make it an important part of their lives

Section D   Short Answer Questions

Directions：*In this section，there is a short passage with five questions or incomplete statements. Read the passage carefully. Then answer the questions or complete the statements in the fewest possible words (not exceeding 10 words).*

Passage 5

"It hurts me more than you." and "This is for your own good." These are the statements my mother used to make years ago when I had to learn Latin, clean my room, stay home and do homework.

That was before we entered the permissive period in education in which we decided it was all right not to push our children to achieve their best in school. The schools and the educators made it easy on us. They taught that it was all right to be parents who take a let-alone policy. We stopped making our children do homework. We gave them calculators, turned on the television, left the *leaching* (过滤) to the teachers and went on vacation. Now teachers, faced with children who have been developing at their own pace for the past 15 years, are realizing we've made a terrible mistake. One such teacher is Sharon Claumpus, who says of her students "so passive" and wonders what happened. Nothing was demanded of them, she believes. Television, says

Claumpus, contributes to children's passivity. "We're not training kids to work anymore," says Claumpus, "we are talking about a generation of kids who've never been hurt or hungry. They have learned somebody will always do it for them. Instead of saying go look it up, you tell them the answer. It takes greater energy to say no to a kid."

Yes, it does. It takes energy and it takes work. It's time for parents to end their vacation and come back to work. It's time to take the car away, to turn the TV off, to tell them it hurts you more than them but it's for their own good. It's time to start telling them no again.

31. How are children described in the passage?

_____

_____

32. Why are children becoming more inactive in study?

_____

_____

33. According to the passage, what attitude used the author's mother to have towards learning?

_____

_____

34. What did the author mean by "permissive period in education"?

_____

_____

35. What's the main idea of the passage?

_____

_____

Notes and Explanations

Passage 1

Explanations

1. [N] 第二段第三句提到 This depends on "active exploration", which is not provided for when children are passengers in cars. (Such children may see more, but they learn less.)孩子们乘车的时候不能主动探索周围的世界，他们在车上做的更多的也许是观察周围的世界,学到的东西要少一些。故可得出答案为 No。

2. [N] 第一段第三句提到 However, allowing our cities to be dominated by cars has progressively eroded children's independent mobility. 得知允许汽车在我们的城市大量存在逐渐破坏了孩子们的活动独立性。从第一段第五句 In recent surveys, when parents in some cities were asked about their own childhood experiences, the majority remembered having more opportunities for going out on their own, compared with their own children today. 在最近的调查中,一些城市中的家长被问及他们自己的童年经历时,他们中间大多数还记得与现在他们自己的孩子相比,他们有更多的机会独立出行。所以答案为 No。

3. [Y] 第二段第三、四句提到 This depends on "active exploration", which is not provided for when children are passengers. (Such children may see more, but they learn less.) Not only is it important that children be able to get to local play areas by themselves, but walking and cycling journeys to school and to

other destinations provide genuine play activities in themselves. 孩子们乘车时学到的知识少了。不仅能够独自到附近玩耍对于孩子们来说很重要,而且走路、骑车去上学或去其他地方给他们提供真正的娱乐活动也很重要。意思与题目完全是一致的。所以答案为 Yes。

4. [NG] 第二段第四句提到 Not only is it important that children be able to get to local play areas by themselves, but walking and cycling journeys to school and to other destinations provide genuine play activities in themselves. 走路、骑车去上学能给他们提供真正的娱乐活动。但是并没有说明孩子们是否真正经常走路、骑车去上学。所以答案为 Not Given。

5. [N] 第三段提到 There are very significant time and money costs for parents associated with transporting their children to school, sport and to other locations. 家长们花费大量的时间和金钱送孩子们上学,参加体育活动和到其他地方。所以答案为 No。

6. [Y] 第四段第一句提到 The reduction in children's freedom may also contribute to a weakening of the sense of local community. 孩子们自由活动的减少可能也会导致他们对本地社区的了解程度的减弱。意思与题目完全是一致的。所以答案为 Yes。

7. [N] 第六段第一、二句提到 As individuals, parents strive to provide the best upbringing they can for their children. However, in doing so, (e. g. by driving their children to sport, school or recreation) parents may be contributing to a more dangerous environment for children generally. 家长们想方设法以最佳的方式养育孩子(开车送孩子们去上学,参加体育或娱乐活动),但这样做可能给孩子们普遍带来更危险的环境。所以答案为 No。

8. 第七段第一句提到 In many parts of Dutch cities, some traffic-calmed precincts in Germany, residential streets are now places where cars must give way to pedestrians. 现在在德国的一些交通不繁忙的地区,居民区街道要求汽车(行驶时)必须给行人让路。从而得出答案为 **residential streets**。

9. 第七段第四句提到 One of the most important aspects of these European cities, in terms of giving cities back to children, has been a range of "traffic calming" initiatives, aimed at reducing the volume speed of traffic. 为了把城市还给孩子们,这些欧洲城市采取很多积极办法,其中重要方面之一是采取交通管制来减少车流量和速度。从而得出答案为 **traffic calming**。

10. 最后一段第一句提到 Modifying cities in order to enhance children's freedom will not only benefit children. 为了孩子们的自由而改变城市现状,从中受益的不仅仅是孩子们(也包括其他人)。从而得出答案为 **modified**。

Passage 2

Notes

1. by means of (Line 2, Para. 3)
此短语的意思是"通过……;用……方法"。例如:
She could not speak, but made her wishes known by means of signs.
虽然她不会说话,但通过打手势让别人了解她的心愿。

2. resort to (Line 4, Para. 3)
resort to 表示"利用,求助于,诉诸"。例如:
When his wife left him he resorted to drink. 妻子离开他后,他借酒浇愁。
She had to resort to the law to deal with that case. 她不得不诉诸法律来解决那个案子。

3. ... is of... origin... (Line 1, Para. 4); ... is of constant utility... (Line 2, Para. 4)
这个句型为 be ＋ of ＋ noun,相当于 be ＋adj.,例如:
This issue is of great importance. (相当于 This issue is very important.)这个问题非常重要。
The book is of value now. (相当于 The book is very valuable now.)本书非常有价值。

4. ... such ground involves... (Line 1～2, Para. 4)

involve 在这句话中意思是"就得……;就需要……"。例如:

Taking the job involves working on weekends. 接受这份工作就得在周末上班。

Marrying him involves living abroad. 嫁给他就得到国外去居住。

5. ... in two major respects... (Line 3～4, Para. 5)

respect 在这里意思是"方面",前面常与介词 in 连用,构成 in... respect,例如:in one respect, in no respect, in several/many/all respects 等短语。例如:

This room is fine except in one respect—what can I sit on? 这个房间什么都好,除了一点——我坐哪儿呢?

6. ... it is superior to... (Line 5, Para. 5)

be superior to 意思是"优于……,比……好"。superior 是形容词,但没有比较级和最高级,后跟介词 to 表示比较。用法相同的词还有 inferior, junior, senior。例如:

This instrument is superior to that one. 这种仪器比那种好。

The socialism is superior to the capitalism. 社会主义比资本主义优越。

He thinks he's superior to us because his father's an important man.

他以为他父亲是大人物,他就高人一等。

Explanations

11. [C] 语法规则要求此处应填一个单数名词作宾语。根据第一句话的意思"话语是一种交流的方式"可以判断 method 符合句意。method 意思是"方式"。

12. [A] 语法规则要求此处应填一个动词＋ed 形式(过去分词)作定语修饰 sounds。只有选项 A 是该形式。根据上下文的意思,应该是"喉咙、舌头和嘴唇等发出的声音",所以 produced 符合句意。produce 意思是"发出"。

13. [K] 语法规则要求此处应填一个名词和 writing 作并列主语。这句话的意思是"当(人的)听力被阻断或无法接收到声音时可以用写字或……来代替有声交流"。根据常识,除了写字还可以用手势来交流。gesture 意思是"手势",符合句意。

14. [H] 语法规则要求情态动词 can 后面应填一个动词原形。选项 E、H 是动词原形。根据下文的解释可以判断 converse 符合句意。converse 意思是"谈话,交流"。

15. [L] 语法规则要求此处应填一个形容词作定语修饰 conversation。根据上下文的意思,but 在此构成两种情况的对比。La Gomera 的居民可以用响亮的口哨声来交流。对于一般的交谈他们用正常的西班牙口语,但是当距离使交流变得不方便或不可能时,他们就借助于这种吹口哨来交流的形式,他们这种形式叫 silbo。因此 ordinary 符合句意。ordinary 意思是"一般的,正常的"。

16. [D] 语法规则要求此处应填一个单数名词作主语。参见上题解释,distance 符合句意。distance 意思是"距离"。

17. [F] 语法规则要求此处应填一个形容词构成 make＋名词＋形容词的结构。根据后面的 impossible 可以判断所填词汇是一个表示否定意义的形容词。选项中 inconvenient 是否定形容词。参见第 15 题解释,inconvenient 符合句意。inconvenient 意思是"不方便的"。

18. [O] 语法规则要求此处应填一个形容词作表语。根据上下文的意思,"当风很小或没有风时"应该是"有利的条件",所以 favorable 符合句意。favorable 意思是"有利的"。

19. [I] 语法规则要求此处应填一个副词修饰句子的谓语。选项中只有选项 I 是副词。根据上下文的意思,practically 符合句意。practically 意思是"实际上"。

20. [M] 语法规则要求此处应填一个形容词作定语修饰 Spanish。这句的意思是"口哨和西班牙口语一样快",根据第三段第二句的提示也可以判断 spoken 符合句意。spoken 意思是"口头的"。

Passage 3

Notes

1. fare (Line 1，Para. 2)

在这里 fare 表示"结果，发生"，是不及物动词，相当于 to turn out；happen，作此义解时通常其主语是 it。例如：

It fared ill with them. 他们的结果很糟糕。

The unions will fare badly if the government's plan becomes law.

如果政府的计划经立法通过，工会的遭遇会很惨。

2. ...more than satisfied with... (Line 5，Para. 2)

more than... 是正式的表达方式，表示"万分，非常"。例如：

We were more than happy to hear of your escape! 我们听说你逃了出来，高兴得不得了！

3. whet (Line 8，Para. 2)

whet 在这里作"促使"讲，本意是"磨，磨快"的意思。例如：

whet a knife 磨刀

whet the public's appetite for upcoming new issues 促使公众更加热衷于即将出现的问题

The episode has whetted their interests. 这一插曲提高了他们的兴趣。

4. book (Line 1，Para. 3)

book 在这里是动词，作"预订"讲。例如：

to book seats on a plane 订飞机座位

You'll have to book up early if you want to see that show. 你要看那场表演的话，要早一点订座。

5. For the remainder of the year... (Line 3～4，Para. 3)

remainder 指"剩余物或剩余人"，这里指"一年中除了上文提到的 spring and summer 的其他时候"。例如：

The remainder of the food will do for tomorrow. 剩下的食物够明天吃的。

Ten people in our class are Arabs and the remainder are Germans.

我们班上有 10 个阿拉伯人，其他的是德国人。

Explanations

这是一份 The Goode's Hotels' Organization 的年度报告。GHO 是英国一个经营饭店服务业的公司，有多家酒店分布在英国各地。这份报告详细总结了 1991 年公司财务等方面的情况。通过这份报告，我们可以看到 20 世纪 90 年代初期英国经济不景气给酒店业造成的冲击有多严重。

21. A) 细节题。答案见第一段...affected us as well as other businesses。选项 A 中的 the entire line 指的是整个酒店行业。选项 B 中的 the worst one 并不等于 not one of the best；选项 C 与倒数第二段中的 We have not reduced staffing levels at any of the hotels... 意思不符；第三段第一句话和第四段提到与选项 D 相关的一些内容，但不能得出此结论。

22. D) 推断题。第二、三、四段中的 three London hotels，eighteen seaside hotels 和 nine hotels situated in country 相加等于 30。

23. B) 推断题。经济不景气往往使人们收入减少，甚至造成失业。因此，人们会相应降低消费水平，选择入住比较便宜的旅馆、旅社。A、C、D 各项都不对。

24. C) 细节题。报告中的五个百分比中四个(40%，30%，29%，15%)都表示下降率，只有第三段中的 20% 表示的是空房率。

25. C) 细节题。这篇文章涉及四个 general points。其中 A、B、D 三项分别可在第一、最后一段和第五段中找到出处。将 C 项带到第六段中核查，情况正好相反。所以答案选 C 项。

新世纪英语丛书

Passage 4

Notes

1. . . . are so involved with. . . (Line 3，Para. 1)

   involved 是形容词，表示"与……有密切关系的"。例如：

   He is deeply involved with her and feels he must marry her. 他和她感情很深，因此他觉得应该娶她。

2. prospective (Line 1，Para. 2)

   prospective 表示"未来的，将来的"。例如：

   achieve the prospective results 达到预期的结果

   a prospective client 可能成为客户的人

   mankind in prospective 未来的人类

3. rather than (Line 3，Para. 2)

   rather than 是并列连词，意思是"而不是……"，常连接两个相同的语法成分。例如：

   Tom ought to go rather than Mary. 不是玛丽，而是汤姆应该去。

   These shoes are comfortable rather than pretty. 这鞋不好看但是很舒服。

   He ran rather than walked. 他跑步而不是步行。

4. in this light (Line 1，Para. 4)

   这个短语表示"在这方面"或"从这点来看"，light 表示"方面，观点，看法"。例如：

   Viewed in this light, the problem seemed less important. 从这点来看，这个问题好像不那么重要。

   The workers and the employers look at difficulties in quite a different light.

   工人们和雇主对困难的看法截然不同。

5. fit into (Line 4，Para. 4)

   fit into 也作 fit in，表示"适合于……"。例如：

   He doesn't fit into this position at all. 他根本不适合这个职位。

6. play an important role in . . . (Line 7，Para. 4)

   这个短语表示"扮演（重要的）角色，起（重要的）作用"。例如：

   to play the role of Hamlet 扮演哈姆雷特的角色

   Words play a tremendous role in your everyday life. 话语在人们的日常生活中起着非常重要的作用。

Explanations

　　这篇文章主要讲述了计算机网络给我们的电子信息产业带来了无限的生机和广阔的前景，但同时也造就了一批令全世界胆战心惊的"新新人类"——电脑黑客。作者借助几位业内人士的看法，从一个全新的角度，论述了电脑给人类生活带来的好处以及电脑黑客的发展未来。

26. D）主旨题。全文涉及了对黑客现象的不同看法。前两段为一种观点，即黑客的表现和形成的原因；后两段为另一种观点，即计算机游戏的好处和黑客的可转变性与发展性。

27. D）细节性问题。第一段第一句中提到导致黑客们奇异行为的原因在于对计算机的强烈控制欲，原文中用的是 the sense of power over the machine ultimately corrupts the computer hackers，与选项 D 相符。

28. B）词汇题。根据上下文，孩子们通过计算机和计算机玩具来努力探寻人与计算机之间的细微差别及密切联系，选项 B 与之意思最接近。

29. A）主旨题。这是一道对作者的观点、态度的判断题。从计算业内人士的观点、实际的例子及文章的结论等综合来看，作者倾向于认为黑客现象或许并不是一件坏事。

30. C）推断题。答案参见后两段。从 Turkic 教授的阐述来看，年轻人玩计算机主要是想表现他们的智力和能力。

Passage 5

Keys

31. They are passive.

32. Because they watch TV too often.

33. Children should be pushed to achieve their best.

34. A time allowing children to do what they wish to.

35. It's time to be more strict with our children.

Notes

1. It hurts me more than you. (Line 1, Para. 1)

   more than 后面省略了 it hurts。这句话的意思是：我比你还痛心。

2. This is for your own good. (Line 1, Para. 1)

   这句话的意思是"这是为你好"。for one's good 意思是"为……好，为……的利益"。

3. These are the statements my mother used to make years ago... (Line 1~2, Para. 1)

   used to 意思是"过去常常"。这句话的意思是：这些是很多年前我妈妈常说的话。

4. Now teachers, faced with children who have been... at their own pace... (Line 5~6, Para. 2)

   这句话的意思是"现在，老师们面对那些在过去 15 年中以自己的方式长大的孩子们，意识到我们犯了一个严重的错误"。who 引导的定语从句使用了现在完成进行时，at one's own pace 表示"以自己的方式"。

5. Television... contributes to children's passivity. (Line 8~9, Para. 2)

   这句话的意思是"电视更加助长了孩子们的懒惰和被动"。其中 contribute to sth. 意思是"有助于，助长"。例如：

   Air pollution contributes to respiratory diseases. 空气污染会引起呼吸道疾病。

Unit 2

Section A Skimming and Scanning

Directions：（略）

Passage 1

Preserving Our Planet

1. Despite decades of scientific research, no one yet knows how much damage human activity is doing to the environment. Humans are thought to be responsible for a large number of environmental problems, ranging from global warming to ozone depletion. What is not in doubt, however, is the devastating effect humans are having on the animal and the plant life of the planet.

2. Currently, an estimated 50,000 species become extinct every year. If this carries on, the impact on all living creatures is likely to be profound, says Dr. Nick Middleton, a geographer at Oxford University. "All species depend in some way on each other to survive. And the danger is that, if you remove one species from this very complex web of interrelationships, you have very little idea about the knock-on effects on the ecosystem. So, if you lose a key species, you might cause a whole flood of other extinctions."

3. Complicating matters is the fact that there are no obvious solutions to the problem. Unlike global warming and ozone depletion—which, if the political will was there, could be reduced by cutting gas emissions—preserving bio-diversity remains an *intractable*（棘手的）problem.

4. The latest idea is "sustainable management". This means humans should be able to use any species of animal or plant for their benefit, provided enough individuals of that species are left alive to ensure its continued existence.

5. Sustainable management is seen as a practical and economical way of protecting species from extinction. Instead of depending on largely ineffective laws against illegal hunting, it gives local people a good economical reason to preserve plants and animals. In Zimbabwe, for instance, there is a sustainable management project to protect elephants. Foreign tourists pay large sums of money to kill these animals for sport. This money is then given to the inhabitants of the area where the hunting takes place. In theory, locals will be encouraged to protect elephants, instead of hunting them illegally—or allowing others to do so—because of the economic benefit involved.

6. This sounds like a sensible strategy, but it remains to be seen whether it will work. With corruption popular in many developing countries, some observers are suspicious that the money will actually reach the people it is intended for. Others wonder how effective the locals will be at stopping illegal hunters.

7. There are also questions about whether sustainable management is practical when it comes

to protecting areas of great bio-diversity such as the world's tropical forests. In theory, the principle should be the same as with elephants-allow logging companies to cut down a certain number of trees, but not so many as to completely destroy the forest.

8. Sustainable management of forests requires controls on the number of trees which are cut down, as well as investment in replacing them. Because almost all tropical forests are located in countries which desperately need income from logging, there are few regulations and incentives to do this. In fact, for loggers, the most sensible economic approach is to cut down as many trees as quickly as possible.

9. One reason is the stable price of most commercial tree species in tropical forests. Typically, they rise in value annually by, at most, four to five per cent. Contrast this with interest rates in most developing countries, where investors can typically expect returns of 15 per cent or more. Clearly, it makes no economic sense to delay harvests.

10. One solution might be to verify wood which comes from sustainably managed forests. In theory, consumers would buy only this wood and so force logging companies to go "green" or go out of business. Unfortunately, unrestricted logging is so much more profitable that wood from managed forests would cost up to five times more—an increase that consumers, no matter how "green", are unlikely to pay.

11. For these reasons, sustainable management of tropical forests is unlikely to become widespread in the near future. This is disheartening news. It's estimated these forests contain anything from 50 to 90 per cent of all animal and plant species on earth. In one study of a five-square-kilometer area of rain forest in Peru, for instance, scientists counted 1,300 species of butterfly and 600 species of bird. In the entire continental United States, only 400 species of butterfly and 700 species of bird have been recorded.

12. Scientists Professor Norman Myers sees the situation as a tremendous "experiment we're conducting with our planet". "We don't know what the outcome will be. If we make a mess of it, we can't move to another planet. It's a case of one planet, one experiment."

1. This passage mainly talks about the experiment humans are conducting with our planet.

2. All species are members of a very complex web of interrelationships.

3. Removing one species from the planet might cause 50,000 species extinct every year.

4. We haven't found satisfactory solutions to the problem of preserving bio-diversity.

5. The political will might help reduce global warming and ozone depletion.

6. The sustainable management will be widespread in the near future.

7. The sustainable management results in the rapid increase of species of animal.

8. Humans should be responsible for environmental problems: global warming, ozone depletion and _____.

9. The animal protected in Zimbabwe is _____.

10. The area of great bio-diversity is _____.

Section B Discourse Vocabulary Test

Directions：（略）

Passage 2

It's tough life being a schoolchild these days. There are so many politicians, social scientists and educationists crowding round his desk to   11   their different philosophies on his young mind that it's a   12   he has any time left for reading, writing and arithmetic.

Alcohol is the newest subject on his curriculum. An alcoholism   13   was of the firm opinion that children should begin receiving rational " 14 " about beer, wine and spirits, from their parents or teachers, when they reach the age of ten or eleven. The idea is that children should not be left to find out about drink for themselves at a later age, in case they find out the wrong things. Tell them young and they won't make mistakes later.   15   the same theory applies to their sex education. All sorts of traumas have been recorded in adolescents who have had the   16   of finding out about sex themselves. Clearly they need to be   17   from such a spontaneous discovery by learning in advance what sex is all about.

As if this wasn't enough, the poor child is nowadays   18   to a range of adult rituals of which in the old days he could have remained in *blissful*（有福的）ignorance until he finished his education. *Leaflets*（传单）are pushed into his locker urging him to join the Young Socialists. National Union of School Students' brochures arrive, suggesting he think up an   19   and then campaign for it in school hours with sit-ins, walk-outs and whatever tactics are   20 .

Even his lessons are becoming politicized. Library boards and school boards condemn some of the children's classics given him in reading classes because of their sexist discrimination. Is there nothing that children can be left to find out for themselves? Perhaps one thing at least—that life cannot be taught in the classroom: it teaches its own lessons in its own time.

A) wonder	I) exactly
B) knowledge	J) experience
C) expert	K) exposed
D) successful	L) necessary
E) impress	M) issue
F) audience	N) protected
G) guidance	O) link
H) subject	

Section C Reading in Depth

Directions：（略）

Passage 3

Do we need laws that prevent us from running risks with our lives? If so, then perhaps laws are needed prohibiting the sale of cigarettes and alcoholic drinks. Both products have been known to kill people. The hazards of drinking too much alcohol are as bad as or worse than the hazards of smoking too many cigarettes. All right then, let's pass a law closing the liquor stores and the bars in this country. Let's put an end once and for all to the ruinous disease from which as many as 10 million Americans currently suffer—alcoholism.

But wait. We've already tried that. For 13 years, between 1920 and 1933, there were no liquor stores anywhere in the United States. They were shut down—abolished by an *amendment* (修正案) to the Constitution (the 18ᵗʰ) and by a law of Congress (the Volstead Act). After January 20, 1920, there was supposed to be no more manufacturing, selling, or transporting of "intoxicating liquors". Without any more liquor, people could not drink it. And if they did not drink it, how could they get drunk? There would be no more dangers to the public welfare from drunkenness and alcoholism. It was all very logical. And yet prohibition of liquor, beer, and wine did not work. Why?

Because, law or no law, millions of people still liked to drink alcohol. And they were willing to take risks to get it. They were not about to change their tastes and habits just because of a change in the law. And gangs of liquor smugglers made it easy to buy an illegal drink—or two or three. They smuggled millions of gallons of the outlawed beverages across the Canadian and Mexican borders. Drinkers were lucky to know of an illegal bar that served Mexican or Canadian liquor. Crime and drunkenness were both supposed to decline as a result of prohibition. Instead people drank more alcohol than ever: often poisoned alcohol.

On December 5, 1993, they *repealed* (撤销) prohibition by *ratifying* (批准) the 21ˢᵗ Amendment to the Constitution.

21. Which of the following was NOT a characteristic reason for the proposal of the 18ᵗʰ Amendment to the Constitution ?

A) There would be no further danger to the public from alcoholism.

B) People would not become drunk or create a public nuisance.

C) There would be a rise in the cost of alcoholic beverages.

D) Without liquor, people would not drink.

22. During Prohibition, illegal alcohol was _____.

A) sold openly

B) no longer a temptation

C) a major factor in the passage of the Volstead Act

D) brought across the Mexican and Canadian borders

23. During Prohibition, people _____.

A) lived in fear of the law

B) were willing to risk arrest for the pleasure of liquor

C) recklessly endangered their communities

D) were respectful of the legal sanctions placed on them

24. When enacting the prohibition laws, government officials assumed that _____.

A) every American would buy alcohol illegally

B) all criminal activities would cease

C) patrols of the Canadian border would halt the sale of alcohol

D) the social threat from drunkenness would decline

25. It can be inferred from the passage that _____.

A) the Congress was wise to repeal Prohibition

B) the Prohibition Era was characterized by a decrease in crime and drunkenness

C) during Prohibition, most Americans stopped drinking

D) laws should be passed to ban the sale of alcoholic beverages

Passage 4

In technologically advanced societies, the enormous consumption of energy per head is one aspect of the ever-increasing pressure man is placing on his environment. Early industrial man used three times as much energy as his agricultural ancestor; modern man is using three times as much as his industrial ancestor. If present trends continue, the rate of consumption will have *tripled* (三倍) again by the end of the century. The problem lies in the fact that most of our current energy sources are finite. The hard truth is that a day will come when there is little or no exploitable coal, oil or natural gas anywhere. The sharp rise in the price of oil over the last decade has been unpleasant for many parts of the world but in the long run it is beneficial, partly because it discourages waste and partly because it has forced many nations to seek ways of developing better and more permanent sources of energy.

Energy sources may initially be divided into two kinds: nonrenewable (i. e. finite) and renewable. The former group includes coal, oil, and gas, in the long run, nuclear; the latter hydropower, solar power and wind power. The energy from all these sources ultimately derives from the sun. There is a further source—geothermal—which depends on the earth's own heat. In practice this may be classed as nonrenewable as it is exploitable in only a few places and even that is limited.

There is a second distinction that is often made between conventional and non-conventional energy sources. A conventional energy source is one which is at present widely exploited. In view of the points made in paragraph 1 (above) it will be realized that, broadly, the conventional sources are the non-renewable ones. This is not entirely true, however, as a good deal of oil is locked up in solid form in rock (tar sands and oil shale) and this source, though non-renewable, is also non-conventional, since it has not so far been developed very much.

26. The sentence "The sharp rise in the price of oil... in the long run it is beneficial..." (Line 7~8, Para. 1) means _____.

A) the oil producers will make more money

B) the merchants will benefit a lot

C) the sharp rise will make people save on the use of oil

D) both A and B

27. What's the meaning of "geothermal" (Line 4, Para. 2)?

A) The heat.　　　　　　　　　B) The earth.

C) Temperature.　　　　　　　　D) The heat from the earth.

28. We are warned that _____.

    A) the non-renewable energy source will be less and less

    B) the non-renewable energy will be more and more

    C) there will be no energy source

    D) heat energy will be permanent

29. If we continue to consume energy at the present rate, by the end of the century, we shall have used energy _____.

    A) 6 times as much as the early industrial men

    B) 27 times as much as the agricultural ancestor

    C) 3 times as much as the modern men

    D) 9 times as much as the agricultural men

30. Which of the following is correct according to the passage?

    A) Non-renewable source is more.

    B) Renewable source is little.

    C) There is nothing to do between non-renewable and non-conventional sources.

    D) Oil locked up in solid form in rock is not widely exploited at present.

Section D　Short Answer Questions

Directions：（略）

Passage 5

    Your passport is your official identification as an American citizen. In America, most people never consider obtaining a passport unless they are planning a trip out of the country. A passport is final proof of identity in almost every country in the world. In 1979 almost 15 million Americans held passports. Most of these passports were obtained to travel outside the country because, except for a few Western nations, passports are required to enter every country. And if you travel abroad, you must have a valid passport to reenter the country.

    When traveling abroad, you will need a passport for identification when exchanging dollars for francs or marks or other foreign currency. You may also need your passport to use a credit card, buy an airplane ticket, check into a hotel or *casino* (赌场).

    Don't confuse passports and visas. Whereas a passport is issued by a country to its citizens, a visa is official permission to visit a country granted by the government of that country. For some years, many countries were dropping their visa requirements, but that trend has reversed. Argentina, Brazil, and Venezuela now require visas from U. S. citizens. They may be obtained from the embassy of the country you wish to visit.

    Passport applications are available at passport agency offices in large cities like Boston, New York, or Chicago. In smaller cities, applications are available at post offices and at federal courts. To get your first passport, you must submit the application in person, along with a birth certificate and two pictures.

    Maybe because most Americans use their passports only when traveling and because they are good for five years, many people lose their passports. And every passport is worth thousands of dollars to smugglers or criminals who desire to enter this country illegally or assume a false identity. Travelers should keep their passports in their pockets or pocketbooks at all times; never pack them or leave them in a room or automobile; when you arrive back home, store your passport in a safe or safety deposit box. And report a lost or stolen passport immediately; it is literally your identity.

31. What is the main purpose of this passage?

_____

_____

32. Passports are needed when _____ .

_____

_____

33. Concerning passports and visas, what can we conclude from the passage?

_____

_____

34. What does the passage suggest about the importance of passports?

_____

_____

35. Where should travelers keep their passports?

_____

_____

Notes and Explanations

Passage 1

Explanations

1. [N] 通过快速浏览(skim)文章便可得知本文首先指出人类对环境问题的产生负有不可推卸的责任。然后描绘了人类为保护环境所采取的一些做法,如实施可持续性管理政策。所以答案为 No。

2. [Y] 第二段提到 All species depend in some way on each other to survive. ... So, if you lose a key species, you might cause a whole flood of other extinctions. 所有物种在某种程度上彼此依靠才能生存。……如果失去一种主要的物种,可能会引起大量其他物种的灭绝。所以答案为 Yes。

3. [N] 第二段第一句和最后一句提到 Currently, an estimated 50,000 species become extinct every year. ... So, if you lose a key species, you might cause a whole flood of other extinctions. 目前估计每年大约有 50 000 种物种绝迹。……如果失去一种主要物种,可能会引起大量其他物种的灭绝。所以答案为 No。

4. [Y] 第三段第一句提到 Complicating matters is the fact that there are no obvious solutions to the problem. 得知使问题复杂的是没有明确的解决问题(保护生物多样性)的办法。所以答案为 Yes。

5. [Y] 第三段第二句提到 Unlike global warming and ozone depletion-which, if the political will was there, could be reduced by cutting gas emission-preserving bio-diversity remains an intractable problem. 与全球变暖和臭氧大大减少等环境问题不一样,保护生物多样性仍然是一个棘手的问题,因为如果政府干预减

少煤气的排放,全球变暖和臭氧层减少等环境问题可以减少。所以答案为 Yes。

6. [N] 第十一段第一句提到 For these reasons, sustainable management of tropical forests is unlikely to become widespread in the near future. 对于热带森林进行的可持续性管理办法不可能在不远的将来普及。所以答案为 No。

7. [NG] 第五段第一、二句提到 Sustainable management is seen as a practical and economical way of protecting species from extinction. Instead of depending on largely ineffective laws against illegal hunting, it gives local people a good economical reason to preserve plants and animals. 人们把可持续管理视为一种保护物种使之免于绝迹的实际而又经济的办法。它使当地人们可以为了经济上的原因而去保护动植物,而不是依靠在很大程度上难以奏效的反对非法偷猎的规章制度。但没有提及本题中的命题,所以答案为 Not Given。

8. 第一段第二、三句提到 Humans are thought to be responsible for a large number of environmental problems, ranging from global warming to ozone depletion. What is not in doubt, however, is the devastating effect humans are having on the animal and plant life of the planet. 人们认为人类应该为一系列环境问题负责,从全球变暖到臭氧大大减少。然而有一点是毫无疑问的,即人类正对地球上的动植物的生活产生极大的破坏作用。从第二段第一句 Currently, an estimated 50,000 species become extinct every year. 得知目前,估计每年大约有 50,000 种物种绝迹。从而得出答案为 **species extinction**。

9. 第五段第三句提到 In Zimbabwe, for instance, there is a sustainable management project to protect elephants. 在津巴布韦有可持续管理项目来保护大象。从而得出答案为 **elephants**。

10. 第七段第一句提到 There are also questions about whether sustainable management is practical when it comes to protecting areas of great bio-diversity such as the world's tropical forests. 当涉及保护多生物地区时,如世界热带森林,可持续管理是否仍然切实可行,人们也有一些疑问。从而得出答案为 **tropical forests**。

Passage 2

Notes

1. impress...on... (Line 2, Para. 1)
▷在这里用 impress sth. on sb. 表示"给某人留下深刻的印象"。例如:
I'll impress one thing on you. 我要你记住一件事。
We should impress on the young people that pride goes before a fall. 我们应该让年轻人记住骄兵必败。
▷impress 还可以用于其他句型。例如:
I was impressed by his prodigious talent. 他那过人的才干给我留下了深刻的印象。
He impressed me as an honest man. 他给我的印象是他是个老实人。

2. in case (Line 4, Para. 2)
这里 in case 意思是"以免……,以防万一"。例如:
Be quiet in case you wake the baby. 轻点儿,别把孩子弄醒。
Keep the window closed in case it rains. 把窗户关好以防下雨。
It may rain, you'd better take an umbrella in case. 可能要下雨,你最好带把伞,以防万一。

3. apply to (Line 5, Para. 2)
此短语意思是"适用"。例如:
This rule applies to freshmen only. 此项规定仅仅适用于大学一年级的学生。
This price concession will not apply to any item after that date.
过了那个日期,这一价格折扣对任一款将不再有效。

4. in advance (Line 8, Para. 2)

此短语意思是"预先,事先"。例如:

You ought to have told me in advance. 你本该事先告诉我的(但你没有)。

He had known of this plan in advance. 他事先就知道这项计划。

You must pay \$100 in advance. 你必须预付100美金。

5. ...is exposed to... (Line 1, Para. 3)

expose 是及物动词,常常用于被动语态,表示"使……处于……作用(或影响)之下"。例如:

Children should be exposed to good books. 孩子们应该接触好的书籍。

People should be aware of the dangers of exposing children to violence and sex on TV.

人们应该意识到儿童接触有关暴力和色情电视节目的危害。

People should be exposed to new ideas. 人们应该接触新思想。

6. ...could have remained... (Line 2, Para. 3)

could have + p. p. (过去分词)表示一种遗憾,翻译成"本来能够……,但没有能……"。例如:

I could have saved that boy, but I didn't. 我本来能够救那个男孩,但我没有。

You could have finished that test, but why you didn't? 你本来能够完成那次考试,为什么你没完成呢?

Explanations

11. [E] 语法规则要求此处应填一个动词原形构成动词不定式,并和 on 搭配构成动词短语。选项 E、M、O 是动词原形。根据第一段的意思"现在有太多的政客、社会学家和教育家挤在学校课桌旁想要把他们不同的观点强加在孩子头脑中",可以判断 impress 符合句意。固定短语搭配"impress...on..."意思是"给……留下印象"。

12. [A] 语法规则要求此处应填一个单数名词。第一段的意思是"学生要想有时间来阅读、写作或做算术题,那简直是令人不可思议的事",由此可以判断 wonder 符合句意。wonder 意思是"令人惊讶的事,令人不可思议的事"。

13. [C] 语法规则要求此处应填一个单数名词作主语。根据上下文可以判断持有这种观点的应该是 expert。expert 意思是"专家"。

14. [G] 语法规则要求此处应填一个名词作 receiving 的宾语。根据上下文,孩子在了解啤酒、红酒和烈酒方面应得到父母和老师的指导,所以 guidance 符合句意。guidance 意思是"指导"。

15. [I] 语法规则要求此处应填一个副词作状语修饰 the same。选项中只有选项 I 是副词。"exactly the same theory"指的是前一句话"Tell them young and they won't make mistakes later"。exactly 意思是"确切地"。

16. [J] 语法规则要求此处应填一个名词作宾语。根据后面的介词 of 引导的短语可判断本句话的意思是"自己弄懂性的经历或体验"。experience 意思是"经历或体验",符合句意。

17. [N] 语法规则要求此处应填一个动词+ed 形式构成不定式的被动语态,并和 from 搭配作 need 的宾语。选项 K、N 是该形式。protected 可以和 from 搭配。protect 意思是"被保护,不受……侵害",符合句意。

18. [K] 语法规则要求此处应填一个动词+ed 形式构成被动语态并和 to 搭配使用。选项 K、N 是该形式。根据上下文判断 exposed 符合句意。be exposed to 意思是"被置于……中,暴露于……下"。

19. [M] 语法规则要求此处应填一个单数名词作宾语。根据动词短语 think up 的意思(想出,编造出),其后面接续的宾语应选 issue。issue 意思是"问题"。

20. [L] 语法规则要求此处应填一个形容词。根据上下文推断此处的意思应是"任何必要的办法,策略",因此,necessary 符合句意。necessary 意思是"必要的"。

Passage 3

Notes

1. ... prevent us from running risks... (Line 1, Para. 1)

   prevent sb. from doing sth. 意思是"阻止、妨碍某人做某事"。例如：

   The rain prevented us from playing tennis 那场雨使我们不能打网球了。

   That did not prevent us from getting on very well together. 那并未妨碍我们在一起和睦相处。

2. ... running risks ... (Line 1, Para. 1)

   run 的意思非常多，在这里与 risks 搭配，run risks 也作 take risks (Line 2, Para. 3)，意思是"冒险"。例如：

   run the risk of discovery 冒被发现的危险

   run a chance of being killed 冒被杀的危险

3. put an end to (Line 5, Para. 1)

   意思是"结束……，停止……"，在这里 to 是介词。同义的短语还有：come to an end, make an end of sth. 例如：

   We should put an end to this foolish quarrel. 我们应该停止这场无谓的争吵。

   Let's put an end to the arms race. 让我们停止军备竞赛吧。

   The discussion was put an end to by his sudden arrival. 他的突然到来使讨论停止了。

   The wind put and end to the pier. 大风把码头毁了。

4. once and for all (Line 5, Para. 1)

   也作 once for all，意思是"一劳永逸地，一次了结地；永远地，彻底地"。例如：

   We had decided to settle the matter once and for all. 我们已经决定彻底地解决这个问题。

5. They were not about to change their tastes... (Line 2, Para. 3)

   be about to do 意思是"将要，刚要"。例如：

   They are just about to leave. 他们刚要离开。

   In that case we may be about to witness a historic clash.

   那样的话，我们就将可能目睹一场历史性的冲突。

6. as a result of (Line 6, Para. 3)

   意思是"作为……的结果，由于……"。例如：

   She died as a direct result of that accident. 她的死是那次事故的直接结果。

   As a result of what we saw we decided to change the rules.

   鉴于我们所看到的情况，我们决定要更改规则。

Explanations

本文是一篇议论文，讲述了美国历史上的几次禁酒令的颁布情况。通过分析，可见禁酒令并不能使大家真正禁酒，所以最后国会撤销了禁酒令。

21. C) 细节题。作者在第二段倒数几句提到...people could not drink it. ... There would be no more dangers to public welfare from drunkenness and alcoholism，但文章中没有提到 There would be a rise in the cost of an alcoholic beverage。

22. D) 细节题。答案出自文章的第三段 They smuggled millions of gallons of the outlawed beverage across the Canadian and Mexican borders. Drinkers were lucky to know of an illegal bar that served Mexican or Canadian liquor.

23. B) 细节题。答案出自文章的第三段的最后两句话 Crime and drunkenness were both supposed to

decline as a result of prohibition. Instead people drank more alcohol than ever—often poisoned alcohol。这两句话说明了人们宁愿犯罪也要喝酒。

24. **D**）细节题。文章的第三段倒数第二句话 Crime and drunkenness were both supposed to decline as a result of prohibition 对这个问题解释得很清楚。

25. **A**）推断题。答案出自文章第二段的最后两句话 It was all very logical. And yet prohibition of liquor beer, and wine did not work. 和文章第三段的头两句话 Because, law or no law, millions of people still liked to drink alcohol. And they were willing to take risks to get it. 由此我们可以看出,国会撤销禁酒令是非常明智的。

Passage 4

Notes

1. ... will have tripled... (Line 4, Para. 1)

will have + p. p.(过去分词)是将来完成时,表示将来某一时刻某动作已经完成或某事情已经发生。例如:

By the end of this year I'll have saved £1,000. 到今年年底我将存有 1 000 英镑了。

He will have had his exam by 18 December. 他 12 月 18 号就将考完试了。

By this summer we'll have been here for five years. 到今年夏天我们到这里就将满 5 年了。

2. ... lies in... (Line 5, Para. 1)

lie in 意思是"在于……,由于……",原文中这句话的意思是"问题在于我们目前的能源来源是有限的"。例如:

The root of all these events lay in history. 所有这些事件的根源都在于历史。

3. in the long run (Line 8, Para. 1; Line 2, Para. 2)

此短语意思是"最终,从长远来看,毕竟,终究"。例如:

In the long run automation will be of great benefit to us all.

从长远来看,自动化必将给我们大家带来很多好处。

You will succeed in the long run. 最终你必将成功。

4. ... derives from... (Line 3, Para. 2)

此短语意思是"来源于(vi.),由……获得(vt.)"。例如:

He derives a lot of pleasure from meeting new friends. 他从结交新朋友中获得许多乐趣。

We can derive English "chauffeur" from French. 我们可以把英语中 chauffeur 一词的来源追溯到法语。

The word "DERIDE" derives from the Latin "de" ("down") and "ridere" ("to laugh").

Deride 一词来源于拉丁文的 de(下)和 ridere(笑)。

5. lock up (Line 5, Para. 3)

此短语意思是"上锁,封锁,监禁,禁闭",在这句话里意思是"存在于……"。例如:

Don't forget to lock up before you leave home. 离家之前别忘了锁门。

They locked him up in the room but he broke out of it. 他们把他锁在屋里,但他还是逃走了。

Since all his capital is locked up in land, he cannot help you.

既然他所有的资金都投资在地产上,他自然帮不了你。

6. so far (Line 6, Para. 3)

此短语意思是"到目前为止"。例如:

The weather has been hot so far this summer. 到目前为止,今年夏天的天气一直很热。

This is likely to be the biggest conference so far. 这可能是迄今为止规模最大的一次会议了。

Explanations

本文是一篇说明文,从长远的观点分析了能源的消耗,并介绍了可再生能源与不可再生能源、传统能源与非传统能源的区别。

26. **C)** 细节题。第一段最后一句提到"石油价格上涨一方面能抑制浪费,另一方面使许多国家寻找更好更持久地开发能源的办法",这句话中没有提到石油生产者经商赚钱的事,因此选 C 项。

27. **D)** 词汇题。参见第二段第四句,第二个破折号后 which depends on the earth's own heat,因此选 D 项。

28. **A)** 细节题。从字面上理解,不可更新能源当然会越用越少,第一段第五句提到总有一天可开发的能源如煤、石油、天然气会用完。文章中没有提到选项 B、C 和 D,因此选 A 项。

29. **B)** 细节题。文章第一段提到早期从事工业者以从事农业的祖先 3 倍的速度消耗能源,现代人又以早期从事工业者 3 倍的速度消耗能源。照现在的消费趋势,到本世纪末能源消耗量又是文章中提到的"目前"的 3 倍。所以现在以 27 倍于从事农业的祖先的速度消耗能源。

30. **D)** 细节题。不可再生能源如煤、石油、天然气是有限的,因此选项 A 可排除;可再生能源包括太阳能,此种能源是大量的,因此选项 B 可排除;不可更新能源与非传统能源之间是有关系的,文中就列举了石油的例子。石油以固体形式存在于沥青与页岩之中,尽管是不可再生能源,它也是非传统能源,只是因为没有开发罢了,因此选项 C 被排除。

Passage 5

Keys

31. To provide information about passports.

32. exchanging currency, using credit cards, checking into hotels, etc.

33. Passports are more important than visas.

34. Most people don't realize how important passports are.

35. In their pockets or pocketbooks.

Notes

1. ...except for a few Western nations, passports are required every country. (Line 4~5, Para. 1)

   这句话的意思是:除了几个西方国家,要想进入其他所有国家,必须要有护照。except for 意思是"除了……"。例如:

   We had a good time, except for the weather. 我们玩得很高兴,除了天公不作美。

2. To get your first passport, you must submit the application in person... (Line 3, Para. 4)

   in person 意思是"亲自"。例如:

   It is unnecessary to do everything in person. 不必事必躬亲。

3. ...along with a birth certificate and two pictures. (Line 3~4, Para. 4)

   along with sth. /sb. 意思是"和……在一起"。例如:

   He went on the journey along with his two friends. 他和他的两个朋友一起踏上旅程。

   She placed in the drawer the bank notes, along with the change and receipts.

   她把银行票据连同找回的零钱和收据一起放进抽屉。

4. ...and because they are good for five years, many people lose their passports. (Line 1~2, Para. 5)

   good 在这句话中意思是"有效的"。例如:a good contract 有效的合同

5. Travelers should keep their passports in their pockets or pocketbooks at all times... (Line 4, Para. 5)

   at all times 意思是"随时,总是"。例如:

   We must be ready at all times to fight against the terrorism. 我们必须随时准备与恐怖主义作斗争。

Unit 3

Section A   Skimming and Scanning

Directions：（略）

Passage 1

Forest Fires：A Major Disaster

1. In the decade that ended in 1950, more than 1,824,000 forest fires occurred in the United States. They occurred at the rate of about 500 per day. They burned over an average of 21,622,000 acres each year, an area larger than the state of Maine. They caused direct damage to timber and property estimated at $ 392,000,000. They took scores of human lives.

2. The great majority of forest fires, especially in the East and South, are attacked with adequate manpower and equipment, such fires are fairly easy to control. But nearly every small forest fire is possibly a big one. If a combination of dry weather and high winds occur, a forest fire may spread with explosive violence, roaring through the trees faster than a man can run, A really bad forest fire is a terrifying thing. It will destroy nearly everything in its path.

3. That was what happened when the Peshtigo fire in Wisconsin in 1847 wiped out whole settlements and killed 1,500; when the great Idaho fires of 1910 wiped out several million acres of virgin timber in a few days. It happened when the Tillamook fire in Oregon in 1933 killed as much timber as was cut in the entire United States the preceding year. It happened in Maine in 1947 when forest fires destroyed more than 800 homes. It can happen again. Given the right combination of weather and fuels, big and destructive forest fires are still possible in many parts of the world.

4. A surface fire, consuming the dry leaves, some trees, and shrubs and bushes on the forest floor, may not kill many of the larger trees, but it kill seedlings and small trees. Most fires start as surface fires but may develop into other types.

5. Sometimes fires burn deep below the surface in the thick layer of decayed leaves or needles, or in such soils that have become dry. Giving off very little smoke between surface outbreaks, such "good fires" may burn days or weeks before being discovered, and it is difficult to know when they may safely be declared out. Ground fires are common in northern forest regions. These fires usually kill most of the trees in their way, for although they burn slowly they produce great heat beneath the surface.

6. It is usually the "crown fire", or combined surface and crown fire, that causes the greatest timber and property damage, and loss of human life. Such a fire is usually the start of a surface fire jumping across open fields or large rivers. Crown fires occur mostly in *coniferous* （针叶树的） forests, for the green leaves of hard woods are not easily get on fire. These fires may, however, run through forests of mixed hardwoods and conifers. Usually they create showers of flying *embers*

（燃灰）which set fires far in advance. Crown fires may kill all the trees over wide area; they may destroy farm homes and villages.

7. Losses of merchantable timber and property are direct, and readily apparent. Forest fires, however, cause many damages not so easily recognized. Fire may kill the tiny young trees in a forest and to destroy the mature timber crop of 20, 50, or 100 years hence. Fire may alter the character of a forest. As a result of fire, for example, a forest in which valuable pines or spruces grew may in time become mostly a poor growth of inferior species. Repeated fires have turned many millions of acres of forest land in the United States into unproductive wasteland.

8. Even a small, smoky surface fire may leave fire scars on the trunks of trees, where wood diseases may enter. Fire-weakened trees may be attacked by insects, or more easily felled by the wind.

9. Storm runoff is greatly accelerated when fires burn the vegetation and surface plants on steep slopes. A flood that caused $347,000 worth of damage in Salt Lake City in 1945 came directly from a 600-acre burned area on the grass-and-bush-covered hills north of the city. The Montrose, California, flood of 1934, that caused $5 million damage and took 34 lives, came from a watershed technicians found ample evidence would have been held back until after the flood peaks had passed and damage would have been less if the plant and forest cover in the upland watersheds had not been destroyed, mainly by forest fires.

10. Fires have weakened the ability of watersheds in many parts of the United States to absorb rainfall and hold back runoff. Along with unwise land clearing and other watershed abuses, fire is responsible for a vast amount of flood damage, for worse problems of water supply, and for the *sediment*（沉淀物）in reservoirs, stream channels, and harbors with millions of tons of sand or earth carried away from the land.

11. Forest fires kill many game animals and birds. Wood ashes washed into streams after a fire sometimes kill larger numbers of fish. Destruction of the vegetation along stream-banks may cause water temperatures to rise and make the stream unfit for certain fish. Sedimentation from fire-damaged watersheds has ruined many good fishing streams.

12. Many railroad lines, high ways, and telephones and telegraph lines pass through forest areas, and fires can therefore break up business communications and railroad and truck transportation.

13. Losses such as these, and many other indirect losses caused by forest fires, are not easily measured in dollars. But they represent a huge waste on the resources and manpower of the nation. To the losses caused by fires must be added the cost of controlling them, to keep the damages from mounting to an even greater total.

14. Unquestionably, fires raging through the forest rank with floods, earthquake, and tornadoes as major *calamities.*（灾祸）

1. In winter when the weather is dry, forest fire tends to occur more seriously.

2. Of the three kinds of forest fires, the least dangerous is the surface fire.

3. Even a small, smoky fire may injure trees in that it may cause the trees to be infected with certain diseases.

4. The heat that is produced by ground fires can benefit plants.

5. Fires can be harmful even to the fish in the streams in that they destroy the cooling shade along the banks of the stream.

6. The fires change the course of the streams.

7. The article tells us how forest fires can be controlled.

8. Forest fires can turn vast areas of forest land into _____.

9. The fire that causes the greatest damage is _____.

10. Forest fires may cause great damage to timber and property, and even the _____ of human lives.

Section B Discourse Vocabulary Test

Directions：（略）

Passage 2

Eye contact is a nonverbal ___11___ that helps the speaker "sell" his or her ideas to an audience. Besides its persuasive powers, eye contact helps hold listeners' interest. A ___12___ speaker must ___13___ eye contact with an audience. To have good *rapport* (关系) with listeners, a speaker should maintain direct eye contact for at least 75 percent of the time. Some speakers focus exclusively in their notes. Others gaze over the heads of their listeners. Both are likely to lose ___14___ 's interest and esteem. People who maintain eye contact while speaking, whether from a *podium* (演讲台) or from across the table, are "regarded not only as exceptionally well-disposed by their target but also as more believable and earnest".

To show the *potency* (作用，效力) of eye contact in daily life, we have only to consider how passers-by behave when their glances happen to meet on the street. At one ___15___ are those who smile to each other, and at the other who feel ___16___ and immediately look away. To make eye contact, it seems, is to make a certain ___17___ with someone.

Eye contact with an audience also lets a speaker know and monitor the listeners. It is, in fact, ___18___ for analyzing an audience during a speech. Visual *cues* (暗示) from the audience can ___19___ that a speech is dragging, that the speaker is dwelling on a particular point for too long, or that a particular point requires further explanation. As we have pointed out, visual ___20___ from listeners should play an important role in shaping a speech as it is delivered.

A) indicate	I) maintain
B) technique	J) principle
C) extreme	K) essential
D) successful	L) feedback
E) manufacture	M) awkward
F) audience	N) individual
G) conscious	O) link
H) subject	

Section C　Reading in Depth

Directions：（略）

Passage 3

　　Although marriage customs vary greatly from one culture to another, the importance of the institution is universally acknowledged. Infant marriage, prevalent in places such as India and Melanesia, is a result of concern for family, caste, and property alliances. Levirate, the custom by which a man might marry the wife of his deceased brother, was practiced chiefly by the ancient Hebrews, and designed to continue a family connection that was already established. Sororate, a custom which is still practiced in remote parts of the world, permits a man to marry one or more of his wife's sisters, usually if she has died or cannot have children. *Monogamy*（一夫一妻制）, the union of one man and one woman, is the *prototype*（原型，典型）of human marriage and it's the most widely accepted form, predominating also in societies in which other forms of marriage are accepted. All other forms of marriage are generally classed under *polygamy*（一夫多妻制）.

　　In most societies, marriage is established through a contractual procedure, generally with some sort of religious *sanction*（约束）. Most marriages are preceded by a betrothal period, during which various rituals, such as exchanges of gifts and visits, lead to the final wedding ceremony and make the claims of the partners public. In societies where arranged marriages still predominate, families must negotiate *dowries*（嫁妆）, future living arrangements and other important matters before marriage can be arranged.

　　Because marriage arouses apprehension as well as joy, Hindus, Buddhists, and many other communities consult *astrologers*（占星家）before and after marriages are arranged to avoid unlucky times and places. In some countries, including Ethiopia, it was long customary to place an armed guard by the bridal couple during the wedding ceremony to protect them from *demons*（魔鬼）. An exchange of rings or the joining of hands frequently represents the new bonds between the married couple, as in the United States and many other countries. Finally, the interest of the community is expressed in many ways, through feasting and dancing, the presence of witnesses, and the official sealing of marriage documents.

21. According to the passage, _____ is widespread in the whole world.
　　A) infant marriage　　　　　　　　　B) levirate
　　C) sororate　　　　　　　　　　　　D) monogamy

22. It is still a universal practice _____.
　　A) for a man to marry his sister-in-law
　　B) for newly married couples to wear disguises
　　C) for a man to marry one or more of his wife's sisters
　　D) for a couple to go through a certain contractual procedure to get married

23. If a man has four wives, the marriage belongs to _____.
　　A) polygamy　　　B) levirate　　　　C) sororate　　　D) monogamy

24. Which of the following is NOT true?
    A) The bridal couple may ask a guard to stand before their house for one year to protect them.
    B) The couple may exchange some thing before the marriage.
    C) The two families may negotiate dowries before marriage.
    D) The parents of the couple may visit each other.

25. Some couples consult astrologers before arranging their marriage because _____.
    A) they want to avoid unlucky things
    B) it's a very popular custom to observe
    C) it's part of the ceremony to follow
    D) they are told to do so

Passage 4

Adam Smith was the first person to see the importance of the division of labor and to explain part of its advantages. He gives as an example the process by which pins were made in England.

One man draws the wire, another strengthens it, a third cuts it, a fourth points it, a fifth *grinds* (研磨) it at the top to prepare it to receive the head. To make the head requires two or three distinct operations. To put it on is a separate operation, to *polish* (擦亮) the pins is another. It is even a trade by itself to put them into the paper. And the important business of making pins, in this manner, is divided into about eighteen distinct operations, which in some factories are all performed by different people, though in others the same man will sometimes perform two or three of them.

Ten men, Smith said, in this way, turned out twelve pounds of pins a day or about 4,800 pins *apiece* (就每个而论). But if all of them had worked separately and independently without division of labor, they certainly could not each of them have made twenty pins in a day and perhaps not even one.

There can be no doubt that division of labor, provided that it is not taken too far, is an efficient way of organizing work. Fewer people can make more pins. Adam Smith saw this but he also took it for granted that division of labor is in itself responsible for economic growth and development and that it accounts for the difference between expanding economies and those that stand still. But division of labor adds nothing new, it only enable people to produce more of what they already have.

26. According to the passage, Adam Smith was the first person to _____.
    A) take advantage of the division of labor
    B) introduce the division of labor into England
    C) understand the effects of the division of labor
    D) explain the causes of the division of labor

27. Adam Smith saw that the division of labor _____.
    A) enabled each worker to make pins more quickly and more cheaply
    B) increased the possible output per worker
    C) increased the number of people employed in factories
    D) improved the quality of pins produced

28. Adam Smith mentioned the number 4,800 in order to _____.

    A) show the advantages of the division of labor

    B) show the advantages of the old craft system

    C) emphasize how powerful the individual workers were

    D) emphasize the importance of the increased production

29. According to the writer, Adam Smith's mistake was believing that division of labor _____.

    A) was an efficient way of organizing work

    B) was an important development in methods of production

    C) inevitably led to economic development

    D) increased the production of existing goods

30. "Provided that it is not taken too far" (Line 1, Para. 4) means _____.

    A) if work is done near the factory   B) if the factory is not too big

    C) if it is not led to extremity   D) if workers don't have to go a long way

Section D   Short Answer Questions

Directions:（略）

Passage 5

Looking ahead to 2010, it appears financially impossible to accommodate 85,000 new students in classrooms at public four-year universities. Fortunately, such an approach is not necessary. Indeed, it's not even appropriate.

Several forces are riding to the rescue. The two most important are distance learning and community and technical colleges. These will not eliminate the traditional setting where *bachelor's* (学士) and graduate degrees are earned. But they will be able to handle much of the growth in enrollments and the demand for higher education.

"When faced with a problem created by technology, apply more technology," a late journalist once asserted. Higher education seems to be an example. New learning technology is a crucial tool in teaching new technical skills.

William Richardson, president of Johns Hopkins University, praised "Western Governors' University"—a virtual *institution* (虚拟大学) that uses the Internet and other information technology to overcome the vast distances of the West and reach people with education. "Just as the extremely controlled high school of old was perfect training for an assembly-line work force, so today's college is equally appropriate as a setting for a society whose members must acquire and manage knowledge from a wide variety of sources," he notes.

Eastern Washington has long been a leader in this movement. For the past decade, Spokane's Education Service District 101 has brought the best teachers in the region to rural classrooms via satellite uplink. Washington State University (WSU) president Sam Smith reports that, during the same period, WSU managed a one-third increase in students with only 2% more faculty.

It's been done by holding growth at the main campus almost flat, setting up three branch campuses, locating learning at community colleges, and offering an extended degree program where students learn at home. In each case, technology is used to extend the "reach" of faculty.

The other cost-effective strategy is reliance on community and technical colleges. Here, Washington State has an edge. Its public two-year colleges provide the most extensive coverage in the nation. Jean Floten, president of Bellevue Community College, notes the system served 425,000 adult enrollees last year—a tenth of the state's adult population. Almost half were there for job training versus 40 percent for academic preparation.

31. According to the author, to enroll more students, universities have to do many things except to _____.
    _____ _____ _____ _____
    _____ _____ _____ _____

32. What are the two most important forces "riding to the rescue" according to the second paragraph?
    _____ _____ _____ _____
    _____ _____ _____ _____

33. According to the passage, what is new learning technology referred to?
    _____ _____ _____ _____
    _____ _____ _____ _____

34. According to paragraph 4, in order to cope with the new problem, what should we do?
    _____ _____ _____ _____
    _____ _____ _____ _____

35. Which aspect of education is mainly discussed in the text?
    _____ _____ _____ _____
    _____ _____ _____ _____

Notes and Explanations

Passage 1

Explanations

1. [NG] 第二段第三句提到 If a combination of dry weather and high winds occur, a forest fire may spread with explosive violence, roaring through the trees faster than a man can run. 如果天气干燥,风势很大,森林大火会急剧蔓延,呼啸着掠过树木,速度超过人跑的速度。但没有提及本题中的命题,所以答案为 Not Given。

2. [Y] 通过快速浏览文章便可得知本文描述了森林火灾的三种类型、各自的特点以及所产生的危害。所以答案为 Yes。

3. [Y] 第八段第一句提到"甚至火势微弱的火灾可在树干上留下疤痕,疾病就从这些疤痕处入侵"。所以答案为 Yes。

4. [N] 第五段最后两句提到 Ground fires are common in northern forest regions. These fires usually kill most of the trees in their way, for although they burn slowly they produce great heat beneath the surface. 地表火在北部林区很常见。这些火情通常会使火道上的大多数树木死亡,因为尽管它们燃烧很慢,却从地表下面产生大量的热量。所以答案为 No。

5. [Y] 从第十一段第三句 Destruction of the vegetation along stream-banks may cause water temperatures to rise and make the stream unfit for certain fish. 得知小溪岸边植被的破坏可使溪水温度升高,使某些鱼类不适合在小溪里生存。所以答案为 Yes。

6. [NG] 第十一段描述森林火灾对猎物、鸟类及鱼类的危害和影响,但没有提及本题中的命题,所以答案为 Not Given。

7. [N] 通过快速浏览文章(skim)便可得知本文只描述了森林火灾的三种类型、各自的特点以及所产生的危害和影响,并没有讲如何控制森林火灾。所以答案为 No。

8. 从第七段最后一句提到 Repeated fires have turned many millions of acres of forest land in the United States into unproductive wasteland. 可以得出答案为 **unproductive wasteland**。

9. 快速浏览文章便可得知本文描述了森林火灾的三种类型各自的特点以及所产生的危害。从而得出答案为 **the crown fire**。

10. 第一段提到 They caused direct damage to timber and property estimated at $392,000,000. They took scores of human lives. 从而得出答案为 **loss**。

Passage 2

Notes

1. ... focus exclusively in their notes. (Line 4~5, Para. 1)
   这句话的意思是"有的演讲者只盯着自己的演讲稿看",exclusively 是副词,意思是"只,仅仅,专门"。例如:
   This room is for women exclusively. 这个房间只供妇女使用。
   The article was written exclusively for *Newsweek*. 这篇文章是专门为《新闻周刊》撰写的。
   He is exclusively employed on repairing cars. 他受雇专门修理汽车。

2. ... are regarded as... (Line 7, Para. 1)
   regard... as... 意思是"认为,把……当作"。例如:
   I regard him as my brother. 我把他当作我的兄弟。

I regard him as stupid. 我认为他是傻瓜。

She regarded him as being without principles. 她认为他是没有原则的人。

3. ...happen to...（Line 2，Para. 2）

happen 后接不定式，意思是"碰巧，恰巧"。例如：

I happen to know that linguist. 我正好认识那位语言学家。

I happened to look in that direction and caught him in the act of doing it.

他正做那事的时候，我恰巧朝那个方向看。

4. ...the speaker is dwelling on...（Line 3，Para. 3）

dwell on 意思是"老是想着……；详述，强调；凝视"等。在原文中意思是"演讲者在某一点上过于强调"。过去式、过去分词是 dwelt。例如：

It is no use dwelling on the past. 老是想着过去是没有用的。

He didn't dwell on the details of the matter. 他没有详述事情的细节。

The principal dwelt on traffic safety in his talk. 校长在讲话中强调了交通安全。

Explanations

11. [B] 语法规则要求此处应填一个单数名词作表语。根据上下文的意思，"目光交流/接触是一种非言语的（交际）方法"。technique 意思是"手段，方法"。

12. [D] 语法规则要求此处应填一个形容词作定语修饰名词 speaker。根据前一句话的意思判断本句的意思是"一个成功的发言人必须要和听众保持目光交流"。successful 意思是"成功的"，符合句意。

13. [I] 语法规则要求情态动词 should 后应该填一个动词原形。根据上下文判断此处的意思是"发言人应该至少有百分之七十五的（发言）时间和听众保持直接的目光交流。"maintain 意思是"保持"，符合句意。

14. [F] 语法规则要求此处应填一个表示人的名词作定语。选项中只有 F 项是表示人的名词。此文从开篇就一直强调发言人和听众之间目光交流的重要性。文章第一段开头的几句都出现了 audience 一词，因此不难判断此处应是 audience。这句话的意思是"两者都会使听众失去（对发言人的）兴趣和尊重"。

15. [C] 语法规则要求此处应填一个单数名词与介词 at 搭配使用。这里作者举了街头路人的目光凑巧碰在一起时发生的两种情况。作者使用了一对介词短语"At one...，and at the other..."。可以判断 extreme 符合句意。extreme 意思是"一端，极端"。

16. [M] 语法规则要求此处应填一个形容词作系动词 feel 的表语。根据下文路人的表现是"马上把目光移开了"可以判断 awkward 符合句意。awkward 意思是"尴尬的，不好意思的"。

17. [O] 语法规则要求此处应填一个单数名词构成 make ＋ 名词 ＋ with 的结构。此句的意思是"和别人的目光接触似乎使人和别人有了某种联系"，因此 link 符合句意。make link with 意思是"和……产生联系"。

18. [K] 语法规则要求此处应填一个形容词构成 It is ＋ 形容词 for sb./sth. 的结构。根据上下文的意思可以推断出本句的意思是"目光交流在发言（过程）中是分析听众的必要手段"，因此可以判断 essential 符合句意。essential 意思是"基本的，必需的"。

19. [A] 语法规则要求情态动词 can 后应该填一个动词原形。根据所填词汇的宾语从句判断 indicate 符合句意。indicate 意思是"表明，显示、暗示"。

20. [L] 语法规则要求此处应填一个名词作主语。根据上下文的意思，此处的意思应该是"听众的目光反馈"，因此 feedback 符合句意。feedback 意思是"反馈"。

Passage 3

Notes

1. ... prevalent in places... (Line 2，Para. 1)

prevalent 意思是"普遍，流行，盛行"。例如：

Colds are very prevalent in winter. 感冒流行于冬季。

Smog is more prevalent in urban centers. 烟雾在市中心更为普遍。

2. lead to (Line 3，Para. 2)

此短语意思是"导致，引起……后果"。例如：

A bad cold can lead to pneumonia. 重感冒可能会导致肺炎。

These evening courses will lead to an academic degree. 这些夜校课程读完就有可能得到学位。

3. ... make the claims of... (Line 4，Para. 2)

此短语意思是"宣称，宣布，声称"。例如：

He made the claims that he had been there. 他声称他到过那里。

Don't make claims to know what you don't know. 不要不懂还非声称自己都懂。

He made no claims to sound scholarship. 他并不自认为自己有多大学问。

4. as well as (Line 1，Para. 3)

此短语意思是"也，和"，as well as 前、后常常连接并列结构，表示并列关系。例如：

On Sundays，his landlady provided dinner as well as breakfast.

每个星期天，他的女房东除早饭外还供应他正餐。

Hiking is good exercise as well as fun. 徒步旅行很有趣，也是很好的锻炼。

In theory as well as in practice，the idea is unsound. 这个主意在理论上和实践中都站不住脚。

5. ... it was long customary to place... (Line 3，Para. 3)

it is / was customary to do sth. 意思是"……是合乎习俗的，习惯上应做……"。例如：

It is customary to exchange gifts at Christmas. 圣诞节时人们互赠礼物是一种习俗。

During the Spring Festival it is customary for Chinese people to eat dumpling.

在春节期间中国人吃饺子是一种习俗。

Explanations

本文是一篇说明文，介绍了古今世界各地的不同的婚俗风情。读者从本文的说明中对此话题可略知一二。

21. **D）**细节题。答案参见第一段后半部分。一夫一妻制是比较普遍的。选项 A、B、C 谈到的三种类型只在某些地区而不是在全世界盛行。

22. **D）**细节题。参见第二段第一句。选项 A 不对，从第一段可知，这只是古希伯来人的婚俗；选项 B 不对，从第三段可知，这只是在某些国家流行，如：埃塞俄比亚。选项 C 不对，参见第一段，这只是存在于边远地区的婚俗。

23. **A）**细节题。答案参见第一段最后一句，意思是除了前面提到的是一夫一妻制，后面所讲的其他形式一般属于一夫多妻制。

24. **A）**细节题。根据第二段所述，夫妇婚前要交换信物、谈论嫁妆、双方家长互访，因此选项 B、C、D 都正确。选项 A 不对是因为根据第三段，新婚当天可能有警卫守护，但不是一年，所以答案选 A 项。

25. **A）**细节题。参见第三段第一句话，这句话的意思是"结婚既让人高兴也让人忧愁"，所以有人婚前、婚后求助于占星术，为的是躲过不吉利的时间和地点。

Passage 4

Notes

1. ... division of labor... (Line 1，Para. 1)

此短语意思是"劳动分工"。与此相似的结构例如：division of the profits 利润的分配，division of responsibility 责任的分担。

2. ..., which in some factories are all performed by different people... (Line 4~5，Para. 2)

这里的 which 引导的是一个非限定性定语从句，指代的是前面的 eighteen distinct operations。

3. turn out (Line 1，Para. 3)

这里 turn out 意思相当于 produce，表示"生产，产出"。例如：

The factory can turn out 100 cars a day. 这家工厂每天生产 100 辆汽车。

4. ... twelve pounds of pins a day... (Line 1，Para. 3)

这里的 pound 是重量单位，100 pounds 等于 45.36 千克，所以这里的 twelve pounds 大概等与 5.4 千克。所以原文中讲：史密斯说，按这种方式，10 个人每天能生产出 12 磅的大头针，大概每个人平均一天做 4 800 个。

5. There can be no doubt that ... (Line 1，Para. 4)

doubt 在这里作名词，要注意 doubt 的用法。如果 doubt 前面是否定的，其同位语从句用 that 引导。作动词用时，肯定句里其宾语从句用 whether 或 if 引导，用 that 引导时意思是"恐怕不会……"。否定句里其宾语从句用 that 引导。例如：

There is no doubt that he is guilty. 毫无疑问他一定有罪。

There is no doubt that he will come. 毫无疑问他一定会来。

I doubt whether he will come. 我怀疑他是否会来。

I doubt that he will come. 我恐怕他不会来。

I don't doubt that he will come. 毫无疑问他会来。

6. ..., provided that it is not taken too far, ... (Line 1，Para. 4)

provided that（也作 provided），意思是"假如，倘若"。例如：

I will go，provided that you go too. 如果你去的话，我就去。

Provided that there is no opposition, we shall hold the meeting here.

假如没有异议的话，我们就在此举行会议。

7. ... took it for granted that... (Line 3，Para. 4)

原形为 take it for granted that...，意思是"认为……理所当然"，其结构为 take something/someone for granted。例如：

I take it for granted that we will win. 我理所当然地认为我们会赢。

I take it for granted that we should build the new roads. 我认为我们修新路是理所当然的。

8. ... is responsible for... (Line 3，Para. 4)

be responsible for 表示"对……负责任"。例如：

Who is responsible for breaking the mirror? 镜子是谁打破的？（谁对此负责？）

9. ... account for... (Line 4，Para. 4)

account for 意思是"解释，说明"。例如：

He could not account for his foolish mistake. 他无法解释他犯的愚蠢错误。

Explanations

著名的经济学家 Adam Smith 的劳动力分工学说至今还在经济领域内被广泛使用，如流水化生产线、专业化大生产等。本文夹叙夹议,先介绍了这一理论是如何出现的,它的具体内容是什么,然后对其进行评述,最后指出 Adam Smith 本人认识上的错误。

26. **C)** 细节题。根据在第一段。选择项中将 see the importance of 换成了 understand the effects of。

27. **A)** 细节题。文章中并没有谈及 division of labor 与 B、C、D 各项的关系,第三段的具体的数字对比和第四段的 is an efficient way of organizing 为此选择提供了依据。

28. **A)** 细节题。答案在第三段。"每天生产 4 800 个、20 个和甚至一个也没有"三个数字形成鲜明的对比,旨在说明劳动力分工的巨大优势。

29. **C)** 态度题,是对作者观点、态度的提问。答案在第四段,作者用 take it for granted 来暗示 Adam Smith 的错误。应注意作者用词中隐含的观点和态度。

30. **C)** 词汇题。too far 等于 extreme。

Passage 5

Keys

31. enlarge their campuses
32. Distance learning and community and technical colleges.
33. The Internet and other information technology used in education.
34. Provide knowledge through diverse means.
35. Cost-effective strategies.

Notes

1. Looking ahead to 2010, it appears... appropriate. (Para. 1)
   这段话的意思是:展望 2010 年,在公立四年制大学里扩建能容下 85 000 个新生的校舍在资金上是不可能的。幸运的是,这样的办法也是不必要的。事实上,它甚至是不合适的。

2. Several forces are riding to the rescue. (Line 1, Para. 2)
   这句话的意思是:有几种力量起了补救作用。rescue 在这里是名词,意思是"补救,营救,抢救"。例如:
   Our car couldn't start, but a friend came to the rescue and drove us home.
   我们的车无法启动,一位朋友开车赶来把我们送回了家。
   When memory fails, he has his notes to come to his rescue. 记忆力不管用时,他有笔记可以救急。

3. When faced with a problem created by technology, apply more technology... (Line 1, Para. 3)
   这句话的意思是:当面对由技术引发的问题时,应该应用更多的技术。

4. New learning technology is a crucial tool in teaching new technical skills. (Line 2~3, Para. 3)
   这句话的意思是:新的学习方法在教授新的技术性的技能时是一个关键的工具。(根据第四段的介绍,我们可知道这种 New learning technology 指的是互联网和其他信息技术)。

5. It's been done by holding growth... almost flat, setting up three... home. (Line 1~3, Para. 6)
   flat 在这句话中是形容词,作 growth 的宾补语,意思是"平稳的,无变化的"。这句话的意思是:保持主校区的学生数量基本不变,建立三个分校,使学习集中于社区大学,并向学生提供能在家学习的各种各样的学位课程计划,这些措施使 WSU 的学生人数增长了 1/3,而教师只增加了 2%。

Section A   Skimming and Scanning

Directions：（略）

Passage 1

Family Sociology

The basic family structures

The structure of the family, and the needs that the family fulfills vary from society to society. The nuclear family—two adults and their children—is the main family unit in most western societies. In others, especially in Asian societies, it is a subordinate part of an extended family unit, which also consists of grandparents and other relatives. A third type of family unit, which is becoming more prevalent, is the single-parent family, in which children live with an unmarried, divorced, or widowed mother or father.

History and evolution of the family unit

The family unit began primarily as an economic unit; men hunted, while women gathered and prepared food and tended children. Infanticide and *expulsion*（驱逐）of the *infirm*（体弱，虚弱）who could not work were common. Later, with the advent of Christianity, marriage and childbearing became central concerns in religious teaching. However, after the Reformation, which began in the 1500s, the purely religious nature of family ties was partly abandoned in favor of civil bonds. Today, most western nations now recognize the family relationship as primarily a civil matter rather than a religious one.

The modern family

1. The modern family differs from earlier traditional forms, primarily in its functions, composition, and life cycle and in the roles of husbands and wives. Many of the functions that were once performed by or within the traditional family unit are now performed by or within community institutions, e. g., economic production (work), education, and recreation. In the modern family, members now work in different occupations and in locations away from the home. Education is provided by the state or by private groups. Organized recreational activities often take place outside the home. The family is still responsible for the socialization of children. Even in this capacity, however, the influence of peers and of the mass media has assumed a larger role.

2. Family composition in industrial societies has also changed dramatically. The average number of children born to a woman in the United States, for example, fell from 7. 0 in 1800 to 2. 0 by the early 1990s. Consequently, the number of years separating the births of the youngest and the oldest children has declined. This has occurred in conjunction with increased longevity. In earlier times, marriage normally dissolved through the death of a spouse before the youngest child

left home. Today husbands and wives potentially have about as many years together after the children leave home as before.

3. During the 20th century, extended family households declined in prevalence. This change is associated particularly with increased residential mobility and with diminished financial responsibility of children for aging parents, as pensions from jobs and government-sponsored benefits for retired people became more common.

4. By the 1970s, the prototypical nuclear family had yielded somewhat to modified structure including the one-parent family, the stepfamily, and the childless family. One-parent families in the past were usually the result of the death of a spouse. Now, however, most one-parent families are the result of divorce, although some are created when unmarried mothers bear children. In 1991, more than one out of four children lived with only one parent, usually the mother. Most one-parent families, however, eventually became two-parent families through remarriage.

5. A stepfamily is created by a new marriage of a single parent. It may consist of a parent and children and a childless spouse, a parent and children and a spouse whose children live elsewhere, or two joined one-parent families. In a stepfamily, problems in relations between non-biological parents and children may generate tension; the difficulties can be especially great in the marriage of single parents when the children of both parents live with them as *siblings*(兄弟,姐妹).

6. Childless families may be increasingly the result of deliberate choice and the availability of birth control. For many years, the proportion of couples that were childless declined steadily as venereal and other diseases that cause *infertility*（不能生育）were conquered. In the 1970s, however, the changes in the status of women reversed this trend. Couples often elect to have no children or to postpone having them until their careers are well established. Since the 1960s, several variations on the family unit have emerged. More unmarried couples are living together, before or instead of marrying. Some elderly couples, most often widowed, are finding it more economically practical to cohabit without marrying.

World trends

1. All industrial nations are experiencing family trends similar to those found in the United States. The problem of unwed mothers—especially very young ones and those who are unable to support themselves—and their children is an international one, although improved methods of birth control and legalized abortion have slowed the trend somewhat. Divorce is increasing even where religious and legal *impediment*（阻碍）to it is strongest.

2. Unchecked population growth in developing nations threatens the family system. The number of surviving children in a family has rapidly increased as infectious diseases, famine, and other causes of child mortality have been reduced. Because families often cannot support so many children, the reduction in infant mortality has posed a challenge to the nuclear family and to the resources of developing nations.

1. Due to changes in function, the modern family is weaker than earlier traditional forms.

2. Some elderly couples prefer living together without marriage because it is more practical.

3. Peer influence and mass media have assumed a larger role in the socialization of children.

4. During the 20th century, extended family households became more common.

5. Presently, most western countries view the family relationship as essentially a civil matter.

大学英语4级阅读与简答（新题型）

6. The family unit first began as a product of religious teaching.

7. Divorce is slowly decreasing, especially where religious and legal impediment are strongest.

8. Childless families may be increasingly the result of deliberate choice and the availability of _____.

9. Unchecked population growth in developing nations threatens the _____.

10. The main family unit in most western societies is the _____.

Section B   Discourse Vocabulary Test

Directions：（略）

Passage 2

Most students have little __11__ experience. The interview should hold little terror. If you are still __12__, help is at hand. Your Careers Service will arrange practice interviews and firms often advertise for mock interviewees and will pay you for the __13__.

So you are about to have your first interview with the company of your dreams—how do you make a good __14__? First, take care about your __15__ appearance. Interviewers will realize that you cannot __16__ expensive, quality clothes but they will not be impressed if your clothes are untidy and your hair is dirty. No one is too poor to afford soap. Second, don't forget the importance of body language. Make sure your entrance is *deliberate*（从容的）, and shake the interviewer's hand __17__, but don't crush it. Maintain eye contact, smile and try to relax.

Initially, you will probably be asked open-ended questions relating to your application form: interests, courses and so on. This is your cue to begin talking, so don't answer in monosyllables and clam up. Make sure you answer the questions and don't be afraid of stopping to think before speaking. At the end of the interview you will probably be asked if you have any questions. It is advisable to have a list of them prepared, as intelligent *queries*（疑问）convey interest.

Second round interviews can last anything between a few hours and two days spent at a hotel. Here your communication, leadership and __18__ skills will be assessed. You might have to give a presentation, chair a meeting and __19__ various topics. In addition, companies often ask you to sit tests, some of which examine your mathematical and problem-solving skills, while others test your personal and communication skills.

These interviews are intended to give you the __20__ to shine. Try to relax and enjoy it, you will not be at your best if you let your nerves take over. Just remember, if you are not accepted, then you probably would not have enjoyed the work anyway. Just try to make the most of the interviews.

A）meeting	I）maintain
B）interview	J）social
C）experience	K）privilege
D）nervous	L）personal
E）individual	M）firmly
F）impression	N）opportunity
G）conscious	O）discuss
H）afford	

Section C　Reading in Depth

Directions：（略）

Passage 3

There are all kinds of reasons for wanting to be your own boss. Some people like the idea of there being no one in authority over them, telling them what to do, saying their work is not up to standard, turning down their ideas, or insisting on methods that seem pointless. Others are attracted by the thought of deciding their own hours, or days, of work.

Running your own business gives you the status of being self-employed, perhaps also of being a Company Director. There is the general feeling of independence, and that your income and perhaps even your way of life is in your own hands. Some are attracted to the idea of starting a small enterprise and making it grow much as a gardener tends his *plot*（小块土地）and makes a number of plants come to maturity, each in turn creating further growth.

If you are your own boss, say some people, work is much more pleasant. You can get someone else to do the less interesting jobs and you are not *bogged*（使陷入困境）down in annoying details. Work becomes easier too, because you can get someone else to do the more difficult tasks.

Many others want to set up a little business of their own to occupy their spare time, and as a pleasant way of earning extra money from work they like doing.

These are just a few of the reasons commonly given. Some have good sense behind them; others are based on completely false ideas. Most contain some element of truth which gets *magnified*（放大，扩大）out of all proportion, and seized upon without it being borne in mind that there are other points to consider as well.

As with so much else in life, running an enterprise of your own *entails*（使蒙受，需要）disadvantages as well as advantages. It is surprising how rarely people stop to consider in real details just what the drawbacks are, yet this is an essential first step for anyone thinking about whether it is even practicable for him to be his own boss.

21. Which of the following is NOT the reason some people want to be their own boss, as mentioned in the selection?

A）There are always people telling them what to do and how to do.

B）Their good suggestions are frequently declined by their bosses.

C) They get extremely low pay, and have slim chance to be promoted.

D) There is no chance for them to decide how long to work.

22. Which of the following statements can't be inferred from the selection ?

A) Some people have much spare time after work and they want to kill them.

B) Some people are having the work they don't like best.

C) Being your own boss might offer you a new life.

D) If you want to start your own business, you can only start it small.

23. The author suggests in this selection that _____.

A) being your own boss is far better than to be employed

B) the reasons commonly given by those who want to be their own bosses are pretty sound

C) the wish to run their own enterprises is seriously considered and thus reasonable

D) the very first thing to start your own business is to evaluate the possibility and probability

24. The word "drawbacks" (Line 3, Para. 6) means _____.

    A) real reasons   B) advantages

    C) small enterprises   D) disadvantages

25. According to the contextual plot of the selection, the next paragraphs to come after this selection will most probably talk about _____.

A) the making of your own bosses

B) the reasons for misleading illusions and disadvantages of being your own bosses

C) how to start your own small enterprises

D) what to do in the first step and the other steps

Passage 4

The character of the English is essentially middle-class. There is a sound historical reason for this, for, since the end of the eighteenth century, the middle classes have been the dominant forces in our community. They gained wealth by the Industrial Revolution, political power by the reform bill of 1832; they are connected with the rise and organization of the British Empire; they are responsible for the literature of the 19th century. *Solidity*（稳健）, caution, *integrity*（正直）, efficiency, lack of imagination, *hypocrisy*（伪善）, these qualities characterize the middle classes in every country, but in England they are national characteristics also, because only in England have the middle classes been in power for one hundred and fifty years. Napoleon, in his rude way, called us "a nation of shopkeeper". We prefer to call ourselves "a great commercial nation"—it sounds more dignified but the two phrases amount to the same. Of course there are other classes: there is an *aristocracy*（贵族）, there are the poor. But it is on the middle-classes that the eye of the critic rests—just as it rests on the poor in Russia and on the aristocracy in Japan. Russia is symbolized by the peasant or by the factory worker; Japan by the *samurai*（武士阶层）; the national figure of England is Mr. Bull with his top hat, his comfortable clothes, his *substantial*（结实的）stomach, and his substantial balance at the bank.

Just as the heart of England is the middle classes, so the heart of the middle classes is the public school system. This extraordinary institution is local. It does not even exist all over the British Isles. It is unknown in Ireland, almost unknown in Scotland, and though it may inspire other great institutions, it remains unique, because it was created by the Anglo-Saxon middle classes, and can flourish only where they flourish. How perfectly it expresses their character—far better, for instance, than does the university, into which social and spiritual complexities have already entered. With its boarding houses, its *compulsory*（强制的）games, its system of *prefects*（学校的级长）and *fagging*（做苦工）, its insistence on good form and on group spirit, it produces a type whose weight is out of all proportion to its numbers.

26. In calling the British "a nation of shopkeeper", Napoleon _____.
    A) held them in contempt   B) was making an objective observation
    C) was praising them to the sky   D) did not understand them at all

27. The two phrases—"a nation of shopkeeper" and "great commercial nation" are _____.
    A) dramatically opposite in meaning   B) exaggerations
    C) fair criticisms of British society   D) not dissimilar in nature

28. The writer thinks that the Japanese society is better represented by its _____.
    A) middle class   B) aristocracy
    C) poor people   D) working class

29. Which of the following statements about the British universities is true?
    A) It is not as good as the middle class in explaining the English national character.
    B) It is basically middle class in character.
    C) It fails to give a clear picture of the English national character.
    D) It is also central in representing the English national character.

30. We can infer from the passage that _____.
    A) the British prefer to wear top hat better than any other people
    B) only Britain has middle-class people
    C) there are more middle-class people in British Ivory Tower than in society
    D) most of the British belong to the middle classes

Section D   Short Answer Questions

Directions：（略）

Passage 5

As the traditional Christmas and New Year hangover clears, finding a job might be the last thing on your mind. With Britain in the throws of an economic depression, it is important to start job hunting now, rather than to wait until July when the majority of the best jobs will have been snapped up. You may think that concentrating purely on finals would be best, but unless you are considering an *academic career*（学术生涯）, then you could find yourself with a good degree but no job comes in October. So, drag yourself away from your books and come along to the Milk Round.

The Spring Milk Round takes place between January and March each year. College careers services arrange graduate recruitment programs whereby companies visit universities and *polytechnics*（理工学院）in order to hunt down graduate trainees. The Milk Round is considered to be an effective and convenient method of recruitment.

Students are put in contact with companies who have expressed a firm interest in employing graduates from their institution or maybe from just one course. Interviews are held on campus, saving a lot of traveling, which is particularly relevant at this stage in your academic career.

To participate in the Milk Round, it is advisable to first find out from your career service which companies are coming to your institution. You will then be able to gather information about individual companies and jobs on offer. Application forms can be obtained from your career service.

It is important to prepare thoroughly in advance. David Warrell from Ford Motor Company advises students: "Sort out what you want to do and why you want to do it. Once this has been decided, find out which companies will give what you want." The next step is to find out as much as you can about the company.

When filling out application forms, remember that recruitment managers will be looking for someone who can prove that they have the appropriate skills for the job—these will not necessarily be academic. You must be able to demonstrate that you are suited to the career you have applied for.

31. According to the passage, what is probably the best timing for job-hunting in Britain?

_____ _____ _____

_____ _____ _____

32. According to the context, what does "recruitment" in the second paragraph probably mean?

_____ _____ _____

_____ _____ _____

33. What is beyond the responsibilities of the college career service?

_____ _____ _____

_____ _____ _____

34. When does the Milk Round usually take place according to the passage?

_____ _____ _____

_____ _____ _____

35. What is crucial while filling in the application form?

_____ _____ _____

_____ _____ _____

Notes and Explanations

Passage 1

Explanations

1. 〔NG〕The modern family 部分第一段第一句提到 The modern family differs from earlier traditional forms, primarily in its functions, composition, and life cycle and in the roles of husbands and wives. 现代家庭与早期传统形式不同,主要表现在家庭功能、构成、生命周期及夫妻在家庭的作用这几个方面。但没有提及本题中的命题,所以答案为 Not Given。

2. 〔Y〕The modern family 部分第六段最后一句提到 Some elderly couples, most often widowed, are finding it more economically practical to cohabit without marrying. 一些丧偶的老年朋友发现与伴侣同居而不结婚更加经济。所以答案为 Yes。

3. 〔Y〕The modern family 部分第一段最后一句提到 Even in this capacity, however, the influence of peers and of the mass media has assumed a larger role. 甚至在这方面,来自同龄人和媒体的影响起着更大的作用。所以答案为 Yes。

4. 〔N〕The modern family 部分第三段第一句提到 During the 20th century, extended family households declined in prevalence. 在 20 世纪大家庭减少,不再像以往那么普遍。所以答案为 No。

5. 〔Y〕History and evolution of the family unit 部分最后一句提到 Today, most western nations now recognize the family relationship as primarily a civil matter rather than a religious one. 当今大多数西方国家把家庭关系认作是民事而不是宗教方面的事情。所以答案为 Yes。

6. 〔N〕History and evolution of the family unit 部分第一句提到 The family unit began primarily as an economic unit; men hunted, while women gathered and prepared food and tended children. Later, with the advent of Christianity, marriage and childbearing became central concerns in religious teaching. 家庭单位首先以经济单位的形式开始;男人狩猎,女人采集、准备食物和照顾小孩儿。后来,随着基督教的出现,婚姻和生育成为宗教教育中主要关注的内容。所以答案为 No。

7. 〔N〕World trends 部分第一段最后一句提到 Divorce is increasing even where religious and legal impediment to it is strongest. 甚至在宗教和法律约束极强的地方,离婚的人也越来越多。所以答案为 No。

8. 通过"childless families"、"deliberate choice"、"availability"等词,在文章倒数第三段中找到原文"Childless families may be increasingly the result of deliberate choice and the availability of birth control."从中得到答案为 **birth control**。

9. 从最后一段第一句 Unchecked population growth in developing nations threatens the family system. 得到答案为 **family system**。

10. 从第一段第二句 The nuclear family—two adults and their children—is the main family unit in most western societies. 得到答案为 **nuclear family**。

Passage 2

Notes

1. ... at hand... (Line 2, Para. 1)
此短语意思是"near in time or place",是一种正式的表达方式,可译为"在手边,在附近,供使用"。例如:
the evidence at hand 手中的证据
When she writes, she always keeps a dictionary at hand. 她写作时总放本词典在手边。

新世纪英语丛书

Your question is not related to the matter at hand. 你的问题与目前审议的事无关。

▷另外,这个词组还表示"即将到来的"。例如:

A major international crisis is at hand. 一个严重的国际危机即将到来。

The great day is at hand. 重要的日子要到了。

2. ...clam up... (Line 3, Para. 3)

此短语意思是"保持沉默,拒不开口"。例如:

clam up on somebody 拒绝和某人谈话

She clammed up whenever I mentioned her husband. 每当我谈到她丈夫,她就不说话了。

3. ...ask you to sit tests... (Line 3~4, Para. 4)

sit 在这里是及物动词,表示"参加考试,应试",常用于英式英语,作不及物动词时意义相同,但后常接介词 for。例如:

He's sitting his bar finals. 他正参加律师资格考试的复试。

to sit one's A-levels 参加高级课程的考试

sit for university entrance 参加大学入学考试

4. ...are intended to... (Line 1, Para. 5)

intend 在这里是及物动词,表示"计划,打算,想要",通常后面接续为 intend to do 或 intend doing 或 intend that... 例如:

I've made a mistake though I didn't intend to. 虽然不是有意,但我还是犯了错。

I intend to go (going). 我打算(想)要去。

I intend them to go. 我的意思是要他们去。

I intend that they should go. 我的意思是他们应该去。

5. ...be at your best... (Line 2, Para. 5)

此短语意思是"在最佳状态中"。此句型可为:be at one's/its best。另外还有"在全盛时期"的意思。例如:

I am never at my best in the early morning. 我一向无法在大清早处于最佳状态。

Come and see Hangzhou at its best. 请在杭州景色最美的时候来游览。

the days when Spain was at her best 西班牙的国力全盛时期

6. ...take over... (Line 2, Para. 5)

take over 原意是"接管,接收",在这里意思是"取而代之,取得领导地位"。这句话的意思是"如果你让紧张的神经占了上风,你就不会处于最佳状态"。例如:

Movies are going down and television is taking over in the West.

在西方,电影业每况愈下,电视业正在取而代之。

Microfilms might even take over the libraries one day. 微缩胶卷有朝一日可能会取代图书馆。

7. ...make the most of... (Line 3, Para. 5)

此短语意思是"尽量利用,获得最大利益",亦作"make the best of..."。例如:

He doesn't do well because he doesn't make the most of his ability. 他做得不好是因为没尽全力。

Tom studies hard. He wants to make the most of his chance to learn.

汤姆学习很努力。他要充分利用学习机会。

Explanations

11. [B] 语法规则要求此处应填一个单数名词作定语。根据下文的提示此处应是 interview。interview 意思是"面试"。

12. [D] 语法规则要求此处应填一个形容词作表语。根据前一句的意思可以判断此句的意思是"如果你还感到忐忑不安,随时可以求助"。nervous 意思是"紧张的",符合句意。

13. [K] 语法规则要求此处应填一个名词作介词 for 的宾语。此句提到职业服务公司会安排面试练习、常常做广告招收模拟求职者并为此支付工资。privilege 意思是"特有的机会,难得的事",符合句意。

14. [F] 语法规则要求此处应填一个单数名词做宾语。由于上下文一直说的是如何在自己(心目中)理想的公司做好面试,因此此处应填 impression。make a good impression 表示"留下好印象",符合句意。

15. [L] 语法规则要求此处应填一个形容词作定语修饰 appearance。下一句的意思是"面试者知道你可能买不起昂贵的、质量很好的衣服,但如果你衣着不整,头发很脏,他们不会留下什么好印象"。由此可以判断这里应填 personal。personal appearance 意思是"个人外表"。

16. [H] 语法规则要求情态动词 can 后应填一个动词原形。选项 H、I、O 是动词原形。afford 常与 can 或 cannot 连用,表示"买得/不起",符合句意。

17. [M] 语法规则要求此处应填一个副词作状语修饰 shake the interviewer's hand。只有选项 M 是副词。firmly 意思是"坚定地,有力地",可以修饰握手的状态,符合句意。

18. [J] 语法规则要求此处应填一个形容词作定语修饰 skills。根据上下文的意思,在宾馆考察的应该是"交际能力、领导才能和社交能力",因此 social 符合句意。social skills 意思是"社交能力"。

19. [O] 语法规则要求此处应填一个动词原形与 give 和 chair 并列,并与宾语 topics 搭配。能和 topics 搭配的动词是 discuss。discuss 意思是"讨论"。

20. [N] 语法规则要求此处应填一个名词作 give 的直接宾语。此句的意思是"这些面试目的在于给你闪光的机会"。opportunity 的意思是"机会",符合句意。

Passage 3

Notes

1. ... up to standard... (Line 2～3, Para. 1)

up to 在这里意思是"接近于,达到,赶得上……"。例如:

He could not live up to their expectations. 他无法达到他们的期望。

If your goods are up to sample, they should sell readily in the market.

如果你们的货物和样品的质量一样好,那么它们在市场上应该有很好的销路。

The team did not play up to its best today. 那个球队今天发挥得不是最好。

2. ... turning down their ideas... (Line 3, Para. 1)

turn down 意思是"拒绝某人或其请求、意见、求婚等"。例如:

I was turned down for the job. 我想做这份工作而遭拒绝。

to turn down a job 拒绝一份工作

turn down sb.'s offer of help 拒绝某人提供的帮助

She turned him down; she won't marry him. 她拒绝了他的求婚,她不肯嫁给他。

3. ... or insisting on methods that... (Line 3, Para. 1)

insist on 意思是"坚持"。例如:

He insists on his innocence. 他坚持他是无罪的。

Parents always insist on the importance of being honest. 父母总是强调诚实的重要性。

He insists on driving her home. 他坚持要用车送她回家。

4. ... each in turn creating further growth. (Line 5, Para. 2)

in turn 在此处意思是"转而,反过来"。例如:

Theory is based on practice and in turn serves practice. 理论以实践为基础,反过来又为实践服务。

5. ... others are based on completely false ideas. (Line 1～2, Para. 5)

be based on 意思是"以……为基础",主动语态为 base...on/upon sth. 例如:

They always base their conclusions on facts. 他们总是把结论建立在事实的基础上。

His evidence is based upon hearsay. 他是以道听途说为依据。

6. ...out of all proportion... （Line 3, Para. 5）

out of (all) proportion 意思是"对……来说过分、离谱"。例如：

The fine was out of all proportion to the seriousness of the offence.

罚金对于所犯过失的严重性来说，实在是太重了。

His story was exaggerated out of proportion. 他的故事夸张得太离谱了。

Don't get things out of proportion. 别把事情弄得太过分了。

He knew that the situation was all out of proportion now, but he couldn't help it.

他知道局面已不可收拾，但也爱莫能助。

7. ...and seized upon without it being borne in mind that... （Line 3, Para. 5）

and 后面省略了 gets，与上句的 gets magnified 并列，gets 是系动词，相当于 is。seize upon 的意思是"利用"，seize 后面常与 on 或 upon 连用。例如：

seize upon an occasion 利用一次机会

He would seize upon any excuse to justify himself. 他会利用任何借口来为自己辩解。

Explanations

　　我们每个人都会碰到这样的事情：在工作中总会有人对你指手画脚，自己的好主意总是被否定，老板或上司总会让你做一些你不喜欢并且毫无意义的事情。那么你可曾想过自己当老板？如果想过，为什么有这样的想法？自己当老板是否真的像大家想的那样只有快乐没有忧愁呢？在这篇文章中作者回答了这些问题，对自己当老板的好处进行了剖析。这是一篇精彩的议论文。

21. **C)** 细节题。这个问题问的是哪个选项不是人们想自己当老板的原因。在第一段所说的各种原因中，分别提到了 telling them what to do 和 insisting on methods that seem pointless；turning down their ideas；以及 deciding their own hours, or days, of work；而选项 C 中所述的"低报酬，提升机会渺茫"在本文中未提到。

22. **D)** 推断题。根据第四段 to occupy their spare time, work they like doing，我们可以推断出选项 D 是正确答案。根据第二段 and perhaps even your way of life 可排除选项 C。尽管文中有 starting a small enterprise, a little business 之说，却并没有肯定只能这样做，所以得不出选项 D 中的结论。

23. **D)** 细节题。第三段并非暗示，而是明确指出自己做老板的种种好处，所以选项 A 被排除。第五段说以上给出的理由有些很有意义，另一些是基于错误的想法，考虑不周而离谱，所以选项 B 和 C 可被排除。在第六段中，作者用这样一句话 yet this is an essential first step for anyone thinking about whether it is even practicable for him to be his own boss 来建议大家如果想自己当老板，要先考虑是否可行。因此选 D 项。

24. **D)** 词汇题。在文中作者指出，那些想自己当老板的人往往看到的只是事情的好处和优点，而未考虑其负面的因素。在第六段使用 drawbacks 一词来替换 disadvantages，以避免重复。

25. **B)** 推断题。这个问题问的是根据文章结构，如果接下来讨论，那么该论述什么内容。通过对全文结构脉络的分析，我们可以清楚地看到：第一段到第四段讲为什么人们想自己当老板。第五段分析有这种想法的人考虑得不全面，第六段指出应该考虑周全，不仅考虑优点，还应考虑其负面因素。那么接下来要谈的应该是分析产生这种片面考虑问题的原因并详细分析各种弊端了。因此选项 B 最合理。

Passage 4

Notes

1. . . . they are responsible for the literature of the 19th century. (Line 4~5, Para. 1)

be responsible for 在这里表示"对……有功的"。例如：

He is responsible for the unity of his nation. 他对民族团结有功。

2. . . . because only in England have the middle classes been in. . . (Line 7~8, Para. 1)

这句话里 only 放在句首，修饰状语，句子是采用倒装句语序，并且使用部分倒装。例如：

Only then could the work be seriously begun. 只有那时这工作才能真正开始。

Only in this way can our honor be saved. 只有这样才能保住我们的荣誉。

3. . . . two phrases amount to the same. (Line 10, Para. 1)

amount to 意思是"（在意义、效果、价值等方面）等同，接近"。to 是介词。原文中意思是"这两个短语意思基本相同"。例如：

This amounts to doing the whole thing over again. 这等于要把整个事情重做一遍。

Her standards amounted to perfection. 她的标准等于要求事事完美。

4. But it is on the middle-classes that the eye of the critic rests. . . (Line 11~12, Para. 1)

这是一个强调句式，在 it is. . . that. . . 中，强调了状语 on the middle classes；rest on 在这句话中意思是"停留在，集中在，落在……上"。这句话的意思是：可是中产阶级才是批评家们集中关注的对象。例如：

His eyes rested on the new sofa. 他的目光落在那张新沙发上。

Their argument rests on who should pay for that damage.

他们的争议主要集中于谁应该为那个损失做出赔偿。

5. Russia is symbolized by. . . (Line 12~13, Para. 1)

symbolize 意思是"以……为象征，以……为标志"。例如：

A dove symbolizes peace. 鸽子象征着和平。

A nation is symbolized by its national flag. 国家是以其国旗为象征的。

Explanations

作为一个民族，英国人都具有哪些特性呢？与其他民族相比，为什么他们会有这些特性呢？本文通过对比英国人和其他民族，深刻地阐述了中产阶级对英国社会、教育及民族特性的影响。通过作者深入浅出地剖析，使我们对英国及英国人有了更进一步的了解。本文属于议论文。

26. A）推断题。在第一段中间部分提到，拿破仑将英国蔑称为"小店主的国家"，此评价虽然粗鲁，但却道出了英国社会的阶级特征——中产阶级即小资产阶级占主导地位。接下来的一句话讲英国人自称自己的国家是"伟大的商业国家"。所以拿破仑的说法显然带有一种蔑视的意味，作者用插入语 in his rude way 来提示我们，因此选 A 项。hold sth. in contempt 意思是"蔑视，瞧不起"。

27. D）词汇题。参见第一题的解释。两种说法在实质上没什么区别，只是口吻、民族感情不同而已。

28. B）细节题。答案参见第一段末尾。长期以来，日本大和民族一直实行帝制，武士阶级作为贵族的一分子主导着其民族特性。因此选 B 项。

29. A）细节题。答案参见第二段后半部分。中产阶级思想是英国社会的核心，也是公立学校的核心。但由于大学还包含了更复杂的社会和精神层面的因素，其民族特性就不那么明显了。

30. D）推断题。从第一段第一句和最后一句、第二段第一句看出，尽管英国还有其他阶级，但中产阶级是主要力量 dominant force，代表民族形象 national figure，是英国的核心。从拿破仑的话和英国人对自身的评价也可得出此结论。

Passage 5

Keys

31. From Christmas to early spring.
32. To get students in the company as new employees.
33. To pass Milk Round.
34. In the late winter and early spring.
35. To show what you are able to do.

Notes

1. With Britain in the throws of... rather than to wait until snapped up. (Line 2~4, Para. 1)

这句话的意思是：因为英国正处在经济萧条时期，所以圣诞节过后就开始找工作很重要，而不是一直等到七月，那时大部分好工作将被抢没了。when 引导的限定性定语从句修饰 July，will have been snapped up 是将来完成时的被动语态，表示"将来某一时间将要被完成的动作"，snap up 意思是"抓住，拿光，抢购一空"。例如：

snap up a chance 抓住机会

Shoppers crowded into downtown stores, snapping up once-rationed consumer goods.

顾客们拥入市中心的商店，抢购曾是定量供应的消费品。

2. Students are put in contact with companies who have... course. (Line 1~2, Para. 3)

这句话的意思是：学生们被安排与一些公司联系，这些公司非常想聘用从这所学院或许只是从某一门课程毕业的学生。

3. To participate in the Milk Round, it is advisable to... institution. (Line 1~2, Para. 4)

这句话的意思是：要想参加人才招聘会，最好先从毕业分配服务处了解清楚哪些公司将会来你们学院。to participate in sth. 意思是"参加，参与"。

4. It is important to prepare thoroughly in advance. (Line 1, Para. 5)

这句话的意思是：事先做好充分准备是很重要的。in advance 意思是"事先，提前"。

5. Sort out what you want to do and why you want to do it. (Line 2, Para. 5)

这句话的意思是：想好你要做什么工作以及为什么你要做这个工作。sort out 本意是"整理，挑出"。例如：

It takes me some time to sort out my thoughts before I can start writing. 下笔之前，我得花些时间整理思路。

Sort out the washing into white and colored materials. 把要洗的东西分成白色和有色两类。

Unit 5

Section A   Skimming and Scanning

Directions：（略）

Passage 1

Lessons from the Titanic

1. From the comfort of our modern lives we tend to look back at the turn of the twentieth century as a dangerous time for sea travelers. With limited communication facilities，and shipping technology still in its infancy in the early nineteen hundreds，we consider ocean travel to have been a risky business. But to the people of the time it was one of the safest forms of transport. At the time of the Titanic's maiden voyage in 1912，there had only been four lives lost in the previous forty years on passenger ships on the North Atlantic crossing. And the Titanic was confidently proclaimed to be unsinkable. She represented the *pinnacle*（顶点）of technological advance at the time. Her builders，crew and passengers had no doubt that she was the finest ship ever built. But still she did sink on April 14，1912，taking 1,517 of her passengers and crew with her.

2. The RMS Titanic left Southampton for New York on April 10，1912. On board were some of the richest and most famous people of the time who had paid large sums of money to sail on the first voyage of the most luxurious ship in the world. Imagine her placed on her end：she was larger at 269 meters than many of the tallest buildings of the day. And with nine decks，she was as high as an eleven storey building. The Titanic carried 329 first class，285 second class and 710 third class passengers with 899 crew members，under the care of the very experienced Captain Edward J. Smith. She also carried enough food to feed a small town，including 40,000 fresh eggs，36,000 apples，111,000 1bs of fresh meat and 2,200 1bs of coffee for the five-day journey.

3. RMS Titanic was believed to be unsinkable because the *hull*（船体）was divided into sixteen watertight compartments. Even if two of these compartments flooded，the ship could still float. The ship's owners could not imagine that，in the case of an accident，the Titanic would not be able to float until she was rescued. It was largely as a result of this confidence in the ship and in the safety of ocean travel that the disaster could claim such a great loss of life.

4. In the ten hours prior to the Titanic's fatal collision with an iceberg at 11：40 pm，six warnings of icebergs in her path were received by the Titanic's wireless operators. Only one of these messages was formally posted on the bridge；the others were in various locations across the ship. If the combined information in these messages of iceberg positions had been plotted，the ice field which lay across the Titanic's path would have been apparent. Instead，the lack of formal procedures for dealing with information from a relatively new piece of technology，the wireless，meant that the danger was not known until too late. This was not the fault of the Titanic crew.

Procedures for dealing with warnings received through the wireless had not been formalized across the shipping industry at the time. The fact that the wireless operators were not even Titanic crew, but rather contracted workers from a wireless company, made their role in the ship's operation quite unclear.

5. Captain Smith's seemingly casual attitude in increasing the speed on this day to a dangerous 22 knots or 41 kilometers per hour, can then be partly explained by his ignorance of what lay ahead. But this only partly accounts for his actions, since the spring weather in Greenland was known to cause huge chunks of ice to break off from the *glaciers* (冰川). Captain Smith knew that these icebergs would float southward and had already acknowledged this danger by taking a more southerly route than at other times of the year. So why was the Titanic traveling at high speed when he knew, if not of the specific risk, at least of the general risk of icebergs in her path? As with the lack of coordination of the wireless messages, it was simply standard operating procedure at the time. Captain Smith was following the practices accepted on the North Atlantic, Practices which had coincided with forty years of safe travel. He believed, wrongly as we now know, that the ship could turn or stop in time if an iceberg was sighted by the lookouts.

6. There were around two and a half hours between the time the Titanic collided into the iceberg and its final submersion. In this time 705 people were loaded into the twenty lifeboats. There were 473 empty seats available on lifeboats while over 1,500 people drowned. These figures raise two important issues. Firstly, Why there were not enough lifeboats to seat every passenger and crew member on board. And secondly, why the lifeboats were not full.

7. The Titanic had sixteen lifeboats and four collapsible boats which could carry just over half the number of people on board her maiden voyage and only a third of the Titanic's total capacity. Regulations for the number of lifeboats required were based on outdated British Board of Trade regulations written in 1894 for ships a quarter of the Titanic's size, and had never been revised. Under these requirements, the Titanic was only obliged to carry enough lifeboats to seat 962 people. At design meetings in 1910, the shipyard's managing director, Alexander Carlisle, had proposed that forty eight lifeboats be installed on the Titanic, but the idea had been quickly rejected as too expensive. Discussion then turned to the ship's *décor* (陈设,布景), and as Carlisle later described the incident: "we spent two hours discussing carpet for the first class cabins and fifteen minutes discussing lifeboats."

8. The belief that the Titanic was unsinkable was so strong that passengers and crew alike clung to the belief even as she was actually sinking. This attitude was not helped by Captain Smith, who had not acquainted his senior officers with the full situation. For the first hour after the collision, the majority of people aboard the Titanic, including senior crew, were not aware that she would sink, that there were insufficient lifeboats or that the nearest ship responding to the Titanic's distress calls would arrive two hours after she was on the bottom of the ocean. As a result, the officers in charge of loading the boats received a very half-hearted response to their early calls for women and children to board the lifeboats. People felt that they would be safer, and certainly warmer, aboard the Titanic than perched in a little boat in the North Atlantic Ocean. Not realizing the *magnitude* (程度) of the *impending* (即将来临的) disaster themselves, the officers allowed several boats to be lowered only half full.

9. Procedures again were at fault, as an additional reason for the officers' reluctance to lower the lifeboats at full capacity was that they feared the lifeboats would buckle under the weight of 65 people. They had not been informed that the lifeboats had been fully tested prior to departure. Such procedures as assigning passengers and crew to lifeboats and lifeboat loading drills were simply not part of the standard operation of ships nor were they included in crew training at this time.

10. As the Titanic sank, another ship, believed to have been the Californian, was seen motionless less than twenty miles away. The ship failed to respond to the Titanic's eight distress rockets. Although the officers of the Californian tried to signal the Titanic with their flashing Morse lamp, they did not wake up their radio operator to listen for a distress call. At this time, communication at sea through wireless was new and the benefits not well appreciated, so the wireless on ships was often not operated around the clock. In the case of the Californian, the wireless operator slept unaware while 1,500 Titanic passengers and crew drowned only a few miles away.

11. After the Titanic sank, investigations were held in both Washington and London. In the end, both inquiries decided that no one could be blamed for the sinking. However, they did address the fundamental safety issues which had contributed to the enormous loss of life. As a result, international agreements were drawn up to improve safety procedures at sea. The new regulations covered 24 hour wireless operation, crew training, proper lifeboats drills, lifeboat capacity for all on board and the creation of an international ice patrol.

1. The enormous loss of life on the Titanic was primarily caused by inadequate equipment, training and procedures.

2. Nobody had thought of installing enough lifeboats to accommodate all the passengers and crew in the event of an emergency.

3. Captain Smith didn't inform his officers of the true situation because he didn't want to cause a panic.

4. The lifeboats would have buckled if they had been fully loaded.

5. After the Titanic sank, the lifeboats which were not full should have returned to rescue as many people from the water as they could.

6. The Captain of the Californian could have brought his ship to the rescue if he had realized that the Titanic was sinking.

7. The sinking of the Titanic prompted an *overhaul* (细密检查) of standard operating procedures which made ocean travel much safer.

8. In 1910, the proposal that forty eight lifeboats be installed on the Titanic met quick objection because of high _____.

9. On Titanic, there were not enough lifeboats to seat every passenger and crew member and the officers agreed to lower the boats only _____.

10. International agreements were put forward to improve _____ at sea.

Section B Discourse Vocabulary Test

大学英语 4 级阅读与简答（新题型）

新世纪英语丛书

Directions：（略）

Passage 2

What happens to someone living in a different culture? The experience can be like riding a *roller coaster* （云霄飞车）. People can ___11___ both *elation* （兴高采烈） and depression in a very short period. They *vacillate* （犹豫不定） between loving and hating the new country. Often, but not always, there is an initial period when ___12___ feel enthusiasm and excitement. The cultural differences they experience at first can be fascinating rather than troubling. At first, there is often a high level of interest and ___13___ because the newcomers are eager to become ___14___ with the new culture. Life seems exciting, novel, *exotic* （异国的）, and stimulating. However, after a while, the newness and strangeness of being in another country can ___15___ emotions in a ___16___ way. Many people in a new culture do not realize that their problems, feelings, and mood changes are common.

When people are immersed in a new culture, "culture shock" is a ___17___ response. They should anticipate that they will probably feel bewildered and disoriented at times. This is normal when people neither speak the language nor understand the details of daily behavior. The newcomer may be unsure, for example, about when to shake hands or when to embrace. In some cases, it may even be difficult to know when a person means "yes" or "no".

After all, people can become overwhelmed when ___18___ of everything that was once familiar. The adult trying to become familiar with another culture may feel like a child. Stress, *fatigue* （疲劳） and tension are common ___19___ of culture shock. In most cases, however, at least a partial adjustment takes place. This adjustment (even if incomplete) allows the newcomer to function and sometimes succeed in the new country. ___20___, there are many examples of successful adjustment among refugees, immigrants, and others who have settled in the United States. Many have made very notable contributions to American society.

A) positive	I) motivation
B) negative	J) principle
C) newcomers	K) influence
D) appearances	L) familiar
E) Certainly	M) keen
F) deprived	N) symptoms
G) conscious	O) typical
H) experience	

Section C   Reading in Depth

Directions：（略）

Passage 3

More and more, the operations of our businesses, governments, and financial institutions are controlled by information that exists only inside computer memories. Anyone clever enough to *modify*（修改，更改）this information for his own purposes can *reap*（收获）substantial reward. Even worse, a number of people who have done this and been caught at it have managed to get away without punishment.

It's easy for computer crimes to go undetected if no one checks up on what the computer is doing. But even if the crime is detected, the criminal may walk away not only unpunished but with a glowing recommendation from his former employers.

Of course, we have no statistics on crimes that go undetected. But it's disturbing to note how many of the crimes we do know about were detected by accident, not by systematic inspections or other security procedures. The computer criminals who have been caught may have been the victims of uncommonly bad luck.

For example, a certain *keypunch*（打孔机）operator complained of having to stay overtime to punch extra cards. Investigation revealed that the extra cards she was being asked to punch were for dishonest transactions. In another case, dissatisfied employees of the thief tipped off the company that was being robbed.

Unlike other lawbreakers, who must leave the country, commit suicide, or go to jail, computer criminals sometimes escape punishment, demanding not only that they not be charged but that they be given good recommendations and perhaps other benefits. All too often, their demands have been met.

Why? Because company executives are afraid of the bad publicity that would result if the public found out that their computer had been misused. They hesitate at the thought of a criminal boasting in open court of how he *juggled*（欺骗）the most *confidential*（机密的）records right under the noses of the company's executives, accountants and security staff. And so another computer criminal departs with just the recommendations he needs to continue his crimes elsewhere.

21. It can be concluded from the passage that _____.
    A) it is still impossible to detect computer crimes today
    B) people commit computer crimes at the request of their company
    C) computer criminals escape punishment because they can't be detected
    D) computer crimes are the most serious problem in the operation of financial institutions

22. It is implied in the third paragraph that _____.
    A) most computer criminals who are caught blame their bad luck
    B) the rapid increase of computer crimes is a troublesome problem
    C) most computer criminals are smart enough to cover up their crimes
    D) many more computer crimes go undetected than are discovered

23. Which of the following is mentioned in the passage?

 A) A strict law against computer crimes must be enforced.

 B) Companies usually hesitate to uncover computer crimes to protect their reputation.

 C) Companies will guard against computer crimes to protect their reputation.

 D) Companies need to impose restrictions on confidential information.

24. What may happen to computer criminals once they are caught?

 A) With a bad reputation they can hardly find another job.

 B) They may walk away and easily find another job.

 C) They will be denied access to confidential records.

 D) They must leave the country or go to jail.

25. The passage is mainly about _____.

 A) why computer criminals are often able to escape punishment

 B) why computer crimes are difficult to detect by systematic inspections

 C) how computer criminals manage to get good recommendations from their former employers

 D) why computer crimes can't be eliminated

Passage 4

   It is a *sheer* (绝对的) chance that the moon, because of its size and *orbit* (轨道), neatly covers the sun during a total eclipse like a plug in a drain. For scientists, it is nothing less than heaven-sent luck. The sun is so bright that most early solar research had to be done during eclipses. Space stations and the *coronagraph* (日冕仪), a telescope that produces an artificial eclipse, have changed that. But still, researchers from Russia, Brazil, Japan, the U. S. and other countries *fanned out* (扇形展开) across Asia last week for a few fleeting seconds of quality observation time useful for a range of disciplines.

   Many were trying to determine the exact diameter of the sun, which remains unknown. On Borneo, Professor John Parkinson of University College London wanted an exact timing of the eclipse's duration, which, together with information about the size and distance of the moon, could determine the figure for the sun's size. Indian scientists took a different approach: they sought a *precise* (精确的) measurement of the shadow cast on the earth. Three Indian air force planes were deployed with cameramen and scientists to examine the shadow. Separately, a pair of MiG—25 *fighters* (米格-25战斗机) were fitted with equipment to photograph the sun corona and the dust rings around it. They traveled along the path of the eclipse at 3,000 km/h, gaining several precious minutes of observation denied researchers stuck on the ground.

   On earth, communications experts measured radio waves in an attempt to determine the exact change in the density of the atmosphere at different stages of the blackout. Botanists measured changes in plants as the light dimmed and temperatures dropped. Zoologists watched for unusual behavior among birds, fish and *orangutans* (猩猩). In ancient times eclipses *dispersed* (驱散) armies in the midst of fierce battles; today they attract fresh troops carrying not swords or guns but cameras and computers.

26. The first sentence of the text means that it's rare that _____.

A) the moon shelters the sun partially

B) the moon blocks the sun completely

C) the earth shadows the moon neatly

D) the earth just covers the moon

27. Which of the following happened during the eclipse?

A) Professor Parkinson took pictures of the sun and its dust rings.

B) British scientists went near to the moon's shadow and studied it.

C) Indian fighters flew at high speed to see how long the eclipse lasted.

D) Indian scientists measured the shadow of eclipse cast on the earth.

28. The writer seems to suggest that a total eclipse is _____.

A) quite unusual

B) common in history

C) less useful than an artificial one

D) harmful to plants and animals

29. From the second paragraph we learn that _____.

A) even now we can't say for sure how large the moon is

B) it is difficult to determine how long an eclipse will last

C) the sun's size is still something to be estimated and decided

D) the moon's shadow denies researchers enough time for observation

30. According to the writer, what would ancient people possibly do during an eclipse?

A) People would rush out of their dwellings to see it.

B) People would watch for unusual behaviors of animals.

C) People would fight an even more fierce battle.

D) People would be terribly scared and flee for shelter.

Section D   Short Answer Questions

Directions：（略）

Passage 5

Nervous about meeting your father-in-laws? Worried about year-end bills? Talk about it. Share your anxiety. By voicing your fear, you can begin to clarify and understand it. Sometimes, too, a listener (especially one who has experienced the same problem) can eliminate the sense of isolation that may *compound* (混合) stress.

"Often what causes stress and tension are the things we keep inside," says J. Ross, an associate director at a psychiatric center. Ross suggests talking to someone who really listens and has your best interests at heart. But watch sudden impulses to talk. If you decide to talk about a sensitive problem, you might want to wait an hour to see whether talking still feels right. If so, go ahead. If not, what then? Write down your feelings in a letter and then throw the letter away. To relieve anxiety at 3 a. m. , get out of bed, write down the problem and say you will deal with it at 9:30 in the morning. By scheduling "worry time", Elkin says, you're deciding to deal with the problem.

When anxiety strikes, the heart races and breathing becomes shallow and rapid. But by breathing slowly and deeply, you can calm yourself almost instantly. The technique is simple. Slowly breathe in through your nose, *expending*（支出）your *abdomen*（腹部）and then your *rib*（肋骨）*cage*（骨架）. Next, release the breath through your nose, more slowly than you took it in, and silently say "Relax" or "Let go".

Once you've mastered this, you may be able to train yourself to relax on hint, says Jeffrey A. Migdow, co-author of Take a Deep Breath. Set times for yourself to breathe deeply for a minute or two throughout the day—whenever the phone rings, for example. Then, when you get home, try the deep breathing for ten minutes. After a little practice, breathing slowly and deeply during tense moments could become automatic.

31. It is implied in the passage that stress can _____.

　　_____

　　_____

32. What are the two ways mentioned to deal with stress?

　　_____

　　_____

33. What should you do if you don't feel like talking about stress to others?

　　_____

　　_____

34. According to the author, a phone call can _____.

　　_____

　　_____

35. What is the passage mainly about?

　　_____

　　_____

Notes and Explanations

Passage 1

Explanations

1. [Y] 通过快速浏览(skim)文章中便可得知本文指出泰坦尼克号海难的主要原因是船本身设备未达要求、船上人员缺乏训练及紧急救援步骤不熟练。故可得出答案为 Yes。

2. [N] 第七段第四句提到 At design meetings in 1910, the shipyard's managing director, Alexander Carlisle, had proposed that forty eight lifeboats be installed on the Titanic, but the idea had been quickly rejected as too expensive. 在 1910 年的设计会上, 船厂的管理经理 Alexander Carlisle 建议在泰坦尼克号上安装 48 条救生船, 但是这个建议很快因费用太高而被否决。所以答案为 No。

3. [NG] 第八段第一、二句提到 The belief that the Titanic was unsinkable was so strong that passengers and crew alike clung to the belief even as she was actually sinking. This attitude was not helped by Captain Smith, who had not acquainted his senior officers with the full situation. 人们坚信泰坦尼克号不会沉没, 甚至船体真正发生下沉时全体乘客及船员仍然坚持他们的想法。船长 Smith(和人们的感觉一样)没有使高级船员们熟悉整个情况。但没有提及本题中的命题, 所以答案为 Not Given。

4. [N] 第九段第一、二句提到 ... an additional reason for the officers' reluctance to lower the lifeboats at full capacity was that they feared the lifeboats would buckle under the weight of 65 people. They had not been informed that the lifeboats had been fully tested prior to departure. 官员们不愿意把满员的救生船放下去的另一原因是他们害怕救生船承受不住 65 个人的重量。他们未被告知救生船在出发之前已进行了充分测试。所以答案为 No。

5. [NG] 第八段最后一句提到 Not realizing the magnitude of the impending disaster themselves, the officers allowed several boats to be lowered only half full. 官员们自己都没意识到即将来临的灾难的危险程度, 只允许放下几条装载仅半满的救生船。但没有提及本题中的命题, 所以答案为 Not Given。

6. [Y] 通过"Californian"一词, 快速浏览(scan)第十段便可得知如果 Californian 号的船长意识到 Titanic 号要沉没了他会把船驶来进行救援。第二句提到 The ship failed to respond to the Titanic's eight distress rockets. Although the officers of the Californian tried to signal the Titanic with their flashing Morse lamp, they did not wake up their radio operator to listen for a distress call. 最后一句指出 In the case of the Californian, the wireless operator slept unaware while 1,500 Titanic passengers and crew drowned only a few miles away. Californian 号的无线操作员在熟睡, 没有对来自泰坦尼克号的 8 个求救信号做出反映, 既没意识到泰坦尼克号上的 1,500 名乘客及船员在几英里外的海域遇难。意思与题目完全是一致的。所以答案为 Yes。

7. [Y] 最后一段谈到人们对海难进行了调查。本段第三句提到 However, they did address the fundamental safety issues which had contributed to the enormous loss of life. As a result, international agreements were drawn up to improve safety procedures at sea. 避免重大海难事故须完善海上行驶安全措施。所以答案为 Yes。

8. 第七段第四句提到 At design meetings in 1910, the shipyard's managing director, Alexander Carlisle, had proposed that forty eight lifeboats be installed on the Titanic, but the idea had been quickly rejected as too expensive. 在 1910 年的设计会上, 船厂的管理经理 Alexander Carlisle 建议在泰坦尼克号上安装 48 条救生船, 但是这个建议很快因费用太高被否决。所以答案为 **expense**。

9. 第八段最后一句提到 Not realizing the magnitude of the impending disaster themselves, the officers allowed several boats to be lowered only half full. 官员们自己都没意识到即将来临的灾难的危险程度, 只允许放下几条装载仅半满的救生船。所以答案为 **half full**。

10. 最后一段第四句提到 As a result, international agreements were drawn up to improve safety procedures at sea. 结果，国际条例制定出改善海上行驶的安全措施。所以答案为 **safety procedures**。

Passage 2

Notes

1. What happens to someone... (Line 1，Para. 1)

   sth. happens to sb. 意思是"某事发生在某人身上"。例如：

   If anything happens to him，let us know. 如果他发生了什么意外，请通知我们。

   What has happened to your arm? It's all swollen. 你的手臂怎么了？肿得好厉害。

2. ... to become familiar with the new culture. (Line 6～7，Para. 1)

   become familiar with sth. 也作 be familiar with sth.，意思是"对……很熟悉；通晓……"。例如：

   I'm quite familiar with the book. 我通晓这本书。

   He is quite familiar with English. 他通晓英语。

   I'm quite familiar with his family. 我对他的家庭成员很熟悉。

3. at times (Line 2，Para. 2)

   at times 意思是"时不时地；有时"。例如：

   At times I feel that I want to leave this job. 有时我不想做这份工作。

   At times I want to commit suicide. 有时我想自杀。

4. after all (Line 1，Para. 3)

   after all 放在句首、句中或句尾，意思是"毕竟，究竟，终究"。例如：

   After all，what is it that prevents her going to the meeting? 究竟是什么使她不去参加会议呢？

   The day turned out fine after all. 最终天还是转晴了。

   This is，after all，the least important part of the problem. 这毕竟是问题中最无足轻重的部分。

5. ... may feel like a child. (Line 2，Para. 3)

   feel like 后接名词，意思是"好像就是……"；后接动名词时意思是"想做……"。例如：

   When I realized what a stupid mistake I had made，I felt like a fool.

   当我发现自己犯了一个极其愚蠢的错误时，我觉得自己就是一个大笨蛋。

   It feels like years. 感觉好像已有很多年了。

   I don't feel like taking a tour. 我不想去旅游。

6. Many have made very notable contributions to... (Line 6～7，Para. 3)

   意思是"很多人已经做出了令人瞩目的贡献"，make contribution to 表示"给……作贡献，捐献"。例如：

   You should make contribution to your homeland. 你应该为祖国作贡献。

   Every week I give a small contribution to the church. 我每星期都给教堂捐点钱。

Explanations

11. [H] 语法规则要求情态动词 can 后应填一个动词原形。选项 H、K 是动词原形。根据上文和本句话的意思可以判断 experience 符合句意。experience 作动词用，意思是"经历，体验"。

12. [C] 语法规则要求此处应填一个名词作 when 引导的定语从句的主语。谓语动词的形式要求主语是复数名词。选项 C、D、N 是复数名词。根据上下文的意思，本句话意思是"初来的人感到高兴和兴奋"。另外，后面两句中也提到了 newcomer，因此 newcomer 符合句意。

13. [I] 语法规则要求此处应填一个单数名词和 interest 并列作介词 of 的宾语。选项 I、J 是单数名词。本句话的意思是"因为初到者渴望熟悉新的文化，所以他们起初很有兴趣和动力"。motivation 意思是"动力"，符合句意。

14. [L]语法规则要求此处应填一个形容词和 with 搭配成词组作表语。能够和 with 搭配的是 familiar。词组"become familiar with..."意思是"变得熟悉……",符合句意。

15. [K]语法规则要求情态动词 can 后应填一个动词原形。选项 H、K 是动词原形。这句话的开头使用了 However,表明意思有了转折。可以根据此句前半部分的意思"经过一段时间,在另一个国家的新鲜(感)和陌生(感)"推断出后面的意思应该是"负面/消极地影响情感",因此此处填 influence。

16. [B]语法规则要求此处应填一个形容词作定语修饰 way,构成介词短语 in a...way。选项 A、B、G、L、M、O 是形容词。根据对上题的解释也可以判断 negative 符合句意。negative 意思是"负面的,消极的"。

17. [O]语法规则要求此处应填一个形容词作定语修饰 response。本句话上下文中分别用了 common,normal 等词,由此可以判断此处应填 typical。typical 意思是"典型的"。本句话的意思是"当人们浸入一种新的文化时,'文化休克'是一种典型的反应"。

18. [F]本句话的状语从句省略了主语和 be 动词。语法规则要求此处应填一个动词＋ed 形式构成被动语态。选项中只有选项 F 是该形式。be deprived of 意思是"被剥夺"。符合句意。此句用 After all 来开头,表示提醒读者以下情况是人之常情,"毕竟,当人们曾经熟悉的东西被剥夺时,人们是难以承受的"。

19. [N]语法规则要求此处应填一个复数名词作表语。选项 C、D、N 是复数名词。此句提到的"压力,疲劳和紧张"都应该是"文化休克的常见症状"。symptoms 意思是"症状,病症",符合句意。

20. [E]语法规则要求此处应填一个副词作状语修饰谓语。选项中只有选项 E 是副词。上一句提到"初到者如果适应环境就能(在社会中)有用,甚至在新的国家获得成功",因此,接下来的语气应该是非常肯定的,所以 certainly 符合句意。

Passage 3

Notes

1. ... have managed to... (Line 4, Para. 1)

manage to do sth. 意思是"设法做到……;努力完成……"。例如:

He would manage to come and talk to us if possible. 如果可能他会尽量赶来与我们谈谈。

It is heavy, but I can manage to carry it. 东西很重,但我能拿得动。

2. ... get away without punishment. (Line 4~5, Para. 1)

意思是"不受惩罚就逃脱了"。get away 意思是"逃脱,逃离"。例如:

The thief got away in the dark. 贼趁天黑逃跑了。

You should not get away from your duty. 你不应该逃避责任。

3. ... were detected by accident... (Line 2, Para. 3)

by accident 意思是"碰巧,偶然,无意中"。例如:

The gun went off by accident. 枪意外走火。

I met my former girlfriend on the street by accident the other day.

那天我碰巧在街上遇到了我从前的女朋友。

She stepped on his toe by accident. 她无意中踩了他的脚。

4. ... dissatisfied employees of the thief tipped off the company... (Line 3~4, Para. 4)

介词 of 在这里表示同位关系,连接两个名词,意思是"就是,等于……",一般不翻译。例如:

the City of New York 纽约市

the art of painting 绘画艺术

at the age of eight 在 8 岁的时候

▷词组 tip off 意思是"泄露消息"。

5. ... demanding not only that they not be charged but that they be given... (Line 2~3, Para. 5)

demand 等表示"请求,命令,建议"等的一类动词后面接 that 引导的宾语从句时,多用动词原形做宾语从句的谓语动词,是虚拟语气。这类动词主要有:suggest, demand, insist, ask, advise, propose, urge, vote, request, desire, move(提议), decreed(规定), order, recommend, require, intend(打算), petition(恳求)等。例如:

She petitioned the king that her son be pardoned. 她恳求国王宽恕她的儿子。

He ordered that the man be released. 他命令释放那个人。

I move that we accept the proposal. 我提议通过这项提案。

I advise that he go at once. 我建议他马上就去。

6. ... right under the noses of... (Line 3~4, Para. 6)

此短语意思是"就在……的鼻子底下,当着……的面",汉语常用"就在……的眼皮底下"。例如:

The book you are looking for is right under your nose. 你要找的书就在你的眼皮底下。

The action was taken right under the noses of the enemy. 行动就在敌军眼皮底下进行。

Explanations

　　本文是一篇议论文,对时下比较热门的话题——计算机犯罪进行了讨论,举例说明利用计算机犯罪的情况并分析了为什么这种罪犯不但可以不受惩罚,反而可以轻而易举地得以继续犯罪。

21. D) 推断题。根据文章第二、三段可排除选项 A 和 C;根据全文内容,选项 B 明显错误;根据文章第一段,正确答案应是 D 项。

22. D) 推断题。第三段第三句话 The computer criminals who have been caught may have been the victims of uncommonly bad luck,意思是"被抓到的罪犯都是非常罕见的运气不好的人",意即大多数罪犯都未被抓到。所以可以推断出 D 项正确。第三段未提到选项 A、B 和 C。

23. B) 判断题。根据文章最后一段可排除选项 A、C 和 D。

24. B) 细节题。根据第二段的最后一句话、第五段和第六段最后一句可知 B 项是正确答案。选项 A、C 和 D 与文章意思相反。

25. A) 主旨题。本文主要给我们举例说明利用计算机犯罪的情况并分析了这种罪犯不但可以不受惩罚,反而可以轻而易举地得以继续犯罪的原因。第一段是主题段,提出计算机罪犯可以轻而易举地逃脱惩罚;第二至第四段说明第一个原因,即计算机犯罪很难被发现;第五至第六段说明第二个原因,即为了公司的声誉,公司主管即使发现了计算机罪犯也不会惩罚他们,反而还要给他们提供推荐及其他的好处。

Passage 4

Notes

1. It is a sheer chance that..., neatly covers the sun... (Line 1~2, Para. 1)

sheer chance 意思是"偶然的机会"。sheer 是形容词,意思是"完全的,绝对的,十足的"。例如:

sheer nonsense 一派胡言

He knew the secret by sheer chance. 他发现了这个秘密纯属偶然。

He won his position by sheer ability. 他全凭能力赢得了这个职位。

2. ... it is nothing less than heaven-sent luck. (Line 2~3, Para. 1)

这句话的意思是"这简直就是上天给予的好运"。nothing less than 也作 no less than,意思是"与……同等重要,无异于;简直又是……;恰恰,正是……"。例如:

It is nothing (no) less than a scandal. 这简直就是一桩丑闻。

His words are nothing less than nonsense. 他的话简直就是胡说八道。

The plan is nothing less than subversive. 这项计划完全是颠覆性的。

3. ... were fitted with equipment to... (Line 7, Para. 2)

be fitted with 意思是"给……安装设备"。例如：

The door is fitted with a new handle. 门已经装上了新把手。

The room was fitted with bulletproof windows. 我们已经给房间安装上了防弹窗。

4. ...in an attempt to determine... （Line 1, Para. 3）

be in an attempt to do sth. 意思是"企图做……，尝试做……"。例如：

He was in an attempt to escape. 他试图逃跑。

She is in an attempt to break the world record. 她想打破这项世界记录。

5. ...in the midst of fierce battles... （Line 5, Para. 3）

in the midst of sth. 意思是"在……当中；正当……时候"，在原文中是"正当……时候"的意思。例如：

There is a spy in the midst of us. 在我们当中有一个间谍。

I could not recognize him in the midst of crowd. 在人群当中我无法认出他。

He knocked at the door in the midst of our quarreling. 正当我们吵架之时他来敲门。

Explanations

这是一篇说明文。在这篇科普文章中，作者告诉我们世界各地的科学家正在用最新的方法和设备，借助日食这一奇妙的自然现象，来对太阳的大小以及日食对动植物的影响进行研究。

26. B）细节题，也考察个别词汇。第一句原文用的是 neatly covers，与选项 B 中的 blocks completely 意思相同，都有"完全覆盖，全部遮挡"的意思。

27. D）细节题。答案参见第二段。根据第二段第三句话 Indian scientists took a different approach：they sought a precise measurement of the shadow cast on the earth. 可以知道 D 项是正确答案，印度科学家要准确测量日全食投射在地球上的阴影。

28. D）推断题。第一段第一句话明确提到选项 A 的内容，而本题使用 suggest，意思是"暗含什么意思"，所以排除选项 A；选项 B 与选项 A 意思相反，也不符合题意，明显不对；文章第三段提到植物学家和动物学家在日食发生时观察到了植物的变化和动物的异常行为，由此可推断出正确答案为 D 项。

29. C）细节题。根据第二段第一句话，太阳的直径还不为人所知，所以选 C 项。

30. D）细节题。根据第三段最后一句话 In ancient times eclipses dispersed armies in the midst of fierce battles；... 可知古代人对日食缺乏了解，因此会产生恐惧心理：日食发生时，正在激烈战斗的士兵都会四下溃散，所以选 D 项。

Passage 5

Keys

31. cause a sense of isolation

32. Talking about it or breathing slowly and deeply.

33. Persuade yourself not to think about it all the time.

34. make breath shallow and rapid

35. How to deal with stress.

Notes

1. By voicing your fear, you can begin to clarify and understand it. （Line 2, Para. 1）

这句话的意思是：说出你的担心，你就能开始明白理解它了。voice 在这句话中作及物动词，意思是"大声说出，表露出"。例如：

The chairman voiced the feeling of the meeting when he demanded more pay.

主席要求加薪之举道出了与会者的心声。

2. But watch sudden impulses to talk. (Line 3，Para. 2)

这句话的意思是：但是要注意突然想与人倾诉的愿望。

3. If you. . . wait an hour to see whether talking still feels right. (Line 3~4，Para. 2)

这句话的意思是：如果你决定谈论一个敏感的话题,也许你会想再等一个小时看看这种谈话感觉是否对劲。

4. . . . more slowly than you took it in . . . (Line 4，Para. 3)

take in 意思是"吸进……；让……进入,接纳,吸收"。例如：

get rid of the stale and take in the fresh 吐故纳新

Tankers were taking in cargoes of finished oil products. 油船正在装石油成品。

5. Once you've mastered this, you may be able to train. . . on hint. . . (Line 1，Para. 4)

这句话的意思是：一旦你掌握了这个方法,你也许就能训练自己有意识地放松。once 意思是"一旦"。例如：

Once you show any fear，he will attack you. 一旦你表现出恐惧,他就会攻击你。

Once printed，this dictionary will be very popular. 一旦出版,这本词典将会非常畅销。

Unit 6

Section A   Skimming and Scanning

Directions：（略）

Passage 1

Zoo Conservation Programs

1. One of London Zoo's recent advertisements caused me some irritation, so patently did it distort reality. Headlined without zoos you might as well tell these animals to get stuffed, it was bordered with illustrations of several endangered species and went on to *extol*（颂扬）the myth that without zoos like London Zoo these animals "will almost certainly disappear forever". With the zoo world's rather mediocre record on conservation, one might be forgiven for being slightly skeptical about such an advertisement.

2. Zoos were originally created as places of entertainment, and their suggested involvement with conservation didn't seriously arise until about 30 years ago, when the Zoological Society of London held the first formal international meeting on the subject. Eight years later, a series of world conferences took place, entitled "The Breeding of Endangered Species", and from this point onwards conservation became the zoo community's buzzword. This commitment has now been clearly defined in The World Zoo Conservation Strategy（WZCS, September 1993）, which—although an important and welcome document—does seem to be based on an unrealistic optimism about the nature of the zoo industry.

3. The WZCS estimates that there are about 10,000 zoos in the world, of which around 1,000 represent a core of quality collections capable of participating in coordinated conservation programs. This is probably the document's first failing, as I believe that 10,000 is a serious underestimate of the total number of places *masquerading*（假装, 伪装）as zoological establishments. Of course it is difficult to get accurate data but, to put the issue into perspective, I have found that, in a year of working in Eastern Europe, I discover fresh zoos on almost a weekly basis.

4. The second flaw in the reasoning of the WZCS document is the naïve faith in places in its 1,000 core zoos. One would assume that the *caliber*（能力, 才能）of these institutions would have been carefully examined, but it appears that the criterion for inclusion on this select list might merely be that the zoo is a member of a zoo federation or association. This might be a good starting point, working on the premise that members must meet certain standards, but again the facts don't support the theory. The greatly respected American Association of Zoological Parks and Aquariums（AAZPA）has had extremely *dubious*（怀疑的）members, and in the UK the Federation of Zoological Gardens of Great Britain and Ireland has occasionally had members that

have been roundly *censured* （责难，批评）in the national press. These include Robin Hill Adventure Park on the Isle of Wight，which many considered the most notorious collection of animals in the country. This establishment，which for years was protected by the Isle's local council （which viewed it as a tourist *amenity* （休闲去处），was finally closed down following a damning report by a *veterinary* （兽医的）inspector appointed under the terms of the Zoo Licensing Act 1981. As it was always a collection of dubious *repute* （名声，名誉），one is obliged to reflect upon the standards that the Zoo Federation sets when granting membership. The situation is even worse in developing countries where little money is available for redevelopment and it is hard to see a way of incorporating collections into the overall scheme of the WZCS.

5. Even assuming that the WZCS's 1,000 core zoos are all of a high standard—complete with scientific staff and research facilities，trained and dedicated keepers，accommodation that permits normal or natural behavior，and a policy of cooperating fully with one another—what might be the potential for conservation? Colin Tudge，author of Last Animals at the Zoo （Oxford University Press，1992），argues that "if the world's zoos worked together in cooperative breeding programs，then even without further expansion they could save around 2,000 species of endangered land *vertebrates*(脊椎动物)". This seems an extremely optimistic proposition from a man who must be aware of the failings and weaknesses of the zoo industry—the man who，when a member of the council of London Zoo，had to persuade the zoo to devote more of its activities to conservation. Moreover，where are the facts to support such optimism?

6. Today approximately 16 species might be said to have been "saved" by captive breeding programs，although a number of these can hardly be looked upon as resounding successes. Beyond that，about a further 20 species are being seriously considered for zoo conservation programs. Given that the international conference at London Zoo was held 30 years ago，this is pretty slow progress，and a long way off Tudge's target of 2,000.

1. London Zoo's advertisement are dishonest.

2. Zoos made an insignificant contribution to conservation up until 30 years ago.

3. The WZCS document is not known in Eastern Europe.

4. Zoos in the WZCS select list were carefully inspected.

5. No one knew how the animals were being treated at Robin Hill Adventure Park.

6. Colin Tudge was dissatisfied with the treatment of animals at London Zoo.

7. The number of successful zoo conservation programs is unsatisfactory.

8. The objective of the WZCS document is to identify zoos suitable for _____ practice.

9. One of the factors that led the writer to doubt the value of the WZCS document is the _____ of money in developing countries.

10. Given that the international conference at London Zoo was held 30 years ago, the present zoo conservation programs is pretty _____.

Section B　Discourse Vocabulary Test

Directions：（略）

Passage 2

Heat loss by sweating depends on the fact that when a liquid *evaporates*（蒸发）, it __11__ an enormous quantity of heat from its surroundings. Therefore, when 1 ml. of sweat evaporates, a great deal of heat is absorbed from the __12__ of the body in contact with it. This heat transfer occurs even if the __13__ is hotter than the body.

Two factors __14__ the rate of evaporation of sweat, and therefore the effectiveness of sweating as a method of cooling the body. The first is the __15__ of movement of air surrounding the body. The second is the amount of water vapor in the air that surrounds the body.

When air moves over the surface of water, the amount of evaporation is greatly increased. For this reason, sweat evaporates very __16__ on windy days, and the rate of heat loss by sweating is much more than on a still day. This accounts for the fact that hot still days are much less __17__ than hot windy days. In contrast, the sweat evaporates very rapidly on hot windy days, and cools the body quickly and __18__ .

The second __19__ is the amount of *water vapor*（水蒸气）in the air—the *humidity*（湿度）. When air is carrying the maximum amount of water vapor that it can hold, it is said to be 100% saturated with water vapor. The __20__ humidity of the air is said to be 100%. Under these conditions the air cannot carry any water, so no water can evaporate. When the relative humidity is high, therefore, sweat cannot evaporate. Instead, it forms large drops and runs off your skin without cooling you.

When the air is very dry and carries no water at all, the relative humidity is said to be 0%. It is obvious that under these conditions, evaporation will be much more rapid. Therefore, sweating will be much more effective as a method of losing heat from the body. On a hot dry day, sweat evaporates as soon as it is formed, and you feel reasonably cool even though the temperature of your environment is very high.

A) absorbs	I) maintain
B) rapidly	J) relative
C) reason	K) comfortable
D) surface	L) effectively
E) affect	M) environment
F) efficiently	N) individual
G) conscious	O) factor
H) amount	

Section C Reading in Depth

Directions：（略）

Passage 3

There is a new type of small advertisement becoming increasingly common in newspaper classified columns. It is sometimes placed among "situations *vacant*（空缺的）", although it does not offer anyone a job, and sometimes it appears among "situations wanted", although it is not placed by someone looking for a job either. What it does is to offer help in applying for a job.

"Contact us before writing your application", or "Make use of our long experience in preparing your curriculum *vitae*（履历表）or job history", is how it is usually expressed. The growth and *apparent*（显然的）success of such a specialized service is, of course, a reflection of the current high levels of unemployment. It is also an indication of the growing importance of the curriculum vitae (or job history), with the suggestion that it may now qualify as an art form in its own right.

There was a time when job seekers simply wrote letters of application. "Just put down your name, address, age and whether you have passed any exams", was about the average level of advice offered to young people applying for their first jobs when I left school. The letter was really just for openers, it was explained, everything else could and should be saved for the interview. And in those days of full employment the technique worked. The letter proved that you could write and were available for work. Your eager face and intelligent replies did the rest.

Later, as you moved up the ladder, something slightly more sophisticated was called for. The advice then was to put something in the letter which would distinguish you from the rest. It might be the aggressive approach. "Your search is over. I am the person you are looking for", was a widely used trick that occasionally succeeded. Or it might be some special feature specially designed for the job in view.

There is no doubt, however, that it is the increasing number of applications with university education at all the process of engaging staff that has led to the greater importance of the curriculum vitae.

21. The new type of advertisement which is appearing in newspaper columns _____.
    A) informs job hunters of the opportunities available
    B) promises useful advice to those looking for employment
    C) divides available jobs into various types
    D) informs employers that people are available for work

22. Nowadays a demand for this specialized type of service has been created because _____.
    A) there is a lack of jobs available for artistic people
    B) there are so many top-level jobs available
    C) there are so many people out of work
    D) the job history is considered to be a work of art

23. In the past it was expected that first-job hunters would _____.
    A) write an initial letter giving their life history

B) pass some exams before applying for a job

C) have no qualifications other than being able to read and write

D) keep the detailed information until they obtain interview

24. Later, as one went on to apply for more important jobs, one was advised to include in the letter _____.

A) something that would attract attention to one's application

B) a personal opinion about the organization one was trying to join

C) something that would offend the person reading it

D) a lie that one would easily get away with telling

25. The job history has become such an important document because _____.

A) there has been an increase in the number of jobs advertised

B) there has been an increase in the number of applicants with degrees

C) jobs are becoming much more complicated nowadays

D) the other processes of applying for jobs are more complicated

Passage 4

During past ages dramatic changes have taken place inside the earth. And changes are still going on today. They show themselves in the occurrence of earthquakes, in the outbursts of volcanoes, and in the uplift of mountain ranges.

In outward appearance, the earth is a nearly *spherical* （球形的） ball with a *radius* （半径） of 6,350 kilometers. Internally the earth consists of two parts, a core and a *mantle* （地幔,地核与地壳之间的部分,主要由氧和硅构成,占地球体积的 80%）. The core is made of rather dense stuff. The materials at the center of the earth is at least thirteen times as heavy as ordinary water, while at the outer parts of the core the material is about ten times as heavy as ordinary water.

The mantle possesses a thin outer *crust* （地壳） that is *exceptional* （异常的） in being composed of a particularly light kind of rock. Over the continents of the world this *crustal* （硬壳,外壳） rock is about thirty-five kilometers thick, while over the oceans it is at most only two or three kilometers thick. Below the crustal layer comes a different, dense rock, probably of a basic *silicate* （硅酸盐） variety. Indeed apart from the thin outer crust, the rocks of the whole mantle are of a basic silicate variety right down to the *junction* （结合处） with the core, at a depth below the surface of about 2,900 kilometers. As we go inwards to greater and greater depths, the density of rocks of the earth's mantle increases. The density immediately below the outer crust is about 3.3 times that of water. We may compare this with a density of 4.0 at a depth of 500 kilometers, 4.5 at 1,000 kilometers, about 5.0 at 2,000 kilometers, and with about 5.6 at the surface of the core, which is at a depth of 2,900 kilometers.

The last of these values is important. We are now saying that in the part of mantle immediately outside the core, the density is about 5.6 times that of water. On the other hand immediately inside the core the density is about 9.7. This means that at the surface of the core there is not only a change from liquid on the inside to solid on the outside, but there is also a very considerable change in the density of material, from 9.7 on the inside to 5.6 on the outside. This change gives an important clue to the nature of the material in the core.

26. Changes inside the earth show themselves in the forms of _____.

    A) the happening of earthquakes   B) the eruption of volcanoes

    C) the uplift of mountains   D) all of the above

27. According to the passage, the diameter of the earth is about _____.

    A) 6,350 kilometers   B) 12,700 kilometers

    C) 3,450 kilometers   D) 6,900 kilometers

28. The word "dense" (Line 4, Para. 3) could possibly mean _____.

    A) flat   B) sensitive   C) thick   D) oval

29. The great change in the density of the material inside and outside the core throws light on

    _____.

    A) the nature of the material in the core

    B) the pressures occurring inside the earth

    C) the shape of the earth

    D) the density of the material at the depth of 500 kilometers inside the core

30. The passage mainly informs the reader _____.

    A) the changes inside the earth   B) the interior of the earth

    C) the composition of the mantle   D) the appearance of the core

Section D   Short Answer Questions

Directions：（略）

Passage 5

    Advances in technology have helped more of the world's population live better and longer—and that's part of our problem. Better health standards have kept larger numbers of people alive. The world's population is now almost four billion and expected to double in 25 years. Growing population and slowly rising living standards have increased our need for food at the rate of 30 million tons per year. As a result, the world's *stockpile*（库存）of food is declining by about 10 million tons per year.

    What can be done? At present we are cultivating only 3.5 billion acres of farmland out of a worldwide total of 7.8 billion acres. New acreage can be brought under *cultivation*（耕作），although the most favorable lands are already in use. The costs in clearing, transportation, and *irrigation*（灌溉）of developing only 20 million acres of land are estimated at about $ 400 billion and could run as much as $1 trillion!

    Land reform in some areas might be of help. New foods from the sea are also a possibility, but this is limited by pollution and by too intensive fishing in recent years. New varieties of seeds are still being developed, but the process is slow and costly. Fertilizer production must also be expanded, particularly in the less-developed countries.

    Reduction of waste would also help relieve the food shortage. Decreased *consumption*（消费）in the developed nations could increase the quantities distributed to needy nations. For example, the United States uses the equivalent of seven pounds of grain in the production of one pound of meat. Reducing meat consumption would free this for shipment abroad. It is estimated that the average person in poor countries consumes four hundreds pounds of grains per year, in contrast to the citizen of North America who consumes a ton (about one hundred pounds of which is in the form of beer or whiskey).

31. Given the present growth rate of the world's population and our ability to produce food, what does the author think is the most serious problem?
_____ _____ _____ _____ _____
_____ _____ _____ _____ _____

32. It is implied in the passage that the food production in the world is now increasing by
_____.
_____ _____ _____ _____ _____
_____ _____ _____ _____ _____

33. What is the main difficulty in increasing the world's farmland?
_____ _____ _____ _____ _____
_____ _____ _____ _____ _____

34. By the statement that North Americans consume about a ton of grain per year the author means that _____.
_____ _____ _____ _____ _____
_____ _____ _____ _____ _____

35. What would happen if Americans reduce their consumption of meat?
_____ _____ _____ _____ _____
_____ _____ _____ _____ _____

Notes and Explanations

Passage 1

Explanations

1. [Y] 第一段第一句提到 One of London Zoo's recent advertisements caused me some irritation, so patently did it distort reality. 伦敦动物园最近有很多广告,我对其中一个很不满,它显然歪曲了事实。故可得出答案为 Yes。
2. [Y] 第二段第一句提到 Zoos were originally created as places of entertainment, and their suggested involvement with conservation didn't seriously arise until about 30 years ago, when the Zoological Society of London held the first formal international meeting on the subject. 动物园最早是给人们提供娱乐的地方,30 年前人们才开始对其进行了保护,那时动物协会第一次举办了这个方面的国际会议。所以答案为 Yes。
3. [NG] 第二段最后一句提到 This commitment has now been clearly defined in The World Zoo Conservation Strategy (WZCS, September 1993), which—although an important and welcome document—does seem to be based on an unrealistic optimism about the nature of the zoo industry. 这种投入从世界动物园保护法的出现清楚反映出来,尽管这个文件很重要并受到欢迎,它却似乎建立在一种对

动物园行业本质特点盲目的乐观之上。但没有提及本题中的命题，所以答案为 Not Given。

4. [N] 第四段第二句提到 One would assume that the caliber of these institutions would have been carefully examined，but it appears that the criterion for inclusion on this select list might merely be that the zoo is a member of a zoo federation or association. 人们会认为这些动物园的能力已接受了认真检查，但是被列入名单的标准似乎是这个动物园可能只是某个动物园协会的一个成员。所以答案为 No。

5. [N] 第四段第四、五句提到 The greatly respected American Association of Zoological Parks and Aquariums（AAZPA）has had extremely dubious members，and in the UK the Federation of Zoological Gardens of Great Britain and Ireland has occasionally had members that have been roundly censured in the national press. This include Robin Hill Adventure Park on the Isle of Wight，... 具有很大权威性的机构 American Association of Zoological Parks and Aquariums（AAZPA）有一些有问题的会员，而英国的 The Federation of zoological Gardens of Great Britain and Ireland 也偶尔会有一些成员遭到全国新闻媒体的批评，其中包括 Robin Hill Adventure Park. 所以答案为 No。

6. [NG] 第五段第三句提到 This seems an extremely optimistic proposition from a man who must be aware of the failings and weaknesses of the zoo industry—the man who，when a member of the council of London Zoo，had to persuade the zoo to devote more of its activities to conservation. 这似乎是非常乐观的建议，因为作为伦敦动物园委员会的成员，Colin Tudge 一定意识到动物园业内存在的缺陷和不足，他不得不说服伦敦动物园加大投入来保护动物。但没有提及本题中的命题，所以答案为 Not Given。

7. [Y] 第六段第一句提到 Today approximately 16 species might be said to have been "saved" by captive breeding programs，although a number of these can hardly be looked upon as resounding successes. 目前，虽然有很多项目不能认为很成功，但是据说在园中饲养项目中大概有 16 种动物被拯救过来。从而得出答案为 Yes。

8. 第二段第二句提到 Eight years later，a series of world conferences took place，entitled "The Breeding of Endangered Species"，and from this point onwards conservation became the zoo community's buzzword. 八年以后，举行了一系列的以养殖濒危动物为主题的国际会议，从此，保护动物在众多动物园业中成为流行词汇。从而得出答案为 **conservation**。

9. 第四段谈到 WZCS 项目的第二个不足。最后一句提到 The situation is even worse in developing countries where little money is available for redevelopment and it is hard to see a way of incorporating collections into the overall scheme of the WZCS. 从中得出答案为 **lack**。

10. 从第六段最后一句 Given that the international conference at London Zoo was held 30 years ago，this is pretty slow progress，and a long way off Tudge's target of 2,000. 可以得出答案为 **slow progress**。

Passage 2

Notes

1. ... in contact with... （Line 3，Para. 1）

   in contact with 这个介词短语在句中作后置定语，修饰 body，意思是"与之相关的，有联系的"。这句话的意思是：因此，当一毫升的汗水蒸发的时候，人体表面大量热量被随之带走。例如：

   be in contact with sb. 与某人接触（联系）

   come in/into contact with the enemy 与敌人发生遭遇

   lose all contact with reality 完全脱离现实

   have much personal contact with sb. 和某人有很多私人交往

2. ... even if the environment ... （Line 4，Para. 1）

   even if 意思是"即使；虽然"。例如：

   I'll come even if it rains. 即使下雨我也会来的。

Even if you dislike ancient monuments, Warrick Castle is worth a visit.

即使你不喜欢古迹，但瓦里克城堡还是值得一看的。

3. This accounts for the fact that... （Line 3，Para. 3）

account for 意思是"解释，说明"。例如：

account for one's actions 为自己的行为做出解释

That accounts for it. 原来是这么一回事。

4. In contrast... （Line 4，Para. 3）

in contrast 意思是"相比之下"。例如：

It was windy yesterday. In contrast, it seems quite warm today.

昨天是个大风天，相比之下，今天好像非常暖和。

5. ...it is said to be...saturated with water vapor. （Line 2～3，Para. 4）

这句话的意思是：当空气中携带了它所能含有的水蒸气的最大值时，人们即称空气百分之百地饱含了水蒸气。

6. ...even though... （Line 4，Para. 5）

even though 与 even if 意思相同，表示"虽然；尽管"，这句话的意思是：尽管你周围的温度很高，你也会感觉有点儿凉快。例如：

I believe you're on duty—even though you are in plain clothes. 我相信你在值勤——尽管你穿着便衣。

Explanations

11. [A] 语法规则要求此处应填一个动词的第三人称单数形式作谓语。只有选项 A 是此形式。第二句话中出现的 is absorbed 提示 absorbs 符合句意。absorb 意思是"吸收"。此句的意思是"当液体蒸发的时候，它从周围环境中吸收大量的热。因此，当一毫升的汗水蒸发时，其所附着的体表大量的热量就被吸收了。"

12. [D] 语法规则要求此处应填一个名词作介词 from 的宾语。选项 C、D、H、M、O 是名词。根据句意可以推断此处应该填 surface。surface 这里意思是"体表"。

13. [M] 语法规则要求此处应填一个单数名词作主语。这句话的意思是"即使周围温度比身体本身（温度）还高，这种热量转移照样发生"。environment 意思是"周围环境"，符合句意。

14. [E] 语法规则要求此处应填一个动词原形作谓语。选项 E、I 是动词原形。根据上下文可见，文章分析了影响汗水蒸发速度的两个因素。affect 意思是"影响"，符合句意。

15. [H] 语法规则要求此处应填一个修饰不可数名词 water 的名词。前一句中用了 the amount of movement of air surrounding the body，本句用 the amount of water vapor in the air that surrounds the body。所以 amount（数量）符合句意。

16. [B] 语法规则要求此处应填一个副词作状语修饰谓语。选项 B、F、L 是副词。根据前一句的意思"当有空气从水面吹过时，蒸发量大大增加"可以判断有风的日子里汗水蒸发应该很快。rapidly 符合句意。

17. [K] 语法规则要求此处应填一个形容词构成形容词比较级。选项 G、J、K 是形容词。根据前一句的意思"很热又没风的日子里，汗水蒸发慢"可以推断"很热但是有风的日子"舒服。comfortable 意思是"舒服的，舒适的"，符合句意。

18. [L] 语法规则要求此处应填一个副词和 quickly 并列作状语修饰 cools the body。选项 B、F、L 是副词。由于在"虽热但有风的日子"汗水蒸发得非常快，因此后半句意思应是"汗液的蒸发使身体迅速而有效地凉爽下来"。另外，在第二段第一句提到 effectiveness of sweating，在第五段第三句又提到 sweating will be much more effective，因此此处应选副词 effectively。effectively 意思是"有效地，有作用地"。

19. [O] 语法规则要求此处应填一个单数名词作主语。与第二段第一句相呼应，第四段分析了影响汗水蒸发速度的第二个因素——空气中的水蒸气的数量，即湿度，因此 factor（因素）符合句意。

20. ［J］语法规则要求此处应填一个形容词作定语修饰 humidity。选项 G、J、K 是形容词。前一句已提到 relative humidity(相对湿度),因此此处仍填 relative。

Passage 3

Notes

1. ... applying for a job. (Line 4, Para. 1)

apply for 意思是"申请;请求",尤其指书面形式的请求,申请,通常用 apply to sb. for sth. 表示"向……申请……"。例如:

apply for a job (citizenship, credit) 申请职位(国籍,信用贷款)

They applied to him for help. 他们向他求援。

2. Make use of... (Line 1, Para. 2)

make use of sth. 意思是"使用,利用"。例如:

Industry is making increasing use of robots. 工业领域正越来越多地使用机器人。

He made good use of his spare time. 他的业余时间利用得很好。

3. Later, as you moved up the ladder, ... (Line 1, Para. 4)

这句话的意思是:再以后,当你申请更重要的职位时,就需要写更高级的求职信了。ladder 本意是指"梯子",在这里是指"阶梯,上升的层次"。move up the ladder 意指"申请更重要的职位"。

4. ... was called for. (Line 1, Para. 4)

call for 意思是"需要"。例如:

The situation calls for immediate action. 当前的情况需要立即采取行动。

5. ... distinguish you from the rest. (Line 2, Para. 4)

distinguish 作及物动词,常用于句型"distinguish...from...",表示"区分,辨别,分清"。例如:

These are some features that distinguish spoken English from written English.

这是区别英语口语和书面语的一些特征。

distinguish facts from rumors 辨别事实和传闻

distinguish right from wrong 分清是非

6. There is no doubt that... (Line 1, Para. 5)

这个句型表示"毫无疑问……",类似的表达方式有:there is no denying that... 等。例如:

There is no doubt that we will win the match in the end. 毫无疑问我们最终会赢得这场比赛。

7. ... it is... that... (Line 1~3, Para. 5)

这是一个强调句式,强调的部分是主语,这句话的意思是:正是因为求职者中有大学学位的人越来越多,所以一个人的履历表才越来越重要。

Explanations

这是一篇说明文。本文介绍了一种新型的广告,它既不是人找工作,也非工作找人,而是帮助你如何找工作。

21. **B)** 细节题。根据文章第一段最后一句话"What it does is to offer help in applying for a job."可判断出选项 B 为正确答案。根据第一段第二句话"... although it does not offer anyone a job..."可判断选项 A 是不对的;根据第一段第二句话"... although it is not placed by someone looking for a job either..."可判断出选项 D 是错误的;选项 C 在原文中找不到根据。所以答案为 B 项。

22. **C)** 细节题。这道题问的是社会需要这种特殊服务的原因是什么。根据文章第二段第二句话"The growth and apparent success of such a specialized service is, of course, a reflection of the current high levels of unemployment."可知这种新型广告出现的原因主要是有大量的人失业,选项 C 中的 out of

work 与原文中的 unemployment 同义,所以选 C 项。

23. **D)** 细节题。根据文章第三段第一句话"There was a time when job seekers simply wrote letters of application. . . just for openers. . . everything else could and should be saved for the interview."可知过去对于第一次找工作的人来说应该做的是 D 项。

24. **A)** 细节题。根据文章第四段"Later, as you moved up the ladder, something slightly more sophisticated was called for. . . which would distinguish you from the rest. . . it might be some special feature. . ."可知更高级的求职信要求有独特的地方,以使自己能与其他人有所区别,从而更具有吸引力。原文中 move up the ladder 意思是"申请更重要的职位"。

25. **B)** 细节题。根据文章第五段的内容". . . it is the increasing number of applications with university education at all the process of engaging staff that has led to the greater importance of the curriculum vitae."可知正是因为求职者中有大学学位的人越来越多,所以一个人的履历表才越来越重要了,所以选 B 项。只是选项 B 中把原文的 university education 换成了 degrees,问题题干中把 the curriculum vitae 换成了 job history,这种说法在第二段第一句话中也出现过,两者表示的意思完全相同。

Passage 4

Notes

1. . . . consists of two parts. . . (Line 2, Para. 2)

   consist of 意思是"组成,构成,存在"。例如:

   The house consists of six rooms. 这栋房子由六个房间组成。

   That area's future weather pattern might consist of long, dry periods.

   那个地区未来的天气可能会出现长期的干旱。

2. The core is made of. . . (Line 3, Para. 2)

   be made of 意思是"由……制成",表示可看出原料;如果看不出原料,就应该用 be made from。例如:

   The table is made of wood. 桌子是木头做的。

   The bread is made of corn. 面包是小麦做的。

3. The mantle possesses a thin . . . light kind of rock. (Line 1~2, Para. 3)

   这句话的意思是:地幔外部是地壳。地壳与地幔不同,由岩石构成。

   compose 意思是"构成,组成",常用过去分词作表语,后跟 of 搭配,例如:

   Steel is composed of iron and a number of other elements. 钢是由铁和其他几种金属合成的。

4. . . . at most. . . (Line 3, Para. 3)

   at most 意思是"至多,不超过"。例如:

   There is only at most room for one person. 至多只有可容一人的空间。

   She's at most 25 years old. 她至多 25 岁。

5. Indeed apart from. . . (Line 5, Para. 3)

   apart from 意思是"除……以外"。例如:

   He lives entirely alone, apart from the rats, bats, and moths.

   他一个人住,只有老鼠、蝙蝠和飞蛾跟他做伴。

Explanations

这是一篇科普类的说明文。通过我们熟知的地表的变化,说明了地球内部的结构与变化。

26. **D)** 细节题。答案参见文章第一段第三句话 They show themselves in the occurrence of earthquake, in the outbursts of volcanoes, and in the uplift of mountain ranges,这句话告诉我们地球内部的变化在地表上的表现包括地震、火山喷发和山脉的上升隆起。因此只能选 D 项。前三个选项都不全面,所以不对。

27. **B**）细节题。根据文章第二段第一句话 the earth is a nearly spherical ball with a radius of 6 350 kilometers,可知地球的半径为 6 350 公里,直径(diameter)应该是 12 700 公里。所以选 B 项。

28. **C**）词汇题。根据文章第三段第二句话 over the continents of the world this crustal rock is about thirty-five kilometers thick, while over the oceans...kilometers thick,可知接下来的这句话中 dense 修饰 rock,应该与上文的 thick 同义,所以选 C 项。

29. **A**）细节题。根据第四段最后一句话 This change gives an important clue to the nature of the material in the core,可知地核内外的物质密度的变化正好说明了地核内物质的特性。所以选 A 项。

30. **B**）主旨题。本文以地球内部的大小、结构、物质密度和地表变化等为主线展开说明,对地表的变化的说明主要是为了说明其内部的变化,所以应选 B 项。

Passage 5

Keys

31. Food shortage in the near future.

32. 20 million tons per year

33. Its high cost.

34. much of this is used in the production of meat

35. They can export more grain to other countries.

Notes

1. As a result, the world's stockpile of food is declining by... (Line 5, Para. 1)

   as a result 意思是"结果是……"。例如:

   He is always lazy in his studies. As a result, he failed in the final examination.

   他学习很懒惰,结果期末考试没及格。

2. At present we are cultivating only 3.5 billion acres of farmland out of...acres. (Line 1~2, Para. 2)

   这句话的意思是:目前,我们能耕种的农田只有 35 亿英亩,而全世界的总数有 78 亿英亩。out of 在这句话中意思相当于 from,表示"从……中"。例如:

   wake up out of a deep sleep 从熟睡中醒来

3. The costs in clearing, ... are estimated at about...and could run as $1 trillion! (Line 3~5, Para. 2)

   在这句话中 run 的意思是"价格为,使花费"。例如:

   This watch runs $100. 这块手表的价格为 100 美元。

   The car repair will run you a couple of hundred at least. 修理这辆汽车至少要花掉你两三百块钱。

4. Land reform in some areas might be of help. (Line 1, Para. 3)

   这句话的意思是:有些地区的土地改革也许是有用的。be of help 相当于 be helpful。

5. New varieties of seeds are still being developed, but... (Line 2~3, Para. 3)

   这句话使用了现在进行时的被动语态,意思是"人们正在开发各种各样的新品种"。

Unit 7

Section A   Skimming and Scanning

Directions：（略）

Passage 1

By Their Colors You Shall Know Them

1. Colors divide Europeans, just as languages. The confident Germans like their bright and sharp, ruby red, vermilion, pine green. The sophisticated Italians like olive green, pumpkin ecru. The cautious British feel at home with navy blue and brown.

2. Never mind 1992: a Europe sans frontiers colorwise remains a distant prospect. Fashion companies that sell in more than one country need to be alert to different national tastes in color.

3. What causes a color to be more popular in one country? "Climate and skin color," says Philippa Watkins, a senior lecturer in textiles at the Royal College Of Art in London: "The long Italian summer, and olive skins of the people are perfectly suited to deep, rich colors or very bright colors." However, color forecasters are speculating that if the greenhouse effect produce lasting climatic change, national color preferences could radically *reorientate* (重新认识).

4. The recent succession of sunny summers in Britain has already prompted sales of very bright colors, once considered unsuitable for our gray skies.

5. There are more deep-rooted forces at work, too, linked to each nation's history, geography and religion. Why do the Greeks love blue? Blue is the color of the Greek flag and Greek *Orthodoxy* (传统,常规). But it is also the color of the Greek sky most of the year, and the famously beautiful Aegean.

6. The expert color forecasters try to bear in mind national preferences. "By their very nature, European-wide color predictions are something of a compromise," says Stephen Higginson, who coordinates the International Color Authority's bi-annual publication. "Each country will emphasize different parts of the *palette* (调色板) we produce."

7. Often, it's the mix of colors that makes all the differences. A young French yuppie mixes greens and purples in a manner that seems quite starting to British eyes. I am convinced that Daniel Hechter's use of green explains why the well-known French designer has never made much headway on this side of Channel.

8. The problem is that just as soon as ground rules about a nation's sense of color have been drawn up, they have to be rewritten. Peter Lefevre, a leading authority on color with the International Wool Secretariat in Paris, points out that the French once believed that it was bad luck to wear green.

9. Color is changing before our eyes. Think pink, and think again. Pink came of age in the

Thirties under the tutelage of Elsa Schiaparelli. With the invention of "shocking pink", the Italian fashion designer did away with the color's longtime association with sweet, docile femininity. Her pink "shocked" because it was of an unimagined vibrancy: a hot, bold color for a *brash* (鲁莽的) new age.

10. Half a century on, pink is different. Schiaparelli's brand of pink no longer "shocks". That pink that was so amazed in the Thirties seems tame indeed alongside the sizzling shades now on offer. After living through the colors of the psychedelic Sixties, and more than one revival of eye-dazzling neons and day-glo brights, we are all turning into color trippers.

11. Many of the new fashion colors—the ones will be wearing next spring—were bright beyond belief in Florence this month at Pitti Tmmagine Filati, the yarn trade exhibition. Here fashion manufacturers were playing their seasonal game of trying to predict the market, and the color specialists had run out of superlatives for such a *profusion* (丰富, 大量) of vibrant reds, yellows and purples. International Textiles, the trade monthly, found the best description: felt-tip colors.

12. Pre-guessing colors is a tricky, inexact business. Color sells clothes, but no one knows for sure what will sell, and when. The unwary retailer who puts a range of pastel cardigans into the shops in April might make heavy losses if it rains throughout the month.

13. Forecasters have to take into account a broad diversity of themes, which may influence the customers' choice. These range from intangibles—something in the air, the international *zeitgeist* (时代思潮)—specifics such as important designers' collections, exhibitions or popular films (Out of Africa prompted a surge in demand for the colors of the *savannah* (热带草原)).

14. The key colors for fashion and interiors are determined by a handful of color experts, who spend their time traveling the world picking up inspiration and trying to spot trends. They meet twice a year to predict the colors the Europeans will all want to wear, or be surrounded by, two years hence. Their ideas are, in turn, picked up and developed by yarn manufacturers.

15. It is often suggested that we British have an undeveloped sense of color. A stroll down any town high street on a Saturday morning can be depressing: there is every color of rainbow, garishly mixed in a manner calculated to offend the sensibilities of the purist. But the picture is more encouraging than it seems. Recent years have seen a quiet revolution in our sense of color, marked by a greater willingness on the part of retailers such as Marks and Spencer, BHS and Habitat to explore and experiment.

16. Judie Buddy, a leading American color specialist who has been living in Europe since the Sixties, remembers to put yellow in a spring fashion range. "They threw me out of the door."

17. In 1980, Littlewoods was equally skeptical about Ms. Buddy's suggestions for a range of peach-colored knitwear. But it sold well. "We did sweaters in peach, baby *turquoise* (蓝绿色) blue and soft buttercup yellow," she recalls, describing the tones with the ease that comes naturally to color professionals.

18. Designers, both in fashion and interiors, are now working with color with more sophistication. Graig Leeson, a young Englishman who designs for Reporter, one of Italy's most successful man's wear labels, says: "Once upon a time, there was red and green and yellow. Now designers are exploring tones rather than the obvious primary colors."

19. Mr. Leeson is now playing with blue, a very popular color for this summer. "The base color is blue, but it's blue with 20 different tones; more like aquamarine, eggshell blue, petrol blue, denim blue."

20. This new sophistication may, perhaps, hold the key for the future of color. Hand in hand with the development of ever-brighter colors, the next decade will see a movement towards greater sophistication and subtlety in fashion colors. After all, can pink get that much pinker?

1. Colors are as important as languages in Europe.
2. The Italians' favorite color is olive green and pumpkin and ecru, which reflect their character of being vigorous.
3. Pink became popular in the Thirties because it was no longer only associated with femininity.
4. Color predictors are sure what will sell well in the fashion market.
5. National color sense changes more quickly at present than in the past.
6. The colors promoted by Julia Buddy were easily accepted by the British retailers.
7. The designers are now looking more closely at mixing different tones for future designs.
8. The British national color preference indicates that they behave with great _____.
9. The color experts meet to predict the European color fashion _____ every year.
10. The British bad color sense is _____.

Section B   Discourse Vocabulary Test
Directions：（略）

Passage 2

Currencies have a market, the foreign exchange market. Here, pounds sterling, U. S. dollars, Swiss francs, Italian lire, etc. are bought and sold. We ought to add that the foreign exchange market is a "market" only in the ___11___ sense of the term. It ___12___ of the foreign exchange departments of most of the banks acting either on their own or on their clients' ___13___. There are, in addition, the foreign exchange brokers who act as specialized firms in the field.

Practically, all dealing is done by telephone or teleprinter in the offices of the ___15___ brokers. These brokers are in ___14___ touch with both their opposite broker and the banks. The slightest variation in exchange rate anywhere in the world is watched for possible action. If there are no restrictions on movement of capital between countries, actions are to be taken which will include the rapid shifting of funds between ___16___ centers to take ___17___ of profitable price *differentials* （差额）.

The freedom of trade in currencies is at ___18___ somewhat restricted by a variety of exchange controls which are still enforced by many countries. The demand in one country, say England, for a foreign currency ___19___ from the desire for imports from another country, say, France. The pound sterling-French francs price is mainly *regulated* （调节） by interested parties in either country wanting to buy them, or sell to the other. The strength of the pull in either direction settles price of the currencies in terms of one another. This is how in a free exchange market the rate is arrived at.

Needless to say, there are __20__ more than two countries trading with one another. This somewhat complicates the establishment of exchange rates, because not only pounds, sterling and French francs but also, for example, U. S. dollars, Indian rupees, and Canadian dollars will all *simultaneously* (同时) be in relationship to one another.

A) extent	I) care
B) constant	J) reasonable
C) widest	K) financial
D) account	L) present
E) exchange	M) results
F) consists	N) normally
G) conscious	O) seldom
H) advantage	

Section C   Reading in Depth

Directions：（略）

Passage 3

The American comedy actress Whoopi Goldberg is all voice, *dreadlocks* (满头细长发辫) and teeth. And how came the name Whoopi Goldberg? Well, she was born Caryn Johnson, but discovered that it was not a name people remembered. Following the American saying "making whoopee", which means having fun, she gave herself the name Whoopi Goldberg, and began to be noticed.

Whoopi Goldberg (42), is a very busy woman—she's listed in Variety as the fifth busiest star in film production. Her first major film was Steven Spielberg's adaptation of the Alice Walker's novel The Color Purple in 1985, for which she earned a Golden Globe Award and an Academy Award nomination. Since then, she's had many big-screen assignments, starring in such films as Ghost, Jumpin' Jack Flash, Clara's Heart, The Long Walk Home, Sister Act, made in America and giving voice to animated characters in Disney film The Lion King. Her performance as a deceitful *fortune-teller* (算命人) in the 1990 film Ghost won her both a Golden Globe and an Oscar for Best Supporting Actress. Her TV performances have included acting as host for a late-night talk show The Whoopi Goldberg Show, appearing in many television specials and having a role for seasons in the TV series Star Trek：The Next Generation. Whoopi Goldberg aims to be a "working actor" for many years, but all this fame and fortune was a long time coming.

As proof of her *versatility* (多才多艺), the *comedienne* (喜剧女演员) has appeared in films of extremely diverse character. Ghost had the returning spirits of dead people causing laughter and chaos in the lives of their surviving relatives, while in Jumpin' Jack Flash, directed by Penny Marshall, Goldberg played an odd computer operator who gets ridiculously caught up in a web of international scheme. Two of her big comedies have been Sister Act, in which she played a witness to a crime who has to hide as a nun in a *convent* (修道院), and Eddie, a basketball comedy.

Now she's "made it". Whoopi Goldberg's determined to stick around. "I have a lot to do in Hollywood," she says. "I'm an actor; I'm a *chameleon* (变色龙), and I can do anything . . ."

21. The author thinks that one of Whoopi Goldberg's most noticeable features is _____.
    A) her voice   B) her name
    C) the prizes she won   D) her versatility

22. Whoopi Goldberg won an Oscar because of her performance in _____.
    A) The Color Purple   B) Sister Act
    C) The Lion King   D) Ghost

23. Whoopi Goldberg won fame and fortune _____.
    A) when she used her original name Caryn Johnson
    B) soon after she adopted the name Whoopi
    C) at the time she performed in The Color Purple
    D) after she struggled for a long time

24. The expression "made it" (Line 1, Para. 4) most likely means _____.
    A) more to fight for   B) been lucky
    C) been successful   D) worked hard

25. We can infer from the passage that _____.
    A) it's tough for a black actress to be successful in America
    B) all voice, dreadlocks and teeth are the necessities for a comedy star
    C) a decent name alone can make you shinning in Hollywood
    D) Whoopi Goldberg has great expectation and determination

Passage 4

There was no Churchillism, no Heathism, nor Callaghanism. Margaret Thatcher is the only Prime Minister to have had her own "ism". But what is Thatcherism? Has it been a consistent ideology or merely household budgeting on a national scale? Does it amount to a philosophy or is it just one woman's political style?

Certainly, she has made her party more ideological. Lord Hailsham of St. Marylebone once said: "Conservatives do not believe that political struggle is the most important thing in life the simplest among them prefer for hunting, the wisest, religion." With an almost Maoist *fervor* (热诚,炽热), however, Mrs. Thatcher has taken her party on a long march of reform through institutions of British society: the union, the civil service, education, the health service and the law.

Warrior rather than healer, she has set in train what she sees as a libertarian movement to extend personal choice and create an enterprise society in which the state leaves people free to spend more of their own money and managers are free to manage without being prey to the constant demands of trade union leaders. Thatcherism has been based on simple slogans such as "sound money". As Nigel Lawson, the former Chancellor of the Exchequer, said, the inflation rate is judge and jury for her governments. Thatcherism has looked to the creation of strong defense and a strong economy, not just for their *intrinsic* (固有的;内在的) merits, but to restore national self-confidence and Britain's reputation in the world. The simple slogans have lived throughout it all: The Enterprise Economy, Stand On Your Own Two Feet, Making Britain Great Again and, of course, those famous Victorian Values.

Thatcherism has been about free markets and a belief in individual responsibility. Mrs. Thatcher and her' ministers have sought to educate Britain; out of what they see as the dependency culture, to end the common belief that the solving of problems was always up to them—the council, the government, the authorities. Mrs. Thatcher has encouraged the belief that there is a limit to government responsibilities. Her ability to win elections against a background of high unemployment argues that she succeeded to some extent in that.

26. Through this article, the writer intends to _____.

    A) demonstrate that Thatcherism is a style rather than a philosophy

    B) stress that Thatcherism has amounted to a philosophy

    C) comment on Thatcherism both philosophically and stylistically

    D) attack Thatcherism either as a philosophy or as a style

27. Which of the following can be the best description of Mrs. Thatcher's political style?

    A) Household budging.   B) Warrior rather than healer.

    C) Judge and jury.   D) Stand on your own two feet.

28. Which of the following is NOT encouraged by Thatcherism?

    A) The entire social problems should wait for the government to deal with.

    B) The conservative should be more ideological.

    C) The individual British should be able to spend freely as much his own money as possible.

    D) National self-confidence and good reputation of Britain should be restored.

29. The word "it" in the sentence "The simple slogans have lived throughout it all" (Line 8, Para. 3) refers to _____.

    A) the simple slogans

    B) national self-confidence and Britain's reputation in the world

    C) libertarian movement

    D) Thatcherism

30. From the figurative use of "a long march" (Line 4, Para. 2), we may infer that the author means _____.

    A) the libertarian movement shall be tough and last for long

    B) Mrs. Thatcher is going to lead a long march in Britain

    C) Britain should learn from Mao

    D) in Britain, there are also snowy mountains and grassland to cross

Section D　Short Answer Questions

Directions：（略）

Passage 5

Boxing is a sport in which two fighters battle with their fists. In ancient Greece, boxing was a popular amateur competitive sport and was included in the first Olympian Game. In ancient Rome，boxers often wore the *metal-studded*（镶嵌）leather hand covering with which they *maimed*（使残废）and even killed their opponents，sometimes as part of *gladiatorial*（角斗士的）spectacles. The sport declined in popularity after the fall of the Roman Empire. In the 18th century, boxing was revived in London in the form of *bare-knuckle*（膝关节的，骨关节的）prizefighters in which the contestants fought for money and fame.

The boxers wear gloves and fight in a square called a ring. A good *bout*（回合）between two fighters is a fast，violent display of strength and skill. The boxers throw powerful punches as each tries to dominate his opponent. At the same time，each boxer must guard his head and body against the other's punches by *dodging*（躲避）or blocking the blows. There are several ways to win a fight. The action may range all over the ring as the fighters weave about or press forward to create openings for blows. Good boxers must be strong，quick，skillful，and in excellent physical condition. They also should have the courage and determination to fight in spite of pain and exhaustion. Boxers fight as amateurs or professionals. Most amateurs compete as members of an organization or a team，and some box in tournaments. Amateurs may not accept money for boxing. Professionals fight for money and are often called prizefighters.

Boxing began thousands of years ago，and for much of its history it was an extremely brutal sport. Modern boxing enjoyed great popularity in the United States from the 1920's through the 1940's. However，spectator interest in the sport of boxing then began to decline. Today，only the top professional championship bouts and competition in boxing during the Olympic Games regularly draw widespread attention from the public. Boxing has been criticized as a dangerous sport because of the possibility of injury. However，rules attempt to reduce the chances of damage to boxers. Fighters must wear protective equipment and a doctor must be present. Beginning in the 1980's，most professional fights were reduced from 15 to 12 rounds to cut down on injuries due to *fatigue*（疲乏）in late rounds.

31. According to the passage, where do the boxers fight with each other?

    _____ _____ _____ _____ _____

    _____ _____ _____ _____ _____

32. What is the essential quality of a boxer?

    _____ _____ _____ _____ _____

    _____ _____ _____ _____ _____

33. According to the passage, a good bout between two fighters should be _____.

    _____ _____ _____ _____ _____

    _____ _____ _____ _____ _____

34. What is the opposite meaning of "amateur" in paragraph 2?

    _____ _____ _____ _____ _____

    _____ _____ _____ _____ _____

35. In which country in history is boxing the most dangerous?

    _____ _____ _____ _____ _____

    _____ _____ _____ _____ _____

Notes and Explanations

Passage 1

Explanations

1. [NG] 第一段第一句提到 Colors divide Europeans, just as languages. 正如语言一样, 颜色把欧洲人分成多个部分。但没有提及本题中的命题, 所以答案为 Not Given。

2. [N] 第一段第三句提到 The sophisticated Italians like olive green, pumpkin ecru. 老道的意大利人喜欢橄榄绿和棕黄色。所以答案为 No。

3. [Y] 第九段第三、四句提到 Pink came of age in the Thirties under the tutelage of Elsa Schiapareli. With the invention of "shocking pink", the Italian fashion designer did away with the color's longtime association with sweet, docile femininity. 三十年代在 Elsa Schiapareli 的引导下, 粉色成为一种很成熟的颜色。随着"惊艳粉色"的出现, 意大利时装设计师去除粉色长久以来与女性温柔、温顺气质相关的思想。所以答案为 Yes。

4. [N] 从第十二段第二句 Color sells clothes, but no one knows for sure what will sell, and when... 得知颜色能促进服装的销售。但没人能准确知道什么能畅销、什么时候畅销。所以答案为 No。

5. [NG] 通过快速浏览文章, 便可得知不同国家的人们由于受气候、肤色等因素的影响偏爱特定的颜色, 但他们的颜色喜好在一些复杂因素的影响下也会变化。但没有提及本题中的命题, 所以答案为 Not Given。

6. [N] 从第十六段 They threw me out of the door. 得知答案为 No。

7. [Y] 第十八段最后一句提到 Now designers are exploring tones rather than the obvious primary colors. 现在设计师在努力探索各种复杂的色调而不是些简单的颜色, 与本题中的命题意义相同, 所以答案为 Yes。

8. 第一段最后一句提到 The Cautious British feel at home with navy blue and brown. 谨慎小心的英国人钟爱深蓝色和棕色。可以得出答案为 **caution**。

9. 从第十四段第二句 They meet twice a year to predict the colors the Europeans will all want to wear, or be surrounded by, two years hence. 可以得出答案为 **twice**。

10. 从第十五段第一句 It is often suggested that we British have an underdeveloped sense of color. 和第三句 But the picture is more encouraging than it seems. Recent years have been a quiet revolution in our sense of color, ... 可以得出答案为 **improving**。

Passage 2

Notes

1. Here, pounds sterling, ... Italian lire... (Line 1～2, Para. 1)
这句话介绍了几个国家的货币单位: sterling 是以英镑为基准的英国货币; pound sterling 是英镑; Swiss francs 是瑞士法郎; lire 是意大利的货币单位"里拉"。

2. ... most of the banks acting either on their own or on their clients' account. (Line 4, Para. 1)
act on/upon 意思是"遵照……行事, 奉行"。例如:
act on principles 遵照原则办事
act on a guess 根据猜测行事

3. These brokers are in constant touch with both their opposite broker and the banks. (Line 2, Para. 2)
这句话的意思是: 这些经纪人和对方经纪人或银行经常保持联系。opposite 在句中的意思是"(另一单位)与自己职位相等的人"。be in touch with 意思是"和……有联系"。例如:

We can be in touch with the world through Internet. 我可以通过互联网和全世界联系。

4. If there are no restrictions... price differentials. (Line 3～6, Para. 2)

这句话的意思是：如果对国与国之间的资本流动没有任何限制，那么很多交易将会进行，包括金融中心之间资金的快速流通转换，利用可观的差价赚取利润。take advantage of 意思是"利用"。例如：

take full advantage of the exceptional opportunities in exports 充分利用出口方面的难得的机会

We had better take advantage of the warmer weather by going for a walk this afternoon.

我们最好趁着天气暖和今天下午出去散散步。

5. The demand in one country, say England... say, France. (Line 2～3, Para. 3)

say 在这两句话中都表示举例子，这种用法的 say 常用作插入语，是副词，意思是"例如"。例如：

any gas, say oxygen, 任何气体，例如氧气

Explanations

11. [C] 语法规则要求此处应填一个形容词作定语修饰 sense。选项 B、C、G、J、K 是形容词。根据下两句的解释，"It consists of... in the field"，这里应是"最广义上的定义"，widest 符合句意。

12. [F] 语法规则要求此处应填一个动词的第三人称单数形式作谓语。选项 F、M 是该形式。这句话解释了"market"一词的定义范围，短语 consist of 意思是"由……组成（或构成）"，符合句意。

13. [D] 语法规则要求此处应填一个名词和介词 on 搭配成短语 on one's...。选项 A、D、E、H、I、L 是名词。这句话意思是"大多数银行的外汇部门要么代表自己的利益要么代表他们客户的利益"。词组 on one's account 意思是"为了……的利益"，符合句意。

14. [B] 语法规则要求此处应填一个形容词作定语修饰 touch 并构成短语 in... touch with...。根据上下文推断，这些经纪人应该是要经常和他们（所要交易的）对方经纪人或银行打交道。constant 意思是"经常的，反复的"，符合句意。in constant... touch with 意思是"保持长久联系"。

15. [E] 语法规则要求此处应填一个名词作定语说明 rate 的种类。根据上下文提示，此处应该说的是汇率的变化，在第四段第二句提到了 the establishment of exchange rates（汇率的建立），所以 exchange 符合句意。exchange rate 意思是"汇率"。

16. [K] 语法规则要求此处应填一个形容词作定语修饰 centers。根据上下文推断，这里应是金融中心之间的资金流动。financial 意思是"金融的，财政的"，符合句意。

17. [H] 语法规则要求此处应填一个名词作 take 的宾语并构成词组 take... of。care 和 advantage 可以和 take 搭配构成短语。take advantage of 意思是"利用"，符合此处的意思"利用价格差来赚钱"。

18. [L] 语法规则要求此处应填一个名词作介词 at 的宾语并构成介词短语。at present 意思是"目前，现在"，符合句意。

19. [M] 这句话主语是 The demand in one country，谓语应该是一个动词的第三人称单数形式。词组"result from…"意思是"是……的结果；作为……的结果而产生"，符合句意。

20. [N] 语法规则要求此处应填一个副词作状语修饰谓语。选项 N、O 是副词。根据上下文推断，这句话讲的是通常会有两个以上的国家进行交易。normally 意思是"通常，正常情况下"，符合句意。

Passage 3

Notes

1. ... is all voice... (Line 1, Para. 1)

注意这句话中 all 的用法。当它与表示人体部位或与之相关的名词连用时，表示"以……为主要特色，显著突出的"。例如：

His face was all eyebrows. 他脸上两条眉毛又粗又浓。

be all eyes and ears 凝眸注视，洗耳恭听

2. ... she was born Caryn Johnson, but discovered that it was not a name people remembered. (Line 2~3, Para. 1)

这句话的意思是：她出生后取名卡恩·约翰逊,但她发现这个名字人们记不住。

3. Since then, ... and giving voice to... The Lion King. (Line 4~6, Para. 2)

give voice to 意思是"给……配音"。big-screen 意思是"大片",screen 意思是"电影"。

4. ... won her... for Best Supporting Actress. (Line 7~8, Para. 2)

Best Supporting Actress 意思是"最佳女配角"。

5. Now She's "made it". (Line 1, Para. 4)

make it 在口语中常用,表示"达到预定目标;办成,做到;成功,发迹"。例如:

The charts showed we had made it, and big. 图表表明我们成功了,而且非常成功。

Tell him I want to see him tonight, at my house if he can make it. 告诉他我要见他,行的话就在我家。

He wants to make it as a writer. 他想作为作家而一举成名。

6. ... determined to stick around. (Line 1, Para. 4)

stick around 意思是"逗留,留下;继续努力,坚持"。例如:

If you are going to be out I ought to stick around. 如果你要出去,我就得留下。

Stick around for a while, he will soon be back. 再等一会儿,他马上就会回来了。

Explanations

　　本文是一篇记叙文,简要地介绍了美国喜剧女明星乌比·戈德堡成功的过程,她演过的主要影片、其中的角色以及她的表演风格。在文章末尾还转述了她对自己的评价及对未来的期望。她的多才多艺在很多影片中体现出来,如《人鬼情未了》、《修女也疯狂》、《紫色》等,并给观众留下了深刻的印象。

21. A) 细节题。这个问题问的是美国喜剧女明星乌比·戈德堡最显著的特点之一是什么。答案参见文章第一段第一句话。这句话介绍了她的三大显著点:大嗓门,细长的发辫,满嘴大牙。选项 A 正是其中之一,所以答案为 A 项。根据这句话选项 B、C 和 D 都可被排除。

22. D) 细节题。答案参见第二段中部 Her performance as a deceitful fortune-teller in the 1990 film Ghost won her both... for Best Supporting Actress.

23. D) 细节题。根据第二段最后一句... but all this fame and fortune was a long time coming,答案应选 D 项。

24. C) 词汇题。make 一词有成功、做成的意思,在口语中常用 make it 表示"成功,发迹;办成,做到",所以应选 C 项。

25. D) 推断题。全文并未提及作为黑人使她成功更艰难,所以选项 A 被排除;大嗓门、细长的发辫、满嘴大牙等作为一个演员的个体特征并不能成为作为喜剧明星整个行业的必要素质,所以选项 B 被排除;单凭一个好名字又怎么能在强手如云的好莱坞赢得成功呢? 所以选项 C 被排除。根据文章最后一段可推断出乌比·戈德堡有远大的志向和决心,所以答案是 D 项。

Passage 4

Notes

1. Has it been a... on a national scale? (Line 2~3, Para. 1)

这句话的意思是:它是一个一贯的牢固的思想体系还是一个纯粹的全国规模的家庭计划? scale 意思是"大小,规模,范围",on... scale 意思是"以……为规模;在……范围内"。例如:

on a large scale 大规模地

the mobilization of women for work on an unprecedented scale 以前所未有的规模动员妇女参加工作

on the nationwide scale 在全国范围内

2. Does it amount to a philosophy... (Line 3, Para. 1)

amount to 意思是"等于,就是"。例如:

Your words amount to a refusal. 你的话等于就是拒绝。

His debts amount to over £1,000. 他的债务总计达 1 000 英镑。

3. ... the simplest among them prefer..., the wisest, religion. (Line 2~3, Para. 2)

这是一个省略句。为了避免重复,the wisest 后面省略了相同的谓语和状语,完整的句子应该是:... the wisest among them prefer for religion. 这句话的意思是:在保守党中思想最简单的人喜欢狩猎,最明智的人喜欢宗教。

4. Warrior rather than healer, she has set in train what she sees as a libertarian movement... leaders. (Line 1~4, Para. 3)

这句话的意思是:撒切尔夫人是个战士,而不仅仅是可以治愈病人的医生,她开始了一场她认为是自由派的运动来实现她的个人选择,并创造了一个企业社会;在这个社会里国家让人民自由地多花他们自己的钱,公司经理们更自由地去进行管理而不用担心自己成为那些工会领导们经常盯着的对象。

set/put sth. in train 意思是"把……安排妥当或开始实施某事;……在进行中",原文中这句话 set 的宾语太长,所以把宾语移到了 in train 的后面。例如:

Much was set in train during those eight weeks. 在那 8 个星期里做了很多事情。

5. Thatcherism... "sound money". (Line 4, Para. 3)

sound 在这里是"牢固的,稳固的",是形容词。例如:

a sound economy 稳固的经济

sound investment 可靠的投资

6. ... the former Chancellor of the Exchequer, said,... her governments. (Line 5~6, Para. 3)

Chancellor of the Exchequer 是英国的财政大臣,the Exchequer 是英国的财政部。例如:

In Britain the Chancellor of the Exchequer mainly deals with taxes and government spending. 在英国财政大臣主要掌管税务和政府的开支。

7. Thatcherism has looked to..., not just for..., but to... (Line 6~7, Para. 3)

▷look to 意思是"指望,依靠,寄希望于……"。例如:

Don't look to him for help. 不要指望他来帮忙。

He looks to others to structure time for him. 他总是希望他人来给他安排时间。

▷not... but... 表示"不是……,而是……"。这句话的意思是:撒切尔主义曾寄希望于建立强大的国防和强有力的经济,并不只是因为这两方面本身的优点,还因为她想重新恢复英国国民的自信心和英国在全世界的名声。

Explanations

我们对曾任英国前首相的撒切尔夫人的名字早已耳熟能详。她在英国执政长达 11 年,还喊出了"撒切尔主义"的口号。但大多数人可能对她的这个主义在英国都实行了哪些政策、效果如何还不太了解。本文是一篇议论文,通过对撒切尔主义的介绍和评价,对在英国政坛连任三届的撒切尔夫人也作了一番评论。

21. C) 主旨题。通读全文可知,无论是作者本人的论述还是引述他人的评价都是围绕着撒切尔夫人的领导哲学和风格展开的,所以应选 C 项。

22. B) 细节题。根据第三段第一句话 Warrior rather than healer, she has... leaders,可知这是对撒切尔夫人政治风格最好的描述,所以应选 B 项。

23. A) 细节题。根据第二段第一句话可知,选项 B 是被鼓励的;根据第三段的内容... the state leaves people free to spend more of their money 和... not just for..., but to restore national self-confidence and Britain's reputation in the world. 可知,选项 C 和 D 也是被鼓励的;根据最后一段第二句话可知,选项 A 是不被鼓励的,相反这种 dependency culture 是要被改变的。所以答案应选 A 项。

大学英语 4 级阅读与简答(新题型)

24. **D**）细节题。根据上、下文可知 it 在这里指的是上句话的主语 Thatcherism。

25. **A**）推断题。撒切尔夫人在以保守著称的英国实行改革，所遇到的困难和阻力可想而知，所以把她的这场改革比喻成中国的长征，意思是喻指其过程既漫长又艰辛，所以应选 A 项。

Passage 5

Keys

31. In a ring.

32. Being quick, skillful and strong.

33. a fast, violent display of strength and skill

34. Professional.

35. Ancient Rome.

Notes

1. In the 18th century, boxing was revived... in the form of... the fame. (Line 5~7, Para. 1)

   这句话的意思是：到了十八世纪，拳击在伦敦又流行了起来。拳击手们赤膊上台，为金钱和荣誉而战。

   revive 可做及物动词和不及物动词，意思是"复苏，复兴……"。例如：

   to revive an old custom 恢复旧习俗

   Interest in ancient music has revived recently. 最近古代音乐又流行起来了。

2. They also should have the courage... in spite of pain and exhaustion. (Line 7~8, Para. 2)

   这句话的意思是：尽管他们浑身伤痛，筋疲力尽，但是还要有勇气和决心搏斗下去。in spite of 后面接名词或相当于名词的名词短语，表示"尽管，不管，不顾"。例如：

   In spite of what you say, I still believe he is honest. 不管你说什么，我还是相信他是诚实的。

3. However, rules attempt to reduce the chances of damage to boxers. (Line 6~7, Para. 3)

   这句话的意思是：但是，（人们制定）很多规则试图减少对拳击手受伤的可能性。attempt to do sth. 表示"尝试，试图，企图"。例如：

   He attempted to escape, but was caught again. 他试图逃跑，但还是被抓住了。

4. Beginning in the 1980's, most... to cut down on injuries due to fatigue... (Line 7~9, Para. 3)

   ▷cut down on sth. 意思是"减少或降低"，介词 on 可省略。例如：

   The doctors have told me to cut down (on) smoking and drinking. 医生叫我少抽烟，少喝酒。

   ▷due to sth. 意思是"由于，因为"。例如：

   His illness was due to the bad food. 他生病的原因是食物不好。

   His absence was due to the storm. 他不能来是因为有暴风雨。

Unit 8

Section A   Skimming and Scanning

Directions：（略）

Passage 1

A New Learning Tool

1. Students at 62 large university campuses across the United States can take heart: They may never have to take notes in a lecture again.

2. An upstart Internet venture calling itself http://www.studentu.com is hiring students this semester and paying them to take notes in as many as core courses per campus.

3. The note-takers post their jottings electronically, within 24 hours, on a central web site.

4. Among the dozens of notes already listed are those taken Tuesday during Professor John Syer's course on world politics at California State University in Sacramento and on Aug.24 during Professor Robert Schwebach's lecture on financial markets at Colorado State University.

5. The service, which first went on-line Wednesday, is free.

6. And the *stenographers*（速记员）, most of them hired through their fraternities and enrolled in the courses, are paid $300 a semester to open their notebooks to the world.

7. The creator of the site, Oran Wolf, a 27-year-old graduate of the University of Texas at Austin, who hopes to earn a profit partly through advertising, said he started the service to help students *augment*（增加）their own notes or to help them catch up after a sick day.

8. But he conceded that his offerings could be abused by those with less legitimate excuses, like chronic oversleeping or lingering hangovers.

9. "I definitely don't believe students should skip class," Mr. Wolf said this week from his Houston office, as he admitted that he, too, on occasion, had done just that.

10. "It is important for them to attend the class, use this information as supplements to the course and if they do that, they are going to get A's."

11. There is no shortage of critics who believe that the arrival of Mr. Wolf's venture—along with other web sites that sell sample term papers and synopses of great books—signals nothing less than the erosion of liberal education, if not civilization.

12. But Mark Edmundson, a professor of English at the University of Virginia, one of the schools where Mr. Wolf has set up shop, thinks the problem lies more with universities—than on those trying to beat the system.

13. "There's something *sleazy*（肮脏的）about students taking notes and selling them on the web," Mr. Edmundson said.

14. "But if you can buy the notes and satisfy the course requirements, maybe the course

大学英语4级阅读与简答（新题型）

should have been distributed as a book, rather than having this *charade*（猜字游戏）of somebody standing up and going through a lecture that, for all purposes, doesn't change from year to year, and doesn't allow students the possibility of discussion."

15. Peter Wood, a professor of anthropology and the associate *provost*（院长）at Boston University, which is also on Mr. Wolf's list, said the university might consider taking legal action once notes from the school appear on the site—which, as of Wednesday, they had not.

16. "I am troubled by it because I, like thousands of faculty members, spent a great deal of time developing my courses within a specific intellectual context, a context that I control," he said.

17. Mr. Wolf said the seeds of his idea were first sown while he was studying economics at Austin, when he had occasionally taken advantage of a similar service there: For $30 per class, a private note-taking firm would arrange for him to get paper copies of any notes that he might have missed.

18. After graduating in 1995 and moving to Houston, he learned that university there had no such service, and so he founded his own. Initially taking 10 hours of notes a day himself, he quickly expanded his operation to include about 3,000 subscribers—they, too, paid $30 for each of 120 classes—and about 40 note-takers.

19. Mr. Wolf said professors at the University of Houston were initially *wary*（警惕的，小心的）of helping him and his note-takers gain access to classes, if they were not enrolled.

20. But he said he won them over when they realized that attendance did not drop as a result.

21. When Mr. Wolf discovered that such services were rare on other campuses, he said he decided to take his operation national.

22. With an investment from New Strategy, a Houston company that has nurtured other web companies, and rolling banner of advertisements that includes the Capital One Visa Platinum Card, Mr. Wolf began recruiting note-takers at fraternities at 62 of the largest colleges and universities throughout the United States.

23. Because he has assembled his operation so quickly, using students already in courses, Mr. Wolf said he would not be asking professors for permission to broadcast their notes.

24. Thus, many are likely to be as surprised as Professor Syer at Sacramento who learned from a reporter Wednesday that his introduction to the world's 10 largest countries had been reproduced by an *anonymous*（匿名的）note-taker for all to see.

25. "I'm not unalterably opposed to this *dissemination*（传播）," he said.

26. "I'd just like to know how wide my audience is. I'm going to get up there and take on the policies of the U. S. government, the policies of the Indonesian government, the policies of the Chinese government."

27. "If I think this is something that is going to be quoted globally," he said, "it may change what I say."

1. Students who wish to visit the web site offering notes of major college courses must pay a fee.
2. Mr. Wolf used to oversleep chronically.
3. Many people believe that the kind of service offered by Mr. Wolf is detrimental to the education

of arts.

4. Professor Mark Edmundson believes that such web sites pose a major threat to the present educational system.

5. Students who take notes for Mr. Wolf were denied access to classes.

6. By broadcasting notes without permission from the professors, Mr. Wolf might get involved in lawsuits.

7. Professor Syer was indignant when he learned that notes of his lecture were posted on the Internet.

8. The note-takers post their jottings _____, within 24 hours, on a central web site.

9. Wolf considered it vital for the students to use the information on the site as _____ to the course.

10. Peter Wood considered it _____ to have the notes from his university appear on the site.

Section B   Discourse Vocabulary Test

Directions：（略）

Passage 2

The World Health Organization (WHO) says as many as 10 __11__ persons worldwide may have the *virus*（病毒）that __12__ AIDS. Experts believe about 350 thousand persons have the __13__ . And one million more may get it in the next five years. In the US, about 50,000 persons have died with AIDS. The country's top __14__ official says more than 90 percent of all Americans who had the AIDS virus five years ago are dead.

There is no __15__ for AIDS and no *vaccine*（疫苗）medicine to prevent it. However, researchers know much more about AIDS than they did just a few years ago. We now know that AIDS is caused by a virus. The virus invades healthy cells, including white blood cells that are part of our __16__ system against disease. It takes control of the __17__ cell's genetic material and forces the cell to make a copy of the virus. The cell then dies. And the viral particles move on to __18__ and kill more healthy cells.

The AIDS virus is __19__ in a person's body fluids. The virus can be passed sexually or by sharing instruments used to take drugs. It also can be __20__ in blood products or from a *pregnant*（怀孕）woman with AIDS to her developing baby.

Many stories about the spread of AIDS are false. You can't get AIDS by working or attending school with someone who has the disease. You can't get it by touching drinking glasses or other objects used by such persons. Experts say no one has gotten AIDS by living with, caring for or touching an AIDS patient.

There are several warning signs of an AIDS infection. They include always feeling tired, unexplained weight loss and the uncontrolled *expulsion*（排除）of body wastes. Other warning signs are the appearance of white areas on the mouth, dark red areas of skin that don't disappear and a higher than normal body temperature.

A）causes	I ）invade
B）carried	J ）passed
C）cure	K）essential
D）million	L）influence
E）medicine	M）healthy
F）disease	N）individual
G）defense	O）medical
H）subject	

Section C　Reading in Depth

Directions：（略）

Passage 3

One of the teacher's rewards is that he is using his mind on valuable subjects. All over the world people are spending their lives either on doing jobs where the mind must be kept numb all day, or else on highly rewarded activities which are boring. One can get accustomed to operating an adding-machine for five and a half days a week, or to writing advertisements to persuade the public that one brand of cigarettes is better than another. Yet no one would do either of these things for its own sake. Only the money makes them tolerable. But if you really understand an important and interesting subject, like the structure of the human body or the history of the World Wars, it is a genuine happiness to explain them to others, to welcome every new book on them, and to learn as you teach.

With this another reward of teaching is very closely linked. That is the happiness of making something. When the pupils come to you, their minds are only half-formed, full of black space and vague notions and oversimplification. You do not merely insert a lot of facts, if you teach them properly. It is not like injecting 500 CC of *serum*（血液）, or giving a year's *dose*（一剂药,剂量）of vitamins. You take the living mind, and mould it. It resists sometimes. It may lie passive and apparently refuse to accept anything you print on it. Sometimes it takes the mould too easily, and then seems to melt again and become featureless. But often it comes into helping to create a human being. To teach a boy the difference between truth and lie in print, to start him thinking about the meaning of poetry or patriotism, to hear him hammering back at you with the facts and arguments you have helped him to find, sharpened by himself and fitted to his own powers, gives the sort of satisfaction that an artist has when he makes a picture out of black *canvas*（画布）and chemical colorings, or a doctor when he hears a sick pulse pick up and carry the energies of new life under his hands.

21. What makes people tolerant of boring jobs is _____.

　　A) the job itself　　　　　　　　　　B) the money

　　C) the significance of the job　　　　D) the fact that it can keep the mind numb

22. According to the author, it is a genuine happiness _____.

 A) to earn a lot of money

 B) to do highly rewarded jobs where the mind must be kept numb

 C) to spend one's life on operating an adding-machine

 D) to use one's mind on valuable subjects

23. Teaching a pupil properly _____.

 A) means taking and molding the living mind

 B) is just to insert a lot of facts in the mind

 C) is just like injecting 500 CC of serum

 D) should be the same as giving a year's dose of vitamins

24. Which of the following is NOT implied in the passage?

 A) The teacher is an "engineer" who moulds the mind as he works.

 B) Pupils are always ready to accept what you teach them.

 C) A teacher helps to create a human being.

 D) Teaching isn't a kind of easy work.

25. The author refers to an artist and a doctor _____.

 A) because an artist can make a picture and a doctor can hear sick pulse

 B) in order to make people know how a teacher feels when he succeeds in creating a human being

 C) because both the artist and the doctor were once students

 D) in order to show the fact that students can become good doctors and artists

Passage 4

Although one might not think so from some of the criticism of it, advertising is essential to the kind of society in which people in the United Kingdom, and a very large part of the world at large, live. Advertising is necessary as a means of communicating with others. It is also a way of telling people about the goods and services that are offered. If it were not for advertising, some goods information would never reach the ears of many people. Advertising helps a great deal to raise the people's standard of living.

In talking about advertising, one should not think only in terms of a *commercial* (商业广告) on television, or an advertisement in the newspapers or periodicals. In its widest sense, advertising includes many other activities such as packaging, shop displays and even the spoken word of the salesman. After all, the roots of advertising are to be found in the market place.

For many years it was thought that it was enough to produce goods and supply services. It is only more recently that it has become increasingly understood that the production of goods is a waste of resources unless those goods can be sold at a fair price within a reasonable time span. In the competitive society in which we live, it is essential that we go out and sell what we have to offer, and advertising plays an important role in this respect, whether selling at home or in export markets.

About 2 percent of the U. K. *gross* (总数) national product is spent on advertising. But it must not be thought that this advertising tries to sell goods to consumers who do not want them. Of course, advertising does try to attract the interest of the potential consumer, but if the article purchased does not match up to the standards that the advertising suggests that it will, it is obviously unlikely that the article will sell well.

26. According to the passage, which of the following is true?

A) Talking about advertising, one should not merely associate with commercials on the TV and advertisements in the newspaper and magazines.

B) Without advertisements, people still can have the information of products through other forms of media.

C) For a long time it has been understood that the production of goods is a waste of resources until they are sold at a certain price within certain time.

D) All advertisements are trying to push goods to consumers who want them and who don't want them.

27. As a means of communication, advertising tells people of _____.

A) the goods they produced

B) the services they offered

C) the only way to raise their standard of living

D) the products and services being supplied

28. Which of the following is NOT a form of advertising?

A) Commercials during the intervals of TV series.

B) Well-designed packaging.

C) Salesmen in the supermarkets.

D) Shop displays in the window.

29. Advertising is essential _____.

A) for goods to be sold in foreign countries

B) for goods to be sold in other places within the country

C) for goods to be sold in its production place

D) all of the above

30. According to the passage, an article of goods will sell well as long as it has _____.

A) standard quality   B) just-so-so quality and good advertisements

C) well designed advertisements   D) both A and C

Section D   Short Answer Questions

Directions:（略）

Passage 5

The concept of information superhighway has been around for more than a decade, but until 1993 it was merely a technological imagination. Today information superhighway has become an everyday topic and is making its entry into our lives.

Information superhighway is an *unprecedented*（空前的，史无前例的）nationwide, or worldwide, electronic communications network that connects everyone to everyone else, and provides just about any sort of electronic communication imaginable. Hook up your computer to the Internet and you are on your information superhighway. The purpose of information superhighway is to provide remote electronic banking, schooling, shopping, taxpaying, game playing, video conferencing, movie ordering, medical *diagnosing*（诊断）, etc. Information superhighway will make many things you do easier and more convenient. For example, instead of calling your friends one by one to tell them the party is canceled, you'll simply send a single e-mail message to everyone at once. And if you live in a rural area far from a major hospital, *telemedicine* （远程医疗）may allow a specialist in London to diagnose you without your having to travel farther than to your local physician's clinic. Information superhighway may also pull together newspaper and magazine articles from around the world on a particular topic of your own interests. If you like to shop with someone who lives in another city, you may call him or her and then do some shopping together for an hour or two.

Whether you like it or not, information superhighway will change the way we live.

31. What time has the imagination of information superhighway become true?

   _____ _____ _____ _____

   _____ _____ _____ _____

32. According to Para. 2, information superhighway is, in fact, _____.

   _____ _____ _____ _____

   _____ _____ _____ _____

33. In order to "run" on the superhighway of information, what do you need to do first?

   _____ _____ _____ _____

   _____ _____ _____ _____

34. What are the typical features of information superhighway?

   _____ _____ _____ _____

   _____ _____ _____ _____

35. The phrase "do some shopping" in the last sentence of Paragraph 2 properly means _____.

   _____ _____ _____ _____

   _____ _____ _____ _____

Notes and Explanations

Passage 1

Explanations

1. [N] 第五段提到 The service, which first went on-line Wednesday, is free. 这种最早在星期三开始的网上服务是免费的。可以得到答案为 No。

2. [NG] 第八段提到 But he conceded that his offerings could be abused by those with less legitimate excuses, like chronic oversleeping or lingering hangovers. 他承认他提供的课堂笔记可能被那些因睡过头或酒后头晕等很多不合理的理由而缺课的学生滥用。但没有提及本题中的命题,所以答案为 Not Given。

3. [Y] 第十一段提到 There is no shortage of critics who believe that the arrival of Mr. Wolf's venture—along with other web sites that sell sample term papers and synopses of great books—signals nothing less than the erosion of liberal education, if not civilization. 有很多批评家认为 Mr. Wolf 的网上课程笔记服务及其他出售论文和名著概要的网站的出现若不是对文明的破坏,就是对人文学科的腐蚀。所以答案为 Yes。

4. [N] 第十二段提到 But Mark Edmundson, a professor of English at the University of Virginia, one of the schools where Mr. Wolf set up shop, thinks the problem lies more with universities than on those trying to beat the system. Mark Edmundson 认为问题与其说是在于那些人试图破坏教育体制不如说在于学校。所以答案为 No。

5. [N] 第十九段提到 Mr. Wolf said professors at the University of Houston were initially wary of helping him and his note-takers gain access to classes, if they were not enrolled. Houston 大学的教授们在最初的时候谨慎地给他提供帮助,让那些记课程笔记但不是注册在内的学生听课。所以答案为 No。

6. [Y] 第十五段提到 Peter Wood, a professor of anthropology and the associate provost at Boston University, which is also on Mr. Wolf's list, said the university might consider taking legal action once notes from the school appear on the site. Boston 大学副院长、人类学教授 Mr. Wood 也在 Mr. Wolf 列的单子上。他说一旦有来自学校课程的笔记出现在网上,大学可能会采取法律行动。所以答案为 Yes。

7. [N] 从第二十五段"I'm not unalterably opposed to this dissemination," he said. 得知"Professor Syer 对于网上传播有关他的课程笔记的做法并不是绝对反对。"所以答案为 No。

8. 从第三段 The note-takers post their jottings electronically, within 24 hours, on a central web site. 得出答案为 **electronically**。

9. 第十段提到 It is important for them to attend the class, use this information as supplements to the course and if they do that, they are going to get A's. Wolf 认为学生上课很重要并可把网上的笔记当作课程学习的补充。如果能做到的话,学生一定能取得优秀的成绩。从中得出答案为 **supplements**。

10. 第十五段提到 Peter Wood, a professor of anthropology and the associate provost（院长）at Boston University, which is also on Mr. Wolf's list, said the university might consider taking legal action once notes from the school appear on the site. Boston 大学副院长、人类学教授 Mr. Wood 也在 Mr. Wolf 列的单子上。他说一旦有来自学校课程笔记出现在网上,大学可能会采取法律行动。从而得出答案为 **illegal**。

Passage 2

Notes

1. The country's top medical... dead. (Line 4~5, Para. 1)

这句话的意思是:美国医疗部门的高级官员说,五年前感染艾滋病毒的美国人百分之九十多现在已经去世了。

2. There is no cure... and no vaccine medicine to prevent it. (Line 1，Para. 2)

cure 意思是"治疗或治愈的方法;补救办法,对策"。例如:

Scientists have so far failed to provide a cure for the common cold.

到目前为止,科学家仍未能提供治疗普通感冒的药物。

At present there seems no cure for rising prices and falling living standards.

目前对物价上涨和生活水平降低似乎还没有对策。

3. Experts say no one has gotten AIDS by living with, caring for... patient. (Line 3~4，Para. 4)

care for 在这句话中意思是"照料"。例如:

He's very good at caring for sick animals. 他很善于照料生病的动物。

Explanations

11. [D] 语法规则要求此处应填一个数量词修饰 persons。选项中只有 D 项是数量词。根据第一段第三句的"And one million more..."可以判断 million 符合句意。

12. [A] 语法规则要求此处应填一个动词的第三人称单数形式作谓语。只有选项 A 是该形式。根据这句话的意思"世界卫生组织称全世界有多达一千万的人染有导致艾滋病的病毒",causes(导致)符合句意。

13. [F] 语法规则要求此处应填一个名词作 have 的宾语。这句话的意思是"专家认为有三十五万人有这种病",根据上下文可知,这种病指的是艾滋病。所以 disease 疾病符合句意。

14. [O] 语法规则要求此处应填一个形容词修饰 official。选项 K、M、N、O 是形容词。根据上下文的意思,medical(医学的、医术的)符合此处意思"医疗卫生官员"。

15. [C] 语法规则要求此处应填一个单数名词。根据上下文的意思,此处意思应该是"没有能治愈艾滋病的治疗办法",cure 意思是"治疗,治愈",符合句意。

16. [G] 语法规则要求此处应填一个形容词或名词作定语修饰 system。这句话中提到了白细胞,根据常识白细胞是人的自身抗病防御系统的一部分。defense(防御)符合句意。defense system 意思是"防御系统"。

17. [M] 语法规则要求此处应填一个形容词作定语修饰 cell。根据上句话"The virus invades healthy cells"可推断这里应选 healthy。

18. [I] 语法规则要求此处应填一个动词原形构成动词不定式作 move on 的结果状语。只有选项 I 是动词原形。根据上文"The virus invades healthy cells"可推断这里 invade(侵入)符合句意。

19. [B] 语法规则要求此处应填一个动词的过去分词形式构成被动语态。选项 B、J 是该形式。根据上下文的意思,此处应该是"艾滋病毒由人的体液携带",所以 carried 符合句意。

20. [J] 语法规则要求此处应填一个动词的过去分词形式构成被动语态。前一句话"The virus can be passed..."和本句中的 also 表明这里应选 passed。

Passage 3

Notes

1. One can get accustomed to operating... (Line 3，Para. 1)

get/become/be accustomed to 意思是"适应……,习惯于……",to 是介词,后面接名词或动名词。例如:

We are accustomed to working hard. 我们习惯了努力工作。

My eyes soon got accustomed to the darkness. 我的眼睛很快适应了黑暗。

2. Yet no one would do either of these things for its own sake. (Line 5~6，Para. 1)

for one's (own) sake 意思是"为了……的缘故,为了……的利益",sake 意思是"理由,缘故,利益"。这句

话的意思是:没有人只是为了工作本身的缘故而做这些事。例如:

for safety's sake 为了安全起见

for the country's sake 为了国家的利益

3. With this another reward of teaching is very closely linked. (Line 1, Para. 2)

这是一个部分倒装句,为了强调 with it 把这部分状语提前,正常的语序应是:Another reward of teaching is very closely linked with this. 这句话的意思是:教书的另一个回报与此密切相关。be linked with 意思是"与……相关联"。例如:

The two clues are closely linked with each other in this case. 在这个案子中这两条线索紧密相连。

4. But often it comes into helping to create a human being. (Line 7~8, Para. 2)

come into helping 意思是"开始起作用"。例如:

come into fashion/being/power/existence/force/consideration 开始流行/形成/掌权/存在/生效/考虑

5. To teach a boy the difference between truth and lie in print... (Line 8, Para. 2)

in print 意思是"以印刷的形式出版的",修饰名词时作后置定语,这里是指"书上印的(真理和谎言)"。例如:

see one's name in print 看见某人的名字出现在出版物中

the book in print 已出版的书

Explanations

这是一篇议论文,用许多生动形象的比喻论述了教师的回报是什么。相信作为老师或学生的读者读过后会对教和学之间的关系和师生关系有新的认识。

21. B) 细节题。根据第一段第五句 Only the money makes them tolerable. 和其上下文可知,使人们能容忍文中提到的枯燥工作的因素只有金钱,所以答案是 B 项。

22. D) 细节题。根据第一段第一句话和最后一句话,我们可知道作者的观点很明确:教师真正的幸福就是用心培养学生、传授知识,同时又能教学相长。所以答案应是 D 项。根据第一段其他选项是作者认为很枯燥的事,所以不对。

23. A) 细节题。根据第二段第六句话 You take the living mind, and mould it. 可知,答案是 A 项。教书意味着塑造人。根据第二段第四句 You do not merely insert a lot of facts, if you teach them properly. 可知,如果你会教书育人,就不该只硬塞给学生一些事实,而是启发他们去思考、分析,然后自己决定是接受还是拒绝,所以选项 B 不对;根据第二段第五句可知选项 C 和 D 都不对,故都被排除。

24. B) 推断题。根据文章第二段第六句可推断出老师教书育人,所以是人类灵魂的工程师,所以选项 A 是正确的。根据文章第二、三、六和第十句 But it comes into helping to create a human being. 可推断出选项 C 是正确的。从整个第二段的论述以及拿老师与艺术家和医生作类比,可推断出选项 D 是正确的。只有选项 B 在文中意思是不对的,第二段第七句和第八句表明学生有时会和老师作对,甚至反抗,有时确实毫无成效,所以学生们并非总是接受老师的教育的。

25. B) 细节题。作者在文章末段最后一句使用类比来说明当老师成功地塑造了一个人才时那种满足感和成就感(give the sort of satisfaction),正如画家在黑色画布上用颜料画出图画以及医生听到患者由于自己的及时救助而康复时的心情一样,所以应选择 B 项。选项 A 只是提到了这两种职业的从业特点,而不是作者作类比的目的,所以不对;选项 C 和 D 很明显不对,是干扰项,可排除。

Passage 4

Notes

1. ... advertising is essential to... at large, live. (Line 1~3, Para. 1)

▷这句话的意思是:广告对于生活在像英国或整个世界上很大一部分的人们来说是必不可少的。

at large 意思是"大多数,整个"。例如:

The people at large want peace. 大多数人都想要和平。

▷society at large 整个社会

Recently there has been unrest in the country at large. 近来全国发生了动乱。

2. If it were not for advertising. . . many people. (Line 4~5,Para. 1)

这个句子用了虚拟语气,意思是:要不是有广告,一些商品的信息永远都不会为人所知。

3. In its widest sense, advertising. . . salesman. (Line 2~4,Para. 2)

▷sense 在这里意思是"意义,含义",通常使用句型 in. . . sense,in the widest sense 意思是"最广义地说"。

例如:

This word can be used in several senses. 这个词可以有几种解释。

▷literature in the broad sense 广义文学

He cannot be called a writer in the strict sense of the word. 严格地说,他不能被称为作家。

4. It is only more recently that it has. . . time span. (Line 1~3,Para. 3)

这是一个强调句式。被强调的部分是状语。这句话的意思是:直到近来人们才越来越认识到如果商品不能在一定的时间段内以一个合理的价格销售出去,那么这种商品的生产就是一种资源的浪费。

5. . . . but if the article. . . it is. . . unlikely that. . . well. (Line 3~5,Para. 4)

▷match up to 意思是"与……期待的一样好"。例如:

It wasn't a bad holiday, but the weather didn't match up to our hopes.

假期过得还不错,但天气不如我们希望的好。

▷It is unlikely that. . . 意思是"……是不可能的",这句话的意思是:广告的确吸引了一些潜在顾客的兴趣,但是如果顾客买到的商品并不像广告上说的那么好,那么很明显这种商品的销路就不会很好。

Explanations

这是一篇议论文。文章以英国为背景,论述了各种形式的广告及其作用。读过本文,读者应对广告有一个全新的了解。

26. **A)** 细节题。根据第一段倒数第二句话 If it were not for advertising. . . people. 可知,选项 B 是不对的;根据第三段第二句话可知,选项 C 是不对的;根据第四段的第二句和第三句可知,选项 D 是不对的;根据第二段的内容可知,选项 A 是正确的。

27. **D)** 细节题。根据第一段第三句 It is a way of telling people about the goods and services that are offered. 可知,答案是 D 项。

28. **C)** 细节题。根据第二段的内容可知选项 A、B、D 都是广告的不同形式,只有选项 C 不是。另外根据第二段第二句的末尾 even the spoken word of the salesman 可知是指售货员所说的话也属于广告的一种形式,但不是售货员本人。所以选项 C 不属于广告的形式。

29. **D)** 细节题。根据第三段最后一句话可知选项 A、B、C 的内容都是广告起作用的地方,所以应选 D 项,囊括前三个选项,概括全面。

30. **D)** 细节题。根据第四段最后一句可知:产品畅销的原因与好的商品质量、好的广告宣传是密切相关的,两者缺一不可,所以应选 D 项。

Passage 5

Keys

31. After 1993.

32. a way of electronic communication

33. Buy a computer and hook it up to the Internet.

34. Making things we do easier and more convenient.

35. buying things from shops by using a computer at home

Notes

1. The concept of... decade，but until 1993 it was merely... imagination.（Line 1～2，Para. 1）

   这句话的意思是:信息高速路的概念已经存在了十多年了,但是在 1993 年以前,它还只是一个技术上的设想。be around 意思是"存在"。

2. Hook up your computer to the Internet and...（Line 3～4，Para. 2）

   这句话的意思是"把你的计算机连接到互联网上,你就……"。

3. And if you live in a rural area... farther than to your local physician's clinic.（Line 8～9，Para. 2）

   这句话的意思是:如果你住在远离大医院的乡下,那么远程医疗可以让一位伦敦的专家来为你诊断,这样你就不必走很远的路去城里就医而是只需到当地医生的诊所就可以了。

4. Information superhighway may also pull... interests.（Line 9～11，Para. 2）

   这句话的意思是:信息高速路还可以把全世界关于某一个你特别感兴趣的话题的报纸或杂志的文章收集在一起。

Unit 9

Section A   Skimming and Scanning

Directions：（略）

Passage 1

Hospital Team Excels in HR Leadership

1. St Andrew's War Memorial Hospital is a 229-bed acute care private hospital with 870 employees that has a commitment to providing compassionate quality care, which stems from the Christian ideals of the Uniting and Presbyterian Churches.

2. St Andrew's dedication to patient care is defined as "Total Personal Care"—a concept that goes beyond the traditional boundaries of patient/doctor/hospital relationships. It also refers to the relationship between employer and employee and the importance placed on happy, satisfied, and motivated staff.

3. The private health care industry has been dealing with rapid change. As the number of privately insured patients declines, private hospitals face increased competitive pressures to achieve greater efficiencies. This, combined with major structural changes to the Queensland health system, including "co-locating" private and public hospitals, has made the health sector turbulent and challenging.

4. When the present chief executive officer, Vaughan Howell, joined St Andrew's three years ago, he assessed this environment and, anticipating the changes, made plans for the future. Howell led an extensive review of the organization, beginning with its mission, vision, and values, and continuing through its core business, organization structure, and culture, and management processes, from which emerged a plan for significant change.

Mission, vision, values

1. The review started with a market research project to find out customers perceptions of the quality of care provided through assigning an organizational "personality". The research outlined a personality that the public identified with St Andrew's and it was an image that needed some improvement.

2. As a result, the concept of "Total Personal Care" was developed. It is an *ethos*（准则）describing the holistic approach that St Andrew's takes towards patient care. It involves providing a highly personalized standard of care that extends beyond a patient's stay in hospital and includes personalized pre- and post-hospitalization programs, *rehabilitation*（恢复，修复）, education, family/community involvement, and emotional and spiritual support. It stresses the importance of not only providing clinical expertise and the latest technology, but first and foremost, a caring attitude.

3. Through the review process, the mission, vision, and the values were rewritten. They now read：

Mission: To provide for the health care needs of the community, giving expression to the Christian values of the Presbyterian and Uniting Churches both as a provider of direct patient care and as a part of the wider health care community.

Vision: To earn a reputation for excellence in health care. This will be accomplished by the compassionate and effective delivery of appropriate acute health care services to our community, technological advances, continuous quality improvement, and sharing our achievements with the wider health care community through teaching and research. Through the development of highly specialized clinical services we aim to be regarded throughout Queensland and beyond as a leader in our fields.

4. The four value statements were derived from the mission and vision and were created following a widely consultative process. They are:

Our focus is our customers, both internal and external.

We will strive to be the leader in our fields.

We will take personal responsibilities for our actions.

We will constantly re-evaluate our services.

Strategic planning

1. But how do mission, vision, and values become the platform for a workable strategic plan? St Andrew's has attempted to take these elements and pragmatically link them to bottom-line performance by *aligning* (使一致) organization-wide strategic goals and performance indicators.

2. Planning of these linkages at board and senior management level was supplemented by several stakeholder focus groups. As key customers, doctors and patients were involved to ensure their expectations remained central in establishing our future path, more than 200 employees also took part in this process, and their input was invaluable in relating the vision back to the workplace.

3. Following *endorsement* (赞同,认可) of the strategic direction, departmental action plans were aligned and agreed, and then detailed through individual action plans. The Organization Development Team (ODT) designed, introduced, and monitored this process so that any gaps could be addressed and any inconsistencies between departmental plans and the strategic plan could be remedied. The action planning process has now developed to the point where almost all employees—from the CEO to entry-level employees—have a specific individual action plan to guide their work.

Performance management

1. These ideas and concepts are not new, and the creation of "feel-good" slogans and mottoes is not hard. What is difficult is translating those ideas into measurable behaviors and integrating them into business operations. This was pursued through the careful use of key performance indicators in action planning and a performance management that incorporated the values and clarified accountabilities.

2. St Andrew's performance management system moves away from the subjective, ratings-based annual appraisal to a regular, ongoing system of performance management. It begins with the initial hiring of a new employee. The position description lists the values as required "attitudes", which are key selection criteria.

Reward and recognition

1. The values are affirmed and reinforced through the reward and recognition system, which allows any employee to formally recognize a fellow employee or team who demonstrate exceptional examples of the values of St Andrew's.

2. These examples are acknowledged across the organization and culminate in the annual celebration of the Staff Achievement Awards. The type of reward and recognition is driven by the employee and varies depending on their personal preference. St Andrew's is sensitive to the fact that some employees prefer to limit their public recognition.

Employer values

1. It is important to acknowledge how critical it is that the organization's systems and processes reflect the same values that staff is expected to demonstrate individually. Competition between the various private hospitals to recruit and retain the best personnel is fierce. To ensure St Andrew's maintains a reputation for being a preferred employer, the concept of Total Personal Care also extends to the staff. The ODT, with the support of the whole organization, has implemented many initiatives designed to support the values as well as maximize job satisfaction.

2. By promoting Total Personal Care as a theme, St Andrew's has succeeded in motivating staff by encouraging their individual dedication and commitment to their jobs.

1. St Andrew's War memorial Hospital is a private hospital with the best personnel in the field.

2. St Andrew's "Total Personnel Care" represents the traditional opinion of patient/doctor/ hospital relationship.

3. The private hospitals face increased competitive pressures because of the decrease in the number of privately insured patients.

4. The market research showed that St Andrew's had a perfect image in the public.

5. New mission focuses on delivering health care services to the community.

6. The delivery of community health care services, technological advances and quality improvement will help St Andrew's to earn a reputation for excellence.

7. The elite employee recognized by staff will get bonus in the annual celebration of the Staff Achievement Awards.

8. In strategic planning, St Andrew's has attempted to link mission, vision and values to _____ performance.

9. ODT was responsible for addressing any gaps and remedying any inconsistencies between departmental plans and strategic plan and all employees have a specific _____ action plan to guide their work.

10. Because of the stiff competition to recruit and retain the best personnel, St Andrew's has recognized the importance of providing Total Personal Care to _____ to keep a reputation of being a preferred employer.

Section B Discourse Vocabulary Test

Directions：（略）

Passage 2

These are two complementary ways of processing a text. They are both used whenever we read: sometimes one predominates, sometimes the other, but both are needed. And, though ___11___ unconscious processes, both can be adopted as ___12___ strategies by a reader approaching a difficult text.

In top-down processing, we draw our own ___13___ and experience—the predictions we make, based on the *schemata*（图解，概要）we have acquired—to understand the text. As we see, this kind of processing is used when we ___14___ assumptions and draw inferences. We make conscious use of it when we try to see the ___15___ purpose of the text, or get a rough idea of the pattern of the writer's argument, in order to make a ___16___ guess at the next step. We might compare this approach to an eagle's eye view of the landscape.

In bottom-up processing, the reader builds up a meaning from the black marks on the page recognizing letters and words, working out sentence structure. We can make conscious use of it when an initial reading leaves us confused. ___17___ we cannot believe that apparent message was really what the writer intended; this can happen if our world knowledge is ___18___, or if the writer's point of view is very different from our own. In that case, we must *scrutinize*（细看，详查）the vocabulary and *syntax*（句法）to make sure we have grasped the plain sense ___19___. Thus bottom-up processing can be used as a corrective to "tunnel vision"（seeing things only from our own limited point of view）. Our image of bottom-up processing might be a scientist with a magnifying glass examining the ecology of a certain *transect*（横断面）—a tiny part of the landscape the eagle surveys.

Although logically we might expect that we ought to understand the plain sense if we are to understand anything else, in practice a reader ___20___ shifts from one focus to another: now adopting a top-down approach to predict the probable meaning, then moving to the bottom-up approach to check whether that is really what the writer says. This has become known as interactive reading. Both approaches can be *mobilized*（调动，动员）by conscious choice, and both are important strategies for readers.

A) indicate	I) reasoned
B) normally	J) Perhaps
C) interpret	K) overall
D) successful	L) feedback
E) intelligence	M) awkward
F) audience	N) inadequate
G) conscious	O) correctly
H) continually	

Section C   Reading in Depth

Directions：（略）

Passage 3

The letter that the Navy recently received from a sailor's wife was full of *anguish*（剧痛）in describing the couple's transfer from Great Lakes to San Diego. On the trip across the country with their 2-month-old son, they limited themselves to one meal a day, stayed at the cheapest motels and still spent hundreds of dollars more than they received from the Defense Department in travel allowance. This dramatizes what *Pentagon*（五角大楼）officials rate as the most serious problem facing the nation's armed forces—a pay *squeeze*（紧缺）.

In the words of Adam Thomas B. Hayward, chief of naval operations："The *talent drain*（人才流失）occasioned by inadequate compensation is clearly the single most serious concern I have about the present state of the Navy." The readiness of the Air Force, Army and Marine Corps is similarly *impaired*（减少）as the armed forces lose out increasingly to the civilian job market. In all four of the services, voluntary enlistment for the first time has fallen short of targets，while the career re-enlistment rate has nose-dived over the past few years.

These trends are forcing a re-examination of popular assumptions about military compensation. There has long been a widely accepted notion that even military pay fell behind civilian wages, the *perks*（免费）of service（such as free accommodation）in the armed forces would more than make up for the difference. Pentagon officials say that is no longer true.

As military pay has declined relative to civilian wages, there has also been erosion of many of the perks, such as housing allowance, free medical benefits and cut-rate groceries. A recent Pentagon study shows that, as a result of the combined impact of *inflation*（通货膨胀）and pay ceilings, the real buying power of the salaries received by men and women in the armed services has fallen by 11 percent since 1972, the year of the last big catch-up raise.

In addition, Pentagon officials say the compensation many military people get for special duties also has failed to keep up with inflation. For example, the flight pay, which was once rated at 45% of base pay, has not been changed since 1964. It is now equivalent to only 12% of an *aviator's*（飞行员）base pay. Compensation for overseas duty has not changed since 1949, and the family separation allowance remains at the $30-a-month level established in 1963.

21. The letter from a sailor's wife was cited in order to _____ .

    A) provide evidence of normal decline in the army

    B) serve as the starting point of the author's argument

    C) add variety to the author's style of writing

    D) prepare the reader for widespread popular concern

22. The word "occasioned"(Line 2, Para. 2) means here _____ .

    A) brought about   B) chanced upon

    C) alleviated   D) fabricated

23. The armed forces in the US suffer greatly from talent drain due to _____ .

    A) the irreversible impairment to the readiness of the army

B) the sharp reduction of military compensation in the past

C) the fall of the morale of people in the military services

D) the decline of military pay compared with civilian earnings

24. It has long been assumed that the perks of servicemen _____.

A) have declined relative to those enjoyed by civilians

B) will well exceed their service payments and allowance

C) can well compensate for their salary gap with civilians

D) have made little difference for their income

25. It can be inferred from the text that _____.

A) military pay was significantly raised in 1972

B) military compensation has shrunk by 11 ％ since 1972

C) flight pay used to be 12％ for an aviator's base pay

D) family separation allowance did not start until 1963

Passage 4

The most interesting architectural phenomenon of the 1970s was the enthusiasm for refurbishing older buildings. Obviously, this was not an entirely new phenomenon. What is new is the *wholesale* (大规模的) interest in reusing the past, in recycling, in adaptive *rehabilitation* (修复,复原). A few trial efforts, such as Ghirardelli Square in San Francisco, proved their financial *viability* (可行性) in the 1960s, but it was in the 1970s, with strong government support through tax incentives and rapid *depreciation* (折旧,贬值), as well as growing interest in ecology issues, that recycling became a major factor on the urban scene.

One of the most comprehensive ventures was the restoration and transformation of Boston's eighteenth century Faneuil Hall and the Quincy Market, designed in 1824. This section had fallen on hard times, but beginning with the construction of a new city hall immediately *adjacent* (邻近的), it has returned to life with the intelligent reuse of these fine buildings under the design leadership of Benjamin Thompson. He has provided a marvelous setting for dining, shopping, professional offices, and simply walking.

Butler Square, in Minneapolis, exemplifies major changes in its complex of offices, commercial space, and public *amenities* (环境、房屋等的舒适) carved out of a massive pile designed in 1906 as a hardware warehouse. The exciting interior *timber* (木材,木料) structure of the building was highlighted by cutting light courts through the interior and adding large *skylights* (天窗).

San Antonio, Texas, offers an object lesson for numerous other cities combating urban decay. Rather than bringing in the *bulldozers* (推土机), San Antonio's leaders rehabilitated existing structures, while simultaneously cleaning up the San Antonio River, which *meanders* (曲折前进) through the business district.

26. What is the main idea of the passage?

A) During the 1970s, old buildings in many cities were recycled for modern use.

B) Recent interest in ecology issues has led to the cleaning up of many rivers.

C) The San Antonio example shows that bulldozers are not the way to fight urban decay.

D) Strong government support has made adaptive rehabilitation a reality in Boston.

27. What is the space at Quincy Market now used for?

A) Boston's new city hall.

B) Sports and recreational facilities.

C) Commercial and industrial warehouses.

D) Restaurants, offices, and stores.

28. When was the Butler Square building originally built?

A) In the eighteenth century.

B) In the early nineteenth century.

C) In the late nineteenth century.

D) In the early twentieth century.

29. What is the author's opinion of the San Antonio project?

A) It is clearly the best of projects discussed.

B) It is a good project that could be copied in other cities.

C) The extensive use of bulldozers makes the project unnecessarily costly.

D) The work done on the river was more important than the work done on the buildings.

30. The passage states that the San Antonio project differed from those in Boston and Minneapolis in which of the following ways?

A) It consisted primarily of new construction.

B) It occurred in the business district.

C) It involved the environment as well as buildings.

D) It was designed to combat urban decay.

Section D   Short Answer Questions

Directions：（略）

Passage 5

Children who are never, or seldom, *spanked* （打屁股） do better on some intelligence tests than children who are frequently *smacked* （拍打,掌击）.

Why? Maybe parents who do not spank their children spend more time talking to, and reasoning with them, suggest researchers. "Some parents think this is a waste of time, but research shows such verbal parent-child interactions enhance the child's *cognitive* （认知的） ability," says Murray Straus of the University of New Hampshire. His team studies more than 900 children aged from 1 to 4 at the start of the trial in 1986. They were given tests of cognitive ability, which is the ability to learn and to recognize things, in 1986 and again in 1990.

They then accounted for factors such as whether the father lived with the family, how many children there were in the family, how much time the mother spent with the child, *ethnic* （种族的） group, birth weight, age and gender. They watched mothers with their children and questioned them about *corporal punishment* （体罚）. They found that the more the children were spanked or otherwise physically punished, the lower their scores on the test. The cognitive ability of the children who were not spanked in either of the two sample weeks increased while the cognitive ability of the children who were frequently spanked decreased.

"The children who were spanked didn't get dumber，" Straus said. "What the study showed is spanking is associated with falling behind the average rate of cognitive development，not an absolute decrease in cognitive ability." It seemed parents who did not hit their children reasoned more with them to control their behavior. They found the less corporal punishment mothers in this sample had used the more cognitive stimulation they provided to the child.

There is a trend against slapping and spanking children in the United States，but studies show most parents still hit their children. Straus suggested there should be an awareness campaign. If parents knew the risk they were exposing their children to when they spank，he believed millions would stop.

31. What is the effect if children are frequently spanked?

_____

_____

32. Cognitive ability is the ability _____.

_____

_____

33. How can children's cognitive ability be enhanced?

_____

_____

34. How long did Straus's study last?

_____

_____

35. Why do most parents still hit their children，though there is a trend against spanking children in the United States?

_____

_____

Notes and Explanations

Passage 1

Explanations

1. [NG] 第一段第一句提到 St Andrew's War Memorial Hospital is a 229-bed acute care private hospital with 870 employees that has a commitment to providing compassionate quality care，which stems from the Christian ideals of the Uniting and Presbyterian Churches. St Andrew's War Memorial Hospital 是一所有着 870 名医护人员和 229 个床位的私立紧急救护医院，有责任提供热情优质的服务。但没有提及本题中的命题，所以答案为 Not Given。

2. [N] 第二段提到 St Andrew's dedication to patient care is defined as "Total Personal Care"—a concept that goes beyond the traditional boundaries of patient/doctor/hospital relationships. It also refers to the

relationship between employer and employee and the importance placed on happy, satisfied, and motivated staff. (Total Personal Care)"全部个人看护"是指医院医护人员对病人的周到热情的看护,它超越传统的病人、医生、医院之间关系的界限。它还指雇主和雇员的关系以及对员工的幸福、满意度和工作积极性的关注。所以答案为 No。

3. [Y] 第三段第二句提到 As the number of privately insured patients declines, private hospitals face increased competitive pressures to achieve greater efficiencies. 随着私人购买医疗保险病人数量的减少,为获得更高的效率,私立医院面临的压力不断增加。所以答案为 Yes。

4. [N] Mission, vision, values 部分第一段第二句提到 The research outlined a personality that the public identified with St Andrew's and it was an image that needed some improvement. 调查归纳出大众认定的在 St Andrew's 工作的医护人员身上表现出的品质特点。其医护人员的形象还需一些改进。所以答案为 No。

5. [Y] Mission, vision, values 部分第三段提到 Mission: To provide for the health care needs of the community, giving expression to the Christian values of the Presbyterian and Uniting Churches both as a provider of direct patient care and as a part of the wider health care community. 任务:为社区人们的健康提供服务,实现基督教和基督教长老会教规中规定的任务即给病人提供直接的治疗,给社区的人们提供较为广泛的健康保健服务。所以答案为 Yes。

6. [Y] Mission, vision, values 部分第三段提到 Vision: To earn a reputation for excellence in health care. This will be accomplished by the compassionate and effective delivery of appropriate acute health care services to our community, technological advances, continuous quality improvement, and sharing our achievements with the wider health care community through teaching and research. 设想(目标):为了获得良好的声誉和实现健康保健事业的完美发展,用热情有效的方法给社区的人们提供适当的医疗服务,确保技术上的发展,不断提高质量,通过教学和科研与其他保健机构分享我们的成果。所以答案为 Yes。

7. [NG] Reward and Recognition 部分第二段提到 These examples are acknowledged across the organization and culminate in the annual celebration of the Staff Achievement Awards. 这些优秀人员的工作在整个机构得到认可,他们并在一年一度的优秀员工奖励大会上得到大张旗鼓的表彰。但没有提及本题中的命题,所以答案为 Not Given。

8. 通过"strategic planning"、"mission"、"vision"、"values"等词,从 Strategic planning 部分第一段第二句 St Andrew's has attempted to take these elements and pragmatically link them to bottom-line performance by aligning (使一致) organization-wide strategic goals and performance indicators. 可以得出答案为 **bottom-line**。

9. 通过"ODT"、"gaps"、"inconsistencies"、"departmental plan"、"strategic plan"等词,从 Strategic planning 部分第三段第二句 The Organization Development Team (ODT) designed, introduced, and monitored this process so that any gaps could be addressed and any inconsistencies between departmental plans and the strategic plan could be remedied. The action planning process has now developed to the point where almost all employees—from the CEO to entry-level employees—have a specific individual action plan to guide their work. 可以得出答案为 **individual**。

10. 通过"competition"、"personnel"、"reputation"、"preferred employer"等词,从 Employer Value 部分第一段第二句 Competition between the various private hospitals to recruit and retain the best personnel is fierce. To ensure St Andrew's maintains a reputation for being a preferred employer, the concept of Total Personal Care also extends to the staff. 得出答案为 **the staff**。

Passage 2

Notes

1. And, though normally unconscious...a difficult text. (Line 3～5, Para. 1)
这句话在 though 引导的让步状语从句中省略了主语和谓语。完整的句子应是:And, though they are

大学英语 4 级阅读与简答〈新题型〉

normally... 这句话的意思是:虽然通常是无意识的过程,但当读者解读一篇比较难的文章时会有意识地采用两种阅读技巧。

2. We make conscious use of it when we try to see... (Line 3~4, Para. 2)

make conscious use of 意思是"有意识地使用……",make use of 意思是"使用,利用"。例如:

He made good use of his spare time. 他业余时间利用得很好。

3. We might compare this approach to an eagle's eye view of the landscape. (Line 5~6, Para. 2)

这句话的意思是:我们也许可以把这种方法比作鹰在空中鸟瞰大地风景。这时鹰看到的是大地的全貌,而我们看到的是文章大意。其中 compare sth. to sth. 意思是"把……比作……"。例如:

We compare our body to a machine. 我们把自己的身体比作一台机器。

Shakespeare compares life to a voyage. 莎士比亚把人生比作航程。

4. In that case, we must... to make sure we have... correctly. (Line 5~6, Para. 3)

这句话的意思是:在这种情况下,我们必须仔细揣摩词汇意义与句法意义以确保我们准确无误地掌握其基本意思。make sure 意思是"确保,明确,弄清楚"。例如:

He went around making sure that all the windows were closed.

他巡视了一遍,以确保所有的窗子都关上了。

We should start early if we want to make sure of getting there in time.

如果我们想确保及时到那儿就该早点动身。

5. Our image of bottom-up processing might be a... surveys. (Line 8~10, Para. 3)

我们这种从下向上的阅读可能像一位科学家手拿放大镜仔细看某一横截面的生态分布——就好像鹰鸟瞰大地时观察一小部分地方。

Explanations

11. [B] 语法规则要求此处应填一个副词作状语修饰 unconscious。选项 B、H、J、O 是副词。根据上下文的意思"虽然通常情况下是无意识的过程,但读者在阅读比较难的文章时,可把它们作为有意识的阅读策略",因此此处 normally 符合句意。normally 意思是"通常情况下"。

12. [G] 语法规则要求此处应填一个形容词作定语修饰名词 strategies。选项 D、G、K、M、N 是形容词。此处与上半句的 unconscious 形成对比,因此 conscious 符合句意。另外,在第二段第三句也提到了"We make conscious use...",意思是"有意识的"。

13. [E] 语法规则要求此处应填一个名词作 draw 的宾语。选项 E、F、L 是名词。这句话的意思是"在从上往下的阅读过程中,我们要调用自己的聪明才智和经验"。intelligence(智慧)符合句意。破折号后面是同位语,解释前面的意思"我们要自己推测文章的意思",因此应选 E 项。

14. [C] 语法规则要求此处应填一个动词原形作状语从句的谓语。选项 A、C 是动词原形。根据上下文的意思,本句意思应是"当我们解读假设和推断结论时,可使用这种方法"。interpret 意思是"理解,解释",符合句意。

15. [K] 语法规则要求此处应填一个形容词作定语修饰 purpose。根据下半句"or get a rough idea..."的解释,此处应该是 overall。overall 意思是"整体的,全部的"。

16. [I] 语法规则要求此处应填一个形容词作定语修饰 guess。根据上下文的意思"大概了解了作者的论点后,下一步应是做出合理的推论"。因此应选 reasoned。reasoned 意思是"合理的"。

17. [J] 语法规则要求此处应填一个副词作状语修饰谓语。这句话是对上句"We can make conscious use of it when an initial reading leaves us confused"的解释,perhaps(也许)符合句意。

18. [N] 语法规则要求此处应填一个形容词在条件状语从句中作表语。根据上下文的意思,此处应该是"我们的知识不够"。inadequate(不够的)符合句意。

19. [O] 语法规则要求此处应填一个副词作状语修饰谓语。根据此句的意思"我们仔细查看词汇和句法就是为了确保自己已经正确理解了(文章)大意"。correctly 意思是"正确地"。

20. [H] 语法规则要求此处应填一个副词作状语修饰 shifts。根据下文中的"now...then..."可以判断
continually 符合句意。continually 意思是"不断地;反复地"。

Passage 3

Notes

1. This dramatizes what Pentagon officials rate...squeeze. (Line 5~6, Para. 1)
   这句话的意思是:这被五角大楼官员们视为是(美国)国家军队所面临的最严重的问题——工资紧缺问题更加恶化。what 加上后面的成分构成名词短语作动词 dramatizes 的宾语,rate 在这句话中意思是"认为,视为"。

2. The readiness of the Air Force,...job market. (Line 3~4, Para. 2)
   这句话的意思是:随着部队人才越来越多地流向地方人才市场,人们越来越不愿意参军。

3. In all four of the services, voluntary...short of targets...few years. (Line 4~6, Para. 2)
   short of 意思是"短缺,缺少"。例如:
   They don't appear to be short of money. 他们看起来好像不缺钱。

4. There has long been...make up for the difference. (Line 2~4, Para. 3)
   这句话的意思是:长期以来人们一直认为军人的工资比平民低,但是他们享受的各种福利(如军中的免费食、宿)完全可以弥补其工资与平民工资的差别。
   ▷more than 意思是"远远超出,完全"。例如:
   Some of the stories were really more than could be believed. 有些故事实在是不能相信。
   ▷make up for 意思是"弥补,补偿"。例如:
   make up for the lost time/an omission/a mistake 弥补失去的时间/遗漏/失误
   Do you think her beauty can make up for her stupidity? 你认为她的美貌能弥补她的愚蠢吗?

5. ...as a result of the combined impact of inflation and pay ceilings... (Line 3, Para. 4)
   ▷as a result of 后面接原因,意思是"由于……;作为……的结果"。例如:
   He got lung cancer as a result of heavy smoking. 他因为吸烟太多得了肺癌。
   ▷ceiling 在这句话中意思是"(价格、工资等的)最高限度;最大限额",pay ceiling 就是工资的最高限额。例如:
   a price ceiling 价格的最高限度
   fix/put/set a ceiling on sth. 对……规定最高限额

6. It is now equivalent to only 12% of an aviator's base pay. (Line 3~4, Para. 5)
   be equivalent to sth. 意思是"相当于……;与……相等的"。例如:
   The misery of such a position is equivalent to its happiness. 这种职位的甘苦差不多(相当)。
   vitamin dosage equivalent to the minimum daily requirement 相当于每日最少需要量的维生素剂量

Explanations

这是一篇议论文。本文通过一封海员妻子的书信、一段海军高级将领的话、美国五角大楼官员的话以及最近一项五角大楼研究,说明美国军人津贴降低、军费紧张的问题,并分析了出现这种现象的原因、其现状及其不良影响,如人才流失、兵源不足等。

21. D) 推断题。文中未提及选项 A 和 C。第一段引用的海员妻子的信不是论点,而是文章的引言,作用是引出下文,所以排除选项 B。只有选项 D 符合作者的意图。

22. B) 词汇题。occasion 和选项 B 中的 chance 作名词都表示"偶尔、偶然的机会",作动词都表示"偶然发生,偶尔引起"。选项 A 意思是"引起";选项 C 意思是"减轻,缓和";选项 D 意思是"制造,捏造,伪造"。

23. **D)** 细节题。根据文章第二段第一句和第四段第一句可知,美国军队人才流失是因为与平民相比,军人津贴相对减少,所以答案应是 D 项。选项 A 是军人津贴减少的后果,不是原因。文中未提及选项 B 和 C。

24. **C)** 细节题。这个问题实际上就是对第三段第二句话的解释,只不过原文的 There has been a widely accepted notion that... 被换成了另外一种说法 It has long been assumed that...,所以答案是选项 C。这句话的意思是:长期以来人们误以为军人享受的各种福利完全可以弥补其工资与平民工资的差别。

25. **A)** 推断题。根据文章第四段最后一句话可判断选项 A 是正确的;选项 B 的主语错了,应该是军人实际工资的购买力自从 1972 年下降了 11％;根据文章最后一段第二句可知选项 C 是错的;根据文章最后一句可知选项 D 是错的。

Passage 4

Notes

1. ... but it was in the 1970s, with... on the urban scene. (Line 5～7, Para. 1)
这句话是强调句式。被强调的部分是状语 in the 1970s, with... issues。这句话的意思是:直到 20 世纪 70 年代,随着政府通过税务方面的刺激和快速贬值而进行的强有力支持,以及人们对生态问题的兴趣逐渐增加,重修(旧建筑)才成为城市建设中的一个主要的方面。

2. ... it has returned to life with the intelligent reuse of... (Line 4, Para. 2)
return to life 意思是"重新恢复了生机,焕然一新",这句话的意思是:因为在本杰明·汤普森领导设计下,对这些优秀的建筑物进行了巧妙的重新启用,使其焕然一新。

3. The exciting interior timber... was highlighted by... skylights. (Line 3～4, Para. 3)
highlight 在这里是及物动词,意思是"使显著,使突出"。例如:
Growing economic problems were highlighted by a slowdown in oil output.
石油产量的下降使日益增多的经济困难更加突出了。

4. San Antonio,... other cities combating urban decay. (Line 1, Para. 4)
这句话的意思是:得克萨斯州的圣·安东尼奥市为其他正在与城区衰旧作斗争的城市提供了实际的经验。

5. Rather than bringing in..., the business district. (Line 2～4, Para. 4)
rather than 在这里表示否定,意思是"不是……"。例如:
He ran rather than walked. 他跑步而不是步行。
这句话的意思是:San Antonio 的领导们既修复了现有的建筑,没有使用推土机,而且同时清理了 San Antonio River,使其在城市的商业区蜿蜒流过。

Explanations

这是一篇论说文。文章谈及 20 世纪 70 年代人们对整修旧建筑的热情,并举例说明了各种重修的结果。

26. **A)** 主旨题。综观全文,第一段是主题段,第一句是主题句,接下来的三段举例说明了主题段,所以答案应选 A 项。

27. **D)** 细节题。根据文章第二段可排除选项 A、B 和 C。根据第二段最后一句话可确定答案是 D 项。

28. **D)** 细节题。根据文章第三段第一句可知最早设计建造的时间是 1906 年,所以应是选项 D。

29. **B)** 推断题。根据文章第四段第一句话可知作者认为 San Antonio 的做法为其他城市作了榜样,所以应选 B 项。而选项 C 说大量使用推土机使工程花费大与文章内容不符。文中未提及选项 A 和 D。

30. **C)** 推断题。根据文章最后一段,San Antonio 的领导们没有使用推土机就修复了原有的建筑,同时又清理了 San Antonio River,使其在城市的商业区蜿蜒流过。可见是既兼顾了环境又整修了旧建筑,所以应选 C 项。

Passage 5

Keys

31. The rate of their cognitive development fall behind.
32. to learn and to recognize things
33. By talking to and reasoning with them.
34. Two weeks.
35. Because parents haven't realized the risk.

Notes

1. They found that the more... the lower their scores on the test. (Line 4~5, Para. 3)

   这句话使用了"the more... the more..."句型，意思是"越……越……"，这句话的意思是：他们发现孩子被打屁股或其他体罚的次数越多，他们测验的成绩就越低。

2. What the study showed is spanking is associated with... ability. (Line 1~3, Para. 4)

   What the study showed is 后面省略了 that，be associated with sth. 意思是"把……和……联系起来，和……有关"。例如：

   The doctrine of Evolution is naturally associated with the name of Darwin.

   人们很自然地将进化论和达尔文这个名字联系起来。

3. They found the less corporal... the more cognitive stimulation... the child. (Line 4~5, Para. 4)

   这句话使用了"the more... the more..."句型，意思是"越……越……"，这句话的意思是：他们发现在这次实验中母亲使用的体罚越少，她们给孩子提供的认知方面的刺激就越多。

4. If parents knew the risk they were exposing their children to when... (Line 2~4, Para. 5)

   the risk 后省略了定语从句的关系代词 that，expose sb. to sth. 意思是"使某人置于……之中"。这句话的意思是：如果父母们知道他们打孩子屁股时孩子所遭遇的危险，他们就不会再这样（打孩子）了。

Unit 10

Section A　Skimming and Scanning

Directions：（略）

Passage 1

European Museums Open Door to Corporate Donors

1. Paris, Nov. 11—in another era, it would have seemed normal for a leading British museum to be given art by a wealthy collector. Yet it was a sign of today's very different times that Sir Nicholas Serota, director of the Tate, was seen to score a major *coup*（成功的行动）when he recently persuaded two dozen British artists to donate works from their studios to fill holes in the Tate's contemporary collections.

2. True, the donors will also benefit：museums remain the gateway to *posterity*（子孙, 后代）. But Sir Nicholas had something else in mind when he welcomed the "remarkably generous" gesture：such is the crisis in government financing for British museums that their acquisitions budgets can no longer match market prices. In the case of the Tate, its buying power is about 5 percent of what it was two decades ago. In this, British museums are hardly alone. Few visitors realize that continental Europe's museums, too, spend much of their time and energy these days begging for money to cover not only acquisitions, but also salaries, conservation and even security guards. And they are doing so as government cultural budgets are being squeezed across the region.

3. So has the time come for European museums to look beyond entrance charges, restaurants and gift shops for much-needed extra cash? Is this the moment when corporate sponsorship of major arts institutions finally becomes respectable in Europe? The answers seem obvious. How else can museums remain vigorous?

4. And yet what is being proposed is not universally welcomed. In fact, in much of Europe, the issue is *meshed*（编织, 使缠住）*in ideology*（意识形态）. As with health care and education, culture is seen as a public right that governments have a duty to satisfy. Further, corporate sponsorship of the arts motivated by public relations, not *altruism*（利他主义）, is viewed as somehow *tainted*（腐败的）, especially to cultural officials raised in a *statist*（国家主义者）tradition.

5. This contrasts dramatically with the American approach. In the United States, most museums were born of civil society, they were filled with art *bequeathed*（遗赠）by *philanthropists*（慈善家）, and they are sustained by private donations. A common American view is that government *meddling*（干预）, symbolized by a culture ministry, poses a greater threat to cultural freedom than any amount of corporate involvement.

6. In practice, though, opinions among experts are not quite so sharply defined. American museum directors, who dedicated most of their time to fund-raising, often speak enviously of the enormous government *subsidies*（补助金，资助金）channeled into Europe's museums. And in Europe, some museum directors express admiration for the independence and large *endowments*（捐赠，捐助）enjoyed by American institutions. So perhaps a third way is possible.

7. In a sense, it already exists in Britain. Ten years ago, after being neglected during the Thatcher years, Britain's museums *embarked*（开始，从事）on a huge modernization program using grants from profits from a new national lottery. The lottery covered, say, half a project's cost, with the balance raised privately. Thanks to tax incentives, this worked well enough to create the Tate Modern and to *refurbish*（翻修，革新）Tate Britain, the British Museum and other museums.

8. Similar cost-sharing occurs with major exhibitions, as companies provide money in exchange for prominent display of their names. Where the system is not working, as Sir Nicholas pointed out, is in day-to-day administration and acquisitions, with government subsidies at a standstill, the lottery shifting its attention from the arts and the private sector playing no role. One idea backed by British museums is for donations of art to be made tax-deductible to discourage collectors from selling treasures abroad.

9. While British has taken a lead in exploring new ways of financing museums, those in mainland Europe who have long resisted the principle of corporate sponsorship are fighting a losing battle. In recent years, almost every major European museum has opened a development or sponsorship bureau. Today, it is a rare temporary exhibition that does not receive some corporate contribution. And governments are encouraging the trend.

10. The Prado in Madrid is a case in point. Traditionally, the Spanish government paid for culture, but now it wants commercial partners and is wooing them with tax incentives. The Prado has had to adjust. It now receives $ 3. 2 million over four years from each of two major sponsors, Fundachion Winterthur, the philanthropic arm of a large insurance group, and Banco Bilbao Vizcaya Argentaria, Spain's No. 2 bank, yet these and other private contributors still cover only 7 percent of its budget.

11. A greater test lies ahead. A government board has set a 2008 target for the Prado to finance 40 percent of its budget through corporate donations, entrance charges, food outlets, gift shops and other merchandising. This means doubling its non-government revenues in just five years—and it understands it can do so only by moving closer to what one museum official called the "Anglo-Saxon model" of private-sector collaboration.

12. As in Spain, what is also forcing museums in, say, Germany, Italy and the Netherlands to court banks and businesses is a tightening of government cultural budgets. As corporate boards respond, however, a new problem arises: sponsors are naturally attracted to the most popular museums and the splashiest exhibitions. Thus, if government grants are frozen across the board in the expectation of private money, smaller and regional museums will inevitably suffer.

13. Yet even in France, where governments have long been jealously controlled culture, change is under way. A 2003 law offering tax breaks to companies buying art treasures for national museums is already bringing results. Last month, the Carrefour retail group donated 130 Italian

大学英语 4 级阅读与简答（新题型）

Renaissance drawings, 25 destined for the Louvre. The Louvre's director, Henri Loyrette, noted that the value of recent donations had already exceeds his annual acquisitions budgets. He has also begun looking abroad for financial assistance: earlier this year, he created a nonprofit group, American Friends of the Louvre, for this purpose.

14. There are other reasons for optimism—the French oil giant Total has given $ 5. 8 million toward restoration of the Louvre's Apollo Gallery, while Nippon Television in Japan is financing the museum's new "Mona Lisa" gallery-but also for caution. With notable exceptions like Total, Carrefour and LVMH Moet Hennessy Louis Vuitton, most French companies are simply not used to supporting "good causes." The big difference is that the government has begun urging them to do so.

15. Though still in its infancy in Europe, then, corporate sponsorship looks set to grow. But how far? Continental museums are now ready to welcome private money, but they are in no mood to surrender any *autonomy* (自治，自主) and are not eager to follow the "Anglo-Saxon" example of naming new extensions or galleries after generous donors. Conversely, in exchange for checks, sponsors may want more *fiscal*(财政的) incentives, surer promises of glory, maybe even seats on a board. What is clear is that a third way of financing museums is being tested. All that is missing is agreement on the rules of the game.

1. Recently some British artists decided to donate their works of art to the British Museum.

2. The urgent problem confronting British museums is that it is difficult to find commercial partners.

3. Besides government subsidies, European museums have still such sources of income as entrance charges, food outlets, and gift shops.

4. Companies contribute money to exhibitions in exchange for prominent display of their names.

5. Some European museums are envious of the independence and large endowments enjoyed by American institutions.

6. American museum directors struggle to get financial help from overseas countries.

7. In Britain, the profits from a new national lottery played a major role in helping the museums restore.

8. In much of Europe, culture is traditionally seen as a public right and museums are supposed to be paid by _____.

9. In the United States, most museums are sustained by _____.

10. In order to discourage collectors from selling treasures abroad, British museums proposed donations of arts be made _____.

Section B   Discourse Vocabulary Test

Directions：（略）

Passage 2

Computers and specifically computer networks have created ___11___ for crime that never existed before, and, as a result, the police and justice departments are becoming ___12___ concerned about the growing number of computer users who are gaining ___13___ to private or secret information. It's a problem that is on the rise worldwide. Statistics are showing a trend toward ___14___ computer crime every year.

As we all know, the information that passes through computer networks can be ___15___ and even dangerous if the wrong people get access to it. *War Games*, a 1980s movie, illustrates this point very well. In *War Games*, a young high school boy gains access to the United States' computerized military defense system with the intention of playing a game, but ends up nearly starting a ___16___ war. This theme is, of course, exaggerated. It is very unlikely that anyone, much less a high school boy, could penetrate the US military security system, which limits access to sensitive networks within the government.

But the idea behind the movie is a disturbing one. People can and, in fact, are using their *expertise* (专门技术) in computer ___17___ to break into computer networks and are causing a lot of ___28___ and, even worse, are committing crimes and exposing others to danger. The point is that computer crime is very real and dangerous.

Computer criminals, known as hackers, ___19___ fall into three categories: those who are out for gain, usually material or financial; those who are just plain *malicious* (恶毒的,坏心肠的) and they are trying to hurt someone or cause someone more work; and those who ___20___ do it for the fun or the challenge and don't want to hurt anyone, even though, in fact, they might. The most dangerous by far are those who are out for material or financial gain. This kind of hacking also causes the biggest problems.

A) access	I) maintain
B) increasingly	J) principle
C) nuclear	K) sensitive
D) successful	L) feedback
E) operations	M) basically
F) more	N) individual
G) simply	O) inconvenience
H) opportunities	

Section C   Reading in Depth

Directions:（略）

Passage 3

The constitutional requirements for holding *congressional* (国会的) office in the United States are few and simple. They include age (twenty-five years of age for the House of Representatives, thirty for the Senate); citizenship (seven years for the House, nine years for the Senate), and residency in the state from which the officeholder is elected. Thus, the constitutional gateways to congressional office holding are fairly wide.

Even these minimal requirements, however, sometimes arouse controversy. During the 1960s and 1970s, when people of the post-Second World War "baby boom" reached maturity and the Twenty-sixth *Amendment*（修正案）(permitting eighteen years olds to vote) was *ratified*（批准）, unsuccessful efforts were made to lower the eligible age for senators and representatives.

Because of Americans' geographic mobility, residency sometimes is an issue. Voters normally prefer candidates with longstanding ties to their states or districts. In his 1978 reelection campaign, for instance, Texas Senator John Tower effectively accused his opponent, Representative Robert Krueger, of having spent most of his life "overseas or in the East" studying or teaching—a charge taken seriously in Texas. Well-known candidates sometimes succeed without such ties. New York voters elected to the Senate Robert F. Kennedy (1965~1968) and Daniel Patrick Moynihan (1977) even though each had spent much his life time elsewhere. While members of the House of Representatives are not bound to live in the district from which they are elected, most do so prior to their election.

In the Senate, the "one person, one vote" rule does not apply. Article I of the Constitution assures each state, regardless of population, two Senate seats, and article V guarantees that this equal representation cannot be taken away without the states' consent. The founders *stipulated*（规定）that senators be *designated*（任命）by their respective state *legislatures*（立法机关）rather than by the voters themselves. Thus, the Senate was designed to add stability, wisdom, and *forbearance*（克制）to the actions of the popularly elected House. This distinction between the two houses was *eroded*（有变化）by the Seventeenth Amendment (1913), which provided for the direct popular election of senators.

21. With what topic is the passage primarily concerned?
    A) The founding of Congress.
    B) The congressional process of making laws.
    C) The division of power in Congress.
    D) The factors involved in the election of congressional members.
22. The author mentions all of the following as requirements for holding congressional office EXCEPT _____.
    A) age   B) place of residency
    C) citizenship   D) country of birth
23. The number of senators from each state is stipulated by _____.
    A) the Twenty-sixth Amendment
    B) the population in the state
    C) Article I of the Constitution
    D) local legislation
24. Which of the following can be inferred about Robert Krueger?
    A) He was born on the East Coast.
    B) He defeated John Tower.
    C) He spent most of his life in Texas.
    D) He was not elected to the United States Senate in 1978.
25. Which of the following candidates is eligible to be elected to the United States Senate from the

state of New York?

A) Candidate one—twenty-four years old, natural citizen, lifelong New York resident.

B) Candidate two—twenty-nine years old, United States citizen for eleven years, New York resident for ten years.

C) Candidate three—thirty-five years old, United States citizen for twelve years, New York resident for one year.

D) Candidate four—forty years old, United States citizen for eight years, New York resident for twenty years.

Passage 4

Alarmed by a 20-year decline in student achievement, American schools are considering major *upheavals*（剧变）in the career structure of teacher. School boards are planning to abandon traditional salary schedules and single out outstanding teachers for massive pay rises. The lucky few will be called "master teachers" and earn as much as $40,000 a year instead of the present average of $19,000.

The idea is regarded with deep suspicion by the United States' biggest teachers' union, the National Education Association and the American Federation of Teachers. They say the creation of a *cadre*（结构）of elite teachers will sour professional relationships and encourage teachers to compete rather than cooperate. They also question whether a fair way can be devised to tell which teachers really do perform better than their colleagues.

But heightened public anxiety about secondary education appears to have given the master teacher concept unstoppable political *momentum*（力量，势头）. Florida and Tennessee are racing to introduce ambitious statewide master teacher schemes before the end of the year. Less *grandiose*（宏大的）proposals to pay teachers on the basis of merit instead of seniority have already been implemented in countless school districts and the Secretary of Education Mr. Terrell Bell recently promised substantial incentive grants to states which intend to follow their example.

Low pay is believed to be the single most important reason for the flight from teaching. The average salary of a teacher in the United States is just under $19,000, much less than that of an engineer（$34,700）and not much more than that of a secretary（$16,500）. To make ends meet it is common for teachers to take second jobs in the evening and in their summer holidays. Women, who used to make up the *bulk*（大多数）of teacher candidates are turning to better paid professions.

The unions insist that the answer to this problem is to increase the basic pay of all teachers, but most states would find that too expensive. They would be better able to afford schemes that confine pay increases to a small number of exceptional teachers. Champions of the idea say it would at least hold out the promise of high pay and status to bright graduates who are confident of their ability to do well in the classroom, but are deterred by the present teachers opportunities for promotion.

26. The passage is mainly concerned with _____.

A) American education

B) American teachers

C) decline in American students' achievements

D) a great change in respect to teachers' pay

27. Which of the following is irrelevant to present salary schedules in American schools?

A) Women are turning away from teaching positions.

B) Most teachers take second jobs in their spare time.

C) The public anxiety increases about secondary education.

D) Competitive spirits are fostered among teachers.

28. "Master teachers" are selected because _____.

A) they can get a much higher salary

B) state budges are tight

C) they are senior in their career

D) the US biggest teachers unions doubt most teachers' professional merits

29. What can not be inferred from the passage?

A) The teachers unions hold that the solution to the problems of American education lies in the increase of basic pay for all the teachers.

B) Brilliant graduates refuse to become teachers for the lack of opportunity in promotion.

C) The state governments approve of the "master teacher scheme".

D) The "master teacher scheme" has changed job views of some bright graduates.

30. What is most likely discussed in the following paragraphs?

A) New teaching methodology.

B) Ways to judge teachers' performance.

C) Opinions from teachers' unions on teachers' pay increases.

D) How teachers can be prevented from taking jobs in industry and business.

Section D   Short Answer Questions

Directions：（略）

Passage 5

The advantages and disadvantages of a large population have long been a subject of discussion among economists. It has been argued that the supply of good land is limited. To feed a large population, inferior land must be cultivated and the good land worked intensively. Thus, each person produces less and this means a lower average income, than could be obtained with a smaller population. Other economists have argued that a large population gives more scope for specialization and the development of facilities such as sports, roads and railway, which are not likely to be built unless there is a big demand to justify them.

One of the difficulties in carrying out a worldwide birth control program lies in the fact that official attitudes to population growth vary from country to country depending on the level of industrial development and the availability of food and raw materials. In the developing country where a vastly expanded population is pressing hard upon the limits of food, space and natural resources, it will be the first concern of government to place a limit on the birthrate, whatever the consequences may be. In a highly industrialized society the problem may be more complex. A decreasing birthrate may lead to unemployment because it results in a declining market for manufactured goods. When the pressure of population on housing declines, prices also decline and the building industry is weakened. Faced with considerations such as these, the government of a developed country may well prefer to see a slowly increasing population, rather than one which is stable or in decline.

31. What may a small population mean?
_____
_____

32. According to the passage, what will a large population provide?
_____
_____

33. What will happen to the people in a developed country if the birthrate goes down?
_____
_____

34. What can you infer from the last sentence?
_____
_____

35. Why is it no easy job to carry out a general plan for birth control throughout the world?
_____
_____

Notes and Explanations

Passage 1

Explanations

1. [N] 第一段第二句提到 Yet it was a sign of today's very different times that Sir Nicholas Serota, director of the Tate, was seen to score a major coup when he recently persuaded two dozen British artists to donate works from their studios to fill holes in the Tate's contemporary collections. Tate 博物馆馆长成功地说服二十四名艺术家把他们创作室里的作品捐赠给 Tate 博物馆作为现代艺术品收藏。所以答案为 No。

2. [N] 第二段第五句提到 Few visitors realize that continental Europe's museums, too, spend much of their time and energy these days begging for money to cover not only acquisitions, but also salaries, conservation and even security guards. And they are doing so as government cultural budgets are being squeezed across the region. 很少有参观者意识到欧洲的博物馆最近花很多时间和精力来寻求经费以获得珍品、支付工资、维护博物馆以及雇佣保安。他们这样做是因为在整个欧洲政府消减了文化预算。所以答案为 No。

3. [Y] 通过快速浏览第二段得知欧洲的博物馆最近花很多时间和精力在寻求经费以获得珍品、支付工资、维护博物馆以及雇佣保安。另外,第三段第一句提到 So has the time come for European museums to

look beyond entrance charges, restaurants and gift shops for much-needed extra cash? 欧洲的博物馆除了从门票、餐厅、礼品店获得经费外，去寻求大量额外的经费的时代到来了吗？可以得知，门票、餐厅、礼品店是欧洲博物馆的经费来源。所以答案为 Yes。

4. [Y] 第八段第一句提到 Similar cost-sharing occurs with major exhibitions, as companies provide money in exchange for prominent display of their names. 由于公司名字能在大型展览上获得突出的展示，所以很多公司会提供经济赞助来分担费用。所以答案为 Yes。

5. [Y] 第六段第三句提到 And in Europe, some museum directors express admiration for the independence and large endowments enjoyed by American institutions. 在欧洲，一些博物馆馆长羡慕美国的博物馆能够享受独立和得到大量捐赠。所以答案为 Yes。

6. [NG] 第六段第二句提到 American museum directors, who dedicated most of their time to fund-raising, often speak enviously of the enormous government subsidies channeled into Europe's museums. 因为要花费大量时间筹集资金，美国博物馆馆长们往往会羡慕欧洲博物馆享有大量的政府资助。但没有提及本题中的命题，所以答案为 Not Given。

7. [N] 第七段最后一句提到 Thanks to tax incentives, this worked well enough to create the Tate Modern and to refurbish Tate Britain, the British Museum and other museums. 所以答案为 No。

8. 第四段第三句提到 As with health care and education, culture is seen as a public right that governments have a duty to satisfy. 从而得出答案为 **governments**。

9. 从第四段第二句...and they (American museums) are sustained by private donations. 得出答案为 **private donations**。

10. 从第八段最后一句 One idea backed by British museums is for donations of art to be made tax-deductible to discourage collectors from selling treasures abroad. 得出答案为 **tax-deductible**。

Passage 2

Notes

1. ...who are gaining access to private or secret information. (Line 3~4, Para. 1)
   gain/have access to sth. 意思是"有接近或进入的机会"，to 是介词，后面要接名词、代词或动名词。例如：
   gain access to a country's trading ports 获得进入一个国家贸易港口的权利

2. It's a problem that is on the rise worldwide. (Line 4, Para. 1)
   be on the rise 意思是"（价格等）在上涨，在上升；（数字、数量等）在增加，在增长，在加剧"；在文章中是第二个意思。这句话的意思是：这是一个在世界范围内都在加剧的问题。例如：
   Industrial demand for fuel is on the rise. 工业对燃料的需求正在增长。
   It was darkening and the street tension was on the rise. 天渐渐黑了，街上的紧张气氛在加剧。

3. ...but ends up nearly starting a nuclear war. (Line 4~5, Para. 2)
   end up 意思是"结束，告终"，后面可接名词或动名词，表示"以……结局"。例如：
   He ended up head of the firm. 他最终成为这家公司的主管。
   Wasteful people usually end up in debt. 挥霍浪费的人往往最后负债累累。
   Somewhat to his own surprise he ended up designing the whole car and putting it into production.
   令他自己都有点吃惊的是他最终竟设计了整辆汽车并把它投入生产。

4. It is very unlikely that anyone, much less a high school boy... (Line 5~6, Para. 2)
   much less (still less) 意思是"更不用说，更何况"。例如：
   She wouldn't take a drink, much less stay for dinner. 她连饮料都不喝，更不用说留下来吃饭了。

5. ...even worse, are committing crimes and exposing others to danger. (Line 3, Para. 3)

commit crime 意思是"犯罪",commit 作及物动词,表示"犯(罪),做(傻事、错事、坏事等)"。例如:
commit murder/adultery/suicide 凶杀/通奸/自杀

Explanations

11. [H] 语法规则要求此处应填一个名词作宾语。选项 A、E、H、J、L、O 是名词。根据这句话的意思"计算机尤其是计算机网络为前所未有的犯罪提供了机会"。opportunities 意思是"机会",符合句意。

12. [B] 语法规则要求此处应填一个副词作状语修饰 are concerned about。选项 B、G、M 是副词。根据本句中的"the growing number"和下句中的"It's a problem that is on the rise worldwide",此处应选 B 项。increasingly 意思是"越来越多地,更加"。

13. [A] 语法规则要求此处应填一个名词作 gain 的宾语并与介词 to 搭配使用。能与 to 搭配的是选项 A。根据第二段的第三句提示,此处应该是 access。gain access to 意思是"接近,得到"。

14. [F] 语法规则要求此处应填一个形容词作定语修饰 computer crime。选项 D、F、K 是形容词。上文用了 growing number 和 on the rise。这里应该是 more。

15. [K] 语法规则要求此处应填一个形容词作表语。根据第二段最后一句,此处应选 K 项。sensitive 意思是"敏感的"。

16. [C] 语法规则要求此处应填一个作定语的词说明 war 的种类。根据电影内容此句的意思应该是"这个男孩本来只是想玩游戏,结果差点引发一场核战争"。所以选项 C 符合句意。

17. [E] 语法规则要求此处应填一个名词作介词 in 的宾语。此句的意思是"人们实际上正用他们计算机操作方面的专门技术来攻入计算机网络"。所以 operations(操作)符合句意。

18. [O] 语法规则要求此处应填一个名词作 cause 的宾语。根据下文中的"even worse"可以判断此处应选表示否定的 inconvenience。inconvenience 意思是"不方便"。

19. [M] 语法规则要求此处应填一个副词修饰 fall into。这句话的意思"黑客基本上可分为三类"。basically 意思是"基本上",符合句意。

20. [G] 语法规则要求此处应填一个副词作状语修饰 do it for fun。根据这句话的意思"这类人只是想玩玩或挑战记录,而并不想伤害他人"判断,simply 符合句意。simply 在这里是"只,仅仅"的意思。

Passage 3

Notes

1. During the 1960s and 1970s, ...post-Second World War "baby boom"... (Line 1~2, Para. 2)
第二次世界大战结束后,美国数百万士兵退伍复员并充分就业,工农业发展迅速,人们对未来充满了信心。这期间美国的出生率很高,历史上称为 baby boom(婴儿潮)。到了 20 世纪 60 和 70 年代,婴儿潮时期出生的孩子已长大成人。

2. ...John Tower effectively accused his opponent...of having spent...teaching... (Line 3~4, Para. 3)
accuse sb. of sth. 意思是"指控,控告某人……"。例如:
They publicly accused her of stealing their books. 他们公开指控她偷窃他们的书。

3. While members of the House of Representatives are not bound to live... (Line 7~8, Para. 3)
be bound to 意思是"注定,一定,必然……"。例如:
He is bound to refuse. 他一定会拒绝。
The plan is bound to fail. 这个计划注定会失败。
There are bound to be such accidents. 这样的事故必然会发生。

4. ...most do so prior to their election. (Line 8~9, Para. 3)
prior to 意思是"在……以前,先于;优先于"。例如:
two days prior to the summit 首脑会议前的两天

5. The founders stipulated that senators be designated by their...themselves. (Line 3~5，Para. 4)

stipulate 意思是"规定，约定"，这句话的宾语从句中使用了谓语为动词原形的虚拟语气，其他用法如后面接正常语气也有。例如：

It is stipulated that no one could live in an office building except the janitor.

按规定除门卫外他人一律不得住在办公楼。

Explanations

这是一篇说明文。全文主要向我们介绍了进入美国国会两院(参议院和众议院)的要求，并举例说明了各个因素对选举所造成的影响。

21. D) 主旨题。第一段是主题段，介绍了影响候选人进入美国国会两院(参议院和众议院)的因素，后面几段进一步解释说明了主题段内容，所以应选 D 项。其他选项本文根本没有提及。

22. D) 细节题。第一段提到了前三个选项，文章未提到选项 D，所以答案应是 D 项。

23. C) 细节题。根据文章最后一段第二句话可知正确答案是 C 项。

24. D) 推断题。根据文章第三段第三句可推断出被控告的 Robert Krueger 肯定是失败了，未能入选参议院，所以选项 D 正确。

25. C) 推断题。根据第一段所讲的三个条件：年龄、公民身份、居住时间来判断，只有选项 C 中的 3 号候选人符合从纽约州入选美国参议院的条件。选项 A 和 B 都是年龄不到 30 岁，不符合条件；选项 D 作为美国公民的时间不够，应在 9 年以上。

Passage 4

Notes

1. ...and single out outstanding teachers for... (Line 3，Para. 1)

single out sb. for...意思是"单独挑出某人……"。例如：

Why did you single out Peter for punishment? 你为什么单单惩罚彼德？

2. ...to pay teachers on the basis of merit instead of seniority... (Line 4，Para. 3)

这句话的意思是：很多学校开始根据老师们的业绩而不是根据他们的资历发薪水。

3. To make ends meet it is common for teachers to... (Line 3~4，Para. 4)

to make ends meet 意思是"使收支相抵，量入为出；勉强维持生计"。这句话的意思是：为了勉强维持生计，老师们在晚上或在暑假兼职是很常见的。

4. Women, who used to make up the bulk of teacher candidates are turning to... (Line 5，Para. 4)

这句话的意思是：那些原本是构成教师职业大军主力的女性也转向了薪水更高的职业。

其中 used to 意思是"过去常常"，make up 意思是"构成，组成"。例如：

He used to walk in the park in the morning. 他过去常常早晨在这个公园散步。

Ten chapters make up this volume. 这卷书由 10 章组成。

5. They would be better able to afford...confine pay increases to...teachers. (Line 2~3，Para. 5)

confine...to...意思是"使……局限于……；限制……在……以内"。例如：

You'd better confine your talk to ten minutes. 你最好把你的讲话限制在 10 分钟以内。

Explanations

这是一篇议论文。文章就美国目前教师的薪金过低问题进行了分析，指出目前造成教师跳槽、难以吸引好的毕业生从教和学生成绩下降的原因与教师低工资关系很大，所以应尽快改善和提高教师的待遇。对打算给老师增加工资的"精英教师计划"也做了介绍。

26. **D）** 主旨题。通读全文,可知这篇文章主要讲应尽快解决教师工资过低的问题,如实施"精英教师计划",所以选 D 项。其他选项与本文主题无关。

27. **D）** 细节题。选项 A 和 B 在第四段最后两句都有明确叙述,所以是相关的;选项 C 在第三段第一句也有明确叙述,所以也是相关的;只有选项 D 的内容与现在美国的教师工资计划不相关。

28. **B）** 细节题。根据第五段第一、二句话可知,因为资金有限,只能给一小部分老师涨工资,所以才想出了"精英教师计划",因此答案是 B 项。

29. **D）** 推断题。选项 A 的根据在第五段第一句;选项 B 的根据在第五段最后一句;选项 C 的根据在第三段第二句和最后一句;我们在文中找不到选项 D 的根据,所以答案是 D 项。

30. **B）** 推断题。文章从几个方面论述了给老师增加工资的必要性,但如何根据老师们的表现和业绩来挑选 master teacher 呢? 接下来应从这一点展开,所以应选 B 项。选项 A 与本文内容无关;选项 C 已在本文第二段有明确叙述,所以不需再赘述;选项 D 是如何防止教师在其他领域找工作即跳槽,也与本文主题不相关。

Passage 5

Keys

31. Higher productivity and a higher average income.

32. A chance for developing facilities like sports and transportation system.

33. They will perhaps go out of work.

34. Slowly rising birthrate perhaps is good for a developed nation.

35. Different governments have different views of the question.

Notes

1. It has been argued that the supply of good land is limited. (Line 2, Para. 1)

"It has been argued that..."意思是"有人说……",往往用这种被动语态来表示"很多人认为的观点",类似的说法与结构有 It has been said that... (或 It is said that...), It has been reported that... (或 It is reported that...)等。

2. Thus, each person produces less and this means... population. (Line 3~4, Para. 1)

这句话的意思是:那么,每个人生产的东西就更少,这就意味着和人口少的国家相比,(人口多的国家的)人均收入更低。

3. One of the difficulties in carrying out... lies in the fact that... raw materials. (Line 1~3, Para. 2)

这句话很长,但主语不难找到,即:one of the difficulties,谓语是 lies in,宾语是 the fact,后面是 that 引导的从句作 the fact 的同位语。这句话的意思是:实施这种世界范围的控制生育计划困难之一是由于各国的工业发展水平以及食物和原材料的供应状况不同,各国对于人口增长的态度也不同。

4. A decreasing birthrate may lead to... results in a declining market for... goods. (Line 6~8, Para. 2)

lead to 意思是"导致",result in 意思也是"导致,引起……结果",这句话的意思是:出生率的降低也许会导致失业问题,因为低出生率导致市场对商品需求的下降。

5. Faced with considerations such as these, ... may well prefer to see..., rather than... (Line 9~11, Para. 2)

这句话开头省略了 be,实际上是 The government of a developed country is faced with...另外,may well 后跟动词原形,表示"也许"。这句话的意思是:基于这样的考虑,发达国家也许更愿意看到人口的缓慢增长,而不是人口稳定或下降。

Unit 11

Section A   Skimming and Scanning

Directions: (略)

Passage 1

Children's Ideas about Rainforest

1. Adults and children are frequently confronted with statements about the alarming rate of loss of tropical rainforests. For example, one graphic illustration to which children might readily relate is the estimate that rainforests are being destroyed at rate equivalent to one thousand football fields every forty minutes—about the duration of a normal classroom period. In the face of the frequent and often vivid media coverage, it is likely that children will have formed ideas about rainforests — what and where they are, why they are important, what endangers them — independent of any formal tuition. It is also possible that some of these ideas will be mistaken.

2. Many studies have shown that children harbor misconceptions about "pure", curriculum science. These misconceptions do not remain isolated but become incorporated into a *multifaceted* (多方面的), but organized, conceptual framework, making it and the component ideas, some of which are erroneous, more robust but also accessible to modification. These ideas may be developed by children absorbing ideas through the popular media. Sometimes this information may be erroneous. It seems schools may not be providing an opportunity for children to re-express their ideas and so have them tested and refined by teachers and their peers.

3. Despite the extensive coverage in the popular media of the destruction of rainforests, little formal information is available about children's ideas in this area. The aim of the present study is to start to provide such information, to help teachers design their educational strategies to build upon correct ideas and to displace misconceptions and to plan programmes in environmental studies in their schools.

4. The study surveys children's scientific knowledge and attitudes to rainforests. Secondary school children were asked to complete a questionnaire containing five open-form questions. The most frequent responses to the first question were descriptions which are self-evident from the term "rainforest". Some children described them as damp, wet or hot. The second question concerned the geographical location of rainforests. The commonest responses were continents or countries: Africa (given by 43% of children), South America (30%), Brazil (25%). Some children also gave more general locations, such as being near the Equator.

5. Responses to question three concerned the importance of rainforests. The dominant idea, raised by 64% of the pupils, was that rainforests provide animals with habitats. Fewer students responded that rainforests provide plant habitats, and even fewer mentioned the *indigenous* (本土的) populations of rainforests. More girls (70%) than boys (60%) raised the idea of rainforest as animal habitats.

6. Similarly, but at a lower level, more girls (23%) than boys (5%) said that rainforests provided human habitats. These observations are generally consistent with our previous studies of pupils' views about the use and conservation of rainforests, in which girls were shown to be more sympathetic to animals and expressed views which seem to place an *intrinsic* (内在的,本质的) value on non-human animal life.

7. The fourth question concerned the causes of the destruction of rainforests. Perhaps encouragingly, more than half of the pupils (59%) identified that it is human activities which are destroying rainforests, some personalizing the responsibility by the use of terms such as "we are". About 18% of the pupils referred specifically to logging activity.

8. One misconception, expressed by some 10% of the pupils, was that acid rain is responsible for rainforest destruction; a similar proportion said that pollution is destroying rainforests. Here, children are confusing rainforest destruction with damage to the forests of Western Europe by these factors. While two fifths of the students provided the information that the rainforests provide oxygen, in some cases this response also embraced the misconception that rainforest destruction would reduce atmospheric oxygen, making the atmosphere incompatible with human life on Earth.

9. In answer to the final question about the importance of rainforest conservation, the majority of children simply said that we need rainforests to survive. Only a few of the pupils (6%) mentioned that rainforest destruction may contribute to global warming. This is surprising considering the high level of media coverage on this issue. Some children expressed the idea that the conservation of rainforests is not important.

10. The results of this study suggest that certain ideas *predominate* (控制,支配) in the thinking of children about rainforests. Pupils' responses indicate some misconceptions in basic scientific knowledge of rainforests' ecosystems such as their ideas about rainforests as habitats for animals, plants and humans and the relationship between climatic change and destruction of rainforests.

11. Pupils did not volunteer ideas that suggested that they appreciated the complexity of causes of rainforest destruction. In other words, they gave no indication of an appreciation of either the range of ways in which rainforests are important or the complex social, economic and political factors which drive the activities which are destroying the rainforests. One encouragement is that the results of similar studies about other environmental issues suggest that older children seem to acquire the ability to appreciate, value and evaluate conflicting views. Environmental education offers an arena in which these skills can be developed, which is essential for these children as future decision-makers.

1. The plight of the rainforests has largely been ignored by the media.

2. Children only accept opinions on rainforests that they encounter in their classrooms.

3. It has been suggested that children hold mistaken views about the "pure" science that they study at school.

4. The fact that children's ideas about science form part of a larger framework of ideas means that it is easier to change them.

5. The study involved asking children a number of yes/no questions such as "Are there any rainforests in Africa?"

6. Girls are more likely than boys to hold mistaken views about the rainforests' destruction.

7. Most children think people are responsible for the loss of rainforests.

8. The study reported here follows on from a series of studies that have looked at _____.

9. The most common response to the question about the importance of the rainforests is that _____.

10. The children's most frequent response when asked the rainforests are founded _____.

Section B Discourse Vocabulary Test

Directions：（略）

Passage 2

Good sense is the most equitably ___11___ thing in the world, for each man considers himself so well provided with it that even those who are most ___12___ to satisfy in everything else do not usually wish to have more of it than they have already. It is not ___13___ that everyone is mistaken in this; it shows, rather, that the ___14___ to judge rightly and separate the true from the false, which is essentially what is called good sense or reason, is by ___15___ equal in all men, and thus that our opinions differ not because some men are better *endowed*（赋予）with reason than others, but only because we direct our thoughts along different paths, and do not consider the same things, for it is not enough to have a good mind: what is most important is to apply it rightly. The greatest souls are ___16___ of the greatest *vices*（恶行）; and those who walk very slowly can advance much further, if they always keep to the direct road, than those who run and go astray.

For my part, I have never ___17___ my mind to be more perfect than average in any way. I have, in fact, often wished that my thoughts were as quick, or my ___18___ as precise and distinct, or my memory as capacious or prompt, as those of some other men. And I know of no other qualities than these which make for the perfection of the mind; for as to reason, or good sense, inasmuch as it alone makes us men and ___19___ us from the beasts, I am quite willing to believe that it is whole and entire in each of us, and to follow in the common opinion of the philosophers who say that there are ___20___ of more or less only among the accidents, and not among the forms, or natures, of the individuals of a single species.

A) difficult	I) distributed
B) imagination	J) differences
C) distinguishes	K) nature
D) presumed	L) identified
E) ability	M) consideration
F) capable	N) easy
G) able	O) arranged
H) likely	

Section C   Reading in Depth

Directions：（略）

Passage 3

According to a recent survey, employees in many companies today work longer hours than employees did in 1979. They also take shorter vacations. It seems that Americans are working harder today than ever before. A management consultant, Bill Meyer, decided to find out. For these days, he observed an investment banker hard at work. Meyer wrote down everything the banker did during his long workday—the banker worked 80 hours a week. At the end of three-day period, Meyer reviewed the banker's activities with him. What did they find out? They discovered that the man spent 80 percent of his time doing busy work. For example, he attended unnecessary meetings, made redundant telephone calls, and spent time packing and unpacking his two big briefcases.

Apparently, many people believe that the more time a person spends at work, the more she or he accomplishes. However, the connection between time and productivity is not always positive. In fact, many studies indicate that after a certain point, anyone's productivity and creativity begin to decrease. Furthermore, it is not always easy for individuals to realize that their performance is falling off.

Part of the problem is understandable. When employers evaluate employees, they often consider the amount of time on the job in addition to job performance. Employees know this. Consequently, they work longer hours and take less vacation time than they did nine years ago. Although many working people can do their job effectively during a regular 40-hour work week, they feel they have to spend more time on the job after normal working hours so that the people who can promote them see them.

A group of head-hunters were asked their opinion about a situation. They had a choice of two candidates for an executive position with an important company. The candidates had comparable qualifications for the job. For example, they were both reliable. One could do the job well in a 40-hour work week. The other would do the same job in an 80-hour week just as well. According to a head-hunting expert, the 80-hour-a-week candidates would get the job. The time this candidate spends on the job may encourage other employees to spend more time at work, too. Employers believe that if the employees stay at work later, they may actually do more work.

21. What is the main idea of the passage?

    A) Many people work long hours but not always do more work.

    B) Most people can get work done by working longer hours.

    C) Most Americans work 80 hours a week, and some work longer.

    D) Many Americans in 1979 took longer vacations than they do today.

22. What was the purpose of Bill Meyer's investigation?

    A) To find out everything the banker did in his workday.

    B) To find out whether Americans are working harder than ever before.

C) To prove Americans are not working harder than ever before.

D) To prove Americans are now doing a lot of unnecessary work.

23. In Para. 2, "after a certain point" means _____.

    A) after all the work is finished

    B) after the studies are completed

    C) after working a certain number of hours

    D) after they come back from vacations

24. What was the head-hunters' opinion of the situation?

    A) Those who work long hours are likely to get the job.

    B) Those who could help other employees with their work may get the job.

    C) Those who are doing more work are likely to get the job.

    D) Those who could make better use of time in their work could get the job.

25. According to the passage, which of the following is NOT true?

    A) Most Americans today are working longer hours and have less vacation time.

    B) Some people work more than 40 hours a week because they hope to get a promotion.

    C) Employees are often judged by their job performance and the amount of time on the job.

    D) The more time a person spends at work, the more he or she accomplishes.

Passage 4

This book is written especially for students in an attempt to present the material that is most useful and interesting to them. Previous courses in chemistry are not necessary for the understanding of the material, although those students who have had high school chemistry will find that a review of the inorganic section will better enable them to master the organic and biochemistry sections that follow.

The author has felt that in the past there was an important selection of material from inorganic, organic, and biochemistry in the majority of the textbooks of chemistry for nurses. The tendency has been to develop the inorganic chemistry to such an extent that organic and biochemistry are covered too briefly. The recent advances in biochemistry and their widespread application to the practice of medicine and nursing have considerably altered the situation. Not only is biochemistry more closely allied to the practical chemistry of medicine and nursing but it is also of more interest to the student. In the author's experience the response to biochemistry has always been more favorable than to the other sections. Within the brief period allotted to chemistry, therefore, the sections on inorganic, organic, and biochemistry should be so arranged that a good share of the time is spent in the study of biochemistry. This book presents mainly those fundamentals of inorganic and organic chemistry that are necessary for the understanding of the section on biochemistry.

The fundamental points suggested in the Curriculum Guide are included in the book, with some additions in the biochemistry section. The author feels that a study of urine, vitamins, nutrition, and hormones is so obviously a part of biochemistry that at least the fundamentals should be included in this course.

The book has been planned in such a way that it may be adapted to various courses in chemistry. The material suggested by the Curriculum Guide is covered in the first nineteen chapters and may be used in accelerated courses or where minimum time is allotted to chemistry. When the time allotted to the course is sixty to ninety hours the entire contents of the book may be used to advantage. While the book has been written especially to fit the needs of Schools of Nursing, it could readily be applied in instances where students are required to take but one course in chemistry.

The apathetic attitude of nonprofessional students toward a course in inorganic chemistry may well be overcome by the proper presentation of material selected from inorganic, organic, and biochemistry.

26. This piece of writing is _____.
    A) the record of an introductory speech   B) professor's letter to his students
    C) from a school announcement   D) a preface to a course book

27. To read this book, _____.
    A) one must first review his high school courses
    B) previous courses in chemistry is necessary
    C) a good mastery of biochemistry is essential
    D) one needn't have studied chemistry before

28. In the author's experience, the students are most interested in _____.
    A) chemistry as a whole   B) inorganic chemistry
    C) organic chemistry   D) biochemistry

29. The definitions in this book are _____.
    A) hard to understand   B) frightfully lengthy
    C) hard to remember   D) simple and clear

30. Paragraph 4 suggests that one characteristic of this book is its _____.
    A) adaptability to various needs   B) vividness of the language
    C) simplicity in presentation   D) complexity of the plot

Section D   Short Answer Questions
Directions：（略）

Passage 5

Opinion polls are now beginning to show an unwilling general agreement that, whoever is to blame and whatever happens from now on, high unemployment is probably here to stay. This means we shall have to find ways of sharing the available employment more widely.

But we need to go further. We must ask some fundamental questions about the future of work. Should we continue to treat employment as the norm? Should we not rather encourage many other ways for self-respecting people to work? Should we not create conditions in which many of us can work for ourselves, rather for an employer? Should we not aim to revive the household and the neighborhood, as well as the factory and the office, as centers of production and work?

The industrial age has been the only period of human history in which most people's work has taken the form of jobs. The industrial age may now be coming to an end, and some of the changes in work patterns which it brought may have to be reversed. This seems a discouraging thought. But, in fact, it could offer the prospect of a better future for work. Universal employment, as its history shows, has not meant economic freedom.

Employment became widespread when the enclosures of the 17th and the 18th centuries made many people dependent on paid work by depriving them of the use of the land, and thus of the means to provide a living for themselves. Then the factory system destroyed the cottage industries and removed work from people's homes. Later, as transport improved, first by rail and then by road, people traveled longer distances to their places of employment until, eventually, many people's work lost all connection with their home lives and the places in which they lived. Meanwhile, employment put women at a disadvantage. It became customary for the husband to go out to paid employment, leaving the unpaid work of the home and family to his wife.

All this may now have to change. The time has certainly come to switch some effort and resources away from the impractical goal of creating jobs for all, to the urgent practical task of helping many people to manage without full-time jobs.

31. What do the recent opinion polls agree unwillingly?

_____ _____ _____ _____

_____ _____ _____ _____

32. Why does the author ask some fundamental questions in the second paragraph?

_____ _____ _____ _____

_____ _____ _____ _____

33. What did the arrival of the industrial age mean?

_____ _____ _____ _____

_____ _____ _____ _____

34. As a result of the enclosures of the 17th and 18th centuries, _____.

_____ _____ _____ _____

_____ _____ _____ _____

35. What conclusion can we draw from the last paragraph about the creation of jobs for all?

_____ _____ _____ _____

_____ _____ _____ _____

Notes and Explanations

Passage 1

Explanations

1. [N] 第三段第一句提到 Despite the extensive coverage in the popular media of the destruction of rainforests, little formal information is available about children's ideas in this area. 尽管大众媒体对于雨林遭到破坏进行了广泛的报道,但是有关孩子们对此的看法却没有什么正式的报道。故答案应为 No。

2. [N] 第二段第三句提到 These ideas may be developed by children absorbing ideas through the popular

media. 孩子们可能会从大众媒体得到这些(有关雨林的)知识。可以得知孩子们不仅可以从学校,还能从其他途径了解有关雨林的知识。因此正确答案为 No。

3. [Y] 第二段第一句提到 Many studies have shown that children harbor misconceptions about "pure", curriculum science. 很多研究显示,孩子对纯粹的、课堂上学到的科学知识抱有误解。所以答案为 Yes。

4. [NG] 第二段第二句提到 These misconceptions do not remain isolated but become incorporated into a multifaceted, but organized, conceptual framework, making it and the component ideas, some of which are erroneous, more robust but also accessible to modification. 孩子们对于雨林的错误观念中有一些是可以修正的。这不是本题表达的命题,因此本题的答案应为 Not Given。

5. [N] 第四段第一、二句提到 The study surveys children's scientific knowledge and attitudes to rainforests. Secondary school children were asked to complete a questionnaire containing five open-form questions. 这项研究调查孩子们对于雨林的科学知识和态度。中学生们要求完成一份有五个开放式问题的调查问卷。所以答案应为 No。

6. [NG] 第五、六段涉及了男生和女生对雨林的看法,但是只说明了女孩有更多的同情心,而没有提及她们更有可能对雨林有错误观念。故正确答案应为 Not Given。

7. [Y] 第七段第二句提到 Perhaps encouragingly, more than half of the pupils (59%) identified that it is human activities which are destroying rainforests, some personalizing the responsibility by the use of terms such as "we are". About 18% of the pupils referred specifically to logging activity. 令人感到鼓舞的是,59%的学生认为是人类的活动在破坏雨林,一些人还用"我们"这个词使责任更加个人化。大约 18%的学生特别强调了伐木。所以答案为 Yes。

8. 从第四段第一句 The study surveys children's scientific knowledge and attitudes to rainforests. 得出答案应为 **children's understanding (scientific knowledge and attitudes to) of rainforests**。

9. 第五段第二句提到 The dominant idea, raised by 64% of the pupils, was that rainforests provide animals with habitats. 64%的学生认为的首要问题是雨林为动物们提供的栖息地。可以得出答案为 **without rainforests some animals would have nowhere to live**。

10. 第四段倒数第二句提到 The commonest responses were continents or countries: Africa (given by 43% of children), South America (30%), Brazil (25%). 故答案应为 **in Africa**。

Passage 2

Notes

1. ... and separate the true from the false... (Line 4, Para. 1)

   separate the true from the false 辨别是非

   separate... from... 意思是"使……与……分离;使分开"。例如:

   He separated the big apples from the small ones. 他把大苹果和小苹果区分开来。

   A fence separated the cows from the pigs. 围栏把牛和猪隔开。

2. ... is by nature equal in all men... (Line 5, Para. 1)

   ▷by nature 意思是"生性,本性上"。例如:

   I'm an optimist by nature. 我生来是个乐天派。

   Cats are by nature very clean. 猫生来就喜欢干净。

   ▷in nature 则意思是"本质上,事实上"。例如:

   Her problem was personal in nature. 她的问题本质上属于个人问题。

   It's not in her nature to do anything rude; she's polite by nature.

   事实上她不会做任何鲁莽的事,她本性很有礼貌。

3. ... if they always keep to the direct road, than those who run and go astray. (Line 10, Para. 1)

▷keep to 在此意思是"限于某一位置或停留"。例如：

Traffic in Britain keeps to the left. 英国的交通一律靠左。

▷此外，keep to 还可表示"坚持，保持；固守（习惯等）"。例如：

keep to the style of struggle and plain living 保持艰苦奋斗的作风

▷go astray 意思是"迷路；走上歧途，堕落"。例如：

The boy went astray with his bad companions. 这个男孩随坏伙伴们走上歧途。

▷另外 go astray 还可以当"搞错"讲。例如：

I must have gone astray somewhere in my calculations. 我一定在计算过程中的哪一步搞错了。

4. For my part, I have never presumed... (Line 1, Para. 2)

for one's part 意思是"至于某人；对某人说来"。例如：

For my part, I have no objection. 至于我，没什么反对意见。

For my part, I found the meeting most fruitful. 对我而言，我认为这次会议很有收获。

5. And I know of no other qualities than these which make for the perfection of the mind; for as to reason, or good sense, inasmuch as it alone makes us men and distinguishes us from the beasts, I am quite willing to believe that... (Line 3~6, Para. 2)

▷know of 意思是"听说过"。例如：

I know of the man, but I have never met him. 我听说过那个人，但从未见过面。

▷make for 在文中意思是"有助于，促进"，另外还有"向……方向前进"的意思。例如：

Cultural exchange makes for better understanding. 文化交流促进相互理解。

It started raining, so she made for the nearest shelter. 开始下雨了，她朝最近的避雨处跑去。

▷as to 意思是"关于，至于"。例如：

As to that, I haven't decided yet. 至于那件事，我还未决定。

He was at a loss as to how to explain it. 他全然不知该如何解释这件事。

▷inasmuch as 意思是"因为"。

distinguish... from... 意思是"把……和……区别"。例如：

Speech distinguishes man from the other animals. 人类有别于其他动物在于人会说话。

▷be willing to do/that... 意思是"愿意做……"。例如：

We are willing to help you. 我们愿意帮助你。

Are you willing that he should be admitted into our club? 你愿意他加入我们的俱乐部吗？

Explanations

11. [I] 语法规则要求此处应填一个形容词和 most 构成形容词的最高级形式修饰 thing。根据下文"for each man considers himself so well provided with it that..."可以判断作者要表达的意思是每个人被赋予的判断是非的能力是均等的，所以应选择 I 项。

12. [A] 语法规则要求 be + most 后面应填形容词最高级形式。根据该句话的上文 even those who are... do not usually wish to have more of it than they have already，可以判断此处应选择 A 项。

13. [H] 语法规则要求此处应填一个形容词；根据此句的 that everyone is mistaken in this 和上文意思可判断这里应填 likely。It is not likely that ... 是一常用句型，意为"……是不可能的"。

14. [E] 语法规则要求此处应填一个名词作 that 引导的宾语从句的主语，选项 B、E、J、K、M 都是名词；根据下文 to judge rightly and separate the true from the false 可知选项 E 既符合语法规则又符合句意要求。

15. [K] 语法规则要求介词 by 后面应跟一个名词；根据上文判断此处应填 nature。by nature 为固定短语，意为"生来"。

16. [F] 语法规则要求系动词 be 后面应填一个形容词和 of 构成固定搭配的短语;选项中的形容词只有 capable 可以和 of 搭配使用,而且符合句意要求。

17. [D] 语法规则要求此处应填一个动词 + ed 形式和 have 构成现在完成时态。选项中的动词 + ed 形式 中只有选项 D 符合句子意思"从来没有想过自己比一般人更完美"。

18. [B] 语法规则要求此处应填一个名词。该句中作者先后提到 mind, thoughts 和 memory。B 项 imagination 和这些词的意思相近,所以是正确答案。

19. [C] 语法规则要求由 it 作主语的句子的谓语应该和句中 makes 一样是一般现在时的第三人称单数形式。只有选项 C 符合此条件;distinguish...from 意为"将……与……区分开来",意思上符合上下文要求。

20. [J] 语法规则要求 there be 结构中 be 是 are 时,后面应该是名词复数形式。选项中的名词中只有选项 J 是名词复数形式,而且在意思上也符合上下文要求。

Passage 3

Notes

1. According to a recent survey... (Line 1, Para. 1)

   according to 意思是"根据,按照"。例如:

   according to a recent survey 根据最近的一次调查

   according to the change of circumstances 随着情况的改变

2. Meyer wrote down everything... (Line 4, Para. 1)

   write down 意思是"记下,写下"。例如:

   I wrote down his telephone number in my notebook. 我在笔记本上记下他的电话号码。

   Write your idea down while it's clear in your mind. 趁你的想法清楚时赶快把它写下来。

3. ...that the man spent 80 percent of his time doing busy work. (Line 7, Para. 1)

   ▷"spend + 时间 + (in) doing"是一种常用的句子结构,意思是"花费时间(或金钱)做某事"。例如:

   He spent his summer vacation reading and fishing. 他看书、钓鱼度过了暑假。

   ▷spend 的另一常见用法是"spend + 金钱 + on sth."意思是"把钱花在……上"。例如:

   She spent all her savings on a new car. 她将全部积蓄花在一辆新车上。

4. ...the more time a person spends at work, the more she or he accomplishes. (Line 1~2, Para. 2)

   形容词比较级的一种特殊用法,由"the + 形容词比较级, the + 形容词比较级"构成,意思是"越……,越……"。例如:

   The more you practice, the better you can speak English. 你练得越多,你的英语说得越好。

   The more I see of her, the less I like her. 我越了解她,越不喜欢她。

5. Furthermore, it is not always easy for individuals to realize that their performance is falling off. (Line 4~5, Para. 2)

   fall off 的字面含义为"从……掉落"。引申意思是"降低,下降;减少"。例如:

   The top button fell off the coat. 大衣最上面的纽扣掉了。

   Membership of the club has fallen off this year. 今年俱乐部的会员减少了。

6. ...they often consider the amount of time on the job in addition to job performance. (Line 1~2, Para. 3)

   in addition to 意思是"除了……之外"。例如:

   In addition to apples you asked for, I bought you some oranges. 除了你要的苹果外,我还给你买了橘子。

   He speaks French in addition to Germany. 除了德语外他还说法语。

7. head-hunter (Line 1, Para. 4)

   意思是"物色人才的人,猎头"。head-hunt 为动词,意思是"物色"。

8. The candidates had comparable qualifications for the job. (Line 2～3，Para. 4)

comparable 在文章中相当于 similar，即来应聘该工作的候选人资历相当。

Explanations

本文首先由一份调查指出如今许多公司雇员的工作时间都比 1979 年长，休假时间却比 1979 年短。似乎美国人现在的工作比以往任何时候都辛苦，事实果真如此吗？管理顾问 Bill Meyer 决心弄明白这个问题。观察、记录一位努力工作的投资银行家在三天内所做的事情。结果发现此人 80% 的时间都在瞎忙。文章指出许多人在时间与工作效率的关系上存在误区——认为一个人在工作上花的时间越多，他的成绩就越大。实际上，时间与工效之间的关系并不总是成正比的。

21. **A)** 主旨题。文章第一段论述了美国公司里存在的一种现象：人们花在工作上的时间比以前长了，休假的时间却短了。第二段提出了本文的主题：工作时间和工作效率并不总成正比，然后分析了出现这种现象的原因。所以答案应是 A 项。

22. **B)** 细节题。根据文章第一段第三、四句话可以断定答案是 B。选项 A 并不是他调查的目的，只能说是调查的手段。选项 C 违背文章主题，文中没有涉及。选项 D 是 Bill Meyer 调查中发现的问题，不是调查的目的。

23. **C)** 词汇题。after a certain point 中的 point 应指"（时间上的）一点"，因此 after a certain point 的确切解释应是"在工作若干个小时后"。其他选项都不符合全句所要表达的含义。

24. **A)** 细节题。根据文章第四段第七句 According to a head-hunting expert，the 80-hour-a-week candidate would get the job. 判断，答案应为 A 项。选项 B、C 和 D 都不是物色人才的专家的观点。

25. **D)** 推断题。选项 A 实际上是文章第一段的前两句话。选项 B 是文章第三段的内容。选项 C 是文章第三段的主题句。即老板在衡量职员时，不仅要考虑他的工作表现，还要考虑他在工作上所花费的时间。选项 D 来自文章第二段 Apparently，many people believe that the more time a person spends at work，the more she or he accomplishes. However，the connection between time and productivity is not always positive. ，however 后面所说的是事实——时间与生产率之间的关系并不总是成正比的。因此答案是 D 项。

Passage 4

Notes

1. ... although those students who have had... will better enable them to master the organic and biochemistry sections that follow. (Line 3～5，Para. 1)

who 引导的定语从句修饰 those students。本句的意思是：尽管中学学过化学的同学会发现复习无机化学能使他们更好地掌握以后要学的有机化学及生物化学。

enable sb. to do sth. 意思是"使某人能够做某事"。例如：

enable every student to develop morally，intellectually and physically

使每个学生在德、智、体几方面都能得到发展。

The new contract enables us to demand whatever we want. 根据新合同我们想要什么就可以要什么。

2. The tendency has been to develop the inorganic chemistry to such an extent that organic and biochemistry are covered too briefly. (Line 2～4，Para. 2)

▷to such an extent that 意思是"到……程度，如此……以至于……"，extent 常与介词 to 搭配。例如：

to some (a certain) extent 在某种程度上

to a great (large) extent 大部分，大大地

▷cover 意思是"覆盖，遮盖；行过（路程）"。例如：

The ground was covered with snow. 雪覆盖着地面。

He wants to cover 100 miles by dark. 他要在天黑前走 100 英里。

▷在本句中 cover 意思是"包含,包括",还可表示"涉及"。例如:

Her report covered all aspects of the problem. 她的报告涵盖了这个问题的各个方面。

The doctor's speech covered the history of medicine from Roman times to the present day.

医生的演讲涉及了从罗马时代到今天的医学史。

3. ... *that it may be adapted to various courses in chemistry.* (Line 1,Para. 4)

▷adapt sth. to 意思是"使适应……,使适合……"。例如:

He found he could not adapt his way of life to the company.

他发现他的生活方式无法适应公司的要求。

▷adapt oneself to 意思是"适应……"。例如:

The girl was quick to adapt herself to new circumstances. 女孩很快适应了新环境。

4. *The apathetic attitude of nonprofessional students toward a course in inorganic chemistry may well be overcome by...* (Para. 5)

本句的意思是:也许可以通过从无机化学、有机化学和生物化学中选择适当的材料进行讲授来消除非专业学生对无机化学课程的反感。

apathetic 意思是"冷淡的,冷漠的"。

另外注意 attitude 意思是"态度,看法"时与 to, towards 搭配。例如:

an attitude to labor 劳动观念

We must take a correct attitudes towards criticism from masses. 对于群众的批评我们应持正确的态度。

Explanations

本文是一篇说明文,介绍了一本护士学校所用的化学教材。文章介绍了教材的适用对象,教材内容以及如何使用这本教材。

26. **D)** 推断题。这篇文章主要写的是一本书的内容、作者写这本书的目的及这本书的适用范围。因此这篇文章应是一本书的序言,选项 D 为正确答案。

27. **D)** 细节题。文章第一段的第二句话明确指出学习本书对是否学过化学方面的课程不做特别要求,因此选项 D 正确。其他选项与文章内容不符。

28. **D)** 细节题。根据文章的第二段第五句,即 In the author's experience the response to biochemistry has always been more favorable than to the other sections. 根据作者自己的经验,学生对于生物化学部分的反馈总好过其他部分。因此学生更感兴趣的应该是生物化学(biochemistry)。

29. **D)** 推断题。从文章第一段可以看出书中所下的定义应是 simple and clear。因为这本书对是否学过化学方面的课程不做特别要求,其他选项均与文章内容不符。

30. **A)** 细节题。文章第四段第一句话 The book has been planned in such a way that it may be adapted to various courses in chemistry 也是这一段的主题句,由此可以看出选项 A 是正确答案。其他选项内容均与文章内容不符。

Passage 5

Keys

31. High unemployment exists.

32. Because he wants us to re-examine our thinking about work.

33. It means the changes in work patterns.

34. employment became widespread

35. It is possible to create jobs for all.

Notes

1. ... from now on... (Line 2，Para. 1)

   意思是"从现在开始,从今以后"。例如:

   I will be more careful in examination from now on. 从今以后考试时我会更加细心。

2. The industrial age may now be coming to an end... (Line 2，Para. 3).

   come to an end 意思是"告终,结束"。例如:

   Their meeting came to an end at midnight. 他们的会开到半夜才结束。

   The year is coming to an end. 这一年就要过去了。

3. ... made many people dependent on paid work by depriving them of the use of the land，and thus of the means to provide a living for themselves. (Line 1~3，Para. 4)

   ▷be dependent on 形容词短语,意思是"依靠,依赖;取决于"。例如:

   Success is dependent on the results of this examination. 成功与否取决于这次考试的结果。

   ▷depend on 为动词短语,意思是"依靠,依赖"。例如:

   His wife and children all depend on him. 他的妻子、儿女都依靠他生活。

   Don't depend on others，you have to do it by yourself. 不要依赖别人,你要靠自己。

   ▷deprive...of... 意思是"夺去,剥夺"。例如:

   The criminal has been deprived of his rights. 犯人的权利被剥夺了。

   She has been deprived of her eyesight for many years. 她失明已经多年了。

4. ... many people's work lost all connection with their home lives and the places in which they lived. (Line 5~6，Para. 4)

   lose connection with 意思是"与……失去联系"。have connection with 意思是"与……有关,有联系"。例如:

   They lost connection with each other because of the World War Ⅱ. 由于二战,他们彼此失去了联系。

   He has no connection with that prank. 他与那恶作剧无关。

5. ... leaving the unpaid work of the home and family to his wife. (Line 8，Para. 4)

   leave sth. to sb. 意思是"把……留给某人"。例如:

   She left her estate to the orphanage. 她遗赠地产给孤儿院。

   His uncle left him a large fortune. / His uncle left a large fortune to him. 他叔叔留给他一大笔财产。

6. The time has certainly come to switch some effort and resources away from the impractical goal of creating jobs for all，to... (Line 2~3，Para. 5)

   switch sth. to sth. 意思是"转变,更换,变换(位置)等"。例如:

   They switched the location of the movie to Hainan Island. 他们把这部电影的外景地改到海南岛。

   He secretly switched to a different company. 他秘密跳槽到别的公司。

Unit 12

Section A   Skimming and Scanning

Directions:（略）

Passage 1

Lost for Words

1. In the Native American Navajo nation, which sprawls across four states in the American south-west, the native language is dying. Most of its speakers are middle-aged or elderly. Although many students take classes in Navajo, the schools are run in English. Street signs, supermarket goods and even their own newspaper are all in English. Not surprisingly, linguists doubt that any native speakers of Navajo will remain in a hundred years' time.

2. Navajo is far from alone. Half the world's 6,800 languages are likely to vanish within two generations—that's one language lost every ten days. Never before has the planet's linguistic diversity shrunk at such a pace. "At the moment, we are heading for about three or four languages dominating the world," says Mark Pagel, an evolutionary biologist at the University of Reading. "It's a mass extinction, and whether we will ever *rebound*（回弹）from the loss is difficult to know."

3. Isolation breeds linguistic diversity: as a result, the world is peppered with languages spoken by only a few people. Only 250 languages have more than a million speakers, and at least 3,000 have fewer than 2,500. It is not necessarily these small languages that are about to disappear. Navajo is considered endangered despite having 150,000 speakers. What makes a language endangered is not just the number of speakers, but how old they are. If it is spoken by children it is relatively safe. The critically endangered languages are those that are only spoken by the elderly, according to Michael Krauss, director of the Alassk Native Language Center, in Fairbanks.

4. Why do people reject the language of their parents? It begins with a crisis of confidence, when a small community finds itself alongside a larger, wealthier society, says Nicholas Ostler, of Britain's Foundation for Endangered Languages, in Bath. "People lose faith in their culture," he says. "When the next generation reaches their teens, they might not want to be induced into the old traditions."

5. The change is not always voluntary. Quite often, governments try to kill off a minority language by banning its use in public or discouraging its use in schools, all to promote national unity. The former US policy of running Indian reservation schools in English, for example, effectively put languages such as Navajo on the danger list. But Salikoko Mufwene, who chairs the Linguistics department at the University of Chicago, argues that the deadliest weapon is not

government policy but economic globalization. "Native Americans have not lost pride in their language, but they have had to adapt to socio-economic pressures,"he says. "They cannot refuse to speak English if most commercial activity is in English."But are languages worth saving? At the very least, there is a loss of data for the study of languages and their evolution, which relies on comparisons between languages, both living and dead. When an unwritten and unrecorded language disappears, it is lost to science.

6. Language is also intimately bound up with culture, so it may be difficult to preserve one without the other. "If a person shifts from Navajo to English, they lose something," Mufwene says. "Moreover, the loss of diversity may also deprive us of different ways of looking at the world,"says Pagel. There is mounting evidence that learning a language produces physiological changes in the brain. "Your brain and mine are different from the brain of someone who speaks French, for instance," Pagel says, and this could affect our thoughts and perceptions. "The patterns and connections we make among various concepts may be structured by the linguistic habits of our community."

7. So despite linguists' best efforts, many languages will disappear over the next century. But a growing interest in cultural identity may prevent the direct predictions from coming true. "The key to fostering diversity is for people to learn their ancestral tongue, as well as the dominant language,"says Doug Whalen, founder and president of the Endangered Language Fund in New Haven, Connecticut. "Most of these languages will not survive without a large degree of bilingualism," he says. In New Zealand, classes for children have slowed the erosion of Maori and rekindled interest in the language. A similar approach in Hawaii has produced about 8,000 new speakers of Polynesian languages in the past few years. In California, "apprentice"programs have provided life support to several indigenous languages. Volunteer "apprentices" pair up with one of the last living speakers of a Native American tongue to learn a traditional skill such as basket weaving, with instruction exclusively in the endangered language. After about 300 hours of training they are generally sufficiently fluent to transmit the language to the next generation. But Mufwene says that preventing a language dying out is not the same as giving it new life by using it every day. "Preserving a language is more like preserving fruits in a jar," he says.

8. However, preservation can bring a language back from the dead. There are examples of languages that have survived in written form and then been revived by later generations. But a written form is essential for this, so the mere possibility of revival has led many speakers of endangered languages to develop systems of writing where none existed before.

1. The Navajo language will die out because it currently has too few speakers.

2. A large number of native speakers fail to guarantee the survival of a language.

3. National governments could do more to protect endangered languages.

4. The loss of linguistic diversity is inevitable.

5. Most of Navajo speakers are teenagers and the middle-aged.

6. People reject the language of their parents because they lose their faith in the culture.

7. Preservation can not bring a language back from the dead.

8. The great variety of languages came about largely as a result of _____.

9. One factor which may help to ensure that some endangered languages do not die out completely is people's increasing appreciation of their _____.

10. Some speakers of endangered languages have produced writing systems in order to help secure _____.

Section B   Discourse Vocabulary Test

Directions：（略）

Passage 2

Carnegie Hall, the famous concert hall in New York city, has again __11__ a restoration. While this is not the first, it is certainly the most __12__ in the building history. As a result of this new restoration, Carnegie Hall once again has the quality of sound that it had when it was first built.

Carnegie Hall __13__ its existence to Andrew Carnegie, the wealthy owner of a steel company in the late 1800s. The hall was finished in 1891 and quickly gained a __14__ as an excellent performing arts hall where accomplished musicians gained fame. __15__ its reputation, however, the concert hall suffered from several detrimental renovations over the years. During the Great Depression, when fewer people could __16__ to attend performances, the directors sold part of the building to commercial businesses. As a result, a coffee shop was opened in one corner of the building, for which the builders replaced the brick and terra cotta walls with windowpanes. A renovation in 1946 __17__ damaged the acoustical quality of the hall when the makers of the film Carnegie Hall cut a gaping hole in the dome of the ceiling to allow for lights and air vents. The hole was later covered with short curtains and a fake ceiling, but the hall never sounded the same afterwards.

In 1960, the violinist Issac Stern became __18__ in restoring the hall after a group of real estate developers unveiled plans to demolish Carnegie Hall and build a high-rise office building on the site. This threat spurred Stern to rally public support for Carnegie Hall and encourage the City of New York to buy property. The movement was successful, and the concert hall is now owned by the city. In the __19__ restoration, builders tested each new material for its sound qualities, and they replaced the hole in the ceiling with a dome. The builders also restored the outer walls to their original appearance and closed the coffee shop. Carnegie has never sounded better, and its prospects for the future have never looked more __20__.

A) excellent	I) extensive
B) involved	J) temptation
C) afford	K) undergone
D) Despite	L) spite
E) seriously	M) owes
F) recently	N) musical
G) reputation	O) current
H) promising	

Section C Reading in Depth

Directions：（略）

Passage 3

The idea of helping people comes naturally to most of us. If we see a blind person getting off a bus, we watch to make sure that he is in no danger of falling. Members of a family help one another, with particular care for the very young and the elderly.

There are many people who have nobody near to see their need for help and often nobody to give it even when the need is known. The old, the handicapped, the homeless and friendless—these are the people for whom help may not come, because nobody sees. It may not have occurred to you that you are in a position to help. Community service means helping the people around you. Organizations exist which try to make sure that someone sees when help is needed and does something about it. These organizations depend on voluntary help to carry out a wide variety of tasks, volunteers giving up a little of their spare time to lend a hand.

If you wish to take part in this worthwhile activity, what sort of things would you do? Think of the people most in need of help and the ways in which help can be given. Much of the community services is concerned with the care of the elderly and the handicapped. Old people cannot always redecorate their homes. Household repairs, cleaning, preparing food or taking care of the garden may all prove difficult.

Handicapped people may be young or old. People confined to wheelchairs cannot go out unless somebody takes them. Blind children may love swimming but they need a sighted swimmer to go with them. Some handicapped people may be unable to go out at all and a visitor is then more than welcome.

What do you do if you want to help? Your school may have contact with an outside organization or, indeed, run a community service scheme itself. In many towns there is a committee called the Council of Social Service and it will be able to tell you about voluntary activities in the area. The Citizens' Advice Bureau and the Women's Royal Voluntary Service are other sources of information, as is the public library. Churches, the Scouts and other youth organizations can tell you about their activities. If you join such a group, you will bring pleasure and hope to people who need your help.

21. The author's purpose in writing this passage is to explain _____.

    A) why it is necessary for us to help others

    B) how to help others

    C) who most need help

    D) what community service is

22. The main idea of Para. 2 is that _____.

    A) many people need help, but nobody sees and gives it

    B) the organizations must depend on voluntary help

    C) special help should be given to those who cannot easily get help

D) it is necessary to form organizations to give help to those who need it

23. Which of the following statement is NOT true?

    A) The work of community service takes volunteers little time.

    B) It is natural for most people to help others.

    C) Voluntary help is needed in many places.

    D) Community service means a lot to those who need help.

24. Those who most need help from community service are _____.

    A) the old and young   B) the old and handicapped

    C) the homeless and friendless   D) old women

25. If you want to lend a hand and need the necessary information, you may go to _____.

    A) your school   B) a social service committee

    C) the library and churches   D) any of the above

Passage 4

Imagine eating everything delicious you want with none of the fat. That would be great, wouldn't it?

New "fake fat" products appear on store shelves in the United States recently, but not everyone is happy about it. Makers of the products, which contain a compound called *olestra*, say food manufacturers can now eliminate fat from certain foods. Critics, however, say the new compound can rob the body of essential vitamins and *nutrients* (营养物) and can also cause unpleasant side effects in some people. So it's up to consumers to decide whether the new fat free products taste good enough to keep eating.

Chemists discovered *olestra* in the late 1960s, when they were searching for fat that could be digested by infants more easily. Instead of finding the desired fat, the researchers created a fat that can't be digested at all.

Normally, special chemicals in the *intestines* (肠) "grab" molecules of regular fat and break them down so they can be used by the body. A molecule of regular fat is made up of three molecules of substances called fatty acids.

The fatty acids are absorbed by the intestines and bring with them the essential vitamins A, D, E, and K. When fat molecules are present in the intestines with any of those vitamins, the vitamins attach to the molecules and are carried into the bloodstream.

Olestra, which is made from six to eight molecules of fatty acids, is too large for the intestines to absorb. It just slides through the intestines without being broken down. Manufactures say it's that ability to slide unchanged through the intestines that makes *olestra* so valuable as a fat substitute. It provides consumers with the taste of regular fat without any bad effects on the body. But critics say *olestra* can prevent vitamins A, D, E, and K from being absorbed. It can also prevent the absorption of *carotenoids* (类胡萝卜素), compounds that may reduce the risk of cancer, heart disease, etc.

Manufacturers are adding vitamins A, D, E, and K as well as carotenoids to their products now. Even so, some nutritionists are still concerned that people might eat unlimited amounts of food made with the fat substitute without worrying about how many calories they are consuming.

26. We learn from the passage that *olestra* is a substance that _____.

    A) contains plenty of nutrients

    B) makes foods fat-free while keeping them delicious

    C) renders foods calorie-free while retaining their vitamins

    D) makes food easily digestible

27. The result of the search for an easily digestible fat turned out to be _____.

    A) just as anticipated   B) commercially useless

    C) quite unexpected   D) somewhat controversial

28. *Olestra* is different from ordinary fats in that _____.

    A) it facilitates the absorption of vitamins by the body

    B) it passes through the intestines without being absorbed

    C) it helps reduce the incidence of heart disease

    D) it prevents excessive intake of vitamins

29. What is possible negative effect of *olestra* according to some critics?

    A) It may increase the risk of cancer.   B) It may impair the digestive system.

    C) It may spoil the consumers' appetite.   D) It may affect the overall fat intake.

30. Why are nutritionists concerned about adding vitamins to *olestra*?

    A) People may be induced to eat more than is necessary.

    B) It may trigger a new wave of fake food production.

    C) It may lead to the over-consumption of vitamins.

    D) The function of intestines may be weakened.

Section D   Short Answer Questions

Directions：（略）

Passage 5

All that we really need to plot out the future of our universe are a few good measurements. This does not mean that we can sit down today and outline the future course of the universe with anything like certainty. There are still too many things we do not know about the way the universe is put together. But we do know exactly what information we need to fill in our knowledge, and we have a pretty good idea of how to go about getting it.

Perhaps the best way to think of our present situation is to imagine a train coming into a switchyard. All of the switches are set before the train arrives, so that its path is completely determined. Some switches we can see, others we cannot. There is no ambiguity if we can see the setting of a switch: we can say with confidence that some possible futures will not materialize and others will. At the unseen switches, however, there is no such certainty. We know the train will take one of the tracks leading out, but we have no idea which one. The unseen switches are the true decision points in the future, and what happens when we arrive at them determines the entire subsequent course of events.

When we think about the future of the universe, we can see our "track" many billions of years into the future, but after that there are decision points to be dealt with and possible fates to consider. The goal of science is to reduce the ambiguity at the decision points and find the true road that will be followed.

31. According to the passage, it is difficult to be certain about the distant future of the universe because we _____.

_____

_____

32. The author compares our present situation to _____.

_____

_____

33. According to the author, if we can see the setting of a switch, then we can be sure of _____.

_____

_____

34. What does "decision points" refer to in the passage?

_____

_____

35. Simply put, the goal of science is to make us more certain about _____.

_____

_____

Notes and Explanations

Passage 1

Explanations

1. [N] 第三段第四句提到 Navajo is considered endangered despite having 150,000 speakers. 尽管有 15 万人在说纳瓦霍语,它还是濒临灭绝。与其他很多语言相比,讲纳瓦霍语的人数很多。因此答案应为 No。

2. [Y] 第三段第五、六句提到 What makes a language endangered is not just the number of speakers, but how old they are. If it is spoken by children it is relatively safe. 使一种语言面临失传危险的并不在于说这种语言的有多少人,而是这些人的年龄。如果孩子们在使用这种语言,它就是相对安全的。故正确答案为 Yes。

3. [NG] 第五段第二句提到 Quite often, governments try to kill off a minority language by banning its use in public or discouraging its use in schools, all to promote national unity. 通常政府都会通过禁止在公共场合使用和阻止在学校使用来消灭少数民族语言,以促进国家统一。再者,后面的内容并没有提及政府对少数民族语言的保护,因此答案应为 Not Given。

4. [Y] 通过浏览文章的主体部分可以得知随着社会的融合和经济文化的发展,很多少数民族语言的消失成了一种无法挽回的潮流,因此本题的正确答案为 Yes。

5. [N] 第一段第二句提到 Most of its speakers are middle-aged or elderly. 大多数讲(纳瓦霍语)的都是中老年人。因此,正确答案应为 No。

6. [Y] 从第四段得知人们拒绝自己父母的语言首先是因为面对更大更富足的社会而对自己的文化失去信心。故正确答案为 Yes。

7. [N] 最后一段第一句提到 However, preservation can bring a language back from the dead. 保护可以使一种语言起死回生。故正确答案是 No。

8. 第三段第一句指出 Isolation breeds linguistic diversity.（地域的）孤立造成了语言的多样性。从而得出答案是（**geographical**）**isolation**。

9. 第七段第二句提到 But a growing interest in cultural identity may prevent the direct predictions from coming true. 然而，对于文化特性不断增长的兴趣可能有助于阻止（少数民族语言）灭绝的预言成为现实。从中得知，**cultural identity** 为本题的答案。

10. 从最后一段第二、三句 There are examples of languages that have survived in written form and then been revived by later generations. But a written form is essential for this, so the mere possibility of revival has led many speakers of endangered languages to develop systems of writing where none existed before. 可以知道，保存濒临灭绝的语言的最有效的方法就是把它们变成文字。因此，本题的正确答案应为 **the survival of their mother tongue**。

Passage 2

Notes

1. Carnegie Hall (Line 1, Para. 1)

   卡内基音乐厅，位于美国纽约市，著名的演奏会场。

2. Carnegie Hall owes its existence to Andrew Carnegie... (Line 1, Para. 2)

   owe...to... 在此意思是"把……归功于，受恩于"。例如：

   She owes her good health to her regular life. 她把健康归功于生活有规律。

   I owe it to the doctor that I am still alive. 我把自己至今还活着归功于那位医生。

3. Despite its reputation, however, the concert hall suffered from several detrimental renovations over the years. (Line 3~4, Para. 2)

   ▷despite 意思是"不管"，介词，比相同含义的 in spite of 更正式。例如：

   Despite the traffic jam he arrived here on time. 尽管交通堵塞，他仍然按时到达这里。

   Despite the bad weather we enjoyed our holiday. 尽管天气不好，我们假期仍然过得很愉快。

   ▷suffer from 意思是"受苦，患病；遭受损害"。例如：

   His health suffered terribly from heavy drinking. 他的健康因过度喝酒而严重受损。

   He is suffering from a bad cold. 他严重感冒。

   That big city suffered from heavy earthquake. 那个大城市因地震而遭到严重破坏。

4. During the Great Depression, when fewer people could afford to attend performances... (Line 4~5, Para. 2)

   can/be able to afford sth./to do 意思是"担负得起（费用，损失，后果等）；抽得出（时间）"。例如：

   In accomplishing your task, you cannot afford the waste of a single minute.

   你们在完成任务时，一分钟也不能浪费。

   He told me that the firm could not afford to pay such large salaries.

   他告诉我公司支付不起如此巨额的工资。

5. As a result, a coffee shop was opened in one corner of the building... (Line 6~7, Para. 2)

   ▷as a result 意思是"作为结果，因此"。例如：

   He had stuttered since his childhood and as a result talked very little.

   他从儿时起就口吃，因此很少说话。

We follow up the suggestions, and have had satisfying experiences as a result.

我们接受了建议,因而得到了满意的结果。

▷as a result of sth. 意思是"因为,由于;作为……的结果"。例如:

As a result of the accident, Tom couldn't walk for six months. 由于意外事故,汤姆六个月不能走路。

We couldn't afford to borrow money for a house as a result of the rise in interest rates.

因为利率提高,我们借不起钱买房子。

6. In 1960, the violinist Issac Stern became involved in restoring the hall... (Line 1, Para. 3)

be involved in... 在此意思是"使卷入,使陷入",另外还可表示"使专注,专心"。例如:

be involved in trouble 卷入纠纷

Many workers were involved in the strike. 许多工人参加了罢工。

He was involved in working out a plan. 他专心地制订计划。

Explanations

11. [K] 语法规则要求此处应填一个动词 + ed 形式(过去分词)构成现在完成时态。选项 B、K 是动词 + ed 形式。选项 K undergone(经历,经受)在意思上符合上下文要求。

12. [I] 语法规则要求 the most 后面应该填一个形容词构成形容词的最高级形式,选项中符合上下文意思要求的是 I 项 extensive(大面积的,覆盖范围大的)。

13. [M] 语法规则要求此处应填一个动词作 Carnegie Hall 的谓语,并且应该用第三人称单数形式,这个动词和后面的 to 构成固定搭配的短语。选项 M 符合这两个条件;owe...to 意为"应感激,应该把……归功于",符合上下文意思要求。

14. [G] 语法规则要求此处应填一个名词或代词作句子的宾语,这个词在语义上应该能够和 gain 搭配使用。选项中能够和 gain 搭配的只有 reputation 意思是"获得名声",符合上下文意思的要求。

15. [D] 语法规则要求句首单词的第一个字母应该大写。选项中只有 D 项的第一个字母是大写的,上下文的意思要求这里应该填一个表示让步意义的介词,所以 D 项在上下文意思上也符合要求。

16. [C] 语法规则要求情态动词 could 后面应跟动词原形。选项 C 符合此条件;could afford to do sth. 意为"能负担得起(费用、损失、后果等)",符合上下文意思的要求。

17. [E] 语法规则要求这里应该填一个副词来修饰动词 damaged,选项 E seriously(严重地)既符合这个条件,又符合上下文意思的要求。

18. [B] 语法规则要求此处应填一个形容词和 in 构成固定搭配的短语,选项 B involved 可以和 in 搭配使用,意为"使卷入、陷入",符合上下文意思要求。

19. [O] 语法规则要求此处应填一个形容词来修饰 restoration。选项中符合上下文意思要求的形容词是 H 项 current,意为"有希望的,有前途的"。

20. [H] 语法规则要求此处应填一个形容词构成形容词比较级。根据句子前半部分的意思,此处应填 promising。promising 意思是"有前途的,有希望的",常和 future 搭配使用。

Passage 3

Notes

1. The idea of helping people comes naturally to most of us. (Line 1, Para. 1)

come to sb. 意思是"被某人记起、想起"例如:

It suddenly came to him that he had been wrong all the time.

他突然意识到他一直都在坚持错误的观点。

Suddenly the words of the song came to me. 我突然想起了歌词。

2. If we see a blind person getting off a bus, we watch to make sure that he is in no danger of falling. (Line

1～2, Para. 1)

▷see sb. doing sth. 意思是"看见某人正在做某事"。其他动词像 watch，hear，listen to，observe 等也可用于该结构中。例如：

I saw him reading a novel when I came into the room. 我进屋时看见他正在看一本小说。

I saw them arguing in the middle of the street. 我看见他们在马路中间争论不休。

▷see sb. do sth. 意思是"看见某人做某事(强调过程)"。例如：

I saw him cross the street. 我看见他过马路。

She was seen to go into the cinema. 有人看见她走进电影院。

▷make sure (of) 意思是"确定,查明；确保,务必"等。例如：

Will you make sure that she returned? 请你查明她是否真的回来了,好吗？

Make sure that you pick me up at five at the airport. 你一定要五点到机场接我。

▷in (no) danger of 意思是"置身于……危险中"。例如：

She was seriously ill and in danger of losing her life. 她病得很重,有生命危险。

While in danger of being attacked by two gunmen, she was surprisingly calm.

在面临两个持枪歹徒袭击的危险时刻,她冷静得令人惊讶。

3. It may not have occurred to you that you are in a position to help. (Line 3～4, Para. 2)

▷occur to sb. 意思是"某人想起(想法、念头)"。例如：

Did it ever occur to you that you would go abroad? 你没有想过你可以出国吗？

▷另一个常用结构为 it occurs(ed) to sb. that... 例如：

It never occurred to me for a moment that you meant that. 我从未想到你是这个意思。

▷be in a position to do sth. 意思是"能够做某事"。例如：

Perhaps I shall be in a position to help you next week. 也许下周我能够帮你。

The poor family was in no position to bring up the four children.

那个穷苦的家庭不能把四个孩子抚养成人。

4. These organizations depend on voluntary help to carry out a wide variety of tasks, volunteers giving up a little of their spare time to lend a hand. (Line 6～7, Para. 2)

▷volunteers giving up a little of their spare time to lend a hand 为分词独立结构。

a variety of 意思是"各种各样的,不同的"。例如：

a collection of a variety of butterflies 收集各式各样的蝴蝶

The girls come from a variety of different backgrounds. 女孩子们来自不同的家庭。

▷lend a hand (to sb.) with sth. 意思是"帮助(某人)做……"。例如：

Would you like to lend me a hand with the sofa? 你能帮我搬一下沙发吗？

We must lend a hand with his problem. 我们必须帮他解决问题。

5. If you wish to take part in this worthwhile activity, what sort of things would you do? (Line 1, Para. 3)

take part in 意思是"参加,参与"。例如：

take an active part in a debate 积极参与讨论

They invited me to take part in their celebration. 他们邀请我参加他们的庆祝活动。

6. Think of the people most in need of help and the ways in which help can be given. (Line 1～2, Para. 3)

in need of 意思是"需要"。例如：

He felt lonely and in need of companionship. 他觉得很孤单,需要人陪伴。

The whole house is in need of repairing. 整幢房子需要修理。

7. Much of the community services is concerned with the care of the elderly and the handicapped. (Line 2～3, Para. 3)

be concerned with 意思是"涉及,关于……"。例如：

The chapter is concerned with changes that are likely to take place.

这一章节涉及可能要发生的变化。

His new book is concerned with Africa. 他的新作是关于非洲的。

8. People confined to wheelchairs cannot go out unless somebody takes them. (Line 1~2, Para. 4)

confine (to) 意思是"限制,使局限于……"。例如:

They succeeded in confining the fire to a small area. 他们成功地把火势控制在小范围内。

The man confined himself to five cigarettes a day. 那个人限制自己每天吸五支烟。

9. ...as is the public library. (Line 5, Para. 5)

as is/was/does/did + 名词(或代词)等,意思是"与…… 一样"。例如:

She plays the piano, as does her mother. 她和她母亲一样会弹钢琴。

I voted Labor, so did my husband. 我和丈夫都投了工党的票。

Explanations

这篇文章的主题是社区服务,文章内容涉及什么是社区服务,什么样的人需要社区服务,怎样提供社区服务等。

21. D) 主旨题。文章第一段是引言,第二段作者点出了全文的主题——社区服务。选项 A 是第一段主题,选项 B 是第五段主题,选项 C 是第二、三段主题,而这三个选项都是围绕选项 D 展开的,所以正确答案应是 D 项。

22. D) 推断题。第二段的主题是讲述建立社区服务机构和为需要的人提供帮助的必要性。其他选项只是该段落的细节,不是主题,因此 D 项是正确答案。

23. A) 细节题。在文章第二段最后一句 volunteers giving up a little of their spare time to lend a hand. 中的 a little of their spare time 和选项 A 中的 little time 在意思上有着质的区别,其他选项在文章中均已涉及,因此 A 项是正确答案。

24. B) 细节题。文章的第二段、第三段、第四段均涉及了选项 B。选项 A、选项 C 和选项 D 在文章中没有提到,故不正确。

25. D) 细节题。在文章第五段中可以看到选项 A(你所在的学校)、选项 B(社会服务委员会)、选项 C(图书馆及教堂),因此正确答案应为选项 D(上述任何地方)。

Passage 4

Notes

1. ... say food manufacturers can now eliminate fat from certain foods. (Line 2~3, Para. 2)

eliminate 意思是"排除,消除"。可与 from 连用。例如:

eliminate the false and retain the true 去伪存真

She has been eliminated from the swimming race because she did not win any of the practice races.

她已被取消了参加游泳比赛的资格,因为她在训练中没有得到名次。

2. Critics, however, say the new compound can rob the body of essential vitamins and nutrients... (Line 3~4, Para. 2)

rob sb. /sth. of 意思是"从……夺走……,使失去……"。例如:

rob a man of his money 抢人钱财

The shock robbed her of her speech. 她震惊得说不出话来。

3. So it's up to consumers to decide whether the new fat free products taste good enough to keep eating. (Line 5~6, Para. 2)

▷It's up to sb. to do... 是一常用句型,意思是"是某人的责任,由某人决定"。例如:

It's up to him to decide it. 那件事由他决定。

It's up to us to give them all the help we can. 我们有责任全力帮助他们。

▷另外作为一个短语,还可以表示"胜任,适于;直到"等含义。例如:

be up to standard 符合标准

He is not up to his work. 他不胜任他的工作。

up to now 直到现在

4. Normally，special chemicals in the intestines "grab" molecules of regular fat and break them down so they can be used by the body. (Line 1~2, Para. 4)

▷break down 在文中的意思是"把……分解"。例如:

Sugar and starch are broken down in the stomach. 糖和淀粉在胃中分解。

▷break down 的常见含义为"(机械等)出故障,毁坏;(人)身体出毛病,(健康)衰弱"。例如:

The car broke down on the way home. 在回家的路上汽车抛锚了。

You (Your health) will break down if you work too hard. 如果工作过度身体会垮掉。

5. Manufacturers are adding vitamins A，D，E，and K as well as carotenoids to their products now. (Line 1, Para. 7)

add...to 意思是"增加,增添"。例如:

Please add my name to the list. 请在名单上加上我的名字。

The news added to his anxiety. 这条消息增添了他的忧虑。

Explanations

该篇文章的主题是最近出现在美国市场上的低脂肪食品。主要介绍了这种食品的发现、人体对它的吸收过程以及它的优缺点。文章还提到了对这种食品持反对意见的人的理由。

26. **B)** 推断题。olestra 去除了食品中的脂肪,保留了食物的美味。文章第二段第二句指出生产这种含有 olestra 的食物的人说他们已从食物中去除了脂肪;最后一句谈到消费者根据食品的味道来决定是否长期食用,换言之,消费者并没有发现这种新食品不好吃。因此选项 B 正确。其他选项均与文章内容不符。

27. **C)** 推断题。文中第二段说化学家们在六十年代末想找到易于婴儿消化的一种脂肪,结果却找到了根本不能消化的 olestra,因此选项 C 正确。选项 A 与文章意思相反;文章未提到选项 B 和选项 D。

28. **B)** 细节题。文章第六段第一、第二句说到 Olestra, which is made from six to eight molecules of fatty acids, is too large for the intestines to absorb. It just slides through the intestines without being broken down. ,由此可确定选项 B 正确。选项 A 和 C 与文中意思相反。文章未提及选项 D。

29. **A)** 推断题。文章第六段最后一句说 olestra 阻止了类胡萝卜素和其他一些化合物被人体吸收,而这些化合物会减少癌症和心脏病的发生,由此得出答案是 A 项。文中未提到选项 B、C 和 D。

30. **A)** 推断题。根据文章最后一段最后一句 Even so, some nutritionists are still concerned that people might eat unlimited amounts of food made with the fat substitute without worrying about how many calories they are consuming. ,可以推断 A 项正确。其他选项文章均未提到。

Passage 5

Keys

31. are not sure how the universe is put together

32. a train coming into a switchyard

33. what will happen in our future

34. the unseen possibilities that determine our future

35. the future

Notes

1. All that we really need to plot out the future of our universe are a few good measurements. (Line 1, Para. 1)

plot out 意思是"划分，规划"。例如：

plot out one's time 规划时间

New residential districts are all plotted out. 新居住区的范围都已划定。

2. This does not mean that we can sit down today and outline the future course of the universe with anything like certainty. (Line 2～3, Para. 1)

sit down 意思是"坐下，就座"，在此意思是"坐下来进行商讨或谈判"。例如：

Suddenly he sat down on the ice. 他突然在冰上摔了一跤。

They decided to sit down and straighten out their differences.

他们决定坐下来谈判，明确彼此之间的分歧。

3. There are still too many things we do not know about the way the universe is put together. (Line 3～4, Para. 1)

▷put together 在此意思是"装配(零件等)，组合，拼凑"。例如：

The broken edges of the plate were put together with glue. 用胶水把盘子的碎边粘了起来。

I'm learning how to put together a watch as well as how to take it apart.

我不但学习怎样把一只表拆开，而且还在学习怎样把它组装起来。

▷另外 put together 还可表示"整理(思想、思绪、意见等)"。例如：

Please wait a few minutes; I must put my thoughts together before I give you a definite reply.

请等几分钟，我必须整理出头绪来才能给你明确的答复。

4. ... and we have a pretty good idea of how to go about getting it. (Line 4～5, Para. 1)

go about 在此意思是"着手进行，着手处理，从事"。例如：

Go about your business. 做你自己的事吧。

I'm afraid he is not going about his work in the right way. 我想他着手工作的方法可能不大对头。

5. Perhaps the best way to think of our present situation is to imagine a train coming into a switchyard. (Line 1～2, Para. 2)

▷imagine (sb. /sth.) doing... 意思是"想象(某人、某物)做……"。例如：

He didn't imagine becoming a writer in his childhood. 孩提时代他没有想过成为一名作家。

I can't imagine her marrying him. 我无法想象她和他结婚。

▷switchyard 意思是"(铁路)调车场，编组站"。在此则指"(铁路的)转辙器"。

6. ... but after that there are decision points to be dealt with and possible fates to consider. (Line 2, Para. 3)

deal with 意思是"对待、处理(事情，问题，紧急情况)等"。例如：

She knows well how to deal with children. 她非常了解怎样和孩子相处。

I think this problem should be dealt with quickly. 我认为这个问题应及早处理。

Unit 13

Section A　Skimming and Scanning

Directions：（略）

Passage 1

Playing is a Serious Business

1. Playing is a serious business. Children *engrossed*（吸引）in a make-believe world，fox cubs play-fighting or kittens teasing a ball of string aren't just having fun. Play may look like a carefree and exuberant way to pass the time before the hard work of adulthood comes along，but there's much more to it than that. For a start，play can even cost animals their lives. Eighty per cent of deaths among juvenile fur seals occur because playing pups fail to spot *predators*（掠夺者，食肉动物）approaching. It is also extremely expensive in terms of energy. Playful young animals use around two or three per cent of their energy *cavorting*（嬉闹），and in children that figure can be closer to fifteen per cent. "Even two or three per cent is huge," says John Byers of Idaho University. "You just don't find animals wasting energy like that," he adds. There must be a reason.

2. But if play is not simply a developmental *hiccup*（打嗝），as biologists once thought，why did it evolve? The latest idea suggests that play has evolved to build big brains. In other words，playing makes you intelligent. Playfulness，it seems，is common only among mammals，although a few of the larger-brained birds also indulge. Animals at play often use unique signs—tail-wagging in dogs，for example—to indicate that activity superficially resembling adult behavior is not really in earnest. A popular explanation of play has been that it helps juveniles develop the skills they will need to hunt，mate and socialize as adults. Another has been that it allows young animals to get in shape for adult life by improving their respiratory endurance. Both these ideas have been questioned in recent years.

3. Take the exercise theory. If play evolved to build muscle or as a kind of endurance training，then you would expect to see permanent benefits. But Byers points out that the benefits of increased exercise disappear rapidly after training stops，so any improvement in endurance resulting from juvenile play would be lost by adulthood. "If the function of play was to get into shape," says Byers， "the optimum time for playing would depend on when it was most advantageous for the young of a particular species to do so. But it doesn't work like that." Across species，play tends to peak about halfway through the suckling stage and then decline.

4. Then there's the skills-training hypothesis. At first glance，playing animals do appear to be practicing the complex maneuvers they will need in adulthood. But a closer inspection reveals this interpretation as too simplistic. In one study，behavioral ecologist Tom Caro，from the University of California，looked at the predatory play of kittens and their predatory behavior when

they reached adulthood. He found that the way the cats played had no significant effect on their hunting prowess in later life.

5. Earlier this year, Sergio Pellis of Lethbridge University, Canada, reported that there is a strong positive link between brain size and playfulness among mammals in general. Comparing measurements for fifteen orders of mammal, he and his team found larger brains (for a given body size) are linked to greater playfulness. The converse was also found to be true. Robert Barton of Durham University believes that, because large brains are more sensitive to developmental stimuli than smaller brains, they require more play to help mould them for adulthood. "I concluded it's to do with learning, and with the importance of environmental data to the brain during development," he says.

6. According to Byers, the timing of the playful stage in young animals provides an important clue to what's going on. If you plot the amount of time a juvenile devotes to play each day over the course of its development, you discover a pattern typically associated with a "sensitive period" a brief development window during which the brain can actually be modified in ways that are not possible earlier or later in life. Think of the relative ease with which young children — but not infants or adults — absorb language. Other researchers have found that play in cats, rats and mice is at its most intense just as this "window of opportunity" reaches its peak.

7. "People have not paid enough attention to the amount of the brain activated by play," says Marc Bekoff from Colorado University. Bekoff studied *coyote* (山狗) pups at play and found that the kind of behavior involved was markedly more variable and unpredictable than that of adults. Such behavior activates many different parts of the brain, he reasons. Bekoff likens it to a behavioral *kaleidoscope* (万花筒), with animals at play jumping rapidly between activities. "They use behavior from a lot of different contexts — predation, aggression, reproduction," he says. "Their developing brain is getting all sorts of stimulation."

8. Not only is more of the brain involved in play than was suspected, but it also seems to activate higher cognitive processes. "There's enormous cognitive involvement in play," says Bekoff. He points out that play often involves complex assessments of playmates, ideas of *reciprocity*(互惠) and the use of specialized signals and rules. He believes that play creates a brain that has greater behavioral flexibility and improved potential for learning later in life. The idea is backed up by the work of Stephen Siviy of Gettysburg College. Siviy studied how bouts of play affected the brain's levels of a particular chemical associated with the stimulation and growth of nerve cells. He was surprised by the extent of the activation. "Play just lights everything up," he says. By allowing link-ups between brain areas that might not normally communicate with each other, play may enhance creativity.

9. What might further experimentation suggest about the way children are raised in many societies today? We already know that rat pups denied the chance to play grow smaller brain components and fail to develop the ability to apply social rules when they interact with their peers. With schooling beginning earlier and becoming increasingly exam-orientated, play is likely to get even less of a look-in. Who knows what the result of that will be?

1. Children use around two or three per cent of their energy cavorting.

2. The latest idea suggests that play has evolved to build big brains.

3. Tom Caro found that the way the cats played had significant effect on their hunting prowess in later life.

4. Earlier this year, Sergio Pellis reported that there is a strong positive link between brain size and playfulness among mammals in general.

5. People have not paid enough attention to the intelligence activated by play.

6. Not only is more of the brain involved in play than was suspected, but it also seems to activate higher cognitive processes.

7. With schooling beginning earlier and becoming increasingly exam-orientated, play is likely to play a more important role in brain development.

8. If play evolved to build muscle or as a kind of endurance training, then you would expect to see _____.

9. Other researchers have found that play in cats, rats and mice is at its most intense just as this "window of opportunity" _____.

10. By allowing link-ups between brain areas that might not normally communicate with each other, play may enhance _____.

Section B　Discourse Vocabulary Test
Directions：（略）

Passage 2

The three types of secondary education in the United States have been provided by the Latin grammar school, the academy, and the public high school. The first of these was colonial __11__. It began in New England with the establishment in 1635 of the Boston Free Latin School. The curriculum __12__ mainly of the classical languages, and the purpose of this kind of school was the preparation of boys for college, where most of them would be fitted for ministry.

The academy began in the early 1750's with Benjamin Franklin's school in Philadelphia, which later became the University of Pennsylvania. It __13__ generally to about the middle of the nineteenth century, except in the southern states where the public high school was late in __14__ and where the academy continued a principal means of __15__ education even after 1900. The academy was open to girls as well as to boys, and it provided a wide curriculum than the Latin grammar school had furnished. It was designed not only as a preparation for college but also for practical life in __16__ and business activities. Although its wide educational values were evident and are recognized as important __17__ to secondary education in this country, the academy was never considered a public institution as the public high school has come to be.

The public high school had its __18__ in Massachusetts in 1821 when the English Classical School was established in Boston. In 1827, that state *enacted*（颁令，制定）the first state-wide public high school law in the United States; by 1850, they were also to be found in many other states.

Just as the curriculum of the academy grew out of that of the Latin grammar school, so the curriculum of the public high school developed out of that of the academy. The public high school in the United States is a *repudiation*（抛弃）of the aristocratic and selective principle of the European educational __19__ . Since 1890, enrollments in secondary schools, __20__ in public high schools, have practically doubled in this country every ten years.

A) made	I) intended
B) resource	J) consisted
C) institution	K) contributions
D) extended	L) secondary
E) commercial	M) public
F) education	N) developing
G) origin	O) tradition
H) mainly	

Section C Reading in Depth

Directions：（略）

Passage 3

Sisal（西沙尔麻）and cotton are the two outstanding exports at *Dar es Salaam*（达累斯萨拉姆，坦桑尼亚首都）. Sisal has for many years been the leading export in terms of volume. Since 1959 over 100,000 harbor tons have been exported each year. Sisal thus constitutes approximately one quarter of the total volume of exports passing through the port, but the commodity is not so important as it is at *Tanga*（坦噶，坦桑尼亚东北部港市）. There has been a rapid increase in cotton exports during the past decade, largely because of increased production in the Lake Region of Tanzania and the encouragement of the Tanzanian Government. Market conditions in the Far East and in Europe are good, and there is likely to be further increase in cotton exports through Dar es Salaam. Increases in cotton exports have been paralleled by increases in exports of oil seed and seed cake, largely a by-product of cotton.

Exports of coffee through Dar es Salaam are slight and variable compared with those through Mombassa; this results from the varying quantities moving through Tanzania from Rwanda, Burundi and the Congo, and from the fact that most of the coffee crop from northern Tanzania passes through Mombassa. Grains are occasionally important. Ten exports are increasingly important, and exports of cashew *nuts*（腰果）, castor seed and canned meat are also rising. Cotton easily takes first place among the commodities exported through Dar es Salaam in terms of value.

The most noteworthy feature of the export traffic of Tanga is that there is only one major commodity involved. Exports of sisal, which rose in 1963 to record level of 231,105 harbor tons, constituted in that year 88 percent of the total volume of exports through the port of Tanga, and 72 percent of the total volume of traffic handled at the port. The importance of sisal exports at Tanga reflects the fact that sisal constitutes the leading industry of Tanzania. Other commodities exported through Tanga are comparatively of very minor significance, although exports of tea, canned meat and timber have risen in recent years.

21. It is suggested in the passage that cotton exports through Dar es Salaam will probably increase because _____.

    A) they have been rapidly increasing over the last ten years

    B) the Tanzania Government has been encouraging the Lake Region to grow more

    C) the demand for cotton in Europe and the Far East is growing

    D) exports of oil seed and seed cake have increased

22. It is implied that exports of oil seed and seed cake have increased because _____.

    A) of Tanzania Government encouragement

    B) market conditions in the Far East are good

    C) they are as important in Dar es Salaam as they are in Mombassa

    D) of increases in cotton production

23. The most important difference between Tanga and Dar es Salaam is that Tanga, unlike Dar es Salaam, _____.

    A) only exports one major commodity

    B) exports only seven different commodities

    C) exports only $17,000,000 worth of commodities

    D) has timber and canned meat exported through it

24. Why are sisal exports at Tanga very important?

    A) Because sisal is popular with people.

    B) Because sisal plays a leading role in the industry of Tanzania.

    C) Because Tanga exports more principal commodities than Dar es salaam.

    D) Because sisal is more important than cotton at Tanga.

25. Which of the following do you think may best serve as the title of this passage?

    A) Principal Export Commodities Through Tanga and Dar es Salaam

    B) The Value of Principal Commodities Exported

    C) Exports of Sisal and Cotton

    D) The Importance of the Export

Passage 4

Disney World, Florida, is the biggest amusement resort in the world. It covers 24.4 thousand acres, and is twice the size of Manhattan. It was opened on October 1, 1971, five years after Walt Disney's death, and it is a larger, slightly more ambitious version of Disneyland near Los Angeles.

Foreigners tend to associate Walter Disney with Snow White and the Seven Dwarfs, and with his other famous cartoon characters, Mickey Mouse, Donald Duck and Pluto, or with his nature films, whose superb photography is spoiled, in the opinion of some, by the *vulgarity*（粗俗）of the commentary and musical background.

There is very little that could be called vulgar in Disney World. It attracts people of most tastes and most income groups, and people of all ages, from toddlers to grandpas. There are two expensive hotels, a golf course, forest trails for horseback riding and rivers for canoeing. But the central attraction of the resort is the Magic Kingdom.

Between the huge parking lots and the Magic Kingdom lies a broad artificial lake. In the distance the towers of Cinderella's Castle, which like every other building in the Kingdom is built of solid materials. Even getting to the Magic Kingdom is quite an adventure. You have a choice of transportation. You can either cross the lake on a replica of a Mississippi paddle-wheeler, or you can glide around the shore in a streamlined monorail train.

When you reach the terminal, you walk straight into a little square which faces Main Street. Main Street is late 19th century. There are modern shops inside the buildings, but all the facades are of the period. There are hanging baskets full of red and white flowers, and there is no traffic except a horse-drawn streetcar and an ancient double-decker bus. Yet as you walk through the Magic Kingdom, you are actually walking on top of a network of underground roads. This is how the shops, restaurants and all the other material needs of the Magic Kingdom are invisibly supplied.

26. When did Walt Disney die?

    A) In 1971.   B) In 1976.   C) In 1966.   D) In 1900.

27. The main attraction of Disney World is _____.

    A) The Magic Kingdom   B) The Seven Dwarfs

    C) Mickey Mouse   D) Donald Duck

28. Reaching the Magic Kingdom is _____.

    A) easy   B) difficult   C) dangerous   D) adventurous

29. When one visits this biggest amusement in the world, one will find _____.

    A) it just wastes his time   B) it is relatively cheap

    C) it is very expensive   D) it is vulgar

30. Why is Disney World the most famous amusement resort?

    A) It is funny.   B) It is interesting.

    C) It is the biggest one.   D) It is the most expensive.

Section D　Short Answer Questions

Directions：（略）

Passage 5

The quality of taped recordings was for many years worse than that of *gramophone*（留声机）records. But it gradually caught up as the equipment was improved. By 1940 tape recorders of an advanced design were being produced, suitable for professional use but not for the home. Then in 1947, American manufacturers took those large, heavy machines that ate up tape at the rate of thirty inches per second and began to turn them into a real rival to the gramophone. They reduced the size and weight, lowered the running speed, raised the sound quality and increased the playing time far beyond the four minutes which at that time represented the gramophone record's maximum.

The record industry's answer to this threat was to introduce the long-playing record, which not only gave much longer continuous recordings than before but also better wear and durability and much better quality. The increase in sound quality on gramophone records was mainly due to tape recorders being used to make better original recordings. So strong as it may seem, tape recorders helped to save the record industry from the threat of tape recorders.

Since 1950 tape has led the way, not only in quality but by producing the first really successful stereo recordings, by making recording a hobby available to all, and by bringing a vast new industry of music into the record catalogues for the ease with which music can be recorded on to tape. It has also opened the way for many compositions ignored in the expensive days of the disc.

Sound technicians worked away at the problems of magnetic recording until they were able to produce a seven inch spool holding 1,200 feet tape which was pulled across the magnetic pickups at the speed of only fifteen inches per second. They might have stopped at this point but, as science is the land where nothing is regarded as perfect, they did not.

They devised three ways of increasing the playing game—by developing thinner tape so that more could be wound on to a spool, by running the tape at a slower speed so that it took longer to reach the end, and by recording more than one track along the tape. The next step was double-play tape, followed by triple-play and, the most recent advance, quadruple-play tape which is thinner than human hair.

31. The quality of tape recordings gradually caught up because of _____.
   _____ _____ _____ _____ _____

   _____ _____ _____ _____ _____

32. Really good stereo recordings began to appear in _____.
   _____ _____ _____ _____ _____

   _____ _____ _____ _____ _____

33. What did the record industry do when the tape recorder became a threat?
   _____ _____ _____ _____ _____

   _____ _____ _____ _____ _____

34. Apart from longer playing time, the long-playing record gave _____.
   _____ _____ _____ _____ _____

   _____ _____ _____ _____ _____

35. Why did sound technicians continue to work hard after they had achieved great success with the tape recorder?
   _____ _____ _____ _____ _____

   _____ _____ _____ _____ _____

Notes and Explanations

Passage 1

Explanations

1. ［N］第一段第七句提到 Playful young animals use around two or three per cent of their energy cavorting（嬉闹），and in children that figure can be closer to fifteen per cent. 贪玩的小动物用百分之二、三的能量翻腾跳跃，儿童则用去百分之十五的能量。故正确答案为 No。

2. ［Y］第二段第二句提到 The latest idea suggests that play has evolved to build big brains. 最新的发现认为游戏的发展有助于大脑成长。所以答案为 Yes。

3. ［N］第四段最后一句提到 He found that the way the cats played had no significant effect on their hunting prowess in later life. 他发现小猫游戏的方式对它们日后捕捉猎物的威力没有显著的影响。因此得出正确答案为 No。

4. ［Y］第五段第一句提到 ... there is a strong positive link between brain size and playfulness among mammals in general. 总的来说，哺乳动物脑子的大小与它们的游戏水平成正比。故正确答案为 Yes。

5. ［Y］第七段第一句提到 People have not paid enough attention to the amount of the brain activated by play. 人们还没有充分地认识到游戏所激发的智慧。因此答案是 Yes。

6. ［Y］第八段第一句提到 Not only is more of the brain involved in play than was suspected，but it also seems to activate higher cognitive processes. 不仅游戏中的大脑活动比人们猜测得要多，而且游戏还能激发更高的认知能力。故正确答案为 Yes。

7. ［N］最后一段倒数第二句提到 With schooling beginning earlier and becoming increasingly exam-orientated，play is likely to get even less of a look-in. 随着上学年龄越来越早和以考试为中心的教育方式，游戏可能变得很平庸、没有什么前途了。所以得出答案为 No。

8. 第三段第二句提到 If play evolved to build muscle or as a kind of endurance training，then you would expect to see permanent benefits. 如果游戏发展到可以锻炼肌肉或者成为一种耐力训练，人们就可以发现长期的益处了。从这里可以得到答案 **permanent benefits**。

9. 从第六段最后一句 Other researchers have found that play in cats，rats and mice is at its most intense just as this "window of opportunity" reaches its peak. 可以找到本题的答案 **reaches its peak**。

10. 第八段最后一句提到 By allowing link-ups between brain areas that might not normally communicate with each other，play may enhance creativity. 通过把那些通常不能相互沟通的大脑区域联系起来，游戏可以提高创造力。因此本题的答案为 **creativity**。

Passage 2

Notes

1. The curriculum consisted mainly of the classical languages... （Line 4，Para. 1）

   ▷consist of 意思是"由……构成、组成"。例如：

   This club consists mostly of more than 300 members. 这个俱乐部由 300 多位会员组成。

   His job consists of helping old people who live alone. 他的工作包括帮助独居老人。

   ▷另外注意 consist in 意思是"在于"。例如：

   The beauty of the plan consists in its simplicity. 这个计划妙就妙在简明扼要。

   consist with 意思是"与……一致、符合"。例如：

   Theory should consist with practice. 理论应与实践相一致。

2. ... where most of them would be fitted for ministry. (Line 5，Para. 1)

这句话的意思是：他们中的大多数人都适合做神职人员或政府官员。

fit sb. for sth. /to do 意思是"使（人）能适合……，使（人）能……"。例如：

Vocational training will fit them for a good job. 职业训练使他们能够得到一份好工作。

His height fitted him for basketball. 他身材高适合打篮球。

3. It was designed not only as a preparation for college but also for practical life in commercial and business activities. (Line 6~7，Para. 2)

not only... but also... 意思是"不但……，而且……"。例如：

Not only did he teach in school，but he wrote novels. 他不但在学校教书，而且还写小说。

The nurse was not only competent but also kind. 那个护士不但能干而且亲切。

4. ... and are recognized as important contributions to secondary education in this country... （Line 8，Para. 2）

recognize... as... 意思是"正式承认，认定，认可"。例如：

be recognized as the legitimate representative 被承认为合法代表

He was recognized as an heir by all of his relatives. 他被所有的亲属认定为继承人。

Explanations

11. [C] 语法规则要求此处应填一个单数名词作表语。选项中的名词和前一句中的 school 和 academy 意思相关的是 institution。因此选项 C 既符合语法规则又符合上下文意思要求。

12. [J] 语法规则要求此处应填一个动词的过去式形式和 of 构成一个短语，选项中的过去时动词能够和 of 搭配的有 made 和 consisted。consist of 意思是"由……构成（或组成）"，符合上下文意思要求。

13. [D] 语法规则要求此处应填一个动词的过去式和介词 to 搭配作谓语，选项中符合该条件并符合上下文意思要求的只有 D 项 extended（延续，延伸）。

14. [N] 语法规则要求介词 in 后面应跟名词或动名词作宾语，选项中的名词或动名词中在意思上符合上下文要求的是 N 项，本句话的意思是南方各州的公立学校发展滞后。

15. [L] 语法规则要求此处应填一个形容词来修饰名词 education，文章上文中已提到 19 世纪中叶北方的 academy school（中等专科学校）已发展成为大学，而南部各州的 academy school 则发展缓慢，到 20 世纪初仍旧延用中等教育的模式。根据意思的要求这里应选 L 项。

16. [E] 语法规则要求此处应填一个形容词或名词和 business 并列修饰 activities，既符合语法规则又符合上下文意思的是 E 项 commercial（商业的）。

17. [K] 语法规则要求此处应填一个名词与 important 一起作 as 的宾语。这个条件状语从句的主语是复数名词，所以这里填的应该也是一个复数名词。选项中只有 K 项 contributions（贡献）是复数名词，且意思上符合上下文的要求。

18. [G] 语法规则要求此处应填一个名词与 its 一起作 has 的宾语，上文中介绍前两种中等教育形式时首先介绍的都是这种教育形式出现的时间和地点，这一段介绍第三种形式时仍是如此，所以 G 项 origin（起源，开端）符合意思的要求。

19. [O] 语法规则要求此处应填一个名词和 the European educational 一起做介词 of 的宾语。从前一句话的意思得知符合本句话意思的是 tradition（传统）。

20. [H] 语法规则要求此处应填一个副词来修饰介词短语 in public high schools。选项中只有 H 项 mainly（主要地）是副词，而且意思上也符合上下文的要求。

Passage 3

Notes

1. Sisal has for many years been the leading export in terms of volume. （Line 2，Para. 1）

这句话的意思是"很多年来西沙尔麻的出口在数量上都处于领先地位。"

▷in terms of 意思是"在……方面,从方面……（说来）"。例如:

in terms of theory 在理论上

in terms of manpower 在人力方面

Mary is a top student in terms of math in her class. 玛丽在他们班数学最好。

In terms of money we're quite rich，but not in terms of happiness.

在金钱方面我们很富有,但论及幸福就不然了。

▷in terms of 还有"根据,按照"的意思。例如:

consider problems in terms of the people's interests 从人民利益出发来考虑问题

think in terms of materialist dialectics 按照唯物辩证法进行思考

2. ... and there is likely to be further increase in cotton exports through Dar es Salaam. （Line 8，Para. 1）

▷There is likely to be 意思是"可能会有……"。例如:

There is likely to be a rain tonight. 今晚可能会下雨。

▷likely 的另一个常用句型是 It is likely that...，表示"可能会（有,发生）……"。例如:

It is likely that he will be late. 他可能会迟到。

3. Exports of coffee through Dar es Salaam are slight and variable compared with those through Mombassa；this results from the varying quantities... （Line 1～2，Para. 2）

▷variable 意思是"易变的,变化无常的"。例如:

a man of variable temper 反复无常的人

The weather is variable in autumn. 秋天的天气变化无常。

▷另外请注意 varied 和 various 这两个词形相近的词。

varied 表示"多变的,多样的",如:lead a full and varied life 过丰富多彩的生活,a varied economy 多种经营的经济。

various 表示"不同的,多方面的,不止一个的",如:at various times 在不同的时代,various branches of knowledge 多方面的知识,for various reasons 由于种种原因。

▷compare with 意思是"与……比较起来,较之……"。例如:

Compared with his father, he is tall. 与他父亲比起来,他算是很高了。

I'm afraid my work compares poorly with his. 我想我的工作同他的工作相比要差得多。

▷另外在表示"可与……相比时",compare with 常用于否定句。例如:

My works don't compare with yours. 我的作品不能和你的相比。

▷result from 意思是"由……造成;因……产生"。例如:

The terrible accident resulted from his carelessness. 那桩可怕的意外事故因他的疏忽大意而起。

Their success resulted from self-reliance and hard work. 他们的成功是自力更生、艰苦奋斗的结果。

▷result in 则表示"结果（为）……,导致,引起等"。例如:

His careless speech resulted in much argument. 他过于草率的发言引起诸多争议。

These safety measures will result in the reduction of work accidents. 这些安全措施将减少工伤事故。

4. Other commodities exported through Tanga are comparatively of very minor significance... （Line 5～6，Para. 3）

比较而言,从 Tanga 出口的其他商品就不怎么重要了。该句中的 be of minor significance 表示"不怎

新世纪英语丛书

重要,没多大意义。"

be of 常常与 importance, value, significance, help 等词连用,表示"具有该性质、特征"。

Explanations

本文是一篇说明文,介绍了坦桑尼亚的两个重要港口城市坦噶和达累斯萨拉姆及其出口产品。

21. C) 细节题。从第一段第四句 Market conditions in the Far East and in Europe are good, and there is likely to be further increase in cotton exports through Dar es Salaam. 可以看出,在欧洲及远东,对棉花的需求在增长。因此选项 C 最符合题意。

22. D) 推断题。第一段最后一句 Increases in cotton exports have been paralleled by increases in exports of oil seed and seed cake, largely a by-product of cotton. 指出棉花出口量的提高同时也促进了棉花籽和油渣饼出口量的增加。

23. A) 细节题。从第三段第一句 The most noteworthy feature of the export traffic of Tanga is that there is only one major commodity involved. 可以确定 Tanga 只有一种主要产品出口,即 sisal,因此选项 A 正确。

24. B) 细节题。从第三段第三句 The importance of sisal exports at Tanga reflects the fact that sisal constitutes the leading industry of Tanzania. 可以判断 sisal 的生产是 Tanzania 的主要工业。因此选项 B 正确。

25. A) 主旨题。文章主要介绍了坦噶和达累斯萨拉姆两个港口的产品出口情况。文章没有涉及选项 B、D,选项 C 只是文中涉及的细节问题,故 A 项是正确答案。

Passage 4

Notes

1. Disney World, Florida, is the biggest amusement resort in the world. (Line 1, Para. 1)

▷resort 在此作名词,意思是"常去之地,胜地"。例如:

He would like to go to the summer resort to spend his holiday. 他想到避暑胜地去休假。

▷resort 还可作动词,resort to 为常用短语,表示"求助,诉诸"。例如:

resort to force 诉诸武力

He resorted to his friend for help. 他请求朋友帮忙。

2. ... and it is a larger, slightly more ambitious version of Disneyland near Los Angeles. (Line 3~4, Para. 1)

这句话的意思是:它的形式和洛杉矶附近的迪斯尼乐园一样,但规模更大、设计更大胆。

ambitious 意思是"雄心勃勃的,有野心的"。

3. Foreigners tend to associate Walter Disney with Snow White and the Seven Dwarfs... (Line 1, Para. 2)

tend to do sth. 意思是"易于……,往往会……"。例如:

People under stress tend to express their full range of potential.

处于压力下的人容易发挥自己全部的潜力。

He tends to get angry when people oppose his plan. 别人反对他的计划时,他总会很生气。

Plants tend to die in hot weather if you don't water them. 如果不浇水,植物在炎热天气很容易枯死。

4. ... in the opinion of some, by the vulgarity of the commentary and musical background. (Line 3~4, Para. 2)

这句话是被动语态,意思是:一些人认为那些自然风光片的一流的摄影被解说及背景音乐的粗俗给毁了。

Explanations

本文简要介绍了世界上最大的娱乐胜地——迪斯尼世界。阅读本文后我们可以了解到迪斯尼世界的概况,特别是其中最主要的娱乐场所魔术王国。

26. **C**) 推断题。由第一段可知 Disney 世界建于 1971 年,即 Walt Disney 去世五年后(It was opened on October 1, 1971, five years after Walt Disney's death)。因此可以推断出选项 C 正确,即 Walt Disney 于 1966 年去世。

27. **A**) 细节题。根据第三段最后一句话 But the central attraction of the resort is the Magic Kingdom. 可以确定正确答案是 A 项,其他选项均不符合题意。

28. **D**) 细节题。根据文章第四段第三句 Even getting to the Magic Kingdom is quite an adventure. 可以得出正确答案是 D 项。

29. **B**) 推断题。根据文章第三段前两句 There is very little that could be called vulgar in Disney World. It attracts people of most tastes and most income groups, and people of all ages, from toddlers to grandpas. 可以判断其消费对一般人来说不会很贵,也并不庸俗,因此选项 C、D 不对,选项 A 在文中没有涉及,因此选项 B 是正确答案。

30. **C**) 细节题。文章第一句就告诉我们迪斯尼世界是世界上最大的娱乐胜地,其他选项在文中没有涉及,因此选项 C 是正确答案。

Passage 5

Keys

31. the improvement of the equipment
32. 1950
33. It produced the long-playing records.
34. better wear and durability and much better quality
35. Because they were never satisfied.

Notes

1. But it gradually caught up as the equipment was improved. (Line 2, Para. 1)

   ▷catch up 在此意思是"跟上"。例如:

   They started five minutes ago; we must do all we can to catch up.

   他们在五分钟之前就出发了,我们必须全力以赴赶上去。

   Go on in front. I'll soon catch you up. 你先走,我就会赶上你的。

   ▷另一常用短语为 catch up with sb. /sth. 意思是"赶上……"。例如:

   He caught up with the parade and walked behind. 他赶上了游行队伍,跟在后面走。

   He managed to catch up with the other students in his class. 他设法赶上了班上的其他同学。

2. ... suitable for professional use but not for the home. (Line 3, Para. 1)

   (be) suitable for 意思是"对……合适,适当"。例如:

   This toy is not suitable for young children. 这个玩具不适合小孩玩。

   Is she suitable for the job? 她适合做那项工作吗?

3. Then in 1947, American manufacturers took those large, heavy machines that ate up tape at the rate of thirty inches per second and... (Line 3~5, Para. 1)

   这句话的意思是:随后在 1947 年,美国制造业开始将这些每秒钟走 30 英寸、又大又重的录音机变成了留声机的真正对手。

▷eat up 在此意思是"迅速通过……"。例如：

The little red car ate up the soggy miles. 那辆红色小汽车一会儿就驶过了那段数英里长的泥泞的路。

Thirty minutes in the car ate up the distance between the two shipyards.

乘 30 分钟汽车就赶完了两座船厂之间的路程。

▷另外 eat up 还有"吃完，吃光；耗尽（钱财，时间等）"的意思。例如：

Eat up your dinner before it gets cold. 趁热把饭吃完。

Her savings have been eaten up by illness. 她的积蓄因生病全给用光了。

4. The increase in sound quality on gramophone records was mainly due to tape recorders being used to make better original recordings. (Line 3~4, Para. 2)

due to 意思是"因为，由于"。例如：

Her absence was due to the storm. 她缺勤是因为有暴风雨。

His illness was due to bad food. 他生病是因为吃了变质的食物。

5. Sound technicians worked away at the problems of magnetic recording until they were able to produce a seven inch spool holding 1,200 feet tape which was pulled across the magnetic pickups at the speed of only fifteen inches per second. (Line 1~3, Para. 4)

这句话的意思：技术精湛的专家们没有停滞不前，而是继续研究磁带录音中存在的问题，直到他们能够生产一种七英寸大小的录音磁带。这种磁带可以缠绕 1 200 英尺长的胶带，胶带以每秒 15 英寸的速度通过唱头。

▷work away 意思是"不停地继续工作"。例如：

I found him working away in his office. 我发现他在办公室一直不停地工作。

He is still working away at his homework. 他还在做家庭作业。

▷spool 在此指"录音胶带的线轴"。

6. Since 1950, ... (Line 1, Para. 3)

这一段的意思是：从 1950 年开始录音磁带就在质量上一直领先于留声机唱片，而且首次真正成功地进行了立体声录音。除此以外，录音磁带还使录音发展成大众业余爱好成为可能。不仅如此，将音乐录制到录音磁带上还使一个庞大的新兴音乐产业变成轻而易举的事，这就使人们因留声机昂贵而未能欣赏到的作品得以面世。

Unit 14

Section A   Skimming and Scanning

Directions:（略）

Passage 1

Micro-enterprise Credit for Street Youth

"I am from a large, poor family and for many years we have done without breakfast. Ever since I joined the Street Kids International program I have been able to buy my family sugar and buns for breakfast. I have also bought myself decent second-hand clothes and shoes." Said Doreen Soko. "We've had business experience. Now I'm confident to expand what we've been doing. I've learnt management, and the way of keeping money so we save for reinvestment. Now business is a part of our lives. As well, we didn't know each other before—now we've made new friends." Said Fan Kaoma. (Participants in the Youth Skills Enterprise Initiative Program, Zambia)

Introduction

Although small-scale business training and credit programs have become more common throughout the world, relatively little attention has been paid to the need to direct such opportunities to young people. Even less attention has been paid to children living on the street or in difficult circumstances. Over the past nine years, Street Kids International (S. K. I.) has been working with partner organizations in Africa, Latin America and India to support the economic tires of street children. The purpose of this paper is to share some of the lessons S. K. I. and our partners have learned.

Background

Typically, children do not end up on the streets due to a single cause, but to a combination of factors: a dearth of adequately funded schools, the demand for income at home, family breakdown and violence. The street may be attractive to children as a place to find adventurous play and money. However, it is also a place where some children are exposed with little or no protection to exploitative employment, urban crime, and abuse.

Children who work on the streets are generally involved in unskilled, labor-intensive tasks which require long hours, such as shining shoes, carrying goods, guarding or washing cars, and informal trading. Some may also earn income through begging, or through theft and other illegal activities. At the same time, there are street children who take pride in supporting themselves and their families and who often enjoy their work. Many children may choose entrepreneurship because it allows them a degree of independence, is less exploitative than many forms of paid employment, and is flexible enough to allow them to participate in other activities such as education and domestic tasks.

Street Business Partnerships

大学英语 4 级阅读与简答（新题型）

S. K. I. has worked with partner organizations in Latin America, Africa and India to develop innovative opportunities for street children to earn income.

• The S. K. I. Bicycle Courier Service first started in the Sudan. Participants in this enterprise were supplied with bicycles, which they used to deliver parcels and messages, and which they were required to pay for gradually from their wages. A similar program was taken up in Bangalore, India.

• Another successful project, The Shoe Shine Collective, was a partnership program with the Y. W. C. A. in the Dominican Republic. In this project, participants were lent money to purchase shoe shine boxes. They were also given a safe place to store their equipment, and facilities for individual savings plans.

• The Youth Skills Enterprise Initiative in Zambia is a joint program with the Red Cross Society and the Y. W. C. A. Street youths are supported to start their own small business through business training, life skills training and access to credit.

Lessons learned

The following lessons have emerged from the programs that S. K. I. and partner organizations have created.

• Being an entrepreneur is not for everyone, nor for every street child, ideally, potential participants will have been involved in the organization's programs for at least six months, and trust and relationship-building will have already been established.

• The involvement of the participants has been essential to the development of relevant programs. When children have had a major role in determining procedures, they are more likely to abide by and enforce them.

• It is critical for all loans to be linked to training programs that include the development of basic business and life skills.

• There are tremendous advantages to involving parents or guardians in the program, where such relationships exist. Home visits allow staff the opportunity to know where the participants live, and to understand more about each individual's situation.

• Small loans are provided initially for purchasing fixed assets such as bicycles, shoe shine kits and basic building materials for a market stall. As the entrepreneurs gain experience, the enterprises car be gradually expanded and consideration can be given to increasing loan amounts. The loan amounts in S. K. I. programs have generally ranged from US$30-$100.

• All S. K. I. programs have charged interest on the loans, primarily to get the entrepreneurs used to the concept of paying interest on borrowed money. Generally the rates have been modest (lower than bank rates).

Conclusion

There is a need to recognize the importance of access to credit for impoverished young people seeking to fulfill economic needs. The provision of small loans to support the entrepreneurial dreams and ambitions of youth can be an effective means to help them change their lives. However, we believe that credit must be extended in association with other types of support that help participants develop critical life skill as well as productive businesses.

1. Any street child can set up their own small business if given enough support.

2. In Some cases, the families of street children may need financial support from S. K. I.

3. Only one fixed loan should be given to each child.

4. The children have to pay back slightly more money than they borrowed.

5. Some children may earn income through begging, or through theft and other illegal activities.

6. S. K. I. has worked with partner organizations in Latin America, Africa and Japan to develop innovative opportunities for street children to earn income.

7. Small loans are provided initially for purchasing fixed assets such as bicycles, shoe shine kits and basic building materials for a market stall.

8. The main purpose of S. K. I. is to give business training and loans to _____.

9. Children end up living on the streets because of _____.

10. In order to become more independent, street children may _____.

Section B   Discourse Vocabulary Test

Directions: (略)

Passage 2

Laziness is a sin, everyone knows that. We have probably all had lectures __11__ out that laziness is immoral, that it is wasteful, and that lazy people will never __12__ to anything in life. But laziness can be more __13__ than that, and it is often caused by more complex reasons than simple wish to avoid work. Some people who appear to be lazy are suffering from much more __14__ problems. They may be so distrustful of their fellow workers that they are unable to join in any group task for fear of ridicule or fear of having their ideas stolen. These people who seem lazy may be paralyzed by a fear of __15__ that prevents fruitful work. Or other sorts of fantasies may prevent work; some people are so busy planning, sometimes planning great deals or fantastic __16__, which they are unable to deal with whatever "lesser" work is on hand. Still other people are not avoiding work; strictly __17__, they are merely procrastinating—rescheduling their day.

Nevertheless, laziness can actually be helpful. Like procrastinators, some people may look lazy when they are really thinking, planning, contemplating, researching. We should all remember that some great __18__ discoveries occurred by chance or while someone was "goofing off". Newton wasn't working in the orchard when the apple hit him and he devised the theory of gravity. All of us would like to have someone "lazy" build the car or stove we buy, __19__ if that "laziness" were caused by the worker's taking time to check each steps of his work and to do his job right. And sometimes being "lazy"—that is, taking time off for a rest—is good for the overworked student or executive. Taking a rest can be particularly helpful to the athlete who is trying too hard or the doctor who's simply working himself overtime too many evenings at the clinic. So be careful when you're __20__ to call somebody lazy. That person may be thinking, or planning his or her next book.

A) failure	I) account
B) harmful	J) beneficial
C) scientific	K) particularly
D) amount	L) pointing
E) saying	M) practical
F) serious	N) tempted
G) achievements	O) success
H) speaking	

Section C　Reading in Depth

Directions:（略）

Passage 3

One of the most important social developments that helped to make possible a shift in thinking about the role of public education was the effect of the baby boom of the 1950's and 1960's on the schools. In the 1920's, especially in the Depression conditions of the 1930's, the United States experienced a declining birth rate—every thousand women aged fifteen to forty-four gave birth to about 118 live children in 1920, 89. 2 in 1930, 75. 8 in 1936, and 80 in 1940. With the growing prosperity brought on by the Second World War and the economic boom that followed it, young people married and established households earlier and began to raise larger families than had their predecessors during the depression. Birth rates rose to 102 per thousand in 1946, 106. 2 in 1950, and 118 in 1955. Although economics was probably the most important determinant, it is not the only explanation for the baby boom. The increased value placed on the idea of the family also helps to explain this rise in birth rates. The baby boomers began streaming into the first grade by the mid-1940's and became a flood by 1950. The public school system suddenly found itself overtaxed. While the number of the school children rose because of the wartime and postwar conditions, these same conditions made the schools even less prepared to cope with the flood. The wartime economy meant that few new schools were built between 1940 and 1945. Moreover, during the war and in the boom times that followed, large numbers of teachers left their profession for better paying jobs elsewhere in the economy.

Therefore, in the 1950's and 1960's, the baby boom hit the antiquated and inadequate school system. Consequently, the "custodial rhetoric" of the 1930's and early 1940's no longer made sense, that is, keeping youths aged sixteen and older out of the labor market by keeping them in school could no longer be a high priority for an institution unable to find space and staff to teach younger children aged five to sixteen. With the baby boom, the focus of educators and of laymen interested in education inevitably turned toward the lower grades and back to basic academic skills and discipline. The system no longer had much interest in offering nontraditional, new and extra services to older youths.

21. What does the passage mainly discuss?

A) The teaching profession during the baby boom.

B) Birth rates in the United States in the 1930's and 1940's.

C) The impact of the baby boom on public education.

D) The role of the family in the 1950's and 1960's.

22. The word "it" in the sentence "it is not the only explanation for the baby boom."(Line 9~10, Para. 1) refers to _____.

    A) 1955   B) economics

    C) the baby boom   D) value

23. The public schools of the 1950's and 1960's faced all of the following problems EXCEPT _____.

    A) a declining number of students

    B) old-fashioned facilities

    C) a shortage of teachers

    D) an inadequate number of school buildings

24. According to the passage, why did teachers leave the teaching profession after the outbreak of the war?

    A) They needed to be retrained.

    B) They were dissatisfied with the curriculum.

    C) Other jobs provided higher salaries.

    D) Teaching positions were scarce.

25. The "custodial rhetoric" (Line 2, Para. 2) refers to _____.

    A) raising a family

    B) keeping older individuals in school

    C) running an orderly households

    D) maintaining discipline in the classroom

Passage 4

The destruction of our natural resources and contamination of our food supply continue to occur. Largely because of the extreme difficulty in *affixing* (把……固定) legal responsibility on those who continue to treat our environment with reckless abandon. Attempts to prevent pollution by legislation, economic incentives and friendly persuasion have been met by lawsuits, personal and industrial denial and long delays—not only in accepting responsibility, but more importantly in doing something about it.

It seems that only when government decides it can afford tax incentives or production sacrifices is there any initiative for change. Where is industry's and our recognition that protecting mankind's great treasure in the single most important responsibilities? If ever there will be time for environment health professionals to come to the frontlines and provide leadership to environmental problems, that time is now.

We are being asked, and, in fact, the public is demanding that we take positive action. It is our responsibility as professionals in environmental health to make the difference. Yes, the ecologists, the environmental activists and the conservationists serve to communicate, stimulate thinking and promote behavioral change. However, it is those of us who are paid to make decisions to develop, improve and enforce environmental standards, I submit, who must lead the charge.

We must recognize that environment health issues do not stop at city limits, country lines, state or even federal boundaries. We can no longer afford to be tunnel-visioned in our approach. We must visualize issues from every perspective to make the objective decisions. We must express our views clearly to prevent media distortion and public confusion.

I believe we have a three-part mission for the present. First, we must continue to press for improvements in the quality of life that people make for themselves. Second, We must investigate and understand the link between environment and health. Third, we must be able to communicate technical information in a form that citizens can understand. If we can accomplish these three goals in this decade, maybe we can finally stop environmental degradation, and not merely hold it back. We will then be able to spend pollution dollars truly on prevention rather than on bandages.

26. We can infer from the first two paragraphs that the industrialists disregard environmental protection chiefly because _____.

A) they are unaware of the consequences of what they are doing

B) they are reluctant to sacrifice their own economic interests

C) time has not yet come for them to put due emphasis on it

D) it is difficult for them to take effective measures

27. The main task now facing ecologists, environmental activists and conservationists is _____.

A) to prevent pollution by legislation, economic incentives and persuasion

B) to arouse public awareness of the importance of environmental protection

C) to take radical measures to control environmental pollution

D) to improve the quality of life by enforcing environmental pollution

28. The word "tunnel-visioned" (Line 2, Para. 4) most probably means "_____".

A) narrow-minded   B) blind to the facts

C) short-sighted   D) able to see only one aspect

29. Which of the following, according to the author, should play the leading role in the solution of environmental problems?

A) Legislation and government intervention.

B) The industry's understanding and support.

C) The efforts of environmental health professionals.

D) The cooperation of ecologists, environmental activists and conservationists.

30. Which of the following is true according to the last paragraph?

A) Efforts should be exerted on pollution prevention instead of on remedial measures.

B) More money should be spent in order to stop pollution.

C) Ordinary citizens have no access to technical information on pollution.

D) Environmental degradation will be stopped by the end of this decade.

Section D   Short Answer Questions

Directions：（略）

Passage 5

Most Americans spend far more of their leisure time with the mass media than in any other occupation. In addition, most of us hear, see or read some of the media while engaged in other activities. Thus an extremely large number of our waking hours are spent with the mass media. Of all the media, television is clearly dominant, with newspapers a close second, at least as a source of news and other information. Our exposure to all media is important, however, because all of them contribute materials for the construction of that world in our heads. For most people, increased use of one medium does not decrease the use of another. In fact, in certain cases, and especially for certain purposes, the more one uses one medium, the more likely one is to use others.

There are various factors that can cause you to expose yourself to the media selectively, avoiding much of the material with which you disagree. Some of that selective exposure is probably due to the psychological pressure you feel to avoid the discomfort caused by confrontation with facts and ideas contrary to your beliefs, attitudes, or behavior. However, some selective exposure is not due to the pressure for consistency but to other factors, such as your age, education, and even the area in which you live and the people with whom you associate.

Quite a different sort of factor that affects your media experiences is the social context of exposure: whether you are alone or with others when you are exposed to medium; whether you are at home, at the office, in theater, and so on. These contexts are as much as a potential part of the message you will form as film images on the screen or words on the page. In addition, that social context affects—both directly and indirectly—the media and the media content to which you become exposed. New friends or colleagues get you interested in different things. Other members of the family often select media content that you would not have selected, and you become exposed to it.

These various factors have so much influence on your media exposure that so little of that exposure is planned.

31. Exposure to media is important and people sometimes tend to use more media if _____.
   _____   _____   _____   _____   _____
   _____   _____   _____   _____   _____

32. Why are newspapers considered an important medium according to the passage?
   _____   _____   _____   _____   _____
   _____   _____   _____   _____   _____

33. For one reason or another, people's exposure to the media is often selective and influenced by _____.
   _____   _____   _____   _____   _____
   _____   _____   _____   _____   _____

34. Apart from personal preferences, what determines one's choices of the media and media content?

_____ _____ _____ _____ _____

_____ _____ _____ _____ _____

35. The last sentence of the passage indicates that one's exposure to the media is _____.

_____ _____ _____ _____ _____

Notes and Explanations

Passage 1

Explanations

1. [N] 在 Lessons Learned 部分提到 Being an entrepreneur is not for everyone, nor for every street child, ideally, potential participants will have been involved in the organization's programs for at least six months, and trust and relationship-building will have already been established. 不是每个人,也不是每个流浪儿都可以成为创业者。一般来讲,那些参加活动至少六个月,并且已经建立了信任和关系的人才有可能"。故正确答案为 No。

2. [NG] 通过浏览全文可以看出文章中讲述的 S. K. I. 的资助项目是针对流浪儿的,并没有提及是否资助他们的家庭。因此,正确答案为 Not Given。

3. [N] 在 Lessons Learned 部分提到 As the entrepreneurs gain experience, the enterprises can be gradually expanded and consideration can be given to increasing loan amounts. 随着创业者经验增长,他们的事业可以逐步扩大并可以得到更多的贷款。故答案为 No。

4. [Y] 在 Lessons Learned 部分提到 All S. K. I. programs have charged interest on the loans, primarily to get the entrepreneurs used to the concept of paying interest on borrowed money. Generally the rates have been modest (lower than bank rates). 所有的 S. K. I. 的项目都对贷款收取利息,目的在于让创业者们形成借钱就需要支付利息的观念。利息通常很少(低于银行的利息)。故可得出答案为 Yes。

5. [Y] 在 "Background" 这一段提到 Some may also earn income through begging, or through theft and other illegal activities. 一些孩子通过乞讨或是偷窃和其他非法手段挣钱。从中可以得出答案为 Yes。

6. [N] 在 Street Business Partnerships 这一段提到 S. K. I. has worked with partner organizations in Latin America, Africa and India to develop innovative opportunities for street children to earn income. S. K. I. 与拉丁美洲、非洲和印度的合作组织一起为流浪儿们提供创业机会。故正确答案为 No。

7. [Y] Lessons Learned 提到 Small loans are provided initially for purchasing fixed assets such as bicycles, shoe shine kits and basic building materials for a market stall. 最初的小额贷款用于购买固定资产。例如自行车、擦鞋工具箱和建造市场摊位的基本材料。可以得出答案为 Yes。

8. 在 Introduction 中提到 Over the past nine years, Street Kids International (S. K. I.) has been working with partner organizations in Africa, Latin America and India to support the economic tires of street children. 在过去的九年里,S. K. I. 与在拉丁美洲、非洲和印度的合作机构一起为流浪儿提供经济支持。从而得到答案为 **street children**。

9. 在 Background 中提到 Typically, children do not end up on the streets due to a single cause, but to a combination of factors: a dearth of adequately funded schools, the demand for income at home, family breakdown and violence. 一般来讲,孩子们流落街头并不是由单一因素,而是由许多因素造成的:缺乏资金充足的学校、家庭需要收入、破产和暴力。这些因素其实可以用一个词来归纳:**poverty**。

10. 在 Background 中提到 Many children may choose entrepreneurship because it allows them a degree of

independence, is less exploitative than many forms of paid employment, and is flexible enough to allow them to participate in other activities such as education and domestic tasks. 很多孩子选择创业因为这样他们可以很独立,不用像打工一样被剥削,这种工作的时间很灵活,他们可以参加其他的活动,例如:上学和做家务。因此本题的答案为 **set up their own business**。

Passage 2

Notes

1. ... and that lazy people will never amount to anything in life. (Line 2，Para. 1)
▷amount to 在此意思是"发展成,成长为"。例如:
  If she goes on like this, she will amount to nothing. 如果她一味这样下去,她将一事无成。
▷此外,amount to 还可意思是"共计为;意味着,等于"。例如:
  His suggestion amounts to saying that there is still room for improvement in the work.
  他的建议无异于说这件工作尚有改进的余地。
  His debts amount to over 20,000 dollars. 他的负债超过两万美元。
  His remarks amounted to criticism of me. 他的话等于是批评我。

2. They may be so distrustful of their fellow workers that they are unable to join in any group task for fear of ridicule or fear of having their ideas stolen. (Line 5~6，Para. 1)
▷for fear of 意思是"以免,唯恐"。例如:
  Shut the window for fear of catching a cold. 关闭窗户,以免感冒。
  She hid her jewelry for fear of being stolen. 她把珠宝藏起来以免被偷。
▷另外注意 for fear that 意思是"以免,唯恐",后面跟从句,谓语用虚拟语气 should 加动词原型(或 would be)。例如:
  She hid the jewelry for fear that it would be stolen. 她把宝石藏起来,以免被偷。
  He handled the instrument with care for fear that it should be damaged.
  他小心地操作那仪器,生怕把它弄坏。

3. ... some people are so busy planning... (Line 8，Para. 1)
  be busy (in) doing sth. 意思是"忙于做某事"。例如:
  The students are busy preparing for the final examination. 学生在忙着为期末考试做准备。
  He is busy packing for the journey. 他正忙着为外出旅行打点行装。

4. ... which they are unable to deal with whatever "lesser" work is on hand. (Line 9，Para. 1)
▷deal with 意思是"与……相处,对待,对付;处理"。例如:
  He seemed to be quick-tempered，but was actually not difficult to deal with.
  他似乎性子急躁,但实际上并不难相处。
  Deal with a man as he deals with you. 以其人之道,还治其人之身。
  He is a person who can deal properly with all situations. 他是一个能恰当处理各种局面的人。
▷on hand 意思是"现有的,手头上的;在近处的"。例如:
  I have a large stock on hand. 我手头有大批存货。
  He always has his English dictionary on hand when he studies. 他学习时,总是把英语字典放在手边。

5. We should all remember that some great scientific discoveries occurred by chance or while someone was "goofing off". (Line 2~3，Para. 2)
  occur 意思是"发生"。
  by chance 意思是"偶然地,碰巧"。例如:
  I met her in the street by chance yesterday. 我昨天碰巧在街上遇到她。

大学英语4级阅读与简答〈新题型〉

I met him only by chance. 我只是偶然遇到他。

6. So be careful when you're tempted to call somebody lazy. (Line 9~10，Para. 2)

▷tempt to do 在此意思是"很想做……"。例如：

I feel tempted to say that she is a kind girl. 我很想说她是个善良的女孩。

▷此外，tempt 还可意思是"引诱，诱惑"。例如：

Nothing could tempt me to take such a step. 什么也不能诱使我采取这样一个步骤。

Explanations

11. [L] 语法规则要求此处应填一个能够和 out 搭配的分词来作定语修饰 lectures。选项 E、H、L 都是该形式，但能够和 out 搭配的有选项 H 和 L。根据这句话的意思此处应该选 L 项，point out 意为"指出"。

12. [D] 语法规则要求 will 后面应为动词原形，这个词和 to 构成固定搭配短语。amount to 意为"发展成，成长为"，符合句子意思的要求。

13. [B] 语法规则要求此处应填一个形容词与前面的 more 和后面的 than 构成形容词比较级，上文用 sin，immoral，wasteful 和 amount to nothing 等贬义词来描述懒惰，据此可以断定此处应该也填一个贬义词。选项 B、C、F、J、M 是形容词，但是只有 B 项 harmful（有害的）符合句子意思的要求。

14. [F] 语法规则要求此处应填一个形容词和 more 构成比较级修饰 problems，从后面的三个句子可以断定这个词应该是 serious，意思是"严重的"。

15. [A] 语法规则要求此处应填一个名词来作 of 的宾语，同时这个词又是 that 引导的定语从句的先行词。根据定语从句的意思判断这个词应该是 failure（失败）。

16. [G] 语法规则要求此处应填一个和 deals 并列的复数名词，只有 G 项 achievements（成就）是复数名词，而且符合上下文意思的要求。

17. [H] 语法规则要求此处应填一个词和 strictly 一起构成插入语。选项中能够和 strictly 搭配的只有 speaking，strictly speaking 意为"严格地说"，符合这里意思的要求。

18. [C] 语法规则要求此处应填一个形容词来修饰 discovery。从下一句话中给出的 Newton 的例子可以判断出这里的词应该是 scientific。scientific discovery 意思是"科学发现"。

19. [K] 语法规则要求此处应填一个副词来修饰 if 引导的条件状语从句，选项中只有 K 项 particularly（尤其，特别）是副词，且符合上下文意思的要求。

20. [N] 语法规则要求此处应填一个动词的过去分词构成被动语态结构，根据本句和下一句的意思可以断定这里的词应该是 tempted。be tempted to do sth. 意思是"尝试做某事"。

Passage 3

Notes

1. In the 1920's, especially in the Depression conditions of the 1930's, the United States experienced a declining birth rate — every thousand women aged fifteen to forty-four gave birth to about 118 live children in 1920... (Line 3~5, Para. 1)

birth rate 意思是"婴儿出生率"。这句话的意思是：在二十世纪二十年代，特别是在三十年代的大萧条时期，美国的婴儿出生率下降了。

give birth to 意思是"生产，分娩"。例如：

She gave birth to a fine healthy baby at her late thirties. 她在将近四十岁时生了一个健康漂亮的婴儿。

Lorna gave birth to a daughter yesterday. 昨天洛娜生了一个女孩。

2. With the growing prosperity brought on by the Second World War and the economic boom that followed it, young people married and established households... (Line 5~7, Para. 1)

brought on by the Second World War 在此为过去分词短语作定语，修饰 the growing prosperity，that followed it 作定语，修饰 the economic boom。with 引导的这个结构在句中作状语，表伴随。

bring on 在此意思是"引起，导致"。例如：

Going out in the rain brought on a fever. 冒雨外出致使发烧。

Do you think the border incident will bring on a full-scale war?

你认为这次边境事件会引起一场全面战争吗？

3. The baby boomers began streaming into the first grade by the mid-1940's and became a flood by 1950. (Line 11~12, Para. 1)

stream 在此意思是"蜂拥前进，鱼贯而行"。例如：

They streamed out of the cinema. 他们从电影院鱼贯而出。

Rural residents are streaming to the cities. 农民正在不断涌向城市。

4. The public school system suddenly found itself overtaxed. (Line 12, Para. 1)

overtax 在此意思是"使负担过重"。

find oneself doing/done 意思是"发现自己做/被……"。例如：

He found himself lying in a hospital bed. 他发现自己躺在医院的病床上。

She found herself surrounded by a group of boys. 她发现自己被几个男孩儿围住了。

5. While the number of the school children rose because of the wartime and postwar conditions, these same conditions made the schools even less prepared to cope with the flood. (Line 13~14, Para. 1)

while 在此引导让步状语从句，意思是"尽管"。

cope with 意思是"巧妙地对付、处理"。例如：

He'll cope with all the work. 他将设法处理所有的工作。

She is not a competent driver and can't cope with driving in heavy traffic.

她不是个合格的司机，因此不能应付拥挤的交通状况。

6. Consequently, the "custodial rhetoric" of the 1930's and early 1940's no longer made sense... (Line 2~3, Para. 2)

▷make sense 意思是"有意义，有道理"。例如：

This sentence doesn't make any sense. 这句子毫无意义。

▷make sense of 意思是"弄懂……的意思"。例如：

Can you make sense of this telegram? 你能弄懂这封电报的意思吗？

I can't make sense of his remarks in the meeting. 我没弄明白他在会上讲话的含义。

Explanations

本篇主要讲述二十世纪五六十年代美国的生育高峰对公立学校教育的影响。生育高峰促成了人们对公立学校教育看法的转变。

21. C）主旨题。文章第一段第一句就告诉了我们文章的主题，即促成人们对于公立学校教育作用的看法的转变的重要原因之一是五六十年代的生育高峰对于教育事业的影响。选项 B 不是主题，而是文章主题的一个方面。文章未提及其他两个选项。

22. B）细节题。根据文章第一段第九、十行 Although economics was probably the most important determinant, it is not the only explanation for the baby boom. 可以确定 it 指的是经济 economics，其他选项均不符合句意。

23. A）细节题。根据文章第一段最后两句，可以确定选项 B、C、D 均已涉及，只有选项 A 没有提到。

24. C）细节题。根据文章第一段最后一句话，战争期间及其后的生育高峰期内，许多教师改行从事收入高的工作，可以看出教师改行的原因是选项 C，其他选项均不符合题意。

25. B）词汇题。根据 that is 后面所做出的解释——使十六岁及十六岁以上的年轻人继续待在学校行不通了,因为学校没有校舍,也没有教师来教授五到十六岁的孩子们。由此可以得出 custodial rhetoric 指的是选项 B。

Passage 4

Notes

1. We are being asked, and, in fact, the public is demanding that we take positive action. (Line 1, Para. 3)

▷take action 意思是"采取行动"。例如:

take military action 采取军事行动

take concerted action 采取一致行动

The government had to take action to cope with the general strike.

政府不得不采取行动妥善处理罢工事件。

▷可与 take 搭配的动词短语还有 take measures 采取措施,take steps 采取步骤,采取措施。例如:

They had to take effective measures to improve their work. 他们必须采取有效措施改进工作。

The government decided to take steps to meet the situation. 政府决定采取步骤适应形势。

2. Yes, the ecologists, the environmental activists and the conservationists serve to communicate... (Line 2~3, Para. 3)

serve to do sth. 意思是"对做……有用、有益"。例如:

This agreement will serve to promote the trade between China and Japan.

此项决定将有助于促进中日之间的贸易。

Cultural exchange will serve to promote the understanding between the people in two countries.

文化交流将有助于两国人民的相互了解。

3. I believe we have a three-part mission for the present. First, we must continue to press for improvements in the quality of life that people make for themselves. (Line 1~2, Para. 5)

press for 意思是"逼迫……,催促……"。例如:

press for shorter working hours 强烈要求缩短工作时间

Many workers were involved in the general strike to press for higher wages.

许多工人参加了大罢工,强烈要求提高工资。

4. If we can accomplish these three goals in this decade, maybe we can finally stop environmental degradation, and not merely hold it back. (Line 4~5, Para. 5)

▷hold back 在此意思是"制止,阻止,抵挡"。例如:

They must do something to hold back rushing fans. 他们必须想办法阻止蜂拥而来的慕名者。

There was heavy traffic in the vicinity, she had to hold the children back from running into the streets.

附近车辆行人来往频繁,她不得不阻止孩子跑到街上去。

No one can hold back the wheel of history. 谁也不能阻止历史车轮前进。

▷此外,还可意思是"抑制,控制"。例如:

hold back one's emotion 控制自己的感情

She held back her tears with great difficulty. 她好不容易才忍住眼泪。

Explanations

　　本文首先阐述了环境与健康的关系,认为生态学家及环境保护主义者的主要任务是让人们认识到环保的重要性以及目前所要做的事情。

26. A) 细节题。根据文章第二段第二句可以断定选项 A 正确。其他选项均与文章的意思不符。

27. B) 细节题。答案出自文章第三段第三句 Yes, the ecologists, the environmental activists and the

conservationists serve to communicate, stimulate thinking and promote behavioral change。

28. **D**) 词汇题。根据第四段第二、三句可以判断"tunnel-visioned"是"片面看问题"的意思,因此正确答案是 D 项。

29. **C**) 推断题。在第三段第二句和最后一句,作者指出在解决环境问题上起主要作用的是那些"make decisions"的人,即那些专门研究环保的人。其他选项均不合题意,因此正确答案是 C 项。

30. **C**) 细节题。文章最后一段第四句提出"必须以普通公民可以理解的方式向他们宣传有关环境污染的专业知识"。由此可见正确答案是 C 项。其他选项文中均未提及。

Passage 5

Keys

31. they want to know more of the world

32. Because they are a source of news and information.

33. different factors

34. Social context of exposure.

35. hardly planned

Notes

1. Our exposure to all media is important, however, because all of them contribute materials for the construction of that world in our heads. (Line 5~6, Para. 1)

▷contribute 意思是"提供,捐助,投稿"。例如:

contribute food and clothing for the relief of the poor 捐助食品和衣物救济贫民

I often contributed essays to the school paper. 我经常把文章投到校报。

▷contribute to 为一常用短语,意思是"有助于,(对……)有贡献"。例如:

The construction of the highway will contribute to the growth of the suburbs.
建造高速公路将有助于郊区发展。

A proper amount of exercise will contribute to health. 适度的运动有助于健康。

2. In fact, in certain cases, and especially for certain purposes, the more one uses one medium, the more likely one is to use others. (Line 7~8, Para. 1)

in certain cases 意思是"在特定情况下"。常用其他词组有:

in some cases 在某些情况下

in case 如果,万一

in no case 决不

3. Some of that selective exposure is probably due to the psychological pressure you feel to avoid the discomfort caused by confrontation with facts and ideas contrary to your beliefs, attitudes, or behavior. (Line 2~4, Para. 2)

contrary to sth. 在此意思是"与……相反,违反"。例如:

Contrary to his doctor's advice, he went swimming. 他不听医生的忠告,跑去游泳。

The result is contrary to the expectation. 结果与预料恰好相反。

4. These various factors have so much influence on your media exposure that so little of that exposure is planned. (Para. 4)

have influence on sth. 意思是"对……产生影响"。意思相同的短语还有 have effect on, have impact on 等。例如:

This book had a great influence on his life. 这本书对他的人生影响很大。

Unit 15

Section A　Skimming and Scanning

Directions：（略）

Passage 1

The Problem of Scarce Resources

Section A

　　The problem of how health-care resources should be allocated or apportioned，so that they are distributed in both tile most just and most efficient way，is not a new one. Every health system in an economically developed society is faced with the need to decide（either formally or informally）what proportion of the community's total resources should be spent on health-care；how resources are to be apportioned；what diseases and disabilities and which forms of treatment are to be given priority；which members of the community are to be given special consideration in respect of their health needs；and which forms of treatment are the most cost-effective.

Section B

　　What is new is that，from the 1950s onwards，there have been certain general changes in outlook about tile finitude of resources as a whole and of health-care resources in particular，as well as more specific changes regarding the clientele of health-care resources and the cost to the community of those resources. Thus，in the 1950s and 1960s，there emerged awareness in Western societies that resources for the provision of fossil fuel energy were finite and exhaustible and that the capacity of nature or the environment to sustain economic development and population was also finite. In other words，we became aware of the obvious fact that there were "limits to growth". The new consciousness that there were also severe limits to health-care resources was part of this general revelation of the obvious. Looking back，it now seems quite incredible that in the national health systems that emerged in many countries in the years immediately after the 1939—1945 World War，it was assumed without question that all the basic health needs of any community could be satisfied，at least in principle；the "invisible hand" of economic progress would provide.

Section C

　　However，at exactly the same time as this new realization of the finite character of health-care resources was sinking in an awareness of a contrary kind was developing in Western societies：that people have a basic right to health-care as a necessary-condition of a proper human life. Like education，political and legal processes and institutions，public order，communication，transport and money supply，health care can be seen as one of the fundamental social facilities necessary for people to exercise their other rights as autonomous human beings. People are not in a position to exercise personal liberty and to be self-determining if they are poverty-stricken, or deprived of basic education; or do not live within a context of law and order. In the same way, basic health-care is a condition of the exercise of *autonomy*(自治).

Section D

Although the language of "rights" sometimes leads to confusion, by the late 1970s it was recognized in most societies that people have a right to health-care (though there has been considerable resistance in the United States to the idea that there is a formal right to health-care). It is also accepted that this right generates an obligation or duty for the state to ensure that adequate health-care resources are provided out of the public purse. The state has no obligation to provide a health-care system itself, but to ensure that such a system is provided. Put another way, basic health-care is now recognized as a "public good", rather than a "private good" that one is expected to buy for oneself. As the 1976 declaration of the World Health Organization put it: "The enjoyment of the highest attainable standard of health is one of the fundamental rights of every human being without distinction of race, religion, political belief, economic or social condition." As has just been remarked, in a liberal society basic health is seen as one of the indispensable conditions for the exercise of personal autonomy.

Section E

Just at the time when it became obvious that health-care resources could not possibly meet the demands being made upon them, people were demanding that their fundamental right to health-care be satisfied by the state. The second set of more specific changes that have led to the present concern about the distribution of health-care resources stems from the dramatic rise in health costs in most OECD countries, accompanied by large-scale demographic and social changes which have meant, to take one example, that elderly people are now major (and relatively very expensive) consumers of health-care resources. Thus in OECD countries as a whole, health costs increased from 3.8% of GDP in 1960 to 7% of GDP in 1980, and it has been predicted that the proportion of health costs to GDP will continue to increase. (In the US the current figure is about 12% of GDP and in Australia about 7.8% of GDP)

As a consequence, during the 1980s a kind of doomsday scenario (analogous to similar doomsday extrapolations about energy needs and fossil fuels or about population increases) was projected by health administrators, economists and politicians. In this scenario, ever-rising health costs were matched against static or declining resources.

1. Personal liberty and independence have never been regarded as directly linked to health-care.
2. Health-care came to be seen as a right at about the same time that the limits of health-care resources became evident.
3. In OECD countries population changes have had an impact on health-care costs in recent years.
4. OECD governments have consistently underestimated the level of health-care provision needed.
5. In most economically developed countries the elderly will have to make special provision for their health-care in the future.
6. The state has obligation to provide a health-care system itself, and to ensure that such a system is provided.

7. In a liberal society basic health is seen as one of the indispensable conditions for the exercise of personal autonomy.

8. Between 1950 and 1980 a sharp rise in the cost of _____ existed.

9. It is believed that all the health-care resources the community needed would be produced by _____.

10. People were demanding that their fundamental right to health-care be satisfied by _____.

Section B   Discourse Vocabulary Test

Directions：（略）

Passage 2

　　Are some people born clever, and others born stupid? Or is intelligence developed by our environment and our experiences? Strangely enough, the answer to both these questions is yes. To some extent our intelligence is given us at birth, and an amount of special education can make a genius out of a child born with low intelligence. On the other hand, a child who lives in a boring   11   will develop his intelligence less than one who lives in rich and varied surroundings. Thus the limits of a person's intelligence are fixed at   12 , but whether or not he reaches those limits will depend on his environment. This view, now held by most experts, can be   13   in a number of ways.

　　It is easy to show that intelligence is to some   14   something we are born with. The closer the blood relationship between two people, the closer they are   15   to be in intelligence. Thus if we take two unrelated people at   16   from the population, it is likely that their degrees of intelligence will be completely different. If on the other hand we take two   17   twins they will very likely be as intelligent as each other. Relations like brothers and sisters, parents and children, usually have similar intelligence, and this clearly suggests that intelligence   18   on birth.

　　Imagine now that we take two identical twins and put them in different environments. We might send one, for example, to a university and the other to a factory where the work is boring. We would soon find differences in intelligence   19 , and this indicates that environments as well as birth play a part. This conclusion is also suggested by the fact that people who live in close   20   with each other, but who are not related at all, are likely to have similar degrees of intelligence.

A) extent	I) background
B) identical	J) likely
C) supported	K) environment
D) depends	L) born
E) dependent	M) contact
F) developing	N) research
G) birth	O) random
H) relationship	

Section C   Reading in Depth

Directions:（略）

Passage 3

The American baby boom after the war made unconvincing U. S. advice to poor countries that they restrain their births. However, there has hardly been a year since 1957 in which birth rates have not fallen in the United States and other rich countries, and in 1976 the fall was especially sharp. Both East Germany and West Germany have fewer births than they have deaths, and the United States is only temporarily able to avoid this condition because the children of the baby boom are now an exceptionally large group of married couples.

It is true that Americans do not typically plan their births to set an example for developing nations. We are more affected by women's liberation: once women see interesting and well-paid jobs and careers available they are less willing to provide free labor for child raising. From costing nothing, children suddenly come to seem impossibly expensive.

And to the high cost of children are added the uncertainties introduced by divorce; couples are increasingly unwilling to subject children to the terrible experience of marital breakdown and themselves to the difficulty of raising a child alone.

These circumstances—women working outside the home and the instability of marriage—tend to spread with industrial society and they will affect more and more countries during the remainder of this century. Along with them goes social mobility, ambition to rise in the urban world, a main factor in bringing down the births in Europe in the nineteenth century.

Food shortage will happen again when the reserves resulting from the good harvests of 1976 and 1977 have been consumed. Urbanization is likely to continue with the cities of the developing nations struggling under the weight of twice their present populations by the year 2000. The presently rich countries are approaching a stable population largely because of the changed place of women, and they incidentally are setting an example of *restraint*（限制）to the rest of the world. Industrial society will spread to the poor countries, and aspirations will exceed resources. All this leads to a population in the twenty-first century that is smaller than was feared a few years ago. For those anxious to see world population brought under control the news is encouraging .

21. During the years from 1957 to 1976, the birth rate of the United States _____.

    A) increased   B) was reduced

    C) experienced both falls and rises   D) remained stable

22. What influences the birth rate most in the United States is _____.

    A) highly paid jobs   B) women's desire for independence

    C) expenses of child raising   D) high divorce rate

23. The sentence "From costing nothing, children suddenly come to seem impossibly expensive" (Para. 2) implies that _____.

    A) food and clothing for babies are becoming incredibly expensive

    B) prices are going up dramatically all the time

C) to raise children women have to give up interesting and well-paid jobs

D) social development has made child-raising inexpensive

24. A chief factor in bringing down the births in Europe in the 19ᵗʰ century is _____.

A) birth control

B) the desire to seek fortune in cities

C) the instability of marriage

D) the changed place of women

25. The population in the 21ˢᵗ century, according to the writer, _____.

A) will be smaller than a few years ago

B) will not be as small as people expect

C) will prove to be a threat to the world

D) will not constitute as serious a problem as expected

Passage 4

The government has almost doubled its spending on computer education in schools. Mr. William Shelton, junior Education Minister, announced that the Micro-electronics Education Program (MEP) is to run for two more years with additional funding of at least 9 million.

The program began in 1980, was originally due to end next year, and had a budget of 9 million. This has been raised in bits and pieces over the past year to 11 million. The program will now run until March 1986, at a *provisional* (临时的) cost of around 20 million.

MEP provides courses for teachers and develops computer programs for classroom use of personal computers. It is run in partnership with a Department of Industry program under which British-made personal computers are supplied to schools at half-price.

In that way, virtually every secondary school has been provided with at least one computer at a central cost to the tax payer of under 5 million. The primary schools are now being supplied in a 9 million program which got under way at the turn of the year.

But, as Mr. Shelton admitted yesterday "It's no good having the computers without the right computer programs to put into them and a great deal more is still needed." Hence MEP's new funds.

Mr. Shelton said yesterday that MEP's achievements in curriculum development and teacher training had shown that the computer could be used in all courses. About 15,000 secondary teachers have taken short courses in "computer awareness"—that is a necessary part of the half price computer offer and training materials are now being provided for 50,000 primary teachers. The reasoning behind MEP is that no child now at school can hope for a worthwhile job in the future economy unless he or she understands how to deal with computers—not in a vocational training sense, but in learning the general skill to extract the required information of the moment from the ever-spreading flood.

26. The original MEP program was expected to _____.

A) last two years and cost nine million pounds

B) last four years and cost nine million pounds

C) last two years and cost eleven million pounds

D) last four years and cost eleven million pounds

27. The main aim of MEP is to help curriculum development and _____.

    A) provide personal computers for schools

    B) arrange for cheap computers to be supplied to schools

    C) show teachers to work with classes using computers

    D) train teachers to work with classes using computers

28. Computers have now been introduced _____.

    A) in most secondary schools

    B) in all secondary schools

    C) in most primary schools, at half-price

    D) in most schools, at no expense to the taxpayer

29. The additional grant of money being provided is mainly _____.

    A) part of the agreement to supply computers cheaply

    B) to develop further computer programs for schools

    C) to train 50,000 primary teachers

    D) to provide courses for secondary teachers

30. The reason for the introduction of computers in schools is that _____.

    A) in future, all teaching will be done with computers

    B) computer programmers will have better jobs in future

    C) large number of people will have to be trained as computer programmers

    D) people will need to understand them to obtain information in their work

Section D   Short Answer Questions

Directions:（略）

Passage 5

Public goods are those commodities from whose enjoyment nobody can be effectively *excluded*（被……排斥在外）. Everybody is free to enjoy the benefits of these commodities, and one person's *utilization*（利用）does not reduce the possibilities of anybody else's enjoying the same good.

Examples of public goods are not as rare as one might expect. A flood control dam is a public good. Once the dam is built, all persons living in the area will benefit—regardless of their own contribution to the construction cost of the dam. The same holds true for highway signs or aids to navigation. Once a lighthouse is built, no ship of any nationality can be effectively excluded from the utilization of the lighthouse for navigational purposes. National defense is another example. Even a person who voted against military expenditures or did not pay any taxes will benefit from the protection afforded.

It is no easy task to determine the social costs and social benefits associated with a public good. There is no *practicable*（行得通的）way of charging drivers for looking at highway signs, sailors for watching a lighthouse, and citizens for the security provided to them through national defense. Because the market does not provide the necessary signals, economic analysis has to be substituted for the impersonal judgment of the marketplace.

31. What are public goods according to the author?

　　_____　_____　_____　_____　_____

　　_____　_____　_____　_____　_____

32. How are the first two paragraph organized?

　　_____　_____　_____　_____　_____

　　_____　_____　_____　_____　_____

33. Which words could best explain the meaning of "The same holds true for..." (Line 3，Para. 2)?

　　_____　_____　_____　_____　_____

　　_____　_____　_____　_____　_____

34. According to the passage，is it necessary for a person to pay any money in order to enjoy the protection provided by the national defense?

　　_____　_____　_____　_____　_____

　　_____　_____　_____　_____　_____

35. It can be inferred that finding out the social costs of a public good is _____.

　　_____　_____　_____　_____　_____

　　_____　_____　_____　_____　_____

Notes and Explanations

Passage 1

Explanations

1. ［N］Section C 提到 Like education, political and legal processes and institutions, public order, communication, transport and money supply, health care can be seen as one of the fundamental social facilities necessary for people to exercise their other rights as autonomous human beings. 如同教育、政治和法律程序与条文、公共秩序、通讯、交通和货币供给一样，卫生保健也可被视为人类行使如自主人权之类的其他权利所必需的基本社会设施。所以答案为 No。

2. ［Y］Section C 提到 However, at exactly the same time as this new realization of the finite character of health-care resources was sinking in an awareness of a contrary kind was developing in Western societies: that people have a basic right to health-care as a necessary-condition of a proper human life. 然而，在人们认识到卫生保健资源是有限的同时，在西方社会产生了一种相反的意识：那就是作为人类生活的必要条件，人们拥有卫生保健的基本权利。故可得到答案 Yes。

3. ［Y］Section E 提到 The second set of more specific changes that have led to the present concern about the distribution of health-care resources stems from the dramatic rise in health costs in most OECD countries, accompanied by large-scale demographic and social changes which have meant, to take one example, that elderly people are now major (and relatively very expensive) consumers of health-care resources. 导致对卫生保健资源分配关注的变化源于在大部分 OECD 国家人口增长和社会变化致使医疗费用的激增，例如，老年人成为卫生保健资源的主要消费者。可以得出答案为 Yes。

4. ［NG］Section E 讲述了 OECD 国家在卫生保健资源的投入和消费中面临的问题，但没有提及这些国家低估了所需卫生保健供应的水平。所以答案应为 Not Given。

5. ［NG］在 Section A"Every health system in an economically developed society is faced with the need to decide what proportion of the community's total resources should be spent on health-care; how resources

are to be apportioned; what diseases and disabilities and which forms of treatment are to be given priority; which members of the community are to be given special consideration in respect of their health needs; and which forms of treatment are the most cost-effective."提到发达国家在卫生保健制度的决策中所面临的选择,但并没有提及老年人需要为未来的医疗做特别的准备。故答案应为 Not Given。

6. [N] Section D 提到 The state has no obligation to provide a health-care system itself, but to ensure that such a system is provided. 国家本身没有提供卫生保健系统的义务,但是国家要保证能够提供这样的系统。所以答案为 No。

7. [Y] Section D 提到 As has just been remarked, in a liberal society basic health is seen as one of the indispensable conditions for the exercise of personal autonomy. 正如上文所说的,在一个自由的社会里,基本的医疗保障被视作实现人权的必需条件之一。从而得到答案 Yes。

8. 文章讨论的主题是卫生保健费用的增长和医疗资源的短缺。所以,本题的正确答案为 **health-care**。

9. Section B 提到 Looking back, it now seems quite incredible that in the national health systems that emerged in many countries in the years immediately after the 1939-1945 World War, it was assumed without question that all the basic health needs of any community could be satisfied, at least in principle; the "invisible hand" of economic progress would provide. 毋庸置疑,任何一个群体的基本健康需求都能够得到满足,至少在原则上,经济发展这只"无形的手"能够提供这些基本需求。可以得到答案为 **economic growth**(**progress**)。

10. Section E 提到 Just at the time when it became obvious that health-care resources could not possibly meet the demands being made upon them, people were demanding that their fundamental right to health-care be satisfied by the state. 当医疗资源不能满足需要这个事实变得显而易见的时候,人民就会要求国家来满足他们的基本医疗权利。所以正确答案为 **the state**。

Passage 2

Notes

1. To some extent our intelligence is given us at birth... (Line 2~3, Para. 1)
   to some extent 意思是"在某种程度上"。例如:
   I agree with what you say to some extent. 我在某种程度上同意你的说法。

2. ...is to some extent something we are born with. (Line 1, Para. 2)
   be born with 意思是"生来就有,与生俱来"。例如:
   Confidence is not what we are born with. 信心不是我们生来就有的。

3. Thus if we take two unrelated people at random... (Line 2~3, Para. 2)
   at random 意思是"任意地,胡乱地"。例如:
   The people for the experiment were chosen completely at random. 试验人员完全是随机挑选出来的。
   Please choose any number at random. 请随便选择一个号码。

4. ...we take two identical twins they will very likely be... (Line 4~5, Para. 2)
   identical 在这句话中意思是"完全相同的,完全相似的",identical twins 意思是"同卵双胞胎"。例如:
   Their views on children education are almost identical. 他们对孩子教育所持的观点几乎相同。
   My hat is identical with (to) yours. 我的帽子同你的一模一样。

5. ...people who live in close contact with each other... (Line 4~5, Para. 3)
   be in contact with 意思是"与……有交往,与……有联系"。例如:
   Have you been in contact with him recently? 你最近和他有来往吗?
   I am in contact with a number of schools in the U.S. 我跟美国的许多学校有联系。

Explanations

11. [K] 语法规则要求此处应填一个名词和 a boring 一起作介词 in 的宾语;本句中用了两个句式相同的定语从句,因此可以断定所填词汇应该是 surroundings 的同义词,故选项 K 正确。

12. [G] 语法规则要求此处应填一个名词作介词 at 的宾语。本句话的意思是"人的智力水平在某种程度上是生来就有的"。此处填 birth 正合此意。at birth 意为"在出生时"。

13. [C] 语法规则要求此处应填一个动词 + ed 形式构成被动语态。这句话的意思是"多数专家所持的这个观点可以在很多方面得到支持"。C 项 supported(支持)正合此意。

14. [A] 语法规则要求此处应填一个名词构成固定搭配,to some extent 为固定短语,意为"在某种程度上"。故选项 A 正确。

15. [J] 语法规则要求此处应填一个形容词构成 be + 形容词 + to be(do)的结构。这句话的意思是"血缘关系越亲密智力水平相似的可能性越大",likely 符合此意。be likely to be 意思是"可能是",因此选项 J 正确。

16. [O] 语法规则要求此处应填一个名词作介词 at 的宾语;at random 意为"任意地,随便地",符合句子的意思,故选项 O 正确。

17. [B] 语法规则要求此处应填一个形容词来修饰名词 twins。联系上文中的"completely different"和本句中的 on the other hand 可以判断此处要表达的含义应为"相似的,类似的",故选项 B 正确。

18. [D] 语法规则要求此处应填一个动词和 on 搭配作句子的谓语,句子的主语要求谓语应该是第三人称单数,只有选项 D 符合该要求。depend on 意为"取决于"。

19. [F] 语法规则要求此处应填一个名词或动名词作介词 in 的宾语。本句话的意思是"我们会很快在智力发展方面找到不同,这就说明环境及出生(在智商的形成上)都起作用。"developing 符合句子的意思,intelligence developing 意思是"智力发展"。

20. [M] 语法规则要求此处应填一个名词和 close 一起作介词 in 的宾语,in contact with 意为"与……有联系/来往",in close contact with 则为"与……关系密切",故选项 M 正确。

Passage 3

Notes

1. boom (Line 1, Para. 1)

   boom 意思是"热潮,突然的繁荣";baby boom 意为"生育高峰,婴儿潮"。例如:

   a big travel boom 旅游业的大发展

   a business boom 商业的繁荣

2. ... couples are increasingly unwilling to subject children to the terrible experience... (Line 1~2, Para. 3)

   subject... to 在这里表示"使经受,使蒙受"。例如:

   He was subjected to criticism for his stupid mistakes. 他因犯了愚蠢的错误而遭受责难。

   The location of the island in the middle of the ocean subjects it to frequent hurricanes.

   该岛地处海洋中心,因而常受飓风的袭击。

3. ... during the remainder of this century. (Line 2~3, Para. 4)

   remainder 指"剩余的部分,其余的人",单复数同形,这里指"这个世纪剩余的时间"。例如:

   the remainder of one's life 余生

   Ten people were rescued from the burning building, but the remainder were still inside (of it).

   有 10 人从燃烧的大楼中被救出,其余的人则还困在里面。

4. Along with them goes social mobility... (Line 3, Para. 4)

   本句为倒装句,主语是 social mobility。along with ... 在这里表示"与……一道,与……一起"。这句话意思是:除了这些因素(前面提到的妇女在外工作及婚姻的不稳定),还有社会的流动性。例如:

Supermarkets along with consumers have been hit by inflation.

超级市场与消费者一同遭受通货膨胀的沉重打击。

She placed the bank notes, along with the change and receipts, back in the drawer.

她把钞票连同找回的零钱和收据一起又放回抽屉。

5. Food shortage will happen again when the reserves resulting from the good harvests... (Line 1, Para. 5)

result from 意思是"由……引起，起因于"，resulting from the good harvests... 在本句中做定语，修饰 the reserves。例如：

The terrible accident resulted from his carelessness. 那桩可怕的意外事件因他的疏忽大意而引起。

6. Urbanization is likely to continue... (Line 2, Para. 5)

likely 在这里是形容词，意思是"有可能的，可能发生的"。例如：

He is likely to be late due to the traffic jam. 因为交通阻塞，他可能会迟到。本句话还可以这样表述：It is likely that he will be late due to the traffic jam.

Explanations

　　人口的发展会给全世界的资源造成危机，英国及欧洲发达国家已开始重视这一问题。文章对美国及欧洲一些国家人口出生率下降的原因做了详细的论述，使我们更清楚地认识到人口问题对未来的影响。

21. B）细节题，参见文章第一段第二句。关键在于对本句话的理解，本句意思是"美国及其他富有的国家的人口出生率自 1957 年以来，几乎没有一年不在下降，而且在 1976 年下降得尤其迅速"。由此可知：从 1957 年到 1976 年美国孩子的出生率在下降。

22. B）细节题，根据文章第二段第二句可判断出该题答案为 B 项。

23. C）推断题。此题的关键在于对 impossibly 一词的理解，意思是"无法想象地，非常地"。第二段第二句告诉我们"妇女一旦找到有趣且报酬好的工作，她们便不太愿意花费精力养育孩子。"由此得知 C 项为正确答案。

24. B）细节题。根据文章第四段最后一句话 Along with them goes social mobility, ambition to rise in the urban world, a main factor... 得知，ambition to rise in the urban world 意思与选项 B 一样，所以 B 项为正确答案。

25. D）细节题。根据文章最后一段倒数第二句话 All this leads to a population in the twenty-first century that is smaller than was feared a few years ago. 表明几年前人口问题是人们担忧的问题，这句话不仅指出 21 世纪人口会变少，而且不再成为人们担心害怕的事情。因此，D 项为正确答案。

Passage 4

Notes

1. ... was originally due to end next year... (Line 1, Para. 2)

due 后接不定式，意思是"预定（做）"。例如：

The committee is due to meet on 20 August. 委员会定于 8 月 20 日开会。

2. This has been raised in bits and pieces... (Line 2, Para. 2)

bits and pieces 意思是"零星，七零八碎"。例如：

make a confession in bits and pieces 一点一滴吞吞吐吐地认罪

Let me get my bits and pieces together. 让我来把我的零碎东西归并一下。

3. The program will now run until March 1986, at a provisional cost of around 20 million. (Line 2～3, Para. 2)

at the cost of 意思是"以……为代价"。例如：

He saved the children from the fire at the cost of his own life. 他舍身把孩子们从火中救出。

大学英语 4 级阅读与简答（新题型）

The poor fox escaped from the trap at the cost of a leg. 那可怜的狐狸失去了一条腿,才逃出陷阱。

4. MEP provides courses for teachers and... (Line 1, Para. 3)

   In that way, virtually every secondary school has been provided with... (Line 1, Para. 4)

   provide sth. for sb. 意思是"把某物提供给某人"。provide sb. with sth. 意思是"供给某人某物"。例如:

   They provided food and clothes for the suffers. (或 They provided the suffers with food and clothes.)
   他们提供食物和衣服给受难者。

5. It's no good having the computers without... (Line 1, Para. 5)

   It's no good doing 意思是"即使做……也是没用"。还可表示为:There is no good doing ...

   与 good 此用法相似的词还有 use, sense, point。例如:

   It would be no good taking up the matter now. 现在即使提起那个问题也是没用的。

   It is no use crying over the spilt milk. 覆水难收。

   There is no sense (in) criticizing him. 批评他也没有用。

   There is no point (in) thinking about it. 考虑此事没多大意义。

6. ... but in learning the general skill to extract the required information of the moment from the ever-spreading flood. (Line 7～8, Para. 6)

   extract ... from 意思是"从……得到,从……选取"。例如:

   The newspaper extracted several passages from the speech and printed them on the front page.
   这家报纸从那篇讲话中摘选了几段在头版予以发表。

   How did you manage to extract the information from her? 你是怎样设法从她那儿获得情报的?

Explanations

　　计算机教育在世界各国蓬勃发展,它在生活的各个领域起着越来越重要的作用。MEP 在中小学的发展情况又是如何呢? 在这篇文章中,我们可以看出政府对此事的重视程度。

26. **A)** 细节题。根据文章第二段第一句... was originally due to end next year, and had a budget of 9 million,可以判断出选项 A 为正确答案。

27. **D)** 细节题。根据文章第三段第一句和第六段前两句,可以判断出选项 D 为正确答案。

28. **B)** 细节题。参见文章第四段第一句 virtually every secondary school 表明"几乎每一所中学",如果理解 virtually 一词的意思为"几乎",就能答对本题。

29. **B)** 细节题。根据文章第五段可知选项 B 与文章意思相符。

30. **D)** 推断题。根据文章最后一段最后一句 The reasoning behind MEP is that... from the ever-spreading flood. 可知:如果孩子们不会计算机操作,则不能在未来的经济社会中找到值得做的工作,但操作不是指职业训练,而是学会从繁多的信息中选取需要的信息。由此可以判断选项 D 与文章意思相符。

Passage 5

Keys

31. They are commodities that everybody can utilize.

32. A concept is defined and then examples are given.

33. It can be explained as "The same is true for ."/ "You can get the same benefits from. "

34. No, it is unnecessary.

35. a difficult procedure/task

Notes

1. public goods (Line 1，Para. 1)

   public goods 意思是"公共物品"。第一段阐述了它在经济学上的意义：每个人消费（享用）这种物品而不会导致他人对其消费的减少。

2. ... regardless of their own contribution to... (Line 2～3，Para. 2)

   regardless of 意思是"不管，不顾"。这句话的意思是：一旦水坝建成，居住在这个地区的人们都将获得益处——不管他们对建坝贡献大小。

3. Even a person who voted against ... protection afforded. (Line 6～7，Para. 2)

   vote against 意思是"投票反对"。这句话的意思是：即使一个人反对军用开支或不纳税，他也能得到应有的保护而获得益处。

4. There is no practicable way of charging drivers for... through national defense. (Line 2～4，Para. 3)

   这句话中 charge 后有三个宾语 drivers for looking at high signs，sailors for watching lighthouse and citizens for the security...

5. ... has to be substituted for... (Line 4～5，Para. 3)

   substitute for 意思是"代替"。

Unit 16

Section A   Skimming and Scanning

Directions：（略）

Passage 1

What Is Acute Infection?

1. Acute HIV infection refers to the first stage of infection, the time immediately after a person is infected and before an antibody response to the infection develops. The second stage of infection is *seroconversion*（血清转化）, when a person develops HIV-specific antibodies. During acute HIV infection, there are high levels of virus since the antibody response has not yet developed.

2. Determining acute HIV infection is critical for HIV prevention efforts. Conventional HIV tests do not detect acute infection, yet it is estimated that almost half of new HIV infections may occur when a person with acute infection unknowingly transmits HIV.

3. There is no defined acute *retroviral*（逆转录酶病毒的）syndrome since there are many different symptoms associated with acute HIV infection. After an *incubation*（孵化）period of 1 to 3 weeks, about 50％ of persons with acute HIV infection develop headaches, sore throat, fever, muscle pain, anorexia, rash, and/or diarrhea. The symptoms are generally mild and may span anywhere from days to weeks.

4. It is easy to overlook or miss the signs of acute HIV infection. Half of persons who are acutely infected will never notice any symptoms. Also, the symptoms of acute retroviral syndrome are similar for other common illnesses such as infectious *mononucleosis*（单核细胞增多症）and influenza, which means acute HIV infection often goes undiagnosed.

How is acute infection detected?

1. Acute infection cannot be detected by most routinely used HIV tests. Conventional HIV tests detect HIV-specific antibodies in blood or oral fluids that are produced by the immune system during seroconversion. Therefore, a person who was infected very recently will receive an HIV-negative result using conventional HIV tests.

2. Nucleic acid amplification testing（NAAT）can detect acute HIV infection by looking for the presence of the virus. Because NAAT is expensive to use for each individual specimen, many testing sites are combining HIV-negative blood specimens for testing. This NAAT pooling strategy makes screening for acute HIV infection feasible in settings with low disease incidence but high testing volume.

3. Blood specimens with initial HIV-negative antibody results can be routinely screened using the pooled NAAT strategy to detect acute HIV infection. If a client has an HIV-negative antibody

test but a positive NAAT result for the virus, it is important to have them come back to the clinic for follow-up counseling and repeat testing to confirm HIV infection.

How does it affect prevention?

1. The only way for persons to know that they are HIV+ and take precautions to prevent transmission is to be tested for HIV. However, with most routinely used HIV tests, it may take two months or more after initial infection to receive an HIV+ result. These two months are critical for HIV prevention: it is estimated that almost half of HIV transmissions occur when a person is in this acute HIV infection phase. During acute infection, there are high levels of HIV virus in the body and high viral load has been shown to be associated with increased risk of HIV transmission.

2. If persons are at greatest infectivity during acute infection, it is likely that many persons are transmitting HIV unknowingly during this time. An acutely infected person who receives an HIV-negative antibody test result could be engaging in recommended HIV prevention practices, such as disclosing their status and only having sex or sharing injection equipment with HIV-negative persons, and yet still be transmitting HIV.

3. Persons with acute HIV infection may benefit from enhanced counseling focused on immediate risk reduction strategies and clarification about the conflicting test results. They should also be offered disclosure assistance and partner testing and counseling.

Can acute infection be treated?

1. Treating HIV during the acute infection stage may boost the immune system and slow the progression of HIV disease. One study followed HIV+ persons who started highly active antiretroviral treatment (HAART) in the acute infection stage. These persons had significantly better viral load and CD4 counts, compared to HIV+ persons who began HAART at a later stage.

2. Guidelines for treating HIV infection usually recommend that HIV+ persons who are *asymptomatic* (无症状的) and have low viral loads and strong CD4 counts should wait to begin HAART. It is possible that initiating treatment during acute infection may be beneficial. However, starting HIV medications is a major decision: there are many side effects and toxicities and there are currently no long-term studies on the effectiveness of treatment for acute infection.

What's being done?

1. North Carolina has instituted the Screening and Tracing Active Transmission (STAT) program to identify and manage new HIV infections. As a part of STAT, all tests at publicly funded sites that return HIV-negative using standard testing are re-tested with NAAT. In 2003, NAAT detected an additional 23 cases of HIV infection, a 3.9% increase in the rate of HIV case identification. All 23 persons with acute infection were notified, 21 began HIV medical care, and 48 of their sexual partners received HIV testing, risk reduction counseling and referrals.

2. In 2003, the San Francisco Department of Public Health began to screen for acute HIV infection among persons seeking HIV counseling and testing at the city STD clinic. In 2004, 11 cases of acute HIV infection were detected, reflecting an increase in HIV case detection of 8.8%. Program staff performed contact tracing and partner management for all persons newly diagnosed HIV+.

3. At a hospital Urgent Care Center in Boston, MA, all patients who had symptoms of a viral illness and who reported risk factors for HIV infection were tested for acute HIV infection. Most patients (68%) agreed to be tested for HIV even though they came to the hospital with unrelated concerns. Of 499 patients tested in 2000, 5 had acute HIV infection and 6 had chronic infection. Of the 5 patients with acute HIV infection, 4 returned for their test results, were seen by an HIV physician or nurse and began antiretroviral therapy.

What needs to be done?

1. Acute HIV infection is hard to detect and often goes undiagnosed. Primary care physicians and healthcare workers at emergency rooms, urgent care and STD clinics need education and training on symptoms of acute HIV infection. Clinicians with patients who show signs of viral illness such as influenza or mononucleosis should conduct quick risk assessments for HIV risk and provide referrals to testing and counseling sites as needed.

2. More HIV testing and counseling sites need to test for acute infection, especially in high prevalence areas and high risk settings such as STD clinics. To accomplish this, resources for training, technical assistance and funding need to increase for agencies that provide acute HIV infection testing. State and federal reimbursement protocols, as well as public and private insurance, need to be changed to encourage the use of NAAT.

3. Identifying persons with acute HIV infection can be an effective HIV prevention strategy, as it focuses on persons at greatest risk for transmission. Persons with acute infection may need enhanced post-test counseling, including referrals to medical care and social services such as substance abuse and mental health treatment when appropriate and prevention programs for HIV + persons. Acute infection is also a crucial time for identifying sex and drug use partners and offering disclosure assistance services such as partner notification, counseling, testing and referrals.

1. Acute HIV infection refers to the last stage of infection, the time immediately after a person is infected and before an antibody response to the infection develops.

2. It is easy to overlook or miss the signs of acute HIV infection.

3. Acute infection cannot be detected by any routinely used HIV tests.

4. It is estimated that almost half of HIV transmissions occur when a person is in this acute HIV infection phase.

5. Acute infection can be treated in any stage.

6. Acute HIV infection is hard to detect and often goes undiagnosed.

7. Identifying persons with acute HIV infection can be an effective HIV prevention strategy, as it focuses on persons at greatest risk for transmission.

8. Determining acute HIV infection is critical for _____.

9. The only way for persons to know that they are HIV + and take precautions to prevent transmission is _____.

10. There are currently no long-term studies on the effectiveness of treatment for _____.

Section B   Discourse Vocabulary Test

Directions：（略）

Passage 2

Resources can be said to be scarce in both an ___11___ and in a relative sense: the surface of the Earth is finite, imposing absolute scarcity, but the scarcity that ___12___ economists is the relative scarcity of resources in different users. Materials used for our purpose cannot at the same time be used for other purposes; if the ___13___ of an input is limited, the increased use of it in one manufacturing process must cause it to become less available for other users.

The cost of a product in terms of money may not ___14___ its true cost to society. The true cost, say, the construction of a supersonic jet is the value of the schools and refrigerators that will never be built as a result. Every act of production uses up some of society's ___15___ resources; it means the foregoing of an ___16___ to produce something else. In deciding how to use resources most ___17___ to satisfy the wants of the community, this opportunity cost must ultimately be taken into account.

In a market ___18___ the price of a good and the quantity supplied depends on the cost of making it, and that cost, ultimately, is the cost of not making other goods. The market mechanism *enforces*（加强）this relationship. The cost of, say, a pair of shoes is the price of the leather, the labor, the fuel, and other elements used up in ___19___ them. But the price of these inputs, in turn, depends on what they can produce elsewhere—if the leather can be used to produce handbags that are valued highly by consumers, the price of leather will be bid up ___20___ .

A) quantity	I) economy
B) available	J) producing
C) effectively	K) concerns
D) economist	L) absolute
E) consider	M) likely
F) correspondingly	N) measure
G) opportunity	O) quality
H) productive	

Section C   Reading in Depth

Directions：（略）

Passage 3

Most people have heard of Shakespeare and probably know something of the plays that he wrote. However, not everybody knows much about the life of this remarkable man, except perhaps that he was born in the market town of Stratford-upon-Avon and that he married a woman called Anne Hathaway. We know nothing of his school life. We do not know, for example, how long it lasted, but we presume that he attended the local grammar school, where the principal subject taught was Latin.

Nothing certain is known of what he did between the time he left school and his departure for London. According to a local *legend*（传说）, he was beaten and even put in prison for stealing rabbits and deer from the estate of a neighbouring landowner, Sir Thomas Lucy. It is said that because of this he was forced to run away from his native place. A different legend says that he was apprenticed to a Stratford butcher, but did not like the life and for this reason decided to leave Stratford.

Whatever caused him to leave the town of his birth, the world can be grateful that he did so. What is certain is that he set his foot on the road to fame when he arrived in London. It is said that at first he was without money or friends there, but that he earned a little by taking care of the horses of the gentlemen who attended the plays at the theatre. In time, as he became a familiar figure to the actors in the theatre, they stopped and spoke to him. They found his conversation so brilliant that finally he was invited to join their company.

21. In the early life of Shakespeare, he _____.
    A) attended a public school
    B) lived in London
    C) studied Latin
    D) was put in prison for stealing cattle

22. Why was he forced to leave his native place according to this passage?
    A) Because he didn't want to go to school.
    B) Because he left for London to become famous.
    C) Because he had stolen deer and was beaten.
    D) No one knows for certain.

23. Why can the world be grateful?
    A) He wrote many world-famous plays.
    B) He became a good rider.
    C) He was an actor.
    D) He liked to travel all over the world.

24. "In time, as he became a familiar figure", "in time"(Line 4~5, Para. 3) means _____.
    A) on time
    B) sometimes
    C) some time later
    D) some time

25. The best title is _____.
    A) The Early Life of Shakespeare
    B) Shakespeare's Life in London
    C) Shakespeare's Role in Performance
    D) Shakespeare's Later Life

Passage 4

The temperature of the Sun is over 5,000 degrees Fahrenheit at the surface, but it rises to perhaps more than 16 million degrees at the center. The Sun is so much hotter than the Earth that matter can exist only as a gas, except at the core. In the core of the Sun, the pressures are so great against the gases that, despite the high temperature, there may be a small solid core. However, no one really knows, since the center of the Sun can never be directly observed.

Solar astronomers do know that the Sun is divided into five layers of zones. Starting at the outside and going down into the sun, the zones are the *corona*（日冕）, *chromosphere*（色球层）, *photosphere*（光球层）, *convection zone*（对流层）, and finally the *core*（日核）. The first three zones are regarded as the Sun's atmosphere ends and the main body of the Sun begins.

The Sun's outermost layer begins about 10,000 miles above the visible surface and goes outward for millions of miles. This is the only part of the Sun that can be seen during an eclipse such as the one in February 1979. At any other time, the corona can be seen only when special instruments are used on cameras and telescopes to shut out the glare of the Sun's rays.

The corona is a brilliant, pearly white, filmy light, about as bright as the full Moon. Its beautiful rays are a sensational sight during an eclipse. The corona's rays flash out in a brilliant fan that has wispy spider like rays near the Sun's north and south poles. The corona is thickest at the Sun's *equator*（赤道似的圈、圆）.

The corona rays are made up of gases streaming outward at tremendous speeds and reaching a temperature of more than 2 million degrees Fahrenheit. The rays of gas *thin out*（变弱）as they reach the space around the planets. By the time the Sun's corona rays reach the Earth, they are weak and invisible.

26. Matter on the Sun can exist only in the form of gas because of the Sun's _____.

    A) size   B) age   C) location   D) temperature

27. With what topic is the second paragraph mainly concerned?

    A) How the sun evolved.

    B) The structure of the Sun.

    C) Why scientists study the Sun.

    D) The distance of the Sun from the planets.

28. All of the following are parts of the Sun's atmosphere EXCEPT the _____.

    A) corona   B) chromosphere   C) photosphere   D) core

29. According to the passage, as the corona rays reach the planets, they become _____.

    A) hotter   B) clearer   C) thinner   D) stronger

30. The paragraph following the passage will most likely discuss _____.

    A) the remaining layers of the Sun

    B) the evolution of the Sun to its present form

    C) comparison between the Sun and the Moon

    D) what does the sun do to people

Section D　Short Answer Questions
Directions：（略）

Passage 5

In the late 1960's, many people in North America turned their attention to environmental problems, and new steel-and-glass skyscrapers were widely criticized. Ecologists pointed out that a cluster of tall buildings in a city often overburdens public transportation and parking lot capacities.

Skyscrapers are also excessive consumers, and waster, of electric power. In one recent year, the addition of 17 million square feet of skyscraper office space in New York raised the peak daily demand for electricity by 120,000 kilowatts—enough to supply the entire city of Alnaby, New York, for a day.

Glass-walled skyscrapers can be especially wasteful. The heat loss (or gain) through a wall of half-inch plate glass is more than ten times that through a typical stone wall filled with insulation board. To lessen the pressure on heating and air-conditioning equipment, builders of skyscrapers have begun to use double-covered panels of glass with silver or gold mirror films that reduce strong sunshine as well as heat gain. However, mirror-walled skyscrapers raise the temperature of the surrounding air and affect neighboring buildings.

Skyscrapers put a severe burden on a city's sanitation facilities, too. If fully occupied, the two World Trade Center towers in New York City would alone generate 2.25 million gallons of raw sewage each year—as much as a city the size of Stanford, Connecticut, which has a population of more than 109,000.

Skyscrapers also interfere with television reception, block bird flyways and block up air traffic. In Boston in the late 1960's, some people even feared that shadows from skyscrapers would kill the grass on Boston Common. Still, people continue to build skyscrapers for all the reasons that they have always built them—personal ambition, civic pride, and the desire of owners to have the largest possible amount of rentable space.

31. According to ecologists what do the skyscrapers in North America cause?

_____

_____

32. The exterior surrounding air of a skyscraper is heated by _____.

_____

_____

33. According to the passage, in the 1960's some residents in Boston were concerned with which aspect of the skyscrapers?

_____

_____

34. Where in the passage does the author compare the energy consumption of a skyscraper with that of a city?

_____

_____

35. On what purpose does the author write the passage?

_____

_____

Notes and Explanations

Passage 1

Explanations

1. [N] 第一段第一句提到 Acute HIV infection refers to the first stage of infection, the time immediately after a person is infected and before an antibody response to the infection develops. 急性艾滋病毒感染是

感染的第一个阶段,就在患者被感染之后和对感染的抗体形成之前。故答案为 No。

2. [Y] 第四段第一句提到 It is easy to overlook or miss the signs of acute HIV infection. 急性艾滋病毒感染的迹象是很容易被忽视的。可以得出答案为 Yes。

3. [N] How is acute infection detected 部分第一句提到 Acute infection cannot be detected by most routinely used HIV tests. 大多数例行的、常用的艾滋病毒检查无法查出急性感染。从而得出答案为 No。

4. [Y] 从 How does it affect prevention? 部分第一段第三句 These two months are critical for HIV prevention;it is estimated that almost half of HIV transmissions occur when a person is in this acute HIV infection phase. 可以得出答案为 Yes。

5. [NG] Can acute infection be treated 部分第一段第一句提到 Treating HIV during the acute infection stage may boost the immune system and slow the progression of HIV disease. 在急性感染阶段治疗艾滋病可能会提高免疫系统功能并减缓艾滋病毒的发展。本题的命题没有提到,因此可以得出答案为 Not Given。

6. [Y] What needs to be done 部分第一段第一句提到 Acute HIV infection is hard to detect and often goes undiagnosed. 急性艾滋病毒感染很难被查出,通常也无法诊断。故答案应为 Yes。

7. [Y] 最后一段第一句提到 Identifying persons with acute HIV infection can be an effective HIV prevention strategy, as it focuses on persons at greatest risk for transmission. 诊断急性艾滋病毒感染的病人是艾滋病防治中有效的措施,因为它所针对的病人最有可能传播病毒。因此答案应为 Yes。

8. 第二段第一句提到 Determining acute HIV infection is critical for HIV prevention efforts. 急性艾滋病毒感染的确诊对于艾滋病的预防是至关重要的。从而得到答案:**HIV prevention efforts**。

9. How does it affect prevention 部分第一段第一句提到 The only way for persons to know that they are HIV+ and take precautions to prevent transmission is to be tested for HIV. 对人们来说,要让他们知道自己是艾滋病毒携带者并采取措施防治病毒传播的唯一方法就是进行检查。由此可以得知 **to be tested for HIV** 是本题的正确答案。

10. Can acute infection be treated 部分第二段第三句提到 ...there are many side effects and toxicities and there are currently no long-term studies on the effectiveness of treatment for acute infection. (药物治疗艾滋病)有一些副作用和毒性,目前还没有对于急性感染治疗效果的长期研究。因此本题的正确答案应为 **acute infection**。

Passage 2

Notes

1. The cost of a product in terms of money may not... (Line 1, Para. 2)

in terms of 在这里意思是"根据,按照;从……方面(说来)"。例如:

He thought of everything in terms of money. 他考虑任何事情都从金钱角度出发。

In terms of natural resources, it is one of the poorest countries in Western Europe. 就自然资源而言,这是西欧最穷的国家之一。

2. Every act of production uses up... (Line 3, Para. 2)

use up 在这里意思是"用完,耗尽"。例如:

He has used up all his money. 他花完了所有的钱。

3. ...this opportunity cost must ultimately be taken into account. (Line 5~6, Para. 2)

take into...account 意思是"对……加以考虑",意思与 take account of, take...into consideration 相同。例如:

You must take local customs and conditions into account. 你必须考虑当地的风俗习惯和环境。

When learning a language, we should take account of the differences between our mother tongue and the target language. 我们学习语言时,应该考虑母语与所学习的外国语之间的差异。

4. But the price of these inputs, in turn... (Line 4~5, Para. 3)

in turn 在这句话中的意思是"转而,反过来"。例如:

Theory is based on practice and in turn serves practice. 理论以实践为基础,反过来又为实践服务。

I told him the secret and in turn he told it to Tom. 我告诉了他这个秘密,转而他就告诉了汤姆。

5. ... the price of leather will be bid up correspondingly. (Line 6, Para. 3)

bid up 在这里的意思是"哄抬价钱,竞出高价"。例如:

The house was bid up far beyond its real value. 那座房子的价钱被抬得远远超过其实际价值。

Explanations

11. [L] 语法规则要求此处应填一个形容词作介词 in 的宾语并且在意思上和 relative(相对的)相对,选项中符合此意的是 L 项 absolute(绝对的)。

12. [K] 语法规则要求此处应填一个动词作定语从句的谓语,且应为第三人称单数,只有选项 K 符合这个要求。concerns(使担心,使忧虑)也符合上下文意思的要求。

13. [A] 语法规则要求此处应填一个单数名词作条件状语从句的主语,选项 A、D、G、I、N、O 均是单数名词,但是只有 A 项 quantity(数量)符合句子的意思要求。

14. [N] 语法规则要求此处应填一个动词原形和 may not 一起作句子的谓语。这句话的意思是"并不能用产品的成本来估量它对社会来说的真正成本"。measure(估量,衡量)符合句子的意思。

15. [B] 语法规则要求此处应填一个形容词来修饰名词 resources。这句话的意思是"任何一种生产行为都会用肉社会上的一些可利用资源"。available 意思是"可利用的,有用的",符合句子意思。

16. [G] 语法规则要求此处应填一个名词作介词 of 的宾语,从下一句意思来看,句子的主语 this opportunity 就是指本句中所填的词,所以 G 项 opportunity(机会)符合句子意思。

17. [C] 语法规则要求此处应填一个副词来修饰动词 use,选项 C、F 符合要求。effectively 意为"有效地",correspondingly 意为"相对地,比照地",故选项 C 符合句子意思:在决定如何更有效地使用能源满足社会需求时,最终一定要考虑机会成本。

18. [I] 语法规则要求此处应填一个名词和 a market 一起作介词 in 的宾语;根据主句的意思这里应该填 economy。market economy 意为"市场经济"。

19. [J] 语法规则要求此处应填一个及物的动名词和其宾语 them 一起作介词 in 的宾语,只有 J 项 producing(生产)符合条件,因此 J 项正确。

20. [F] 语法规则要求此处应填一个副词来修饰动词短语 bid up(抬价,提价)。根据这句话的意思,此处应填 correspondingly。correspondingly 意思是"相应地"。

Passage 3

Notes

1. ... but we presume that... (Line 5, Para. 1)

presume 意思是"推测,假定"。例如:

I presume you will be at the meeting. 我推测你将出席会议。

It may fairly be presumed that they are innocent. 完全可以认为他们是无罪的。

2. Nothing certain is known of what he did between the time he left school and his departure for London. (Line 1~2, Para. 2)

departure for 其动词形式为 depart for,意思是"出发到……"。例如:

The plane departed for Paris. 这班飞机要飞往巴黎。

A number of us departed for an outing. 我们当中许多人外出作短途旅游。

3. According to a local legend... (Line 2，Para. 2)

according to 是介词词组，意思是"根据，按照"。例如：

According to the TV，it will be fine today. 根据电视报道，今天是个晴天。

The players are speaking and moving according to the director's instructions.

演员们正按照导演的指示说台词、做动作。

4. What is certain is that he set his foot on the road to... (Line 2，Para. 3)

set foot on 意思是"进入，踏上"。例如：

She has never set foot on foreign soil. 她从未出过国。

He was very happy to set foot on Chinese soil again. 他非常高兴又重新踏上了中国国土。

5. ...as he became a familiar figure... (Line 4～5，Para. 3)

figure 在这里意思是"人物，大人物"。例如：

a great figure in the financial world 金融界的巨头

He was not a political figure but a religious one. 他不是政治人物而是宗教家。

Explanations

众所周知，莎士比亚是欧洲文艺复兴时期晚期英国的一位重要代表人物——著名的剧作家和诗人。他的悲剧《哈姆雷特》(*Hamlet*)中的名言："To be or not to be—that is the question."（"是生还是死——这是个问题"）脍炙人口。而我们对他的早期生活却知之甚少。这篇文章对莎翁的早期生活作了简要概述。

21. C) 细节题。根据文章第一段最后一句话...we presume that...推测出选项 C 与原文相符。而 A 项错在 public school 应为 grammar school。根据第二段第一句可知，他是离开了学校后才到达伦敦，故 B 项不符合题意。根据第二段第二句 according to a local legend 可知，这只是个传说，并非事实，故 D 项也不符合题意。

22. D) 推断题。根据文章第二段，选项 A、B、C 都是人们传说的内容，并非事实，所以可排除掉。D 项为正确答案。

23. A) 推断题。根据文章第三段第二句 What is certain is that he set his foot on the road to fame...可知：至此他开始走上成功之道，逐渐享有声誉。同时，根据对莎士比亚的常识性了解，可判断出 A 项正确。

24. C) 词汇题。根据文章第三段可知，莎士比亚到达伦敦后是一步步走向成功的，尤其是从第三段第三句中 at first，in time（应理解为"后来"），故 C 项为正确答案。

25. A) 文章标题推断题。从全文可看出，作者主要谈论了莎士比亚成名前的生活，所以 A 项为正确答案。

Passage 4

Notes

1. ...despite the high temperature... (Line 4，Para. 1)

despite 意思是"不管，虽然"。例如：

Despite the traffic jam he arrived here on time.

尽管交通阻塞，他仍然准时到达这里。

Despite the shortage of steel，industrial output has increased by five percent. 尽管钢材供应不足，工业产量仍增长了 5%。

2. ...during an eclipse... (Line 2，Para. 3)

eclipse 意思是"（天文）（日、月的）蚀"。例如：

a solar eclipse 日蚀

a lunar eclipse 月蚀

a total eclipse 全蚀

3. Its beautiful rays are a sensational sight during an eclipse. (Line 1~2，Para. 4)

   sensational 意思是"令人激动的，轰动一时的"。例如：

   a sensational landing on the moon 轰动一时的登月事件

   a sensational discovery 引起轰动的发现

4. The corona rays are made up of gases... (Line 1，Para. 5)

   be made up of 意思是"由……组(构)成的"。例如：

   The committee is made up of representatives from all the universities. 该委员会由所有大学的代表组成。

5. The rays of gas thin out... (Line 2，Para. 5)

   thin out 意思是"变薄，变稀，变细，变弱"。例如：

   thin out sb.'s thick hair 把某人的浓发削薄

   The traffic thinned out after 9 o'clock in the evening. 晚上 9 点以后，路上的车辆和行人稀少了。

   The enemy resistance gradually thinned out. 敌人的抵抗逐渐减弱了。

Explanations

　　我们对太阳的结构已有所了解，它从外向里分为五层：日冕层、色球层、光球层、对流层和日核。而且离中心越近温度越高，物质只能以气体形式存在。

26. D）细节题。根据文章第一段第二句 The Sun is so much hotter than the Earth that matter can exist only as gas. 可知，D 项为正确答案。

27. B）推断题。很明显，文章第二段说明了太阳结构：分为五层。故 B 项答案正确。

28. D）细节题。根据文章第二段最后一句话：The first three zones are regarded as the Sun's atmosphere...可知 the first three zones 指上句话提到的 corona（日冕层），chromosphere（色球层）和 photosphere（光球层），所以 D 项为正确答案。

29. C）细节题。根据文章第五段第二句话 The rays of has thin out... 可知 C 项正确。

30. A）推断题。做这类题目，除了了解文章的总体结构之外，主要看最后一段作者论述的内容。文章第四段和第五段详细说明了 corona（日冕层）的情况，由此可知，作者很可能下文将按太阳由外向里的分层结构逐一说明。所以 A 项正确。

Passage 5

Keys

31. They make public traffic and parking places overcrowded.

32. the mirrored walls of the skyscraper

33. The skyscrapers' harmful effects on the city grass.

34. In Para. 2.

35. Tell the bad effects of skyscrapers.

Notes

1. ... turned their attention to environmental problems... (Line 1~2，Para. 1)

   turn attention to 意思是"将注意力转向……"，这句话的意思是：20 世纪 60 年代晚期，北美洲的许多人开始把注意力转向环境问题……

2. ... and new steel-and-glass skyscrapers were widely criticized. (Line 2，Para. 1)

   skyscraper 意思是"高层大楼，摩天大楼"。摩天大楼使人们享受现代生活的同时，也造成了许多负面影响。这篇文章详细地阐述了 skyscraper 的负面影响。

3. Skyscrapers put a severe burden on... （Line 1，Para. 4）

put a burden on 意思是"把重担加在……上"。类似的表达还有：impose a burden on，lay a burden on，place a burden on。例如：

lay (impose) a heavy tax burden on sb. 使某人负担重税

4. Skyscrapers also interfere with television reception... （Line 1，Para. 5）

interfere with 意思是"干扰，妨碍"。这句话的意思是：高层大楼也干扰电视接收。例如：

The noise of the traffic interfered with my sleep. 交通的噪音使我睡不着。

5. ... block bird flyways and block up air traffic. （Line 1~2，Para. 5）

block up 意思是"阻塞，阻碍，挡住"。例如：

My nose has been blocked up. 我的鼻子塞住了。

Unit 17

Section A   Skimming and Scanning

Directions：（略）

Passage 1

How Human Beings Evolved

1. As far as we know the human brain evolved in three main stages. Its ancient and primitive part is the innermost *reptilian*（像爬虫的）brain. Next it evolved the mammalian brain by adding new functions and new ways of controlling the body. Then evolved the third part of the brain, the *neocortex*（新皮层）, the grey matter, the bulk of the brain in two *symmetrical*（对称的）hemispheres, separate but communicating. To a considerable extent it is our neocortex which enables us to behave like human beings.

2. Human emotional responses depend on *neuronal*（神经元集合）pathways which link the right hemisphere to the mammalian brain which in turn is linked to the even older reptilian brain.

3. For human beings, primitive（reptilian）instinctive urges and behavior are overlaid by mammalian care and affection for one's young and human care and affection for one's family and community.

4. So the human brain includes a wide range of emotions, of feelings, of care and affection, and the capability for objective and logical thinking and evaluation.

5. Compared with most, if not all, other animals we also have much longer lifespan and it takes a long time before a human baby becomes an adult, born after nine months in the mother's womb, followed by 4 to 5 years as infant, then 8 to 10 years as child being educated, and say 6 to 9 years as adolescent, about 18 to 25 years old when becoming an adult and independent member of the community.

6. There is a whole scale of behavior from human to the beast-like, from behavior based on affection for the other person to, at the other end, uncontrolled behavior such as rape, and the seduction of the young which I see as another form of rape.

7. Mammalian and human parts of our brain control our reptilian ancestor's instinctive *copulation*（交配）urges. It seems as if rapists and pedophiles do not restrain and control their bottom-level beast-like instincts, and it seems to be these which urge them on.

8. The instinctive sex urge aims to ensure the survival of the species. We have been able to adapt and advance by a process of natural selection and a key characteristic which distinguishes human beings from animals is that we can control the sex urge.

Role of the family

1. Something like 200 million years of evolution are behind us, from reptilian beast through

mammalian animal to human being. Human beings are mammals and are unique in that our children need protecting and bringing up in a humane, emotionally and mentally stimulating environment for between 18 and 21 years, to enable them to mature into socially responsible adults. Men and women co-operate with each other and look after each other and their children, within the family, to do just that.

2. So the role of the family is

• To struggle as a family to survive.

• To protect and support mother and children until children become mature and independent adults capable of providing for themselves.

• To provide a good standard of living and a life of high quality, which includes struggling against oppression and exploitation. And sometimes one has to fight to preserve a good way of life.

• To serve the interests of, and to support, each member of the family. In turn, each member of the family supports the family.

3. Hence human beings work primarily for their family and members of a family stand by, support and help each other in times of need. The family is the basic unit of society and it looks after the interests of all its members, as individuals as well as collectively. This gives great strength to each member of the family in the struggle for daily bread, security and happiness.

Protecting and caring for the next generation

1. There is a genetic difference between men and women. It is women who bear the child and who need protecting and looking after while bearing the child and after childbirth. There clearly are close emotional bonds between mother and child.

2. It is women who generally look after people, after the welfare and well-being of the members of the family. Care, concern, affection and love, feelings and emotions, are important and matter, and women developed, and have, much skill and expertise in such matters. It is generally men who struggle outside the family to secure survival and good living for the family, a struggle for survival in a seemingly hostile environment engineered by other humans.

3. Primarily the family exists to protect and support its young, and this means supporting and looking after the female bearing the child within her body, through birth and while she is protecting and teaching the young how to behave. It is usually the woman whose role it is to ensure the family provides the young with the humane, emotionally and mentally stimulating environment they need to enable them to mature into socially responsible adults. She is assisted in this by her spouse, depending on her needs and depending on his own work. But it is usually the woman who copes with the personal and emotional problems of the family's members and this is challenging, demanding and difficult work demanding social ability and skills as well as care, affection, understanding and concern for people.

4. In the *kibbutzim* (集居区居民), that is in Israel's co-operative settlements, children were brought up communally in age groups, away from their parents. One age group would progress together from *crèche* (托儿所) to nursery and then to school, living together during the week and seeing their parents, or living with their parents, only at weekends.

5. This may have freed both parents for work and defense in the initial struggle for survival. But the practice was continued when successful, possibly to free women for work and so increases

production. But it was done at the expense of the family.

6. Of any group in the country, the kibbutz children consequently showed the highest incidence of mental problems. The kibbutzim have had to backtrack and now give their children a more normal and strengthening family-life experience with their parents.

7. When women are persuaded to regard work outside of the family as more important than caring for the young or the family's members, they are in effect handing over the family's key role to outsiders such as day-care businesses and television program makers. With disastrous results on the way the young perceive home life and adult behavior, tending to condition the young into behaving like fictional and unreal role models, for example concerning sexual behavior, instead of gaining an adult understanding of the reality of living, of family values and relationships, instead of understanding and experiencing socially-responsible behavior caring for and living with other people, instead of seeing adults (parents) behave in socially responsible way struggling in a hostile environment to do the best they can for the young and for each other.

8. The number of young people who run away from home and family, often becoming homeless, placing themselves at a big disadvantage right at the beginning of their lives, speaks for itself.

9. The family needs food and shelter and while the female looks after its young and its people, it is usually the male who struggles outside the immediate family to provide it with an income, with a standard of living, to the best of his ability. He is assisted in this when required by his spouse to an extent which depends on her own work within the family. He struggles outside the family to provide it with a good life against those who wish to profit from the family's needs, against those who wish to exploit, who may even wish to oppress so as to exploit.

10. And there are ways of teaching social responsibility, of teaching the young how to take responsibility for others, how to care for, work with and look after other people. Social responsibility, the caring, giving and sharing with others, the taking on of responsibility for others including conflict management, can be and is being taught.

11. It is in democracies that high standards of living have been achieved. In democracies people can struggle openly for a better life but we see that what has been gained has to be defended and extended.

1. To a considerable extent it is our neocortex which enables us to behave like human beings.
2. Something like 300 million years of evolution are behind us, from reptilian beast through mammalian animal to human being.
3. One of the roles of a family is to make each member get on with others.
4. It is usually the man who copes with the personal and emotional problems of the family's members.
5. According to the author, kibbutzim was done at the expense of the family.
6. The kibbutz children often showed the highest incidence of mental problems.
7. According to the author, women should take more responsibility for the outside affairs instead of looking after the housework.
8. Compared with most, if not all, other animals we also have much longer lifespans and it takes

a long time before a human baby becomes _____.

9. This gives great strength to each member of the family in the struggle for _____.

10. It is women who bear the child and who need protecting and looking after while bearing the child and after _____.

Section B Discourse Vocabulary Test
Directions：（略）

Passage 2

There are many theories about the beginning of drama in Greece. The one most widely accepted today is based on the ___11___ that drama evolved from *ritual*（典礼，仪式）. The argument for this view goes as follows. In the ___12___ , human beings viewed the natural forces of the world, even the seasonal changes, as unpredictable, and they sought, through various means, to control these unknown and feared powers. Those ___13___ which appeared to bring the desired results were then retained and repeated until they hardened into fixed rituals. ___14___ stories arose which explained or *veiled*（遮掩）the mysteries of the rites. As time passed some rituals were ___15___ but the stories, later called myths, persisted and provided material for art and drama.

Those who believe that drama evolved out of ritual also argue that those rites contained the seed of theater because music, dance, masks, and costumes were almost always used. Furthermore, a suitable site had to be provided for performance, and when the entire community did not ___16___ , a clear division was usually made between the "acting area" and the "auditorium". In addition, there were performers, and, since ___17___ importance was attached to avoiding mistakes in the *enactment*（设定）of rites, religious leaders usually assumed that task. Wearing masks and costumes, they often impersonated other people, animals, or supernatural beings, and mimed the desired effect—success in hunt or battle, the coming rain, the revival of the Sun—as an actor might. Eventually such dramatic representations were separated from ___18___ activities.

Another theory ___19___ the theater's origin from the human interest in storytelling. According to this view, tales (about the hunt, war, or other feats) are gradually elaborated, at first through the use of impersonation, action, and dialogue by a narrator and then through the assumption of each of the roles by a different person. A closely related theory traces theater to those dances that are primarily rhythmical and gymnastic or that are ___20___ of animal movements and sounds.

A) abandoned	I) follow
B) assumption	J) treasure
C) political	K) beginning
D) traces	L) end
E) considerable	M) measures
F) Eventually	N) religious
G) considerate	O) participate
H) imitations	

Section C　Reading in Depth

Directions：（略）

Passage 3

How do we measure the economic return to higher education? Typically it is calculated as the difference between average wages of college graduates and those who have not graduated from college. In 1997, for example, college graduates earned an average of 40,508(dollar) versus just 23,970 (dollar) for non-college graduates. Based on these income levels, the economic return to a college education is approximately 69 percent, the difference between the two income levels. But this simple calculation ignores the fact that college graduates tend to come from higher socioeconomic levels, are more highly motivated, and probably have higher IQs than nongraduates. Although these factors influence incomes, they are not the result of college attendance. Therefore the result of the study is an *overstatement*（大话）of the returns to higher education.

More sophisticated analyses adjust for these *extraneous*（外来的）influences. For instance economists Orley Ashenfelter and Alan Krueger, estimate that each year of post-high school education results in a *wage premium*（奖金）of between 15 and 16 percent. Their study is particularly relevant because they examined the earnings differences for identical twins with different education levels, allowing them to control for genetic and socioeconomic factors. Other research puts the wage premium for college graduates at nearly 50 percent.

Unfortunately, you can't spend a college wage-premium. Income levels for the average college graduate have stagnated. After adjusting for inflation, the average income of college graduates holding full-time jobs rose by only 4.4 percent between 1979 and 1997, or at a minuscule annual rate of 0.2 percent. At the same time, workers with only high-school degrees saw their real income plummet by 15 percent. Bottom line: the much-ballyhooed college wage "premium" is due primarily to the fall in inflation-adjusted salaries of workers who haven't been to college.

In fact, if you don't go on to graduate school or are not among the top graduates at one of the nation's elite colleges, chances are your sky-high tuition is buying you no economic advantage whatsoever. In recent decades the flood of graduates has been so great that an increasing proportion have found themselves, within a few years, working as sales clerks, cab drivers, and in other jobs that do not require a college degree. In 1995, approximately 40 percent of people with some college education—and 10 percent of those with a college degree—worked at jobs requiring only high-school skills. That's up from 30 percent and 6 percent, respectively, in 1971.

21. The traditional calculation of the economic return to higher education is inaccurate because _____.

A) it doesn't take into account the changing economic situations

B) it involves small samples

C) it failed to incorporate some aspects which themselves might have added to the earnings of college graduates

D) it does not specify whether non-college graduates have high-school degrees

22. What does the author mean when he says "you can't spend a college wage-premium"(Line 1, Para. 3)?

A) College graduates tend to *stash money away* （存钱）.

B) The economic returns for college graduates have decreased since 1979.

C) The economic returns to higher education have not increased very much since 1979.

D) College graduates could hardly earn enough to pay high living cost.

23. Which of the following statements is NOT true?

A) The economic return to higher education is lower by the more sophisticated analyses than by traditional methods.

B) Results of analyses of college premium differ greatly.

C) Between 1979 and 1997, workers with only high-school degrees saw their real income fall.

D) Graduates from graduate schools have the same economic returns as those from colleges.

24. According to the last paragraph, _____.

A) more and more people go to elite colleges

B) tuition has started to decline

C) there are too many college graduates

D) the quality of college education had declined

25. Which of the following is the topic of the passage?

A) Overestimated College Premium   B) The Payoffs of College Education

C) The Myths of College Education   D) The Decline of College Education

Passage 4

I have no choice but to be skeptical about electronic books, because it isn't technology that's holding up this industry, just common sense. I well recall attending the Magazine Publishers of American conference in Florida about 5 years ago. One of the keynote speakers was CAA's Mike Ovitz, then riding high. He bounded on the stage, clutching some kind of little electronic screen, and proceeded to say that electronic downloads would soon replace the print medium. Notwithstanding the fact that Ovitz has not been wrong about everything he's bet on since leaving CAA, I knew he was wrong then about electronic print downloads.

The e-book, you could argue, is environmentally friendly, which is true, but it is also incredibly counter-intuitive. Computer engineers spend a lot of their time coming up with ways to make computers *ubiquitous* （普遍存在的） in consumer lives, and they've largely succeeded in that, which is part of the point. Many consumers have also been busy rejecting electronic banking, partly because we want a few tactile experiences left in our lives, and handling money is one of those experiences. Reading a book, in a way, is an act of rebellion today. It's a statement that despite the 35 channels coming in on the cable box, the billions of Web sites, and other diversions, you're going to read a book. This is something someone could have done in the 16th century, when the first books were printed in English.

I used to attend a regular "salon" in Manhattan, where Internet people would meet, have dinner and discuss the latest trends. One of the sponsors of these soirees, who worked for a

大学英语 4 级阅读与简答（新题型）

publisher, brought an e-book to the group, and passed it around. Everything about it *bugged*（使烦恼）me; it was characterless, flat and soul-less. One might imagine reading the works of Bill Gates on it, but the thought of reading Thackeray or Dickens or Wilkie Collins or even John Steinbeck on it, is a laughing matter.

In other words, books are more than just words, they have—or used to have—decorative covers, because they are expressions of the author's creativity. That's why some people collect first editions. They want to own the book that was authorized by the writer, an edition he or she might have owned. As books age, they attain a certain *patina*（古色）, redolent of the history the object has been.

26. The author points out at the beginning that _____.
    A) electronic books are constrained by technology
    B) electronic books do not require sophisticated technology
    C) electronic books go against common sense
    D) technology dictates common sense

27. The author acknowledges that _____.
    A) e-books do not pollute the environment
    B) e-books are easy to carry around
    C) e-books will soon replace printed books
    D) e-books will soon go out of fashion

28. The word "tactile" (Line 5, Para. 2) most probably means _____.
    A) creative   B) pleasing to the eye
    C) exciting   D) felt by touch

29. According to the author, which of the following is true of reading such writers as Thackeray or Dickens on an e-book?
    A) The reader can only download part of their works.
    B) The reader does not have to know much about computer.
    C) The reader cannot appreciate the writer's creativity.
    D) The reader may suffer health hazard such as eyesight deterioration.

30. What is the author's main purpose?
    A) To forecast the e-book's future
    B) To make a case against e-books
    C) To suggest alternatives to printed books
    D) To explain why e-books will be the book of the future

Section D   Short Answer Questions
Directions：（略）

Passage 5

The relationship between professional sports clubs and their players is perhaps unlike any other employer-employee relationship in our economy. Nowhere else is a worker's productivity so visible to so many and so easily measured. Productive workers in most firms do not receive the cheers of tens of thousands for a job well done or have the quality of their work publicly reviewed in the press. Likewise, most workers who make a mistake on the job(and who hasn't made a mistake?) do not hear the boss and catcalls of an upset crowd. The productivity of a professional athlete is constantly monitored by fans through a *myriad*(无数的) of statistics-runs batted in, touchdowns scored, field goal percentage, and so on. Although the performance of professional athletes may be objectively measured and compared by the vast quantities of statistics compiled by sports analysts, controversy still surrounds the salaries earned in professional sports.

The general public is still shocked when a star player signs a multimillion dollar contract to play baseball or basketball, yet many professional athletes claim they are underpaid by the team's owners. Further, it is not uncommon for one player to earn 10 or even 20 times more than other players on the same team. Ironically, rules imposed by each of the major sports leagues to promote competition on the playing field contribute to the seemingly inconsistent economics of players' salaries.

31. What is the main characteristic of the professional athletes' performance?

32. How do audience and media monitor professional athletes' performance?

33. What causes controversy about professional athletes?

34. What is the attitude of the general public toward a star player's multi-million dollar contract?

35. What is the byproduct of the rules imposed by the major sports leagues to promote competition on the playing field?

Notes and Explanations

Passage 1

Explanations

1. [Y] 第一段最后一句提到 To a considerable extent it is our neocortex which enables us to behave like human beings. 在相当大的程度上,是新皮层使我们的行为像人类一样。所以答案应为 Yes。
2. [N] Role of the family 部分第一段第一句提到 Something like 200 million years of evolution are behind us, from reptilian beast through mammalian animal to human being. 进化从两亿年前开始,从爬行动物

到哺乳动物再到人。故答案应为 No。

3. [NG] Role of the family 部分第二段提到家庭的功能有四条。但是没有一条提及本题命题，因此，正确答案应为 Not Given。

4. [N] Protecting and caring for the next generation 部分第三段最后一句提到 But it is usually the woman who copes with the personal and emotional problems of the family's members and this is challenging, demanding and difficult work demanding social ability and skills as well as care, affection, understanding and concern for people. 然而，通常是女性处理家庭成员之间的个人和情感问题，这是一个很有挑战性、很有难度的工作，需要社会能力和技巧，还有对他人的关怀、爱护和理解。故答案应为 No。

5. [Y] Protecting and caring for the next generation 部分第五段最后一句提到 But it was done at the expense of the family. （集居区）是以家庭为代价的。所以答案为 Yes。

6. [Y] Protecting and caring for the next generation 部分第六段提到 Of any group in the country, the kibbutz children consequently showed the highest incidence of mental problems. 最终，在任何群体中，集居区的孩子有心理问题的概率是最高的。故答案应为 Yes。

7. [N] Protecting and caring for the next generation 部分第七段提到 When women are persuaded to regard work outside of the family as more important than caring for the young or the family's members, they are in effect handing over the family's key role to outsiders such as day-care businesses and television program makers. 从中可以发现作者并不赞成母亲以放弃教育孩子为代价而外出工作，所以答案应为 No。

8. 第五段第一句提到 Compared with most, if not all, other animals we also have much longer lifespan and it takes a long time before a human baby becomes an adult. 与其他大多数动物相比，我们比它们的寿命长得多，从婴儿成长起来的时间也很长，从而得出答案为 **an adult**。

9. Role of the family 部分第三段最后一句话提到 This gives great strength to each member of the family in the struggle for daily bread, security and happiness. 这使得家庭的所有成员都会为全家的衣食、安全和幸福而努力。故答案应为 **daily bread, security and happiness**。

10. Protecting and caring for the next generation 部分第一段第二句提到 It is women who bear the child and who need protecting and looking after while bearing the child and after childbirth. 是女性孕育了孩子，她们在怀孕的时候和分娩之后需要得到保护和照顾。从而得知 **childbirth** 是正确答案。

Passage 2

Notes

1. The one most widely accepted today is based on... (Line 1~2, Para. 1)

be based on (upon) 意思是"以……为基础"。例如：

You should base your conclusion on careful research. 你应该以审慎的研究为基础而下结论。

The film is based on a novel by D. H. Lawrence. 这部电影是根据 D·H·劳伦斯的一部小说改编的。

2. The argument for this view goes as follows. (Line 2~3, Para. 1)

as follows 意思是"如下"。例如：

The results are as follows. 结果如下。

3. ...later called myths, persisted and... (Line 8, Para. 1)

persist 在这里意思是"持续，留存"。例如：

a melody that persists in the mind 萦回脑际的旋律

characteristics that persist through generations 代代相传的特征

This stormy weather will persist for a couple of days. 这种风雨交加的天气会持续两三天。

4. ...since considerable importance was attached to avoiding mistakes... (Line 5~6, Para. 2)

attach...importance to 在这里意思是"给予重视"。例如：

It is unwise to attach too much importance to the information. 过于重视那个消息是不明智的。

Do you attach any importance to what he said? 你认为他说的话重要吗?

5. ... religious leaders usually assumed that task. (Line 6, Para. 2)

assume 在这里意思是"担任,承担"。例如:

assume an obligation 承担义务

I made a mistake and I will assume responsibility for it. 我犯了错误,我愿意承担责任。

Explanations

11. [B] 语法规则要求此处应填一个名词作介词 on 的宾语。根据下一句中的 this view 可以判断此处应为单数名词形式。assumption 意思是"假定,设想",符合句意。故选项 B 正确。

12. [K] 语法规则要求此处应填一个名词作介词 in 的宾语。从下文中用的表示时间的 as time passed 可以判断这里应该填 beginning。in the beginning 意为"起初,首先",符合句子意思要求。

13. [M] 语法规则要求此处应填一个复数名词和 those 一起作主句的主语。选项 H、M 符合条件;根据前一句的意思这里所填的词应该是 means 的同义词,measure 意思是"方法,措施",符合句子的意思。

14. [F] 语法规则要求此处应填一个副词来修饰整个句子。前文中用了 in the beginning 和 as time passed 来表示时间顺序,这里应该是 eventually(最终),且该词在句首,第一个字母应大写,只有选项 F 符合这三个条件。

15. [A] 语法规则要求此处应填一个动词 + ed 形式和 were 构成被动语态,只有选项 A 符合该要求。abandoned(放弃)和后面的 persisted(坚持)意思相反,符合句子意思的要求。

16. [O] 语法规则要求此处应填一个动词原形作谓语。选项 I、J、L、O 符合该要求。根据主句的意思,这里应该填 participate,意思是"参加,参与",符合上下文意思连贯的要求。

17. [E] 语法规则要求此处应填一个形容词来修饰名词 importance。选项中的形容词中能够和 importance 搭配使用的只有 considerable,意思是"相当的,数量可观的",符合句子意思的要求。

18. [N] 语法规则要求此处应填一个形容词来修饰 activities。符合该要求的选项 C、E、G、N 中可以和 activity 搭配使用的只有 religious。religious activity 的意思是"宗教活动",符合上下文意思的要求。

19. [D] 语法规则要求此处应填一个动词作句子的谓语,句子的单数主语要求谓语是第三人称单数形式。选项 D、M 符合要求。trace 意为"回溯,追溯",更符合句意,因此选项 D 正确。

20. [H] 语法规则要求此处应填一个复数名词作表语。选项 H、M 符合此条件。这句话的意思是"那些舞蹈动作是对动物的动作及声音的模仿"。imitation 意思是"模仿",符合句子的意思。

Passage 3

Notes

1. ... college graduates earned an average of 40,508(dollar) versus... (Line 3, Para. 1)

versus 是介词,意思是"与... 相比,以……为对手"。例如:

the problem of peace versus war 和平还是战争的问题

The match tonight is China versus Japan. 今晚的比赛是中国队对日本队。

2. But this simple calculation ignores the fact... (Line 5~6, Para. 1)

ignore 意思是"忽视,不理会",其形容词形式为 ignorant,常与介词 of 连用,意思是"无知的,不学无术的,没有受教育的"。例如:

The driver ignored the traffic light. 那个司机不理会红绿灯。

I was ignorant of the fact that the boss could be so strict. 我不知道老板居然那样严格。

3. More sophisticated analyses adjust for these extraneous influences. (Line 1, Para. 2)

sophisticated 在这里意思是"复杂的",还可表示"懂事故的,老于事故的"。例如:

a sophisticated computer 精密的电脑

She seems very sophisticated for her age. 她在她的年纪看来似乎非常懂世故。

4. ...chances are your sky-high tuition is... (Line 2, Para. 4)

chances are (that)... 意思是"很可能"。例如:

Chances are that he has heard the news. 他很可能已经听到了这一消息。

5. That's up from 30 percent and 6 percent, respectively... (Line 7, Para. 4)

respectively 意思是"分别地,各自地"。例如:

My brother and I ordered a hot dog and a pizza respectively. 我和我弟弟分别要了热狗和比萨。

Explanations

受过高等教育的人所从事的职业是否比未受过高等教育的人所从事的职业更好呢?我们又该如何衡量两者的价值呢?看看作者是如何分析的。

21. C) 推断题。根据文章第一段第五句 But this simple calculation ignores... than nongraduates. 得知:传统的计算方法忽略了这样的事实:大学毕业生很可能来自社会经济较好的家庭,而且他们的智商很可能比非大学生高。故判断出 C 项为正确答案。

22. C) 推断题。根据文章第三段判断出:从 1979 年开始,高等教育的经济回升事实上并未提高。故 C 项为正确答案。

23. C) 推断题。根据文章第三段,在 1979 年到 1997 年,不论是大学毕业生还是高中毕业的工人们,其经济状况都有下降。C 项与原文意思不符,故选 C 项。

24. C) 推断题。文章最后一段告诉我们:越来越多的大学毕业生也开始从事原先工人们所从事的工作了,由此判断:大学毕业生越来越多了。故选 C 项。

25. A) 文章标题推断题。文章第一段作者就指出高等教育经济回升的衡量是不确切的,是在夸大其词。以下几段作者详细分析了其现象及原因。由此判断 A 项正确。

Passage 4

Notes

1. I have no choice but to be be skeptical about... (Line 1, Para. 1)

be skeptical about/of 意思是"对……怀疑"。例如:

I am skeptical about the team's chances of winning. 我对那支球队的获胜机会表示怀疑。

He was skeptical of the announcement made by the government. 他怀疑政府的宣告(公告)。

2. ...and proceeded to say that... (Line 5, Para. 1)

proceeded to do/with sth. 意思是"开始做"。例如:

After the applause died down, the pianist proceeded to play. 掌声停后,钢琴家开始演奏。

He cleared his throat and then proceeded with his speech. 他清了清嗓子后开始说话(演讲)。

3. Notwithstanding the fact that... (Line 6, Para. 1)

notwithstanding 意思是"虽然,尽管",意思同 in spite of 。例如:

He got drunk at the party notwithstanding his wife's warning.

他不管妻子的警告,仍然在宴会上喝得烂醉。

They traveled on, notwithstanding the storm. 尽管有暴风雨,他们仍然继续赶路。

4. ...coming up with ways to make computers... (Line 2~3, Para. 2)

come up with 在这里意思是"想出、找出(答案、方法、计划)"。例如:

come up with a solution 找出解决办法

He could always come up with a reason for them to linger another month.

他总能想出个理由来让他们再耽搁上一个月。

5. ... but the thought of reading Thackeray or Dickens... is a laughing matter. （Line 5～6，Para. 3）

Thackeray（萨克雷），Dickens（狄更斯），Wilkie Collins（科林斯）是英国小说家，Steinbeck（斯坦贝克）是美国小说家。Thackeray 著有长篇小说《名利场》，Dickens 著有《双城记》、《匹克威克外传》、《大卫·科波菲尔》等。Wilkie Collins 著有《白衣女人》、《月亮宝石》等；Steinbeck 著有《愤怒的葡萄》等。

6. They want to own the book that was authorized by the writer... （Line 3，Para. 4）

authorize 意思是"授权；认可，准许"。例如：

a custom authorized by time 经过漫长岁月业已被认可的习俗

He confidentially authorized me to act for him while he was absent. 他信任地授权我在他不在时代他行事。

Explanations

如今，我们常听到或用到 e-mail，e-book，e-shopping 等词，它们给人类的交流和生活的确带来了很大的方便，但它们真的能完全代替我们传统的生活方式吗？看看作者是怎么看待这个问题的。

26. C）推断题。根据文章第一段第一句可判断出：阻碍电子书籍这项产业的不是技术，而是常识（common sense）。所以 C 项与原文相符。

27. A）细节题。根据文章第二段第一句 The e-book... is environmentally friendly, which is true. 可知，A 项为正确答案。

28. D）词汇题。tactile 意思是"触觉的"，故 D 项为正确答案。

29. C）推断题。文章第三段最后一句和第四段第一句提到：在电子书籍上阅读萨克雷、狄更斯、斯坦贝克等名人的著作是不可能的，而且这些书籍不仅仅是词汇的表述，它们有装饰漂亮的封面，因为它们是作者创造力的表现。由此可知 C 项为正确答案。

30. B）推断题。文章第一段作者指出：怀疑电子书籍；第三段举例说明通过 e-book 读一些名家名著是不可能的，毕竟那样不能领会作者的思想及创造力。由此判断：作者反对 e-book，故 B 项为正确答案。

Passage 5

Keys

31. Closely monitored by audience and media.

32. Through statistics.

33. The salaries.

34. Feel shocked.

35. Greater salary difference.

Notes

1. Likewise, most workers who make a mistake... of an upset crowd. （Line 5～6，Para. 1）

likewise 意思是"同样地"。这句话的意思是：大多数犯了错误的工人听不到老板和同事的奚落声。

2. ... is constantly monitored by fans... （Line 6～7，Para. 1）

monitor 在这里做动词，意思是"监视，监督"。例如：

monitor observance of the declaration 监督宣言的遵守情况

You'll have to monitor your eating constantly. 你一定要经常注意控制饮食。

3. ... when a star player signs a multimillion dollar contract... （Line 1，Para. 2）

sign a contract 意思是"签订合同"，常与 contract 连用的短语还有：

break（violate）a contract 违反合同

cancel a contract 取消合同

make a contract 订立合同

carry out(execute) a contract 履行合同

4. Ironically, rules imposed by... (Line 4，Para. 2)

ironically 意思是"出乎意料地,具有讽刺意味地",在这里表示与上文形成转折、对比。

5. ... contribute to the seemingly inconsistent economics of players' salaries. (Line 5，Para. 2)

contribute to 在这里意思是"成为……的原因;导致",还可作"有贡献,有助于"讲。例如:

Smoking may contribute to lung cancer. 吸烟可能导致肺癌。

The construction of a highway will contribute to the growth of the suburbs.

建造高速公路将有助于郊区的发展。

He contributed $5 to the charity every payday. 他每逢发薪日都捐 5 美元给慈善事业。

Unit 18

Section A   Skimming and Scanning

Directions：（略）

Passage 1

Dominance within the Family

1. Within the family we should see co-operation and teamwork between equals who divide up the work which has to be done between them in a functional way so that each becomes expert and effective in his or her part of what has to be done.

2. But on the whole a family's income is usually earned by the male and income and money pass through his hands to the family. He then may, if he so wishes, use this controlling position to dominate the female. This applies equally well to the female who is a breadwinner, who may then use her controlling position to dominate. And this applies also when the income of one is much larger than that of the other.

3. And both are in the position to use sex as a means of dominating the other, if they so wish, rewarding *compliance*（顺从）with sex, punishing disagreement by withholding sex.

4. Women have at times been persuaded by traditions or beliefs into accepting domination and sometimes exploitation as the norm. And women have in the past been denied education and full equality with men within the family and in the community in which they live.

5. The words "assertiveness" and "asserting" are used at times to indicate that one person is attempting to dominate the other. Dominating and "asserting" put one person's personal gain, likes, dislikes against the other person's interests, introduces conflict and competition into what should be co-operation and teamwork.

6. Considering only women and children, the family protects women and children while children grow to maturity, till children become independent adults. It also protects women from disadvantages resulting from caring for and looking after the family during this period.

7. What keeps the family in place and gives it strength is restricting sex to within marriage. Men are then motivated to marry, to provide and care for wife and children, and themselves gain much strength from doing so.

8. When women are persuaded to make themselves available for sex outside marriage they help to *dismantle*（拆除）not only their own protection and security but also that of their children.

9. In such circumstances the selfish instinctive behaviour of the non-feeling primitive animal is asserting itself, is attempting to dominate, overcome and control human feeling of care, affection, concern for members of one's own family and for other people in human societies.

Living in a hostile environment

10. We have seen that when one member of a family dominates others and when competition, conflict and struggle replace co-operation and teamwork, all the family members suffer as a result.

11. We know that dominating does not work in normal circumstances. Authoritarian organizations are much less effective than participative ones. In authoritarian organizations morale is low, people cease to care and tend to work against each other instead of co-operating with each other for the benefit of the organization, which applies equally well to a family.

12. In the working environment women are just as oppressed and exploited as men are. When women receive lower wages for work of equal value then this is bad for men and women alike. When some people in a group are being underpaid, the pay of the others is being pushed down.

13. Outside the family a struggle is taking place. The breadwinner is competing for work and income on behalf of the family. He is also struggling against those who wish to exploit him (and thus his family) and who oppress so as to exploit.

14. So outside the family we see a widespread struggle against those who wish to dominate other people, against those who want primitive power over others, against those who wish to exploit, against those who may brutally and without feeling oppress human beings so as to exploit them. And "to exploit" includes the whole range of antisocial decisions and activities of those who put profit before people and community.

15. We also saw that on the whole it is men who earn the family's income which then often passes through their hands to the family, and that as a result of the work men do outside the family, it is largely men who gain controlling positions in the working environment.

16. So on the surface it may seem as if it is men who try to dominate women within the family and it is men who oppress and exploit women in the working environment.

17. Anyone who sees men and women co-operating with each other within a family, struggling side by side, back to back, and sees them co-operating with each other and helping each other in the outside working environment, for a more secure and better life for their families, knows how strong and effective they are together.

18. Blaming men as such, within the family and outside it, when women are oppressed and exploited, amounts to putting women against men, to separating them from each other, a "divide so as to conquer" process which weakens both in their joint struggle for a better life. It robs men of the support of their families when they are struggling outside the family against being exploited. It robs women of the support of their families while bringing up children to adulthood, when improving their skills or knowledge when returning to work or to improve the quality of their lives.

19. Dominance and oppression take place within and outside the family, against men and women alike. Both men and women are exploited and oppressed in the working environment to a very considerable degree.

20. What we see in the working environment is a world-wide struggle to achieve a humane way of life, each person, family or community struggling to advance at their own level of development, struggling against those who wish to dominate, exploit, oppress, a struggle whose successful outcome depends on trustful co-operation, companionship and teamwork.

21. Sometimes one has to fight to preserve a good way of life, to prevent others from taking what has been achieved, or one is expected to fight on behalf of those who dominate and exploit.

22. The fighting is usually done by men who are conditioned to fight, *maim*（使残废）and kill. Their training weakens and bypasses humane emotions of care, concern and affection for other people, in effect tends to brutalize them.

23. And we now see in some countries women joining the armed forces, police and security organizations and being trained in somewhat similar ways.

24. Our primitive animal ancestors behaved instinctively. Hunt for food, kill or be killed, fight or flee, copulate, care for own young for a very short and limited period, self before others, regardless of needs of others, marking out and defending territory. Later mammals tend to have feelings, care and affection for their young. Human beings think as well as feel, and care for and look after their young for many years.

25. So conditioning to fight, maim and kill amounts to a throwback to primitive animal behavior, to behavior which puts self before others, a throwback to beast-like behavior for those who attack, to beast-like behavior to counter beast-like behavior for those who defend.

26. But only some people behave in such corrupted ways. There are those many who put people first, who know the difference between human and inhuman behavior, who believe in participative behavior and in democratic government.

27. We saw that casual sex dehumanizes, that it blocks affection and increases cold and selfish behavior against others, that society corrupts itself when promiscuity (casual sex) spreads.

28. The media seem to be concentrating on portraying superstition, violence and casual-sex behavior as acceptable, so strengthening primitive uncaring and antisocial behavior towards others. And images penetrate deeply into the human mind.

29. Sexually explicit and pornographic material would seem to be taking this process even further.

30. So media are at present persuading and conditioning people into thinking that antisocial behavior will not have unpleasant consequences. However, the cost to the community of the kind of negative and antisocial behavior outlined in the sections above, of the lowering of the quality of life, is enormous.

31. What we see is an almost intentional-seeming conditioning towards antisocial behavior which breaks up families and so weakens individuals, and which divides people against each other and so weakens them even further.

32. It looks as if men are being conditioned into opting out of their responsibilities for family, wife and children. Women, on the other hand, are apparently being conditioned into giving away the real support and security they and their children could expect from husband and family, for no real gain.

1. Women have at times been persuaded by traditions or beliefs into accepting domination and sometimes exploitation as the norm.

2. When women receive lower wages for work of equal value then this is good for men.

3. Dominance and oppression take place within and outside the family, against men and women alike.

4. Our primitive animal ancestors cared for own young for a very long period.

5. The fighting is usually done by men who are conditioned to fight, maim and kill.

6. It looks as if men are being forced to opt out of their responsibilities for family, wife and children.

7. According to the author, the dominant position in the family resulted from unequal social status.

8. The family protects women and children while children grow to maturity, till children become _____.

9. When some people in a group are being underpaid, the pay of the others is being _____.

10. So media are at present persuading and conditioning people into thinking that antisocial behavior will not have _____.

Section B　Discourse Vocabulary Test
Directions：（略）

Passage 2

Automation refers to the __11__ of electronic control and automatic operation of productive machinery. It reduces the human factors, mental and physical, in production, and is designed to make possible the manufacture of more goods with fewer workers. The __12__ of automation in American industry has been called the "Second Industrial Revolution."

Labor's concern over automation __13__ from uncertainty about the effects on employment, and fears of major changes in jobs. In the main, labor has taken the view that resistance to technical change is __14__. Eventually, the result of automation may well be an increase in employment, since it is expected that vast industries will grow up around manufacturing, maintaining, and repairing automation equipment. The interest of labor lies in bringing about the __15__ with a minimum of inconvenience and distress to the workers involved. Also, union spokesmen emphasize that the benefit of the increased production and lower costs made possible by automation should be shared by workers in the form of higher wages, more leisure, and improved living __16__.

To protect the interests of their members in the era of automation, unions have __17__ a number of new policies. One of these is the promotion of supplementary unemployment benefit plans. It is __18__ that since the employer involved in such a plan has a direct financial interest in preventing unemployment, he will have a strong drive for planning new installations so as to cause the least possible problems in jobs and job assignments. Some unions are working for dismissal pay agreements, requiring that __19__ dismissed workers be paid a sum of money based on length of service. Another approach is the idea of the "improvement factor", which calls for wage increases based on increases in productivity. It is __20__, however, that labor will rely mainly on reduction in working hours in order to gain a full share in the fruit of automation.

A) unfruitful   I) temporary

B) standards   J) development

C) raise   K) successful

D) emphasized   L) possible

E) arises   M) adapted

F) transition   N) adopted

G) introduction   O) permanently

H) transmission

Section C   Reading in Depth

Directions:（略）

Passage 3

It is natural for young people to be critical of their parents at times and to blame them for most of the misunderstandings between them. They have always complained, more or less justly, that their parents are out of touch with modern ways; that they are possessive and dominant; that they do not trust their children to deal with crises; that they talk too much about certain problems—and that they have no sense of humor, at least in parent-child relationships.

I think it is true that parents often underestimate their teenage children and also forget how they themselves felt when young.

Young people often irritate their parents with their choices in clothes and hairstyles, in entertainers and music. This is not their motive. They feel cut off from the adult world into which they have not yet been accepted. So they create a culture and society of their own. Then, if it turns out that their music or entertainers or vocabulary or clothes or hairstyle irritate their parents, this gives them additional enjoyment. They feel they are superior, at least in a small way, and that they are leaders in style and taste.

Sometimes you are resistant, and proud because you do not want your parents to approve of what you do . If they did approve, it looks as if you are betraying your own age group. But in that case, you are assuming that you are the underdog: you can't win but at least you can keep your honor. This is a passive way of looking at things. It is natural enough after long years of childhood, when you were completely under your parents' control. But it ignores the fact that you are now beginning to be responsible for yourself.

If you plan to control your life, co-operation can be part of that plan, you can charm others, especially your parents, into doing things the way you want. You can impress others with your sense of responsibility and initiative, so that they will give you the authority to do what you want to do.

21. The author is primarily addressing _____ .

     A) parents of teenagers   B) newspaper readers

     C) teenagers   D) those who give advice to teenagers

大学英语 4 级阅读与简答（新题型）

22. The first paragraph is mainly about _____.

    A) the teenagers' criticism of their parents

    B) misunderstandings between teenagers and their parents

    C) the dominance of the parents over their children

    D) the teenagers' ability to deal with crises

23. Teenagers tend to have strange clothes and hairstyles because they _____.

    A) want to irritate their parents

    B) have a strong desire to be leaders in style and taste

    C) have no other way to enjoy themselves better

    D) want to show their existence by creating a culture of their own

24. Teenagers do not want their parents to approve of whatever they do because they _____.

    A) have a desire to be independent

    B) feel that they are superior in a small way to the adults

    C) are not likely to win over the adults

    D) have already been accepted into the adult world

25. To improve parent-child relationships, teenagers are advised to be _____.

    A) obedient   B) responsible   C) independent   D) co-operative

Passage 4

The long years of food shortage in this country have suddenly given way to apparent abundance. Stores and shops are choked with food. *Rationing*（定量供应）is virtually suspended, and overseas suppliers have been asked to hold back deliveries. Yet, instead of joy, there is widespread uneasiness and confusion. Why do food prices keep on rising, when there seems to be so much more food about? Is the abundance only temporary, or has it come to stay? Does it mean that we need to think less now about producing more food at home? No one knows what to expect.

The recent growth of export surpluses on the world food market has certainly been unexpectedly great, partly because a strange sequence of two successful grain harvests in North America is now being followed by a third. Most of Britain's overseas suppliers of meat, too, are offering more this year and home production has also risen.

But the effect of all this on the food situation in this country has been made worse by a simultaneous rise in food prices, due chiefly to the gradual cutting down of government support for food. The shops are overstocked with food not only because there is more food available, but also because people, frightened by high prices, are buying less of it.

Moreover, the rise in domestic prices has come at a time when world prices have begun to fall, with the result that imported food, with the exception of grain, is often cheaper than the home-produced variety. And now grain prices, too, are falling. Consumers are beginning to ask why they should not be enabled to benefit from this trend.

The significance of these developments is not lost on farmers. The older generation has seen it all happen before. Despite the present price and market guarantees, farmers fear they are about to be squeezed between cheap food imports and a shrinking home market. Present production is running at 51 per cent above pre-war levels, and the government has called for an expansion to 60 percent by 1956; but repeated Ministerial advice is carrying little weight and the expansion program is not working very well.

26. Why is there "wide-spread uneasiness and confusion" about the food situation in Britain?
    A) The abundant food supply is not expected to last.
    B) Despite the abundance, food prices keep rising.
    C) Britain is importing less food.
    D) Britain will cut back on its production of food.

27. The main reason for the rise in food prices is that _____.
    A) people are buying less food
    B) imported food is driving prices higher
    C) domestic food production has decreased
    D) the government is providing less support for agriculture

28. Why didn't the government's expansion program work very well?
    A) Because the farmers were uncertain about the financial support the government guaranteed.
    B) Because the farmers were uncertain about the benefits of expanding production.
    C) Because the farmers were uncertain whether foreign markets could be found for their produce.
    D) Because the older generation of farmers were strongly against the program.

29. The decrease in world food prices was a result of _____.
    A) a sharp fall in the purchasing power of the consumers
    B) a sharp fall in the cost of food production
    C) the overproduction food in the food-importing countries
    D) the overproduction on the part of the main food-exporting countries

30. What did the future look like for Britain's food production at the time this article was written?
    A) It looks depressing despite government guarantees.
    B) An expansion of food production was at hand.
    C) British food producers would receive more government financial support.
    D) The fall in world food prices would benefit British food producers.

Section D　Short Answer Questions

Directions:（略）

Passage 5

The question of what children learn, and how they should learn it is continually being debated. Nobody dares any longer to defend the old system, the learning of lessons in a parrot fashion, the grammar-with-a-whip system, and under which, it is thought, children were made to learn passively. The theorists of modern psychology argue that we must understand the needs of children. Children are not just small adults; they are children who must be respected as such.

Well, you may say this is a good idea. But think further. What happens? "Education" becomes the responsibility not of teachers, but of psychologists. What happens then? Teachers worry too much about the psychological implications of their lessons, and forget about the subjects themselves. If a child dislikes a lesson, the teacher feels that it is his fault, not the child's. So teachers worry whether history is "relevant" to modern young children. And do they dare to recount stories about violent battles? Or will this make the children themselves violent? Can they tell their classes about children of different races, or will this encourage racial hatred?

You see, you can go too far. Influenced by educational theorists, who have nothing better to do than write books about their ideas, teachers leave their teacher-training colleges filled with grand, psychological ideas about children and their needs. They make elaborate, sophisticated preparations and try out their "modern methods" on the long-suffering children. Since one "modern method" rapidly replaces another, the poor kids will have had a good bellyful by the time they leave school. Frequently the modern methods are so sophisticated that they fail to be understood by the teachers, let alone the children. And the relaxed discipline may eventually prevent all but a handful of children from learning anything.

31. People do not dare to defend the old system mainly because under the old system _____.

_____　_____　_____　_____　_____

_____　_____　_____　_____　_____

32. What do the modern psychologists maintain?

_____　_____　_____　_____　_____

_____　_____　_____　_____　_____

33. What happens when teachers pay too much attention to the psychology of their lessons?

_____　_____　_____　_____　_____

_____　_____　_____　_____　_____

34. According to theorists of modern psychology, why are violent battles considered as irrelevant to modern young children?

_____　_____　_____　_____　_____

_____　_____　_____　_____　_____

35. According to the passage, the modern methods are understood by neither _____.

_____　_____　_____　_____　_____

_____　_____　_____　_____　_____

Notes and Explanations

Passage 1

Explanations

1. [Y] 第四段第一句提到 Women have at times been persuaded by traditions or beliefs into accepting domination and sometimes exploitation as the norm. 长期以来传统和信仰都在说服女性把被统治甚至被剥削作为一种社会常规。故答案应为 Yes。

2. [N] 第十二段第二句提到 When women receive lower wages for work of equal value then this is bad for

men and women alike. 当女性做（与男性）相同的工作，却得到较低的报酬时，这其实对于男性和女性都不好。所以答案应为 No。

3. [Y] 第十九段第一句提到 Dominance and oppression take place within and outside the family, against men and women alike. 男性和女性都受到了家庭内外的统治和压迫。故答案应为 Yes。

4. [N] 第二十四段提到 Our primitive animal ancestors behaved instinctively. Hunt for food, kill or be killed, fight or flee, copulate, care for own young for a very short and limited period, self before others, regardless of needs of others, marking out and defending territory. 我们原始时代的祖先根据本能行事。捕猎食物，杀人或被杀，战斗或逃亡，交配，在很短、很有限的时间内照顾后代，先己后人，无视别人的需要，占领并保卫自己的领土。所以答案应为 No。

5. [Y] 第二十二段第一句提到 The fighting is usually done by men who are conditioned to fight, maim and kill。那些被训练过的、会打仗、会杀人的男人通常去参与战争。故答案应为 Yes。

6. [N] 最后一段第一句提到 It looks as if men are being conditioned into opting out of their responsibilities for family, wife and children. 看起来男人是出于对家庭、妻子和孩子的责任做出选择，而不是被迫的（forced）。所以答案应为 No。

7. [NG] 通读全文可以发现，文章主要在讨论男性和女性在家庭中的不同地位和他们承担的不同责任。故答案应为 Not Given。

8. 第六段第一句提到 Considering only women and children, the family protects women and children while children grow to maturity, till children become independent adults. 对于妇女和孩子，在孩子成长的过程中，他们会受到保护，直到孩子成为可以独立生活的成年人。从而得出答案为 **independent adults**。

9. 第十二段最后一句提到 When some people in a group are being underpaid, the pay of the others is being pushed down. 当一个群体中的一些人被克扣工资的时候，其他人的薪水也降低了。所以答案应为 **pushed down**。

10. 第三十段第一句提到 So media are at present persuading and conditioning people into thinking that antisocial behavior will not have unpleasant consequences. 现在的媒体在说服人们并使他们相信，反社会的行为不会产生不良的后果。从中得知 **unpleasant consequences** 为本题的正确答案。

Passage 2

Notes

1. Automation refers to the introduction... (Line 1, Para. 1)

   refer to 在这里意思是"指的是"，还可作"谈及；参考，参阅"讲。例如：

   Are you referring to me? 你指的是我吗？

   In his speech, he didn't refer to the problem at all. 在演讲中，他丝毫未触及那个问题。

   If you have some questions, refer to the guidebook. 如果你有问题请参阅旅游指南。

2. Labor's concern over automation arises from... (Line 1, Para. 2)

   arise from 意思是"由（从）……产生（发生）"。例如：

   Accidents can arise from carelessness. 意外事件可能因疏忽而引起。

   New difficulties will arise from the present situation. 目前这种状况将会产生新的困难。

3. In the main, labor has taken the view that... (Line 2, Para. 2)

   in the main 意思是"基本上，大体上"，意思同 in general。例如：

   In the main, the pupils did well in the test. 总的说来，学生在这次考试中成绩不错。

   These businessmen are in the main honest. 这些商人基本上是诚实的。

4. ...he will have a strong drive for planning... (Line 4, Para. 3)

   drive 在这里是名词，意思是"冲动，欲望"。例如：

one's drive for sociability 交际欲

She has tremendous drive toward success. 她有争取成功的强烈欲望。

5. ...which calls for wage increases... (Line 7～8, Para. 3)

call for 在这里意思是"需要"。例如：

This position calls for an experienced secretary. 这一职位需要有经验的秘书来承担。

6. ...labor will rely mainly on reduction... (Line 8, Para. 3)

rely on 意思是"依靠,指望,信赖"。例如：

Don't rely on my seeing you off. 不要指望我为你送行。

We can't rely on her for help. 我们不能指望她帮忙。

You may not rely on the weather report. 天气预报不足为信。

Explanations

11. [G] 语法规则要求此处应填一个名词作介词 to 的宾语。选项 B、F、G、H、J 是名词。其中 introduction 意思是"被采用的东西；刚被引进的东西"，符合句子意思的要求。

12. [J] 语法规则要求此处应填一个名词作句子的主语。句子的谓语要求主语是单数名词。选项 F、G、H、J 符合该要求。development 意思是"发展"，符合上下文意思的要求。

13. [E] 语法规则要求此处应填一个动词作谓语。主语 concern 要求谓语的形式是第三人称单数。选项 E 符合该条件。arise from 意思是"起因于，因……产生(或造成)"，符合句子的意思。

14. [A] 语法规则要求此处应填一个形容词作表语。选项 A、I、K、L 是形容词。unfruitful 意为"无效的,徒劳的"，与句意相符，因此选项 A 正确。

15. [F] 语法规则要求此处应填一个名词作介词 about 的宾语。transition 是"转变,转换,过渡"的意思，与句意相符。

16. [B] 语法规则要求此处应填一个复数名词与 higher wages, more leisure 一起作介词 of 的并列宾语。选项中的名词只有 standards 是复数形式。living standards 意为"生活水平"，符合上下文意思的要求。

17. [N] 语法规则要求此处应填一个动词的过去分词形式构成现在完成时。选项 D、M、N 是该形式。adopt 意为"采用,采纳"，与句子的意思相符，故选项 N 正确。

18. [D] 语法规则要求此处应填一个动词的过去分词形式构成被动语态。emphasize 意思是"强调"。It is emphasized that... 是一常用句型，在这里符合上下文意思的要求。

19. [O] 语法规则要求此处应填一个副词来修饰形容词 dismissed。只有 O 项 permanently(永久地)与此条件相符，意思上也符合上下文的要求。

20. [L] 语法规则要求此处应填一个形容词作表语。It is possible that... 是常用句型，意思是"……是可能的"，符合上下文意思的要求。

Passage 3

Notes

1. It is natural for young people to be critical of... (Line 1, Para. 1)

be critical of 意思是"爱挑剔的,吹毛求疵的"。例如：

That teacher is too critical of his students. 那位老师对学生太过严厉。

Why are you so critical of everything I wear? 你为什么对我穿的每件衣服都这般挑剔？

2. They have always complained, more or less justly... (Line 2, Para. 1)

more or less 意思是"或多或少；有几分"。例如：

All the passengers were more or less wounded in the accident. 在这次事故中，所有乘客或多或少受了伤。

They've more or less finished their work. 他们已差不多完成了工作。

3. ...and that they have no sense of humor... (Line 5, Para. 1)

have a sense of sth. 意思是"有……的感觉(能力、观念)"。例如：

have a sense of shame 有羞耻心

have a sense of responsibility 有责任感

He has no sense of business. 他没有经商意识。

4. ...because you do not want your parents to approve of what you do. (Line 1~2, Para. 4)

approve of 意思是"赞成,许可"。例如：

I can hardly approve of his marriage. 我很难赞成他的婚姻。

Everybody approved of the plans for a new school building. 大家都赞成建造一所新校舍的计划。

5. ...you are now beginning to be responsible for yourself. (Line 5~6, Para. 4)

be responsible for 意思是"对……负责任"。例如：

We are responsible for our own actions. 我们应该对自己的行为负责。

Parents are responsible for their children's safety. 父母应该负责子女的安全。

6. ...you can charm others, especially your parents, into doing things the way you want. (Line 1~2, Para. 5)

charm sb. into doing sth. 意思是"哄某人做某事"。例如：

His daughter charmed him into buying her a car. 他的女儿哄得他为她买了一辆汽车。

John charmed his mother into approving of his plan. 约翰哄得他母亲同意了他的计划。

Explanations

　　"代沟"是一个永远的话题,父母与孩子之间常常产生误解,有时相互抱怨,甚至在当今社会造成家破人亡。这篇文章作者针对十几岁的孩子们,给他们提出建议:如何与父母进行沟通,从而获得父母的支持与理解。

21. **C)** 推断题。从文章第四段和第五段的人称 you, your 推断出:作者是在对孩子们讲话。故选项 C 为正确答案。

22. **A)** 段落主题推断题。文章第一段主要讲到孩子对父母们的抱怨。选项 B、C 只是抱怨内容的一部分;选项 D 断章取义,这句话在文章中的完整理解应为:孩子们抱怨父母不信任他们处理紧急情况的能力。

23. **D)** 推断题。文章第三段主要告诉我们:孩子们穿奇装异服,留奇怪的发型等,主要是向成年人证明他们有自己的文化品味,他们是不可忽视的群体。故选项 D 为正确答案。

24. **A)** 推断题。根据文章第四段可知,如果家长同意他们所为,他们会感到是对自己同龄人的背叛,感到自己是失败者,言外之意,他们想保持自己的东西,想独立。故选项 A 为正确答案。

25. **D)** 推断题。文章第五段第一句 co-operation 即表明选项 D 正确。

Passage 4

Notes

1. ...have suddenly given way to... (Line 1, Para. 1)

give way to 意思是"取代;屈服,让步"。例如：

The company gave way to the workers' demand. 那家公司让步,答应了工人的要求。

Coal gave way to petroleum. 煤炭被石油取代。

2. Stores and shops are choked with food. (Line 2, Para. 1)

be choked with 意思是"噎住,阻塞"。例如：

She was choked with anger. 她气得说不出话来。

The center of the city was choked with cars. 市中心挤满了汽车。

3. ...due chiefly to the gradual cutting down of... (Line 2, Para. 3)

cut down 在这里意思是"缩减,减少……的量"。例如:

The car industry cut down production. 汽车制造业缩减了生产量。

We can't cut down our expenses on the research any more. 我们不能再削减研究的费用了。

4. ... with the exception of grain... (Line 2,Para. 4)

with the exception of 意思是"除……之外"。例如:

She likes all her teachers with the exception of Miss Smith. 除了史密斯小姐外,她喜欢所有的老师。

All the students passed the examinations with the solitary exception of William.

其他所有的学生考试都及格了,唯独威廉例外。

5. ... farmers fear they are about to be squeezed... (Line 2~3,Para. 5)

be about to do 意思是"将要做,正要做"。例如:

The sun is about to set in the west. 太阳快要落山了。

I was about to go to bed,when the phone rang. 我正要上床睡觉,电话铃响了。

Explanations

　　在经济学领域中,"市场"常被喻为"看不见的手",它调节市场价格的运行。同时,政府在一定情况下也会干预经济。这由市场的运行规律所决定。

26. B) 推断题。文章第一段第四句到第一段结束,作者用了一连串的问句提出疑问,由这些问题判断出选项 B 为正确答案。

27. D) 细节题。根据文章第三段第一句 due chiefly to the gradual cutting down of government support for food 可知选项 D 为正确答案。

28. B) 推断题。根据文章第五段第三句 Despite the present price ... a shrinking home market. 推断出:尽管由于目前价格及市场的保障,但农民们还是担心会被便宜的进口食品和市场的缩减而挤垮。所以选项 B 与原文相符。

29. D) 推断题。文章第二段告诉我们:英国和北美这些大的食品出口国的出口量急剧增加,由此推断出这是造成世界其他国家食品价格下降的原因之一。故选项 D 为正确答案。

30. A) 推断题。文章第一段作者对食物丰富带来的问题提出质疑。第二段指出如北美、英国一些大的食品出口国的出口量的增加给世界其他国家造成了影响。第三、第四、第五段又分析了价格的变化对农民的影响及农民们担心的问题。由以上分析判断出选项 A 为正确答案。

Passage 5

Keys

31. children were made to learn passively

32. Children must be understood and respected.

33. They do not pay enough attention to the actual lessons.

34. Because they will make the children themselves violent.

35. teachers nor children

Notes

1. ... children were made to learn passively. (Line 3~4,Para. 1)

make 在此是使役动词,意思是"强迫,迫使",后接不定式短语作宾语补语时省略 to;不定式短语在被动句中作主语补语时 to 不能省略。例如:

They made me repeat the story. 他们逼我又把那事讲了一遍。

He must be made to comply with the rules. 必须强迫他遵守这些规则。

2. ... they are children who must be respected as such. (Line 5, Para. 1)

such 是代词，用以复指前文的 children。例如：

She is a competent leader and has always been regarded as such by her colleagues.

她是个很有能力的领导人，她的同事一向都是这样认为的。

Cricket was boring. Such was her opinion before meeting Ian.

打板球没意思，她在认识伊恩以前就是这种看法。

3. ... they fail to be understood by the teachers, let alone the children. (Line 6～7, Para. 3)

let alone 意思是"更不用说"；在句中作连词，前后连接两个相同成分。例如：

There isn't enough room for us, let alone six dogs and a cat.

连我们的地方都不够，更不用说六条狗和一只猫了。

I haven't decided on the menu yet, let alone bought the food.

我还没有决定吃什么菜呢，更不用说买菜了。

4. And the relaxed discipline may eventually prevent all but a handful of children from learning anything. (Line 7～8, Para. 3)

▷but 意思是"除了……以外"；在句中作介词，常用于否定词（nobody, none, nowhere 等）、疑问词（who, where 等）以及 all, everyone, anyone 等之后。例如：

Everyone was there but him. 除了他之外，所有的人都在。

Nobody but you could be so selfish. 除了你之外，谁也不会这样自私。

▷此外，搭配 nothing but 表示"只能"；anything but 表示"绝不"。例如：

Nothing but trouble will come of this plan. 这个计划只能带来麻烦。

The problem is anything but easy. 这个问题可绝对不容易。

Unit 19

Section A　Skimming and Scanning

Directions：（略）

Passage 1

Parents and Children

1. Sometimes, when Tom Krattenmaker and his 16-year-old daughter, Holland, listen to rock music together and talk about pop culture—interests they both enjoy—he recalls his more-distant relationship with his parents when he was a teenager. "I would never [have said] to my mom, Hey, the new Weezer album is really great—how do you like it?" says Mr. Krattenmaker, of Yardley, Pa. "There was just a complete gap in sensibility and taste, a virtual gulf."

2. Music was not the only gulf. From clothing and hairstyles to activities and expectations, earlier generations of parents and children often appeared to revolve in separate orbits.

3. Today, the generation gap has not disappeared, but it is shrinking in many families. The old authoritarian approach to discipline—a starchy "Because I said so, that's why"—is giving way to a new *egalitarianism*（平等主义）and a "Come, let us reason together" attitude.

4. The result can be a rewarding closeness among family members. Conversations that would not have taken place a generation ago—or that would have been awkward, on subjects such as sex and drugs—now are comfortable and common. And parent-child activities, from shopping to sports, involve an easy camaraderie that can continue into adulthood.

5. No wonder greeting cards today carry the message, "To my mother, my best friend."

6. But family experts caution that the new equality can also have a downside, diminishing respect for parents. "There's still a lot of strict, authoritarian parenting out there, but there is a change happening," says Kerrie Laguna, a mother of two young children and a psychology professor at Lebanon Valley College in Annville, Pa. "In the middle of that change, there is a lot of confusion among parents."

7. Family researchers offer a variety of reasons for these evolving roles and attitudes. They see the 1960s as a benchmark. Dramatic cultural shifts led to more open communication and a more democratic process that encourages everyone to have a say.

8. "My parents were on the 'before' side of that shift, whereas today's parents, the 40-somethings, were on the 'after' side," explains Krattenmaker, news director at Swarthmore College. "It's much easier for 40-somethings and today's teenagers to relate to one another. It's not a total cakewalk for parents these days, because life is more complicated, but 'sharing interests' does make it more fun to be a parent now."

Parents and children as friends

1. "Fun" is, in fact, a word heard far more frequently in families today than in the past, when "duty" and "responsibility" were often operative words.

2. Parents today are more youthful in appearance and attitudes. From blue jeans to blow-dries, their clothes and hairstyles are more casual, helping to bridge the sartorial divide. Those who are athletically inclined also enjoy rollerblading, snowboarding, and rock-climbing with their offspring.

3. For the past three years, Kathy and Phil Dalby of Arnold, Md. have spent at least one evening a week, and sometimes two, at a climbing gym with their three children. "It's great to be able to work together," Mrs. Dalby says. "We discuss various climbs and where the hard parts are. Sometimes that leads to other conversations, and sometimes it doesn't. We're definitely closer."

4. A popular movement with roots in the 1970s, parent effectiveness training, has helped to reshape generational roles. The philosophy encourages children to describe their feelings about various situations. As a result, says Robert Billingham, a family-studies professor at Indiana University, "Parents and children began talking to each other in ways they had not before."

5. On the plus side, he adds, these conversations made parents realize that children may have important thoughts or feelings that adults need to be aware of.

6. But Professor Billingham also sees a downside: Many parents started making decisions based on what their child wanted. "The power shifted to children." Parents said, "I have to focus on making my child happy," as opposed to "I have to parent most appropriately."

7. Other changes are occurring as the ranks of working mothers grow. An increase in guilt on the part of busy parents makes them less eager to spend time disciplining, says Dr. Laguna of Lebanon Valley College.

8. Time-short parents also encourage children's independence, making them more responsible for themselves. They'll say, "We trust you to make the right decisions whether they're ready to assume the responsibility or not," says Billingham.

9. The self-esteem movement of the past quarter-century has also affected family dynamics. Some parents worry that if they tell their child no, or impose limits, it will hurt the child's self-esteem.

10. Yet, parents who don't set rules risk becoming "so powerless in their own homes that they feel out of control and sometimes afraid," cautions Dennis Lowe, director of the Center for the Family at Pepperdine University in Malibu, Calif.

11. He believes that parents—in their eagerness to keep the peace and avoid arguments—miss an opportunity to teach children how to resolve conflicts, rather than simply avoiding them.

12. Although sensitive and democratic parenting has its advantages, Laguna expresses concern about "almost epidemic numbers" of children who have few boundaries or expectations.

13. Dr. Lowe and his wife, Emily, try to maintain structure and boundaries by taking a traditional approach with their children, ages 10 and 14. They also strive for a united front. Challenges arise, he says, when one parent wants an egalitarian relationship with a child, while the other parent wants to set limits.

大学英语 4 级阅读与简答（新题型）

14. "Probably the democratic approach is not bad in and of itself," Lowe says. "It's when it swings so far that it promotes lack of rules and structure and discipline for children. Problems also arise when it promotes *overindulgence* (过分纵容), sometimes in an effort to avoid 'harming' the relationship, rather than teaching children moderation and the limits of life."

15. Overindulgence, Lowe says, can actually be a sign of neglect—neglecting values, neglecting teaching opportunities, and neglecting the relationship. To be successful, people need an appreciation for rules and limits.

16. To give their own children that appreciation, the Lowes discusses everything from the kind of movies the children can watch to what is realistic financially.

17. Lowe sees some parents trying to cultivate friendship with their children even at very early ages. And he knows families where children call parents by their first names. "Rather than 'Mom' or 'Dad,' you have a 7-year-old saying, 'Hey, Gary,' " he explains, adding that a lack of respect for parents could carry over into relationships with teachers, bosses, and others in positions of authority.

Growing understanding

1. Still, encouraging signs exist. Vern Bengtson, who has studied generational changes as coauthor of a forthcoming book, "How Families Still Matter," finds a greater tolerance for divergence between generations today than in the past.

2. "Because of my own rebellion in the '60s, and because of the way I grew out of it, I can better accept my son's desire for independence and the crazy and sometimes rebellious things that he does," says Professor Bengtson of the University of Southern California, Los Angeles. "Based on my experience, he, too, will grow out of it."

3. As Dalby, the rock-climbing mom, looks around at friends and acquaintances, she is heartened to find that many people are far more open with the things they talk about with children. "There are a lot more dangers out there now. It's better to address them yourselves, because somebody will."

4. Where do families go from here? "Parents have to be careful not to totally be their kid's buddy, because they still have to be the authoritarian and disciplinarian," Krattenmaker says.

5. For her part, Laguna would like to see role distinctions that illustrate clearly who the adults are. "I don't think we're swinging back to the 'good old days', when parents ruled and children kept their mouths shut," Billingham says. "We're swinging toward a balance, where parents once again are viewed as parents, and not as peers to their children. Children are being viewed as very loved and valued family members, but without the power or authority of the parents. If we can get this balance, where parents are not afraid to be parents, and parents and children put the family as their priority, we'll be in great shape. I'm very optimistic about the future."

1. There was just a complete gap in sensibility and taste, a virtual gulf existing between Tom Krattenmaker and his parents.

2. Family experts caution that the new equality can also have a downside, diminishing respect for parents.

3. Parents today are more youthful in appearance and attitudes, which is helping to bridge the sartorial divide.

4. Other changes are occurring as the ranks of working hours of fathers grow.

5. Dennis Lowe, director of the Center for the Family at Pepperdine University in Malibu, Calif. believes that parents—in their eagerness to keep the peace and avoid arguments create an opportunity to teach children how to resolve conflicts.

6. In Lowe's mind, some parents trying to cultivate friendship with their children even at very early ages is positive.

7. Billingham holds an optimistic view about the future of generation gap.

8. From clothing and hairstyles to activities and expectations, earlier generations of parents and children often appeared to _____.

9. Parent effectiveness training encourages children to describe their feelings about _____.

10. Some parents worry that if they tell their child no, or impose limits, it will hurt _____.

Section B   Discourse Vocabulary Test

Directions:（略）

Passage 2

Americans often say that there are only two things a person can be __11__ of in life: death and taxes. Americans do not have a corner on the "death" market, but many people feel that the United States leads the world with the worst taxes.

Taxes __12__ of the money which people pay to support their government. There are __13__ three levels of government in the United States: federal, state, and city; therefore, there are three types of taxes.

Salaried people who earn more than a few thousand dollars must pay a certain __14__ of their salaries to the federal government. The percentage varies for individuals. It depends on their salaries. The federal government has a graduated income tax; that is the percentage of the tax increases as a person's income increases. With the high cost of taxes, people are not very happy on April 15, when the federal taxes are due.

The second tax is for the state government. Some states have an income tax __15__ to that of the federal government. Of course, the percentage for the state tax is lower. Other states have a sales tax, which is a percentage __16__ to any item which you buy in that state. Some states use income tax in __17__ to sales tax to raise their *revenues*（税收）. The state tax laws are diverse and confusing.

The third tax is for the city. This tax comes in two forms: property tax and excise tax, which is demanded on vehicles in a city. The cities __18__ these funds for education, police and fire departments, public works and *municipal*（城市的）buildings.

Since Americans pay such high taxes, they often feel that they are working one day each week just to pay their taxes. People always __19__ about taxes. Although Americans have __20__ views on many issues: religious, racial, cultural, and political, they tend to agree on one subject: Taxes are too high.

大学英语4级阅读与简答（新题型）

A) charged   I) assure

B) consist   J) conflicting

C) utilize   K) permanently

D) percent   L) income

E) similar   M) generally

F) complain   N) percentage

G) compose   O) addition

H) sure

Section C   Reading in Depth

Directions：（略）

Passage 3

    A man living absolutely alone in a desert or forest is free from other people; but he is not absolutely free. His freedom is limited in several ways. Firstly, by the things around him, such as wild animals or cliffs too steep to climb. Secondly, by his own needs: he must have sleep, water, food and shelter from extreme heat or cold. Lastly, by his own nature as a man: disease may attack him, and death will certainly come to him sooner or later.

    When men live together, on the other hand, protection against wild animals is easier and they can work together to get food and build shelters; but each man has to give up some of his freedom so that he can live happily with the others.

    When men become organized into very large groups, and civilization develops, it is possible to get freedom from hunger, thirst, cold, heat and many diseases, so that each person can live a happier life than he could if he were living alone; but such a society cannot work successfully unless the freedom of each human being is to some extent limited so that he is kept from hurting others. I am not free to kill others, nor to steal someone else's property, nor to behave in a way that offends against the moral sense of the society in which I live. I have to limit my own freedom myself so that others will not limit it too much: I agree to respect the rights of others, and in return they agree to respect mine.

    The advantages of such an agreement are great: one man can become a doctor, knowing that others will grow food, make clothes and build a house for him, in return for the work he does to keep them healthy. If each man had to grow his own food, make his own clothes, build his own house and learn to be his own doctor, he would find it impossible to do any one of these jobs really well. By working together, we make it possible for society to provide us all with food, clothes, shelter and medical care, while leaving each of us with as much freedom as it can.

21. A man living alone in a desert or forest _____.

    A) is absolutely free   B) feels lonely

    C) has limited freedom   D) enjoys no freedom

22. The author suggests that when men live together _____.

   A) they will have no freedom

   B) they can help each other protect against wild animals

   C) they have to work for their own foods and shelters

   D) everyone's happiness is at the expense of other people's freedom

23. Which of these is NOT true for a man living in an organized society?

   A) He can live a happier life.

   B) He has no such problems as hunger, thirst, cold and many diseases.

   C) He has no freedom to hurt others.

   D) He has to limit his own freedom.

24. According to the passage, to do all his own jobs, one would _____.

   A) enjoy a complete freedom

   B) find it a happy thing to do everything at his own will

   C) find it a very hard job to deal with everything by himself

   D) feel quite fantastic and stimulating

25. We may infer from the passage that the author _____.

   A) is against separation from a civilized society

   B) is for a well-organized society

   C) is against freedom gained at other's expense

   D) denies the existence of many-sided people

Passage 4

Shyness is the cause of much unhappiness for a great many people. All kinds of people describe themselves as shy: short, tall, dull, intelligent, young, old, slim, overweight. Shy people are anxious and self-conscious; that is, they are excessively concerned with their own appearance and actions. Worrisome thoughts are constantly swirling in their minds: What kind of impression am I making? Do they like me? Do I sound stupid? I'm ugly. I'm wearing unattractive clothes.

It is obvious that such uncomfortable feelings must affect people negatively. A person's self-concept is reflected in the way he or she behaves, and the way a person behaves affects other people's reactions. In general, the way people think about themselves has a profound effect on all areas of their lives. For instance, people who have a positive sense of self-worth or high self-esteem usually act with confidence. Because they have self-assurance, they don't need constant praise and encouragement from others to feel good about themselves. Self-confident people are their own best friends. They participate in life enthusiastically and naturally. They are not affected by what others think they "should do". People with high self-esteem are not hurt by criticism; they do not regard criticism as personal rejection. Instead, they view criticism as suggestion for improvement.

In contrast, shy people, having low self-esteem, are likely to be passive and easily influenced by others. They need reassurance that they are doing "the right thing". Shy people are very sensitive to criticism; they feel it confirms their inferiority. They also find it difficult to be pleased by compliments because they believe they are unworthy of praise. A shy person may respond to a compliment with a statement like this one: "You're just saying that to make me feel good. I know it's not true." It's clear that, while self-assurance is a healthy quality, overdoing it is detrimental, or harmful.

26. What is the passage mainly about?

    A) Shyness causes unhappiness.

    B) Shyness affects many people in our society.

    C) Shyness is caused by an unhappy childhood.

    D) Talking to strangers will make one get rid of his shyness.

27. Shy people are unhappy because _____.

    A) they are very sensitive to criticism

    B) they are thought to be inferior to others

    C) they are very difficult to be pleased by compliments

    D) they are constantly troubled by unnecessary worries

28. The word "self-esteem" (Line 5, Para. 2) most probably means _____.

    A) self-respect   B) self-opinion

    C) self-control   D) self-educated

29. It can be inferred from the passage that shy people _____.

    A) have ideas of their own

    B) are inferior to others

    C) are unworthy of praise

    D) need encouragement and praise from others to feel good about themselves

30. Which of the following is NOT true according to the passage?

    A) Shy people are easily hurt by criticism.

    B) Shy people have trouble accepting compliments.

    C) If we think well of ourselves, we'll act with confidence.

    D) People are shy because they care about their appearance and actions.

Section D Short Answer Questions

Directions:（略）

Passage 5

No one knows exactly how many disabled people there are in the world, but estimates suggest the figure is over 450 million. The number of disabled people in India alone is probably more than double the total population of Canada.

In the United Kingdom, about one in ten people have some disability. "Disabled people" in this context are those who are physically handicapped, deaf, hard of hearing, blind, partially sighted, speech impaired, mentally handicapped, or mentally ill. Disability is not just something that happens to other people; as we get older, many of us will become less mobile, hard of hearing or have failing eyesight.

Disablement can take many forms and occur at any time of life. Some people are born with disabilities. Many others become disabled as they get older. There are many progressive disabling diseases. The longer time goes on, the worse they become. Some people are disabled in accidents. Many others may have a period of disability in the form of a mental illness. All are affected by people's attitude towards them.

Disabled people face many physical barriers. Next time you go shopping or to work, visit friends, imagine how you would manage if you could not get up steps, or onto buses and trains. How would you cope if you could not see where you were going or could not hear the traffic? But there are other barriers: prejudice can be even more *formidable* (可怕的) and harder to break down and ignorance inevitable represents by far the greatest barrier of all. It is almost impossible for the able-bodied to fully appreciate what the severely handicapped go through, but the International Year of Disabled People is of enormous value in drawing attention to these barriers and showing that it is the individual person and their ability, not their disability, which counts.

31. How many disabled people are there in the world based on the estimation in the first paragraph?

_____

_____

32. Disabled people may have problems in _____.

_____

_____

33. What kind of people can suffer from some disability?

_____

_____

34. Which three examples of disability are mentioned in the first half of Paragraph 4?

_____

_____

35. The International Year of Disabled People did most in _____.

_____

_____

Notes and Explanations

Passage 1

Explanations

1. [Y] 第一段最后一句提到 There was just a complete gap in sensibility and taste, a virtual gulf.（在父母和孩子之间）确实有着完全不同的情感和品味的代沟——真实的鸿沟。故可得出答案 Yes。

2. [Y] 第六段第一句提到 But family experts caution that the new equality can also have a downside, diminishing respect for parents. 但是研究家庭问题的专家提醒说,这种新的平等会使孩子对父母的尊重减少甚至消失。故答案应为 Yes。

3. [Y] Parents and children as friends 部分第二段第一、二句提到 Parents today are more youthful in appearance and attitudes. From blue jeans to blow-dries, their clothes and hairstyles are more casual, helping to bridge the sartorial divide. 现在的父母在外表和态度上都更加年轻。从牛仔裤到电吹风,他们的服装和发型都更加休闲,这些都有助于缩小他们与孩子在服饰上的区别。因此,答案应为 Yes。

4. [NG] Parents and children as friends 部分第七段第一句提到 Other changes are occurring as the ranks of working mothers grow. 其他的变化在于外出工作的母亲的数量在增加。父亲工作时间增长对家庭的变化并没有提及,故答案为 Not Given。

5. [N] Parents and children as friends 部分第十一段提到 He believes that parents—in their eagerness to keep the peace and avoid arguments—miss an opportunity to teach children how to resolve conflicts, rather than simply avoiding them. Dennis Lowe 认为"那些想要维护家庭的安定而避免争执的父母错过了教会他们的孩子如何解决冲突而不是仅仅逃避冲突的机会"。故正确答案是 No。

6. [N] Parents and children as friends 部分第十七段提到 Lowe sees some parents trying to cultivate friendship with their children even at very early ages. And he knows families where children call parents by their first names. "Rather than 'Mom' or 'Dad', you have a 7-year-old saying, 'Hey, Gary,'"he explains, adding that a lack of respect for parents could carry over into relationships with teachers, bosses, and others in positions of authority. Lowe 发现有些父母在孩子很小的时候就和他们培养友谊。他知道有些家庭中的孩子对父母直呼其名。而不是"妈妈"、"爸爸",七岁的孩子就会说"嗨,格雷"。这种不尊敬父母的行为会对孩子在和老师、老板和其他需要尊敬的人的关系中产生影响。故答案为 No。

7. [Y] Growing understanding 部分第五段最后提到 If we can get this balance, where parents are not afraid to be parents, and parents and children put the family as their priority, we'll be in great shape. I'm very optimistic about the future. 如果我们能达到这样的平衡,父母不再害怕做父母,父母和孩子都把家庭看作最重要的东西,这样就对了。我对未来很乐观。所以答案为 Yes。

8. 第二段第二句提到 From clothing and hairstyles to activities and expectations, earlier generations of parents and children often appeared to revolve in separate orbits. 从服装、发型到行为、理想,以前的父母和孩子都表现地大相径庭。从而得出答案为 **revolve in separate orbits**。

9. Parents and children as friends 部分第四段第二句提到 The philosophy encourages children to describe their feelings about various situations. 这种理念鼓励孩子们在不同的场合描述自己的感觉。故答案应为 **various situations**。

10. Parents and children as friends 部分第九段第二句提到 Some parents worry that if they tell their child no, or impose limits, it will hurt the child's self-esteem. 有的父母担心如果他们对孩子说"不",或对他们加以限制,这样会伤害孩子的自尊心。所以答案是 **child's self-esteem**。

Passage 2

Notes

1. be sure of (Line 1, Para. 1)
▷be sure of 意思是"对……确信"。例如:
The officer is sure of his loyalty to the country. 长官相信他对国家的忠诚。
▷be sure 后面还可以用介词 about。

2. federal, state, and city government (Line 2, Para. 2)
分别指联邦政府、州政府和市政府。

3. vary for individuals (Line 2, Para. 3)
vary for individuals 意思是"因人而异"。
vary 是"改变,变化"的意思。例如:

Her mood varies from day to day. 她的心情天天在变化。

A good driver varies the speed of his car according to the condition of the roads.

优秀的司机会根据路况来变换车速。

4. similar to (Line 1，Para. 4)

similar to 意思是"与……相似"。例如：

Your views on education are similar to mine. 你的教育观点与我的相似。

5. complain about (Line 2，Para. 6)

complain about/of 意思是"抱怨，发牢骚"。例如：

The old lady complained about the noise from the bar to the police. 老妇人向警察抱怨酒吧的噪声。

Don't complain about your job any more. 别再抱怨你的工作了。

Explanations

11. [H] 语法规则要求此处应填一个形容词构成 be ＋ 形容词 ＋ of 结构。选项中能够构成此结构的只有选项 H。be sure of 为意为"对……有把握"，符合句子的意思。因此选项 H 为正确答案。

12. [B] 语法规则要求此处应填一个动词作句子的谓语。主语 taxes 要求谓语动词是动词原形，而且和 of 构成固定搭配的短语，意思应该是"由……构成(或组成)"。选项中 consist 可以和 of 构成固定搭配短语，意思上也符合句子的要求。

13. [M] 语法规则要求此处应填一个副词来修饰 there be 这个结构。选项 K、M 符合该要求。generally 意思是"一般地，通常"，permanently 意思是"永存地，不变地"。generally 符合句意的要求。所以选项 M 正确。

14. [N] 语法规则要求此处应填一个名词作句子的主语。选项 D、L、N、O 是名词。这一段讨论的是所得税占薪水的比例问题。据此可以得知这里应该填 percentage，意思是"百分率，百分比"。

15. [E] 语法规则要求此处应填一个形容词构成形容词短语作定语修饰 an income tax。选项中只有 similar 可以和 to 搭配。similar to 意为"与……相似(或类似)"，符合句子意思的要求。

16. [A] 语法规则要求此处应填一个动词的过去分词形式作形容词用，作 percentage 的定语。只有 A 项 charged(收费)符合该条件。

17. [O] 语法规则要求此处应填一个名词与前面的 in 和后面的 to 构成固定搭配的短语，意思是"除……之外"。选项 O 符合这两个条件。

18. [C] 语法规则要求此处应填一个动词形式作句子的谓语，主语 The cities 要求谓语是动词原形，且应为一般现在时。选项 B、C、F、G、I 均符合该要求，但是只有 utilize(利用)与句意相符，因此 C 项正确。

19. [F] 语法规则要求此处应填一个动词和 about 搭配作句子的谓语。且应为一般现在时，选项中能和 about 搭配的动词只有 complain。complain about 意为"抱怨，埋怨"，意思与文章下文相符，所以 F 项正确。

20. [J] 语法规则要求此处应填一个形容词来修饰名词 views。选项 E、H、J 与该条件符合。conflicting 意思是"相冲突的，相矛盾的"，与下文意思相符，因此 J 项正确。

Passage 3

Notes

1. A man living absolutely. . . (Line 1，Para. 1)

absolutely 意思是"完全地，绝对地"，文中第一句中的两个 absolutely 意思一样，全句译为：一个独自生活在沙漠或森林中不受干扰的人并不完全自由。

2. . . . he must have. . . shelter from . . . cold. (Line 3～4，Para. 1)

shelter from 意思是"作为屏障，庇护所"。shelter 还可用作动词。例如：

The trees shelter the field from the cold wind. 那些树木使田野不受冷风侵袭。

3. ... protection against... (Line 1，Para. 2)

▷意思是"防御，保护"。例如：

This hat will give protection against the sun. 这顶帽子可以遮阳。

▷其动词形式为 protect... against (from)。例如：

In summer，we wear sunglasses to protect our eyes from the strong sunlight.

夏天我们戴太阳镜以遮挡强烈的阳光。

4. ... in return for the work he does... (Line 2，Para. 4)

in return 意思是"作为回报"。例如：

If you give me your photo，I'll give you mine in return. 如果你送我一张照片，我便回赠一张给你。

5. If each man had to grow his own food，... he would find it impossible to do any one of those jobs really well. (Line 3～5，Para. 4)

这是含有虚拟语气的句子，表示对未来情况的一种假设。本句话中 had to 后面有四个不定式短语，to grow his own food，make his own clothes，build his own house and learn to be his own doctor.

Explanations

在文中，作者认为一个人通过与世隔绝而实现绝对的自由是不可能的，人们应该在一个有序的社会中与其他人和平共处，相互帮助，取长补短；尽管会牺牲自己的部分自由，但是这样做是必须的也是值得的。因此他认为一个秩序良好的社会是必要的。

21. C) 细节题。根据文章的第一和第二句：A man living absolutely alone in a desert or forest is free from other people；but he is not absolutely free. His freedom is limited in several ways. 得出正确答案为 C 项。

22. B) 细节题。问的是作者认为人们生活在一起的时候会是怎样的。文章的第二段中说道：When men live together，on the other hand，protection against animals is easier and... 因此 B 项为正确答案。

23. B) 推断题。要求根据文章的内容，做出 true 或 false 的推断。根据文章第三段中提到的 When men become organized into... so that he is kept from hurting others. 四个选项的内容都提到了，但 B 项中 no such problem as 的提法太绝对，与文章中的 possible to get freedom from 在意义上不等同。因此 B 项不符合文章的原意，故为正确答案。

24. C) 推断题。文章第四段中讲到：If each man had to grow his own food，make his own clothes，build his own house and learn to be his own doctor，he would find it impossible to do any one of these jobs really well. 由此可以推断出选项 C 的内容与之最为相近。因此正确答案为 C 项。

25. B) 主旨题。文章前三段的第一句和最后一段都指出一个秩序良好的社会是必要的。所以答案应该是 B 项。

Passage 4

Notes

1. describe... as... (Line 2，Para. 1)

describe... as... 意思是"把……描述成……"。例如：

He described my plan as an unrealistic one. 他把我的计划描述成不切实际的计划。

The poor woman was described as a cruel stepmother by the relatives.

那个可怜的女人被亲戚们描述成了一个残忍的继母。

2. ... they are excessively concerned with... (Line 3，Para. 1)

be concerned with 意思是"对……关心(关注)"。例如:

The mountaineers are concerned with the weather in the Everest. 登山者关注着喜马拉雅山的天气。

The parents are concerned with their son's future. 父母关心他们儿子的前途。

3. It is obvious that... (Line 1, Para. 2)

It is +adj. + that 从句,是一个常用句型,It 为形式主语,真正主语是 that 引导的从句。例如:

It is obvious that the computer plays an important role in modern society.

电子计算机在现代社会的重要作用是显而易见的。

It is necessary that people pay more attention to the environmental protection.

人们对于环境保护给予更多的关注是有必要的。

4. self-worth, self-esteem, self-assurance (Para. 2)

self-worth, self-esteem, self-assurance 分别表示"自我价值,自尊,自信心"。

5. regard...as, view...as (Para. 2)

regard...as, view...as 都是"将……视作……"的意思。例如:

People regard him as the best tennis player in Japan. 人们认为他是日本最好的网球运动员。

The businessman views this difficulty as a new challenge. 商人把这个困难视作一个新的挑战。

6. ...are likely to be... (Line 1, Para. 3)

be likely to 意思是"可能会"。例如:

It is likely to rain tonight. 今晚可能会下雨。

He isn't likely to win. 他不可能会赢。

Explanations

本文分析了害羞产生的原因。由于害羞人们会对自己的一切都感到不满意,因而会对他们的生活产生负面的影响:他们自我评价较低,处世被动消极,情绪易受他人影响。因此过分害羞是有害的。

26. **A)** 主旨题。作者在第一段第一句就提出了本文的主旨:害羞是很多人不快乐的原因。

27. **D)** 细节题。第一段中 Worrisome thoughts are constantly swirling in their minds... 他们的脑海中总是萦绕着一些让人苦恼的想法。因此 D 项为正确答案。

28. **A)** 词汇题。第二段第四句 For instance, people who have positive sense of self-worth or high self-esteem usually act with confidence. 有着积极的自我价值观或者较高的自我评价的人一般做事很有信心。其他选项不符合本句的意思。

29. **D)** 推断题。根据文章的内容,第二段第三到第五句和第三段第二句,自我评价高的人通常很有信心,因此他们不需要别人经常表扬和鼓励来达到良好的自我感觉,相比之下,害羞的人通常做事被动并易受他人影响,需要别人来证实他们做的事情正确无误。因此 D 项为正确答案。

30. **D)** 推断题。根据第一段第三句 Shy people are anxious and self-conscious; that is, they are excessively concerned with their own appearance and actions. 可得知,过分关注自己的外表的行为是害羞的表现,而非害羞的原因。因此 D 项是正确答案。

Passage 5

Keys

31. Over 450 million.

32. hearing, sight, speech, thought processes and mobility

33. All people of all ages can suffer from disability.

34. The three examples are physical disability, blindness and deafness.

35. breaking down the barriers of prejudice and appreciating a person's ability

Notes

1. Some people are born with disabilities.（Line 1~2，Para. 3）

   be born with 意思是"与生俱来"。例如：

   born with a silver spoon in one's mouth 生于富贵之家（谚语）

2. . . . and harder to break down and. . .（Line 4~5，Para. 4）

   break down 意思是"克服，镇压"。例如：

   How can we break down the barriers of fear and hostility which divided the two countries?

   怎样才能消除两个国家人民之间的恐惧与仇恨呢？

   break down resistance/oppositions 镇压抵抗

3. go through（Line 6，Para. 4）

   go through 意思是"经历，遭受某事"。例如：

   She's gone through a difficult time recently. 她最近经历了一段困难时期。

4. . . . enormous value in drawing attention to these. . .（Line 7，Para. 4）

   draw attention to 意思是"引起注意"。例如：

   The fashionable evening dress drew attention to all girls in the party.

   那件时髦的晚礼服吸引了聚会上所有女孩的注意。

Unit 20

Section A   Skimming and Scanning

Directions：（略）

Passage 1

Is Smoking a Major Cause of Lung Cancer in Women

1. Many people think that lung cancer affects mostly men. But even though we hear more about breast cancer, lung cancer is the leading cause of cancer deaths in women. And nearly all lung cancer deaths in women are due to smoking. Quitting smoking now is one important change you can make to improve your lung and overall health and live longer. Former smokers have a lower risk for lung cancer than do current smokers. In one to nine months after quitting smoking, your lungs will function better. And after 10 years, your risk of lung cancer is nearly the same as someone who never smoked.

Should women who smoke be concerned about heart disease?

2. Yes. More women die each year from heart disease than from any other illness. Smoking is the major cause of heart disease in women, especially those younger than age 50. Women who use birth control pills have a much higher risk of heart disease if they smoke. But after just one year of quitting smoking, you reduce your risk of heart disease by half.

Why do women and girls smoke?

3. Women and girls smoke for different reasons. Some women smoke to deal with stress or control weight. Younger women and girls may start smoking as a way of rebelling, being independent, or fitting in with their peers. Tobacco companies use research on how women and girls feel about themselves to influence women and girls to smoke. But there is never a good reason to smoke, and it's best to never start. There are, though, many good reasons to quit smoking. When you quit, your health and quality of life will improve. You also will help safeguard the health of those you live with by not exposing them to second-hand smoke (the smoke released from a lit cigarette or cigar).

Why should I quit smoking?

4. When you quit：

  • Your chances of getting sick from smoking will be less.

  • You will have more energy and breathe easier.

  • If you are pregnant, your baby will get more oxygen and be healthier.

  • Your children and other people in your home will be healthier. Second-hand smoke can cause *asthma*（哮喘）and other health problems.

  • You will have more money to spend on other things.

What are the dangers of second-hand smoke?

5. Second-hand smoke happens when non-smokers inhale other people's tobacco smoke. It includes：

- *Side-stream*（侧流烟，指从香烟或雪茄烟燃端飘出的烟）smoke—smoke that comes directly from a burning cigarette，pipe，or cigar.
- Mainstream smoke — smoke that is exhaled by the smoker.

6. When a cigarette is smoked，about half of the smoke is side-stream smoke. Side-stream smoke contains most of the same chemicals found in the mainstream smoke inhaled by the smoker.

7. People who don't smoke，but are exposed to second-hand smoke，absorb *nicotine*（尼古丁）and other chemicals just as someone who smokes does. Studies have shown that second-hand smoke can cause lung cancer in healthy adults who do not smoke. Children of parents who smoke are more likely to suffer from *pneumonia*（肺炎），*bronchitis*（支气管炎），ear infections，asthma，and SIDS（the sudden death of a baby under age one which cannot be explained）. Mothers who smoke and breastfeed may pass harmful chemicals from nicotine to their baby through breast milk.

What have other women done to quit smoking?

8. Almost half of women who smoke have tried to quit during the past year. Many women have to try two or three times before they are able to quit for good. It's hard work，but don't give up! Millions of women have been able to quit，and you can too!

9. Follow these steps to help you to quit for good：

- Learn how much you depend on nicotine. Knowing how addicted you are to nicotine can help you decide what kind of help you need. Take the Nicotine Addiction Test.
- Get ready to quit by picking a date to stop smoking. Quitting all at once works better than trying to quit a little at a time.
- Write down why you want to quit. Keep this list as a handy reminder.
- Tell loved ones，friends，and coworkers your quit date. Ask them for their support. Ask them not to smoke around you or leave cigarettes out around you.
- Create a fund. Each time you would normally buy a pack of cigarettes，put that saved money in a special place. If you used to smoke one pack per day，after one month，you've saved about $150. Set a goal and reward yourself once you reach that goal.
- Plan for challenges. Think ahead for how you will deal with situations or triggers that will make you want to smoke.

10. Get medicine and use it correctly. There are many medicines that can help you quit and reduce your urge to smoke. You and your health care provider can decide what medicine will work best for you. Always first talk with your health care provider before trying any medicines，especially when you are pregnant or if you have heart problems.

- Be prepared for *relapse*（复发）. Most people start smoking again within the first three months after quitting. Don't give up if this happens to you. Many women try to quit several times before quitting for good. Learn from what helped you and what didn't the last time you tried to quit to increase your chances of success next time. It may help you to keep a craving journal to record when and why you smoke.
- Get more help if you need it. Join a quit-smoking program or support group to help you

quit. Contact your local hospital, health center, or health department for quit-smoking programs in your area. Your state may also provide toll-free quit line phone numbers. Find the number in your state.

Can medicines really help me quit?

11. There are many medicines that can help you quit smoking. So you don't have to do it alone. At first, you may feel depressed, have trouble sleeping, or just not feel like yourself. This means that your body is going through withdrawal, or getting used to not having nicotine. These symptoms only last a few weeks and medicines can help give you some relief. Most help you quit by giving you small, steady doses of nicotine. Using them can double your chances of quitting for good. Talk with your health care provider about which of these medicines is right for you.

12. Nicotine replacement therapy includes nicotine patches, gum, nasal spray, and inhalers. They help lessen your urge to smoke by taking the place of nicotine from cigarettes.

13. In general, when you quit smoking, use the nicotine as a "substitute" for one to two months, then gradually cut down the nicotine until you stop that, too. You can buy patches and gum on your own at a drug store. You need a prescription for the inhaler and nasal spray.

14. Not everyone can use these medicines. If you are pregnant or have heart problems, be sure to talk with your health care provider before using any of them.

1. The passage mainly tells us why and how women should quit smoking.

2. Lung cancer is the leading cause of cancer deaths in women.

3. Smoking is the major cause of heart disease in those women younger than age 50.

4. Some women and girls start smoking because they want to make themselves more fashionable and beautiful.

5. When a cigarette is smoked, about one third of the smoke is side-stream smoke.

6. Trying to quit a little at a time works better than quitting all at once.

7. One fourth people could give up smoking at once after quitting.

8. Quitting smoking now is one important change you can make to improve _____ and live longer.

9. Studies have shown that _____ can cause lung cancer in healthy adults who do not smoke.

10. If _____, be sure to talk with your health care provider before using any of the medicines.

Section B   Discourse Vocabulary Test

Directions：（略）

Passage 2

Americans are people obsessed with child-rearing. In their books, magazines, talk shows, parent training courses, White House conferences, and chats over the back fence, they __11__ debate the best ways to raise children. Moreover, Americans do more than debate their theories; they translate them into __12__. They erect playgrounds for the youngsters' pleasure, __13__ large schools for their education, and train skilled specialists for their welfare. Whole industries in America are __14__ to making children happy, healthy and wise.

But this interest in childhood is __15__ new. In fact, until very recently people considered childhood just a grief, unimportant *prelude*（序幕）to adulthood and the real business of living. By and large, they either __16__ children, beat them, or *fondled*（爱抚）them carelessly, much as we would amuse ourselves with some little dogs. When they gave serious thought to children at all, people either conceived of them as miniature adults or as peculiar, unformed animals.

Through the ages the __17__ of childhood have been as varied as its duration. Actions that would have provoked a beating in one era elicit extra loving care in another. Babies who have been *nurtured*（养育）exclusively by their mother in one generation are left with day-care workers in another. In some places children have been trained to get through __18__ mountain passes, and carry heavy objects on their heads. In other places they have been taught complicated piano *concerto*（协奏曲）.

But diverse as it has been, childhood has one __19__ experience at its core and that is the social aspect of nurture. All children need adults to bring them up. Because human young take so long to become __20__ , we think that civilization may have grown up around the need to feed and protect them.

A) relatively	I) danger
B) dangerous	J) regard
C) ignored	K) independent
D) endlessly	L) depend
E) activity	M) equip
F) experiences	N) common
G) consideration	O) devoted
H) action	

Section C　Reading in Depth

Directions:（略）

Passage 3

Most people feel lonely sometimes but is usually lasts only between a few minutes and a few hours. This kind of loneliness is not serious. In fact, it is quite normal. For some people, though, loneliness can last for years. Psychologists are studying this complex phenomenon in an attempt to better understand long-term loneliness. These researchers have already identified three different types of loneliness.

The first kind of loneliness is temporary. This is the most common type. It usually disappears quickly and does not require any special attention. The second kind, situational loneliness, is a natural result of a particular situation, for example, a divorce, the death of a loved one, or moving to a new place. Although this kind of loneliness can cause physical problems, such as headaches and sleeplessness, it usually does not last for more than a year. Situational loneliness is easy to understand and to predict.

The third kind is the most severe. Unlike the second type, *chronic*（长期的）loneliness usually lasts more than two years and has no specific cause. People who experience habitual loneliness have problems socializing and becoming close to others. Unfortunately, many chronically lonely people think there is little or nothing they can do to improve their condition.

Psychologists agree that one important factor in loneliness is a person's social contacts, i. e., friends, family members, co-workers, etc. We depend on various people for different reasons. However, psychologists have found that the number of social contacts we have is not the only reason for loneliness. It is more important how many social contacts we think or expect we should have. In other words, though lonely people may have many social contacts, they sometimes feel they should have more.

Most researchers agree that the loneliest people are between the ages of 18 and 25. They found that more than 50 percent of the college freshmen were situationally lonely at the beginning of the semester, but had adjusted after a few months. Thirteen percent were still lonely after seven months due to shyness and fear. They felt very uncomfortable meeting new people, even though they understood that their fear was not rational. The situationally lonely freshmen overcame their loneliness by making new friends, but the chronically lonely people remained unhappy because they were afraid to do so.

21. What is the main idea of this passage?

   A) There are three different kinds of loneliness.

   B) Chronic loneliness is the most severe kind.

   C) Researchers want to cure loneliness.

   D) There is some difference between being alone and being lonely.

22. Lonely people have social contacts _____.

   A) because they can ask for help

   B) until they produce good health

   C) but they think they do not have enough

   D) and therefore they can get emotional support from their friends

23. Situational loneliness has made it possible for people _____.

   A) to adjust to their new circumstances

   B) to cause sleeplessness and headaches

   C) to understand that their shyness can not be got rid of

   D) to keep fit

24. "The situationally lonely freshmen overcame their loneliness" （Line 5～6, Para. 5）probably means _____.

   A) they accepted their loneliness   B) they were no longer lonely

   C) they made new friends   D) they improve their condition

25. What does "to do so" （Line 7, Para. 5）mean?

   A) To predict situational loneliness.   B) To have physical problems.

C) To question popularity.   D) To make new friends.

Passage 4

To read a new book, you simply need good light, time and the right frame of mind. But to read a new software package, you need a thousand pounds' worth of hardware, considerable computer knowledge, plenty of time and, most important of all, endless determination.

Generally speaking, all books are very much alike, and the experienced reader has no difficulty coping with an unfamiliar book. But imagine how *frustrating* (令人感到挫折的) it would be if you had to make a mental adjustment, if you had to read in a different way, every time you read a book from a different publisher. Yet this is exactly what it is like when you use a new software package.

You can be engrossed in a good book within a minute, but getting new software running takes ages. Learning to use a new piece of software is like trying to ride a trick bicycle, on which the handlebars have a reverse action. It looks easier than it really is. This is partly because you must first unlearn what you learnt on the last package; no two packages use the control characters on the keyboard in quite the same way. How much easier it would be if there were some standards to which all software writers adhered!

Since you can't rely on your previous experience, the only way to understand your new software package is to rely on the manual. Some software manuals are written with the beginner in mind and have explicit instructions with well-designed exercises that lead you gently on from stage to stage. But most assume that you are already an expert, and have complicated explanations which only confuse and *irritate* (使恼怒) you. All require a full set of fingers and thumbs to mark pages while hunting out information. Yes, perhaps the information is in the manual, but where?

26. How do you probably feel when learning to use a new software package?

    A) frustrated   B) encouraged   C) engrossed   D) dismayed

27. The author mentions the trick bicycle, on which the handlebars have a reverse action, in order to show _____.

    A) how difficult it is to learn to ride a bicycle

    B) it is impossible to learn to ride this bicycle

    C) how difficult it is to learn a new software package

    D) to learn to ride a bicycle is the same thing as to learn a new software package

28. How could a software package become easier to users according to the author?

    A) All software packages are made by the same software company.

    B) The users are familiar with all kinds of software packages.

    C) There are some standards to which all software writers adhere.

    D) There is a committee which examines all software packages.

29. What is the most common problem in software manuals according to the passage?

    A) They have complicated explanations which are quite beyond your understanding.

    B) They are printed in very small characters.

    C) Their instructions and explanations are too simple.

D) They are written with the beginner in mind.

30. We can infer from the passage that the word "explicit" (Line 3, Para. 4) means _____.

A) confusing   B) clear   C) complicated   D) involved

Section D   Short Answer Questions

Directions：（略）

Passage 5

Although few would deny that it's better to be rich than poor, for some people the quest for money is so all-consuming that it extinguishes all other aspects of life.

The cause of the *compulsion* （被迫） to make enormous sums of money varies with the individual, but often money is a substitute for something a person's life lacks. To some, money means security. To some, it means power. To others it means they are going to be able to buy love, and to a fourth group it means competition and winning the game. The belief that money can produce these things often leads to insomnia, heart attacks and problems with a spouse or children.

A tremendous need for power is invariably the bottom line for those driven to make a lot of money. The bigger the pile, the more powerful they think they will feel. Parents and family background also influence a person's pursuit of money. Many people who grew up poor and then made a fortune live in fear that they will lose it. Others strive for money to compete with their wealthy, successful parents. They want to be successful at any price. They do not feel they should enjoy what they have earned.

Making money for its own sake can be *addicting* （上瘾） like high-stakes gambling. Some very wealthy people work so many hours, so hard and at such an intense pace that they totally neglect themselves. They don't eat right. They don't sleep right. They just act as if they were poor, as if they were struggling to make a dime.

Many wealthy people are driven by the need for approval. But they may go out of their ways not to appear wealthy out of fear that they may receive less support from others.

Obsession with money is a man's problem, but with the ranks of female executives growing, the *feverish* （狂热） quest for money is becoming more of "an equal-opportunity" problem. In some ways, women may have the greatest conflict with making money. In society's eyes, financial achievement is not fully satisfying for women. They must also be successful as *nurturers* （教育者）

31. In the author's point of view, money is _____.

    _____   _____   _____   _____   _____

    _____   _____   _____   _____   _____

32. The wrong belief about money can lead to _____.

    _____   _____   _____   _____   _____

33. What is the bottom line of having too much money?

_____ _____ _____ _____ _____

34. A person's pursuit of money is often influenced by _____.

_____ _____ _____ _____ _____

35. Why do many rich people pretend to be poor?

_____ _____ _____ _____ _____

_____ _____ _____ _____ _____

Notes and Explanations

Passage 1

Explanations

1. [Y] 通过浏览文章中的六个黑色小标题,可以发现全文讲述了女性为什么要戒烟和如何戒烟,故答案为 Yes。

2. [Y] 第一段第二句提到 But even though we hear more about breast cancer, lung cancer is the leading cause of cancer deaths in women. 尽管我们对于乳腺癌了解得比较多,然而肺癌才是女性癌症死亡中的首要原因。所以答案为 Yes。

3. [N] 第二段第三句提到 Smoking is the major cause of heart disease in women, especially those younger than age 50. 吸烟是女性心脏病的主要原因,特别是对于那些 50 岁以下的女性。故答案为 No。

4. [Y] 第三段第二、三句提到 Some women smoke to deal with stress or control weight. Younger women and girls may start smoking as a way of rebelling, being independent, or fitting in with their peers. 有些女性吸烟是为了缓解压力和控制体重。年轻的女性把吸烟作为一种反叛、独立和在同龄人中显得时髦而开始吸烟。所以答案是 Yes。

5. [N] 第六段第一句提到 When a cigarette is smoked, about half of the smoke is side-stream smoke. 在吸烟的时候,大约有一半的烟都成了侧流烟。故答案为 No。

6. [N] 第九段提到 Get ready to quit by picking a date to stop smoking. Quitting all at once works better than trying to quit a little at a time. 一次全部戒掉比慢慢戒掉有效。所以答案是 No。

7. [NG] 第十段提到 Be prepared for relapse. Most people start smoking again within the first three months after quitting. Don't give up if this happens to you. Many women try to quit several times before quitting for good. Learn from what helped you and what didn't the last time you tried to quit to increase your chances of success next time. It may help you to keep a craving journal to record when and why you smoke. 大多数人在戒烟的头三个月中就会复吸。如果你也是这样的话,不要放弃。很多女性都是在戒烟很多次后才成功。从上一次戒烟的经历中吸取经验教训会增加你下一次成功的概率。记录你什么时候吸烟和为什么吸烟可能会很有帮助。命题没有被明确提及,故答案为 Not Given。

8. 第一段第四句提到 Quitting smoking now is one important change you can make to improve your lung and overall health and live longer. 现在就戒烟可以使你改善肺功能及全身的健康状况,活得更长。从而得出答案为 **your lung and overall health**。

9. 第七段第二句提到 Studies have shown that second-hand smoke can cause lung cancer in healthy adults who do not smoke. 研究表明二手烟会使那些不吸烟的健康成年人患肺癌。从而得知本题的正确答案是 **second hand smoke**。

10. 最后一句提到 If you are pregnant or have heart problems，be sure to talk with your health care provider before using any of them. 如果你怀孕了或是有心脏问题的话，一定要在用药之前咨询你的医师。从而得知 **you are pregnant or have heart problems** 是本题的正确答案。

Passage 2

Notes

1. Americans are people obsessed with child-rearing. (Line 1, Para. 1)

▷be obsessed with 在本句中的意思是"着迷于……；全神贯注于……"；还可以表示"受到……的困扰"。例如：

He has been obsessed with the constant stomachache. 他一直遭受胃病的困扰。

▷还可以用 obsession with。例如：

His obsession with computer games began six months ago. 他半年前就迷上了电脑。

2. Americans do more than debate their theories；they translate them into action. (Line 3~4, Para. 1)

translate…into… 在本句中的意思是"把……变为……"。本句意思是：美国人不光在讨论理论，他们更多地将理论付诸行动。

3. Whole industries in America are devoted to making children… (Line 5~6, Para. 1)

▷be devoted to 意思是"全心全意地做……，不遗余力地做……"。例如：

She is devoted to the biological study all her life. 她终身致力于生物学研究。

▷还可以用 devotion to sb. /sth. 例如：

a mother's devotion to her children 母亲对子女深深的疼爱

4. conceive of (Line 5, Para. 2)

conceive of 意思是"想象为，认为"。例如：

The ancients conceived of the world as flat. 古人认为地球是平的。

5. Actions that would have provoked a beating in one era elicit extra loving care in another. (Line 1~2, Para. 3)

这个句子中含有虚拟语气，意思是：在一个时代可能会遭到棍棒的行为，在另一个时代却会得到关爱。

6. In some place children… get through dangerous… (Line 4, Para. 3)

get through 意思是"设法做，完成"。例如：

Let's start；there's a lot of work to get through. 开始吧，有大量工作要做呢。

7. But diverse as it has been, … (Line 1, Para. 4)

diverse as it has been 是由 as 引导的让步状语从句，等同于 although it has been diverse。

Explanations

11. [D] 语法规则要求此处应填一个副词来修饰动词 debate。本句话的状语列举了一系列美国人谈论育儿话题的场合。endlessly 意思是"不断地"，与上下文句意相符，因此选项 D 正确。

12. [H] 语法规则要求此处应填一个名词作介词 into 的宾语。action 意思是"动作，行动"。translate them into action 意思是"把它们变为行动"，与句意相符：美国人不仅讨论理论，而且还将理论付诸行动，因此选项 H 正确。

13. [M] 语法规则要求此处应填一个动词与 erect 和 train 一起作并列谓语。而且要用一般现在时。equip 意为"装备，配备"，与句意相符，因此选项 M 正确。

14. [O] 语法规则要求此处应填一个动词的过去分词形式构成 be ＋ 动词 ed ＋ to do/be 的结构。选项 O 符合此条件。be devoted to 意为"致力于……"，与句意相符，因此 O 项正确。

15. [A] 语法规则要求此处应填一个副词来修饰形容词 new。A 项 relatively(相对地)既符合语法要求，又符合上下文意思的要求。

16. [C] 语法规则要求此处应填一个动词的过去式与 beat 和 fondled 一起作句子的并列谓语。选项 C 符合该要求。ignore 意思是"不理睬,忽视",与文章上下文的意思相符。

17. [F] 语法规则要求此处应填一个名词作句子的主语,谓语动词的形式要求主语是复数名词。选项中的名词只有 F 项是复数名词。experience 意思是"经历、经验",与句意相符。

18. [B] 语法规则要求此处应填一个形容词来修饰 mountain passes。选项 B、K、N、O 是形容词。B 项 dangerous(危险的)与文中孩子要接受训练的意思相符,所以 B 项正确。

19. [N] 语法规则要求此处应填一个形容词来修饰 experience。common 意为"共同的",与句中要表示"尽管形式多样,但孩子们有一个共同的经历……"相符,所以 N 项正确。

20. [K] 语法规则要求此处应填一个形容词作表语。independent 意思是"独立的",与上下文的意思相符,因此 K 项正确。

Passage 3

Notes

1. Psychologists are studying this complex phenomenon in an attempt to better understand long-term loneliness. (Line 3~4, Para. 1)

   这句话的意思是:心理学家正在研究这个复杂的现象,试图更好的理解长期孤独感。

   in an attempt to do sth. 意思是"尝试,试图做某事"。例如:

   They made no attempt to escape. 他们并未企图逃跑。

   They failed all their attempts to climb the mountain. 他们攀登那座山的一切尝试都失败了。

2. The second kind, situational loneliness, is a natural result of a particular situation... (Line 2~3, Para. 2)

   a result of 意思是"结果,效果"。例如:

   The flight was delayed as a result of fog. 因有雾该航班晚点了。

3. People who experience habitual loneliness have problems socializing and becoming close to others. (Line 2~3, Para. 3)

   这句话的意思是:那些经历着习惯性孤独感的人在社交和与别人接近方面存在问题。

   who experience habitual loneliness 作定语修饰 people,后面的分词短语 socializing and becoming closing to others 同样作定语修饰 problems。

4. Thirteen percent were still lonely after seven months due to shyness and fear. (Line 3~4, Para. 5)

   ▷due to 意思是"由于,因为(某人或某物)引起"。例如:

   The team's success was largely due to her efforts. 该队能成功在很大程度上是因为她的努力。

   ▷due to 还有"应得的,应支付的"的意思。例如:

   Have they been paid the money due to them? 他们是否得到了应得的钱?

5. They felt very uncomfortable meeting new people, even though they understand that their fear was not rational. (Line 4~5, Para. 5)

   这是一个由 even though 引导的让步状语从句,意为:尽管他们知道他们的恐惧并不理智,然而在见到陌生人的时候,他们还是感到不自在。

Explanations

本文讲述了人们可能会遇到的三种孤独感。心理学家们认为第一种,也就是暂时的孤独感是很正常的;第二种,即情景孤独感通常出现在人们遭受到某些变故之后,但是经过一段时间,这种孤独感会逐渐消失;而第三种,长期的孤独感会影响人们正常的社交。

21. A) 主旨题。文章第一段是主题段,作者在此提出心理学家们将孤独分成了三种。

22. C) 细节题。第四段的后半部分提到心理学家发现感到孤独的人并不是缺乏与别人接触,而是他们觉得自己应该更多地与人交往。因此 C 项为正确答案。

23. **B**）细节题。从第二段的后半部分 Although this kind of loneliness can cause physical problems, such as headaches and sleeplessness,... 可以得出 B 项为正确答案。

24. **B**）词汇题。overcome 是"克服"的意思。选项 C 是他们克服孤独感的途径,因此不是正确答案;选项 A 和 D 不符合文章的意思。

25. **D**）细节题。因为这句话的前一部分说有情景孤独感的人通过交新朋友不再感到孤独,而有长期孤独感的人依然感到不快乐,因为他们害怕去交新朋友。

Passage 4

Notes

1. Generally speaking, all books are very alike, and the experienced reader has no difficulty coping with an unfamiliar book. (Line 1, Para. 2)

   句型 have no difficulty (in) doing sth. 的意思是"毫不费力地做某事"。例如:

   The little boy has no difficulty (in) calculating. 小男孩做算数毫不费力。

2. You can be engrossed in a good book... (Line 1, Para. 3)

   be engrossed in 意思是"全神贯注于"。例如:

   When he is engrossed in his work, no one dare interrupt him. 在他集中精力工作的时候,没人敢去打扰他。

3. Learning to use a new piece of software is like trying to ride a trick bicycle, on which the handlebars have a reverse action. (Line 2~3, Para. 3)

   on which 引导的非限定性定语从句修饰先行词 a trick bicycle, 这句话的意思是:学习使用一个新的软件就像骑一辆车把向前的特技自行车一样,看似容易做起来难。

4. How much easier it would be if there were some standards to which all software writers adhered! (Line 5~6, Para. 3)

   这句话中,作者用了虚拟语气。"如果能有所有的软件编写者都遵循的原则,就会容易很多了",事实上并非如此。

5. But most assume that you are... (Line 4, Para. 4)

   这句话中,most 后面省略了 software manuals。本句意为:大多数软件使用手册都假设你是专家,复杂的解释弄得你一头雾水,让人生气。

Explanations

在这篇文章中,作者对读书和使用软件进行了比较。他认为书本对读者的要求较低,容易满足读者的需要;而软件使用起来较为复杂,各种软件的差异很大,加之大多数软件制造者没有充分估计用户的水平,使用手册编写得过于深奥,使得用户一头雾水、无从下手。

26. **A**）细节题。第二段中作者认为如果每次读不同的出版商出版的书,都得换一种读法,这是很让人受挫的,就像使用新的软件包一样。

27. **C**）细节题。第三段第二、三句讲到,使用一个新的软件就像骑一辆车把向前的特技自行车一样,因此 C 项最符合题意。

28. **C**）细节题。第三段中 How much easier it would be if there were some standards to which all software writers adhered. 作者在这里表达了他的愿望。因此 C 项为正确答案。

29. **A**）推断题。在第四段的后半部分,作者认为软件使用手册过于复杂,没有充分考虑到使用者的水平,影响到软件的使用。B 项提及的并不是主要原因;C 项与原文冲突;D 项断章取义。

30. **B**）词汇题。根据上下文,"有些软件使用手册编写时就考虑到初学者的水平","还配有精心设计的由浅入深的练习",因此 explicit 的意思应该是"清楚,明白"。

Passage 5

Keys

31. a substitute for something a person's life lacks

32. insomnia, heart attacks and problems with a spouse or children

33. The need for power.

34. his parents and family background

35. Because they are afraid they may receive less support from others.

Notes

1. ... for some people the quest for money is... (Line 1~2, Para. 1)

quest for 意思是"追求，寻求"。例如：

the quest for gold/ knowledge/ happiness 勘探黄金/寻求知识/追求幸福

2. ..., but often money is a substitute for something a person's life lacks. (Line 2, Para. 2)

▷substitute for 意为"代替，接替"。例如：

He will be the substitute for me as chairman. 他将接替我担任主席。

I'll never find a substitute for that watch. 我永远也找不到什么东西来代替那块表了。

▷也可以用 substitute A for B 意为"用 A 代替 B"

Can I substitute milk for cream? 我可以用牛奶代替奶油吗？

3. Others strive for money to compete with their wealthy, ... (Line 4~5, Para. 3)

▷strive for 意思是"追求"。例如：

The young man worked very hard to strive for success. 年轻人努力工作以追求成功。

▷compete with 意为"与……竞争"。例如：

Several companies compete with each other to gain the contract. 几家公司为争取一份合同互相竞争。

4. They want to be successful at any price. (Line 5, Para. 3)

at any price 意思是"不惜任何代价"。例如：

The people want peace at any price. 人民不惜任何代价也要争取和平。

5. Making money for its own sake can be addicting... (Line 1, Para. 4)

这个句子的意思是：为了挣钱而挣钱会上瘾。

for sb. /sth. 's sake 意为"为了某人（或某事）（起见）"。例如：

I'll help you for your sister's sake. 看在你姐姐的面子上，我会帮你。

6. They just act as if they were poor, as if they were struggling to make a dime. (Line 3~4, Para. 4)

本句中使用了虚拟语气，分别由 as if 引出。本句意为：他们拼命挣钱好像自己很穷，得为每一分钱努力。

7. In some ways, women may have the greatest conflict with making money. (Line 2~3, Para. 6)

▷have conflict with 意思是"与……冲突，意见不合"。例如：

Mary has a conflict with her parents because of her marriage. 玛丽因为婚姻问题和父母意见不和。

▷conflict 用作动词时，也可以与 with 搭配。例如：

Their account of the event conflicts with ours. 他们对事情的解释与我们的截然不同。

Unit 21

Section A   Skimming and Scanning

Directions：（略）

Passage 1

Children at Work

Rise of child labor

1. Children have been used as workers for thousands of years in countries around the world. The rise of child labor in the United States began in the late seventeen and early eighteen hundreds. Industrialization was a strong force in increasing the number of working children. By 1900, more than two million U. S. children were at work. The 1900 census, which counted workers aged 10 to 15, found that 18. 2 percent of the country's children between those ages were employed. Children worked in factories, mines, fields and in the streets. They also picked cotton, shined shoes, sold newspapers, canned fish, made clothes and wove fabric. Children worked to help support their families.

2. The contribution of a child's income or labor at home can move a family from hunger to bare sufficiency.

3. Parents of child workers are often unemployed or underemployed, desperate for a secure job and income. Yet it is often their children who are offered jobs—because children are cheaper and easier to exploit.

4. Economic development that assures adults a living wage would reduce the need for child labor. Yet in many nations-in-debt lack of resources, a focus on military spending, and unfavorable trade patterns undercut development programs.

Working conditions of child labor

Working conditions were often *horrendous*（可怕的）. Children would work twelve hours a day, six days a week throughout the year. The hours were long, the pay was low and the children were exhausted and hungry. Factory children were kept inside all day long. Children who worked the fields spent long, hot days in the sun or went barefoot in mud and rain. These young workers could not attend school and rarely knew how to read or write.

Lack of Education

Education is the most important factor in ending abusive forms of child labor. Misplaced government priorities and cuts in social spending forced by international lending institutions means diminished support for education. Availability, quality and relevance of education suffer as a result. World-wide some 140 million primary age children are not enrolled in school. School fees (sometimes $6 – 10 per month) often force children to work, while inflexible classroom schedules demand that they choose between work and school.

Movements against child labor

1. Children in the United States continued to work under deplorable conditions until well into the mid-twentieth century. In the early nineteen hundreds, reformers began working to raise awareness about the dangers of child labor and tried to establish laws regulating the practice. In 1904, the National Child Labor Committee was formed. In 1908, the Committee hired Lewis Hine as its staff photographer and sent him throughout the country to photograph and report on child labor. Documenting child labor in both photographs and words, his state-by-state and industry-by-industry surveys became one of the movement's most powerful tools. Often photographing the children looking directly into the camera, Hine brought them face to face with people throughout the country who would rather believe that such poverty and hardship did not exist.

2. The movement against child labor confronted its biggest obstacle when it *lobbied*(游说) for the creation of a federal child labor law that would prohibit the use of child labor, nationwide. At the time, the federal government did not have clear authority to regulate child labor. Legal scholars believed that the U. S. Constitution left the matter of child labor to each State to regulate as it saw fit. Nevertheless, the movement was able to generate strong public support for the federal regulation of child labor. It also succeeded in establishing a Children's Bureau within the United States government in 1912.

3. By 1916, the U. S. Congress had passed its first federal child labor law, which effectively prevented factories and mines from using children under the age of 14. However, the U. S. Supreme Court struck down the law and ruled that it was not within the federal government's authority to regulate child labor. In December of 1918, Congress tried again and passed a second child labor law. This time, it based the law on its powers of taxation rather than its powers of interstate commerce. However, the U. S. Supreme Court again struck down the law for the same reasons.

4. For the next twenty years, the U. S. Congress and the U. S. Supreme court remained at odds over federal regulation of child labor. It wasn't until 1938 that federal protection of working children would be obtained through passage of the Fair Labor Standards Act. Like the first child labor bill, it prohibited the interstate commerce of products or services that were made using children under a certain age. It also established minimum standards and working conditions for the employment children above a certain age. The law was again challenged in the U. S. Supreme Court. However, in 1941, the U. S. Supreme Court reversed its earlier ruling on the 1918 law and upheld the right of the federal government to use its interstate commerce powers to regulate child labor.

Child labor all over the world

1. With the Fair Labor Standards Act and its amendments, the movement to end child labor in the United States accomplished most of what it initially set out to do. The worst abuses of child labor as it existed in the first few decades of the twentieth century are now history. Countless children and their children were saved from deadening exploitation in mines, mills, and factories. But new challenges have arisen both in the United States and abroad. Young people around the world continue to *toil*(苦干) as child laborers. Internationally, two hundred fifty million children

work to help support their families. Africa, Asia, Central America and South America have the highest rates of child labor. There are also a significant number of children who are migrant farm workers and sweatshop workers in the United States.

2. Children weaving carpets develop muscular deformities and respiratory infections from fiber and chemical inhalation. Long hours, regimentation, and sometimes physical and psychological abuse often earns them less than 1% of the eventual retail price.

3. In South Asia a needy family "exchanges" their 8-year old child for a cash loan. The money lender puts the child into bonded labor until the debt is paid. A $10 loan can ensnare a child for life as daily expenses and work errors count against her pennies-a-day income. 20-hour days lead to physical and mental injury, and social deprivation.

4. Often children work with family members to produce food for their own consumption. A growing number work in the export-oriented commercial agricultural sector—demanding and dangerous. As many as 100,000—usually children of migrant workers—labor illegally in U. S. agriculture.

5. Millions of children are "hidden" workers, kept by wealthy families as domestic servants. These children (90% young girls) often are unpaid except for room and board. A day's work for a child as young as 5 years old can average 15—18 hours, and include sexual and emotional abuse.

6. Millions of youth (girls and boys) are lured to urban centers' sex trade for abuse by local customers or foreigners (almost always men). As the threat of AIDS looms, younger and younger children are sought; sometimes the child is as young as 7 years old. In the U. S. , some 100,000 children are involved in prostitution.

7. Some 200,000 children serve as soldiers. Easily trainable and eager to please adult commanders, these children will face a lifetime of unlearning the arts of war if other educational experiences are even available.

1. In the early 1900's, reformers began working to raise awareness about the dangers of child labor.
2. Child labors were allowed to attend night school where they learned reading and writing.
3. The rise of child labor in the United States began in the late 1700's and early 1800's.
4. In 1908, the U. S. Congress hired Lewis Hine as its staff photographer.
5. Children who worked the fields spent long days in the sun or went barefoot in mud and rain.
6. By 1900, more than ten million U. S. children were at work.
7. Presently in America, nearly 28 percent of the children between 16 and 18 are employed.
8. The strong force in increasing the number of working children in the late seventeen and early eighteen hundreds was _____.
9. By 1916, the U. S. Congress had passed its first federal child labor law, which effectively prevented factories and mines from using children _____.
10. _____ have the highest rates of child labor.

Section B   Discourse Vocabulary Test

Directions：（略）

Passage 2

There is one difference between the sexes on which __11__ every expert agrees. Men are more aggressive than women. It shows up in 2-year-olds. It continues through school days and __12__ into adulthood.

Feminists have argued that the *nurturing*（教养）nature of women is not biological in origin，but rather has been *drummed*（灌输）into women by a society. But the signs that it is at least partly inborn are too numerous to __13__. Female *toddlers*（学步的孩子）learn much faster than males just as tiny infant girls respond more readily to human faces. And grown women are far more *adept*（熟练）than men at interpreting facial __14__, such as anger, sadness, and fear.

What difference do such differences make in the real world? Among other things, women appear to be somewhat less __15__ than men. At the Harvard Law School, for instance, female students enter with certificates just as outstanding as those of their male fellows. But they don't __16__ for the "Law Review" in proportionate numbers，a fact some school officials attribute to women's discomfort in the incredibly competitive atmosphere.

Students of management styles have found fewer differences than they expected between men and women who reach leadership positions，perhaps because many successful women __17__ imitate *masculine*（男性的）ways. But an analysis by Purdue social psychologist Alice Eagle of 166 studies of leadership style did find one __18__ difference：men __19__ to be more "autocratic"—making decision on their own—while women tend to consult colleagues and subordinates more often.

The aggression nurturance *gulf*（鸿沟）even shows up in politics. The "gender gap" in polling is real and enduring：men are far more prone to support a strong defense and tough law-and-order measures such as capital punishment，for instance，while women are more __20__ to approve of higher spending to solve domestic social problems such as poverty and inequality.

Applied to the female of the species，the word "different" has，for centuries，been read to mean "inferior". At last，that is beginning to change. And in the end，it's not a question of better or worse. The obvious point is that each sex brings strengths and weaknesses that may check and balance the other；each is half of the human whole.

A）essentially	I）deliberately
B）virtually	J）qualify
C）likely	K）like
D）convenient	L）tend
E）consistent	M）competitive
F）ignore	N）investigate
G）fit	O）persists
H）expressions	

Section C　Reading in Depth

Directions:（略）

Passage 3

If you feel overwhelmed by your college experiences, you are not alone——many of today's college students are suffering from a form of shock.

Lisa is a good example of a student in shock. She is an attractive, intelligent twenty-year-old college junior at a state university. Now, only three years later, Lisa is miserable. She has changed her major four times and is forced to hold down two part-time jobs in order to pay her tuition. She suffers from sleeping and eating disorders and has no close friends. Sometimes she bursts out crying for no apparent reason.

What is happening to Lisa happens to millions of college students each year. As a result, roughly one-quarter of the student population at any time will suffer from symptoms of depression. Of that group, almost half will experience depression intense enough to call for professional help. But many reject that idea, because they don't want people to think there's something wrong with them.

There are three reasons today's college students are suffering more than in earlier generations. First is a weakening family support structure. Today, with high divorce rates and many parents experiencing their own psychological difficulties, the traditional family is not always available for guidance and support.

Another problem is financial pressure. In the last decade tuition costs have *skyrocketed*（猛涨）——up about sixty-six percent at public colleges and ninety percent at private schools. At the same time there has been a cutback in federal aid to students. College loans are now much harder to obtain. Consequently, most students must work at least part-time.

A final cause of student shock is the large selection of majors available. Because of the *magnitude*（重要性）and difficulty of choosing a major, college can prove a time of great *indecision*（犹豫不决）. Many students switch majors. As a result, it is becoming common place to take five or six years to get a degree. It can be depressing to students to be faced with the added tuition costs.

While there is no magic cure-all for student shock, colleges have begun to research into the psychological problems of students, and *upgrade*（提高）their psychological counseling centers to handle the greater demand for services. In addition, stress-management workshops have become common on college campuses. Instructors teach students various techniques for handling stress.

21. Which of the following best expresses the central point of the selection?

　　A) Going to college is a depressing experience for many students.

　　B) Lisa has not enjoyed college because her life has been filled with stress.

　　C) Stress-related problems are increasing on college campuses and schools have responded.

　　D) Colleges should increase their counseling services.

22. Which sentence best expresses the main idea of Paragraph 2?

　　A) Lisa is experiencing a form of shock.

B) Lisa can't decide on a major.

C) Lisa feels she has lost all her good friends.

D) Lisa cries frequently.

23. The author implies that some students who suffer from extreme depression _____.

A) should drop out of college

B) have never done well in school

C) can always handle it on their own

D) are reluctant to get professional help

24. According to Paragraph 7, which of the following methods is not being used by colleges to reduce stress?

A) Upgraded psychological counseling.

B) Psychological research.

C) Lowered tuition.

D) Instructions for students to deal with stress.

25. The author supports his point that college life has become more difficult for students with _____.

A) quotations from experts

B) statistics and reasons

C) information taken from a survey of college dropouts

D) personal experiences

Passage 4

France might be described as an "all-round" country, one that has achieved results of equal importance in many diverse branches of artistic and intellectual activity. The French ideal has always been the man who has a good all-round knowledge, an all-round understanding: it is the ideal of general culture as opposed to specialization.

This is the ideal reflected in the education France provides for her children. By studying this education we in England may learn a few things useful to ourselves even though, perhaps indeed because, the French system is very different from our own in its aims, its organization and its results. The French child, too, the raw material of this education, is unlike the English child and differences in the raw material may well account for differences in the processes employed.

The French child, boy or girl, gives one the impression of being intellectually more *precocious* (早熟的) than the product of the chillier English climate. English parents readily adapt their conversation to the child's point of view and interest themselves more in his games and childish preoccupations. The English are, as regards national character, younger than the French, or, to put it another way, there is in England no deep division between the life of the child and that of the grown man. The art of talking to children in the kind of language they understand is so much an English art that most of the French children's favorite books are translations from the English. French parents, on the other hand, do their best to develop the child's intelligence as rapidly as possible. They have little patience with childish ideas even if they do not go so far as to look upon childhood as an unfortunate but necessary *prelude* (开端) to adult life. Not that they need to force the child, for he usually leads himself willingly to the process, and enjoys the effect of his unexpectedly clever remarks and of his keen judgment of men and things. It is not without significance that the French mother instead of appealing to the child's heart by asking him to be good appeals to his reason by asking him to be wise. Reasonableness is looked for early in France, and the age of reason is fixed at seven years.

26. The author considers that France _____.

    A) specialized in the ideal of general culture

    B) favors the ideal of general culture

    C) is a specialist country in spite of herself

    D) cannot help being a specialist country

27. In comparing French and English education the author indicates that _____.

    A) a great deal can be learnt by both countries

    B) differences should not be looked for only in the methods

    C) the French child needs far more training

    D) the main differences are in the children

28. The passage suggests that the French child _____.

    A) is as he is because of the climate   B) only associates with adults

    C) is forced to behave like an adult   D) is not treated as a child

29. In Paragraph 3, what is said about English books _____.

    A) appears to be somewhat contradictory

    B) is not in any sense a contradiction

    C) suggests that French parents like English children's books

    D) suggests that French parents find these books educational

30. With what conclusion, regarding French mother, is the reader left?

    A) They are the most significant influence in their son's lives.

    B) They equate goodness with reason.

    C) They know how to appeal to what is best in their sons.

    D) They identify wisdom with reasonableness.

Section D   Short Answer Questions

Directions:（略）

Passage 5

    From good reading we can derive pleasure, companionship, experience, and instruction. A good book may absorb our attention so completely that for the time being we forget our surroundings and even our identity. Reading good books is one of the greatest pleasures in life. It increases our contentment when we are cheerful, and lessens our troubles when we are sad. Whatever our main purpose may be in reading, our contact with good books should never fail to give us enjoyment and satisfaction.

    With a good book in our hands we need never be lonely. Whether the characters portrayed are taken from real life or are pure imaginary, they may become our companions and friends. The people we meet in books may delight us either because they resemble human friends whom we hold dear or because they present unfamiliar types whom we are glad to welcome as new *acquaintances* (相识的人). Our human friends sometimes may bore us, but the friends we make in books need never weary us with company. When human friends desert us, good books are always ready to give us friendship, sympathy, and encouragement.

One of the most valuable gifts given by books is experience. Few of us can travel far from home or have a wide range of experience, but all of us can lead varied lives through the pages of books. Whether we wish to escape from the seemingly dull realities of everyday life or whether we long to visit some far-off places, a book will help us when nothing else can. To travel by book we need no bank account to pay our way; no airship or ocean liner or train to transport us; no passport to enter the land of our heart's desire. Through books we may get the thrill of risky adventure without danger. We can climb loft mountains and cross the scorching sands of the desert without hardship. In books we may join the *picturesque* (独特的) peasants in an Alpine village or the kindly natives on a South Sea island. The possibilities of nature, the enjoyment of music, the treasures of arts, the marvels of engineering, are all open to the wonder and enjoyment of those who read.

31. While reading we sometimes forget our surroundings and even our identity because _____.

_____ _____ _____ _____ _____

_____ _____ _____ _____ _____

32. The first sentence in Paragraph 2 means that _____.

_____ _____ _____ _____ _____

_____ _____ _____ _____ _____

33. According to the writer, _____ portrayed in books may become our companions and friends.

_____ _____ _____ _____ _____

_____ _____ _____ _____ _____

34. Why do people like their acquaintances in books all the more?

_____ _____ _____ _____ _____

_____ _____ _____ _____ _____

35. The phrase "to travel by book" means _____.

_____ _____ _____ _____ _____

_____ _____ _____ _____ _____

Notes and Explanations

Passage 1

Explanations

1. [Y] Movements against child labor 部分第一段第二句提到 In the early nineteenth hundreds, reformers began working to raise awareness about the dangers of child labor and tried to establish laws regulating the practice. 十九世纪早期,改革者着手致力于提高人们对童工的危险性的意识,并试图制定法律来规范这种行为。故可以得出答案为 Yes.

2. [N] Working conditions of child labor 部分最后一句提到 These young workers could not attend school and rarely know how to read or write. 这些童工不能上学,基本不会阅读和写字。因此答案为 No。

3. [Y] Rise of child labor 部分第一段第二句提到 The rise of child labor in the United States began in the late seventeen and early eighteen hundreds. 美国童工的兴起是在十七世纪后期和十八世纪的早期。故可以得出答案为 Yes。

4. [N] Movements against child labor 部分第一段中第四句提到 In 1908, the Committee hired Lewis Hine as its staff photographer and sent him throughout the country to photograph and report on child labor。在 1908 年,委员会雇用了刘易斯·海因作为摄影师,并派他在全国范围内拍摄并报告童工的情况。故答案为 No。

5. [Y] Working conditions of child labor 部分第五句提到 Children who worked in the fields spent long, hot days in the sun or went barefoot in mud and rain. 那些在地里工作的孩子们长时间处于太阳的暴晒下,或者光脚走在稀泥和雨水中。故答案为 Yes。

6. [N] Rise of child labor 部分第一段中第四句提到 By 1900, more than two million U. S. children were at work. 到 1900 年,美国有多于两百万的儿童在工作。故答案是 No。

7. [NG] Rise of child labor 部分第一段第五句提到 The 1900 census, which counted workers aged 10 to 15, found that 18. 2 percent of the country's children between those ages were employed. 在 1900 年的人口普查中,年龄在 10 岁到 15 岁之间的儿童中有 18.2% 都在工作。并没有提到 16 到 18 岁的儿童的情况,因此答案是 Not Given。

8. Rise of child labor 部分第一段第三句提到 Industrialization was a strong force in increasing the number of working children. 工业化是导致童工数目增加的重要因素。从而得出答案是 **industrialization**。

9. Movements against child labor 部分第三段第一句提到 By 1916, the U. S. Congress had passed its first federal child labor law, which effectively prevented factories and mines from using children under the age of 14. 到 1916 年,美国国会通过了第一个联邦童工法律,这个法律有效地限制了工厂和矿山雇佣 14 岁以下的儿童。从而得出答案是 **under the age of 14**。

10. Child labor all over the world 部分第一段倒数第二句提到 Africa, Asia, Central America and South America have the highest rates of child labor. 非洲、亚洲、中美洲和南美洲是童工率最高的地区。由此得出答案是 **Africa, Asia, Central America and South America**。

Passage 2

Notes

1. It shows up in 2-year-olds. (Line 2, Para. 1)

show up 意思是"到来,出现"。例如:

It was ten o'clock when he finally showed up. 十点钟时他终于到了。

We are hoping for a full team but only five players showed up.

今天我们希望全体队员都到齐,结果只到了五个人。

2. ...just as tiny infant girls respond more readily to human faces... (Line 4, Para. 2)

respond to 意为"反应,回应"。例如:

She responded to my letter with a telephone call. 她收到了我的信,给我回了个电话。

He responded to my volley with a backhand. 他反手一击,把我的球打了回来。

3. ...a fact some school officials attribute to women's discomfort... (Line 4~5, Para. 3)

attribute sth. to 意为"将……归因于"。例如:

She attributed her failure to bad luck. 她把她的失败归因于运气不好。

His great age is attributed to eating properly. 他的长寿归因于饮食得当。

4. ...men are far more prone to support... (Line 2, Para. 5)

be prone to 意思是"有……倾向的"。例如:

Everybody is prone to make mistakes when he is sleepy. 人在昏昏欲睡时都容易犯错误。

He is prone to lose temper when people disagree with him. 人家一不同意他的意见,他就发脾气。

Explanations

11. [B] 语法规则要求此处应填一个副词修饰形容词 every。选项 A、B、I 是副词。virtually 意思是"几乎,基本上",符合句意。

12. [O] 语法规则要求此处应填一个动词第三人称单数形式与 continues 一起作并列谓语。选项中只有 persists 是这种形式。这句话意思是"这种现象——男子更具有争强好胜心——贯穿在校学习时期并延续到成年时期。"persist 意思是"继续存在",符合句子的意思。

13. [F] 语法规则要求此处应填一个动词原形与 too numerous 构成 too...to... 结构,意思是"太多而不能……"。选项 F、G、J、L、N 都是动词原形。根据上文意思本句要表达的意思是"太多了而不能忽视",ignore 符合这个意思。

14. [H] 语法规则要求此处应填一个复数名词与 facial 一起作动名词 interpreting 的宾语。只有选项 H 是复数名词。facial expressions 意思是"面部表情"。anger, sadness and fear 都属于面部表情,所以选项 H 符合句意。

15. [M] 语法规则要求此处应填一个形容词和 less...than 构成形容词比较级形式。从下文所举的例子中看出,but they don't 与前文形成转折关系,由此推断出女性不如男性具有竞争力,competitive 符合句意,故选 M 项。

16. [J] 语法规则要求此处应该填一个动词原形且这个动词能和 for 搭配使用。选项中的动词原形有选项 F、G、J、L、N。能和 for 搭配使用的有选项 G 和 J。qualify for 意思是"合格",符合句意,故选 J 项。

17. [I] 语法规则要求此处应填一个副词修饰动词 imitate。选项 A、B、I 是副词。前一句话说男女之间有 fewer differences,而后一句话用 but 表示转折,可以推断此处应该填 deliberately,意思是"故意地,有目的地"。

18. [E] 语法规则要求此处应填一个形容词修饰名词 difference。选项 C、D、E、M 是形容词。本句中两次用到词组 tend to,意思是"倾向于,有……趋势",可以推断 consistent 符合本句意思。consistent 意思是"一致的,并立的"。

19. [L] 语法规则要求此处应填一个动词原形作谓语,并且这个动词可以带一个不定式 to consult 作宾语。选项中常带不定式作宾语的是 tend。tend to do sth. 意思是"倾向于做……,有……趋势"。tend to do sth. 也符合 men tend to..., while women tend to... 这一平行结构的要求。

20. [C] 语法规则要求此处应填一个形容词构成 be+形容词+to do/be 的结构。be likely to do/be 意思是"可能",符合上下文意思的要求。

Passage 3

Notes

1. She has changed her major four times and is forced to hold down two... （Line 2～3，Para. 2）

▷be forced to do 意为"被迫做某事"。例如：

She was forced to work ten hours every day for the boss. 她每天不得已要为老板工作 10 个小时。

▷hold down 意思是"保持，做"。例如：

The rate of inflation must be held down. 通货膨胀率必须保持在一定水平。

2. Sometimes she bursts out crying for no apparent reason. （Line 4～5，Para. 2）

burst out doing 意为"突然"。例如：

burst out crying/laughing/singing 突然哭起来/笑起来/唱起来

She burst out laughing after listening to a story. 她听完故事后突然笑了起来。

3. As a result, roughly one-quarter of the student... （Line 1～2，Para. 3）

Consequently, most students must work at least part-time. （Line 5，Para. 5）

▷as a result 和 consequently 都表示"结果，因而"。例如：

My car broke down and consequently/as a result I was late. 我的车坏了，所以我迟到了。

▷as a result of 表示"由于"。例如：

He was late as a result of the traffic jam. 由于交通阻塞，他迟到了。

4. Of that group, almost... to call for professional help. （Line 3，Para. 3）

▷call for 意思是"要求，需要"。例如：

The situation calls for prompt action. 形势所迫，必须立即采取行动。

That rude remark was not called for. 没必要说那么难听的话。

▷这里的 call 还可以用作名词。例如：

The President made a call for national unity. 总统号召全国上下团结起来。

5. It can be depressing to students to be faced with the added tuition costs. （Line 4，Para. 6）

be faced with 意为"面临"。例如：

The new government is faced with a lot of problems. 新政府面临着很多问题。

Explanations

　　本文讲到大学生活使得很多大学生感到不安。有四分之一的大学生会产生压抑的感觉，有时甚至还需要求助于心理医生。作者随后分析了造成这种压抑的三个原因：首先是家庭结构的变化使得父母们忽略了对孩子的帮助；其次是由于学费上涨和政府对学生资助的减少造成了学生的经济压力；第三是专业选择范围的扩大使得学生不断地调换专业而延长了他们的毕业时间，加重了经济负担。

21. C）主旨题。本文首先讲到大学生活使得很多大学生感到不安，然后讲到校方对这一问题的反应和采取的措施。文章第一句就指出了文章的主题。

22. A）推断题。第二段讲述了 Lisa 在中学里是一个非常出色的学生，但是进入大学以后，她换了四个专业，并且不得不靠打两份工来支付学费。Lisa 整天寝食难安，也没有知心朋友，有时还会莫名地大哭。B、C、D 三项说的都是细节，而不是第二段的主题。

23. D）细节题。第三段中说，Of that group, almost half will... to call for professional help，然而很多学生因为不愿让别人认为他们有病而拒绝求助于医生。

24. C）细节题。在第七段中提到了选项 A（增加心理咨询）、选项 B（进行心理研究）、选项 D（指导学生如何减压），没有提到选项 C。

25. B）细节题。文中用了 one quarter，half，sixth-six，ninety 等数字来说明问题，并且分析了出现问题的三个原因,因此 B 项为正确答案。

Passage 4

Notes

1. France might be described as an "all-round" country... (Line 1, Para. 1)

   all-round 的意思是"全面的"。这句话的意思是:法国是一个全面发展的国家,在各种文学艺术和科学技术方面都取得过重大成就。

2. The French child, too, the raw material of this education... (Line 4, Para. 2)

   raw material 的意思是"原材料",这里指教育对象。法国的教育对象与英国的不同,这种差异也许能够说明为什么他们采取的教育方针不同。

3. The French child,... more precocious than the product of the chillier English climate. (Line 1~2, Para. 3)

   这里 the product of the chillier English climate 用来比喻"在英国寒冷的气候中出生的孩子"。

4. ...go so far as to look upon childhood as an unfortunate but... (Line 9~10, Para. 3)

   look upon...as 意思是"把……看作"。例如:

   She looked upon the little girl as her own daughter. 她把那个小女孩看作自己的亲生女儿。

Explanations

　　文章中作者认为法国是一个全面发展的国家,在文学艺术和科学技术方面都很有建树,这是因为法国人一直把培养全面发展的人作为他们的理想。因此在教育孩子的方法上,法国人与英国人有很多的不同之处。而受到民族性格的影响,英国的大人与孩子之间没有语言等方面的明确界限。因此英国与法国的教育差异不仅仅存在于教育方法。

26. **B)** 细节题。第一段第二句讲到法国人总想把孩子培养成知识渊博、多才多艺、善解人意的人。相对于专业化来讲这是一种一般文化中人们的普遍理想。在结尾处说:it is the ideal of general culture as opposed to specialization 所以正确答案应是 B 项。

27. **B)** 主旨题。第二段讲到法国和英国的教育体制有很大区别,如教学目标、教学体制和教学效果等。因此选 B 项。

28. **D)** 推断题。根据第三段第五句 The French parents, on the other hand, do their best to develop the children's intelligence as rapidly as possible.(他们想要尽量缩短童年的时间)可以推断出 D 项最符合题意。

29. **B)** 推断题。第三段中讲到,英国人和孩子进行交流的艺术非常精湛,因此英国的儿童读物也受到了法国儿童的喜爱。因此 B 项为正确答案。

30. **D)** 细节题。文章倒数第二句 It is not without significance that the French mother... 讲到法国的母亲要求孩子通过获得渊博的知识来获得理性,而不是通过循规蹈矩来获得理性,他们这样做并非没有意义。因此正确答案是 D 项。

Passage 5

Keys

31. the book completely absorbs our attention

32. our contact with good books may drive away any loneliness we feel

33. all characters, real and imaginary

34. Because they never weary or desert us.

35. "to take imaginary journeys to the places mentioned in the book"

Notes

1. Whatever our main purpose may be in reading, our contact with good books should never fail to give us enjoyment and satisfaction. (Line 4~6, Para. 1)

▷whatever 引导让步状语，表示"无论什么"。例如：

Whatever happens, don't be surprised. 无论发生什么事，都不要惊讶。

▷fail to 的意思是"未能，不能"。例如：

The car failed to stop at the red light. 那辆汽车在红灯前没有停住。

I failed to see the reason. 我不了解原因。

2. ... good books are always ready to give us friendship... (Line 6~7, Para. 2)

be ready to do sth. / for sth. 意为"愿意，做好准备"。例如：

I am always ready to help you. 我随时都可以帮助你。

The troop were ready for anything. 部队已经做好了一切准备。

3. Few of us can travel far from home or have a wide range of experience... (Line 1~2, Para. 3)

a range of 的意思是"成套，系列，种类"，既可以修饰可数名词，也可以修饰不可数名词。例如：

a whole range of tools/dresses/food 各式各样的工具/服装/食品

The new model comes in an exciting range of colors. 这种新式样有各种鲜艳的颜色。

4. Whether we wish to escape from the seemingly dull realities of... or whether we long to visit some far-off places... (Line 3~4, Para. 3)

long to 意为"希望，渴望"。例如：

She longed to escape from her mother's domination. 她渴望摆脱母亲的控制。

新世纪英语丛书

Unit 22

Section A　Skimming and Scanning

Directions：（略）

Passage 1

Coastline Danger

Tsunami of Papua New Guinea

On July 1, 1998, an unexpected tsunami pounded the northern coastline of Papua New Guinea. In three massive waves, as high as 15 meters, it washed away entire villages, drowned over 2,500 people and left thousands homeless. Survivors of the Papua New Guinea disaster described the tsunami as a wall of water hurling toward shore, averaging 10 meters high and extending about 5 kilometers from front to back. The largest wave swept over the shore at speeds of up to 20 kilometers per hour for more than a minute, before draining away in preparation for the next.

Tsunami of Indonesian island of Sumatra

On the morning of December 26, 2004 a magnitude 9.3 struck off the Northwest coast of the the Indonesian island of Sumatra. The earthquake resulted from complex slip on the *fault*（断层）where the oceanic portion of the Indian Plate slides under Sumatra, part of the Eurasian Plate. The earthquake deformed the ocean floor, pushing the overlying water up into a tsunami wave. The tsunami wave devastated nearby areas where the wave may have been as high 25 meters (80 feet) tall and killed nearly 300,000 people from nations in the region and tourists from around the world. The tsunami wave itself also traveled the globe, and was measured in the Pacific and many other places by tide gauges. Measurements in California exceeded 40 cm in height, while New Jersey saw water level fluctuations as great as 34 cm. Eyewitness accounts, photos, and videos provided unprecedented documentation of the event. To prepare for future tsunamis, we encourage everyone to educate themselves about what they can do now, and in the event that they should ever be threatened by a tsunami.

What is tsunami

1. What are tsunamis? Tsunamis are enormous waves initiated by sudden *seismic*（地震的）events. A tsunami is generated when a large mass of water is displaced suddenly, creating a swell that moves away from its origin. The effect is similar to the ripples that form when a pebble is dropped into a pond but a thousand times larger. A tsunami wave can be 100 to 200 kilometers wide and long. It can reach speeds of 725 to 800 km/hour. It can travel thousands of kilometers across the ocean and maintain a barely noticeable height of less than a half-meter. However, as the tsunami enters the shallow waters of a coastline, it bunches up into a monstrous wall of

seawater that can reach heights of 30 meters and still be many kilometers in length.

2. The impact of such large waves on a shoreline can be devastating. Buildings, bridges, and other structures may be destroyed. Extensive beach erosion commonly occurs. In addition, water may flood areas hundreds of meters inland. The amount of damage depends on the geometry of the coastline as well as the size of the tsunami. Because variations in the shapes of coastal areas can focus or diffuse the energy in a wave, different parts of a coastline may experience very different degrees of damage from a given tsunami. The largest waves, hence the greatest amount of damage, are generally observed in embayment that funnel the waves into a narrow bay.

Causes of tsunamis

1. Tsunamis are frequently caused by underwater earthquakes with a magnitude greater than 7 on the Richter scale. The most dangerous tsunamis are triggered by quakes with a shallow focus that produce extended vibrations and shift the sea floor vertically. Tsunamis are sometimes generated by other *catastrophic*(灾变的) events, such as underwater volcanic explosions. For example, the disastrous eruption of Krakatau that killed more than 30,000 people in 1883 produced waves that were 35 meters high and that traveled thousands of kilometers. Although scientists are not certain exactly how this eruption led to a tsunami, a recent study of sea-floor deposits suggests that water displaced by immense ash flows was the cause. Underwater landslides have also been known to create tsunamis. For instance, the Hawaiian Islands have all experienced enormous landslides in the past, and coastal sediments record evidence of tsunamis that were generated from them.

2. The exact trigger of the Papua New Guinea tsunami is not yet known, although an earthquake was certainly involved. Because the earthquake was relatively small, scientists were somewhat surprised by the disastrous results. One study of seismic data indicated that the earthquake was centered offshore and produced a 2-meter vertical displacement of the sea floor; the conclusion was that this abrupt motion triggered the tsunami. Other evidence indicates that the tsunami was produced by a huge offshore landslide, itself triggered by the earthquake. Eyewitness accounts indicate that the first wave struck shore about 20 minutes after the main shock of the earthquake, too long for the tsunami to have originated from sub-sea faulting during the quake. A slump or landslide typically lags several minutes behind an earthquake and could explain the delay. Further support comes from a 70-second-long rumble recorded in the middle of the Pacific soon after the earthquake. This sound lasted too long to have come from a small aftershock and may have represented a seafloor slide.

Preventing tsunamis

Unfortunately, tsunamis cannot be stopped or prevented. However, effective warning systems might save hundreds of lives. In the United States, the National Tsunami Hazard Mitigation Program has been developed to reduce the impacts of tsunamis along the U. S. Pacific Coast. One goal of this program is to improve the tsunami warning systems. Components of such systems include seismic sensors that ware of large earthquakes and oceanic sensors that detect tsunamis crossing the ocean. Destructive tsunamis need to be detected quickly so that warnings can be issued to allow orderly evacuation of coastal communities in the path of the waves. Of course, evacuation can only save lives if the tsunami is triggered far enough away to give advanced warning.

1. The passage gives a general description of underwater earthquake, underwater landslides and tsunamis.

2. Tsunamis are enormous waves initiated by gradual seismic events.

3. When the tsunami enters the shore, it would form a even bigger wave.

4. The tsunami may even influence the inland miles away from the shore.

5. An underwater earthquake of 5.5 on the Richter scale would definitely cause tsunamis.

6. The exact cause of the Papua New Guinea tsunami is not clear now.

7. One goal of the National Tsunami Hazard Mitigation Program is to reduce the influence caused by the tsunami according to the passage.

8. The speed of the largest wave in the tsunami of Papua New Guinea is _____ for more than a minute.

9. The amount of damage depends on the geometry of the coastline and _____.

10. Besides underwater earthquake, _____ may also cause tsunami.

Section B   Discourse Vocabulary Test
Directions:（略）

Passage 2

The way people hold to the belief that a fun-filled, pain-free life __11__ happiness actually reduces their chances of ever attaining real happiness. If fun and pleasure are equal to happiness, then pain must be equal to unhappiness. But in fact, the __12__ is true: more often than not, things that lead to happiness involve some pain.

As a result, many people avoid the very attempts that are the source of true happiness. They fear the pain __13__ brought by such things as marriage, raising children, professional achievement, religious commitment, self-improvement, etc.

Ask a bachelor why he __14__ marriage even though he finds dating to be less and less satisfying. If he is honest, he will tell you that he is afraid of making a commitment. For commitment is in fact quite painful. The single life is filled with fun, adventure and excitement. Marriage has such moments, but they are not its most __15__ features.

Couples with infant children are __16__ to get a whole night's sleep or a three-day vacation. I don't know any parent who would choose the word "fun" to __17__ raising children. But couples who decide not to have children never know the joy of watching a child grow up or of playing with a grandchild.

Understanding and accepting that true happiness has nothing to do with fun is one of the most liberating realizations. It liberates time: now we can __18__ more hours to activities that can genuinely increase our happiness. It __19__ money: buying that new car or those fancy clothes that will do nothing to increase our happiness now seems __20__. And it liberates us from envy: we now understand that all those who are always having so much fun actually may not be happy at all.

A）lucky	I ）believe
B）chiefly	J ）opposite
C）devote	K）inevitably
D）resists	L）take
E）equals	M）distinguishing
F）cheerful	N）liberates
G）pointless	O）attain
H）describe	

Section C   Reading in Depth

Directions：（略）

Passage 3

Normally a student must attend a certain number of courses in order to graduate, and each course which he attends gives him a credit which he may count towards a degree. In many American universities the total work for a degree consists of thirty-six courses each lasting for one semester. A typical course consists of three classes per week for fifteen weeks; while attending a university a student will probably attend four or five courses during each semester. Normally a student would expect to take four years attending two semesters each year. It is possible to spread the period of work for the degree over a longer period. It is also possible for a student to move between one university and another during his degree course, though this is not in fact done as a regular practice.

For every course that he follows a student is given a grade, which is recorded, and the record is available for the student to show to prospective employers. All this imposes a constant pressure and strain of work, but in spite of this some students still find time for great activity in student affairs. Elections to positions in student organizations arouse much enthusiasm. The effective work of maintaining discipline is usually performed by students who advise the academic authorities. Any student who is thought to have broken the rules, for example, by cheating has to appear before a student court. With the enormous number of students, the operation of the system does involve a certain amount of activity. A student who has held one of these positions of authority is much respected and it will be of benefit to him later in his career.

21. Normally a student would at least attend _____ classes each week.
    A) 36   B) 12   C) 20   D) 25
22. According to the first paragraph an American student is allowed _____.
    A) to live in a different university
    B) to take a particular course in a different university
    C) to live at home and drive to classes
    D) to get two degrees from two different universities
23. American university students are usually under pressure of work because _____.
    A) their academic performance will affect their future careers

B) they are heavily involved in student affairs

C) they have to observe university discipline

D) they want to run for positions of authority

24. Some students are enthusiastic for positions in student organizations probably because _____.

A) they hate the constant pressure and strain of their study

B) they will then be able to stay longer in the university

C) such positions help them get better jobs

D) such positions are usually well paid

25. The student organizations seem to be effective in _____.

A) dealing with the academic affairs of the university

B) ensuring that the students observe university regulations

C) evaluating students' performance by bringing them before a student court

D) keeping up the students' enthusiasm for social activities

Passage 4

Language learning begins with listening. Individual children vary greatly in the amount of listening they do before they start speaking, and late starters are often long listeners. Most children will "obey" spoken instructions some time before they can speak, though the word "obey" is hardly accurate as a description of the eager and delighted cooperation usually shown by the child. Before they can speak many children will also ask questions by gesture and by making questioning noises.

Any attempt to trace the development from the noises babies make to their first spoken words leads to considerable difficulties. It is agreed that they enjoy making noises and that during the first few months one or two noises sort themselves out as particularly *indicative* (表示) of delight, distress, *sociability* (社交) and so on. But since these cannot be said to show the baby's intention to communicate, they can hardly be regarded as early forms of language. It is agreed, too, that from about three months they play with sounds for enjoyment, and that by six months they are able to add new sounds to their store. This self-imitation leads on to deliberate imitation of sounds made or words spoken to them by other people. The problem then arises as to the point at which one can say that these imitations can be considered speech.

It is a problem we need not get our teeth into. The meaning of a word depends on what a particular person means by it in a particular situation; and it is clear that what a child means by a word will change as he gains more experience of the world. Thus the use, say at seven months, of "mama" as a greeting for his mother cannot be dismissed as a meaningless sound simply because he also uses it at other times for his father, his dog, or anything else he likes.

Playful and apparently meaningless imitation of what other people say continues after the child has begun to speak for himself. I doubt, however, whether anything is gained when parents cash in on this ability in an attempt to teach new sounds.

26. Before children start speaking, _____.

A) they need equal amount of listening

B) they need different amounts of listening

C) they are all eager to cooperate with adults by obeying spoken instructions

D) they can't understand and obey adult's oral instructions

27. Children who start speaking late _____ .

A) may have problems with their hearing

B) probably do not hear enough language spoken around them

C) usually pay close attention to what they hear

D) often take a longer time in learning to listen properly

28. A baby's first noises are _____ .

A) a reflection of his moods and feelings

B) an early form of language

C) a sign that he means to tell you something

D) an imitation of the speech of adults

29. The problem of deciding at what point a baby's imitations can be considered as speech

_____ .

A) is important because words have different meanings for different people

B) is not especially important because the changeover takes place gradually

C) is one that can never be properly understood because the meaning of words changes with age

D) is one that should be completely ignored because children's use of words often meaningless

30. According to the passage _____ .

A) parents can never hope to teach their children new sounds

B) children no longer imitate people after they begin to speak

C) children who are good at imitating learn new sounds more quickly

D) even after they have learnt to speak children still enjoy imitating

Section D Short Answer Questions

Directions：（略）

Passage 5

Tea drinking was common in China for nearly one thousand years before anyone in Europe had ever heard about tea. People in Britain were much slower in finding out what tea was like，mainly because tea was very expensive. It could not be bought in shops and even those people who could afford to have it sent from Holland did so only because it was a fashionable curiosity. Some of them were not sure how to use it. They thought it was a vegetable and tried cooking the leaves. Then they served them mixed with butter and salt. They soon discovered their mistake but many people used to spread the used tea leaves on bread and give them to their children as sandwiches.

Tea remained scarce and very expensive in England until the ships of the East India Company began to bring it direct from China early in the seventeenth century. During the next few years so much tea came into the country that the price fell and many more people could afford to buy it.

At the same time people on the Continent were becoming more and more fond of tea. Until then tea had been drunk without milk in it. But one day a famous French lady named Madame de

Sevigne decided to see what tea tasted like when milk was added. She found it so pleasant that she would never again drink it without milk. Because she was such a great lady her friends thought they must copy everything she did so they also drank their tea with milk in it. Slowly this habit spread until it reached England and today very few Britons drink tea without milk.

At first, tea was usually drunk after dinner in the evening. No one ever thought of drinking tea in the afternoon until a *duchess* (公爵夫人) found that a cup of tea and piece of cake at three or four o'clock stopped her getting "a sinking feeling" as she called it. She invited her friends to have this new meal with her and therefore, teatime was born.

31. What is the passage mainly about?

_____ _____ _____ _____ _____

_____ _____ _____ _____ _____

32. Not many people drunk tea before the seventeenth century in England because _____.

_____ _____ _____ _____ _____

_____ _____ _____ _____ _____

33. Madame de Sevigne found tea especially pleasant by _____.

_____ _____ _____ _____ _____

34. What does "tea-time" refer to?

_____ _____ _____ _____ _____

_____ _____ _____ _____ _____

35. According to the passage, what kind of people influenced the habit of drinking tea?

_____ _____ _____ _____ _____

_____ _____ _____ _____ _____

Notes and Explanations

Passage 1

Explanations

1. [N] 通过快速浏览(scan)文章中的几个黑体字标题,便可得知本文重点介绍了海啸的事例、导致海啸的原因以及如何防止海啸。故答案是 No。
2. [N] What is tsunami? 部分第一段第二句提到 Tsunamis are enormous waves initiated by sudden seismic events. 海啸是由突然的地震导致巨大的波浪发生的。故答案是 No。
3. [Y] What is tsunami? 部分第一段最后一句提到 However, as the tsunami enters the shallow waters of a coastline, it bunches up into a monstrous wall of seawater that can reach heights of 30 meters and still be many kilometers in length. 然而,当海啸到了海岸边的浅水地带时,会聚成一道异常巨大的高达 30 米、宽度达到几公里的水墙。故答案是 Yes。
4. [Y] What is tsunami? 部分第二段第四句提到 In addition, water may flood areas hundreds of meters inland. 另外,水能淹没岸边上百米的范围。故答案是 Yes。
5. [N] Causes of tsunami 部分第一段第一句提到 Tsunamis are frequently caused by underwater

earthquakes with a magnitude greater than 7 on the Richter scale. 海啸通常都是由高于里氏 7 级的海底地震引起的。故题干中说里氏 5.5 级的地震一定会引起海啸是错误的。答案是 No。

6. [Y] 在文章 Causes of tsunami 部分的第二段开头提到 The exact trigger of the Papua New Guinea tsunami is not yet known, although an earthquake was certainly involved. 尽管发生了地震,但导致巴布亚新几内亚海啸的确切原因目前还不知道。故答案是 Yes。

7. [N] 最后一部分 Preventing tsunamis 中第四句提到 One goal of this program is to improve the tsunami warning systems. 这个项目的一个目的就是改进海啸预警系统。故答案是 No。

8. 第一部分 Tsunami of Papua New Guinea 中最后一句提到 The largest wave swept over the shore at speeds of up to 20 kilometers per hour for more than a minute. 冲上海岸的最大波浪的速度高达每小时 20 公里。从而得出答案是 **20 kilometers per hour**。

9. 第三部分 What is tsunami? 中第二段第五句提到 The amount of damage depends on the geometry of the coast line as well as the size of the tsunami. 海啸引起的破坏程度取决于海岸线的形状和海啸的大小。由此得出答案是 **the size of the tsunami**。

10. 第四部分 Causes of tsunami 的第一段中分别提到 Tsunamis are sometimes generated by other catastrophic events, such as underwater volcanic explosions. 海啸有时会由其他一些灾难性事件引起,比如海底火山爆发。还有 Underwater landslides have also been known to create tsunamis 海底的山体滑坡也会导致海啸。由此得出答案是 **underwater volcanic explosions, and underwater landslides**。

Passage 2

Notes

1. The way people hold to the belief that a fun-filled, pain-free life... (Line 1, Para. 1)
▷hold to 意为"坚持,遵循"。例如:
She holds to her convictions. 她始终坚持自己的信念。
The mother holds to the idea that her son will come back. 母亲一直认为她的儿子会回来。
▷pain-free 意思是"没有痛苦的",类似的构词还有 ticket-free 免票的,tree-free 没有树的。

2. If fun and pleasure are equal to happiness... (Line 2, Para. 1)
be equal to 意思是"相等的,能胜任的,具有……资格的"。例如:
My heart is not equal to the race. 我的心脏无法承受那场比赛。
He was equal to the occasion. 他能应付那个场面。

3. But in fact, the opposition is true: more often than not, things that lead to happiness involve some pain. (Line 3~4, Para. 1)
more often than not 意思是"多半,通常"。例如:
Nancy comes over on Saturday more often than not. 南茜通常在周六来。

4. As a result, many people avoid the very attempts that are... (Line 1, Para. 2)
very 在这句话中的意思是"正是,正好,就(在)……"。例如:
This is the very book I want. 这就是我想要的书。
At the very moment the phone rang. 正好在那个时候电话响了。

Explanations

11. [E] 语法规则要求此处应填一个动词第三人称单数形式作 that 引导的同位语从句的谓语。选项 D、E、N 是动词第三人称单数形式。根据下一句话 If fun and pleasure are equal to happiness, then pain must be equal to unhappiness. 可以判断出此处应填 equals。

12. [J] 语法规则要求此处应填一个单数名词作句子的主语。选项中只有 J 项单数名词。本句话中 But in

fact，表示转折关系，与前一句话情况相反，opposite 意思是"相反的"，符合句意。

13. [K] 语法规则要求此处应填一个副词修饰过去分词短语 brought by such things as marriage, raising children, professional achievement, religious commitment, self-improvement, etc. 选项 B、K 是副词。根据前一句话 avoid 判断出，许多人想逃避真正幸福的来源，因为他们担心痛苦是不可避免地由婚姻、抚养孩子等带来的，所以 inevitably（不可避免地）符合句意。

14. [D] 语法规则要求此处应填一个动词的第三人称单数形式作 why 引导的宾语从句的谓语。根据后一句话中 he is afraid of making a commitment，可判断出他（单身汉）"拒绝或逃避婚姻"，resists（对抗，抵制）符合句意，故选 D 项。

15. [M] 语法规则要求此处应填一个形容词构成形容词最高级形式。选项 A、F、G、M 是形容词。根据上文 The single life is filled with fun, adventure and excitement. 而婚姻生活也有这样的时刻，但它们不是生活的主流，可以判断出 distinguishing 符合句意，意思是"显著的，突出的"，故选 M 项。

16. [A] 语法规则要求此处应填一个形容词构成 be ＋ 形容词 ＋ to do sth. 的句型。本句话意思是"有婴儿的夫妇晚上能睡一个好觉或度三天假是非常幸运的事情"，lucky（幸运的）符合句意，故选 A 项。

17. [H] 语法规则要求此处应填一个动词原形和 to 构成动词不定式作目的状语修饰 choose the word fun. 选项 C、H、I、L、O 是动词原形，但只有 describe 符合句意"选择词汇来描述某事（物）"。

18. [C] 语法规则要求此处应填一个动词原形和介词 to 搭配作谓语。选项 C、H、I、L、O 是动词原形，能和 to 搭配的是 devote。devote...to... 意思是"专心于……"，符合句意。

19. [N] 语法规则要求此处应填一个动词的第三人称单数形式作谓语。上句话 It liberates time. 和本句话 It liberates money. 应属排比句，句子结构相同。故 liberates 符合句意。

20. [G] 语法规则要求此处应填一个形容词作表语。根据 It liberates money：buying that new car or those fancy clothes that will do nothing to increase our happiness now seems pointless. 可以判断出此处应该填一个贬义词，pointless 意思是"无意义的"，符合句意，故选 G 项。

Passage 3

Notes

1. Normally a student must attend a certain number of courses in order to graduate, and each course which he attends gives him a credit which he may count towards a degree. (Line 1～2, Para. 1)

   count towards 意思是"（按照获得某事物的条件）被包括在内的"。例如：

   These payments will count towards your pension. 你付的这些款项将来会计入你的养老金里。

2. ..., and the record is available for the student to show to prospective employers. (Line 1～2, Para. 2)

   be available for 意为"用作"。例如：

   This machine is not available for washing. 这个机器不是用来洗衣服的。

   The Prime Minister was not available for comment. 首相无暇做出评论。

3. Elections to positions in student organizations arouse much enthusiasm. (Line 4, Para. 2)

   arouse much enthusiasm 意思是"激起很多的热情"。例如：

   The pop singer arouses much enthusiasm among his fans. 这位流行歌手激起了歌迷的极大热情。

4. Any student who is thought to have broken the rules... (Line 6, Para. 2)

   这个句子的意思是：任何被认为违反了纪律的学生，如考试作弊等，都会受到学生法庭的审判。

5. ...and it will be of benefit to him later in his career. (Line 9, Para. 2)

   be of benefit to... 意思是"对……有好处，使……获益"。例如：

   Fluent spoken English will be of benefit to you in your future communication with the foreigners.

   流利的英语口语对你今后与外国人交流有好处。

Explanations

　　本文介绍了美国大学的学分制。美国的大学生们要上一定数量的课程之后才可能得到学分。每一门课程的学分都会记录在案,并且可能在学生求职的时候产生影响,因而学生们对学分非常重视。他们在上课的同时还会争取参加一些学校的组织,以增加自己的影响力,为未来奠定基础。

21. B) 细节题。第一段第三句讲到 A typical course consists of three classes per week for fifteen weeks; while attending a university a student will probably attend four or five courses during each semester. 因此正确答案为 B 项。

22. B) 细节题。第一段最后一句讲到学生在大学阶段,可以在两所不同的大学修学分,但事实上,这种情况并不多见。文章没有提到选项 A、C 和 D,因此 B 项是正确答案。

23. A) 细节题。第二段的第一句讲到,每一门课程都会有成绩,这些成绩会被记录在案,将来学生求职时会用到。第二句 All this imposes a constant pressure and strain of work. 正是本题的题干。

24. C) 推断题。第二段第三句到最后一句讲到学生们热衷于参加学校学生工作,是因为这些学生团体在学校具有一定的影响力,因此 A student who has held one of these positions of authority is much respected and it will be benefit to him later in his career. 从此可以得出 C 项为正确答案。

25. B) 细节题。第二段第四句讲到学生通过向学校当局提出合理建议来有效地维持学校的秩序,违反校规的人将受到学生法庭的审判。因此正确答案为 B 项。

Passage 4

Notes

1. Language learning begins with listening. (Line 1, Para. 1)
▷begin with... 意为"首先,以……开始"。例如:
I have to begin with an apology. 我得首先表示歉意。
▷to begin with 表示"首先,第一"。例如:
I'm not going. To begin with I haven't a ticket, and secondly I don't like the play.
我不去。一来我没票,二来我不喜欢这出戏。

2. Individual children vary greatly in the amount of listening... (Line 1~2, Para. 1)
vary in 意思是"在……方面不同"。例如:
Computers vary widely in price. 计算机的价格差异很大。

3. ...one or two noises sort themselves out as particularly... (Line 3, Para. 2)
sort out 意为"分类,捡出"。例如:
We must sort out the good apples from the bad. 我们一定要将好坏苹果分开。

4. ...they are able to add new sounds to their store. (Line 6~7, Para. 2)
add...to 意思是"增加"。例如:
Will you add more sugar to your coffee? 你的咖啡要多加些糖吗?
Please add my name to the list. 请在名单上加上我的名字。

5. It is a problem we need not get our teeth into. (Line 1, Para. 3)
get one's teeth into 是"积极地、有目的地去做……"的意思。例如:
Now more and more people get their teeth into the problem of environment.
现在越来越多的人热衷于环境问题。

6. ...when parents cash in on this ability in an attempt to teach new sounds. (Line 2~3, Para. 4)
cash in on 意思是"利用,从……获利"。例如:
The shops are cashing in on temporary shortages by raising prices.
商店趁一时缺货而提高价格,以便从中获利。

Explanations

在这篇文章中,作者想告诉我们,婴儿是先学会听之后才开始学说话的。在婴儿刚刚开始发出声音的几个月里,他们用一两种声音来表示自己的快乐和悲伤以及与别人交流。在小孩学会自己说话之后,他们还会很愿意去模仿那些他们并不明白是什么意思的话。但作者对于父母们想要利用这个特点教孩子一些新的声音的做法提出质疑。

26. **B**) 细节题。第一段第二句讲到,在小孩学会说话之前,individual children vary 是 greatly in the amount of listening they do,B 项与这个意思最接近,所以是正确答案。

27. **D**) 细节题。第一段第二句说到...late speakers are often long listeners. D 项解释了这种说法,而 A、B、C 三项则与文章内容不符。

28. **A**) 推断题。第二段第二句说到底 It is agreed that they enjoy making noises and that... and so on. 在婴儿刚刚开始发出声音的几个月里,他们用一两种声音来表示自己的快乐和悲伤以及与别人交流。因此 A 项(作为他的情绪和感情的一种反映)最符合这个意思。而 B、C、D 三项都把这种行为视作语言,不符合文章的原意。

29. **B**) 推断题。根据是第二段最后一句和第三段第一句。

30. **D**) 推断题。最后一段讲到:在小孩学会自己说话之后,他们还会继续模仿那些他们并不明白是什么意思的话。D 项符合这一说法;而 A 和 C 项与此段第二句 I doubt, however, whether anything is gained when parents cash in on this ability in an attempt to teach new sounds. 相关,但内容不符。因此 D 项为正确答案。

Passage 5

Keys

31. Tea drinking in England.

32. it was scarce and very expensive

33. adding milk to it

34. Three or four o'clock in the afternoon when English people usually have tea.

35. The upper circles/class.

Notes

1. ... anyone in Europe had ever heard about tea. (Line 1～2, Para. 1)

   hear about 意为"听到关于某事物的消息"。例如:

   I've just heard about his dismissal. 我刚听到他遭解雇的事。

   You will hear about this later. 这事你就等着瞧吧。

2. ... even those people who could afford to have it sent from Holland... (Line 3～4, Para. 1)

   can/could afford to do 意为"有足够的钱(时间)做"。例如:

   They walked because they couldn't afford to take a taxi. 他们因为坐不起计程车而步行。

3. At the same time people on the Continent were becoming more and more fond of tea. (Line 1, Para. 3)

   the Continent 指"欧洲大陆"。由于英国是由众多岛屿构成的,因此它与欧洲的其他国家有大海相隔。

   become fond of 意为"喜欢上……"。例如:

   He was becoming fond of painting after his retirement. 他退休以后喜欢上了绘画。

4. No one ever thought of drinking tea in the afternoon... (Line 1～2, Para. 4)

   think of 意为"想到,考虑"。例如:What do you think of the play? 你认为那戏剧怎样?

   I can't think of his phone number. 我想不起他的电话号码了。

Unit 23

Section A　Skimming and Scanning

Directions：(略)

Passage 1

How Clean Is the Water?

Plants and animals require water that is moderately pure. They cannot survive if their water is loaded with toxic chemicals or harmful *microorganisms*(微生物). If severe, water pollution can kill large numbers of fish, birds, and other animals, in some cases killing all members of a species in an affected area. Fish and shellfish harvested from polluted waters may be unsafe to eat. People who ingest polluted water can become ill, and, with prolonged exposure, may develop cancers or bear children with birth defects. The major water pollutants can be classed into five categories, each of which presents its own set of hazards.

Petroleum products

Oil and chemicals derived from petroleum are used for fuel, lubrication, plastics manufacturing, and many other purposes. However, these petroleum products often find their way into the water by means of accidental spills from ships, tanker trucks, pipelines, and leaky underground storage tanks. An oil spill has its worst effects when it encounters a shoreline. Oil in coastal waters kills tide pool life and harms birds and marine mammals by causing feathers and fur to lose their natural waterproof quality, which causes the animals to drown or die of cold. Additionally, these animals can become sick or poisoned when they swallow the oil while *preening* (用嘴梳理).

Pesticides and herbicides

1. Pesticides and herbicides are useful for killing unwanted insects and weeds, for instance on farms or in suburban yards. Some of these chemicals are *biodegradable*(生物能分解的) and quickly decay into harmless or less harmful forms, while others are non-biodegradable and remain dangerous for many years. When animals consume plants that have been treated with certain non-biodegradable chemicals, such as DDT, these chemicals are absorbed into the tissues or organs of the animals. When other animals feed on these contaminated animals, the chemicals are passed up the food chain. With each step up the food chain, the concentration of the pollutant increases. In one study, DDT levels in *ospreys*(鱼鹰) were found to be 10 to 50 times higher than in the fish that they ate, 600 times the level in the plankton that the fish ate, and 10 million times higher than in the water. Animals at the top of food chains may, as a result of these chemical concentrations, suffer cancers, reproductive problems, and death.

2. Many drinking water supplies are contaminated with pesticides from widespread

agricultural use. More than 14 million Americans drink water contaminated with pesticides, and the Environmental Protection Agency (EPA) estimates that 10 percent of wells contain pesticides. Nitrates, a pollutant often derived from fertilizer runoff, can cause *methemoglobinemia*(贫血症) in infants, a potentially lethal form of anemia that is also called "blue baby syndrome."

Heavy metals

Heavy metals, such as copper, lead, mercury, and *selenium*(硒), get into water from many sources, including industries, automobile exhaust, mines, and even natural soil. Like pesticides, heavy metals become more concentrated as animals feed on plants and are consumed in turn by other animals. When they reach high levels in the body, heavy metals can be immediately poisonous, or can result in long-term health problems similar to those caused by pesticides and herbicides. For example, *cadmium*(镉) in fertilizer derived from sewage *sludge*(淤泥) can be absorbed by crops. If these crops are eaten by humans in sufficient amounts, the metal can cause liver and kidney damage. Lead can get into water from lead pipes and solder in older water systems; children exposed to lead in water can suffer mental retardation.

Hazardous wastes

Hazardous wastes are chemical wastes that are toxic (poisonous), reactive (capable of producing explosive or toxic gases), corrosive (capable of corroding steel), or ignitable (flammable). If dumped, improperly treated or stored, hazardous wastes can pollute water supplies and cause a variety of illness, birth defects and cancers. Even tiny amounts, over time, can lead to serious health problems. In 1969, the Cuyahoga River in Cleveland, Ohio, was so polluted with hazardous wastes that it caught fire and burned. PCBs, a class of chemicals once widely used in electrical equipment such as transformers, can get into the environment through oil spills and even a small amount can reach toxic levels as organisms eat one another.

Infectious organisms

A 1994 study by the Centers for Disease Control and Prevention (CDC) estimated that about 900,000 people get sick annually in the United States because of organisms in their drinking water, and around 900 people die. Many disease-causing organisms that are present in small numbers in most natural waters are considered pollutants when found in drinking water. Such *parasites*(寄生物) as Giardia lambia and Cryptosporidium parvum occasionally turn up in urban water supplies. These parasites can cause illness, especially in people who are very old or very young, and in people who are already suffering from other diseases. In 1993, an outbreak of Cryptosporidium in the water supply of Milwaukee, Wisconsin, sickened more than 400,000 people and killed more than 100.

Receding Federal Government Commitment law

1. EPA must enforce current laws. Congress should make funding water clean up a top priority.

2. On May 19, just hours before a Congressional vote, the U. S. Environmental Protection Agency withdrew its proposed revision to sewage dumping rules. Hours later, the U. S. House approved an amendment offered by Rep. Bart Stupak (D-MI) and Clay Shaw (R-FL) that would have blocked the policy.

3. Clean Water Action mobilized its members and allies nationwide around the U. S. House

vote; EPA's withdrawal of the policy signaled that Congress heard people's concerns about the economic, health and environmental costs of weakening sewage dumping rules.

4. It remains to be seen whether these victories will withstand continuing pressure for weaker pollution controls and lead to cleaner, safer water over time. That is why Congress must take additional actions over the months and weeks ahead. Clean Water Action and allies are now campaigning to ensure that EPA is permanently blocked from bringing back the agency's ill-conceived sewage dumping rule. Meanwhile, the wins have added momentum for Clean Water Action's longer-term campaign to build support for new investments that would help communities meet urgent cleanup needs.

1. Giardia lambia and Cryptosporidium parvum frequently turn up in urban water supplies.
2. An oil spill causes the most damage when it hits a shoreline.
3. With each step up the food chain, the concentration of a pollutant slightly decreases.
4. Many drinking water supplies are contaminated with pesticides due to widespread agricultural use.
5. A substantial amount of water pollution is caused when tankers routinely and deliberately flush out their oil tanks with seawater.
6. The animals can become sick or poisoned when they swallow the oil while preening (grooming their feathers or fur).
7. When other animals feed on these contaminated animals, the chemicals would not be passed to other animals.
8. Animals at the top of food chains may, as a result of these chemical concentrations, suffer _____.
9. Hazardous wastes are chemical wastes that are _____.
10. Plants and animals cannot survive if their water is loaded with _____.

Section B　Discourse Vocabulary Test
Directions:（略）

Passage 2

Another common type of reasoning is the search for causes and results. We want to know whether cigarettes really do cause lung cancer, what causes *malnutrition*（营养不良）, the decay of cities, or the decay of teeth. We are ___11___ interested in ___12___ s: what is the effect of *sulfur*（硫）or lead in the atmosphere, of oil spills and raw *sewage*（污水）in rivers and the sea, of staying up late on the night before an examination?

Causal reasoning may go from cause to effect or from effect to cause. Either way, we reason from what we know to what we want to find out. Sometimes we reason from an effect to a cause and then on to another effect. Thus, if we reason that because the lights have gone out, the refrigerator won't work, we first ___13___ the effect (lights out) to the cause (power off) and then relate that cause to another effect (refrigerator not working). This kind of ___14___ is called, for short, effect to effect. It is quite ___15___ to reason through an extensive chain of causal relations. When the lights go out we might reason in the following causal chain: lights out-power off-refrigerator not working—temperature will rise; milk will sour. In other words, we ___16___ a succession of effects from the power failure, each becoming the cause of the next.

Causes are classified as necessary, ___17___, or *contributory* (有帮助的). A necessary cause is one which must be present for the effect to occur, as *combustion* (助燃) is necessary to drive a gasoline engine. A sufficient cause is one which can ___18___ an effect unaided, though there may be more than one sufficient cause: a dead battery is enough to keep a car from starting, but faulty *spark* (点火) plugs or an empty gas tank will have the same effect. A ___19___ cause is one which helps to produce an effect but cannot do so by itself, as running through a red light may help cause accident, *pedestrians* (步行者) or other cars in the intersection must also be present.

In establishing or *refuting* (反驳) a causal relation it is usually necessary to show the process by which the *alleged* (所谓的) cause produces the effect. Such an ___20___ is called a causal process.

A) previous	I) diagnose
B) effect	J) common
C) sufficient	K) relate
D) equally	L) cause
E) make	M) explanation
F) produce	N) probably
G) contributory	O) reasoning
H) casual	

Section C   Reading in Depth

Directions：(略)

Passage 3

I hear many parents complaining that their teenage children are rebelling. I wish it were so. At your age you ought to be growing away from your parents. You should be learning to stand on your own two feet. But take a good look at the present rebellion. It seems that teenagers are all taking the same way of showing that they disagree with their parents. Instead of striking out boldly on their own, most of them are clutching at one another's hands for reassurance.

They claim they want to dress as they please. But they all wear the same clothes. They set off in new directions in music. But somehow they all end up huddled round listening to the same record. Their reason for thinking or acting in thus-and-such a way is that the crowd is doing it. They have come out of their *cocoon* (蚕茧) into a larger cocoon.

It has become harder and harder for a teenager to stand up against the popularity wave and to go his or her own way. Industry has firmly carved out a teenager market. These days every teenager can learn from the advertisements what a teenager should have and be. And many of today's parents have come to award high marks for the popularity of their children. All this adds up to a great barrier for the teenager who wants to find his or her own path.

But the barrier is worth climbing over. The path is worth following. You may want to listen to classical music instead of going to a party. You may want to collect rocks when everyone else is collecting records. You may have some thoughts that you don't care to share at once with your classmates. Well, go to it. Find yourself. Be yourself. Popularity will come with the people who respect you for who you are. That's the only kind of popularity that really counts.

21. The author's purpose in writing this passage is to tell _____.

    A) readers how to be popular with people around

    B) teenagers how to learn to decide things for themselves

    C) parents how to control and guide their children

    D) people how to understand and respect each other

22. According to the author, many teenagers think they are brave enough to act on their own, but, in fact, most of them _____.

    A) have much difficulty understanding each other

    B) lack confidence

    C) dare not show that they disagree with their parents

    D) are very much afraid of getting lost

23. Which of the following is NOT true according to the passage?

    A) There is no popularity that really counts.

    B) What many parents are doing is in fact hindering their children from finding their own paths.

    C) It is not necessarily bad for a teenager to disagree with his or her classmates.

    D) Most teenagers claim that they want to do what they like to, but they are actually doing the same.

24. The author thinks of advertisements as _____.

    A) convincing   B) influential   C) instructive   D) authoritative

25. During the teenage years, one should learn to _____.

    A) differ from others in as many ways as possible

    B) get into the right season and become popular

    C) find one's real self

    D) rebel against parents and the popularity wave

Passage 4

The *Enlightenment* (启蒙运动) and the romantic movement of modern European culture stimulated interest in *myth* (神话), both through theories about myth and through new academic disciplines. Although the Enlightenment emphasized the rationality of human beings, it directed attention to all human expressions, including religion and mythology. Enlightenment scholars tried to make sense of the seemingly irrational and fantastic mythic stories. Their explanations included historical evolutionary theories—that human culture evolved from an early state of ignorance and irrationality to the modern culture of rationality—with myths seen as products of the early ages of ignorance and irrationality. Myths were also thought to result from euhemerism, that is, the *divinizing* (神化) of the heroic virtues of a human being. More important than any one theory of mythology, however, was the development of systematic disciplines devoted to the study of mythology. In new fields such as social and cultural anthropology and the history of religions, scholars were forced to come to terms with myths from earlier historical periods outside the Western tradition, and they began to relate the study of myth to a broader understanding of culture and history.

The romantic movement turned to the older Indo-European myths as intellectual and cultural resources. Romantic scholars tended to view myth as an *irreducible* (无法恢复的) form of human expression. For them, myth, as a mode of thinking and perception, possessed prestige equal to or sometimes greater than the rational grasp of reality.

Myth had always been part of classical and theological studies in the West, but during and after the Enlightenment, the concern for myth, revived with new intensity, could be detected in almost all the newer university disciplines—anthropology, history, psychology, history of religions, political science, structural linguistics. Most current theories of myth emerged from one or more of these disciplines.

26. In the first sentence, the word "discipline" is closest in meaning to the word _____.
    A) subject   B) rule   C) study   D) research

27. Which of the following is characteristic of the Enlightenment?
    A) Attention to all human expression.   B) Rational thinking.
    C) Systematic study of human culture.   D) Broad understanding of culture and history.

28. According to historical evolutionary theory, _____.
    A) myths reflect an age of ignorance and irrationality
    B) myths are irreducible form of human expression
    C) myths possess prestige equal to the rational grasp of reality
    D) myths are based on stories though seemingly irrational

29. When scholars began to study myths from other cultures, _____.
    A) they found myths were rational stories
    B) they got a better understanding of myths
    C) they found they were better than Western myths
    D) they began to understand human culture and history

30. Before the Enlightenment, the study of myths was closely related with _____.
    A) anthropology   B) psychology   C) mythology   D) theology

Section D   Short Answer Questions

Directions：（略）

Passage 5

Health care is improving everywhere. Additional kinds of facilities, such as clinics are being built every day. Still, the hospital remains the most prominent health care agency. Small clinics usually cannot afford to maintain all the sophisticated equipment now available for treatment.

Hospitals do not have unlimited bed space for patients. In fact, many hospitals are unable to accommodate all of their patients. As a result, more and more hospitals are developing outpatient or extended care facilities. Rather than enter as an inpatient, the patient visits the hospital only if further *diagnosis* (诊断) or treatment is necessary. In this way, patients who do not require the regular supervision of the hospital staff can still benefit from the facilities available at the hospital. In addition, beds can be reserved for the acutely ill. Patients may even save as much as half of the money they would normally have to pay for inpatient treatment.

Patients who use outpatient services are usually able to walk. Among them are persons who have just completed a hospitality during the acute phase of an illness and who need some follow-up treatment. Patients hospitalized for a heart attack fall into this category.

The elderly also are making greater use of various forms of extended care facilities. Medical advances enable people to live longer, but they often have *chronic* (慢性的) health problems that require constant supervision but not hospitalization. In the United States, Medicare has made it possible for the elderly to take advantage of these health facilities.

Facilities for self-care patients are also included in the outpatient centers. Included are the *post-coronary* (冠状动脉) patient trying to adjust to a new pace of life; and the patient requiring regular x-ray therapy. Each kind of patient is encouraged to live as normal a life as possible, using the hospital's facilities only when necessary. This concept is known as progressive care.

31. Small clinics always find it difficult to maintain all the _____.

_____

_____

32. Not all patients need _____ of the hospital staff.

_____

_____

33. The word "acutely" in paragraph 2 probably means _____.

_____

_____

34. Self-care patients use the hospital's facilities only _____.

_____

_____

35. What might be the best title for this passage?

_____

_____

Notes and Explanations

Passage 1

Explanations

1. [N] Infectious organisms 部分第三句提到…Giardia lambia and Cryptosporidium parvum occasionally turn up in urban water supplies. Giardia lambia 和 Cryptosporidium parvum 两种寄生虫偶尔会出现在城

市的水资源中。故答案是 No。

2. [Y] Petroleum products 部分第三句提到 An oil spill has its worst effects when it encounters a shoreline. 泄露的油被冲到海岸边时会出现最糟糕的情况。故答案是 Yes。

3. [N] Pesticides and herbicides 部分第一段中间提到 With each step up the food chain, the concentration of the pollutant increases. 随着食物链向上发展，污染物的集中也会随之加剧。由此得出答案是 No。

4. [Y] Pesticides and herbicides 部分第二段第一句提到 Many drinking water supplies are contaminated with pesticides from widespread agricultural use. 许多饮用水资源都受到了农业中大量使用的杀虫剂的污染。由此得出答案是 Yes。

5. [NG] Petroleum products 部分第二句提到 However, these petroleum products often find their way into the water by means of accidental spills from ships, tanker trucks, pipelines, and leaky underground storage tanks. 然而，运油船的事故性泄露，油罐、运油管、还有地下储油罐的泄漏都会导致水资源的污染。文章中并没有提及用海水冲刷油罐的问题。由此得出答案是 Not Given。

6. [Y] Petroleum products 部分最后一句提到 Additionally, these animals can become sick or poisoned when they swallow the oil while preening. 另外，这些动物用嘴梳理羽毛时吞咽下的油会导致生病或者中毒。由此得出答案是 Yes。

7. [N] Pesticides and herbicides 部分的第一段提到 When other animals feed on these contaminated animals, the chemicals are passed up the food chain. 当其他动物吃了被污染的动物，那些化学物质会随着食物链传递下去。从而得出答案是 No。

8. Pesticides and herbicides 部分第一段最后一句提到 Animals at the top of food chains may, as a result of these chemical concentrations, suffer cancers, reproductive problems, and death. 由于这些化学污染，在食物链顶端的动物会患上癌症、生育问题或者导致死亡。由此得出答案是 **cancers, reproductive problems, and death**。

9. Hazardous wastes 部分的第一句话提到 Hazardous wastes are chemical wastes that are toxic (poisonous), reactive (capable of producing explosive or toxic gases), corrosive (capable of corroding steel), or ignitable (flammable). 危险的废弃品是指那些有毒、易燃易爆、易腐蚀的化学废弃品。由此得出答案是 **toxic, reactive, corrosive, or ignitable**。

10. 第一段第二句提到 They cannot survive if their water is loaded with toxic chemicals or harmful microorganisms. 如果水里有有毒的化学物质或危害性的微生物，它们就不能生存。由此得出答案是 **toxic chemicals or harmful microorganisms**。

Passage 2

Notes

1. ..., of staying up late on the night before an examination? (Line 4~5, Para. 1)

stay up 意为"醒着，不去睡"。例如：

She promised the children they could stay up for their favorite TV program.

她答应孩子们可以晚点睡，看他们最喜爱的电视节目。

Staying up on the eve of the Spring Festival is an old Chinese tradition. 除夕守岁是中国的古老传统。

2. Causal reasoning may go from cause to effect or from effect to cause. (Line 1, Para. 2)

causal reasoning 意为"因果关系"，cause to effect 意为"从起因到结果"，effect to cause 意为"从结果到起因"。

3. Thus, if we reason that because the lights have gone out, ... to the cause (power off)... (Line 3~4, Para. 2)

▷go out 在这里是"熄灭"的意思。例如：

There was a power cut and all the lights went out. 因停电所有的灯都熄灭了。

▷power off 意思是"停电"。

4. In other words, we diagnose a succession of effects from the power failure... (Line 8~9, Para. 2)

a succession of 意为"一连串的,一系列的"。例如:

a succession of wet days, defeats, poor leaders 一个接一个的阴雨天,失败,不称职的领导人

5. ..., as running through a red light may help cause an accident... (Line 6~7, Para. 3)

run through 意思是"跑步穿过,贯穿"。例如:

All the policemen ran through the bridge to help the broken truck.

所有的警察都跑过桥去帮助那辆抛锚的卡车。

Explanations

11. [D] 语法规则要求此处应填一个副词来修饰形容词 interested。选项 D、N 是副词。根据本文第一句话 Another common type of reasoning is the search for causes and results. 紧接着文章提到我们应该关注原因,由此可以推断出我们同样也应该关注结果,所以 equally(同样地)符合句意。

12. [B] 语法规则要求此处应填一个单数名词名词和后面的三个以 of 开始的介词短语一起作表语。选项 B、M 是单数名词。根据上文的 We are equally interested in effects 推断出 effect 符合本句意思要求。

13. [K] 语法规则要求此处应填一个动词原形和介词 to 搭配作谓语。选项 E、F、I、K 是动词原形。根据本句的主句后半部分出现的 relate... to 可以判断出此处也应该选 relate。

14. [O] 语法规则要求此处应填一个单数名词或动名词作句子的主语。选项 B、M 是单数名词,选项 O 是动名词。根据文章第一句话得知本文讲述另外一种类型的推理。本句话中提到"这种……称为是……",可以判断定此处应选 O 项。

15. [J] 语法规则要求此处应填一个形容词构成 It is+形容词+to do/be 结构。选项 A、C、G、H、J 是形容词。可以用在该结构的是选项 C、H、J。本句话意思应该是"通过一系列的因果关系链进行推理是相当……的"。common(常见的)符合此意。

16. [I] 语法规则要求此处应填一个动词原形作谓语。选项 E、F、I、K 是动词原形。本句意思应该是"我们根据停电判断出一系列的结果"。diagnose(诊断;判断)符合句意。

17. [C] 语法规则要求此处应填一个形容词和 necessary, contributory 并列。本段讲述三种类型的原因。第一句是主题句,第二句解释什么是 necessary cause,第三句解释什么是 sufficient cause,第四句解释什么是 contributory cause。由此可以判断主题句中空白处应该是 sufficient(充分的)。

18. [F] 语法规则要求此处应填一个动词原形作谓语。可以和 effect 搭配使用的是 produce。produce effect 意思是"产生结果",符合句意。

19. [G] 语法规则要求此处应填一个形容词作 cause 的定语。根据本段首句的 contributory 和本句话定语从句中的 helps 推断出,此空应选一个意思对等于 helps 的词意,故选 G 项。

20. [M] 语法规则要求此处应填一个单数名词作主语。根据句意"这样一种……被称作因果过程"可推断出此空应该是表示"推理"或"解释、说明"的词,explanation 符合句意。

Passage 3

Notes

1. At your age you ought to be growing away from your parents. (Line 2, Para. 1)

grow away from 意思是"疏远,离开",这个短语不能用于被动语态。例如:

a teenage girl growing away from her mother 跟自己母亲逐渐疏远的少女

2. You should be learning to stand on your own two feet. (Line 2~3, Para. 1)

这句话的意思是"你应该逐渐学会独立生活"。stand on one's own feet 意思是"自立"。

3. Instead of striking out boldly on their own, most... (Line 4～5, Para. 1)

strike out on one's own 意思是"开始独立生活"。例如：

The children from the poor family strike out on their own earlier. 穷苦出身的孩子更早开始独立生活。

4. But somehow they all end up huddled round listening to the same record. (Line 2～3, Para. 2)

end up 意为"达到某状态,来到某处"。例如：

If you continued to steal you'll end up in prison. 你要是继续行窃终得进监狱。

At first he refused to accept any responsibility but he ended up apologizing.

最初他拒不承担任何责任,到头来还是道了歉。

5. ...for a teenager to stand up against the popularity wave and... (Line 1, Para. 3)

stand up against 意思是"抵制"。例如：

The girl couldn't stand up against the attraction of the big cities. 女孩不能抗拒大城市对她的诱惑。

6. Industry has firmly carved out a teenage market. (Line 2, Para. 3)

carve out 意为"靠勤奋创业或树名声等"。例如：

She carved out a name for herself as a reporter. 她努力工作,成了有名的记者。

7. All this adds up to a great barrier for the teenager... (Line 4～5, Para. 3)

add up to 意为"总计,相当于"。例如：

These numbers add up to 100. 这些数目合计为 100。

These clues don't really add up to very much. 这些线索没有什么实际意义。

Explanations

　　在文章中,作者认为很多家长抱怨自己的孩子很叛逆,然而孩子们对家长的叛逆并不意味着他们可以独立生活,大多数的孩子都是在同龄人中寻求肯定。他们穿式样相同的衣服,听同样的唱片,别人做什么他们就做什么。青少年越来越难于抵制潮流,坚持自己的想法。因此,作者认为鼓励青少年不要盲从、不要随波逐流、保持自我是非常重要的。

21. **B)** 主旨题。文章中多数句子的主语是 teenagers 或 you(指 teenagers),因此可以断定这篇文章是写给 teenagers 的。

22. **B)** 推断题。第一段最后两句讲到尽管孩子们在家长面前表现得非常叛逆,但事实上 Instead of striking out boldly on their own, most of them are clutching at one another's hand for assurance. 他们并不敢独立地面对问题,而是在彼此之间寻找信心。

23. **A)** 推断题。第三段第四句提到了选项 B,最后一段提到了选项 C,第一段后两句和第二段都提到了选项 D,而 A 项的内容与文章最后一句意思相反。

24. **B)** 细节题。第三段第三句 These days every teenager can learn from the advertisements what a teenager should have and be. 说明广告对青少年是具有影响力的。

25. **C)** 推断题。文章最后一段鼓励青少年找回自我、保持自我,这种时尚才真正有价值,因此 C 项为正确答案。

Passage 4

Notes

1. Enlightenment scholars tried to make sense of the seemingly irrational and fantastic mythic stories. (Line 4～5, Para. 1)

make sense of 意思是"理解或弄懂困难的事物"。例如：

Can you make sense of this poem? 你能看懂这首诗吗?

It is very difficult to make sense of the words on that antique. 想要弄懂那件古玩上的文字是很困难的。

2. ... that the human culture evolved from an early state... (Line 6，Para. 1)

evolve from 意思是"进化，逐渐形成"。例如：

All advanced animals are evolved from some simple creatures. 所有的高级动物都是由简单生物进化而来的。

3. Myths were also thought to result from euhemerism ... (Line 8，Para. 1)

result from 意思是"产生，出现"。例如：

His injuries resulted from a fall from the horse. 他从马上摔下来受了伤。

The high productivity results from the improvement of the machine. 机器的改进使得生产力得到了提高。

4. ... scholars were forced to come to terms with myths from earlier historical periods... (Line 11～12，Para. 1)

这句话的意思是：学者们不得不从更早的历史角度来研究神话。

come to terms with 在这里的意思是"研究"。

5. Most current theories of myth emerged from one or more of these disciplines. (Line 4～5，Para. 3)

emerge from 意思是"出现，显现"。例如：

The whale emerged from the water. 鲸鱼从水里浮现出来。

Their conclusion emerged from the basic theories. 他们的结论是从那些基础的理论中得出的。

Explanations

本文介绍了"启蒙运动"前后对于神话研究的不同之处。"启蒙运动"以前神话在西方是古希腊和古罗马文化研究与基督教神学研究的内容之一。启蒙运动主义者把神话看作是远古时代蒙昧与非理性的产物。而在浪漫主义文学时代，神话被视为思想与洞察力的典范。

26. **A)** 词汇题。discipline 是"学科"的意思，因此 A 项为正确答案。

27. **B)** 细节题。第一段第二句 Although the Enlightenment emphasized the rationality of human beings... 告诉我们"启蒙运动"强调的是人的理性，因此 B 项为正确答案。

28. **A)** 细节题。根据第一段第四句 Their explanation included historical evolutionary theories... —with myths seen as products of the early ages of ignorance and irrationality,历史进化论认为人类文明是从早期的蒙昧和非理性逐步进化到现代文明与理性的,因此他们把神话也看作是远古时代蒙昧与非理性的产物。

29. **B)** 细节题。第一段最后一句 In new fields such as social and cultural... and they began to relate the study of myth to a boarder understanding of culture and history 与选项 B 表达的内容相符,所以是正确答案。

30. **D)** 细节题。第三段第一句 Myth had always been part of classical and theological studies in the West, but during and after the Enlightenment, the concern revived with new intensity... 说明在"启蒙运动"以前神话在西方是古希腊和古罗马文化研究与基督教神学(theology)研究的内容。

Passage 5

Keys

31. sophisticated equipment now available for treatment

32. the regular supervision

33. badly

34. when necessary

35. Outpatient Services of Hospitals

Notes

1. Rather than enter as an inpatient，the patient visits the hospital...（Line 3，Para. 2）
   ▷rather than 意思是"而不"。例如：
   I think Tom, rather than you, is to blame. 我认为该受责备的人是汤姆，而不是你。
   ▷rather... than... 意思是"与其说……，不如说……"。例如：
   I am rather bored than tired. 我与其说是疲惫不如说是厌倦。

2. In this way, patients who ... can still benefit from the facilities available at the hospital.（Line 4～5，Para. 2）
   benefit from 意思是"得到好处"。例如：
   I benefited enormously from my father's advice. 我从父亲的忠告中获益匪浅。

3. Patients hospitalized for a heart attack fall into this category.（Line 3，Para. 3）
   fall into 意思是"属于，被归类"。例如：
   This movie falls into a new style, which is modernism. 这部电影属于现代主义风格。

4. The elderly also are making greater use of various forms of extended care facilities.（Line 1，Para. 4）
   ... made it possible for the elderly to take advantage of these health facilities.（Line 3～4，Para. 4）
   make use of 和 take advantage of 在此都表示"利用"。例如：
   The students make use of their spare time to read some classic novels.
   学生们利用业余时间读一些经典小说。
   Human beings should make good use of various natural resources. 人类应该充分利用各种自然资源。
   They took full advantage of the hotel's facilities. 他们充分利用了旅店的设施。

5. Included are the post-coronary patient trying to adjust to a new pace of life...（Line 2～3，Para. 5）
   这是一个倒装句，正常语序应是 The post-coronary patient trying to adjust to a new pace of life are included. adjust to 意思是"适应"。例如：
   It is necessary for a young man to adjust to new environment quickly in the modern society.
   在现代社会年轻人必须能够快速地适应新的环境。

Unit 24

Section A   Skimming and Scanning

Directions：（略）

Passage 1

How to Be a Film Researcher?

1. If you like exploring new territory, research may be just the job for you. A good researcher is an integral part of any production team. Yet, when was the last time you watched an outstanding film and said to yourself afterwards, "That was an incredible piece of work — I wonder who researched it". I would venture to guess that for most people this is not the first question that comes to mind after you watch a film. It is obvious that a producer, director, and editor play significant roles in shaping a film, which is why they tend to receive the most prolific accolades. On the other hand, a good researcher may just be the *unsung*（未唱的） hero of a well-crafted and thought-provoking non-fiction film.

2. To find out more about a researcher's role in the production process, New England Film. com spoke with someone who knows quite a bit about quality programming—NOVA's Senior Science Editor, Evan Hadingham. Unlike many people in this business who have always wanted to make films, Evan started out writing books on archeology and pre-history. In 1986, he applied to a fellowship program that sought to take print science writers and give them 11 months of training in film and television. Apparently, the program struck a chord with Evan because 15 years later he is using his talents on one of the most respected science programs on television. Researching is one of the foremost aspects of his job, and here are a few insider tips he offers on how to be a researcher.

Tip 1：Have wide interests

Be curious. Subject matter can vary widely when you work as a researcher. Quite simply, the broader your interests are the more skills you will be bringing to your work and the more likely you will enjoy your research. In Evan's case, his training as a writer endowed him with journalistic skills that are essential to his job as content editor. Just as research, story-telling, and critical thinking were essential as a writer, they are also essential for a film researcher.

Tip 2：Be critical

Often a researcher is given the task of finding out everything there is to know about a certain subject. A good researcher must be able to sort through information and determine which details are relevant and which are not. This is a lofty task. Being critical also requires an ability to wade through varying interpretations of material in search of those resources that are the least biased.

The researcher then must parlay this information to the rest of the production team, in some ways determining what the producer, writer, and director know about a subject. Processing so much information and presenting it unerringly requires excellent critical thinking skills.

Tip 3: Be self-critical

As Evan put it, part of being critical is being self-critical. Recognizing biases in other people's writings and opinions is important, but recognizing one's own biases is just as important. A good researcher needs to reflect upon his/her own biases, and to be open-minded enough to change his/her point of view if the evidence warrants it.

Tip 4: Strive for complete journalistic accuracy and balance

While NOVA believes in putting significant emphasis on the editorial end of production, not every production company devotes enough time to the research phase of a project. Unfortunately, this often results in factual inaccuracies. To prevent inaccuracies and maintain the highest standard of journalistic integrity, it is imperative that facts are checked and re-checked. Evan refers to this aspect of his position as "good cop, bad cop on content." A capable researcher/content editor asks tough questions about how and where facts were obtained. If necessary, a knowledgeable outside party should be consulted to verify the accuracy of information contained within a script. If you are running on a limited time schedule for research, quickly try to determine who seems to have the most authoritative and least prejudiced view, and then find them and their resources.

Tip 5: Know your sources

For nearly every researcher, a research trip now begins on your desktop. The Internet has become a treasure *trove*(收藏的东西) of information making research faster and easier, and academic resources more accessible. Evan makes use of the Internet primarily by drawing on print stories from reputable science magazines whose back issues are available on-line. "Lexus-Nexus" is another valuable research tool. Be warned, however, that not all material on the web—or anywhere else for that matter—can be trusted. Be a skeptical researcher. In the end, you will at times have to make a judgment call on a source's legitimacy. Evan's advice: make sure to get more than one account of everything.

Tip 6: Finally. Get out there

As Evan emphasized in our interview, research is the ultimate entry point into the film world. You don't have to be a writer, a filmmaker, a historian, a scientist, etc. to be a researcher. You do, however, have to have a good sampling of some of the qualities above and an abundance of enthusiasm and motivation. According to Evan, one of the best *interns*(实习) he ever had at NOVA knew little-to-nothing about filmmaking but had intelligence and eagerness that made her exceptional. Don't feel that you have to limit yourself to film research for experience, rather look beyond film for other outlets. Get experience in writing and researching for print, the Web, and in any other areas you find interesting. A wide-range of talents is crucial to survival in the business.

If you are looking for a way to get some firsthand experience in the film world, or, if you are someone who enjoys the editorial and storytelling function but are not interested in production, research might be the right place for you. Either way, as a researcher you will have a major impact on the story a film tells and will be assisting in communicating knowledge to a much wider audience.

Though a film researcher may not be recognized with the same acclaim that other members of a production team tend to receive, Evan assures me that the best producers understand the critical role a researcher plays in the success of a film. Ultimately, though, research is something that should be rewarding for the researcher. "Research and producing are like a journey of discovery," according to Evan.

1. Film researches receive accolades similar to editors.
2. Production teams need to have good film researchers.
3. Evan started out as a director, failed and then went into research.
4. Being a film researcher is an excellent way to work your way into the movie industry.
5. The author believes research can be interesting because film directors respect and crave your opinion.
6. According to the author, a variety of skills will best aid you in making it in the film business.
7. In doing his/her work, a film researcher must be able to identify biased information.
8. A good researcher is _____ of any production team.
9. A good researcher must be able to sort through information and determine _____.
10. _____ is crucial to a film researcher to survive in the business.

Section B   Discourse Vocabulary Test
Directions：（略）

Passage 2

Either out of ___11___ or discomfort we sometimes express our ___12___ in an unclear way. One key to making your emotions clear is to realize that you most often can summarize them in a few words—hurt, glad, confused, excited, resentful, and so on. In the same way, with a little thought you can probably describe very ___13___ any reasons you have for feeling a certain way.

In addition to avoiding ___14___ length, a second way to prevent confusion is to avoid *over qualifying*（过分修饰）or *downplaying*（不予重视）your emotions—"I'm a little unhappy" or "I'm pretty excited" or "I'm sort of confused". Of course, not all emotions are strong ones. We do feel degrees of sadness and joy, for example, but some communicators have a ___15___ to downplay almost every feeling. Do you?

A third danger to avoid is expressing feelings in a coded manner. This happened most often when the sender is ___16___ about revealing the feeling in question. Some codes are verbal ones, as when the sender hints more or less subtly at the message. For example, an ___17___ way to say "I'm lonesome" might be "I guess there isn't much happening this weekend, so if you're not busy, why don't you drop by?" Such a message is so indirect that the chances that your real feeling will be recognized are slim. For this reason, people who send coded messages stand less of a chance of having their emotions understood—and their needs met.

Finally, you can ___18___ yourself clearly by making sure that both you and your partner understand that your feeling is ___19___ on a specific set of circumstances rather than being *indicative*（指示的）of the whole relationship. Instead of saying, "I resent you," say, "I resent you when you don't keep your ___20___." Rather than "I resent you," say, "I resent you when you don't keep your promises." Rather than "I'm bored with you," say "I'm bored when you talk about your money."

A) emotions	I) excessive
B) miserable	J) uncomfortable
C) confusion	K) tendency
D) indirect	L) promises
E) strong	M) wishes
F) express	N) centered
G) briefly	O) heart
H) qualify	

Section C　Reading in Depth

Directions：（略）

Passage 3

Learning disabilities are very common. They affect perhaps 10 percent of all children. Four times as many boys as girls have learning disabilities.

Since about 1970, new research has helped brain scientists understand these problems better. Scientists now know there are many different kinds of learning disabilities and that they are caused by many different things. There is no longer any question that all learning disabilities result from differences in the way the brain is organized.

You cannot look at a child and tell if he or she has a learning disability. There is no outward sign of the disorder. So some researchers began looking at the brain itself to learn what might be wrong.

In one study, researchers examined the brain of a learning-disabled person who had died in an accident. They found two unusual things. One involved cells in the left side of the brain, which control language. These cells normally are white. In the learning-disabled person, however, these cells were gray. The researchers also found that many of the nerve cells were not in a line the way they should have been. The nerve cells were mixed together.

The study was carried out under the guidance of Norman Geschwind, an early expert on learning disabilities. Doctor Geschwind proposed that learning disabilities resulted mainly from problems in the left side of the brain. He believed this side of the brain failed to develop normally. Probably, he said, nerve cells there did not connect as they should. So the brain was like an electrical device in which the wires were crossed.

Other researchers did not examine brain tissue. Instead, they measured the brain's electrical activity and made a map of the electrical signals. Frank Duffy experimented with this technique at Children's Hospital Medical Center in Boston. Doctor Duffy found large differences in the brain activity of normal children and those with reading problems. The differences appeared throughout the brain. Doctor Duffy said his research gives evidence that reading disabilities involve damage to a wide area of the brain, not just the left side.

21. Which of the following is NOT mentioned in the passage?

    A) Learning disabilities may result from the unknown area of the brain.

    B) Learning disabilities may result from damage to a wide area of the brain.

    C) Learning disabilities may result from abnormal organization of brain cells.

    D) Learning disabilities may result from problems in the left side of the brain.

22. Scientists found that the brain cells of a learning-disabled person differ from those of a normal person in _____.

    A) structure and function   B) color and function

    C) size and arrangement   D) color and arrangement

23. All of the following statements are true EXCEPT that _____.

    A) many factors account for learning disorder

    B) a learning-disabled person shows no outward signs

    C) reading disabilities are a common problem that affects 10 percent of the population

    D) the brain activity of learning-disabled children is different from that of normal children

24. Doctor Duffy believed that _____.

    A) he found the exact cause of learning disabilities

    B) the problem of learning disabilities did not lie in the left side of the brain

    C) the problem of learning disabilities resulted from the left side of the brain

    D) the problem of learning disabilities was not limited to the left side of the brain

25. According to the passage we can conclude that further researches should be made _____.

    A) to help learning-disabled children to develop their intelligence

    B) to help learning-disabled children to develop their brains

    C) to investigate possible influences on brain development and organization

    D) to explore how the left side of the brain functions in language learning

Passage 4

It is indeed unfortunate that in our modern era of technologic and scientific achievement, there is no adequate explanation for a seemingly simple question: "Why do people become too fat and what can be done to prevent it?" About 50 million men and 60 million women between the ages of 18 and 79 are "too fat" and need to reduce excess weight. This amounts to about 377 million kg of excess fat for men and 667 million kg for women, or a total of 1,044 million kg (2,297 million lb) for the United States adult population! If the over-fat men and women dieted by consuming 600 fewer calories each day to reduce to a "normal" value of body fat (achievable in 68 days for men and 101 days for women), the reduced caloric *intake* (摄入量) would equal 5.7 trillion calories. Translating this into fossil fuel energy and considering such factors as the energy required to plant, cultivate, harvest, feed, process, transport, wholesale, retail, acquire, store and cook the food, the annual energy savings would be equal to that required to supply the residential electric demands of Boston, Chicago, San Francisco and Washington D. C. or 13 billion gallons of gasoline to fuel

大学英语 4 级阅读与简答（新题型）

900,000 autos per year. Until recently, the major cause of *obesity*（肥胖）was believed to be overeating. However, if *gluttony*（贪食）and overindulgence were the only factors associated with an increase in body fat, the easiest way to permanently reduce would surely be to cut back on food and drink. Of course, if it were that simple, obesity would soon be eliminated as a major health problem. There are obviously other factors operative such as genetic, environmental, and social influences. However, these causes probably *overlap*（重复）. It seems fairly certain that the treatment procedures devised so far, whether they be diets, surgery, drugs, psychological methods, or exercise, either alone or in combination, have not been particularly successful in solving the problem on a long-term basis. There is, nonetheless, optimism that as researchers continue to investigate the many facets of obesity, as well as to test and quantify various treatment modes, significant progress can be made to conquer this major health problem.

26. The complaint made by the writer in the first few lines of the passage is that _____.
    A) people have failed to solve the important problem of obesity and weight control in our modern era
    B) we spend so much money on technologic and scientific achievement
    C) the problem of obesity and weight control is difficult to solve
    D) the problem of obesity and weight needs to be solved only by doctors

27. The percentage of the excess fat for women in the total amount of excess fat is roughly _____.
    A) 50%   B) 60%   C) 70%   D) 40%

28. How many calories would equal the energy required annually to supply the residential electric demands of Boston, Chicago, San Francisco, and Washington D. C. ?
    A) 13 billion.   B) 5.7 trillion.
    C) Less than 5.7 trillion.   D) More than 5.7 trillion.

29. Which of the following should not be considered in evaluating the cause of an over-fat person?
    A) Indulgence in drinking.
    B) Genetic, environmental, and social factors.
    C) All these factors probably overlap.
    D) Overeating.

30. The writer finally says there is optimism for the treatment of obesity, because _____.
    A) various treatment procedures have been devised so far
    B) the treatment procedures are particularly successful in solving the problem on a short-term basis
    C) exercise alone can be successful in solving this major health problem
    D) significant progress will be made to conquer this major health problem through researchers' efforts

Section D   Short Answer Questions

Directions:（略）

Passage 5

Introductory sociology is not an easy course either to teach or to study. Students bring to the course that degree of knowledge of human behavior is necessary to survive as human beings. They are seldom prepared for the shock of seeing familiar things being written and talked about in an unfamiliar way. From the teacher's side, he or she has been encouraged to nourish a specialty within the field, and most are not prepared to be expert on the dozen or so topics typically covered in an introductory course.

This book is designed to help make both teaching and learning about sociology at an introductory level a little more possible. Its two principal aims are clarity and economy of language, and comprehensiveness of coverage. Responses of students and teachers to the first three editions of this book have suggested a good measure of success in achieving both these aims; this fourth edition attempts to improve on that accomplishment.

Three other features of the book may be *highlighted*（强调）. First, it is electric in theoretical *orientation*（倾向）using relevant insights from various theoretical perspectives. Second, the book is analytic rather than descriptive in approach; it is a book on sociology as a field of study rather than on society as an object of description. Third, the book strives for a balance between the classic and the contemporary in sociological analysis. While our discipline's origins in the work of Weber, Durkheim, Simmel, and Marx are never forgotten, every effort is made to cite the most recent *empirical*（经验主义的）and theoretical publications.

Some topics in this edition were not covered in the last. In the introductory chapter, Weber, Durkheim, and Marx have been given the detailed treatment they deserve as cofounders of the discipline of sociology. I have added a chapter on socialization to give the students an earlier exposure to the "self and society problem". Coverage of the conflict perspective on social reality has been expanded in several ways: by a section on Marx in the social change chapter, by a conflict approach to the study of deviant behavior and, above all, by introducing the power element in human relations in chapters 6 and 7 in the sections on social stratification and minorities.

31. What is the book designed to do?

   _____

   _____

32. The author states the two principal aims of the book in the second paragraph. What are the two aims?

   _____

   _____

33. What type of information is stated in the third paragraph?

   _____

   _____

34. What does the fourth edition attempt to?

_____ _____ _____ _____

_____ _____ _____ _____

35. What does the book strive for?

_____ _____ _____ _____

_____ _____ _____ _____

Notes and Explanations

Passage 1

Explanations

1. ［N］第一段中第五句提到 It is obvious that a producer, director, and editor play significant roles in shaping a film, which is why they tend to receive the most prolific accolades. On the other hand, a good researcher may just be the unsung hero of a well-crafted and thought-provoking non-fiction film. 显而易见，制片人、导演和编剧对一部电影的拍摄都起重要的作用，因此他们都受到大量的赞美。而另一方面，优秀的影片研究者却往往成为一个有着完美剧情、引人深思的影片的幕后英雄。由此可以得出答案是No。

2. ［Y］Tip 2 部分提到 The researcher then must parlay this information to the rest of the production team, in some ways determining what the producer, writer, and director know about a subject. 研究者必须将这些信息传递给摄制组中的其他人，这在某些方面决定了制片人、作者和导演对影片主题的了解。由此可以得出答案是Yes。

3. ［N］第二段第二句提到 Unlike many people in this business who have always wanted to make films, Evan started out writing books on archeology and pre-history. 和那些总是想制作电影的同行不同的是，伊万最初写一些关于考古学和史前史的书。由此得出答案是No。

4. ［Y］Tip 6 第一句提到 As Evan emphasized in our interview, research is the ultimate entry point into the film world. 正如伊万在我们的会谈中强调的，研究工作是进入电影世界的最佳入口。由此得出答案为Yes。

5. ［N］Tip 4 第一句提到 While NOVA believes in putting significant emphasis on the editorial end of production, not every production company devotes enough time to the research phase of a project. 尽管NOVA对于影片制作的编辑阶段很重视，但不是每个制片公司都会在项目的研究阶段投入大量时间。由此得出答案是No。

6. ［Y］Tip 1 第二句提到 Quite simply, the broader your interests are the more skills you will be bringing to your work and the more likely you will enjoy your research. 很简单，你的兴趣越广泛，你就可以在工作中运用更多的技巧，从而会越享受研究的过程。由此得出答案是Yes。

7. ［Y］Tip 3 第二句提到 Recognizing biases in other people's writings and opinions is important, but recognizing one's own biases is just as important. 识别出别人文章和观点中的偏见是十分重要的，但能够识别自己的偏见也是同样重要的。由此得出答案是Yes。

8. 第一段第二句提到 A good researcher is an integral part of any production team. 一个优秀的研究者是任何一个摄制组里不可或缺的部分。由此得出答案是 **an integral part**。

9. Tip 2 第二句提到 A good researcher must be able to sort through information and determine which details are relevant and which are not. 一个优秀的研究者应该能够整理不同的信息，并决定哪些是相关的信息，哪些是无关的信息。由此得出答案是 **which details are relevant and which are not**。

10. Tip 6 最后一句提到 A wide-range of talents is crucial to survival in the business. 多才多艺对于研究者在这个行业里的立足是至关重要的。由此得出答案是 **A wide-range of talents**。

Passage 2

Notes

1. Either out of confusion or discomfort we sometimes express our emotions in an unclear way. (Line 1, Para. 1)

   out of 意思是"来自于,出于"。例如:

   She copied the answer out of his notebook. 她从他的笔记本上抄答案。

   He chose to keep silence out of selfishness. 他出于自私选择了保持沉默。

2. In addition to avoiding excessive length... (Line 1, Para. 2)

   in addition to 后面跟名词或者动名词,表示"除了……之外"。例如:

   He speaks French in addition to English. 他除了英语之外,也会说法语。

   In addition to the names on the list, there are six other applicants.

   除了名单上的名字之外,还有 6 个申请者。

3. I'm sort of confused. (Line 3, Para. 2)

   sort of 意思是"有点,有几分"。例如:

   I'm sort of thought this might happen. 我多少猜到了这件事会发生。

   I felt sort of embarrassed. 我感到有些难为情。

4. A third danger to avoid is expressing feeling in a coded manner. (Line 1, Para. 3)

   a coded manner 意思是"暗示的方式"。

5. This happened most often... the feeling in question. (Line 1～2, Para. 3)

   in question 意为"在谈论的,在议论中的"。例如:

   Who's the woman in question? 大家在谈论的女人是谁?

6. ... why don't you drop by? (Line 5, Para. 3)

   drop by 意思是"顺便到某处一下",这种表达在口语中用的较多。例如:

   Drop by some time. 有空来坐坐。

7. ... that your feeling is centered on a specific set of circumstances rather than being indicative of the whole relationship. (Line 2～3, Para. 4)

   center on 意为"集中于,当作重点"。例如:

   Her research is centered on the social effect of unemployment. 她的研究课题是失业对社会的影响。

   Public interest centers on the outcome of the general election. 公众的注意力集中在大选的结果上。

Explanations

11. [C] 语法规则要求此处应填一个单数名词与 discomfort 并列作介词 of 的宾语。选项 C、K、O 是单数名词。根据本句出现的 discomfort 和 unclear way 可以判断此处应填一个意思和 unclear 对应的词。confusion 意思是"困惑",符合句意。

12. [A] 语法规则要求此处应填一个名词构成 make ＋ 名词 ＋ 形容词的结构。选项中只有 A 项是复数名词。根据上句中的 emotions(复数形式)、unclear 以及本句中的 clear 可以推断此处意思应该是"使感情清晰",所以 emotions 符合句意。

13. [G] 语法规则要求此处应填一个副词来修饰 describe,选项中只有 briefly(简短地)为副词,而且符合句意。

14. [I] 语法规则要求此处应填一个形容词来修饰 length。选项 B、D、E、I、J 是形容词。能够和 length 搭配使用的词只有 excessive。根据本句话中的 avoid 和 prevent confusion 可以推断 excessive 符合句意。excessive 意思是"过分的，过度的"。

15. [K]语法规则要求此处应填一个单数名词构成 have ＋ 名词 ＋ to do sth. 的结构。能够用在这一结构的是 tendency。have a tendency to do sth. 意思是"有做某事的倾向"，符合句意。

16. [J]语法规则要求此处应填一个形容词和 about 搭配作状语从句的表语。能够和 about 搭配的是 uncomfortable。uncomfortable 意思是"不舒服的"，符合句意。

17. [D]语法规则要求此处应填一个形容词来修饰 way。根据本句话所举的例子可以推断 indirect(间接地)符合句意。

18. [F]语法规则要求此处应该填一个动词原形作谓语。选项 F、H 是动词原形。可以和 oneself 搭配使用的是 express。express oneself 意思是"表达自己（的情感）"，符合句意。

19. [N]语法规则要求此处应填一个动词的过去分词形式构成被动语态。选项中只有 N 项符合该条件。be centered on 意思是"围绕……，以……为中心"，符合句意。

20. [L]语法规则要求此处应填一个复数名词。选项 A、L、M 是复数名词。从上文可以得知这里应该填 promises。keep one's promises 意思是"遵守诺言，守信用"，与上文一致。

Passage 3

Notes

1. Four times as many as boys as girls have learning disabilities.（Para. 1）

　four times as many（...）as 意思是"是……的四倍"，这是一个常用的表示倍数的比较结构，比较项是不可数名词时用 as much as。例如

　Our school has three times as much space as my friend's school. 我们学校的面积是我朋友学校的三倍。

2. The nerve cells were mixed together.（Line 5，Para. 4）

　mix together 意思是"混合，拌和"。例如：

　If you mix red and yellow together，you get orange. 把红色和黄色混在一起就是橙色。

　Don't mix business and pleasure together. 不要把正事和娱乐混在一起。

3. The study was carried out under the guidance of Norman Geschwind...（Line 1，Para. 5）

▷carry out 意为"执行，实施"。例如：

　carry out an enquiry/an investigation/a survey 进行查询、调查、勘查

▷under the guidance of 意为"在……的指导下"。例如：

　The postgraduate students finish their thesis under the guidance of their supervisor.

　研究生在导师的指导下完成论文。

4. So the brain was like an electrical device in which the wires were crossed.（Line 4～5，Para. 5）

　本句中有一个由 in which 引导的定语从句，先行词是 an electrical device。这句话的意思是：因此大脑就像一个电线纵横的电器设备。

Explanations

　　文章中分析了几种造成学习障碍的原因。一种研究证实是由于左脑与一般人不同而造成了一些人学习障碍；还有研究人员认为有阅读障碍的人大脑大面积受到损伤，不仅仅限于左脑；Norman 教授的研究表明有学习障碍的人脑细胞的组织结构与别人不同。

21. **A)** 推断题。第六段最后两句提到了选项 B，第五段最后两行提到了选项 C，第四段第三句提到了选项 D。只有 A 项文章没有提及。

22. **D)** 细节题。第四段中后半部分讲到 These cells are normally white. In the learning-disabled person，however，these cells are gray. The researchers also found that... The nerve cells were mixed together.

因此答案是 D 项。

23. **C）** 推断题。第二段第二句讲到 A 项（学习障碍是由多种原因造成的）；第三段第二句讲到 B 项（有学习障碍的人从外表是看不出来的）；第六段第三句讲到 D 项（有学习障碍的孩子的大脑活动与正常孩子不同）。第一段讲到有学习障碍的人占儿童总数的十分之一。所以 C 项是正确答案。

24. **D）** 推断题。Doctor Duffy 的研究表明有阅读障碍的孩子与正常孩子的大脑活动差别很大,这种差异表现在大脑各个部分,而不止限于左脑。因此 D 项为正确答案。

25. **C）** 推断题。因为文章中已经对于学习障碍的原因进行了分析,主要是因为有障碍的人与正常人的大脑不同,因此科学家应该进一步研究的对象应该是 C 项。

Passage 4

Notes

1. ... or a total of 1,044 million kg for the United States ... （Line 5～6）

   a total of 意思是"总数为,总计"。例如:

   There are a total of 13 billion people in China. 中国共有 13 亿人口。

2. However, if gluttony and overindulgence were the only factors associated with an increase in body fat, ...（Line 14）

   associate with 意思是"联系,交往"。例如:

   He seems to associate with criminals. 他好像与不法分子有来往。

   I am associated with the law agency. 我与那家律师事务所有联系。

3. ... the easiest way to permanently reduce would surely be to cut back on food and drink. （Line 15～16）

   cut back 意思是"缩减,削减"。例如:

   You have to cut back on spending. 你必须削减开支。

   The company cut back production by ten percent last year. 公司去年的产量减少了 10%。

4. There is, nonetheless, optimism that ...（Line 21）

   nonetheless 意思是"仍然",是表转折的关系副词。例如:

   They thought it might snow; nonetheless they began to climb the mountain.

   虽然他们心想可能会下雪,但仍然开始登山。

Explanations

作者在文章中提出了一个科学技术如此发达的现代社会无法解决的问题:"为什么人们会变得那么肥胖,怎样做才能防止肥胖"。美国成年人当中的肥胖问题实在让人担忧。造成肥胖的原因不仅仅是饮食过量,它还受到遗传、环境、社会的影响。因此从根本上解决这个问题是很重要的。

26. **A）** 推断题。作者在文章一开始就讲到尽管现代科学技术如此发达,人们却对一个表面看来非常简单的问题"为什么人们变得这么胖,怎样做才能解决这个问题?"束手无策。因此 A 为正确答案。

27. **B）** 细节题。文章第四到第五行讲到在 1,044 million kg fat 中有 667million kg 来自女性,因此 B 项为正确答案。

28. **B）** 细节题。根据文章第八行 the reduced caloric intake would equal 5.7 trillion calories... to fuel 900,000 autos per year. 可以确定正确答案是 B 项。

29. **C）** 细节题。文章倒数第七行指出肥胖不仅仅是饮食过量造成的,还受到遗传、环境、社会的影响。这几个原因分别在 A、B、D 项中列出,C 项不是造成肥胖的原因。

30. **D）** 推断题。文章最后提到 optimism that as researchers continue to investigate the many factors of obesity, as well as to test and quantify various treatment modes, significant progress can be made to conquer this major health problem. 由此可知 D 项是正确答案。

大学英语 4 级阅读与简答（新题型）

Passage 5

Keys

31. Help make both teaching and learning about sociology at an introductory level a little more possible.

32. Clarity and economy of language, and comprehensiveness of coverage.

33. Three other features of the book.

34. Improve on measures of success in achieving both aims.

35. A balance between the classic and the contemporary in sociological analysis.

Notes

1. ..., and most are not prepared to be expert on the dozen or so topics... (Line 5, Para. 1)

   expert on/at/in 意思是"……方面的专家"。例如：

   an expert in/at cooking 烹调专家

   an expert in economics 经济学专家

   She is expert at/in taking care of baby. 她擅长照顾小孩。

2. This book is designed to help make both... (Line 1, Para. 2)

   be designed to 意思是"打算做……用"。例如：

   The new machine is designed to improve the efficiency of productivity.

   设计新机器是为了提高生产效率。

3. Responses of students and teachers to the first three editions of this book... (Line 3~4, Para. 2)

   response to 意思是"回答，回应"。例如：

   There's no response to her cries for help. 她的呼救声没有激起什么回应。

4. Third, the book strives for a balance between... (Line 4, Para. 3)

   strive for 意思是"力争"。例如：

   The ambitious young man strives for his success by hard work.

   雄心勃勃的年轻人在努力工作争取成功。

Section A   Skimming and Scanning

Directions：（略）

Passage 1

Hypnosis：Medical Tool or Illusion？

Measures to hypnosis

The image most people have of the mysterious art of *hypnotism*（催眠术）is of a stage trick. But hypnotists are much more likely nowadays to be scientists seeking ways to probe the subconscious mind, or find a new way to relieve pain. But is hypnosis a real phenomenon? If so, what is it useful for? Over the past few years, researchers have found that hypnotized individuals actively respond to suggestions even though they sometimes perceive the dramatic changes in thought and behavior they experience as happening "by themselves." During hypnosis, it is as though the brain temporarily suspends its attempts to *authenticate*（鉴别）incoming sensory information. Some people are more hypnotizable than others, although scientists still don't know why. To study any phenomenon properly, researchers must first have a way to measure it. In the case of hypnosis, that yardstick is the Stanford Hypnotic Susceptibility Scales. The Stanford scales, as they are often called, were devised in the late 1950s by Stanford University psychologists. One version of the Stanford scales consists of a series of 12 activities—such as holding one's arm outstretched or sniffing the contents of a bottle—that test the depth of the hypnotic state. In the first instance, individuals are told that they are holding a very heavy ball, and they are scored as "passing" that suggestion if their arm sags under the imagined weight. In the second case, subjects are told that they have no sense of smell, and then a vial of ammonia is waved under their nose. If they have no reaction, they are *deemed*（相信）very responsive to hypnosis；if they *grimace*（扮鬼脸）and recoil, they are not.

Principles of hypnosis

1. Researchers with very different theoretical perspectives now agree on several fundamental principles of hypnosis. The first is that a person's ability to respond to hypnosis is remarkably stable during adulthood. In addition, a person's responsiveness to hypnosis also remains fairly consistent regardless of the characteristics of the hypnotist：the practitioner's gender, age and experience have little or no effect on a subject's ability to be hypnotized. Similarly, the success of hypnosis does not depend on whether a subject is highly motivated or especially willing. A very responsive subject will become hypnotized under a variety of experimental conditions and therapeutic settings, whereas a less susceptible person will not, despite his or her sincere efforts. (Negative attitudes and expectations can, however, interfere with hypnosis.)

2. Under hypnosis，subjects do not behave as passive automatons but instead are active problem solvers who incorporate their moral and cultural ideas into their behavior while remaining exquisitely responsive to the expectations expressed by the experimenter. Nevertheless，the subject does not experience hypnotically suggested behavior as something that is actively achieved. To the contrary，it is typically deemed as effortless as something that just happens. People who have been hypnotized often say things like "My hand became heavy and moved down by itself" or "Suddenly I found myself feeling no pain." Many researchers now believe that these types of disconnections are at the bean intent，fail to detect exceedingly painful stimulation or temporarily forget a familiar fact. Of course，these kinds of things also happen outside hypnosis—occasionally in day-to-day life and more dramatically in certain psychiatric and neurological disorders.

Functions of hypnosis

1. Scientists think that hypnosis may relieve pain by decreasing the activity of brain areas involved in the experience of suffering. *Positron*（正电子）emission tomography（PET）scans of horizontal and vertical brain sections were taken while the hands of hypnotized volunteers were *dunked*（泡）into painfully hot water. The activity of *the somatosensory cortex*（大脑皮层的体觉区域），which processes physical stimuli，did not differ whether a subject was given the hypnotic suggestion that the sensation would be painfully hot or that it would be minimally unpleasant. In contrast，a part of the brain known to be involved in the suffering aspect of pain，the anterior cingulated cortex，was much less active when subjects were told that the pain would be minimally unpleasant.

2. Perhaps nowhere has hypnosis *engendered*（造成）more controversy than over the issue of "recovered" memory. Cognitive science has established that people are fairly adept at discerning whether an event actually occurred or whether they only imagined it. But under some circumstances，we falter. We can come to believe（or can be led to believe）that something happened to us when，in fact，it did not. One of the key cues humans appear to use in making the distinction between reality and imagination is the experience of effort. Apparently，at the time of encoding a memory，a "tag" cues us as to the amount of effort we expended；if the event is tagged as having involved a good deal of mental effort on our part，we tend to interpret it as something we imagined. If it is tagged as having involved relatively little mental effort，we tend to interpret it as something that actually happened to us. Given that the calling card of hypnosis is precisely the feeling of effortlessness，we can see why hypnotized people can so easily mistake an imagined past event for something that happened long ago. Hence，something that is merely imagined can become ingrained as an episode in our life story.

Medical benefits of hypnosis

So what are the medical benefits of hypnosis? A 1996 National Institutes of Health technology assessment panel judged hypnosis to be an effective intervention for alleviating pain from cancer and other chronic conditions. Voluminous clinical studies also indicate that hypnosis can reduce the acute pain experienced by patients undergoing burn-wound debridement，children enduring bone marrow aspirations and women in labor. The pain-relieving effect of hypnosis is often substantial，and in a few cases the degree of relief matches or exceeds that provided by *morphine*（吗啡）. Hypnosis can boost the effectiveness of psycho-therapy for disorders such as obesity, insomnia, anxiety and hypertension.

1. Scientists have found out what makes some people easier to hypnotize than others.
2. One version of the Stanford scales—holding one's arm outstretched or sniffing the contents of a bottle—is testing the depth of the hypnotic state.
3. A person who does not recoil from the smell of ammonia is not deeply hypnotized.
4. The practitioner's gender, age and experience have little or no effect on a subject's ability to be hypnotized.
5. Hypnotism can be a substitute for *anesthesia* (麻木).
6. Hypnotism can slow the action of part of the brain.
7. More doctors are learning the technique of hypnotism.
8. During hypnosis, it is as though the brain temporarily suspends its attempts to authenticate _____.
9. To study hypnosis properly, the measure researchers adopt is _____.
10. _____ of hypnosis is often substantial, and in a few cases the degree of relief matches or exceeds that provided by morphine.

Section B   Discourse Vocabulary Test
Directions:（略）

Passage 2

People can be ___11___ to different things—e. g. , alcohol, drugs, certain foods, or even television. People who have such an addiction are—compulsive; i. e. , they have a very powerful psychological need that they feel they must satisfy. According to psychologists, many people are compulsive spenders: they feel that they must spend money. This compulsion, like most others, is irrational—impossible to explain ___12___. For compulsive spenders who buy on credit, charge accounts are even more exciting than money. In other words, ___13___ spenders feel that with credit, they can do anything. Their pleasure in spending enormous amounts is actually greater than the pleasure that they get from the things they buy.

There is even a ___14___ psychology of bargain hunting. To ___15___ money, of course, most people look for sales, low prices, and discounts. Compulsive bargain hunters, however, often buy things that they don't need just because they are cheap. They want to believe that they are helping their budgets, but they are ___16___ playing an exciting game: when they can buy something for less than other people, they feel that they are winning. Most people, experts claim, have two ___17___ for their ___18___: a good reason for the things that they do and the real reason.

It is not only scientists, of course, who understand the ___19___ of spending habits, but also business-people. Stores, companies, and advertisers use psychology to increase business. They consider people's needs for love, power, or influence, their basic values, their beliefs and opinions, and so on in their advertising and sales methods.

Psychologists often use a method called "behavior therapy" to help ___20___ solve their personality problems. In the same way, they can help people who feel that they have problems with money.

A) compulsive   I) nervous
B) private   J) reasons
C) addicted   K) individuals
D) save   L) psychology
E) specially   M) behavior
F) reasonably   N) consider
G) special   O) mental
H) really

Section C   Reading in Depth

Directions：（略）

Passage 3

The military services recently have shown more interest in family issues, including those relating to father-child relationships. This interest parallels the growing recognition by military leaders of the interdependency between military effectiveness and family functioning. It has been found that the extent to which members are satisfied with their family life is reflected in their job performance and is eventually tied to their decision to stay in the military.

This recognition, coupled with the changing image of the military community and family, has helped to provide more support services for military fathers. At the present time, the military services include a number of organizations that provide an impressive range of services and programs for fathers. Among these are Family Support Centers, Chaplain Services, Parent Educating Programs, Child-Care Services, and Recreational Services for fathers and their children. In addition, each service branch has established policies and procedures for handling incidents of child abuse and neglect. A key aspect of these important moves is their focus on prevention rather than punishment and discharge.

Despite military efforts to provide services for families, military fathers have been unwilling in the past to seek services or ask for help with a personal or family problem. They often believe that if they seek help for a problem, they may risk the danger of putting themselves in very unfavorable conditions and thus ruin their careers. As a consequence, military services and programs in recent years have increasingly adopted the concept of reaching out to military fathers to prevent certain problems in their planning efforts.

21. The word "parallels" (Line 2, Para. 1) means _____.
    A) extends side by side with   B) is similar to
    C) grows at the same time as   D) acts as a balance to
22. From the first paragraph we can see that _____.
    A) enjoyable family life is the key to military effectiveness
    B) military leaders are anxious to improve their relationship with their children

C) fathers are usually unwilling to stay in the military

D) enjoyable family life promotes job performance

23. The fundamental goal of the organizations listed in the second paragraph is _____.

A) to prevent crimes on the military

B) to bring about military effectiveness

C) to handle incidents of child abuse and neglect

D) to educate the children in the military

24. The support services described in the passage _____.

A) have done their best to help military fathers

B) have solved all the problems of military fathers

C) have not been functioning efficiently

D) have ruined some people's careers

25. From the last sentence of the passage, we know that _____.

A) access to military services has been made more convenient recently

B) military services have been working hard on some ideological problems

C) more and more people have realized the importance of planning in military services

D) the concept of prevention rather than punishment has been accepted by most people in the military

Passage 4

Today we live in a shadow of AIDS—the terrifyingly modern *epidemic*（传染病）that travels by jet and zeros in on the body's own disease—fighting immune system. More than 15 years after the first rumors of "gay plague" spread through the bathhouses of New York City and San Francisco, nearly 30 million people—gays and straights alike—have been infected by HIV, the virus that causes what has been, until now, an almost invariably fatal disease.

In July, at an international AIDS conference in Vancouver, a virologist named David Ho reported on a most promising experiment. By *administering*（配药）the *protease-inhibitor*（抑制剂）cocktails to patients in the earliest stages of infection, his team seems to have come tantalizingly close to eliminating the virus from the blood and other body tissues. Mathematical models suggest that patients caught early enough might be virus-free within two or three years.

Dr. David Ho was one of a small group of researchers who recognized from the start that AIDS was probably an infectious disease. He performed or collaborated on much of the basic *virology*（病毒学）work that showed HIV does not lie dormant, as most scientists thought, but multiplies in vast numbers right from the start. His insights helped shift the focus of AIDS treatment from the late stages of illness to the first weeks of infection. And it was his team's pioneering work with combination therapy, reported in Vancouver, that first raised hope that the virus might someday be eliminated.

Ho is not, to be sure, a household name—like Bill Clinton, who dominated the front page this year with his masterful comeback victory, or Bill Gates, who deftly extended the scope of his software empire into news, television and the Internet. But some people make headlines while others make history. And when the history of this era is written, it is likely that the men and women who turned the tide on AIDS will be seen as true heroes of the ages. For helping lift a death sentence—for a few years at least, and perhaps longer—on tens of thousands of AIDS sufferers, and for pioneering the treatment that might, just might, lead to a cure, David Dai Ho, M. D. , is *TIME*'s Man of the Year for 1996.

26. What does the word "straights" in line 4 of the first paragraph refer to?

    A) homosexuals   B) heterosexuals

    C) drug takers   D) sportsmen

27. The AIDS virus would destroy our _____.

    A) blood system   B) digestion system

    C) immune system   D) brain

28. Which of the following is correct according to the passage?

    A) Doctors thought AIDS would not spread among people.

    B) The numbers of the HIV virus would always stay in the same amount.

    C) Some patients could recover if they are diagnosed early and receive medical treatment.

    D) Dr. Ho's therapy is not as successful as he said.

29. We can infer from the passage that _____.

    A) Dr. Ho's achievements could not be compared with those of Bill Clinton and Bill Gates

    B) Dr. Ho would be remembered longer than Bill Clinton and Bill Gates

    C) Dr. Ho told the world his successful research on AIDS in America

    D) the most important period to treat AIDS is the last stage according to Dr. Ho

30. The main idea of the passage is _____.

    A) introduction of a new and effective therapy to AIDS

    B) comparison between a famous virologist and Bill Clinton and Bill Gates

    C) some information about AIDS

    D) the details of cocktail therapy

Section D　Short Answer Questions

Directions：（略）

Passage 5

Students who score high in achievement needs tend to make higher grades in college than those who score low. When degree aptitude for college work, as indicated by College Entrance Examination Board Tests, is constant, engineering students who score high in achievement needs tend to make higher grades in college than the aptitude test scores would indicate.

We can define this need as the habitual desire to do useful work well. It is a salient influence characteristic of those who need little supervision. Their desire for accomplishment is a stronger motivation than any stimulation the supervision can provide. Individuals who function in terms of this drive do not "bluff" in regard to a job that they fail to do well.

Some employees have a strong drive for success in their work; others are satisfied when they make a living. Those who want to feel that they are successful have high aspiration for themselves. Thoughts concerning the achievement drive are often prominent in the evaluations made by the typical employment interviewer who interviews college seniors for executive training. He wants to find out whether the senior has a strong drive to get ahead or merely to hold a job. Research indicates that some who do get ahead have an even stronger drive to avoid failure.

31. What is the main subject of this passage?

_____ _____ _____ _____

_____ _____ _____ _____

32. What is interesting about engineering students who score high in achievement needs?

_____ _____ _____ _____

_____ _____ _____ _____

33. According to the passage, what would an individual with a strong drive succeed in?

_____ _____ _____ _____

34. What quality do employment interviewers look for in college seniors for executive training?

_____ _____ _____ _____

_____ _____ _____ _____

35. What motivates some seniors to succeed?

_____ _____ _____ _____

_____ _____ _____ _____

Notes and Explanations

Passage 1

Explanations

1. [N] Measures to hypnosis 部分第六句提到 Some people are more hypnotizable than others, although scientists still don't know why. 一些人比其他人更容易被催眠,但是科学家们至今仍不清楚原因。由此得出答案是 No。

2. [Y] Measures to hypnosis 部分提到 One version of the Stanford scales consists of a series of 12 activities—such as holding one's arm outstretched or sniffing the contents of a bottle—that test the depth of the hypnotic state. 斯坦福度量法的一个版本包括 12 个活动,比如伸出胳膊或嗅瓶子里的气体,这些动作用来测试催眠的深度。由此可得出答案是 Yes。

3. [N] Measures to hypnosis 部分最后提到 In the second case, subjects are told that they have no sense of smell, and then a vial of ammonia is waved under their noses. ... If they grimace and recoil, they are not. 在第二个试验中,受试者被告知他们已经丧失了嗅觉,然后在他们面前挥动氨水瓶。如果他们做鬼脸或者退缩,说明他们并没有被彻底催眠。由此得出答案是 No。

4. [Y] Principles of hypnosis 部分第一段第三句提到 ... the practitioner's gender, age and experience have little or no effect on a subject's ability to be hypnotized. 受试者的性别、年龄和经验对于他/她接受催眠的能力没有或只有很小的影响。由此得出答案是 Yes。

5. [Y] Principles of hypnosis 第二段倒数第二句提到 Many researchers now believe that these types of

disconnections are at the bean intent, fail to detect exceedingly painful stimulation or temporarily forget a familiar fact. 很多研究者相信这种失去感觉的情况是人的大脑的问题,没有察觉到疼痛的刺激或暂时忘记了一个熟悉的事实。这就是麻木的感觉。由此得出答案是 Yes。

6. [N] Functions of hypnosis 部分第一段第一句提到 Scientists think that hypnosis may relieve pain by decreasing the activity of brain areas involved in the experience of suffering. 科学家们认为催眠可以通过减少大脑活动的区域来减轻疼痛感。而不是减慢活动,由此得出答案是 No。

7. [NG] 这篇文章是讨论催眠的方法、原则、功能以及医学功能,并没有提到现在有更多的医生学习催眠的技巧。因此答案是 Not Given。

8. 第一段中第五句提到 During hypnosis, it is as though the brain temporarily suspends its attempts to authenticate incoming sensory information. 在催眠过程中,就好像是大脑暂时减缓了处理感觉信息的过程。由此得出答案是 **incoming sensory information**。

9. 第一段中提到 In the case of hypnosis, that yardstick is the Stanford Hypnotic Susceptibility Scales. 斯坦福催眠感受度量法是研究催眠的尺度。由此得出答案是 **the Stanford Hypnotic Susceptibility Scales**。

10. 最后一段倒数第二句提到 The pain-relieving effect of hypnosis is often substantial, and in a few cases the degree of relief matches or exceeds that provided by morphine. 催眠减轻疼痛的效果是很明显的,在有些案例中舒缓疼痛的效果相当于或超过使用吗啡的效果。由此得出答案是 **The pain-relieving effect**。

Passage 2

Notes

1. People can be addicted to different things... even television. (Line 1, Para. 1)

be addicted to 意思是"有瘾的,上瘾的"。例如:

It doesn't take long to become addicted to these drugs. 服用这些毒品不用很长时间就会上瘾。

My children are hopelessly addicted to television. 我的几个孩子都成了电视迷,简直无可救药了。

2. ... they feel that they must spend money. This compulsion, like most others, is irrational—impossible to explain reasonably. (Line 4~5, Para. 1)

irrational 意思是"荒谬的,没有道理的,没有理智的",反义词是 rational。例如:

The survivors of the crash wandered about in a confused and irrational state.

空难幸存者困惑而失去理智地徘徊着。

His remarks are totally irrational. 他的评论完全没有道理。

3. For compulsive spenders who buy on credit... (Line 5, Para. 1)

buy (sth.) on credit 意思是"赊购"。例如:

If you can't afford to pay cash, buy the furniture on credit. 你如果不能付现金,可以赊购家具。

This shop gives/offers interest-free credit. 这家商店提供无息赊购优惠。

4. To save money, of course, most people look for sales... (Line 1~2, Para. 2)

在这里 sales 意思是"打折"。例如:

This shirt was a bargain—only $10 in a sale. 这件衬衫是便宜货,大减价时只卖 10 美元。

Have the January sales started yet? 元月大减价开始了吗?

5. Psychologists often use a method called "behavior therapy"... (Line 1, Para. 4)

behavior therapy 在这里的意思是"行为治疗",therapy 一般指"(不使用药物或不做手术的)治疗"。类似的说法还有:group therapy, occupational therapy, physiotherapy, psychotherapy, radiotherapy, speech therapy 等。

Explanations

11. [C] 语法规则要求此处应填一个形容词构成 be + 形容词 + 介词的结构。选项 A、B、C、G、I、O 是形容词。本句所举的例子 alcohol，drugs，certain foods or even television 都是可以让人上瘾的东西，所以可以断定 addicted 符合句意。To be addicted to 意思是"沉迷于……，迷恋于……"。

12. [F] 语法规则要求此处应填一个副词作状语修饰 explain。选项 E、F、H 是副词。常与 explain 搭配使用的是 reasonably。根据上文破折号前 This compulsion，like most others，is irrational 可以判断出此处应填一个与 irrational 意思相近（或相同）的词，impossible to explain reasonably 意思是"不能合理解释"，符合句意。

13. [A] 语法规则要求此处应填一个形容词作定语修饰 spenders。此句前一句讲的是 compulsive spenders 的情况，in other words 表明本句话还是讲 compulsive spenders 的情况，所以这里的词应该还是 compulsive。

14. [G] 语法规则要求此处应填一个形容词作定语修饰 psychology。根据下文讲两类消费者讨价还价的情况可以判断出 special（专门的）符合句意。

15. [D] 语法规则要求此处应填一个动词原形构成动词不定式作目的状语。选项 D、N 符合该条件。根据下文的 sales，low prices 和 discounts 可以判断出此处应该是"省钱"的意思，故 save 符合题意。

16. [H] 语法规则要求此处应填一个副词作状语修饰 playing。根据上下文判断出此处还是讲 compulsive spenders 的情况，他们在玩一种激动人心的游戏，由此推断出 really（实际上）符合句意。

17. [J] 语法规则要求此处应填一个复数名词。根据下文中的 a good reason 和 the real reason 可判断出 reasons 符合句意。

18. [M] 语法规则要求此处应填一个名词作介词 for 的宾语。选项 J、L、M 是名词。根据上下文可判断出"买东西"是"大多数人"的一种行为，behavior（行为）符合句意。

19. [L] 语法规则要求此处应填一个单数名词名词作 understand 的宾语。根据下文 stores，companies and advertisersuse psychology to increase business 可判断 psychology 符合句意。

20. [K] 语法规则要求此处应填一个复数名词构成 help ＋ 名词 ＋ do sth. 的结构。根据下文中的 personality problems 可判断出 individuals（个人的）符合句意。

Passage 3

Notes

1. It has been found that the extent to which... their decision to stay in the military. (Line 3~5, Para. 1)
这句话的意思是：人们发现军人对家庭生活的满意程度可以从他们的工作表现中反映出来并最终和他们决定是否留在部队中服役有关。which 引导的是定语从句，修饰 the extent。tie to 意思是"使有联系，使不能离开"。例如：

He is tied to his work. 他不能离开工作岗位。

Perhaps those reasons were tied to the problems arising from the struggle over Western Sahara.
也许那些原因和在西撒哈拉沙漠开战时出现的问题有关。

2. This recognition, coupled with the changing image... (Line 1, Para. 2)
coupled with 意思是"加上，外加"。例如：

The strike, coupled with the floods, was expected to reduce supplies of food drastically.
预计罢工外加洪涝灾害会大大减少食物供应。

Working too hard, coupled with not getting enough sleep, made him ill.
辛勤工作加上睡眠不足使他疾病缠身。

3. As a consequence, military services and programs in recent years... (Line 4~5, Para. 3)
as a consequence（in consequence）意思是"结果"。例如：

We hadn't enough money to pay the bus fare, and as a consequence, we had to walk home.
我们的钱不够付车费，结果我们不得不步行回家。

4. ... have increasingly adopted the concept of reaching out to military fathers... (Line 5, Para. 3)

reach out to 意思是"和……联系,联系群众"。例如:

The movement was a largely unofficial attempt to reach out to the working urban class.

非官方人士企图通过这一运动设法接近城市劳动阶级。

A party which doesn't reach out is like a head without a body.

不联系群众的政党就像有头没有躯干的人体。

Explanations

本文介绍了部队所能提供的有效的家庭服务特别是为军人父亲提供的家庭服务与家庭职能的关系。军人父亲对家庭生活的满意程度体现在工作表现中并最终和他们决定是否留在军中服役有关系。因此近年来的部队服务项目越来越多地考虑到帮助部队成员特别是军人父亲避免和解决一些家庭问题。

21. **C)** 词汇题。根据上下文的意思可以推断 parallels 的意思是"同步增长"。

22. **C)** 推断题。从第一段最后一句推断出如果对家庭生活不满意的话,军人父亲就会考虑离开部队。选项 A 错在 key(关键)一词,家庭生活的影响对军人父亲在部队的表现很重要,但不能因此说是起着关键的作用。选项 B 在没有上下文的情况下意思不够明确,正确信息应为 enjoyable family life promotes job performance in the military。所以正确答案应是 C 项。

23. **B)** 细节题。从第二段第一句可以推断出建立本段列出的服务项目的目的是提供更有效的服务。所以正确答案是 B 项。

24. **A)** 细节题。从第二段第一句和第三段最后一句可以断定本题正确答案是 A 项。

25. **A)** 细节题。考察对句子的理解。从文章最后一句话我们可以得知近年来的部队服务项目越来越多地考虑到以上门服务的方式帮助部队成员特别是军人父亲避免和解决一些家庭问题,因此人们可以更方便地得到这些服务。

Passage 4

Notes

1. gays and straights... (Line 4, Para. 1)

gay 在这里的意思是"同性恋者",straights 在这里的意思是"异性恋者"。

2. ... a virologist named David Ho reported on a most promising experiment. (Line 1~2, Para. 2)

promising 的意思是"大有希望的,很有前途的",反义词是 unpromising。例如:

a promising young singer 大有前途的青年歌手

3. By administering... his team seems to have come tantalizingly close to eliminating the virus from the blood and other body tissues. (Line 2~4, Para. 2)

这句话的意思是:通过将一种抑制剂注入艾滋病早期感染者的体内,他的研究小组好像接近于将血液中的和其他身体组织中的艾滋病病毒清除干净。

come close to 的意思是"靠近,与……接近/相似"。例如:

Come close to each other so that I can get you all in the photograph.

互相靠拢一些,这样我就能够把你们全照进去。

The book comes close to perfection. 这本书几乎完美无缺。

4. ... but multiplies in vast numbers right from the start. (Line 3~4, Para. 3)

这里 right 是副词,放在状语前起加强语气的作用。例如:

Put it right in the middle. 放在正中间。

He was standing right beside me. 他就站在我旁边。

5. For helping lift a death sentence—for a few years... is *TIME*'s Man of the Year for 1996.

(Line 5～8，Para. 4)

这句话的意思是：在近几年甚至更长的时间内，David Ho 博士也许会拯救成千上万的艾滋病患者的生命，也许会首先发现一种治愈艾滋病的方法，为此时代周刊把他视为 1996 年度风云人物。

这里 lift 的意思是"解除，去除"。例如：

The unpopular tax was soon lifted. 那项不受欢迎的税收不久就被废除了。

Explanations

本文主要谈到 David Ho 博士在艾滋病治疗方面的贡献。艾滋病已经成为当今社会最有杀伤力的疾病之一。在温哥华举办的一次国际会议上，Ho 博士提出了新的治疗方法——鸡尾酒疗法。如果在患病的初期进行治疗，可以在两三年内彻底消灭所有病毒。Ho 博士同时指出艾滋病的病毒是可以大量繁殖的。在最后一段，作者把 Ho 博士和 Bill Clinton 以及 Bill Gates 相比较，断言 Ho 博士的贡献经过时间的沉淀会被人们一直记住的。

26. **B）** 词汇题。把 straights 和 gays 比较就可以猜出它的词义是 B 项。

27. **C）** 常识题。第一段第一句明确提到了选项 C。

28. **C）** 推断题。根据第二段内容可以确定正确答案是 C 项。

29. **B）** 推断题。最后一段后半部分作者大力称赞 Ho 博士的成就，由此可以看出 B 项是正确答案。C 项是考察细节，文中提到"Vancouver(温哥华)"是在加拿大，所以不会是在美国。D 项是说在 Ho 博士的治疗过程中，治疗艾滋病最重要的时期是在后期，这和原文是不相符的。

30. **A）** 主旨题。第一段是引言，指出艾滋病的致命性和不可治愈性，第二段介绍了 Ho 博士提出的新的治疗方法，第三段详细介绍了这种治疗方法，最后一段指出这种治疗方法给 Ho 博士带来的荣誉，因此可以确定正确答案是 A 项。

Passage 5

Keys

31. Individual motivation for work.
32. Their grades tend to be higher than those of other students.
33. They would have high aspiration for themselves.
34. High achievement needs.
35. A strong drive to get ahead and avoid failure.

Notes

1. We can define this need as the habitual desire... (Line 1, Para. 2)

define... as... 的意思是"将……定义为……；限定"。例如：

The power of the President are defined in the constitution. 总统的权力在宪法中有明确规定。

2. Some employees have a strong drive for success in their work... (Line 1, Para. 3)

drive 在这里的意思是"驱动力"。例如：

Every serious dancer is driven by notions of perfection, perfect expressiveness, perfect technique.

每个严肃的舞蹈者都为完美的信念、完美的表现力、完美的技巧所驱使。

3. Thoughts concerning the achievement drive are often prominent in the evaluations... (Line 3, Para. 3)

concerning 是介词，意思是"关于，有关"。例如：

Concerning your letter, I am pleased to inform you that you are to receive the order by the end of this week. 关于你的来信，我乐意告诉你，你们将在本周末收到订货。

Unit 26

Section A Skimming and Scanning

Directions：（略）

Passage 1

Is There Water on Mars?

1. Mars (Greek：Ares) is the god of War. The planet probably got this name due to its red color；Mars is sometimes referred to as the Red Planet. (An interesting side note：the Roman god Mars was a god of agriculture before becoming associated with the Greek Ares；those in favor of colonizing and terra-forming Mars may prefer this symbolism). The name of the month March derives from Mars.

2. Mars has been known since prehistoric times. Of course, it has been extensively studied with ground-based observatories. But even very large telescopes find Mars a difficult target, it's just too small. It is still a favorite of science writers as the most favorable place in the Solar System (other than Earth!) for human habitation. But the famous "canals" "seen" by Lowell and others were, unfortunately, just as imaginary as Barsoomian princesses.

3. The first spacecraft to visit Mars was Mariner 4 in 1965. Several others followed including Mars 2, the first spacecraft to land on Mars and the two Viking landers in 1976. Ending a long 20 year hiatus, Mars Pathfinder landed successfully on Mars on 1997 July 4. In 2004 the Marss Expeditioin Rovers "Spirit" and "Opportunity" landed on Mars sending back geologic data and many pictures；they are still operating after more than a year on Mars. Three Mars orbiters (Mars Global Surveyor, Mars Odyssey, and Mars Express) are also currently in operation.

4. Mars' orbit is significantly elliptical. One result of this is a temperature variation of about 30℃ at the sub-solar point between aphelion and perihelion. This has a major influence on Mars's climate. While the average temperature on Mars is about 218 K (-55℃, -67 F), Martian surface temperatures range widely from as little as 140 K (-133℃, -207 F) at the winter pole to almost 300 K (27 ℃, 80 F) on the day side during summer.

5. Though Mars is much smaller than Earth, its surface area is about the same as the land surface area of Earth.

6. A large number of photographs taken by the Mars Global Surveyor spacecraft suggest that even today water may be flowing up from the interior of Mars, and streaming onto the surface—dramatically increasing the likelihood that at least part of the planet is biologically alive. "If this proves to be the case," said Ed Weiler, of NASA's Office of Space science, "it has profound implications for the possibility of life (on Mars)."

7. Finding liquid water on Mars' surface has never been easy—mostly because it simply can't exist there. The modem Martian atmosphere has barely 1% the density of the Earth's, and the planet's average temperature hovers around -55 ℃. In an environment as harsh as this, any water that did appear would either vaporize into space or freeze solid. What scientists studying Mars have always been looking for instead are clues that there was water in the planet's distant past: In fact, they admit that there may have been oceans at one time on Mars.

8. The 65,000 images, which the Surveyor has *beamed*(传回) home since it was launched in 1998, show plenty of channels and terraces on the surface of Mars. But a handful of the pictures took the scientists by surprise. Besides looking fairly new, the channels are mainly located near the poles of Mars, where the temperature is coldest. Scientists have long assumed that if underground water was going to bubble up on Mars, it would have to do so somewhere in the comparatively balmy equatorial zones, where temperatures at high noon in midsummer may approach 20℃. Moreover, the channels are all carved into the cold, shaded sides of slopes.

9. *Paradoxically*(荒谬的), this finding may increase the chances that the *gullies*(沟) are water-related. Any water that appeared on the sunny sides of hills would be likely to evaporate almost instantly. Moisture that seeped out in the shade would form a temporary crest of ice that would last only until the pressure of upwelling water behind it caused it to burst. When it did, there would be a sudden downward *gush*(涌出) that would leave precisely the kind of clear-cut channel Surveyor spotted. If such features were discovered on Earth, said Michael Malin, principal investigator for the Surveyor's camera system, "there would be no question that water would be associated with them."

10. However, there are alternative explanations for these channels and *ridges*(山脊). One school of thought maintains that they could have been caused by "rivers" of silicon dust. The theory goes that millions of years ago, when the molten mass of Mars cooled down, the fast cooling of the surface lava produced extremely small silicon particles. It has been proved that Martian soils contain a large amount of silicon. These particles would then have bonded with the methane gas which was also produced by the cooling process due to the action of ultraviolet light. The silicon combined with methane would then have flowed in much the same way as rivers—from high to low areas. Over a long period of time, the flow would disintegrate rock and form channels or gullies, like those photographed by the Surveyor.

11. Another theory is that the features which seem to be evidence of the action of water whether oceans or rivers—are more likely linked to the planet's volcanoes. Paul Withers of the University of Arizona and Gregory Neumann of the Massachusetts Institute of Technology, think that there is a closer correlation between the sizes of the terraces and seismic activity than the formation of ocean shore lines. They explained that the surface crest of Mars is not formed of a network of plates, like the Earth's, which move over time. Martian volcanoes grew much higher than those on Earth, putting tremendous stress on the crest, and generating the ridges and channels seen in the Surveyor photographs. "In our future work," said Withers and Neumann, "we intend to study the terraces further in order to ascertain what the Martian crust and *lithosphere*(岩石圈) were like at the time the seismic activity led to the formation of the volcanoes."

12. For NASA, the new findings couldn't have come at a better time. After the recent spectacular failures of two unmanned Mars probes, the agency's entire planetary exploration program came under fire. The possibility of a wet Mars, however, suggests that not only might the planet be home to indigenous life, it could also more easily support human life. Visiting astronauts would need water for a variety of purposes, including manufacturing air and perhaps even rocket fuel. Pumping up water available on Mars rather than hauling supplies from earth could dramatically slash the cost of a mission. All this, NASA hopes, will encourage the reluctant Congress to give the green light to future Mars missions, both manned and unmanned.

1. A large number of photographs taken by the Mars Global Surveyor spacecraft suggest that water cannot be flowing up from the interior of Mars nowadays.

2. Finding liquid water on Mars' surface has never been easy—mostly because it is difficult to land on Mars.

3. The average temperature of the Mars hovers around -55 ℃.

4. Besides looking fairly new, the channels are mainly located near the poles of Mars, where the temperature is hottest.

5. Any water that appeared on the sunny sides of hills would be likely to evaporate slowly.

6. One school of thought maintains that they could have been caused by "rivers" of silicon dust.

7. Professors explained that the surface crest of Mars is formed of a network of plates, like the Earth's, which move over time.

8. Scientists studying Mars have always looked for signs that water was once present on _____.

9. The formations discovered by the Mars Global Survey were surprising because they appear _____ of the planet.

10. The new findings may benefit NASA by persuading Congress to _____.

Section B Discourse Vocabulary Test
Directions：（略）

Passage 2

Space is a dangerous place, not only because of meteors but also because of rays from the sun and other stars. The __11__ again acts as our protective blanket on earth. Light gets through, and this is __12__ for plants to make the food which we eat. Heat, too, makes our environment __13__. Various kinds of rays come through the air from outer space, but enormous quantities of radiation from the sun are screened off. As soon as men leave the atmosphere they are __14__ to this radiation but their spacesuits or the walls of their spacecraft, if they are inside, do prevent a lot of radiation damage.

Radiation is the greatest known danger to explorers in __15__. The unit of radiation is called "*Rem*"（雷姆）. Scientists have reason to think that a man can put up with far more radiation than 0.1 Rem without being damaged; the figure of 60 Rems has been agreed on. The trouble is that it is __16__ difficult to be sure about radiation damage. A person may feel perfectly well, __17__ the cells of his or her sex organs may be damaged, and this will not be discovered until the birth of deformed children or even grandchildren.

Missions of the Apollo flights have had to cross belts of high amount of Rems. So far, no dangerous amounts of radiation have been ___18___, but the Apollo missions have been quite short. We simply do not know yet how men are going to get on when they spend weeks and months outside the protection of the atmosphere, working in a space laboratory. Drugs might help to ___19___ the damage done by radiation, but no really ___20___ ones have been found so far.

A) exposed	I) endurable
B) space	J) slowly
C) enormous	K) extremely
D) atmosphere	L) effective
E) essential	M) effect
F) but	N) fatal
G) remain	O) decrease
H) reported	

Section C   Reading in Depth

Directions：（略）

Passage 3

Britain almost more than any other country in the world must seriously face the problem of building upwards, that is to say of accommodation a considerable proportion of its population in high blocks of flats. It is said that the Englishman objects to this kind of existence, but if the case is such, he does in fact differ from the inhabitants of most countries of the world today. In the past our own blocks of flats have been associated with the lower-income groups and they have lacked the obvious provisions, such as central heating, constant hot water supply, electrically operated lifts from top to bottom, and so on, as well as such details, important notwithstanding, as easy facilities for disposal of dust and rubbish and storage places for baby carriages on the ground floor, playgrounds for children on the top of the buildings, and drying grounds for washing. It is likely that the dispute regarding flats versus individual houses will continue to rage on for a long time as far as Britain is concerned. And it is unfortunate that there should be hot feelings on both sides whenever this subject is raised. Those who oppose the building of flats base their case primarily on the assumption that everyone prefers an individual home and garden and on the high cost per unit of accommodation. The latter ignores the higher cost of providing full services to a scattered community and the cost in both money and time of the journeys to work for the suburban resident.

21. We can infer from the passage that _____.
   A) English people, like most people in other countries, dislike living in flats
   B) people in most countries of the world today are not opposed to living in flats

C) people in Britain are forced to move into high blocks of flats

D) modern flats still fail to provide the necessary facilities for living

22. What is said about the blocks of flats built in the past in Britain?

A) They were mostly inhabited by people who did not earn much.

B) They were usually not large enough to accommodate big families.

C) They were sold to people before necessary facilities were installed.

D) They provided playground for children on the top of the buildings.

23. The word "rage" in the sentence "It is likely that the dispute regarding flats versus individual houses will continue to rage on for a long time as far as Britain is concerned." means "_____".

A) be ignored
B) develop with great force
C) encourage people greatly
D) be in fashion

24. Some people oppose the building of flats because _____.

A) the living expenses for each individual family are higher

B) it involves higher cost compared with the building of houses

C) they believe people like to live in houses with gardens

D) the disposal of rubbish remains a problem for those living in flats

25. The author mentions that people who live in suburban houses _____.

A) do not have access to easy facilities because they live away from the city

B) have to pay a lot of money to employ people to do service work

C) take longer time to know each other because they are a scattered community

D) have to spend more money and time traveling to work every day

Passage 4

Where do *pesticides* (杀虫剂) fit into the picture of environmental disease? We have seen that they now pollute soil, water, and food, that they have the power to make our streams fishless and our gardens and woodlands silent and birdless. Man, however much he may like to pretend the contrary, is part of nature. Can he escape a pollution that is now so thoroughly distributed throughout our world?

We know that even single exposures to these chemicals, if the amount is large enough, can cause extremely severe poisoning. But this is not the major problem. The sudden illness or death of farmers, farm workers, and others exposed to sufficient quantities of pesticides are very sad and should not occur. For the population as a whole, we must be more concerned with the delayed effects of absorbing small amounts of the pesticides that invisibly pollute our world.

Responsible public health officials have pointed out that the biological effects of chemicals are cumulative over long periods of time, and that the danger to the individual may depend on the sum of the exposures received throughout his lifetime. For these very reasons the danger is easily ignored. It is human nature to shake off what may seem to us a threat of future disaster. "Men are naturally most impressed by diseases which have obvious signs," says a wise physician, Dr. Rene Dubos, "yet some of their worst enemies slowly approach them unnoticed."

26. Which of the following is closest in meaning to the sentence "Man, however much he may like to pretend the contrary, is part of nature. " (Line 3~4, Para. 1)?

A) Man appears indifferent to what happens in nature.

B) Man acts as if he does not belong to nature.

C) Man can avoid the effects of environmental pollution.

D) Man can escape his responsibilities for environmental protection.

27. What is the author's attitude towards the environmental effects of pesticides?

A) Pessimistic.　　B) Indifferent.　　C) Defensive.　　D) Concerned.

28. In the author's view, the sudden death caused by exposure to large amounts of pesticides _____.

A) is not the worst of the negative consequences resulting from the use of pesticides

B) now occurs most frequently among all accidental deaths

C) has sharply increased so as to become the center of public attention

D) is unavoidable because people can't do without pesticides in farming

29. People tend to ignore the delayed effects of exposure to chemicals because _____.

A) limited exposure to them does little harm to people's health

B) the present is more important for them than the future

C) the danger does not become apparent immediately

D) humans are capable of withstanding small amounts of poisoning

30. It can be concluded from Dr Dubos' remarks that _____.

A) people find invisible diseases difficult to deal with

B) attacks by hidden enemies tend to be fatal

C) diseases with obvious sighs are easy to cure

D) people tend to overlook hidden dangers caused by pesticides

Section D　Short Answer Questions

Directions: (略)

Passage 5

　　Writing in a foreign language at first may seem to be very like writing in your native language, but of course it isn't. The problem stems from more than a mere difference between words or symbols. It is also a matter of the arrangement of words together in a sentence. The words and word groups of one language don't fit together in the same way as the words of another language do. Perhaps even more important, ideas don't fit together the same way from language to language. A Russian, an Egyptian, a Brazilian, and Japanese tend to arrange their ideas on the same subject in quite different ways within a paragraph. These differences exist because each culture has its own special way of thinking. And how a person thinks largely determines how he writes. Thus, in order to write well in English, a foreign student should first understand how English speakers usually arrange their ideas. This arrangement of ideas can be called a thought pattern. And, even though English thought patterns are not native to you, once you understand them you can more easily imitate them. By doing this, you will succeed in writing more effective

English. A basic feature of the English paragraph is that it normally follows a straight line of development. This English thought pattern is important for a writer to understand. The paragraph often begins with a statement of its central idea, known as a topic sentence, followed by a series of subdivisions of the central idea. These subdivisions have the purpose of developing the topic sentence, preparing for the addition of other ideas in later paragraph.

31. What other differences in writing in a foreign language does the author mention besides the difference of words?

_____ _____ _____ _____

_____ _____ _____ _____

32. Why do people from different countries write in different ways?

_____ _____ _____ _____

33. How can we manage to write well in English?

_____ _____ _____ _____

34. What is the use of a topic sentence?

_____ _____ _____ _____

35. An English paragraph is different from an *Oriental* (东方的) paragraph in that the former _____.

_____ _____ _____ _____

Notes and Explanations

Passage 1

Explanations

1. [N] 第六段的第一句提到 A large number of photographs taken by the Mars Global Surveyor spacecraft suggest that even today water may be flowing up from the interior of Mars. 火星观察者飞船拍摄的大量照片显示水仍可能在火星内部流动。由此得出答案是 No。

2. [N] 第七段的第一句提到 Finding liquid water on Mars'surface has never been easy—mostly because it simply can't exist there. 在火星表面发现液态水是很困难的,主要是因为那儿根本不可能有水。由此得出答案是 No。

3. [Y] 第七段第二句提到...the planet's average temperature hovers around -55 ℃. 火星的表面温度始终在零下五十五度左右。由此得出答案是 Yes。

4. [N] 第八段第三句提到 Besides looking fairly new, the channels are mainly located near the poles of Mars, where the temperature is coldest. 除了看上去很新,火星上的沟渠主要位于火星的两极附近,也是温度最低的地方。由此得出答案是 No。

5. [N] 第九段第二句提到 Any water that appeared on the sunny sides of hills would be likely to evaporate almost instantly. 任何出现在山体阳面的水都会立刻蒸发掉。由此得出答案是 No。

6. [Y] 第十段第二句提到 One school of thought maintains that they could have been caused by "rivers" of silicon dust. 一种观点认为沟渠和山脊是由硅的灰尘流造成的。由此得出答案是 Yes。

7. [N] 第十一段第三句提到 They explained that the surface crest of Mars is not formed of a network of plates, like the Earth's, which move over time. 他们解释说火星的表层并不是像地球那样由多年变化形成板状构造。由此得出答案是 No。

8. 第七段第四句提到 What scientists studying Mars have always been looking for instead are clues that there was water in the planet's distant past: In fact, they admit that there may have been oceans at one time on Mars. 科学家们一直都在寻找一些过去火星曾经存在水的蛛丝马迹：事实上，他们承认火星上曾一度有过海洋。文中还提到火星存在地下水的可能，科学家们试图在火星表面发现水。由此得出答案是 **the planet's surface**。

9. 第八段第二、三句提到 But a handful of the pictures took the scientists by surprises. Besides looking fairly new, the channels are mainly located near the poles of Mars, where the temperature is coldest. 但是很多照片都让科学家们很震惊。除了看上去很新，火星上的沟渠主要都位于火星的两极附近，也是温度最低的地方。由此得出答案是 **in the coldest parts**。

10. 最后一句话提到 All this, NASA hopes, will encourage the reluctant Congress to give the green light to future Mars missions, both manned and unmanned. NASA 希望，这些可以敦促犹豫不决的国会对未来的载人和不载人火星计划多开绿灯。由此得出答案是 **allow more Mars missions**。

Passage 2

Notes

1. The atmosphere again acts as... (Line 2, Para. 1)
   act 在这里的意思是"起作用，发生作用，生效"。例如：
   Does the drug take long to act on the nerve center? 这药要过很长时间才对神经中枢发生作用吗？
   A trained dog can act as a guide to a blind person. 经过训练的狗能当盲人的向导。

2. ...but enormous quantities of radiation from the sun are screened off. (Line 4~5, Para. 1)
   screen 在此处的意思是"把……隔开或遮挡"。例如：
   A floppy hat screened her face. 一顶有边的软帽遮住了她的脸。
   Part of the room was screened off as a reception area. 这个房间的一部分被隔开作为接待间。

3. Radiation is the greatest known danger to explorers in space. (Line 1, Para. 2)
   known 在这里的意思是"已知的"。例如：
   He's known to the police. 他是警察所熟知的罪犯。
   Samuel Clemens, known as Mark Twain, became a famous American writer.
   塞缪尔·克莱门斯，笔名是马克·吐温，为美国的著名作家。

4. Scientists have reason to think that a man can put up with far more radiation than... (Line 2, Para. 2)
   put up with 的意思是"忍受，忍耐"。例如：
   I can't put up with your rudeness any more; leave the room.
   我不能再忍受你这种无礼的态度了，请离开这个房间。
   That woman has a lot to put up with. 那个女人要忍受许多困难。

5. ...no really effective ones have been found so far. (Line 5, Para. 3)
   so far 的意思是"至今为止"。例如：
   He's had three wives so far. 至今为止，他已经娶过三个老婆了。
   "Have you met your new neighbor?" "Not so far." "你见过你的新邻居了吗？" "至今还没有。"

Explanations

11. [D] 语法规则要求此处应填一个名词作主语,谓语的形式要求主语是单数名词。选项 B、D、M 是单数名词。根据本句中 acts as our protective blanket on earth 可以推断出 atmosphere(大气层)符合句意。

12. [E] 语法规则要求此处应填一个形容词构成 It/This is + 形容词 + for sb. /sth. to do/be 句型。选项 C、E、I、L、N 是形容词。本句话的意思是"光能穿过大气层,这对植物生产我们吃的食物是必要的",由此判断出 essential(必要的)符合句意。

13. [I] 语法规则要求此处应填一个形容词作 our environment 的补语。根据后面两句话的解释可以判断 endurable(可忍耐的;可生存的)符合句意。

14. [A] 语法规则要求此处应填一个动词的过去分词形式构成被动语态。选项 A、H 是此形式。根据本句的状语从句的意思判断 exposed 符合句意。be exposed to 是意思是"暴露在……下"。

15. [B] 语法规则要求此处应填一个名词作介词 in 的宾语。根据本句话前半部分的意思可以判断 space 符合句意。in space 意思是"在太空中"。

16. [K] 语法规则要求此处应填一个副词作状语修饰 difficult。选项中只有 extremely 和 slowly 可能正确。根据下一句话的解释可以判断 extremely 符合句意,意思是"非常地,极端地"。

17. [F] 语法规则要求此处应填一个连词。选项中只有选项 F 是连词。这两个并列句的意思是相反的,所以 but 符合句意。

18. [H] 语法规则要求此处应填一个动词的过去分词形式构成被动语态。选项中只有 exposed 和 reported 可能正确。根据本句话意思判断 reported(报道)符合句意。

19. [O] 语法规则要求此处应填一个动词原形构成动词不定式。选项 G,O 是动词原形。根据本段的大意可以判断 decrease 符合句意。decrease the damage 意思是"减少损害"。

20. [L] 语法规则要求此处应填一个形容词作定语修饰 ones(drugs)。选项 C、E、I、L、N 是形容词。常和 drugs 搭配使用的是 effective。effective drugs 意思是"有效的药物",符合句意。

Passage 3

Notes

1. It is said that the Englishman objects to this kind of existence, … (Line 3)

   object to 的意思是"反对",to 是介词。例如:

   I strongly object to being treated as a child. 我强烈反对被人当作孩子一样对待。

   They object on religious grounds to this new law. 他们出于宗教原因反对这一新法律。

2. … as far as Britain is concerned. (Line 10~11)

   as far as… is concerned 的意思是"就……而言"。例如:

   As far as we're concerned you can go whenever you want. 就我们而言,你们随时想走都可以走。

   As far as I'm concerned the whole idea is crazy. 依我之见,整个想法真是荒诞之极。

3. Those who oppose… (Line 12)

   oppose 在这里是及物动词,意思是"反对"。例如:

   The proposed new airport will be vigorously opposed by the local residents.

   拟议中的新机场将会受到当地居民的强烈反对。

   The president opposes giving military aid to this country. 总统反对向该国提供军事援助。

Explanations

这篇文章讨论了英国的高层建筑问题。文中提到了高层建筑存在的很多问题,诸如中央供暖、不断的热水供应、从顶层到底层的电梯以及其他的细微之处。而最令人难以忍受的是处理灰尘和垃圾的方便设施与存放婴儿车的地方在一个楼层,孩子们玩耍的运动场在顶楼,烘干层是用来洗衣服的。而那些反对公寓建筑的人则忽略了为一个分散的社区提供一切服务所需的较高费用以及从郊区的住所去上班所花费的的时间与金钱。

21. **B)** 细节题。文章的第二句话讲到据说英国人反对这种建筑的存在,但如果真是这样,英国人的确与当今世界上大多数国家的居民不同。由此可以得出正确答案是 B 项。

22. **A)** 细节题。文中提到"多层公寓一直是与低收入人群联系起来的",因此可以得出 A 项是正确答案。

23. **B)** 细节题。rage 意思是"愤怒",这里加以引申,表示"越发激烈"的意思。

24. **C)** 细节题。文章倒数第二句讲到那些反对公寓建筑的人主要是基于这样一种设想,即所有的人都喜欢有一个独立的房间与花园,由此可以推出答案是 C 项。

25. **D)** 细节题。选项 A、B 和 C 在本文中均未提及,从文章的最后一句可以得出选项 D 才是正确答案。

Passage 4

Notes

1. ... make our streams fishless and our gardens and woodlands silent and birdless. (Line 2~3, Para. 1)
在这句话里,fishless 和 birdless 都表示"没有鱼"和"没有鸟"。作者在这里用表示"没有"的后缀-less 来创造出词语来表达其意图。

2. ... and others exposed to... (Line 3, Para. 2)
expose to 在这里的意思是"暴露"。例如:
Keep indoors and don't expose your skin to the sun. 留在屋里,不要让皮肤在太阳下暴晒。
As a nurse in the war she was exposed to many dangers. 作为战地护士,她置身于各种各样的危险之中。

3. Responsible public health officials have pointed out... (Line 1, Para. 3)
point out 在此处的意思是"指出,指明"。例如:
May I point out that if we don't leave now we shall miss the bus.
我想指出,我们如果现在不走,就会赶不上公共汽车。
I pointed out to him where I used to live. 我把我过去住的地方指给他看。

4. ... "yet some of their worst enemies slowly approach them unnoticed." (Line 6, Para. 3)
approach 在这里的意思是"靠近,接近"。例如:
The time is approaching when we will have to leave. 我们要离开的时刻越来越近了。
He's a good player, but doesn't approach international standard. 他是位好选手,但离国际水平尚远。

Explanations

　　本文谈论杀虫剂对环境的影响。杀虫剂污染土壤、水与食物,并且只要达到一定数量,就会引起极为严重的中毒。负责公众健康的官员已经指出化学品的生理影响会经过较长的时期累积下来,而它对个体的危害则取决于一生中与其接触的多少。人类的本性就是不理会看似在将来会造成灾难的威胁。"人们自然地对那些有明显症状的疾病印象最深,"内科医生 Rene Dubos 博士说,"然而有些最可怕的敌人却在不知不觉中慢慢地来到了身边"。

26. **B)** 细节题。这句的意思是"而人类不论怎样想伪装成非自然的事物,仍是自然的一部分",the contrary 指"与自然相对的人类"。所以可以得出答案是 B 项。

27. **D)** 推断题。第一段中作者提出的几个问题表明他对此事的关注。第二段最后一句 we must be more concerned with... 说明了作者对此事的态度。

28. **A)** 细节题。在第二段的开始,作者提到"只要达到一定数量,就会引起极为严重的中毒",但又指出这还不是主要问题,我们更应注重不断接触少量杀虫剂所导致的潜在后果。由此可见答案是 A 项。

29. **C)** 细节题。在文章的第三段的开头就提到"化学品的生理影响经过较长的时期会累积下来,而它对个体的危害则取决于一生中与其接触的多少"。正是由于这些原因,危险很容易被忽视。因此人类的本性就是不理会看似在将来会造成灾难的威胁。所以人们比较容易忽略与化学品接触造成的潜在后果,因此 C 项是正确答案。

30. **D）** 推断题。根据文章最后一句,Dubos 博士认为"然而有些最可怕的敌人却在不知不觉中慢慢地来到了身边",所以可以看出人们是很容易忽视杀虫剂引起的潜在危险的。

Passage 5

Keys

31. The arrangement of words and ideas.
32. Because they think in different ways.
33. By imitating the English thought pattern.
34. To state/introduce the central idea.
35. follows a straight/direct line of development

Notes

1. The problem stems from more than a mere difference between words or symbols. （Line 2～3）

   stem from... = arise from 意思是"来自或起源于……;由……造成"。例如:

   Correct decisions stem from correct judgments. 正确的决定来源于正确的判断。

   Discontent stems from low pay and poor working conditions. 因工资低、工作条件差而产生不满情绪。

2. A basic feature of the English paragraph is that it normally follows a straight line of development. （Line 12～13）

   a straight line of development 意思是"直线式发展"。

   根据文章介绍,以英语为母语的人的思维特点是直线展开式,英语段落的写作也是直线式发展,即以"主题句 + 细节部分"组成。主题句是对一个段落的概括;而细节则是对主题的阐述和说明。

3. The paragraph often begins with a statement of its central idea, known as a topic sentence, followed by a series of subdivisions of the central idea. （Line 14～16）

   本句的意思是"段落以概括主题思想的主题句开始,随后是说明主题句的一系列细节"。句中 known as a topic sentence 是过去分词短语作后置定语,修饰 statement;followed by a series of subdivisions of the central idea 是过去分词短语作状语,表示伴随情况。

4. These subdivisions have the purpose of developing the topic sentence, preparing for the addition of other ideas in later paragraph. （Line 16～17）

   本句的意思是"这些细节的目的是展开讨论主题句,同时为下一段的阐述做好过渡准备"。句中 developing the topic sentence 是动名词短语,作介词宾语;preparing for the addition of other ideas in later paragraph 是现在分词短语,在意思上与 developing the topic sentence 并列,都表示细节的目的或作用,在形式上作状语,表示伴随情况。

Unit 27

Section A   Skimming and Scanning

Directions：（略）

Passage 1

Measuring Human Behavior

1   What is psychological testing?

Psychological Testing is the measurement of some aspect of human behavior by procedures consisting of carefully prescribed content, methods of administration, and interpretation. The test may address any aspect of intellectual or emotional functioning, including personality traits, attitudes, intelligence, or emotional concerns. Interpretation is based on a comparison of the individual's responses with those previously obtained to establish appropriate standards for the test scores. The usefulness of psychological tests depends on their accuracy in predicting behavior. By providing information about the probability of a person's responses or performance, tests aid in making a variety of decisions.

2   The first intelligence test

The primary drive behind the development of the major tests used today was the need for practical guidelines for solving social problems. The first useful intelligence test was prepared in 1905 by the French psychologists Alfred Binet and Theodore Simon. The two developed a 30-item scale to ensure that no child could be denied instruction in the Paris school system without formal examination. In 1916, the American psychologist Lewis Terman produced the first Stanford Revision of the Binet-Simon scale to provide comparison standards for Americans from age three to adulthood. The test was further revised in 1937 and 1960, and today the Stanford-Binet remains one of tile most widely used intelligence tests.

3   Progress sparked by WW Ⅰ

The need to classify soldiers during World War Ⅰ resulted in the development of two group intelligence tests—Army Alpha and Army Beta. To help detect soldiers who might break down in combat, the American psychologist Robert Woodworth designed the Personal Data Sheet, a forerunner of the modem personality inventory. During the 1930s controversies over the nature of intelligence led to the development of the Wechsler-Bellevue Intelligence Scale, which not only provided an index of general mental ability but also revealed patterns of intellectual strengths and weaknesses. The Wechsler tests now extend from the preschool through the adult age range and are at least as prominent as the Stanford-Binet.

4   Inkblots and story-telling

As interest in the newly emerging field of psychoanalysis grew in the 1930s, two important

大学英语４级阅读与简答（新题型）

projective techniques introduced systematic ways to study unconscious motivation: the Rorschach or *inkblot* (墨水斑点) test—developed by the Swiss psychiatrist Hermann Rorschach —using a series of inkblots on cards, and a story-telling procedure called the Thematic Apperception Test —developed by the American psychologists Henry A. Murray and C. D. Morgan. Both of these tests are frequently included in contemporary personality assessment.

5 Utilization in academic settings

In educational settings, intelligence and achievement tests are administered routinely to assess individual accomplishment and to improve instruction and curriculum planning. Elementary schools use kindergarten and first-grade screening procedures to determine readiness for reading and writing programs. Screening tests also identify developmental, visual, and auditory problems for which the child may need special assistance. If the child's progress in school is unusually slow, or if he or she shows signs of a learning disability or behavior disorder, testing may clarify whether the difficulty is *neurologically* (神经学上的) or emotionally based. Many high schools administer interest *inventories* (目录) and aptitude tests to assist in the students' educational or vocational planning.

6 Obtaining information for clinical purposes

In clinics or hospitals, psychological tests may be administered for purposes of diagnosis and treatment planning. Clinical tests can provide information about overall personality functioning and the need for psychotherapy; testing also may focus on some specific question, such as the presence or absence of organically based brain disorder. Clinical testing usually involves a battery of tests, interpreted as a whole, to describe intellectual and emotional states. Decisions about treatment do not depend exclusively on psychological test results but are based on the judgment of relevant staff members with whom the psychologist collaborates.

7 Employment testing

Tests are also used in industrial and organizational settings, primarily for selection and classification. Selection procedures provide guidelines for accepting or rejecting candidates for jobs. Classification procedures, which are more complex, aim to specify the types of positions for which an individual seems best suited. Intelligence testing is usually supplemented by methods devised expressly to meet the needs of the organization.

8 Present criticism of testing

The major psychological testing controversies stem from two interrelated issues: technical shortcomings in test design and ethical problems in interpretation and application of results. Some technical weaknesses exist in all tests. Because of this, it is crucial that results be viewed as only one kind of information about any individual. Most criticisms of testing arise from the overvaluation of and inappropriate reliance on test results in making major life decisions. These criticisms have been particularly relevant in the case of intelligence testing. Psychologists generally agree that using tests to bar youngsters from educational opportunities, without careful consideration of past and present resources or motivation, is unethical. Because tests tend to draw on those skills associated with white, middle-class functioning, they may discriminate against disadvantaged and minority groups. As long as unequal learning opportunities exist, they will continue to be reflected in test results. The American Psychological Association continues to work actively to monitor and refine ethical standards and public policy recommendations regarding the use of psychological testing.

9 Measuring human behavior in large groups

The Experimental Centre of Euro-control (the European Organization for the Safety of Air Navigation) was built around what was then the first digital Air Traffic Control (ATC) Simulator in the world, and is certainly the most flexible. It is capable of simulating up to 40 working ATC positions simultaneously. A real-time simulation takes three to six weeks, and may involve 20 to 60 exercises, each about 90 minutes long. About 50 megabytes of data are collected by the system software for each exercise, giving exhaustive detail of the activity of the simulated aircraft, and the orders given by the controllers.

Air traffic controllers usually work in pairs on each sector. Although they employ speech communications and gestures to communicate, most of their work is mental, rather than physical. The task is not, strictly speaking, paced, although some activities are triggered by communications from aircraft or adjacent sectors. In normal operations, the controllers organize their workload to anticipate problems and maintain a continuously safe state. The ability of the controllers to cope with the workload is often the decisive factor in fixing the capacity of the system. We are therefore greatly interested in measuring the effects of carrying out air traffic control on the controllers. The methods used must be simple, reliable and labor-economic (we have, at most, five technical assistants to measure up to 40 participants). They must not be intrusive, and they must have some face validity, since controllers' co-operation must be requested, and cannot be demanded. Fortunately, controllers are fully aware of the need to improve methods, and will put up with considerable inconvenience if they are convinced it will have useful results.

1. The first useful intelligence test was prepared in 1905 by Alfred Binet and Theodore Simon.
2. The Stanford-Binet intelligence test is comprised of multiple-choice questions.
3. During WW I, psychologist Robert Woodworth designed the Personal Data Sheet to help detect soldiers who had an especially high level of intelligence.
4. The Wechsler tests are not nearly as prominent as the Stanford-Binet tests.
5. Swiss psychiatrist Hermann Rorschach invented a story-telling procedure called the Thematic Apperception Test.
6. Most criticisms of testing arise from the overvaluation of the inappropriate reliance on test results in making major life decisions, especially in the case of intelligence testing.
7. During the 1930s controversies over the nature of intelligence led to the development of the Stanford-Binet Intelligence Scale.
8. Psychological Testing is the measurement of some aspects of human behavior by procedures consisting of _____.
9. In clinics or hospitals, psychological tests may be administered for purposes of _____.
10. Selection procedures provide guidelines for _____ for jobs.

Section B Discourse Vocabulary Test

Directions：（略）

Passage 2

Psychologists now believe that noise has a ___11___ effect on people's attitudes and behavior. Experiments have ___12___ that in noisy situations (even temporary ones), people behave more irritably and less cooperatively; in more permanent noisy situations, many people cannot work hard, and they ___13___ from severe anxiety as well as other psychological problems. However, psychologists distinguish between "sound" and "noise". "Sound" is ___14___ physically in *decibels* (分贝). "Noise" cannot be measured in the same way because it ___15___ to the psychological effect of sound and its level of "intensity" depends on the situation. Thus, for passengers at an airport who expect to hear airplanes taking off and landing, there may be a lot of sound, but not much noise (that is, they are not bothered by the noise). By ___16___ , if you are at a concert and two people behind you are whispering, you feel they are talking noisily even if there is not much sound. You notice the noise because it ___17___ you psychologically. Both sound and noise can have ___18___ effects, but what is most important is if the person has control over the sound. People walking down the street with earphones, listening to music that they enjoy, are receiving a lot of decibels of sound, but they are probably happy hearing sounds which they control. On the other hand, people in the street without earphones must tolerate a lot of noise which they have no ___19___ over. It is noise pollution that we need to control in order to help people live more ___20___ .

A) complete	I) affects
B) considerable	J) trouble
C) measured	K) control
D) contrast	L) healthy
E) different	M) happily
F) proved	N) negative
G) refers	O) pay
H) suffer	

Section C Reading in Depth

Directions：（略）

Passage 3

Becket not only traveled light, he lived light. In all the world he owned just the clothes he stood up in, a full suitcase and a bank account. Arriving anywhere with these possessions, he might just as easily put up for a month or a year as for a single night. For long stays, not less than a month, he might take a furnished flat, sometimes even a house. But whatever the length, he rarely needed anything he did not have with him. He was, he liked to think, a self-contained person.

Becket had one occasional anxiety: the suspicion that he owned more than that would fit comfortably into the case. The feeling, when it came, was the signal for him to throw something away or just leave it lying about. This was the automatic fate of his worn-out clothes for example. Having no use for choice or variety, he kept just a raincoat, a suit, a pair of shoes and a few shirts, socks and so on; no more in the clothing line. He bought and read many books, and left them wherever he happened to be sitting when he finished them. They quickly found new owners.

Becket was a professional traveler, interested and interesting. He liked to get the feeling of a place by living in it, reading its newspapers, watching its TV, discussing its affairs. Though Becket's health gave him no cause for alarm, he made a point of seeing a doctor as soon as he arrived anywhere. "A doctor knows a place and its people better than anyone", he used to say. He never went to see a doctor; he always sent for one; that, he found, was the quickest way to confidences, which came out freely as soon as he mentioned that he was a writer.

Becket was an artist as well. He painted pictures of his places and, when he had gathered enough information, he wrote about them. He sold his work, through an agent, to newspapers and magazines. It was an agreeable sort of life for a good social mixer, and as Becket never stayed anywhere for long, he enjoyed the satisfying advantage of paying very little in tax.

21. What do we know about Becket's possessions?

    A) He had enough baggage to stay for one night.

    B) He carried all of them around with him.

    C) He had thrown or given them away.

    D) He left most of his things at home when he traveled.

22. Becket took over a flat when _____.

    A) there were no suitable hotels

    B) he meant to stay somewhere for several nights

    C) he was sure of staying a year or more

    D) he expected not to move on for a month at least

23. How did Becket feel about taxation?

    A) It worried him, so he kept moving from place to place.

    B) He hated it, so he broke the tax laws.

    C) He was pleased he could honestly avoid it.

    D) He felt ashamed of not paying taxes.

24. If anything worried Becket, it was _____.

    A) his thought of having too much baggage

    B) his habit of leaving things lying about

    C) the fact that he owned so little

    D) the poor state of his clothes

25. Becket did not keep books because _____.

    A) he had not interest in literature

    B) the books he read belonged to other people

    C) he had no room in his case for them

D) he preferred to give them to his friends

Passage 4

In these days of technological triumphs, it is well to remind ourselves from time to time that living mechanisms are often incomparably more efficient than their artificial imitations. There is no better illustration of this idea than the sonar system of bats. Ounce for ounce and watt for watt, it is billions of times more efficient and more sensitive than the radars and sonar designed by man. Of course, the bats have had some 50 million years of evolution to refine their sonar. Their physiological mechanisms for echo location, based on all this accumulated experience, therefore merit our thorough study and analysis. To appreciate the precision of the bats' echo location, we must first consider the degree of their reliance upon it. Thanks to sonar, an insect-eating bat can get along perfectly well without eyesight. This was brilliantly demonstrated by an experiment performed in the late eighteenth century by the Italian naturalist Lazure Spallanzani. He caught some bats in a bell tower, blinded them, and released them outdoors. Four of these blind bats were recaptured after they had found their way back to the bell tower, and on examining their stomachs' contents, Spallanzani found that they had been able to capture and fill themselves with flying insects. We know from experiments that bats easily find insects in the dark of night, even when the insects emit no sound that can be heard by human ears. A bat will catch hundreds of soft-bodied, silent-flying moths in a single hour. It will even detect and chase *pebbles* (小砾石) tossed into the air.

26. The passage is mainly about _____.
    A) living mechanisms and their artificial imitations
    B) the remarkable sonar system of bats
    C) the deficiencies of man-made sonar
    D) the experiment of "blind-bats"

27. Which of the following statements is true?
    A) Living mechanisms are always more efficient than their artificial imitations.
    B) Bats rely on their sonar system as well as eyesight to eat insects.
    C) The sonar system of bats has had 50 million years to be refined.
    D) People have discovered the bats' sonar system thousands of years age.

28. Lazure Spallanzani demonstrated that a bat can get along well without eyesight through

    _____.
    A) some bats he caught and blinded and released
    B) four of the blind bats finding their way back
    C) the four returned bats he recaptured
    D) the stomachs of the blind bats found to be filled with flying insects

29. Bats find insects in the dark of night with the help of _____.
    A) echoes   B) eyesight
    C) sound wave   D) none of the above

30. It is implied but not stated in the passage that _____.

A) pebbles tossed into the air make no sound that can be heard by human ears

B) a bat will catch hundreds of moths in a single hour

C) insect-eating bats are totally blind

D) the sonar system of bats is as good as man-made sonar

Section D   Short Answer Questions

Directions：（略）

Passage 5

Cigarette smoking is believed by most research workers in this field to be an important factor in the development of cancer of the lungs and the throat and is believed to be related to cancer of the *bladder* （膀胱）and the *oral cavity* （口腔）. Male cigarette smokers have a higher death rate from heart disease than non-smoking males.

Female smokers are thought to be less affected because they do not breathe in the smoke so deeply. The majority of physicians and researchers consider these relationships proved to their satisfaction and say. "Give up smoking. If you don't smoke, don't start". Some competent physicians and research workers—though their small number is *dwindling* （减小）even further—are less sure of the effect of cigarette smoking on health. They consider the increase in *respiratory* （呼吸的）diseases and various forms of cancer may possibly be explained by other factors in the complex human environment—atmospheric pollution, increased nervous stress, chemical substances in processed food, or chemical pesticides that are now being used by farmers in vast quantities to destroy insects and small animals. Smokers who develop cancer or lung diseases, they say, may also, by coincidence, live in industrial areas, or eat more canned food. Gradually, however, research is isolating all other possible factors and proving them to be statistically irrelevant. While all tobacco smoking affects life expectancy and health, cigarette smoking appears to have a much greater effect than cigar or pipe smoking. However, *nicotine* （尼古丁）consumption is not diminished by the latter forms, and current research indicates relationship between all forms of smoking and cancer of the mouth and throat. Filters and low *tar* （焦油）tobacco are claimed to made smoking to some extent safer, but they can only marginally reduce, not eliminate, the hazards.

31. Why are male smokers more affected by smoking than female ones?

    _____   _____   _____

32. What did the author mention in the passage cigarette can do harm to?

    _____   _____   _____

33. What is the author's attitude towards smoking?

    _____   _____   _____

34. It is not certain that cigarette smoking has greater effect on health than _____.

_____　_____　_____　_____　_____

35. What is the authors purpose of writing the passage?

_____　_____　_____　_____　_____

_____　_____　_____　_____

Notes and Explanations

Passage 1

Explanations

1. [Y] 第二部分 The first intelligence test 第二句提到 The first useful intelligence test was prepared in 1905 by the French psychologists Alfred Binet and Theodore Simon. 第一套有用的智力测试题是由法国心理学家 Alfred Binet 和 Theodore Simone 在 1905 年完成的。由此得出答案是 Yes。

2. [NG] 第二部分 The first intelligence test 最后一句提到…today the Stanford-Binet remains one of the most widely used intelligence tests. 时至今日，斯坦福—比耐测试法仍是应用最广的智力测试方法。然而作者并没有提及这个测试方法的形式。由此得出答案是 Not Given。

3. [N] 第三部分 Progress sparked by WWⅠ第二句提到 To help detect soldiers who might break down in combat，the American psychologist Robert Woodworth designed the Personal Data Sheet，a forerunner of the modern personality inventory. 为了帮助察觉战争中可能精神崩溃的士兵，现代性格调查的先驱者、美国心理学家 Robert Woodworth 设计了个人信息问卷。由此得出答案是 No。

4. [N] 第三部分 Progress sparked by WWⅠ最后一句提到 The Wechsler tests now extend from the preschool through the adult age range and are at least as prominent as the Stanford-Binet. 现在参加 Wechsler 测试的人群年龄段已经覆盖了从学龄前儿童到成年人的各个年龄段，效果至少和 Stanford-Binet 一样显著。由此得出答案是 No。

5. [N] 第四部分 Inkblots and story-telling 提到…the Rorschach or inkblot test—developed by the Swiss psychiatrist Hermann Rorschach—using a series of inkblots on cards，and a story-telling procedure called the The matic Apperception Test—developed by the American psychologists Henry A. Murray and C. D. Morgan. Rorschach 测试法或墨水测试法是由瑞士精神病学家 Hermann Rorschach 发明的，是采用将一系列墨水点印在卡片上的方法。另一种测试法是讲故事，这种名为主题接受测试的方法由美国心理学家 Henry A. Murray 和 C. D. Morgan 发明。由此得出答案是 No。

6. [Y] 第八部分 Present criticism of testing 第四句提到 Most criticisms of testing arise from the overvaluation of and inappropriate reliance on test results in making major life decisions. 大部分对于测试的批评来自于在做重要生活决定时对测试结果的过高估计和不适当的依赖。由此得出答案是 Yes。

7. [N] 第三部分 Progress sparked by WWⅠ第三句提到 During the 1930s controversies over the nature of intelligence led to the development of the Wechsler-Bellevue Intelligence Scale. 20 世纪 30 年代关于智力的本质的争论导致了 Wechsler-Bellevue 智力度量法的发展。由此得出答案是 No。

8. 第一部分第一句提到 Psychological Testing is the measurement of some aspect of human behavior by procedures consisting of carefully prescribed content，methods of administration，and interpretation。心理测试是对人类行为的某些方面的测试，过程包括精心设计的指令内容、实施方法和行为解析方法。由此得出答案是 **carefully prescribed content，methods of administration，and interpretation**。

9. 第六部分 Obtaining information for clinical purposes 第一句提到 In clinics or hospitals，psychological

tests may be administered for purposes of diagnosis and treatment planning. 在诊所和医院里,心理测试是为了诊断病情和制订治疗计划而进行的。由此得出答案是 **diagnosis and treatment planning**。

10. 第七部分 Employment testing 第二句提到 Selection procedures provide guidelines for accepting or rejecting candidates for jobs. 选择过程提供了是接受还是拒绝求职者的指导方针。由此得出答案是 **accepting or rejecting candidates**。

Passage 2

Notes

1. ... noise has a considerable effect on people's attitudes... (Line 1)

   effect 的意思是"结果,影响,效果"。例如:

   The disclosures had the effect of reducing the government's popularity.

   揭发的事实产生了降低政府威信的效果。

   The new system will take effect next May. 新制度将在五月起实施。

2. ... and they suffer from severe anxiety as well as... (Line 4)

   suffer from 的意思是"(尤指长期地或习惯性地)患有(疾病),为……所苦"。例如:

   She suffers from headache. 她患头痛病。

   Our business has suffered from lack of investment. 我们的企业苦于缺乏投资。

3. However, psychologists distinguish between "sound" and "noise". (Line 4~5)

   distinguish 表示"分辨"的意思。后面常接 between... and..., sth. from sth. 例如:

   It's important to distinguish between compound interest and simple interest. 分清复利和单利是重要的。

   Small children can't distinguish right from wrong. 小孩子不能明辨是非。

4. People walking down the street with earphones, listening to music that they enjoy, are... (Line 12~13)

   在这句话里 walking down the street with earphones 是现在分词短语做后置定语,修饰 People;listening to music 是现在分词短语作状语,表示伴随情况。

Explanations

11. [B] 语法规则要求此处应填一个形容词作定语修饰 effect。选项 A、B、E、L、N 是形容词。下文所举的种种例子说明噪音对人的影响之大,所以 considerable(相当〈大、多〉的,可观的)符合句意。

12. [F] 语法规则要求此处应填一个动词的过去分词形式构成现在完成时态。选项 C、F 是过去分词形式。experiment 常和 proved(证明)搭配,故选 F 项。

13. [H] 语法规则要求此处应填一个动词原形和介词 from 搭配作谓语。选项 H、K、O 是动词原形。能和 from 搭配使用的是 suffer。suffer from 意思是"遭受",符合句意。

14. [C] 语法规则要求此处应填一个动词过去分词形式构成被动语态。根据下一句中的 be measured 可以判断此处也应该填 measured(测量,衡量)。

15. [G] 语法规则要求此处应填一个动词的第三人称单数形式作谓语。选项 G、I 是该形式。从本句话的意思可以判断 refers 符合句意。refer to 意思是"指的是"。

16. [D] 语法规则要求此处应填一个名词作 by 的宾语构成介词短语。选项 D、J 是名词。可以和 by 搭配的是 contrast。by contrast 意思是"相比之下,相比而言",符合句意。

17. [I] 语法规则要求此处应填一个动词的第三人称单数形式作谓语。根据句意"噪音从心理上影响到你"判断出 affects(影响)符合句意。

18. [N] 语法规则要求此处应填一个形容词作定语修饰 effect。根据上下文,此处应填一个表示否定的词,negative(负面的)符合句意。

19. [K] 语法规则要求此处应填一个名词和 over 搭配使用。选项 D、J 是名词。根据句意可以判断 control

符合句意。have (no) control over 是意思是"（不能）控制"。

20. [M] 语法规则要求此处填一个副词构成副词的比较级修饰动词 live，只有 M 项 happily（幸福地）是副词，而且符合句意。

Passage 3

Notes

1. Becket not only traveled light, he lived light. (Line 1, Para. 1)

   在这句话里第一个 light 的意思是"轻的"，第二个 light 的意思是"轻松的"。例如：

   It's so light a child could lift. 这东西太轻了，孩子都能拿起来。

   light reading 消遣性的读物

2. In all the world he owned just the clothes... (Line 1, Para. 1)

   ▷clothes 意思是"衣服，衣物"，没有单数形式，不能与数词连用，但可用 few, a few, many 等修饰，一件衣服可用 a piece/suit of clothes 来表达。

   ▷cloth 意思是"布，衣料"，为不可数名词，如：a piece of cloth。另一个意思是"布块，桌布，作某种特殊用途的布"，为可数名词，复数为 cloths，如：a table cloth。

   ▷clothing 是衣服的总称，所有的穿着之物，包括帽子、手套等，还可指被子，常与 food 连用，food and clothing 意思是"衣食"。

3. ... he might just as easily put up for a month or a year... (Line 2~3, Para. 1)

   put up 常用的意思有"举起，盖起，投宿，提出"等。例如：

   Scientists have put up a new machine into space to improve telephone connections.

   科学家已把一种新机器放入太空，用来改进电话通讯。

   Another supermarket has been put up near our house. 我家附近又开了一家超市。

   He's going to put up another proposal in the meeting. 他要在会上提出另一条建议。

   Have you put up the tent? 你搭起帐篷了没有？

4. ... not less than a month... (Line 3~4, Para. 1)

   not less than 表示"不少于"，而 no less than 则表示"多达，有……之多"。例如：

   Its estimated population is no less than 182,000. 估计人口多达十八万两千。

5. This was the automatic fate of his worn-out clothes for example. (Line 3, Para. 2)

   worn-out 的意思是"用坏的，穿旧的；精疲力竭的"。例如：

   worn-out shoes 穿破的鞋子

   She was worn-out after three sleepless nights. 三天三夜她都没合眼，被弄得精疲力竭。

Explanations

本文讲述了一个名叫 Becket 的人的生活经历。他四处旅游，只随身携带尽可能少的行李。虽然他随身带的东西已经很少了，但他总是怀疑他带的东西还是多了。而这种念头就是提醒他需要扔掉一些东西的信号。所以他随身携带的衣服就是必不可少的几件。Becket 是一个专业的旅行者，他喜欢住在一个地方，阅读当地的报纸，看当地的电视节目，讨论当地发生的事件。他还喜欢和当地的医生交谈，因为医生最了解当地情况和当地人。他同时又是一个艺术家。他会把他去过的地方画下来，并在收集了足够的信息后，把他的所见所闻写成作品，然后通过经纪人，把他的作品卖给报纸和杂志。

21. B) 细节题。根据第一段第一、二句，Becket 所有的东西都会在旅游时带上。因此答案应该是 B 项。

22. D) 细节题。从第一段第三句 For long stays, not less than a month, he might take a furnished flat, sometimes even a house. 可以得知当他在一个地方决定住上一个月以上时，他才会租房子。所以答案是 D 项。

23. C) 推断题。从文章最后一句话可以得出答案是 C 项，他可以合理地不交税。

24. **A)** 细节题。在文章第二段开头就提到他有一件担心的事,就是"怀疑他带的东西还是多了",所以可以断定答案是 A 项。

25. **C)** 细节题。Becket 之所以不带书是因为他随身携带的东西是尽可能的少,所以他读完一本书后会把书放在原地,不会带走。所以答案是 C 项。

<h2 style="text-align:center">Passage 4</h2>

Notes

1. ...it is well to remind ourselves from time to time that... (Line 1)

   remind sb. of.../that 的意思是"使某人想起……"。例如:

   I must write to Mother—will you remind me? 我得给母亲写信,你提醒我好吗?

   This hotel reminds me of the one stayed in last year. 这家旅馆使我想起我们去年住过的那一家。

2. ...the bats have had some 50 million years of evolution to refine their sonar. (Line 5)

   refine 原意是"净化,提炼",在这句话里的意思是"使……变得更好"。例如:

   Oil has to be refined before it can be used. 石油在使用前必须提炼。

   refined 的意思使"精炼的",但有时还含有贬义的意思,指"(人或行为)(故意显出)有教养的"。例如:

   She's so refined that she always eats cake with a little fork. 她非常文雅,吃蛋糕时一定用小叉子。

3. Their physiological mechanisms for echo location... (Line 5~6)

   echo location 在这里指蝙蝠特殊的利用回声定位的功能。

4. Thanks to sonar... (Line 8)

   thanks to sth. 表示"由于,因为",相当于 because of。例如:

   It was thanks to your stupidity that we lost the game. 我们输掉比赛是由于你的愚蠢。

   It was no thanks to you that we won. 我们不是有了你才赢的。

5. ...an insect-eating bat can get along perfectly well without eyesight. (Line 8)

   get along 的意思是"(勉强)过活;进展"。例如:

   He didn't even offer to help us, but I'm sure we can get along quite well without him.

   他甚至没提出向我们提供帮助,不过我确信没有他的帮助我们也能生活得很好。

   How's the work getting along? 工作进展得如何?

Explanations

本文是讨论蝙蝠的声呐系统。它的声呐系统比人类设计的雷达和声呐系统要有效和敏感得多。由于有了声呐系统,蝙蝠可以在丧失视力的情况下,准确无误的抓住飞虫。在十八世纪,意大利自然学家 Lazure Spallanzani 所做的实验充分地证明了这一点。

26. **B)** 主旨题。本文主要讲述的是蝙蝠非凡的声呐系统的形成及其作用,因此正确答案是 B 项。

27. **C)** 细节题。选项 C 说蝙蝠的声呐系统用了五千万年的时间来进化,这在文中第五行提到了,蝙蝠的声呐系统在长期的生物进化过程中进行演变。选项 A 在文中也到了,但题中的 always 与文中的 often 意义不同。因此正确答案是 C 项。

28. **D)** 细节题。意大利的自然学家 Lazure Spallanzani 发现蝙蝠没有视力仍旧可以捕食,是因为他对抓回来的蝙蝠的胃进行了解剖。因此正确答案是 D 项。

29. **A)** 细节题。蝙蝠在黑暗中捕食主要是依靠回音定位。所以答案是 A 项。

30. **A)** 推断题。根据最后一句话可以得出正确答案是 A 项。

Passage 5

Keys

31. Because male smokers breathe in the smoke deeper than female ones.
32. Lung, mouth, throat, and heart.
33. Critical.
34. atmospheric pollution
35. To explain the influence of cigarette smoking on health.

Notes

1. ... is believed to be related to cancer of... (Line 2, Para. 1)

be related to 的意思是"和……有联系"。例如：

I am related to her by marriage. 我和她有姻亲关系。

The fall in the cost of living is directly related to the drop in the oil price.

生活费用下降直接与石油价格下跌有关。

2. ... these relationships proved to their satisfaction... (Line 2~3, Para. 2)

be proved to one's satisfaction 的意思是"确信，完全相信"。例如：

It has been proved to my satisfaction. 我现在完全相信。

To his satisfaction, the project went on smoothly. 项目顺利进行，他很满意。

3. ... increased nervous stress... (Line 7, Para. 2)

stress 的意思是"压力，重压，紧张"。例如：

stresses and strains of a busy business executive's life 一位繁忙的商界人士生活的紧张和压力

He's under a lot of stress because his wife is very ill. 由于妻子病得很厉害，他的压力很大。

4. ... or chemical pesticides that are... (Line 8, Para. 2)

pesticide 的意思是"杀虫剂"，后缀-cide 表示"杀……"，类似的词还有：insecticide 等。

5. ... they say, may also, by coincidence... (Line 9~10, Para. 2)

by coincidence 意思是"巧合"。例如：

By a curious coincidence, my husband and I have the same birthday.

纯粹是巧合，我丈夫和我是同一天生日。

It is no coincidence that his car was seen near the bank at the time of the robbery.

银行遭劫时，有人看到他的车在附近，这绝不是巧合。

Unit 28

Section A　Skimming and Scanning

Directions：(略)

Passage 1

Should I Be Afraid of This Spider?

Many people are deathly afraid of handling a spider because they fear it may be poisonous. Although almost all spiders are capable of producing *venom*（毒液）, very few species produce harmful bites, and even fewer cause death. Compared to other *venomous*（有毒的）creatures, spiders rank low on the fatality scale. During a typical year in the U. S. , twelve deaths were caused by bees, ten by wasps, fourteen by snakes, and only six by spiders. Learning a little about the spiders that are dangerous might help overcome a *spider-phobia*（恐惧）.

The Black Widow

1. In the U. S. , there are three kinds of spiders which are considered dangerous. They are the Black Widow, the Brown Recluse and the Aggressive House spider. The Black Widow is a small to medium sized spider, easily recognized by its glossy coal-black color and the reddish hourglass marking on the underside of its globe-shaped abdomen. In the northern species, the hourglass may appear incomplete or split into two triangles. The female's body is about half an inch in length, and with her slender legs extended, about an inch and a half. She has eight relatively large eyes arranged in two rows of four. The web she constructs is irregular, tangled, and cris-crossed. Invariably, she builds it outside the house in protected places, like under large rocks or logs, or in holes of dirt embankments, barns, outhouses, and other outbuildings. The Widow spider gets its name from the fact that the female frequently eats her male partner after mating, thus making herself a "widow". Despite its reputation, Black Widows are very timid and are not known to aggressively bite humans unless they are guarding an egg mass or are cornered and pressed. However, the bite of a Widow contains a *neurotoxin*（毒害神经）that interferes with muscle control. The bite causes a lot of pain in the abdomen and limbs and it can result in breathing difficulties and paralysis. In the rare event that death occurs, it is usually by *suffocation*（窒息）.

2. The southern Black Widow and the northern Black Widow are a shiny, jet-black color. The southern Black Widow has a red hourglass marking on the underside of the abdomen and another red spot at the tip end of the abdomen. The northern Black Widow has a row of red spots located in the middle of its back and two reddish triangles resembling an hourglass on the underside of the abdomen. The red Widow spider has a reddish orange head-thorax and legs with a black abdomen. The abdomen may have a dorsal row of red spots with a yellow border. The red Widow

lacks a complete hourglass under the abdomen, but may have one or two red spots. The brown Window spider varies in color from gray to light brown or black. The abdomen has variable markings of black, white, red, and yellow. On the underside of the abdomen the brown Widow has an orange or yellowish-red hourglass marking.

3. The life cycle of the Widow spiders are all similar. The female lays approximately 250 eggs in an egg sac which is about 1/2 to 5/8 inch in diameter. The eggs hatch in 20 days and remain in the egg sac from about four days to one month. The young spiders then molt to the second stage and begin feeding. As the young spiders grow, they construct a loosely woven web and capture progressively larger prey. Male spiders molt three to six times before maturing. The females molt six to eight times and occasionally eat the males after mating. In Florida all the Widows, except the northern Black Widow, breed year-round.

The Brown Recluse

1. The Brown Recluse is a small spider with two unique characteristics. The first is a dark fiddle or violin-shaped marking on its *thorax*(胸部). The second is its six eyes arranged in three pairs that form a semi-circle (most spiders have eight eyes). Its slim light brown to yellow body measures about three eighths of an inch long, and with its slender legs extended, it measures more than an inch. It doesn't always spin a web, but when it does, the web is irregular in shape and can usually be found under logs, stones, or piles of lumber. It is not uncommon for a Recluse to live inside a house in the dark corners of a trunk, among piles of stored clothing, or inside a garage or basement storage area.

2. The Brown Recluse is a shy spider and searches for its insect prey primarily at night. People typically are bitten accidentally while putting on clothes in which the spider is hiding or by rolling onto them while in bed. The physical bite of the Brown Recluse is fairly painless with maybe only a slight stinging sensation being felt. People often do not know when the actual bite occurred. The symptoms from the venom appear about six to eight hours after the bite. The first symptom is a pimple-sized swelling at the bite site. About 12~24 hours after being bitten one may feel *malaise*(不舒服), chills, fever and *nausea*(恶心). The bite usually produces a necrotic (death of tissue) condition followed by deep scaring, which often requires skin *grafts*(移植). The poison also destroys red blood cells and may cause death by liver and/or kidney failure.

Hobo spider

1. The Aggressive House spider, nick-named the "Hobo spider", is a medium sized, long-legged, swift running member of the funnel web spider family. The brown abdomen has a distinctive yellowish *chevron*(回纹状) pattern. The legs are a uniform brown without the darker brown bands that other nonpoisonous funnel web spiders have. Adult Hobo spiders are approximately a half to five eighths of an inch in size. The male spider has *pedipalps*(须肢) between the front legs, which are swollen and are often referred to as "boxing gloves". These spiders build funnel shaped webs in corners of homes as well as on stairs. In the yard, the webs are usually attached to anything that remains stationary near the ground level. Its web is non-sticky by spider standards and serves more as a trip web. Thus, the Hobo spider must pounce upon its prey to capture it before it can get away. This may explain its aggressive nature.

2. Experts call it the Aggressive House spider because it bites with little *provocation*(激怒)

when cornered or threatened. Fortunately, the bite is relatively painless, and often the victim does not even realize that he has been bit. 50% are "dry" bites that do not inject venom. If venom is injected, an immediate redness will develop around the bite; later, it will blister in the center. Within 24 to 36 hours, the blister breaks open, leaving an open, oozing ulceration. This ulceration "scabs" over within three weeks from the initial bite, leaving a permanent scar. In addition to the tissue damage, other symptoms such as headaches, nausea, sweating, and joint pain may be experienced after the bite. In extreme cases, skin graft, amputation, and the possibility of bone marrow failure may occur.

3. On the positive side, the Widow, the Recluse and the Aggressive House spider, can be helpful creatures. They consume enormous numbers of harmful insects. The Widow, in particular, eats troublesome flies and mosquitoes (which carry diseases), locusts, and grasshoppers (which destroy grain crops) and beetles and caterpillars (which defoliate plants and trees). Keeping debris and woodpiles away from living quarters will aid in limiting their food sources and thus decrease the chances of having contact with them.

1. Compared to other poisonous creatures, spiders are the most poisonous.
2. The bite of the Brown Recluse spider is relatively painless.
3. The Black Widow's venom is more dangerous than that of the Brown Recluse spider.
4. Black Widows are very timid but are known to aggressively bite humans.
5. The Hobo spider is timid compared to the female Black Widow spider.
6. Dangerous spiders serve useful purposes.
7. The Brown Recluse is a shy spider and searches for its insect prey primarily at night.
8. In the U. S. , there are three kinds of spiders which are considered dangerous. They are _____.
9. The symptoms from the venom of the Brown Recluse appear about _____ hours after the bite.
10. The Aggressive House spider get its name because it bites with little provocation when _____.

Section B Discourse Vocabulary Test
Directions：（略）

Passage 2

As the __11__ of life continues to increase, we are fast losing the art of __12__. Once you are in the habit of rushing through life, being on the go from morning till night, it is hard to slow down. But relaxation is __13__ for a healthy mind and body.

Stress is a natural part of everyday life and there is no way to avoid it. In fact, it is not the bad thing it is often supposed to be. A certain amount of __14__ is vital to provide motivation and give __15__ to life. It is only when the stress gets out of control that it can lead to poor performance and ill health.

The amount of stress a person can withstand __16__ very much on the individual. Some people are not afraid of stress, and such characters are __17__ prime material for managerial responsibilities, others lose heart at the first sign of unusual difficulties. When __18__ to stress, in whatever form, we react both chemically and physically. In fact we make choice between "flight or fight" and in more primitive days the choices made the difference between life or death. The crises we meet today are __19__ to be so extreme, but however little the stress, it involves the same response. It is when such a reaction lasts long, through continued exposure to stress, that health becomes endangered. Since we can't __20__ stress from our lives (it would be unwise to do so even if we could), we need to find ways to deal with it.

A) stress	I) experience
B) essential	J) obviously
C) control	K) relaxation
D) pace	L) appear
E) purpose	M) depends
F) exposed	N) quickly
G) bear	O) unlikely
H) remove	

Section C   Reading in Depth
Directions：（略）

Passage 3

The significance of trust is that it allows the parties involved in the relationship to indicate how they feel, how they behave, and where they disagree without fear of contradiction or *reprisal* (报复). Trusting relationships encourage people to disclose their plans and perceptions without hurting themselves or others. Hurt, whether real or imagined, is one of the most harmful consequences of personal relationships with other human beings. In situations which you feel that the other person has the power and intent to hurt you, trust diminishes quickly. Thus a climate of distrust appears in your relations with others. Conversely, if I can say whatever comes to my mind without getting hurt, a climate of trust pervades the relationship. Trust is a perceptual phenomenon that evolves from our experiences with others. If trusting were so easy, we would not need to make such a point of its importance in human relationships. To say that a person should trust others is to diminish the difficulty of producing trust. In mutual relationships, both parties must behave toward one another in trusting ways. Even though it hurts in the pit of the *stomach* (心窝), you must trust the other person and encourage him or her to say those things that demand a trusting response. No one likes to get hurt and few like to hurt others, especially not those others who are close to us in person-to-person relationships. We avoid expressing our true feelings lest we become the target of a revenging attack from the other person. If I indicate that I do not appreciate having you smoke in my car, I may love you as a friend or I may become the subject of ridicule for allowing little things like that to bother me. If that happens, I will be less open and less trusting of you the next time.

21. The significance of trust lies in the fact that _____.
    A) trust is not easy to reach between human beings
    B) trust allows people to say whatever comes to their minds
    C) one likes to get hurt
    D) few like to trust others

22. What will NOT happen if a person feels he will be hurt by the other?
    A) Trust diminishes quickly.
    B) He will disclose his plans and perceptions.
    C) A climate of distrust pervades the relationship.
    D) One of the most harmful consequences of personal relationships with others appear.

23. Trust is a phenomenon that _____.
    A) results from our experiences with others
    B) comes from our perceptions
    C) may trust in the pit of the stomach
    D) none of the above

24. People avoid expressing their true feelings because _____.
    A) they become the target of revenging attack from others
    B) they are not so open and trusting others
    C) they do not want to become the target of revenging attack from others
    D) they do not want to lose friends

25. It is implied but not stated in the passage that _____.
    A) people usually do not like to trust those who are close to us
    B) people will usually get reprisal or ridicule for their trust
    C) if trust has been established, it will never disappear
    D) the negative response will usually result in the diminishing of trusting between persons

Passage 4

We buried Donald Brown last May. He was murdered by four men who wanted to rob the supermarket manager he was protecting. Partolman Brown was 61 years old. In just six months he and his wife had planned to retire to Florida. Now there will be no retirement in the sun, and she is alone.

Donald Brown was the second police officer to die since I became Police Commissioner of Boston in 1972. The first was Detective John Schroeder, shot in a *pawnshop* (当铺) robbery in November 1970. John Schroeder was the brother of Walter Schroeder, who was killed in a bank robbery in 1970. Their names are together on the honor roll in Police Headquarters.

At least two of these police officers were shot by a handgun, the kind almost anyone can buy nearly everywhere for a few dollars. Ownership of handguns has become so widespread that this weapon is no longer merely the instrument of crime; it is now a cause of violent crime. Of the 11 Boston police officers killed since 1962, seven were killed with handguns; of the 18 wounded by guns since 1962, 17 were shot with handguns.

Gun advocates are fond of saying that guns don't kill, people do. But guns do kill. Half of the people who commit suicide do so with handguns. Fifty-four percent of the murders committed in 1972 were committed with handguns.

No one can convince me, after returning from patrolman Brown's funeral, that we should allow people to own handguns. I know that many Americans feel deeply and honestly that they have a right to own and enjoy guns. I am asking that they give them up. I am not asking for registration or licensing, or the outlawing of cheap guns. I am saying that no private citizen, whatever his claim, should possess a handgun. Only police officers should.

26. The suggestion the author presents in the passage is that _____.
    A) handguns are the cause of violent crime
    B) handguns are a dangerous weapon
    C) American people's right to own and enjoy guns should be respected
    D) only police officers should possess guns

27. In paragraph 1, the tone of the author is _____.
    A) calm   B) bitter   C) exciting   D) regretful

28. When did the author become Police Commissioner of Boston?
    A) In 1972.   B) In November, 1970.
    C) In 1962.   D) Before 1970.

29. According to the author, which is true of handguns?
    A) They don't kill.
    B) We should not allow people to own handguns.
    C) Anyone can easily buy a handgun at a very high price.
    D) Handguns can't be the cause of violent crime.

30. The passage is mainly aimed to _____.
    A) persuade the government
    B) describe police officers' death
    C) tell the robbers' means to kill policeman
    D) explain means of people's possession of guns

Section D   Short Answer Questions

Directions: (略)

Passage 5

The demand for energy all over the world has resulted in increased production and shipment of oil. Most of the oil is transported in huge tankers. Some of them are the largest ships afloat. If a tanker sinks or is grounded, millions of gallons of oil may escape into the sea. In addition, oil can escape from wells that have been drilled into the sea bottom. A number of serious accidents have already resulted in oil spillage. Sea birds have died in great numbers as their feathers became coated with dirty black oil. Undersea life has also been affected by oil spills.

As the oil resources of the world are beginning to be used up, we may have to turn to atomic energy for power. This creates another problem. If radiation escapes into the atmosphere, radiation pollution will occur. As you have already learned, radiation may have a harmful effect on human health. Sometimes it causes cancer. Some radiation is natural. But man has already added additional radioactive substances to the air as a result of atomic bomb tests. Unless atomic energy plants are built and run with great care, harmful radioactive substances may enter the atmosphere.

Radioactive *Iodine* (碘) 131 and *strontium* (锶) 90 already exist in the atmosphere. They have come from atomic bomb tests. Strontium 90 is a special problem. It has entered the ecological food chains. First taken up by plants, it has entered the bodies of cows who have eaten the plants. Human beings have swallowed it in milk. It settles in the bones of the human body. All humans born after 1961 have an average of 10 times as much strontium 90 in their bones as those born before 1945. On the grassland, the amount is even higher. Grass contains strontium 90 and the deer eat the polluted grass. People who have eaten deer meat have strontium 90 in their bones.

In addition to *sewage* (污水), cities produce many tons of rubbish or junk each day. Bottles, plastic bags, paper, cans, and even junked cars make up much of this waste. Solid waste is an increasing problem. If it is dumped on land, it breeds rats, flies, and mosquitoes, and produces unpleasant smell. One way to handle it is to make clean landfills. Here the rubbish is crushed and covered with soil. This can make land for parks and other useful purposes. But many cities are running out of space for such landfills.

If solid waste could be recycled, it would yield many useful products. Already, cans, bottles, and paper are being recycled in this way in some cities. Like other solutions to the pollution problem, recycling of solid wastes may be expensive. However, something like it will have to be done if our environment is to be preserved.

31. What are the two sources of oil spills on the sea?

_____ _____ _____ _____

_____ _____ _____ _____

32. Why do we not depend mainly on atomic energy at present?

_____ _____ _____ _____

_____ _____ _____ _____

33. Why did people born before 1945 have much less strontium 90 in their bodies?

_____ _____ _____ _____

_____ _____ _____ _____

34. What are junked cars?

_____ _____ _____ _____

35. What does it refer to in the last sentence?

_____ _____ _____ _____

_____ _____ _____ _____

Notes and Explanations

Passage 1

Explanations

1. [N] 第一段第三句提到 Compared to other venomous creatures, spiders rank low on the fatality scale. 相对于其他有毒的生物,蜘蛛在致命毒性榜上排名在后。由此得出答案是 No。

2. [Y] The Brown Recluse 部分第二段第三句提到 The physical bite of the Brown Recluse is fairly painless with maybe only a slight stinging sensation being felt. 被棕隐士咬了之后几乎是没有感觉的,可能会有轻微的刺痛感。由此得出答案是 Yes。

3. [NG] 文章分别介绍了黑寡妇蜘蛛和棕隐士蜘蛛的毒性,并没有对这两种蜘蛛的毒性进行比较。由此得出答案是 Not Given。

4. [N] The Black Widow 部分第一段倒数第四句提到 Black Widows are very timid and are not known to aggressively bite humans unless they are guarding an egg mass or are cornered and pressed. 黑寡妇蜘蛛很胆小,不会主动攻击人类,除非它们在保护卵、被逼急了或被挤压了。由此得出答案是 No。

5. [N] Hobo spider 部分第二段第一句提到 Experts call it the Aggressive House spider because it bites with little provocation when cornered or threatened. 专家们称这种蜘蛛为攻击型室内蜘蛛,因为它们一旦被逼急了或受到威胁,具有很强的攻击性。由此得出答案是 No。

6. [Y] 最后一段第一句提到 On the positive side, the Widow, the Recluse and the Aggressive House spider, can be helpful creatures. 从积极角度来看,黑寡妇蜘蛛、棕隐士蜘蛛、攻击型室内蜘蛛也是有益生物。由此得出答案是 Yes。

7. [Y] The Brown Recluse 部分第二段第一句提到 The Brown Recluse is a shy spider and searches for its insect prey primarily at night. 棕隐士蜘蛛非常害羞,通常都是在夜间出来捕食。由此得出答案是 Yes。

8. The Black Widow 部分第一段第一句提到 In the U. S. , there are three kinds of spiders which are considered dangerous. They are the Black Widow, the Brown Recluse and the Aggressive House spider. 在美国,有三种蜘蛛是危险的。它们是黑寡妇蜘蛛、棕隐士蜘蛛和攻击型室内蜘蛛。由此得出答案是 **the Black Widow, the Brown Recluse and the Aggressive House spider**。

9. The Brown Recluse 部分第二段第五句提到 The symptoms from the venom appear about six to eight hours after the bite. 毒液导致的症状会在被咬后六到八小时显现出来。由此得出答案是 **six to eight**。

10. Hobo spider 部分第二段第一句提到 Experts call it the Aggressive House spider because it bites with little provocation when cornered or threatened. 专家们称这种蜘蛛为攻击型室内蜘蛛,因为它们一旦被逼急了或受到威胁,具有很强的攻击性。由此得出答案是 **cornered or threatened**。

Passage 2

Notes

1. Once you are in the habit of rushing through life... (Line 1~2, Para. 1)

   ▷in the habit of 的意思是"有……习惯,经常爱……"。例如:

   He's in the habit of scratching his head when he's puzzled. 他在困惑的时候总爱挠头。

   I'm in the habit of reading the newspaper at breakfast. 我有吃早饭时看报纸的习惯。

   I'm not in the habit of lending money, but I'll make an exception in this case.

   我通常没有借钱给别人的习惯,但这一回我会破例。

▷out of habit 意思是"出于习惯"。例如：

I smoke only out of habit; I wish I could break the habit of it.

我吸烟只是一种习惯，我希望改掉这个习惯。

2. ...being on the go from morning till night... (Line 2, Para. 1)

这句话是伴随状语，补充说明忙碌的状况。on the go 意思是"一直忙"。go 是名词，意思是"忙碌，奔忙，爱动"。例如：

I'm feeling tired out; I've been on the go ever since 8 o'clock in the morning.

我觉得筋疲力尽。从早晨8点开始我一直在忙碌。

You can't keep small children still, they are always on the go.

你不能让孩子们安静下来，他们总是要动。

3. ...it is often supposed to be. (Line 2, Para. 2)

be supposed to 在这里的意思是"有义务做……，应该"，另外还有其他的意思，如"意图是，打算；一般是"。例如：

You're not supposed to smoke in here. 你不应该在这里吸烟。

This law is supposed to help the poor. 这条法律旨在帮助穷人。

I haven't seen it myself, but it's supposed to be a very good film.

我还没有看过这部电影，但大家认为这是一部很好的电影。

4. In fact we make choice between "flight or fight" and in more primitive days the choices made the difference between life or death. (Line 4~5, Para. 3)

这句话的意思是：实际上我们在逃避与斗争之间做出选择，这种选择在原始时期是一种生死抉择。flight 在此的意思是"逃避"。

Explanations

11. [D] 语法规则要求此处应填一个名词作状语从句的主语，谓语动词的形式要求主语是单数名词。选项 A、D、E、G、I、K 是单数名词。根据后面两句话的意思可以得知本句话的意思是"随着生活节奏的不断加快，我们在迅速失去放松的艺术"。pace 符合句意。the pace of life 意思是"生活的步伐（或节奏）"。

12. [K] 语法规则要求此处应填一个名词作介词 of 的宾语。根据后面两句话的意思可以得知本句话的意思是"随着生活节奏的不断加快，我们在迅速失去放松的艺术"。relaxation 符合句意。the art of relaxation 意思是"放松的艺术"。

13. [B] 语法规则要求此处应填一个形容词和介词 for 搭配构成 be ＋ 形容词 ＋ for sth. 的结构。只有选项 B 是形容词，且可以和 for 搭配使用。be essential for... 意思是"对……是必要的"，符合句意。

14. [A] 语法规则要求此处应填一个名词作主语，谓语动词的形式要求主语的形式是单数名词。根据上文"压力未必是件坏事"判断：适量的压力是件好事。stress(压力)符合题意。

15. [E] 语法规则要求此处应填一个名词作 give 的宾语。根据句意判断此处应填 purpose。give purpose to life 意思是"设定生活的目标"，符合句意。

16. [M] 语法规则要求此处应填一个动词第三人称单数形式作谓语。只有选项 M 是该形式。depend on 意思是"依靠，依赖，取决于"，符合句意。

17. [J] 语法规则要求此处应填一个副词作状语修饰句子的谓语。选项 J、N 是副词。根据句意判断 obviously(显然)符合句意。

18. [F] 本句的状语从句省略了主语和 be 动词。语法规则要求此处应填一个动词的过去分词形式构成被动语态。选项中只有选项 F 是该形式。be exposed to 意思是"暴露在……下"，符合句意。

19. [O] 语法规则要求此处应填一个形容词构成 be ＋ 形容词 ＋ to do/be 的结构。根据下文 so extreme 判断出此处意思是"没那么极端（或严重）"。be unlikely to do 意思是"不可能……"，符合句意。

20. [H] 语法规则要求此处应填一个动词原形和 from 搭配使用。选项中能和 from 搭配使用的动词原形是 remove。remove...from 意思是"从……消除掉",符合句意。

Passage 3

Notes

1. ...it allows the parties involved in the relationship to indicate... (Line 1)

   involve (...) in 的意思是"使……卷入,使……介入"。例如:

   Don't involve other people in your mad schemes! 不要把他人卷进你的疯狂计划中去!

   If I were you I won't get involved in their problems. 我要是你就不去介入他们的问题。

2. Trusting relationships encourage people to disclose their plans... (Line 3)

   disclose 的意思是"公开,揭露,泄露"。例如:

   The judge asked the reporter not to disclose the name of the murder victim.

   法官要求记者不要公开被谋杀者的姓名。

   She disclosed that she had been in prison. 她透露自己曾坐过牢。

3. In situations which you feel that... (Line 5)

   ▷situation 和 conditions 都可以表示"形势,事态,情况"。例如:

   We are studying the economic conditions/situation in several developing countries.

   我们在研究几个发展中国家的经济形势/情况。

   ▷conditions 指"影响日常生活的事物",如食物、工作、住房等;situation 指"更具有普遍意义的东西",诸如政府计划和财政等。

4. In mutual relationships, both parties... (Line 11)

   mutual 的意思是"互相的,彼此的;共同的"。例如:

   I like her and I hope the feeling is mutual. 我喜欢她,希望她也喜欢我。

   an agreement that will be for our mutual benefit 对我们双方都会有利的协议

Explanations

　　本文阐述了信任的意义:它使得双方可以交流所感、所做以及他们的分歧而不用担心产生矛盾或受到报复。信任可以拉近人们之间的关系,而伤害却是人际关系中最有害的结果之一。信任是我们和其他人交往过程中所感觉到的现象。而在现实中要建立信任是很不容易的,双方要以诚相待。没有人喜欢被伤害,只有很少的人喜欢伤害别人。除非我们已经成为别人攻击的对象,否则我们不会表达我们的真实感情。

21. B) 细节题。文章开头就说到信任的意义在于它使得双方可以交流他们所感、他们所做以及他们的分歧而不用担心产生矛盾或受到报复。所以答案是 B 项。

22. B) 细节题。根据第二和第三句话,可以得出选项中不正确的只有 B 项。

23. A) 细节题。根据第六句 Trust is a perceptual phenomenon that evolves from our experiences with others. 可以得出正确答案是 A 项。

24. C) 细节题。根据倒数第三句话 We avoid expressing our true feelings lest we become the target of a revenging attack from the other person. 可以断定正确答案应该是 C 项。

25. D) 推断题。注意 implied,这里是"暗示"的意思,指作者没有直接说出来的话。根据第四句话 In situations which you feel...diminishes quickly. 和倒数第三句话 We avoid expressing our true feelings ... next time. 可以得出选项 D 是正确答案。

Passage 4

Notes

1. In just six months he and his wife... (Line 2~3, Para. 1)

▷in 后面接时间词,表示"在……之后"。例如:

I will be back in two hours. 我会在两小时后回来。

▷比较 by 后面接时间词,表示"到……时"。例如:

I will be back by next May. 我到明年五月会回来。

2. Their names are together on the honor roll... (Line 4, Para. 2)

roll 在这里是名词,意思是"名册",另外 roll 还有"打滚;卷状物;轰隆声等"。例如:

The teacher called the roll. 教师点了名。

a roll of thunder 隆隆的雷声

3. Gun advocates are fond of saying that... (Line 1, Para. 4)

be fond of 的意思是"喜欢;喜爱"。例如:

She has many faults, but we're all very fond of her. 她虽有许多缺点,但我们都喜欢她。

My young nephews are fond of playing practical jokes on me. 我的几个小外甥都喜欢对我恶作剧。

4. ... who commit suicide do... (Line 2, Para. 4)

commit 表示"做"的意思时,通常表示做坏事。另外还有"承担义务"的意思。例如:

to commit a crime/a sin/suicide/murder 犯罪/作恶/自杀/杀人

The government has committed itself to improving health education. 政府决心致力于改善健康教育。

Explanations

这篇文章讨论了当前一个重要的问题——枪支犯罪的问题。文章是从一个波士顿的警察署长的角度来谈论个人手枪的合法性。在文章开头列举了一系列被杀害的警察的例子。在这些殉职的警察中至少有两个是被那种几乎在任何地方花上几美元就可以买得到的手枪所杀害的。所以从被杀害的警察的葬礼回来后没有人能使作者信服允许人们拥有手枪的理由。最后作者呼吁除了警察以外,任何人不得拥有手枪。

26. **D)** 推断题。文章最后一段作者建议禁止除警察以外的任何人拥有手枪,所以正确答案是 D 项。

27. **D)** 推断题。在第一段第四句 In just six months he and his wife had planned to and... she is alone. 里用了 just 和 alone 等词表达了他的惋惜之情,所以答案是 D 项。

28. **D)** 细节题。根据第二段前两句可以断定他至少应该于 1970 年之前当上署长,所以答案是 D 项。

29. **B)** 推断题。选项 A 与第四段内容相左,选项 C 与第三段第一句意思不符,选项 D 与第三段第二句意思不符,只有选项 B 是作者想要表达的意思。

30. **A)** 推断题。作者从一个警察署长的角度分析了很多案例,说明枪支的危害,并建议禁止除警察以外的其他人拥有手枪。从此可以看出他一定是在说服决策部门做出相关决定。所以答案是 A 项。

Passage 5

Keys

31. Oil ships and oil wells.

32. Because we still depend on oil for power now.

33. Because there were no atomic bomb tests then.

34. Useless cars.

35. Recycling of solid wastes.

Notes

1. If a tanker sinks or is grounded, millions of gallons of oil may escape into the sea. (Line 2~3, Para. 1)

In addition, oil can escape from wells that have been drilled into the sea bottom. (Line 3～4, Para. 1)

escape 在此处意思是"泄漏"，后接 from... 意思是"从……泄漏"；后接 into... 意思是"泄漏到……"。例如：

The gas is escaping somewhere. 有个地方在漏气。

Make a hole and let the water escape. 打个孔让水流走。

2. As the oil resources of the world are beginning to be used up, we may have to turn to atomic energy for power. (Line 1～2, Para. 2)

▷use up 意思是"用光；耗尽"。例如：

She used up the chicken bones to make soup. 她把鸡骨头全用来熬汤了。

He has used up all his strength and energy. 他已耗尽了体力和精力。

▷turn to...(for...) 意思是"向……寻求……"。例如：

The more depressed he got, the more he turned to drink. 他情绪越低落就越是借酒浇愁。

The child turned to his mother for comfort. 那孩子向母亲寻求安慰。

3. First taken up by plants, it has entered the bodies of cows who have eaten the plants. (Line 3, Para. 3)

▷take up 在此处意思是"吸收"。例如：

Use blotting paper to take up ink, not your handkerchief. 要用吸墨纸而不是手帕来吸墨水。

When the vacuum cleaner bag is full, it will not take up the dirt from the rug.

如果吸尘器的清洁袋满了，就不会再吸毯子上的灰尘了。

▷first taken up by plants 是过去分词短语，在句中作状语，表示原因。

4. But many cities are running out of space for such landfills. (Line 5～6, Para. 4)

run out of ＝ use up 意思是"用光；耗尽"。run out 也是同义词组，但常用作不及物动词。例如：

Our time is running out. /We are running out of time. 我们剩下的时间不多了。

Unit 29

Section A   Skimming and Scanning

Directions：（略）

Passage 1

Qualities of a Good Mentor（导师）

1. The Graduate College Award for Outstanding Mentoring of Graduate Students is a new award, created upon recommendation of the Graduate Student Advisory Council. The award recognizes exemplary efforts by the graduate faculty in advising and serving graduate students. This award was presented for the first time in 1996～1997.

2. What is it about the nominees and winners that make them regarded as excellent mentors? What special qualities do they have? In the nomination materials—which include letters from students, faculty and essays by the nominees themselves—several characteristics appear repeatedly.

3. As formal mentoring programs gain popularity, the need for identifying and preparing good mentors grows.

4. Can you name a person who had a positive and enduring impact on your personal or professional life, someone worthy of being called your mentor? Had he or she been trained to serve in such a role or been formally assigned to help you? I frequently ask veteran teachers these questions. As you might guess, most teachers with 10 or more years of experience were typically not assigned a mentor, but instead found informal support from a caring colleague. Unfortunately, not all teachers found this support. In fact, many veterans remember their first year in the classroom as a difficult and lonely time during which no one came to their aid.

5. Much has changed in the past decade, however, because many school districts have established entry-year programs that pair beginning teachers with veteran, mentor teachers. In the majority of such cases, the matching occurs before they meet and establish a personal relationship. This prevalent aspect of school-based mentoring programs presents special challenges that are further exacerbated when mentor teachers receive no or inadequate training and only token support for their work. The following six basic but essential qualities of the good mentor are essential for entry-year program mentor teacher training and need to be taught and developed accordingly.

The good mentor is committed to the role of mentoring.

6. The good mentor is highly committed to the task of helping beginning teachers find success and gratification in their new work. Committed mentors show up for, and stay on, the job. Committed mentors understand that persistence is as important in mentoring as it is in classroom teaching. Such commitment flows naturally from a resolute belief that mentors are capable of

making a significant and positive impact on the life of another. This belief is not grounded in naive conceptions of what it means to be a mentor. Rather, it is anchored in the knowledge that mentoring can be a challenging endeavor requiring significant investments of time and energy.

The good mentor is accepting of the beginning teacher.

7. At the foundation of any effective helping relationship is *empathy*（移情作用）. As Carl Rogers (1958) pointed out, empathy means accepting another person without making judgments. It means setting aside, at least temporarily, personal beliefs and values. The good mentor teacher recognizes the power of accepting the beginning teacher as a developing person and professional. Accepting mentors do not judge or reject mentees as being poorly prepared, overconfident, naive, or defensive. Rather, should new teachers exhibit such characteristics; good mentors simply view these traits as challenges to overcome in their efforts to deliver meaningful support.

The good mentor is skilled at providing instructional support.

8. Beginning teachers enter their careers with varying degrees of skill in instructional design and delivery. Good mentors are willing to coach beginning teachers to improve their performance wherever their skill level. Although this seems obvious, many mentor teachers stop short of providing quality instructional support. Among the factors contributing to this problem is a school culture that does not encourage teachers to observe one another in their classrooms. I often ask mentors-in-training whether they could imagine helping someone improve a tennis serve or golf swing without seeing the athlete play and with only the person's description of what he or she thought was wrong.

9. Lacking opportunities for shared experience, mentors often limit instructional support to workroom conversations. Although such dialogue can be helpful, discussions based on shared experience are more powerful. Such shared experiences can take different forms: mentors and mentees can engage in team teaching or team planning, mentees can observe mentors, mentors can observe mentees, or both can observe other teachers. Regardless of the nature of the experience, the purpose is to promote collegial dialogue focused on enhancing teacher performance and student learning.

The good mentor is effective in different interpersonal contexts.

10. All beginning teachers are not created equal, nor are all mentor teachers. This simple fact, when overlooked or ignored by a mentor teacher, often leads to relationship difficulties and diminished support for the beginning teacher. Good mentor teachers recognize that each mentoring relationship occurs in a unique, interpersonal context. Beginning teachers can display widely different attitudes toward the help offered by a mentor. One year, a mentor may work with a beginning teacher hungry for advice and the next year be assigned a beginning teacher who reacts defensively to thoughtfully offered suggestions.

11. Just as good teachers adjust their teaching behaviors and communications to meet the needs of individual students, good mentors adjust their mentoring communications to meet the needs of individual mentees. To make such adjustments; good mentors must possess deep understanding of their own communication styles and a willingness to objectively observe the behavior of the mentee.

The good mentor is a model of a continuous learner.

12. Beginning teachers rarely appreciate mentors who have right answers to every question

and best solutions for every problem. Good mentor teachers are transparent about their own search for better answers and more effective solutions to their own problems. They model this commitment by their openness to learn from colleagues, including beginning teachers, and by their willingness to pursue professional growth through a variety of means. They lead and attend workshops. They teach and enroll in graduate classes. They develop and experiment with new practices. They write and read articles in professional journals. Most important, they share new knowledge and perplexing questions with their beginning teachers in a collegial manner.

The good mentor communicates hope and optimism.

13. In "Mentors: They Simply Believe," Lasley (1996) argues that the crucial characteristic of mentors is the ability to communicate their belief that a person is capable of transcending present challenges and of accomplishing great things in the future. For mentor teachers working in school-based programs, such a quality is no less important. Good mentor teachers capitalize on opportunities to affirm the human potential of their mentees. They do so in private conversations and in public settings. Good mentors share their own struggles and frustrations and how they overcame them. And always, they do so in a genuine and caring way that engenders trust.

1. Most experienced teachers had an official mentor.

2. The early teaching years of most teachers are hard and lonely.

3. Mentors themselves need to be taught how to be good mentors.

4. Universities do not advocate new teacher/experienced teacher mentoring programs.

5. Mentors are committed to their mentees because they are paid to be.

6. Mentors will reject mentees for the reason as the mentee doesn't know anything.

7. A good mentor always remains teachable.

8. The good mentor is highly committed to the task of helping beginning teachers find _____ in their new work.

9. As Carl Rogers (1958) pointed out, empathy means accepting another person without _____.

10. Good mentor teachers recognize that each mentoring relationship occurs in a _____ _____ context.

Section B   Discourse Vocabulary Test

Directions: (略)

Passage 2

In a family where the roles of men and women are not sharply separated and where many household tasks are shared to a greater or lesser extent, notions of making ___11___ are hard to maintain. The pattern of sharing in tasks and in decisions makes for equality, and this in turn ___12___ to further sharing. In such a home, the growing boy and girl learn to accept that ___13___ more easily than did their parents and to prepare more ___14___ for participation in a world characterized by cooperation rather than by the "battle of sexes".

If the process goes too far and man's role is regarded as less important—and that has happened in some cases—we are as badly off as before, only in ___15___. It is time to reassess the role of the man in the American family. We are getting a little tired of "Momism"—but we don't want to ___16___ it for a "neo-popism". What we need, rather, is the recognition that bringing up children involves a partnership of equals. There are signs that psychiatrists, psychologists, social workers, and specialists on the family are becoming more aware of the part men play and that they have decided that women should not receive all the credits—nor all the blame. We have almost given up saying that a woman's place is in the home. We are beginning, however, to analyze man's place in the home and to insist that he does have a place in it. Nor is that place ___17___ to the healthy development of the child. The family is ___18___ enterprise for which it is difficult to lay down rules, because each family needs to work out its own ways for solving its own problems. Excessive authoritarianism has unhappy consequences, ___19___ it wears skirts or trousers, and the ideal of equal rights and equal responsibilities is *pertinent*（与……有关）not only to a ___20___ family, and to a healthy democracy as well.

A) fully
B) maintain
C) leads
D) reverse
E) exchange
F) superiority
G) equality
H) entirely

I) whether
J) increase
K) healthy
L) cooperative
M) accident
N) irrelevant
O) while

Section C　Reading in Depth

Directions：（略）

Passage 3

In the traditional marriage, the man worked at a job to earn money for the family. Most men worked in an office, a factory, or some other places away from the home. Since the man earned the money, he paid the bills. The money was used for food, clothes, a house, and other family needs. The man made most of the decisions. He was the boss.

In the traditional marriage, the woman seldom worked away from the house. She stayed at home to care for the children and her husband. She cooked the meals, cleaned the house, washed the clothes, and did other household work. Her job at home was very important.

In recent years, many couples continue to have a traditional relationship of this kind. The man has a job and earns the money for the family. The woman stays at home and cares for the children and the house. Many Americans are happy with this kind of marriage. But some other Americans have a different impression of marriage and family responsibilities.

There are two important differences in male and female roles now. One is that both men and women have many more choices. They may choose to marry or to stay single. They may choose to work or stay at home. Both men and women may choose roles that are comfortable for them.

A second difference in male and female roles is that within marriage many decisions and responsibilities are shared. The husband and wife may choose to have children, or they may not. If they have children, the man may take care of them some of the time, all of the time, or not at all. The woman may want to stay at home and take care of the children. Or she may want to go to work. Men and women now decide these things together in a marriage. Many married people now share these decisions and the responsibilities of their families.

21. Which of the following is NOT true in the traditional marriage?
    A) Men worked at a job to earn money for the family.
    B) The woman made most of the decisions.
    C) The woman stayed at home to care for the children.
    D) The man paid the bills.

22. In recent years _____.
    A) young couples reject the traditional relationship
    B) the woman has a job and earns the money for the family
    C) the woman doesn't stay at home and care for the children and the house
    D) the role of men and women has begun to change

23. Men and women may now choose all the following EXCEPT to _____.
    A) marry or to stay single
    B) work or to stay at home
    C) have the roles that are comfortable for them
    D) leave their jobs just because they have children

24. The following are all now true EXCEPT _____.
    A) they may choose to have children or not
    B) the man may take care of the children some of the time
    C) the woman may want to go to work
    D) the woman is the most important person in the house

25. Which of the following is NOT true?
    A) The man was the boss in the traditional marriage.
    B) The woman's job at home was very important in the past.
    C) Many Americans still have a traditional marriage.
    D) Everyone tries to get married.

Passage 4

A few years ago it was fashionable to speak of a generation gap, a division between young people and their elders. Parents complained that children did not show them proper respect and obedience, while children complained that their parents did not understand them at all. What had gone wrong? Why had the generation gap suddenly appeared? Actually, the generation gap has been around for a long time. Many critics argue that it is built into the fabric of our society.

One important cause of the generation gap is the opportunity that young people have to choose their own life style. In more traditional societies, when children grow up, they are expected to live in the same area as their parents, to marry people that their parents know and approve of, and often to continue the family occupation. In our society, young people often travel great distances for their educations, move out of the family home at an early age, marry or live with people whom their parents have never met, and choose occupations different from those of their parents.

In our upwardly mobile society, parents often expect their children to do better than they did: to find better jobs, to make more money, and to do all the things that they were unable to do. Often, however, the ambitions that parents have for their children are another cause of the division between them. Often, they discover that they have very little in common with each other.

Finally, the speed at which changes take place in our society is another cause of the gap between the generations. In a traditional culture, elderly people are valued for their wisdom, but in our society the knowledge of a lifetime may become obsolete overnight. The young and the old seem to live in two very different worlds, separated by different skills and abilities.

No doubt, the generation gap will continue to be a feature of American life for some time to come. Its causes are rooted in the freedoms and opportunities of our society, and in the rapid pace at which society changes.

26. The main idea of the first paragraph is that _____.
    A) the generation gap suddenly appeared
    B) the generation gap is a feature of American life
    C) how people can reduce the generation gap
    D) many critics argue over the nature of the generation gap

27. The word "around"(Line 5, Para. 1) means _____.
    A) on all sides   B) in every direction
    C) near   D) in existence

28. Which one is NOT the cause of the generation gap?
    A) Young people like to choose their own life styles.
    B) American society is changing very fast.
    C) Parents place high hopes on their children.
    D) Modern education makes them think differently.

29. In American society, young people often _____.
    A) rely on their parents to make a life
    B) stay with their parents in order to get an opportunity for higher education
    C) seek the best advice from their parents
    D) have very little in common with their parents

30. Which of the following statements is true according to the passage?
    A) Parents should be more tolerable towards their children.
    B) The younger generation should value the older generation for their wisdom.
    C) The generation gap is partly created by the elder generation.
    D) The generation gap should be avoidable in American society.

Section D   Short Answer Questions
Directions：（略）

Passage 5

How men first learnt to invent words is unknown; in other words, the origin of language is a mystery. All we really know is that men, unlike animals, somehow invented certain sounds to express thoughts and feelings, actions, and things, so that they could communicate with each other; and that later they agreed upon certain signs, called letters, which could be combined to represent those sounds, and which could be written down, these sounds, whether spoken, or written in letters we call words.

The power of words, then, lies in their associations—the things they bring up before our minds. Words become filled with meaning for us by experience; and the longer we live, the more certain words recall to us the glad and sad events of our past; and the more we read and learn, the more the number of words that mean something to us increases. Great writers are those who not only have great thoughts but also express these thoughts in words which appeal powerfully to our minds and emotions. This charming and telling use of words is what we call literary *style*（文体）. Above all, the real poet is a master of words. He can convey his meaning in words which sing like music, and which by their position and association can move men to tears. We should therefore learn to choose our words carefully and use them accurately, or they will make our speech silly and *vulgar*（粗俗的）.

31. According to the author, what can we describe about words in the first step of inventing words?

_____   _____   _____   _____

_____   _____   _____   _____

32. What is the power of words?

_____   _____   _____   _____

_____   _____   _____   _____

33. In order not to make our speech silly and vulgar, what should we do?

_____   _____   _____   _____

_____   _____   _____   _____

34. According to the author, how could we increase the number of words that mean something to us?

_____   _____   _____   _____

_____   _____   _____   _____

35. What is the best title of the article?

_____   _____   _____   _____

_____   _____   _____   _____

Notes and Explanations

Passage 1

Explanations

1. [N] 第四段第四句提到 As you might guess, most teachers with 10 or more years of experience were typically not assigned a mentor. 正如你所猜测的那样，大部分有着 10 年或更多年教学经验的教师并没有被指派过导师。所以答案是 No。

2. [Y] 第四段最后一句提到 In fact, many veterans remember their first year in the classroom as a difficult and lonely time during which no one came to their aid. 事实上，大部分的资深教师都记得他们从教的第一年，那是一段艰难而孤独的时期，没有人来帮助他们。由此得出答案是 Yes。

3. [Y] 第五段的最后一句提到 The following six basic but essential qualities of the good mentor are essential for entry-year program mentor teacher training and need to be taught and developed accordingly. 以下六个基本又必不可少的素质对于新导师进行培训计划非常关键，要教给新导师并使之付诸实践。由此得出答案是 Yes。

4. [NG] 第五段的开头提到 Much has changed in the past decade, however, because many school districts have established entry-year programs that pair beginning teachers with veteran, mentor teachers. 在过去的十年里发生了很大变化，因为很多学校都在新教师和有经验的老教师之间建立了组合。并没有提及大学是否赞成这一项目。由此得出答案是 Not Given。

5. [N] 第六段第一句提到 The good mentor is highly committed to the task of helping beginning teachers find success and gratification in their new work. 优秀的导师具有强烈的责任感来帮助新教师在未来的工作中取得成功和获得满足。由此得出答案是 No。

6. [N] 第七段第五句提到 Accepting mentors do not judge or reject mentees as being poorly prepared, overconfident, naive, or defensive. 负责任的导师不能因为新教师缺乏准备、过分自信、天真或者不易接近而去评价或拒绝他们。由此得出答案是 No。

7. [Y] 第十二段的标题提到 The good mentor is a model of continuous learner. 优秀导师是不断学习的楷模。由此得出答案是 Yes。

8. 第六段第一句提到 The good mentor is highly committed to the task of helping beginning teachers find success and gratification in their new work. 由此得出答案是 **success and gratification**。

9. 第七段第二句提到 As Carl Rogers pointed out, empathy means accepting another person without making judgments. 如同 Carl Rogers 指出的那样，移情作用意味着不做评价地接收另一个人。由此得出答案是 **making judgments**。

10. 第十段第三句提到 Good mentor teachers recognize that each mentoring relationship occurs in a unique, interpersonal context. 优秀的导师意识到每个指导关系都是建立在独特而相互配合的人际关系上。由此得出答案是 **unique, interpersonal**。

Passage 2

Notes

1. ... where many household tasks are shared to a greater or lesser extent... (Line 1～2, Para. 1)
to ... extent 的意思是"到……程度"。例如：
I agree with what you say to a certain extent. 我在相当程度上同意你所说的。
The temperature rose to such an extent that the firemen had to leave the burning building.

温度骤升,消防队员不得不离开着火的楼房。

2. ... and this in turn leads to further sharing. (Line 3~4, Para. 1)

in turn 的意思是"依次,轮流,反过来"。例如:

He asked each of us in turn. 他依次向我们每个人发问。

He struggled to free himself from the twisting weeds which in turn wrapped themselves more and more closely round his legs. 他奋力挣脱缠绕着他的杂草,而杂草反过来却把他的双腿越缠越紧。

3. ... a world characterized by cooperation rather than by the "battle of sexes". (Line 5~6, Para. 1)

rather than 这里的意思是"而不是",rather... than 的意思是"宁愿……而不……"。例如:

It's management that's at fault rather than the work-force. 错在资方而不在劳方。

I'd rather play tennis than swim. 我愿去打网球,而不是去游泳。

Rather than cause trouble, he left. 他没有惹麻烦,而是离开了。

4. ... we are as badly off as before, only in reverse. (Line 2, Para. 2)

in reverse 在此的意思是"倒退,退步"。例如:

Please drive the car in reverse until you get out of the garage. 请把车倒出车库。

At first Bob did well in school, but then he started moving in reverse. 开始时鲍勃学得很好,然后就开始退步了。

5. We are getting a little tired of "Momism"—but we don't want to exchange it for a "neo-popism". (Line 3~4, Para. 2)

在这句话里 momism 是一个作者造出来的词,意思是"一切都由女性照顾的原则",而后面的 popism 则是与之相对,同样也是根据文章的意思创造出来的词,意思是"一切都由男性照顾的原则",前缀 neo- 的意思是表示"新"。

Explanations

11. [F] 语法规则要求此处应填一个名词作 make 的宾语。选项 F、G、M 是名词。根据上文 the roles of men and women are not sharply separated 和下文 the pattern of sharing in task 判断出此处应填 superiority。making superiority 意思是"制造不平等",符合句意。

12. [C] 语法规则要求此处应填一个动词的第三人称单数形式作谓语,并和介词 to 搭配使用。只有选项 C 是该形式。lead to 是一个固定搭配词组,意思是"导致,结果是",符合句意。

13. [G] 语法规则要求此处应填一个名词作 accept 的宾语。所填词汇前的 that 提示这个词应该是前面提到过的词。上文提到"男女共同分担家务",可以推断本句的意思是"在这样的家庭中孩子们更容易接受平等的概念"。equality 符合句意。

14. [A] 语法规则要求此处应填一个副词作状语修饰不定式 to prepare。选项 A、H 是副词。prepare 常和 fully 搭配使用。prepare fully for 意思是"为……做好充分准备",符合句意。

15. [D] 语法规则要求此处应填一个名词作介词 in 的宾语。根据本句前半部分判断 reverse 符合句意。in reverse 意思是"倒退"。

16. [E] 语法规则要求此处应填一个动词原形构成不定式 to exchange sth. for sth.。选项 B、E、J 是动词原形。能够和 for 搭配使用的是 exchange。exchange for 意思是"用……交换(或替换)……",符合上下文意思。

17. [N] 语法规则要求此处应填一个形容词和 to 搭配构成 be + 形容词 + to sth. 结构。选项 K、L、N 是形容词。能够和 to 搭配使用的是 irrelevant。本句话意思是"那个位置(男性在家庭中的地位)对孩子的健康成长不是没有关系。" be irrelevant to 意思是"与……不相关(或没关系)",符合句意。

18. [L] 语法规则要求此处应填一个形容词作定语修饰 enterprise。根据本句后半部分的解释可以判断 cooperative 符合句意。a cooperative enterprise 意思是"合作企业"。

19. [I] 语法规则要求此处应填一个连词和 or 搭配使用引导状语从句。选项 I、O 是连词。可以和 or 搭配使用的是 whether。whether...or... 意思是"是……还是……",符合句意。

20. [K] 语法规则要求此处应填一个形容词作定语修饰 democracy。能够和 democracy 搭配使用的是 healthy。根据上文 not only to a healthy family 判断,此处应该是与其并列的结构,所以应填 healthy。

Passage 3

Notes

1. ... he paid the bills. (Line 3, Para. 1)

pay the bill 的意思是"付账"。例如:

Have you paid the phone bill yet? 你付电话费了吗?

The bill for the repairs came to $ 650. 修理费用多达 650 美元。

2. ... and did other household work. (Line 3, Para. 2)

household 在这里是形容词,意思是"家庭的,家用的"。例如:

household expenses 家庭开支

household chores 家庭杂活

3. There are two important differences in... (Line 1, Para. 4)

different 后面可以接很多介词:from, to, than 等。一般教师喜欢用 different from,但非正式英国英语的 different to 和美国英语 different than 也很通用。例如:

Mary and Jane are quite different from each other. 玛丽和简很不一样。

This is a different car from the one I drove yesterday. 这是另外一辆车,不是我昨天驾驶的那一辆。

She's so different to Rebecca. 她与丽贝卡很不一样。

How different life today is than what it was 50 years ago. 现在的生活与 50 年前是多么不同啊!

4. They may choose to marry or to stay single. (Line 2, Para. 4)

single 在这里的意思是"单身的,未婚的"。例如:

a single parent 单亲(独自一人养育儿女的父亲或母亲)

He's still single. 他仍单身。

5. ... within marriage many decisions and responsibilities are shared. (Line 1~2, Para. 5)

share 在这句话里表示"分享,分担"的意思。例如:

We haven't enough books for everyone; some of you will have to share.

我们的书不够一人一本,有些人就得合看一本。

Children should be taught to share their toys. 应该教育孩子们愿意把自己的玩具分给其他孩子玩。

Explanations

　　本文讨论了传统家庭和现代家庭的婚姻观念。在传统的婚姻中,男人工作挣钱来养活家庭,男人是家里的主人,而女人很少离家工作,只是待在家里照顾孩子和家庭。现今在男女角色上有两个重要的不同之处。一个是男人和女人都有更多的选择,他们可以自己选择自己喜欢的角色。另一个不同处是男人和女人在家庭决定和责任方面有了新的分工。

21. **B)** 细节题。根据第一段内容,在传统的观念里,男人占了主导地位,女人仅负责照顾孩子和家庭。选项 B 不是这个意思,所以是正确答案。

22. **D)** 细节题。第四和第五段讲到在近几年里,男人和女人的角色开始改变,所以正确答案是 D 项。

23. **D)** 细节题。第四和第五段讲到如今人们有了更多的选择,选项 A、B 和 C 都有可能做到,所以正确答案是 D 项。

24. **D)** 细节题。第四、五段提到了选项 A、B 和 C,没有提到选项 D。

25. **D)** 推断题。选项 A 说在传统的婚姻里,男人是主人,这是第一段的主题;选项 B 说到妇女的工作在过去是很重要的,这是第二段的主题;选项 C 说很多美国人仍旧保有传统的观念,这是第三段的主题;文中未提及选项 D。

Passage 4

Notes

1. ...it was fashionable to speak of a generation gap... (Line 1,Para. 1)
   speak of 意思是"谈到,谈及",用于否定句时意思是"值得一提,值得称道"。例如:
   We've had no rain to speak of, only a few drops. 我们这里没下过什么像样的雨,只不过是滴几滴。
   The lecturer spoke of many things related to chemistry. 演讲者谈到很多有关化学的事情。

2. What had gone wrong? (Line 3~4,Para. 1)
   go wrong 的意思是"搞错,弄错"。例如:
   The sum hasn't worked out, but I can't see where I went wrong. 总数算不出来,可我不明白错在哪里。
   The party was going well until my parents arrived, then everything went wrong.
   在我的父母到来之前,晚会一直开得很好,之后一切就不对头了。

3. ...the fabric of our society. (Line 5,Para. 1)
   fabric 的意思是"织物,结构"。fabric of society 的意思是"社会结构"。例如:
   The cost of repairing the fabric of the church was very high. 修理这座教堂的房屋结构要花费很多钱。
   The whole fabric of society was changed by the war. 这场战争改变了整个社会结构。

4. ...to marry people that their parents know and approve of... (Line 3,Para. 2)
   approve of 的意思是"赞成,同意,支持"。例如:
   I don't approve of smoking in bed. 我不赞成人们在床上吸烟。
   You made a good decision, and I heartily approve of it. 你做了一个很好的决定,我衷心地表示赞同。

Explanations

本文讨论了代沟的形成原因。在几年前谈起代沟还是一件时髦的事。父母们抱怨孩子们不再尊重和服从他们,而孩子们却抱怨父母根本就不理解他们。实际上代沟早已存在,并已成为了我们现今社会的一部分了。导致代沟的原因可能是:年轻人选择自己生活方式的机会;父母对孩子过大的期望;以及社会过快的变化速度。代沟的根源在于社会的自由度和机会以及社会迅速的变化。

26. **B)** 推断题。是对第一段内容的把握。选项 A 说代沟是突然出现的,这是不正确的,文中提到代沟久已存在了;选项 B 说代沟是美国人生活的特点之一,根据第一段最后一句,许多评论家认为代沟已根植于美国社会结构中了,选项 B 的说法是正确的;选项 C 和 D 文中没有提到。

27. **D)** 细节题。第一段里这句话的意思是代沟是久已存在的,所以 around 在这里的意思应该是选项 D"存在"。

28. **D)** 细节题。第二、三、四段分别叙述了导致代沟的三个原因,选项 D 不是原因之一。

29. **D)** 细节题。选项 A 和选项 B 与第二段后半部分内容不符;选项 C 说年轻人应从父母那儿得到好的建议,但因代沟的存在,他们很少这样做;选项 D 说年轻人和父母只有很少的共同点,这是导致代沟的一个重要的因素。

30. **C)** 推断题。根据文章来看,选项 C 是导致代沟的三个因素之一。

Passage 5

Keys

31. Words did not have written form, at first.

32. Words can associate things in the world with our ideas.

33. We should choose words with care and accuracy.

34. By reading and learning more.

35. The Power of Words.

Notes

1. ... unlike animals, somehow invented certain sounds to... (Line 2, Para. 1)

   somehow 的意思是"以某种方式,不知怎么地"。例如:

   Don't worry; we'll get the lost money back somehow. 别担心,我们总会把丢失的钱找回来的。

   I think she's right but somehow I'm not completely sure.

   我想她是对的,但不知为什么我不是很有把握。

2. ... and that later they agreed upon certain signs... (Line 4, Para. 1)

   certain 在这里是做限定词,意思是"某,某种"。例如:

   There are certain reasons why this information cannot be made public. 有某些原因使得这条消息不能公开。

   When the water reaches a certain level, the pump switches itself off.

   当水位达到一定高度,水泵会自动关闭。

3. The power of words, then, lies in their associations... (Line 1, Para. 2)

   lie in 的意思是"在于,因为,位于"。例如:

   His chief attraction lies in his character, not his looks.

   他的吸引力主要在于他的性格,而不是他的外貌。

   The house lies in a little valley behind the trees. 房子位于树林后的小山谷里。

4. ... the more certain words recall to us the glad... (Line 2~3, Para. 2)

   recall 的意思是"回想,回忆起"。例如:

   a style of film-making that recalls Alfred Hitchcock

   一种使人回想起艾尔弗雷德·希区柯克的电影摄制风格

   I don't recall ever meeting her. 我想不起来曾经见过她。

5. ... and association can move men to tears. (Line 8, Para. 2)

   move 的意思是"使感动"。例如:

   The child's suffering moved us to tears. 这孩子受的苦使我们难过得流泪。

   I was very moved by her sad story. 她的悲惨故事使我深受感动。

Unit 30

Section A Skimming and Scanning

Directions：（略）

Passage 1

Underwater Boats

1. Efforts to build underwater boats began in Europe over 500 years ago. Although the technology was not advanced enough to create a successful submarine, several attempts were made with varying degrees of success. In 1578, English scientist William Bourne wrote of the possible use of ballast tanks (hollow tanks that can be filled with seawater) to enable a submersible boat to descend and rise to the surface, though he never built one himself. In 1620, Comelis Drebbel, a Dutch inventor, created several prototype submersibles resembling two wooden rowboats, one atop the other and bound with leather for a watertight skin. These were propelled by oars that emerged from the hull through watertight openings. Drebbel tested his crafts several times below the Thames River in London, England. Historians consider Drebbel's tests the first practical use of a maneuverable submarine.

2. For the next two centuries, scientists and inventors in America, England, France, Germany, and Italy attempted to create a true submersible warship with little success. In 1776, American inventor David Bushnell designed the Turtle for use against the British ships that were blockading New York. The Turtle was an egg-shaped craft, slightly larger than an adult man, constructed of wood and designed to briefly submerge under an anchored enemy ship. Its one-man crew could propel the craft by vigorously cranking a hand-turned propeller. The boat's weapon was an explosive charge that could be screwed into the underside of the target ship's wooden hull. However, the one and only attempt to use Bushnell's craft failed when its pilot discovered that the British ships had copper-plated hulls.

3. American attempts to develop underwater boats achieved some success during the Revolutionary War and the Civil War. Unfortunately, such boats usually proved more dangerous to their crews than their targets. Only in the 1890s did John Holland and Simon Lake develop practical submersible boats. The U. S. Navy purchased its first submarine from Holland on 11 April 1900, the traditional birthday of the U. S. Submarine Force.

4. In 1800, American inventor Robert Fulton built a 6.4-meter submarine named the Nautilus, which was similar in shape to the modem submarine. Fulton introduced two important innovations: rudders for vertical and horizontal control and compressed air as an underwater supply of oxygen. When submerged, the Nautilus was powered by a hand-operated, four-blade propeller. On the surface, the boat was propelled by means of sails attached to a folding mast.

5. During the latter half of the 19th century, many attempts were made to develop an adequate means of submarine propulsion. Inventors experimented with compressed air, steam, and electricity as power sources. In 1898, American inventor John Philip Holland used a dual-propulsion system to develop the first practical submarine with an efficient source of power. His submarine was equipped with a gasoline engine for surface cruising and an electric motor for underwater power. In 1900, the U. S. government purchased the 16. 2-meter submarine and named it the USS Holland.

6. Quickly adopted by nations throughout the world, improved submarines influenced the course of both world wars, though they remained essentially surface ships able to hide only temporarily under water. During World War Ⅱ, the U. S. force of large, fast, long-range fleet submarines played a major role in winning the Pacific war by sinking so much Japanese shipping.

7. In the ten years after the war, a series of technological innovations, culminating in nuclear propulsion, transformed the submarine into a true underwater boat, faster beneath the surface than above and able to remain submerged indefinitely.

8. At the outbreak of World War Ⅰ in 1914, submarine technology had evolved to the point that the United States, the United Kingdom, Germany and Russia had all developed diesel-powered submarines that could operate on electrical batteries underwater. The German U-boat was the most advanced. With an average of only 30 submarines at sea at any one time, the German U-boat service put a stranglehold on wartime shipping and merchant supply lines, and nearly brought the United Kingdom to its knees in four years of conflict.

9. During World War Ⅱ, Germany continued to develop superior U-boats. The Germans invented the snorkel, a retractable tube that could be extended above the surface of the water to capture air and to release exhaust while the submarine continues to operate unseen 18 meters below the surface. They also created streamlined hull designs and larger electric batteries to enable their submarines to travel at much higher speeds and for longer distances. After Germany surrendered in 1945, both the U. S. and Soviet navies benefited from Germany's advanced submarine technology. Postwar diesel-electric submarines made the most of these innovations, and underwater maneuverability and speed increased.

10. The nuclear age began in the 1950's and it led to the development of nuclear reactor power in submarines to increase range and capability. The first nuclear-powered submarine, the USS Nautilus, was developed by the Americans and launched in 1954. In a trial run conducted in 1955, the Nautilus sailed totally submerged for an incredible distance of 2,170 km in 84 hours. Its underwater cruising speed was more than 20 knots, and since the sub was nuclear-powered, it no longer needed to periodically surface for air or for refueling.

11. During the 1990's, the U. S. Navy began allowing some of its submarines to be used for scientific missions. In 1995, for example, the U. S. Navy allowed civilian scientists to conduct missions below the polar ice caps aboard Sturgeon-class attack submarines. The agreement provided for one mission a year for five years. Access to this underwater region had been restricted for years due to the harshness of the environment, the distance from support stations, and the danger of other military submarines lurking in the area. The submarines used for these scientific expeditions were specially suited for Arctic missions, and provided a rare opportunity for scientists to explore and map the Arctic Ocean

floor, measure ice thickness, and collect water samples. These missions set the stage for cooperation between the Navy and the scientific community on future expeditions.

1. William Bourne built the first practical and maneuverable submarine.
2. Robert Fulton pioneered two important submarine innovations: rudders and compressed air.
3. John Philip Holland developed the first submarine with an efficient source of power.
4. Germany's U-boats destroyed more ships than any other submarine during World War Ⅱ.
5. In 1995, the U. S. Navy allowed some of its Sturgeon-class attack submarines to be used by civilian scientists to conduct missions below the polar ice caps.
6. During World War Ⅰ, Italian submarines put a stranglehold on wartime shipping and merchant supply lines, nearly bringing the United Kingdom to its knees.
7. In 1898, American inventor John Philip Holland invented a submarine with a hand-operated propeller for underwater power and sails for surface cruising.
8. The one and only attempt to use Bushnell's craft failed when its pilot discovered that _____.
9. When submerged, the Nautilus, a 6. 4-meter submarine built by Robert Fulton was powered by _____.
10. In the last decade of last century, the U. S. Navy began allowing some of its submarines to be used for _____.

Section B   Discourse Vocabulary Test
Directions:（略）

Passage 2

In science the meaning of the word "explain" suffers with civilization's every step in search of reality. Science can not really explain electricity, magnetism, and gravity; their effects can be measured and __11__, but of their nature no more is known to the modern scientist than to Thales who first looked into the __12__ of the electrification, rejected the __13__ that man can ever discover what these mysterious forces "really" are. Electricity, Bertrand Russell says, is not a thing, like St. Paul's Cathedral; it is a way in which things behave. When we have told how things behave when they are electrified, and under what __14__ they are electrified, we have told all there is to tell. Until __15__ scientists would have __16__ of such an idea. Aristotle, for example, whose natural science dominated Western thought for two thousand years, believed that man could arrive at an understanding of reality by __17__ from self-evident principle. He felt, for example, that it is a self-evident principle that everything in the __18__ has its proper place, hence one can deduce that objects fall to the ground because that's where they __19__, and smoke goes up because that's where it belongs. The goal of Aristotelian science was to explain why things happen. Modern science was born when Galileo began trying to explain how things happen and thus originated the method of controlled experiment which now forms the basis of __20__ investigation.

大学英语 4 级阅读与简答（新题型）

A）approve	I ）support
B）notion	J ）belong
C）nature	K）scientific
D）disapproved	L）reasoning
E）world	M）universe
F）recently	N）rapid
G）predicted	O）type
H）circumstances	

Section C　Reading in Depth

Directions：（略）

Passage 3

When your parents advise you to "get an education" in order to raise your income, they tell you only half the truth. What they really mean is to get just enough education to provide manpower for your society, but not so much that you prove an embarrassment to your society.

Get a high school diploma, at least. Without that, you will be occupationally dead unless your name happens to be George Bernard Shaw or Thomas Alva Edison, and you can successfully dropout in grade school.

Get a college degree, if possible. With a B. A. , you are on the launching pad. But now you have to start to put on the brakes. If you go for a master's degree, make sure it is an MBA.

Do you know, for instance, that long-haul truck drivers earn more per year than full professors? Yes, the average 1977 salary for those truckers was \$24,000, while the full professors managed to earn just \$23,030.

A Ph. D. is the highest degree you can get. Except for a few specialized fields such as physics or chemistry where the degree can quickly be turned to industrial or commercial purposes, if you pursue such a degree in any other field, you will face a dim future. There are more Ph. D. s unemployed or underemployed in this country than any other part of the world.

If you become a doctor of philosophy in English or history or anthropology or political science or languages or—worst of all—in philosophy, you run the risk of becoming overeducated for our national demands. Not for our needs, mind you, but for our demands.

Thousands of Ph. D. s are selling shoes, driving cars, waiting on table, and endlessly filling out applications month after month. They may also take a job in some high school or backwater college that pays much less than the janitor earns.

You can equate the level of income with the level of education only so far. Far enough, that is, to make you useful to the gross national product, but not so far that nobody can turn much of a profit on you.

21. According to the writer, what the society expects of education is to turn out people who _____.

A) will not be a disgrace to society

B) will become loyal citizens

C) can take care of themselves

D) can meet the nation's demands as a source of manpower

22. Many Ph. D. s are out of job because _____.

A) they are improperly educated

B) they are of little commercial value to their society

C) there are fewer jobs in high schools

D) they prefer easier jobs that make more money

23. The nation is only interested in people _____.

A) with diplomas

B) who specialize in physics and chemistry

C) who are valuable to the gross national product

D) both A and C

24. Which of the following is NOT true?

A) Bernard Shaw didn't finish high schools, nor did Edison.

B) One must think carefully before pursuing a master degree.

C) The higher your education level, the more money you will earn.

D) If you are too well-educated, you'll be overeducated for society's demands.

25. The writer sees education as _____.

A) a means of providing job security and financial security and a means of meeting a country's demands for technical workers

B) a way to broaden one's horizons

C) more important than finding a job

D) an opportunity that everyone should have

Passage 4

There are various ways in which individual economic units can interact with one another. Three basic ways may be described as the market system, the administered system, and the traditional system.

In a market system individual economic units are free to interact each other in the market place. It is possible to buy commodities from other economic units or sell commodities to them. In a market, transactions may take place via barter or money exchange. In a barter economy, real goods such as automobiles, shoes, and pizzas are traded against each other. Obviously, finding somebody who wants to trade my old car in exchange for a sailboat may not always be an easy task. Hence, the introduction of money as a medium of exchange eases transactions considerably. In the modern market economy, goods and services are bought or sold for money.

An alternative to the market system is administrative control by some agency over all transactions. This agency will issue edicts or commands as to how much of each kind of goods and services should be produced, exchanged, and consumed by each economic unit. Central planning may be one way of administering such an economy. The central plan, drawn up by government, shows amounts of each commodity produced by the various firms and allocated to different households for consumption. This is an example of complete planning of production, consumption, and exchange for the whole economy.

In a traditional society, production and consumption patterns are governed by tradition: every person's place within the economic system is fixed by parentage, religion, and custom. Transactions take place on the basis of tradition, too. People belonging to a certain group of *caste* (种姓制度,印度世袭制度) may have an obligation to care for other persons, provide them with food and shelter, care for their health, and provide for their education. Clearly, in a system where every decision is made on the basis of tradition alone, progress may be difficult to achieve, a *stagnant* (停滞的) society may result.

26. What is the main purpose of the passage?

    A) To outline constructing types of economic system.

    B) To explain the science of economics.

    C) To argue for the superiority of one economic system.

    D) To compare barter and money-exchange markets.

27. The word "real" in "real goods"(Line 3～4, Para. 2) could best be replaced by _____.

    A) high quality　　B) concrete　　　　C) utter　　　　　D) authentic

28. According to the passage, a barter economy can lead to _____.

    A) rapid speed of transactions　　　B) misunderstandings

    C) inflation　　　　　　　　　　　　D) difficulties for the traders

29. According to the passage, who has the greatest degree of control in an administered system?

    A) Individual households.　　　　　B) Small businesses.

    C) Major corporations.　　　　　　D) The government.

30. Which of the following is not mentioned by the author as a criterion for determining a person's place in a traditional society?

    A) Family background.　　　　　　B) Age.

    C) Religious belief.　　　　　　　D) Custom.

Section D　Short Answer Questions

Directions：（略）

Passage 5

The advantages and disadvantages of a large population have long been a subject of discussion among economists. It has been argued that the supply of good land is limited. To feed a large population, inferior land must be cultivated and the good land worked intensively. Thus, each person produces less and this means a lower average income than could be obtained with a smaller population. Other economists have argued that a large population gives more scope for specialization and the development of facilities such as ports, roads and railways, which are not likely to be built unless there is a big demand to justify them.

One of the difficulties in carrying out a world-wide birth control program lies in the fact that official attitudes to population growth vary from country to country depending on the level of industrial development and the availability of food and raw materials. In the developing country where a vastly expanded population is pressing hard upon the limits of food, space and natural resources, it will be the first concern of government to place a limit on the birthrate, whatever the consequences may be. In the highly industrialized society the problem may be more complex. A decreasing birthrate may lead to unemployment because it results in a declining market for manufactured goods. When the pressure of population on housing declines, prices also decline and the building industry is weakened. Faced with considerations such as these, the government of a developed country may well prefer to see a slowly increasing population, rather than one which is stable or in decline.

31. What does a small population mean to productivity and average income?

_____ _____ _____ _____ _____

_____ _____ _____ _____ _____

32. According to the passage, a large population will provide a chance for developing _____.

_____ _____ _____ _____ _____

_____ _____ _____ _____ _____

33. In a developed country, people would perhaps go out of work if _____.

_____ _____ _____ _____ _____

_____ _____ _____ _____ _____

34. According to the passage, what is slowly rising birthrate perhaps good for?

_____ _____ _____ _____ _____

_____ _____ _____ _____ _____

35. Why is it no easy job to carry out a general plan for birth control throughout the world?

_____ _____ _____ _____ _____

_____ _____ _____ _____ _____

Notes and Explanations

Passage 1

Explanations

1. [N] 第一段第三句提到 In 1578, English scientist William Bourne wrote of the possible use of ballast tanks (hollow tanks that can be filled with seawater) to enable a submersible boat to descend and rise to the surface, though he never built one himself. 在 1578 年,英国科学家 William Bourne 提出了利用沉浮箱(可以装满海水的空箱子)使船下潜和上浮的可能性,但他自己并没有制造这样一个沉浮箱。由此得出答案是 No。

2. [Y] 第四段第二句提到 Fulton introduced two important innovations: rudders for vertical and horizontal control and compressed air as an underwater supply of oxygen. Fulton 引入了两个重要的改进:可以控制水平和垂直方向的舵和提供水下氧气供应的压缩空气。由此得出答案是 Yes。

3. [Y] 第五段第三句提到 In 1898, American inventor John Philip Holland used a dual—propulsion system to develop the first practical submarine with an efficient source of power. 在 1898 年,美国发明家 John Philip

Holland 使用双推进系统改进第一个具有有效推进力的实际可行的潜水艇。由此得出答案是 Yes。

4. [NG] 第八段第二句提到 The German U-boat was the most advanced. 德国的 U 型潜艇是最先进的。但文中并没有提到德国潜艇摧毁了多少对手的船。由此得出答案是 Not Given。

5. [Y] 第十一段第二句提到 In 1995, for example, the U. S. Navy allowed civilian scientists to conduct missions below the polar ice caps aboard Sturgeon-class attack submarines. 在 1995 年，美国海军允许非军事科学家在鲟鱼号攻击潜水艇上进行极地冰盖水下的研究工作。由此得出答案是 Yes。

6. [N] 第八段第三句提到 With an average of only 30 submarines at sea at any one time, the German U-boat service put a stranglehold on wartime shipping and merchant supply lines, and nearly brought the United Kingdom to its knees in four years of conflict. 在任何时候，德国在海域内平均都有 30 艘潜水艇，它的 U 型潜艇在战争时期牢牢地控制了航道和货物运输线，在四年的对抗时间内，狠狠地打击了英国的军队。由此得出答案是 No。

7. [N] 第五段第四句提到 His submarine was equipped with a gasoline engine for surface cruising and an electric motor for underwater power. 他的潜水艇配备了水上使用的汽油引擎和水下使用的电力马达。由此得出答案是 No。

8. 第二段最后一句提到 However, the one and only attempt to use Bushnell's craft failed when its pilot discovered that the British ships had copper-plated hulls. 当驾驶员发现英国船只有铜制的外壳后，唯一使用 Bushnell 船只的努力也失败了。由此得出答案 **the British ships had copper-plated hulls**。

9. 第四段第三句提到 When submerged, the Nautilus was powered by a hand-operated, four-blade propeller. 当下潜时，Nautilus 船使用一种手动的四片推进器使之前进。由此得出答案是 **a hand-operated, four-blade propeller**。

10. 第十一段第一句提到 During the 1990's, the U. S. Navy began allowed some of its submarines to be used for scientific missions. 在二十世纪九十年代，美国海军开始允许一些潜水艇用作科学研究工作。由此得出答案是 **scientific missions**。

Passage 2

Notes

1. In science the meaning of the word "explain" suffers with civilization's every step in search of reality. (Line 1~2)

   这句话的意思是：在自然科学中 explain 的意思随着文明社会寻找真实的每一步而不断变化。

   suffer 意思是"为……而受苦"。例如：

   He suffered for his carelessness. 他因粗心而吃了亏。

   The child suffers from measles. 这小孩得了麻疹。

2. Science can not really explain electricity, magnetism, and gravity;... rejected the notion that man can ever discover what these mysterious forces "really" are. (Line 2~5)

   这句话的意思是：自然科学并不能解释电、磁场和引力是怎么回事，但可以测量和预测其影响。至于其本质，就是在当代科学家中也没有人知道得比泰士勒更多。他曾首次研究电的本质，不赞成人类能够发现这些神秘力量到底是什么这一说法。

3. Until recently scientists would have disapproved of such an idea. (Line 8)

   disapprove 的意思是"不赞成；不同意"。例如：

   I am sorry I must disapprove of your action. 很抱歉，我必须指责你的行动。

   Animal conservationists disapprove of experimenting on animals. 动物保护主义者不赞成用动物做试验。

Explanations

11. [G] 语法规则要求此处应填一个动词过去分词构成被动语态。选项 D、G 是这种形式。根据上文对科学的解释,此处 predicted(预示)符合句意。

12. [C] 语法规则要求此处应填一个名词作介词 into 的宾语。选项 B、C、E、H、M、O 是名词。根据本句话中提到的 nature 判断此处应填 nature,意思是"本质,属性"。

13. [B] 语法规则要求此处应填一个名词作 rejected 的宾语。根据本句的定语从句的前半部分和所填词汇的同位语从句的内容判断 notion 符合句意。notion 意思是"观念",reject the notion 是惯用搭配。

14. [H] 语法规则要求此处应填一个名词作介词 under 的宾语。根据本句话意思判断 circumstances 符合句意。under...circumstances 是一个固定搭配词组,意思是"在……情况下"。

15. [F] 语法规则要求此处应填一个副词和 until 搭配作状语修饰句子的谓语。只有选项 F 是副词。根据上下文的意思可以判断本句话意思是"直到最近科学家们才对这个观点提出反对意见"。recently 符合题意。until recently 意思是"直到最近"。

16. [D] 语法规则要求此处应填一个动词 + ed 形式和 have 构成完成时态。根据上文和后面所举的例子判断 disapproved 符合句意。disapproved of 是一个固定搭配词组,意思是"不赞同"。

17. [L] 语法规则要求此处应填一个动名词和 from self-evident principle 搭配作介词 by 的宾语。选项中只有 reasoning 是动名词。根据本句和下一句所举例子判断 reasoning(推理)符合题意。

18. [M] 语法规则要求此处应填一个名词作介词 in 的宾语。本句话意思是:宇宙中的任何物体都有它自己固定的位置。由此判断 universe(宇宙)符合题意。

19. [J] 语法规则要求此处应填一个动词原形作表语从句的谓语。选项 A、I、J 是动词原形。本句话中 that 引导的两个宾语从句的句式相同,所以可以断定 belong(属于)符合句意。

20. [K] 语法规则要求此处应填一个形容词作定语修饰 investigation。选项 K、N 是形容词。根据前文 the method of controlled experiment 推断出此处应该填 scientific。scientific investigation 意思是"科学探索"。

Passage 3

Notes

1. When your parents advise you to "get an education"... (Line 1, Para. 1)

advise 的意思是"建议(做某事),通知"。例如:

The doctor advised me to take more exercise. 医生嘱咐我多加锻炼。

We are to advise you that the matter is under consideration. 此事已在讨论中,特此通知。

2. ...unless your name happens to be George Bernard Shaw or Thomas Alva Edison... (Line 1~2, Para. 2)

happen to 意思是"碰巧"。例如:

Do you happen to know his new telephone number? 你可知道他的新电话号码?

I happened to be in the market yesterday when a fire started. 昨天发生火灾时,我正好在市场里。

3. If you go for a master's degree, make sure it is an MBA. (Line 2, Para. 3)

▷make sure 意思是"弄清楚;确保"。例如:

Make sure he writes it down. 让他一定记下来。

▷另外关于 sure 的其他常用词组还有:for sure 确切地;毫无疑问地。例如:We'll win for sure. 我们肯定会获胜。to be sure 确实;当然。

4. Not for our needs, mind you, but for our demands. (Line 3, Para. 6)

这句话的意思是:你需要注意的不是我们需要什么,而是我们需求什么。mind 在本文里的意思是"注意,留意"。例如:

Mind the holes in the road. 当心路上的坑坑洼洼。

Explanations

本文讨论了受教育程度和收入的关系。受教育程度高收入不一定就高。很多专业不好的博士还在做一些收入很低的工作。必须使自己对整个国民生产总值能做出一定的贡献才可以提高收入。

21. **D）** 细节题。根据文章第一段第二句可以推断本题正确答案是 D 项。

22. **B）** 细节题。第五段到第七段论述了有些博士生找不到工作的原因。

23. **C）** 推理题。文章最后一段讲到对国民生产总值有贡献就够了，否则即使学历高也不会有人认为你对社会有价值，所以正确答案是 C 项。

24. **C）** 细节题。第二、三、六段分别说明选项 A、B 和 D 是正确的，根据第四段内容，选项 C 不正确。

25. **A）** 推断题。选项 B 在文中没有提到；选项 C 的观点是作者不赞成的；选项 D 并不是本文的主要分析点；选项 A 恰当地说明了作者对教育的看法。

Passage 4

Notes

1. There are various ways in which individual economic units can interact with one another. (Line 1, Para. 1)

   interact 中的 inter-是前缀，意思是"在一起，交互"。例如：

   interaction 交互作用；intercommunication 交际。

2. ... finding somebody who wants to trade my old car in exchange for a sailboat... (Line 4~5, Para. 2)

   ▷in exchange for 意思是"以……换"。例如：

   He is giving her French lessons in exchange for her teaching him English. 他教她法语，她教他英语，互教互学。

   ▷exchange 也可作动词，用于搭配 exchange... for...。例如：

   The deputy manager exchanged the company's interest for his personal honor.

   这个代理经理为了个人荣誉而出卖了公司的利益。

3. Hence, the introduction of money as a medium of exchange eases transactions considerably. (Line 6, Para. 2)

   这句话的意思是：因此，引入作为交易媒介的货币就在相当大的程度上减少了交易的麻烦。

4. This agency will issue edicts or commands as to how much of each kind of goods... (Line 2, Para. 3)

   as to 的意思是"关于；至于"。例如：

   I don't know anything as to the others. 至于其他，我一无所知。

Explanations

本文介绍了经济个体之间的三种经济体制。第一种是市场经济，第二种是计划经济，还有一种是传统的方式。在传统方式下，个人的经济实力是由其出身决定的。某些享有特权的人要担负提供其他人衣、食、健康、教育等各方面的条件。这种传统的方式很显然会妨碍社会的进步。

26. **A）** 主旨题。第一段简要介绍了三种经济体制。第二、三、四段分别较详细地介绍了这三种经济体制。

27. **B）** 词汇题。根据本句中所举的具体例子（汽车、鞋子等）可以确定 real 的意思是"具体的"。

28. **D）** 细节题。在文章的第二段的后半部分提到，易货交易很麻烦，所以货币才应运而生。因此答案是 D 项。

29. **D）** 细节题。根据第三段第四句 The central plan, drawn up by government, shows... 可以得出正确答案应该是 D 项。

30. **B）** 细节题。文章最后一段第一句提到在传统的经济体制中，个体的经济实力是由他/她的出身、宗教信仰和传统来决定的。所以正确答案是 B 项。

Passage 5

Keys

31. Higher productivity, and a higher average income.

32. transport system

33. the birthrate is decreasing

34. A developed nation.

35. Because different governments have different views of the question.

Notes

1. To feed a large population, inferior land must be cultivated and the good land worked intensively. (Line 1~2，Para. 1)

    inferior 常与 to 连用,意思是"次的,劣等的,较劣的",反义词是 superior。例如:

    No inferior products should be allowed to pass. 决不允许放过任何次品。

2. ...official attitudes to population growth vary from country to country... (Line 2，Para. 2)

    vary from...to... 意思是"从……到……不等;在……到……之间变动"。例如:

    The temperature varies from time to time. 温度常常变化。

    Her health varies from good to rather weak. 她的身体时好时坏。

3. ...it will be the first concern of government to place a limit on the birthrate... (Line 5，Para. 2)

    place/set a limit on/to 意思是"对……限制"。例如:

    We must set a limit to the expense of the trip. 我们一定得限制旅行的开支。

图书在版编目(CIP)数据

大学英语 4 级阅读与简答(新题型)/刘宇慧,张俊梅主编. 上海:华东理工大学出版社,2007.8
(新世纪英语丛书)
ISBN 978 - 7 - 5628 - 2068 - 0

Ⅰ.大…　Ⅱ.①刘…②张…　Ⅲ.英语-阅读教学-高等学校-自学参考资料　Ⅳ.H319.4

中国版本图书馆 CIP 数据核字(2007)第 057749 号

新世纪英语丛书

大学英语 4 级阅读与简答(新题型)

主　　编/刘宇慧　张俊梅
策划编辑/王耀峰
责任编辑/李清奇
责任校对/李　晔
封面设计/大象设计　金　丹
出版发行/华东理工大学出版社
　　　　地　　址/上海市梅陇路 130 号,200237
　　　　电　　话/(021)64250306(营销部)
　　　　　　　　　(021)64251904(编辑室)
　　　　传　　真/(021)64252707
　　　　网　　址/www.hdlgpress.com.cn
印　　刷/句容市排印厂
开　　本/787mm×1092mm　1/16
印　　张/24.5
字　　数/787 千字
版　　次/2007 年 8 月第 1 版
印　　次/2007 年 8 月第 1 次
印　　数/1 - 7050 册
书　　号/ISBN 978 - 7 - 5628 - 2068 - 0/H·610
定　　价/29.80 元

(本书如有印装质量问题,请到出版社营销部调换。)